THE
DESERT
PRINCE

By Peter V. Brett

Novels

The Painted Man

The Desert Spear

The Daylight War

The Skull Throne

The Core

Short Stories And Novellas

The Great Bazaar and *Brayan's Gold*

Messenger's Legacy

Barren

THE
DESERT
PRINCE

PETER V.
BRETT

HARPER
Voyager

Harper*Voyager*
An imprint of HarperCollins*Publishers* Ltd
1 London Bridge Street
London SE1 9GF

www.harpercollins.co.uk

HarperCollins*Publishers*
1st Floor, Watermarque Building, Ringsend Road
Dublin 4, Ireland

First published by HarperCollins*Publishers* 2021
1

A catalogue record for this book is available from the British Library

ISBN: 978-0-00-830977-0 (HB)
ISBN: 978-0-00-830978-7 (TPB)

Set in Fournier MT Pro

Printed and Bound in the UK using 100% Renewable Electricity at CPI Group (UK) Ltd

MIX
Paper from
responsible sources
FSC™ C007454

For Cassandra

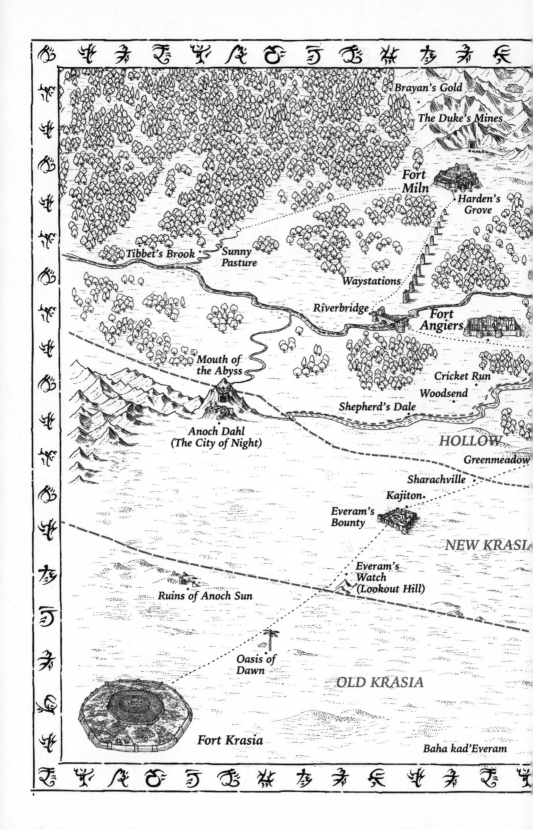

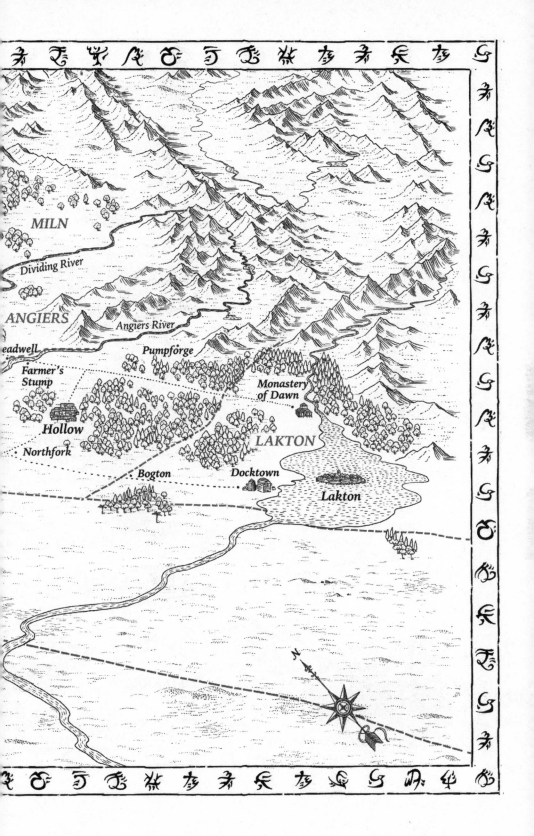

Temple of
Sharik Hora

The
Holy City

Palace
of the
Sharum Ka

Training
Grounds

Middle City

FORT
KRASIA

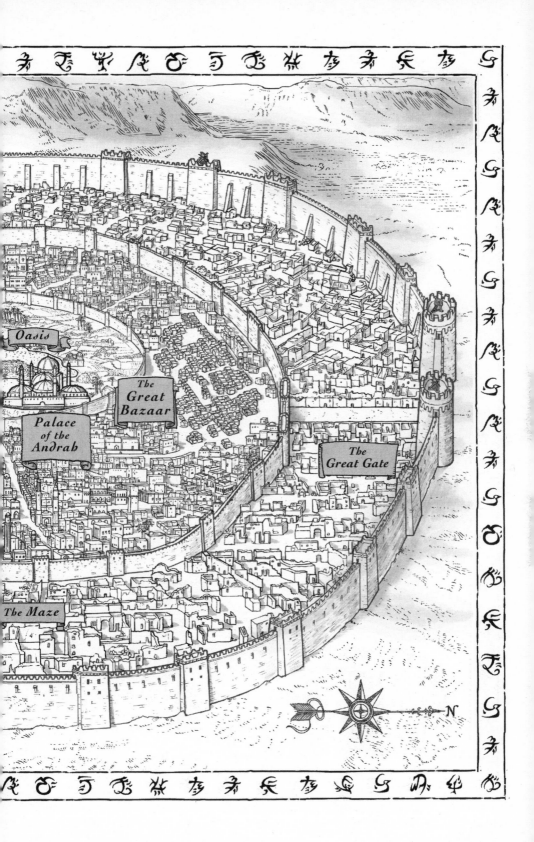

Oasis

The
Great
Bazaar

Palace
of the
Andrah

The
Great
Gate

The Maze

N

CONTENTS

THE
DESERT
PRINCE

I

I AM OLIVE

349 AR

M Y HEAD JERKS as Micha pulls a lock taut while she sections
and plaits my long black hair. I'm used to it. I can't remember a time I wasn't being yanked around to meet expectations.

"Hold still," Grandmum Elona snaps, putting another dusting on
the brush. "Almost powdered your eyeball."

"What's the point of painting my face," I grumble, "when I have to
go dressed in a canvas tarp?"

Elona laughs. "There's always time for the powder kit." I know she
means it. I've never seen Grandmum looking anything less than perfectly put together. She finishes my eyes and gets to work on my lashes.
"You're princess of Hollow. Might have to put on the same potato sack
as the other apprentices, but those girls look up to you. Can't settle for
being anything less than the prettiest one in the room."

"Mistress Darsy is going to give a test today in Herb Lore," I say. "I
need time to compare notes with Selen."

"Tsst!" Micha hisses her disapproval. "You should have thought of
that last night, sister."

Micha and I share a father, Ahmann Jardir, who sits atop the throne
of Krasia, the vast and powerful empire to the south. Thesa and Krasia
were at war before I was born. Some folk say they would be still, if not

for me. Mother says that's nonsense, but not so much that she'll let me visit Father's court. Most of what I know about my people I learned from Micha and my instructors in school.

Micha was raised in Krasia, evidenced by the modest black robes covering everything save her hands and face. She, too, has powdered her cheeks and painted her lips, though the only ones who will see it are the people in this room and Micha's wife, Kendall. Micha is beautiful by anyone's standards, but when she leaves the privacy of my chambers, she will drape a white marriage veil over the lower half of her face.

With more than thirty summers, Micha is twice my age, and has always been more nanny than sister. The duchess always makes time if I want to see her, but her attendants and counselors hover, and I'm left feeling like I'm holding up some urgent decision. Micha is the one who does my hair, scrubs my back, and escorts me everywhere. I love her and she loves me, but I am still a child to her, and her rules can be smothering.

"That good-for-nothing daughter of mine ent gonna be much help with your test, anyway," Grandmum says. "Selen's as bright as she is pretty, and that ent a lot. Besides, you're the duchess' daughter. Who cares about some herb gathering test?"

"The duchess," I say. "If I get a single answer wrong . . . night, even if I get one right but not right *enough*, I'll never hear the end of it."

Grandmum chuckles. "Ay, that sounds like my Leesha. Still think you should be more worried about the practice ring than Herb Lore. Only just stopped powdering that bruise on your cheek."

"Selen threw a lucky punch." It's the truth, if not the whole truth. Selen throws a lot of lucky punches. She's Captain Wonda's prized student. "It was gone overnight."

"Still had a shadow in the morning." Grandmum isn't one to give in, even when she's wrong. "And that ent the point. Got guards everywhere. What do you need to be scrapping in the yard for?"

"*Sharusahk* is more fun than Herb Lore," I say. "At least I'm good at fighting."

"Known a lot of folks that were good at fighting over the years," Grandmum says. "Funny how few of them are still around to keep the rest of us company."

"A princess is always a target for her family's enemies," Micha cuts in. "Someday the guards may not be with her, and Olive will be glad to know how to defend herself."

I resist the urge to roll my eyes. What does Nanny Micha know of fighting? I've never seen her so much as step on a bug. She doesn't even eat meat. "You're a princess, too. Why don't you have to fight?"

"The Kaji tribe has many princesses," Micha says. "If something happens to me, there are dozens to take my place. Hollow has only you to succeed your mother."

There is no sadness in her tone—she could be talking about the weather. Still, the words settle heavy on my shoulders. Micha's mother was low in the pecking order of Father's many wives. Micha wasn't much older than me when she was sent from the famed summer palaces of Krasia to live in cold, rainy Thesa among people once her enemy, playing nursemaid to her littlest sister.

Does she resent her exile? I certainly would, but Micha has never so much as hinted dissatisfaction with her life. She's happier in Hollow than I am.

"Finished," Micha pronounces.

"And here." Elona gives a last swipe of red to my lips. "Pucker."

I press my lips together, evening the color as I look in the mirror. For all my talk of hurry, I can't help but smile at Grandmum's handiwork. I'm a fair hand with the brush, but Elona—famously averse to work—is an artist with the powder kit. I have my father's olive skin, uncommon this far north, but she's matched it perfectly, smoothing my skin and adding natural-looking accents to my high cheeks and sharp jaw.

Blue eyes are a rarity in Krasia, but they're not unheard of. Someone in Father's family must have had them, because mine are the same sky blue as Elona's. They contrast with my dark complexion, but she's framed them with shadows and thickened the lashes, making the flash of color explode.

Micha's plaits form a perfect crown around my head, weaving together into a long braid in back. Elegant enough to suit even the duchess, yet secure for the practice yard.

"You've got a weaver's touch with hair, girl." Elona reaches to tug at my sister's scarf. "Yet you keep your own wrapped up like a washerwoman."

Micha doesn't like anyone touching her headscarf, but she says nothing, simply drawing back out of reach. Sometimes I think I'm the only person in the world not terrified of Grandmum Elona. "You know why."

She does, but it makes no difference. Grandmum is never so alive as when she's talking about something that makes everyone uncomfortable.

"Ay," Elona snorts, "it's *unseemly* to tempt men with something they can't have. Like that ent the whole point! Can't wrap men around your finger without putting their heads in a spin."

"I need no men on my finger," Micha says.

"Nor anywhere else." Elona laughs. "How is Kendall?"

Nanny Micha is usually so outspoken, but she gets shy when anyone mentions her wife. Kendall Demonsong is Mother's royal herald. Kendall is boisterous and charming, clad in vibrantly colored motley, often with cuts modest Micha must find scandalous, but the two of them are more in love than anyone I know.

Micha drops her eyes. "My *jiwah*," she uses the Krasian word for wife, "is well, thank you."

She holds a coarse blue Gatherer's apprentice dress for me to step into. The fabric is dark and absent of design, woven more for warmth and stain resistance than comfort.

The cloth scratches at my skin, and I hate it, and everything it represents. This isn't who I am. Night, sometimes even I don't know who I am, but I know I'm not this.

I slip into sensible brown canvas shoes, comfortable and forgettable, whether in garden soil or university halls.

I know every cobbler in Hollow by name, and have an entire room full of shoes. Boots and sandals, heels and flats. A shoe for every outfit and occasion, made from polished leather, fine silk, or snakeskin.

But most days, I have to wear *canvas*, because that's what Mother wore as an apprentice, thirty summers ago.

"Eyes shut." Grandmum sprays a cloud of perfume and I walk through it as she taught me. "Don't want folk spinning tales about how the princess of Hollow smells after *sharusahk* practice."

"Nonsense," I say. "I sweat roses and cinnamon."

Grandmum cackles, smoothing the coarse shoulders of the dress.

"Even in a potato sack, you're still the prettiest girl in Hollow, like your mum before you." She winks. "Like your grandmum, back in her day."

"You're still first," I say, only partly in jest. Grandmum is on the shady side of sixty, but her hair is still black as night, a perfect contrast with her smooth, pale skin. She has powder and dye and low necklines working for her, but so does every other woman at court. Even the younger ones don't draw attention like Elona Paper.

"Charming as a Jongleur." Elona takes my arms and leans in, kissing the air beside my cheeks so as not to muss the powder on my face. Grandmum fights with every other woman she meets, but for some reason I've always kept on her good side, and I'm happy for it.

I snatch my books and hurry from my chambers, Elona and Micha trailing behind.

My aunt Selen is waiting in the hall downstairs. She's three months younger than I am. They put our cribs in the same room, and we've been inseparable ever since.

Selen is the only person I know whose existence is as much a scandal as my own. Grandmum's affair with General Gared is the stuff of Jongleurs' tales, and nearly broke two marriages. Grandda Erny seems to have gotten used to it. Selen's stepmother Emelia, not so much.

Grandmum takes one look at Selen's hair and sniffs. Elona's hair is lustrous black like the deep of night, and General Gared was said to have hair as yellow as the sun in his youth, but Selen's is uneven, with bright spots that approach blond and dull patches that are closer to brown. "Couldn't let your maid run a comb through that bird's nest before you braided it?"

"Then where would the birds live?" Unable to please her mother, Selen has learned to take pleasure in displeasing her. She turns to me. "Did you ask the duchess about the borough tour?"

The tour comes once a year on Summer Solstice—a chance for children coming of age to see the far reaches of the duchy. The tour visits each of the massive greatwards that protect Hollow from demonkind before venturing beyond their protection for a visit to the borderlands.

"She ent going, and neither are you." Grandmum sounds angry. The only thing worse than displeasing her is ignoring her. "Got everything you need here in the capital, and hot water in pipes. Seeing how the unwashed bumpkins live is overrated, and don't get me started about sleeping on the ground."

"It will be exciting." Selen continues to ignore her mother, baiting her on purpose. "Who knows, we might even see a demon!"

I roll my eyes. Selen and I have spoken to a lot of returning tourists over the years, and none have ever seen more than a bush rattled by the breeze. Everyone knows the demons were wiped out in the war.

"Didn't have greatwards when I was your age," Elona says. "Seen a lifetime's worth of demons. You ent missing much."

Selen crosses her arms. "Da already said I can go."

"Ay, is that right?" Elona puts her hands on her hips. "Just see about that."

"Says you're welcome to come by if you want to discuss it." Selen's eyes glitter with delight as Grandmum's scowl deepens. They both know Elona won't dare visit General Gared's house. If there's anyone in the world who's a match for Grandmum, it's Selen's stepmother Emelia.

"He's gonna have to come out of hiding sooner or later," Elona growls, but she lets it go at that, turning on her heel to stomp off. Selen makes a rude gesture at her back.

"Tsst," Micha hisses. "The Evejah teaches us gloating cheapens a victory, and invites Everam to teach us a lesson in humility."

"Ay, maybe," Selen agrees, "but night if it doesn't feel good."

"I don't understand why you always need to pick a fight," I say to Selen as we hurry out to the courtyard.

"Maybe you'd get your way once in a while, if you picked more," Selen says.

A carriage is waiting to take us to Gatherers' University. Wonda Cutter, captain of Mother's house guard, is chatting with the driver.

"Mornin', Olive." Wonda gives me a warm smile. Her small eyes are set over an oft-broken nose on a heavy, scarred face. Captain Wonda is bigger than all but the tallest men in Cutter's Hollow, and even in peacetime, she takes her work seriously, always wearing her wooden breastplate and bristling with weapons.

A quiver of arrows is secured at her back, along with her unstrung bow. I've seen how fast she can string it if she senses trouble, and she takes the archery ribbon every Solstice Festival. There's a long knife on her thigh, and a spear harnessed crosswise with the bow on her back. Not some elegant fencing spear for festival games, this is a short, brutal thing, designed for one purpose. Folk still whisper about Wonda's exploits in the demon war.

She looks around, then reaches into her pocket, producing two small twists of paper. "Snuck you two some sugar candy, but don't tell your mum you got it from me."

The gift says everything a person needs to know about Captain Wonda. She loves us, would give her life for us, but we'll always be children to her.

"Sunny!" Selen snatches her candy and has it out of the wrapper and into her mouth in one smooth move.

"Thanks, Won." I take my candy, slipping it into a pocket of my dress. I feel bad seeing her look of disappointment when I don't eat it right away like Selen. I love Captain Wonda and want her to be happy, but I'm not a child anymore.

"What are you doing here?" I ask. It's rare for Wonda to leave my mother's side.

"Oh, ay." Captain Wonda rubs the back of her neck, no longer meeting my eyes. "Just passing through and saw the carriage. Figured I'd see you off."

She's a terrible liar, but I don't press. Captain Wonda may be clumsy at keeping Mother's secrets, but she keeps them, for the most part.

Wonda turns to go, then pauses, as if remembering something. "By the way, yur mum is stopping by the university, later." She doesn't wait for a reply, turning back and marching swiftly up the stairs. "See you in the practice yard."

"What was that about?" Selen asks.

"A warning," I say.

The new stableboy, Perin, sets the steps so we can climb into the carriage. Perin is very tall, with a jaw I've caught myself staring at more than once. Grandmum called him a young colt, leering when she said it.

Selen throws him a wink as he closes the door.

"What was that?" I ask.

"What was what?" Selen's mouth twitches, barely containing her smile.

I nod slightly at Micha, raising a questioning brow. My sister will happily gossip about everyone, but we all know she reports everything Selen or I do to Mother.

Selen shrugs, the smile breaking out across her face. "We kissed for three hours yesterday!"

I gape. "You did not."

"Tsst!" Micha wrinkles her nose. "The boy shovels your stables. He would not make a worthy husband."

"Ent looking for a husband," Selen laughs. "Just a warm pair of lips."

I turn to Micha. "Please don't tell Mother."

"Phagh." Micha waves a hand. "If I told your mother every time Selen kissed a boy, I would have time for nothing else."

Selen barks at that. I frown, jealous of her freedom. It's easier to think of Micha as *our* nanny, since she's cared for both of us since we were in nappies, but Micha is here for me, not Selen. She would never keep a secret like that for me, or let a boy close enough to kiss in the first place. I think I'm the only girl in class who's never done it. Selen . . . well, I've lost count.

I hug my Herb Lore book to my chest, staring out the carriage window.

Selen gives my shoulder a shove. "Ay, what's itching you?"

"Nothing," I say, but Selen crosses her arms. She knows me too well. "Demonshit."

She'd talk to me about it. It's nothing we haven't discussed a thousand times, but Micha is listening. "I'm just worried about the exam."

Selen blinks. "What exam?"

"Headmistress Darsy never goes more than ten days without a surprise test," I say. "Today's the tenth."

The corner of Selen's mouth curls. "So there *might* be an exam."

The morning's anxiety comes rushing back. Wonda said Mother would visit today, and it makes me all the more sure a test is coming. Mother always makes time after a test to "discuss" my errors.

"I'm not ready," I say. "I want to compare notes, not kissing stories."

Selen sighs. "Ten minutes of cramming ent going to make much difference for either of us. You're better at this than you think. You'll be all right."

"All right isn't good enough."

Selen rolls her eyes. "The duchess will be disappointed no matter what you do. That's how mums are." Selen's voice becomes higher, haughtier, in perfect imitation of Elona. *"Best study hard, girl, because you ent much to look at!"*

"That's nonsense," I say. Selen takes after her father with a heavy jaw and broad shoulders. I'm taller than most boys our age, but Selen has inches on even me, and her arms and back ripple with muscle. She actively resists the powder kit, and even when Grandmum manages to wrestle her into the vanity chair, she's apt as not to scrub her face clean at the next opportunity.

Selen is more handsome than pretty, but only Grandmum is vain enough to think her a disappointment to look at.

"Know it is," Selen says. "You've always been the pretty one, but I like the way I look, and there ent a shortage of boys happy to kiss me, so who cares what Mum thinks? You'd be happier if you stopped caring, too."

I look down my nose at her. "You still care what the general thinks."

Selen snorts. "Ay, but it doesn't keep me from doing what I want. Yesterday while I was kissing Perin in the stable, Da walked in to give Rockslide an apple."

I look up, and Selen's expression is triumphant. She has my full attention now. "General Cutter caught you?" I wonder why Perin isn't lying on a hospit bed.

Selen's nose wrinkles. "Dodged it by a horse's tail. Hid in the one place he wouldn't look."

I cover my eyes. "Creator, no."

"Dung stall!" Selen's smile is infectious. "Perin wasn't so interested in kissing when I came out smelling like a fertilizer cart."

Micha howls, and laughter bursts from my lips. For a moment, I forget classwork, forget my mother, and remember why I love Selen. She must have been fit to burst, holding in that story while I whined about a test that might not even happen.

"Will you sneak down to see him again?" I hate the excitement I feel, living vicariously through Selen's stories. I wish I could have stories of my own.

"Feh." Selen flicks a finger. "Only so many times you can explain to the washerwoman why your Seventhday dress reeks of horse shit."

"Ay?" I can't hide the disappointment in my voice. "Perin isn't the brightest ward, but he's sunny to look upon."

Selen shrugs. "Kissed him already. First kiss is always the best. Second time they start talking, and it's all headaches from there."

I suppress a twinge of envy, shaking my head. "So worldly at fifteen summers."

"Says the girl who's never kissed anyone." Selen means the words wryly, but she sees the look on my face and her mocking expression softens.

"I can't just go around kissing boys like you," I say.

"Ent always boys," Selen reminds me. "Remember when I gave Sandy Pasture a kissing lesson and she followed us around for two weeks?"

"Maybe it was because you kept giving her lessons," I say.

Selen smirks. "Ay, might have something there. Point is, that's the duchess talking. Teenagers are supposed to sneak around their parents and kiss. I do. Why can't you?"

My eyes flick to Micha, who at least has the courtesy to stare out the window. I can't remember the last time a boy my own age got within ten feet of me without her appearing to interpose herself.

But it's more than just Micha and Mother being overprotective. More even than worry over the gossip that would run through the palace if the duchess' daughter was caught kissing the stableboy.

It's because kissing leads to more.

2

BOTH

"I WANT TO SPAR."

It was a perfectly reasonable request. I was tired of endlessly practicing *sharukin* against empty air without understanding how the gentle movements applied to fighting.

I was five.

"Absolutely not," Mother said.

"The general said Selen can do it." I said the words with triumph, certain I had Mother in an inescapable logic trap.

She dismissed it with a swish of her hand. "I don't care what Gared Cutter says. He's not your father."

"Selen's brother Steave spars." I tried to keep the pleading from my voice, but I knew I was failing. "He's only three."

Mother began rubbing at her temple—never a good sign. "I don't approve of that, either, but it's different with boys."

"Why?" I demanded. "Because he has a pecker? I've got one, too. Why aren't I a boy?"

Even now, I remember how the duchess' normally serene face suddenly tensed. "Oh, poppet. Do you want to be?"

I didn't have an answer for that. At least, not one I thought would get me what I wanted. But I sensed Mother wavering. I crossed my arms and kept my eye on the target. "I want to spar."

But Mother's mind was elsewhere. She knelt to put herself at my level, crown of warded electrum glittering in her hair. She touched my face, her eyes serious and a little sad.

"Whether you spar has nothing to do with being a girl, or a boy," Mother said. "These days those things mean less than they used to, and for you, least of all."

I didn't understand. "What does that mean?"

"It means you are my daughter," the duchess said, "but you are also my son."

"Huh?"

I look back and wish I'd been more articulate, but the words made no sense. I'd known I was different from Selen since we were infants in the bath, but I never gave the fact we peed differently any more thought than the different colors of our hair, eyes, or skin. What did any of it matter? The ways we were alike outweighed the differences.

"You were to be twins," Mother went on. "Two eggs fertilized at the same time—a boy and a girl."

The words were almost too much to close my head around, but I didn't question the claim. Back then it never occurred to me that Mother could be wrong about anything. "What happened?"

"Shortly after you were conceived, a demon prince tried to kill your father, and nearly succeeded. His First Wife Inevera and I had no choice but to use *hora* magic to save him."

That story, I knew already. It was a legend in Mother's keep. Everyone knows the duchess and the Damajah hate each other, but it is said they hold peace because of that night.

"I don't understand." The words felt feeble even to my young self—insufficient to convey the breadth of the feeling. I had only the vaguest notion of what conception meant, and Mother was hinting at something beyond.

"When you work magic to your will, some of it flows through you," Mother said. "The energy can make you stronger for a time. Faster. It heightens senses and speeds healing."

I tilted my head, still confused.

Mother's throat constricted, as if forced to swallow an unpleasant cure. "In that moment, one egg absorbed the other."

I remember staring at her for a long time before responding. "I . . . ate my brother?" It was too big a concept to fully grasp—huge and terrifying, but less so than the one that followed. "Or . . . did I eat my sister?"

"No one 'ate' anyone!" I don't know what response Mother had been preparing for, but this didn't seem to be it. "What does it matter, who absorbed who?"

The answer seemed obvious. "How else can I know who I am?"

"You are not your brother, or your sister," Mother said. "You are both—the sum of everything either might be."

Questions began to accumulate in my head, but I sensed the most important one, even then. "If I didn't eat anyone, why do we keep it secret?"

Mother sighed, straightening my hair and smoothing my dress as she spoke. "Because there isn't anyone quite like you, Olive. Magic made something nature could not. You can bear children or father them, and that will mean different things to different folk. If your father's heirs fear you have a claim to the Skull Throne of New Krasia, there's no telling what they might do."

None of this meant much to me. Mother's worry was distant, like a cloud on the far horizon. I looked at my hands, my arms, my body. Everything was familiar, and yet somehow new. "I'm not a girl?"

"You are what you want to be," Mother said. "And no matter what, I love you and will always be there for you. If you want to stay a girl, I will support you. If you choose to be a boy, I will support you. If you want to announce to the world you are both, I will support you."

Mother took my arms, squeezing gently. "But some of those choices are more difficult paths to walk, and you need to understand that. If you are a girl, your father's people will seek to marry you. If you are a boy, they may seek to harm you, or take you away from me."

That struck home where the other warnings had not. I didn't understand everything, but I knew I didn't want to be taken away from Mother.

"What do you *want* to be?" Mother asked.

I thought of Selen's younger brothers, always running after us— sticky, lumbering, and loud. I thought of our friend Darin Bales, his hair a tangle, clothes ill-fitting, dirt under his nails. Uncle Gared—thick and hairy, smelling of sweat and ale.

Then I remembered playing dress-up with Grandmum, learning her paints and powders, trying on dresses and jewels. I thought of Mother, the most powerful person in Hollow, looking fabulous in her elaborate dresses, with a crown of warded electrum glittering in her hair.

"I want to be a girl."

Mother took my hand. "Then that is what you are, all anyone need know, unless you decide otherwise. The world will try to fit you into one of two boxes, but one day I hope you will outgrow them both."

I pulled my hand back. "Then you'll let me spar."

This time, I had her.

GRANDMUM TOOK ME back to my room afterward. I was still humming with excitement at having changed Mother's mind, but beneath the rush of victory, a pool of questions about myself was quietly growing.

"About time she gave you that talk," Elona said. "Been on her about it for years."

"Really?" I can't hide my surprise. Grandmum knows I have a boy's parts, as well as a girl's. Changed my nappies when I was a baby. But we never talk about it.

"That thing between your legs is the key to a kingdom," Grandmum said.

"I don't want a kingdom," I told her, and I meant it. "They say Mother could have been queen of Thesa, but she chose not to."

"If she'd had a pair of stones, she would have," Elona said. Even at five I was used to this kind of talk from Grandmum. She never spoke down to us the way Mother and the other adults did. "I've got higher hopes for you."

The words made no sense. "My stones will make me brave?" I certainly didn't feel brave.

"Ent the stones, themselves. It's . . . " she rolled a hand in the air, ". . . male energy. Men take what they want. Anyone gets in their way, they swat them aside. My daughter has the biggest stick in Thesa, but she refuses to swing it."

"What if she just didn't want to be queen?" I asked.

Elona scoffed. "Your mum is a priss, but she likes telling folk what to do too much to turn down a crown. Just couldn't bring herself to bully the other dukes and duchesses into giving her one."

"She must have had a reason," I insisted. It never occurred to me then that Mother could be wrong about anything.

Grandmum looked me over. "Ay, maybe. You'd be more dangerous if you were the eldest child of a queen."

I laughed, more in surprise than humor. "Dangerous? I'm just a kid."

"For now," Elona says. "But it won't always be that way. Some secrets you can carry around forever, like a knife in your pocket. Others are like a blade in your hand. Longer you hold, the deeper they cut. Better to let folk know who you are now, so they have time to get used to the idea before you're old enough to be dangerous."

"Mother said people might try to hurt me if we did," I said. "Or take me away."

"You're a ripping princess, Olive." Grandmum shrugged. "Going to be a target no matter what."

The words sent a shock of fear through me. The danger hadn't quite felt real, but now, with Elona confirming it, I had an urge to run and hide.

Grandmum must have seen it on my face, because she laid a hand on my arm, squeezing gently. "Ent no one getting at you here, Olive Paper. But if this scares you, we can double the watch."

The suggestion offered little comfort. "There's already guards everywhere. Will they put them in my room, next?"

Grandmum cackled. "They can put a few in mine!"

Her laughter made me feel a little less afraid. Grandmum Elona was like that. She'd slap you with the truth, then rub away the sting. I wanted her approval as much as anyone's, and I knew she wanted me to agree, but it didn't feel right. "Mum says if I want to be a girl, then I am."

Elona looked at me a long time, then nodded. "Ay, if that's how you want it." She tugged at a lock of hair that had come loose from my braid. "Come along to the vanity, then. Time I started teaching you a woman's weapons."

3

—·—

COMPROMISE

I SEE THE STACK of papers on Headmistress Darsy's desk, and my stomach cramps like it does in the days before my flow comes. I was right about the test.

"What are we going to do?" I whisper. "I can't keep my own garden alive, much less recite the seven cures."

I wish I was exaggerating. Herb Lore has always bored me, and why not? I can't apply the seven cures to my own experience. Whatever Mother's magic did to me in her belly, I'm not like my peers in more ways than just biology. I'm stronger and quicker to heal than anyone my age has a right to be, I've never been sick, and I've no interest in fertility tea.

Mother cites the curious mind as the highest virtue, preferring textbooks to novels, but I'll take Jak Scaletongue adventures over old herb gathering journals and history books every time.

The other girls are already chattering in their seats, but they fall silent when Selen and I arrive. They've saved us space, filled seats circling our favored chairs like a nest around two eggs.

The three boys in the class sit together in the back of the room, vastly outnumbered. Before Mother opened the doors of Gatherers' University to all genders, male Herb Gatherers were rare, and often derided as inferior to their female counterparts. Most Gatherers would refuse male apprentices, and even patients were wary, relegating most male practitioners to research positions. Even now, they are uncommon, and none hold positions of power at the university and hospit.

"Hello, boys," Selen says as we pass. I'm the conventionally pretty one, with perfect hair and powdered face, but she's the one their eyes follow.

It's no different when we get to our seats. The other girls keep a respectful distance from my personal space, but with Selen, they lean in.

I can't blame them. Selen is nearly as royal as I am, sister to the duchess and daughter of a baron, but her self-confidence and unflappable good spirits infect everyone around her. Other girls want to be near her. They want to *be* her.

Sometimes, I want to be her, too. I wonder what it feels like, to be so sure of who you are that others are drawn into your orbit.

"Summer Solstice is next week," Minda says. She's the oldest of us at sixteen, with a round face and a warm smile. Her hair is tied back with a simple blue ribbon. "Are you going on the borough tour?"

"Mum didn't want me to, but Da gave permission anyway." Selen holds up her little finger. "Got the general wrapped up tight."

Everyone laughs, but then the eyes turn to me, and my stomach clenches tighter than it did at the sight of the exam papers. "I haven't spoken to the duchess about it, yet."

I'm afraid to ask, if I'm honest about it. Thirteen summers is old enough to go on the annual borough tour, but Mother has refused to let me go for the last two years. Even with Selen going, I don't have much hope for a change.

Invoking my mother has the desired effect, and the eyes fall away. The ones who aren't terrified of Duchess Paper worship her. Many do both in equal measure.

"I kissed Perin the stableboy," Selen volunteers, pulling all the attention back to herself. She gives me a secret smile and I nod my thanks for the save.

"Aprons on." Before Selen can recount her odoriferous exploits, Headmistress Darsy walks in carrying a huge tray of plants in thick clay pots. Her gray-shot hair is pinned in a tight bun, and she carries the heavy tray effortlessly in hands thick from decades spent setting bones. Darsy was Mother's apprentice once upon a time, another of the surrogates she's surrounded me with to make up for her lack of time. I love her like an aunt, even as I disappoint her as a student.

We pull our aprons—heavy, pocketed things filled with dry herbs and tools—over plain blue apprentice dresses, leaving our seats to meet the headmistress at the planting table.

"We need to re-pot this stiffroot," Darsy says. "Does anyone know why?"

The other girls pause. Even *I* know the answer, so the rest of them must, but everyone gives me time to raise my hand first. Grandmum says it's because they know I will be duchess one day and want to gain favor. I want to believe it is because they are my friends, but the truth is I don't really have any friends other than Selen. Not ones who truly know me.

"Olive." Headmistress Darsy points as I lift my hand.

"Because stiffroot tendrils spread quickly," I say, "and will crack even the thickest clay in time."

"Correct!" Headmistress Darsy beams at me. "The force of stiffroot tendrils is slow, but enormous. Enough to break even these reinforced pots." She gives one of the pots a solid rap with her heavy teacher's rod. "You'll need to twist each stem a few times to break the tendrils free of the clay before you can work it from the soil."

Minda is the first to take a plant. She's a big girl and strong, and she grasps the base of the stem properly, but her face reddens as she strains to pull the roots free. I look around, seeing the other girls and boys struggling similarly. Even Selen gives a grunt, failing on the first pull.

I take my own plant, gripping the pot firmly with one hand as I grasp the stalk with the other. I twist and yank hard. The stiffroot flies free in a spray of dirt, even as the reinforced clay shatters beneath my clutching fingers.

My classmates gape at me, and I resist the urge to flee. I've always been stronger than the others, but sometimes I forget how much. Soil covers my dress and freshly plaited hair, ruining all Micha and Elona's work. I look like a fool.

"Carefully, child!" Darsy moves quickly to my side "Ent pulling a stump out of the ground. Did you cut yourself?"

I should have. I felt the sharp clay slicing across my palm. Anyone else would need stitches, if not surgery, but I know without looking that my skin is unbroken.

"I'm fine." I try to pull away, not wanting further attention, but the headmistress' meaty hands envelop mine, gently examining.

A crash draws everyone's attention. I look up and see Selen standing over a shattered pot, dirt and stiffroot all over the classroom floor.

"Creator, did everyone grease their fingers this morning?!" Having assured herself I am not bleeding, Darsy lifts her skirts and hurries over to Selen, my accident forgotten.

Selen catches my eye, and I know without a word spoken that she threw her pot to the stone floor on purpose before the others could think too much on what I'd done.

I can't imagine what I would do without her.

I step away to the scrub basin to wash as the others finish potting, losing much of Elona's powder work in the process.

The apprentice dress and apron are designed to resist soil and come passably clean with a brushing. Not so, my hair. Undoing the braids would take the rest of class and leave me looking even more disheveled. I try to shake them out without much success. I can feel the dirt tickling my scalp, damp and gritty. I feel humiliated, but I do what Elona would and return to my seat with my head held high, just as Headmistress Darsy lays out the exam I knew was coming.

I know more answers than not, but it doesn't matter if I can brew a perfect sleeping draft from tampweed and skyflower, or identify a dozen seeds by their shapes. The only answers the duchess will notice will be the ones I miss.

"Think I did all right," Selen murmurs after we lay down our pens and Darsy collects the papers. "You?"

"Remember me fondly when Mother kills me," I tell her.

Selen laughs like a swan, a snap to her long neck and a sound more honk than giggle. "Can't be that bad."

"When you passed the flamework exam, your da whooped and swept you off your feet," I say. "I scored higher, but when I told Mother she lectured me for two hours over the dangers of the one question I got wrong."

"Da's just happy I can read," Selen says. "Says he couldn't do more than sign his name till he had thirty summers."

As if on cue, Minda gasps and all the apprentices sit up straight, backs arched and eyes forward. I look up and sigh. The duchess has paid an impromptu visit.

Striking coincidence, that it's just after an exam.

The apprentices bow their heads and spread their skirts as my mother, Duchess Leesha Paper, enters the classroom. Her eyes flick over me, taking in the smudges on my dress and the state of my hair.

"Leesha." Darsy pushes to her feet and curtsies.

"Oh, enough of that." The duchess waves the gesture away and opens her arms for an embrace. This, too, is practiced protocol. A message to the apprentices that Headmistress Darsy is in the duchess' favor. Even Selen doesn't call her Leesha, and they're sisters.

Darsy embraces Mother, but does not linger. "Didn't know you were planning a visit."

"Just passing by." The duchess glances at the exam papers on Darsy's desk. "How are your students progressing?"

Darsy's eyes flick to me, and for one terrible moment, I imagine her handing my mother my exam to grade right in front of the class.

But she doesn't. "Got a lot of fine young Gatherers in this batch, I think. Olive's always first to raise her hand, but they've all got talent."

The words are all true, after a fashion, but the duchess raises a brow at the planting table. The floor's been swept clean, but her pale blue eyes drift over the shards of clay in the waste bin. "Problems repotting the stiffroot?"

"My fault," Selen cuts in before Darsy can reply. She holds up her big hands. "Don't know my own strength, sometimes."

"Just like your father." The duchess smiles at Selen, and my friend beams in spite of herself. Mother's compliments have that effect, all the more precious for their rarity. I can't remember the last time she smiled like that at me.

The duchess looks back to Darsy. "Would you mind if I borrowed my daughter a short while, Headmistress?"

"Of course not." Darsy curtsies, and my stomach knots again.

I KEEP CLOSE to the windows as we walk the halls of Gatherers' University, trying not to stare at the delicate warded spectacles hanging from a silver chain around Mother's neck.

Her magic doesn't work in sunlight. No magic does. Sun burns the power away, which is why demons—creatures of innate magic—only used to come up from the safety of the Core at night.

The duchess is a witch, though she hates that word. It's a science to her, if rather unlike what we learn in Herb Lore and Chemics class. She isn't the kind of witch that stars in Jongleurs' tales—cackling and putting curses on folk in need of a lesson—Mother's wardings protect Hollow from demons.

Or so they say. I've never seen a coreling, alive or even recently dead. Just old demonbones kept in darkness to preserve their power. The war against demonkind ended before I learned to walk. The few corelings to survive the Deliverer's purge were banished to the edge of Mother's greatwards and hunted down by General Gared's Cutters.

But whatever the fate of the corelings, the duchess' magic is real. Her demonbone dice are carved with wards of prophecy, letting her Read what is and what might be. I've seen her predict fire, flood, and drought with uncanny accuracy. A ready brigade here, a levee there, an order to lay in extra stores one season, and Mother averted all those disasters, keeping her people sheltered with clean water and full bellies.

I've never seen her use the wand she wears at her belt for more than drawing wards of light and sound to brighten a room or make herself heard before a crowd, but I've read histories—and seen more than one painting—of her using it to throw fire and lightning at corelings during the war. Exaggerations, I'm sure, but too many folk claim to have borne witness to dismiss the tales entirely.

But it's the spectacles I hate the most. Magic radiates up from the Core, but every living thing carries a bit of it inside them. The wards of sight etched around the lenses allow Mother to see magic as a soft glow, including each person's individual aura. Auras are as personal as their fingerprints, yet as fluid as lakewater, shifting with our thoughts and feelings throughout the day.

With her wardsight, the duchess can Read a person's aura to spot a lie or omission as easily as she might page through one of her dry books of old world science. Sometimes she seems to pluck a thought right out of your head.

I'm never alone as it is, never unguarded, never free to sneak around and kiss like Selen. My thoughts are the only privacy I have left.

"You pulled too hard on the pot and broke it," Mother notes as we walk.

So much for the protection of sunlight. Even without her spectacles, the duchess can see through me.

"It was an accident." I know before they pass my lips that the words are insufficient to stem the coming lecture. Nothing can. Mother's lectures are like the rain. Inevitable. Unavoidable.

"You have to be more careful, Olive," Mother says. "If folk realize how strong you are, they may find it . . . unnatural."

"Aren't I?" I ask.

"Nonsense," Mother chides. "What kind of talk is that?"

"Then why must I hide it?" I demand.

"Because the less attention you draw, the safer you are," Mother says. "You'll have plenty of attention next summer, like it or not."

The words make me swallow my retort. "What happens next summer?"

"Sixteen summers is old enough to approach," the duchess reminds. "Next spring, the Angierians will begin sending calling cards and invitations to balls, and the Krasian matchmakers will form a line at my gate. Duchess Ariane is chomping at the bit to introduce you to her grandson Rhinebeck."

"Introduce?" I've been exchanging letters with Prince Rhinebeck since we were children.

"As a suitor," Mother says. "Even Duchess Elissa of Miln has some young prince in mind if we're interested."

"Men will come court . . . me?" I am incredulous, but there is a tinge of excitement at the prospect of suitors. It's one thing to sneak off with a stableboy, and another to walk in the gardens with a boy everyone considers a good match. I wonder if Rhinebeck is handsome.

But in my heart, I know it isn't that simple. Even if Rhinebeck shines on me like the sun, there's no telling what he'll do on the wedding night when he realizes I'm not like other women.

"I'm not ready to promise anyone" is all I can manage.

"Of course not," Mother agrees. "You're far too young. You've never even kissed anyone."

You would know. I struggle to keep calm as even this small fantasy of freedom is snatched away. "You were promised at thirteen. Grandmum told me."

"Ay, she would know," Mother echoes my own thoughts. "It was her ripping idea, and ended in disaster."

I'd say that's reason enough not to let one's mother make the decision, but I don't have the courage. "When *will* I be old enough?"

Mother looks me over, choosing her words carefully. "A few more summers, I beg."

I blow a slow breath from my nostrils, trying to hide the blend of anger and disappointment.

"Can I at least go on the borough tour with the other girls?"

Mother wrinkles her nose. "I don't think that's a good idea. There's too much happening at court. The Majah tribe have opened their border for the first time since you were born. We're hosting their diplomats in a fortnight to negotiate their entry into the Pact of the Free Cities. If you want to tour the boroughs after that, I can have a team—"

"I don't want a team." The duchess blinks as I cut her off. "I don't want servants and bodyguards and First Minister Arther himself teaching the history of each town we visit."

Mother puts her hands on her hips. "Then I think you're missing the point of the borough tour. It's a rite of passage—"

"You're the one missing the point!" I cut in again, and this time the look on Mother's face is decidedly less patient. "Of course, the tour is about learning the history of the duchy," I allow, carefully measuring my tone, "but that's not why it's a rite of passage. It's about being away from home with your friends. It's about being out from under your parents' thumb for a few days to see the towns. To sleep in portable ward circles in the wild lands beyond the greatwards."

"You'll be with friends," Mother says. "Selen, and Micha . . . "

I stop walking. Mother continues for two strides, then stops and turns, irritation showing for the first time. "Selen is going with the other girls. General Gared gave permission. Micha is my nanny."

"Micha is your sister," Mother corrects, but I only fold my arms.

"Fine," the duchess snaps. "You can't go because it's too dangerous. The other girls, even Selen, don't have assassins hunting them."

"Mother, please." I roll my eyes.

She moves quickly. Quicker than even I can react. Her hand cups my chin, forcing me to meet her eyes. I try to resist, but I'm not the only one who's strong. Mother's fingers are like ice, cold and unyielding. I know she would never hurt me, but she is frightening, nonetheless.

"This is serious, Olive. An assassin could be on you just as quickly. Quicker, in fact, and they won't just cup your chin."

I try to pull away, but Mother lets go of my chin and takes my arm. To an observer it might be a simple, motherly gesture, but her free hand is touching her wand, and even with my strength, her grip is like carved marble as she steers me into an empty classroom, closing the door behind us.

"Show some respect for your sister," the duchess snaps. "She's devoted her life to caring for you."

She's right, but Mother wields the guilt like a lash, trying to distract me. I yank my arm free, striding across the room to stand by the window. Even indirect sunlight is an effective shield against Mother's powers.

"And show some respect for me," the duchess says, "when I tell you the demons are *not* all gone like the Tenders say—banished by the Deliverer. Without the protection of the greatward, you will be vulnerable."

I lower my eyes, trying to look respectful, like I understand the danger. But I don't. I've never so much as glimpsed a wind demon silhouetted against the sky. No one has seen a coreling in years. They've become ale stories, like talking nightwolves or fairy pipkins.

Mother says that when the Deliverer purged the demons from Thesa, he took much of the world's magic with him. Without demons—or their bones—to power wardings, the magic of items faded—unable to fully recharge. There were few folk left with magic of note anymore, beyond my parents, and . . .

"Won't the Warded Children be there to guide and protect us?"

Mother looks like someone put lemon in her tea. The Warded Children were an experiment of hers during the war. The Deliverer tattooed wards on his flesh, the symbols Drawing and holding magic that the tales say gave him fantastical powers. Mother tried to replicate it, with . . . mixed results. It gave them power, but the magic changed them, as it did me. The Children live in the wilds beyond the greatwards now, patrolling the borderlands.

"The Warded Children cannot be trusted," Mother says. "Even the good ones can turn feral if they encounter a demon, and Renna Bales isn't there to hold their leash. With Solstice falling on new moon this year, that's not a risk I'm prepared to take."

I blink. Folk speak of the Warded Children like forest gods, too wild for polite society but devoted to a life of service, Thesa's first line of defense. The idea they might not be trustworthy is unthinkable.

That, or Mother is just trying to scare me.

"Fine, send the guards!" I throw up my hands. "Send Captain Wonda if you must. But let me go with my friends."

Mother uses two fingers to massage her temple. It's a sign she's getting a headache, which means I am either winning or about to lose spectacularly.

"You'll ride in the royal carriage," Mother says.

"But—!" I begin. Putting me in the royal carriage will separate me from the others more than an army of Hollow Soldiers.

"No buts," Mother says. "It's armored. Selen, Micha, and Lord Arther will ride with you, Captain Wonda out front with half a dozen Hollow Lancers. As you visit the boroughs you can get out for walking tours and shopping with your classmates, but Wonda and Micha will accompany you at all times."

I press my lips together. It's not what I imagined, but it's better than being left behind. Far better. For once, I can leave the capital, leave Mother, and see something of the world for myself.

"And you'll stay behind on the overnights beyond the greatward," the duchess finishes.

I feel my eyes bulge as I take in the words. "Even with an armored carriage, Wonda, Arther, and half a dozen lancers, I still can't go on a ripping camping trip?"

I'm ready to say more, but Mother cuts me off with a raised finger. "I'm offering a compromise, Olive. I suggest you take it."

"Did you ask?" Selen is waiting outside Headmistress Darsy's classroom when I return, the other girls already dismissed.

"We need to hurry," I say. "Favah will have my hide if I'm late."

"Take it the answer was no?" Selen says as we quickstep down the halls. Running is prohibited, but the two of us can put on considerable speed without breaking academic decorum.

"It wasn't no." I watch excitement blossom on Selen's face, and hate that I am about to quash it. "But it wasn't exactly a yes. I can't go beyond the wards."

Selen stops short. "But that's the best part!"

I grab her arm and pull her back into motion. It's one thing to argue with Mother, and quite another to cross Dama'ting Favah. I can be reckless at times, but I am not an utter fool.

"The duchess is worried I'll get eaten by a demon."

Selen honks a laugh. "No one's seen a demon since we were in nappies! And even if one did find us, Wonda would have a warded arrow through its skull before it got close enough to pounce."

"I made all of these same points to Mother, but it didn't do much good." Before I can say more, the great bell rings. "Night."

The halls are empty as I abandon decorum and break into a run, appearing in Favah's doorway a moment later. The ancient Krasian priestess kneels on a pillow at the center of the room, eyes closed. She is swathed from head to toe like Micha, but instead of black, Favah wears robes and scarves of pure white.

"An extra hour in the Chamber of Shadows for lateness." Favah doesn't look up from her meditation or even open her eyes. She understands Thesan, but I've never heard her use it, speaking only in her native Krasian.

A crack of her wand across my knuckles I could weather, but there is nothing worse than the Chamber of Shadows. Below the crypts below the basements of the university, the chamber is suffocatingly deep. There are no lights, only wards of sight like those on Mother's spectacles to let me see in magic's strange spectrum as I etch items with wards of power under Favah's close supervision.

"I was in a meeting with Mother," I dare to say.

"The desert allows no excuses," Favah's voice is serene, "and neither do I."

"Ay, she would know," Selen whispers. "She's older than sand."

I suppress a smile, but not quick enough as Favah's eyes snap open, fixed on Selen. "I can punish you as well, Selen vah Gared, but I'll leave that to Dama'ting Jaia. Princess Olive does not need an escort to class from one already late for her own."

"See you in the sparring yard." Selen scurries down the hall, more to escape Favah than for fear of the Krasian Studies teacher. Jaia is far less strict.

The room is dark as I shut the door behind me. The windows are covered in thick curtains, blocking all outside light. Favah still kneels on a pillow on the floor, the dim lamp before her providing the only illumination.

"An hour for being late, and two more for your disrespect," she says as I kneel on the thin pillow across from her.

Could she have heard Selen's whispered words? It seems impossible. The old woman would need ears like a bat. Perhaps some spell allows her to hear across rooms. Like Mother, Favah is a formidable witch. I resolve to take greater care opening my mouth near her class.

The other girls take Krasian Studies with Dama'ting Jaia, learning the language and culture of our southern neighbors. The twelve tribes of Krasia lived for thousands of years in and about the walled city of Fort Krasia, the Desert Spear. Two decades ago, my father, Ahmann Jardir, led them out of the sands to conquer the green lands in a bid to levy troops for the demon war.

A peace was forged before he made it this far north, but apart from the Majah tribe, who took their spoils of war and returned to Desert Spear, the Krasians never gave up the lands they had taken. New Krasia has flourished in the years since.

Jaia is a priestess of Everam, whom my father's people believe to be the Creator, but she is young, and shaped by her decades in the green lands. She married a Hollower, assimilating more than most of her people. Behind her veil, her eyes are always smiling.

Not so, ancient Favah. The aged priestess is one of Mother's most trusted advisors, and Father made her my personal tutor to ensure I understood my heritage. Unlike other instructors, eager to praise me and curry favor with Mother, nothing I do is good enough to please Favah.

While Selen and the other girls have fun learning the culture of my father's people—cooking Krasian dishes, celebrating Krasian holidays, and making conversation in the language—Favah indoctrinates me in the secrets of the *dama'ting* priestesses, which consist mostly of prayer, wardcraft, field surgery, and enough books of prophecy to make my head spin. I can stabilize a warrior before they bleed out, but I don't know a single Krasian dance.

I've never seen Favah smile. Even on the rare occasions when she removes her veil, the deep lines of her face are always pinched in judgment. The crone is said to be more than a century old, an easy rumor to believe. Her limbs are little more than bones with a tough coating of sinew, every vein visible under thin translucent skin.

But Favah still greets each morning with *sharusahk*, her poses strong as a statue. Her memory is sharp, reaching across a century as easily as one might flip to a desired section of a well-read book.

"Take out your dice."

I am quick to comply, laying a clean cloth before me and pulling a thick velvet pouch from an apron pocket. I spill seven clay dice, each with a different number of faces, onto the pristine white silk.

Favah scoops up the dice with a practiced hand, rolling the rough clay in her fingers. "Pathetic. Fifteen years old, and you have yet to complete a passable set of clay. In Krasia, you would have been thrown from the Dama'ting Palace by now."

I should be so fortunate. I no more wish to be a seer than an Herb Gatherer, and even if I were to somehow manage both, Mother and Favah will still find ways to be disappointed in me. I'd rather visit the abyss than spend three hours in the Chamber of Shadows, straining to make sense of wardsight as I struggle to mold and carve dice of clay.

But as with most things in my life, there is nothing to do but endure. The only person who can override Favah is Mother, and I can't imagine she ever would. She laughed the one time I complained that Favah cracked my knuckles with her wand.

"My old teacher Bruna had a bigger stick than Favah, and used it twice as often," the duchess said. "Every swat was a lesson I never forgot."

Favah hands the dice back to me, producing her own set. These are not crude clay. They were carved from the black bones of a demon the better part of a century ago. The worn surfaces shine like polished obsidian, but every facet, every symbol, remains sharp.

Favah slips the *hanzhar* from her belt. I know from experience the curved Krasian blade is sharp as a razor. She drives the point into her thumb, smearing blood across some of the wards.

"Everam, giver of light and life, your children need answers." The dice begin to glow as she shakes them, distributing the blood. "Will it rain tomorrow?"

She throws with force, but a skilled hand. None of the dice stray from the cloth as they flare with magic that jerks them unnaturally out of their spins.

Favah glances at the throw, grunts, and sits back. She waves a hand for me to begin seeking an answer to her question in the scattering of symbols before me.

I squint at the throw. I know the meanings of all the wards, but what they tell me is gibberish. There are no facing symbols for air, or water, or anything remotely useful in predicting the weather.

Favah scowls as I reach for my textbook. I ignore her look, trying to buy time. Rain readings are vital in the desert where these arts began. There are detailed sections on such foretellings, but even these are little help. It seems each seer had their own way of reading the dice, and the methods are often at odds with one another. Reading from the center, there is darkness gathering, which might mean rain clouds. Reading from north to south, the darkness dissipates.

"Well?" Favah prompts.

"It . . . will," I guess. The odds could be worse.

"Are you certain?" Favah asks.

I blow out a breath. "No."

Favah nods. "You should have trusted that instinct. You'd be no worse off flipping a coin than making a prediction based on this throw."

"But . . . the magic," I say. What is the point of all this, if a throw cannot be trusted? There are questions I would ask, about who I am, about what I am meant to be, but it seems pointless to spend years mastering an art just to make an educated guess at the answers.

"The magic imprints off the question," Favah says, "on our lips and in our hearts. We do not always know the right question."

"So if you don't ask if you might be trampled by a horse . . . " I prompt.

"The *alagai hora* will volunteer nothing," Favah says. "Rain is a delicate balance of elements, not a constant like sunrise. Many times, it takes more than one throw to circle to an answer built off so many variables."

She scoops her dice up in a practiced hand. "Tell me, Olive vah Leesha, what should I ask next?"

"If you should take an umbrella tomorrow?" I ask.

Favah makes a dry sound in her throat that just might be a chuckle.

I DREAD THE hours in the Chamber of Shadows, but I put it from my mind, relieved to be free of the oppressive darkness of Favah's classroom. Selen and the others are changing into *sharusahk* robes when I join them.

I dread this part of the day, but Selen immediately moves to my side, blocking me from the others' view as I turn my back and slip off my dress. The other girls wear simple cotton undergarments that are easy to remove, but I wear a traditional Krasian bido—a length of silk woven many times between my legs and over my hips. I say it is to honor my heritage, but truer is I feel safer bound up tight, lest one of the other girls notice my body is different from theirs.

I can't help but glance around the room, seeing that difference increase as we grow older. Already, my classmates are filling out—Minda looks a woman grown, and others are not far behind. Mother and Grand-mum are similarly curved, but I just seem to be getting taller and more muscular.

Mother thinks it's the balance of my female and male hormones. My flow has come and my voice is deeper than I'd like, but I have neither hair on my chin nor a woman's curves. Mother says I may develop either, or both, late, or not at all.

"How bad was it?" Selen asks as I pull on the loose pants and robe we wear in the practice yard.

"A scolding," I say, "and three hours in the chamber."

"Three hours?!" Selen exclaims. "Night! Just for being a few seconds late?"

"One for being late," I say, "and two more for smirking when you said she was old as sand."

Selen rubs the back of her neck. "Ay, sorry about that."

"We're even." I lay a hand on her arm. "Thanks for dropping that flowerpot."

"It was nothing," Selen says. "Couldn't pull the corespawned root free, anyway."

Wonda is already in the yard when the apprentices file out. The big woman has taken off her armor and laid her weapons aside, but she looks no less dangerous in loose-fitting cotton. Traditional *sharusahk* robes are black or white, but hers are forest green, symbolic of her fighting style, mixing Krasian hand-to-hand combat techniques with Thesan boxing. Favah calls it sacrilege, but I've never seen Wonda lose a match, even against Krasian warriors of note. She waits balanced on one leg, the other foot flat against her thigh, steady as a tree.

We assemble silently in the yard, standing in even rows. Wonda drops her foot to the ground, and we mirror her bow. Then the forms, known as *sharukin*, begin.

Many of the poses are Krasian: Embracing the Heavens. Filling the Basin. Asp's Strike. Lonely Minaret. Others are *sharukin* of Wonda's own design: Wind Breaks the Branch. Felling the Tree. Harvest Reap.

We move as one, breathing and flowing from pose to pose in a reflection of our teacher. The movements are gentle, but I feel myself begin to sweat as they tax muscles and push flexibility to its limits.

Mother insists all Herb Gatherers learn the poses. Another relic from the war, but I've always enjoyed *sharusahk*, practicing since I first learned to walk. The forms are the one time of day my mind stops racing and I can be at peace.

It ends all too soon. Wonda straightens and bows to the class again. "Find your partners, girls."

Selen and I immediately link up. We're larger than the other apprentices, and none would dare spar with the princesses of Hollow in any event. I wouldn't mind, but while my forms are more precise, Selen has always been better at applying them to combat. Wonda gives a whistle and the other girls watch as Selen and I trade kicks and punches, probing blows easily blocked as we circle each other.

"Better watch out." I wink, trying to distract her. "My powder's already ruined, so I've got no reason to hold back."

Selen honks, knowing the game. "Come at me. I'll give you another shiner like last week."

"Elona is still mad about that," I say. Nothing gets under her skin like her mother.

"Ay," Selen growls, "but when you hit me so hard my ear swelled up like a cauliflower, she thought it was a grand joke."

With sudden speed and intent, she rushes in, reaching for my thigh. I'm quick to counter, but it was a ruse and I curse myself as Selen shifts targets, taking hold of the collar of my robe. She pivots smoothly, using my own weight and momentum to flip me onto my back.

I try to scramble away, but Selen has a firm grip on my sleeve, jerking my hand out from under me. My cheek slams into the dirt of the practice yard, soiling my face for the second time today.

Selen never stops moving, swinging a leg around my neck in a submission hold I don't have the leverage to break. I heave, and hear apprentices gasp as I get all the way to my feet, dragging Selen up with me. Still she keeps the hold, hanging upside down as her thighs continue to squeeze, cutting off breath and blood. At last I stagger and tap her leg. Immediately she lets go, and I gasp in a breath.

"Good work, Sel," Wonda says as I punch the ground in frustration. "Olive, you were watching her hands when you should have been watching her feet. Minda and Ulana, you're next up."

I watch her feet, but Selen wins the next match, as well. The third time we attempt a simultaneous takedown. Both of us end up on the floor, but not in the way either intended. Wonda calls it a draw.

I don't understand it. I'm stronger than Selen, but even if I were willing to cut loose in front of the other girls, I'm not sure it would matter. I get the feeling Selen is holding back, as well.

"Should have seen that throw comin', Olive," Wonda says after the other girls have been dismissed. "Got to know when to take your time and when to get aggressive. Life might depend on it someday."

I know she means well, but it's been a long day of disappointing my teachers, and I don't know how much more I can take. Micha's braiding has held, but I pull the tie and shake out my hair, trying to work out some of the dirt as I let it fall over the scrape where my cheek hit the ground.

Wonda notes the move. "Used to wear my hair like that, too." She waves her fingers at the scars on one side of her face. "Covers things all right, but makes you feel ashamed over somethin' you ought not. Gonna have a shiner there, but you earned it, workin' hard. One time, Drillmaster Kaval twisted my arm so hard my shoulder went black and blue for two weeks."

She has a strange notion of encouragement, but I take the point and pull back my hair. I don't want people to see the mark. It's a sign of my failure, and no doubt Grandmum will have something to say about it, but I'm tired of being ashamed. I may never be enough for Mother or Favah, but at least Captain Wonda knows I'm trying.

Wonda gives an approving nod and smiles. "Yer mum says I get to take you on the borough tour. Gonna be fun, even if we can't go beyond the greatward."

"Are the wild lands that dangerous?" I ask. "Should Selen and the others worry about getting cored?"

"Bah." Wonda waves a hand. "Ent missin' as much as you think, Olive. Cutter patrols did in all the corelings near the greatwards while you were still in nappies. Yur uncle Gared and I saw it done ourselves. Once or twice a year some coreling wanders into the borderlands, but you'd have to march days for even a chance at seeing one. Warded Children do for those before anyone even hears about it. Ent ever seen one on a borough tour, no matter what kids whisper in the school-yard."

"But it's too dangerous for me, even with the captain of Mother's house guard at my side?" I raise an eyebrow, hoping pride will get the better of her and she'll let me go once we're out from under Mother's prying eyes.

Wonda looks uneasy, but her voice deepens. "Night's always dangerous, Olive, and you can't be too careful on new moon. Yur mum said no, and that's that."

It's an important reminder. Wonda loves me. She believes in me. But like everyone else, she is Mother's creature, and will keep my leash taut, even when she admits there's nothing to be afraid of.

THE REST OF the day follows much the same pattern. I'm overwhelmed by all the equations in Chemics class, but manage to hold my own in Biology. Then it's over to the Warders' Academy.

A reverse of Herb Lore, Warding class is mostly boys, but Selen isn't one to sit in back when she's outnumbered. She takes a seat in their center and spins the tale of the bruise on my face into something to rival an ale story of the demon war. Her punch a last-ditch effort that only delayed my inevitable victory.

The bookish boys hang on her every word until the instructor, my grandfather Erny, raps his cane and sets us to work.

He comes to stand over my workbench as I struggle to carve a wind demon ward into the soft clay of a roofing tile before it's fired. Demons vary depending on terrain, and a ward for corelings of one type won't stop those of another.

I know the wards for the basic demon types—rock, wind, wood, flame, water, mimic, and mind—by heart, and a hundred more besides. With a needle and thread, I can embroider wardwork designs that make my dresses the envy of other girls, and even earn the occasional compliment from Mother.

But as in the Chamber of Shadows, I am clumsy with the tools in the warding shop, as apt to break whatever I'm warding as get it right.

"Smoother strokes, Olive." Erny's voice is endlessly patient, but still

I feel I am disappointing him. "This isn't stitching. Visualize the ward and commit to each line in one motion." He takes a fresh tile, carving out the symbol with quick, efficient movements.

The ease of his cut makes me not want to work while he's watching, so I ask a question, instead. "Why do we still ward roofing tiles, if the greatward protects us?"

"Humanity forgot how to ward once because the demons went quiet, and it nearly cost us everything when they returned," Grandda says. "Won't forget again, if we're smart."

"They went quiet for three thousand years," I say, not sure I even believe the story, myself. "That's a long time to remember."

Erny sighs. "We do what we can, Olive. The rest is up to the Creator."

"ENT FAIR." SELEN paces the tiles as I scrub my face at the end of the day. "The hike is safe enough for every teenager in the duchy, but you have to spend it locked in the nearest inn."

"You don't have to tell me." I check the mirror, pleased to note the scrape on my cheek has already faded. I've always been a quick healer. "You'll be lucky to escape Mother's bubble, yourself."

Selen's mouth opens. "How's that?"

I smile ruefully. "The duchess promised I would have my friends to keep me company."

Selen shakes her head. "Da may be some big hero of the demon war, but he ent ever seen a fight like the one he'll get if he goes back on his promise to let me go beyond the wards, no matter what the duchess says."

"It doesn't matter what he wants, Sel. If the duchess gives an order, Uncle Gared will follow it."

Selen crosses her arms. "He does and I'll steal away anyway."

I raise an eyebrow. "And how will you manage that?"

"Same way you should." Selen drops her voice, even though we're alone. "Slip a drop of tampweed and skyflower into Wonda's and Micha's tea the night before. That little and they won't even taste it. Won't put them to sleep right away, but when it does, they'll be out till noon.

Hike starts at dawn. We can be miles from the greatward before they wake."

Selen speaks with confidence, but I shake my head before it can infect me. "The guides will know we're not allowed. Everyone in Hollow knows what we look like."

"As girls," Selen says.

I blink. "Ay, what's that?"

"I can raid Da's armory for a couple breastplates and helms." She winks. "I'll get Perin to hide them under the carriage. We slip off and join some group of bumpkins just off the farm. Boys don't have to fight to go on the borough tour like us girls. They get a pat on the shoulder and a loan of Da's armor. No one will look twice at us."

My stomach clenches with nervous excitement as I realize she's right. Wonda herself might not recognize us in breastplates and helms.

"There will be the Core to pay when we get back."

Selen shrugs. "Ent gonna throw us in the dungeon, Olive. Same song as always. We say we're sorry and promise never to do it again. Maybe a whipping if they're really mad. Walk on tiptoe for a couple weeks, and then it's forgotten."

Selen is right. General Gared didn't want her going on the borough tour at first, either. She's spent her whole life wrestling with her father for rights and freedoms he gave without thought to her younger brothers. Since that day we wanted to spar, she's fought for every step, the same as I have.

If you choose to be a boy, I will support you, Mother promised, that day.

But it was a false choice. I had no idea what it meant to be treated like a boy then. Even now, strapped tight in my bido weave, I don't fully understand it.

Perhaps it's time to learn.

4

I AM DARIN

My name is Darin Bales, and everyone says my da saved the world.

It's fine, I guess. He died before I was born so I don't really miss him, and I've no shortage of family—blood and otherwise.

Saving the world is the kind of reputation that can stick to a family. Folk I've never met give me gifts and let me get away with just about anything. But sometimes I catch them staring, like they're expecting me to do something amazing.

And when I don't, I can smell their disappointment.

Mam tried to keep me from the worst of it. Brought me back to Tibbet's Brook, the village on the edge of nowhere where she and Da grew up. Most of the folk here have ale stories about Da, too, but they didn't know him in the war. Instead they embellish childhood antics into legends worthy of a Jongleur's tale, taking pride in having known the Deliverer when he was knee-high.

Sometimes it feels like everyone knew my da except me.

I feel dawn coming without even looking at the window. It is still full dark by most folk's reckoning, but my night eyes can see the coming light wash color through the sky.

I don't like sunrise. The light stings as it takes away my night eyes, leaving me half blind until sunset. I feel the sun's heat on my skin like the touch of a hot skillet. I burn easily if I forget to cover up.

Most of the world wakes with the sun. Plants tilt and insects buzz to life as their flowers open. Animals rouse and people wake. I hear every footstep, the sound of countless creatures stretching and rising and clomping about in search of breakfast. I smell every food, every bodily function, every lather of soap.

All of it, all at once. So much that it can be overwhelming if I don't take care.

I want to flee, but first, like every morning, there's chores.

I step over the threshold of Grandda Jeph's farmhouse before the cock crows. The yard is safe, but Grandda doesn't like me doing chores too early. Says it upsets the animals.

I snatch the cloth-lined wicker basket from its spot by the door and run to the chicken coop, ignoring the squawks of protest as I snatch eggs and am gone before the birds even realize I'm there, juggling them into the basket.

Grandda doesn't like me juggling the eggs, but I need the practice if I'm to become a Jongleur. I've given this a lot of thought. Other jobs just seem like too much work, and no one looks twice when a strange Jongleur comes to town. I could go somewhere no one knows me, and they just treat me like regular folk. And if they figure it out, I go somewhere else.

I open the henhouse door and leave a scattering of seed in the yard, then dash indoors to leave the eggs on the kitchen counter while the house still sleeps. An instant later I'm on a stool beneath the first of the cows. They're no less surprised than the hens as I blur through their stalls, but happy for a quick, efficient milking.

The windows of the farmhouse are still dark as I leave the milk in the coldhouse and rush to the rest of my chores. Feedbags for the horses and slop for the pigs. The wellhouse, the curing shed, the smokehouse, the silo. Like a wind blowing through the farm, I pay each a hurried visit, racing against the dawn.

The old rooster stirs. I hate that bird. It inhales just as I finish filling the firebox—the last of my chores. I cover my ears and flee, getting as much distance as I can before it begins to shriek.

I CUT OVERLAND through fallow fields and thick stands of trees, keeping to the shade as much as I can. I skip over a wide stream, seeing faint indentations worn into the stones by generations before me. Reckon my da was one of them. This is the most direct route from the farm to Town Square. Stepping where he used to step, like reading his old journals, lets me know a little bit of him.

The sun is only a sliver on the horizon when I reach Town Square, but the smell of Aunt Selia's butter cookies is already in the air. She's left a tray of them by her window to cool. My mouth waters and my stomach grumbles to life.

Selia Barren is Town Speaker and head of the militia in Tibbet's Brook. She ent really my aunt, but Mam always says family's about more than blood. The other kids call her Old Lady Barren. Everyone's scared of her, except me.

I scamper up her wall and peek in the window. The kitchen is empty. Quickly I stuff a cookie into my mouth, letting it overwhelm my senses. In an hour they will stiffen into the hard, crumbly biscuits Aunt Selia likes with her tea, but fresh from the oven, they are still warm, fragrant, and soft. The recipe is simple, letting the butter rule without confusing it with too many other flavors. I use both hands to stuff more into my pockets.

"Darin Bales, I knew it was you, stealing my cookies!"

I freeze as Selia storms into the kitchen. I should have scented her as she lay in wait, but I was too focused on the smell of the cookies.

"Sorry, Aunt Selia," I try to say, but my teeth are full of cookie, and it comes out "thorry and thelia."

Her expression doesn't change, but her scent changes from irritation to amusement, and I can see the muscles around her mouth twitch. "You could just ask, Darin. I've never denied you a cookie."

It's true, but Selia always offers the oldest cookies, yesterday's batch that sits in the crock on her table.

I swallow. "Better when they're fresh."

Selia crosses her arms. "You could still come in and ask."

I glance over my shoulder at the rising sun. "Ent got time." I snatch another cookie and set off running before she can shout.

The school bell rings, but I put my hood up, keeping to the shade as much as I can on the run to Soggy Marsh. Still, the light stings my eyes and makes me dizzy.

The Marsh gets an unfair reputation. When folk think of it, they think of the rice paddies—wet, bug-infested, and smelly. But the outskirts of the wetlands are actually quite nice, with lots of fishing holes and cool shady spots far from folk. Perfect for sleeping away the heat of morning.

I wake past midday, feeling refreshed. I finish the cookies in my pocket as I go down to the swimming hole to cool off. After a quick swim I climb a tree and take out my pipes, testing the reeds. One of the notes is sour. I close my eyes and run my thumb over the reed. There's a hairline crack.

At the water's edge I cut a new reed, then return to my perch and take out my tuning kit. I shape the reed and treat it with quick-drying resin, then carefully unweave the rough cord that binds the pipes tightly together. By the time I clean them all, the resin is dry and I replace the sour reed. Lashing them back together to act as a single unit is tricky, but I've done it so many times now it's become second nature.

Again I test the notes. Satisfied this time, I begin to play.

I hear voices, soon after. Marsh kids released from the schoolhouse for the day, come down to swim.

There's laughter as they hear my music. They spin around, staring up at the trees, trying to guess where the music is coming from.

"Schoolmam's given up on you comin' back, Darin Bales!" Ami Rice calls. "She don't even call you on the roll anymore!"

I make my tune a little more playful, laughing through the music. Nothing could drag me back to the chaos of that crowded classroom.

"Come swimming with us!" Rej Marsh calls. "We promise there won't be math!"

The others laugh. They don't mean it cruelly. I can smell the playfulness. Their invitation is genuine. It always is, and that makes me happy.

But I never go.

The other kids in the Brook ent mean, but they don't understand me, either. Ent the math or the spelling that drove me out, or any of them. It's all of them. The noise, the smells, the constant chatter. It was being inside with everyone in close, squeezing the air around me.

It's better this way—safe in the trees, away from the splashing and shrieking, but present with my music. Sometimes they call out requests and sometimes I oblige, but mostly they act like I'm not there, and that's fine with me.

The sun is setting as I circle back to Grandda's farm for supper. I love dusk as much as I hate the dawn. Even indirect sunlight feels like a great fist, squeezing me throughout the day. But now that pressure is receding and it's like waking up, feeling my senses expand and my powers return.

I'm almost home when I see fresh scars in the bark of a tall tree, throbbing with escaping heat.

My eyes flick around, noting similar marks on other trees as I follow the path to where the creature dropped down to the ground, leaving two great taloned footprints in the dirt.

Wood demon.

For the most part, corelings come in two types—Regulars and Wanderers. Regulars tend to hunt the same area every night. Wanderers roam about, following spoor trails and sound in search of prey. They can range for miles, coming in and out of a region.

Tibbet's Brook was too far away to get purged of demons like the Free Cities did when Da destroyed the demon hive. But there were less out here to begin with, and Aunt Selia's militia cleared out all the Regulars years ago.

Still, every once in a while a Wanderer finds its way onto someone's property. If it finds prey, there's a chance it might become a Regular. It's hard to imagine one wandering so close to the farm's greatward without drawing attention, but these prints are barely a day old.

Demons hate sunlight even more than I do. My skin burns easily, but they burst into flame. Like me, I expect they feel morning's weight pressing on them long before the dawn. To escape they use their magic to dissipate, becoming insubstantial as they flee back underground using one of the natural vents magic uses to flow up from the Core.

But even Wanderers are creatures of habit. Whatever vent a coreling uses to escape the sun will be the same one it rises from the next night, which means the demon is still in the area.

I take a deep breath and blow it slowly out my nostrils. Today had been such a quiet day. I have to tell everyone about this, but I already know what they'll say.

When your da saves the world, folk have expectations.

I BUSY MYSELF in the barn, but it's really just an excuse to get out of the house. I'd rather listen in on the adults from here than sit there and have them talk like I'm invisible.

Aunt Selia and her wife, Lesa, came out to the farm when she got news of the Wanderer. Figured she'd call me out for stealing her butter cookies while she was here, but she din't.

"Boy's got to learn to do things for himself, Ren," Grandda says.

Mam snorts. "How many summers did you have again, Jeph Bales, the first time you stood up to a demon on your property?"

"Too many, and you know it." Grandda strikes a match, puffing at his pipe. "Like to think I raised my kids to be better than me."

Mam doesn't have a reply to that. "What do you think, Hary? Darin ready for this?"

"Boy knows all the songs, backward and forward," Master Roller says. "Just . . . needs a bit of confidence."

Ay, that's a sunny way of putting it.

It ent that I'm scared of corelings, exactly. Been wandering around alone at night since I was old enough to walk. Come across demons plenty of times.

But I'm smart enough to avoid them. They want me to use my pipes to call one right to me.

"Only way to get confident at a thing is to do it," Selia says. "Ent going to be by himself. Hary and me will be right there with him."

"New moon tomorrow," Mam notes.

Selia scoffs. "Ent seen more than the occasional Wanderer around these parts in ten years. Let the boy show what he can do."

"Ay, all right," Mam says at last. "Reckon it's time Darin started learning the family business."

5

MAJAH

THE ROYAL CARRIAGE doesn't stand out as much as I feared. Here in the capital, other powerful families have sent their children on the borough tour in carriages much more garish.

Mother prefers efficient simplicity over ornate design. Her carriage is dignified, if plain, but it is designed to withstand demon talons and Milnese flamework weapons alike. Beneath the polished wood veneer of its panels and roof, the carriage is comprised of specially warded glass, stronger, thinner, and lighter than steel.

But while the carriage doesn't stand out, Mother's cavalry surrounding the cart does. The Hollow Lancers have always been flamboyant like their leader, Captain Gamon, with colorfully lacquered wooden armor under bright blue tabards and yellow capes, feathers in their helms.

I always thought they looked quite fine prancing through maneuvers in the yard, lances standing in precise lines like the bristles of a fine brush. But here, they shout my presence at a time I want nothing more than anonymity. Selen's plan won't work if everyone on the entire tour's got one eye on us.

We lead a procession that grows and grows as we wind through Cutter's Hollow.

Teens are gathering today in every borough. The tourism minister estimates over a thousand in the group from the capital alone. For some it is their first time away from home. Others have made it an annual tradition, a state-funded excuse to travel and shop. A small army of vendors follow the tour, in addition to those in the countless market squares we'll encounter along the way.

A select few tourists ride horses or travel in carriages, but most walk, or crowd together in the backs of mule carts.

The streets of Cutter's Hollow curve and loop, punctuated by irregular plazas, fields, and stands of trees. Even the buildings have shapes and sizes that defy practical architecture.

This is not the work of some mad civil engineer. From above, the odd shapes form the lines of Mother's greatwards—lines of power that Draw ambient magic and shape it into a forbidding that no demons can abide.

"Our first stop will be New Rizon, the site of the most famous confrontation in the Battle of New Moon in 333 AR."

First Minister Arther is in his glory, making the carriage his personal classroom as he recites the history of the boroughs of Hollow Duchy. It's so boring I almost wish I'd stayed behind.

I look out the window and see Minda and our other classmates as they follow on foot. I watch enviously as they laugh and mingle with a group from the Warders' Academy.

"It was here that Arlen Bales was seen glowing in the night sky as he Drew power from the first greatward, throwing fire and lightning at the demon horde."

"That can't possibly be honest word," Selen says. I'm inclined to agree, though there are paintings of the event in every Holy House from here to Krasia.

"I didn't witness it personally," Arther admits, "but I heard accounts from those who did, and I saw the Deliverer's magic firsthand. This is not conjecture. It is verified historical fact."

Selen and I share a look, but neither of us argues further.

"The battle was the first test of the greatwards your mother built to shelter the refugees from Krasia's advance," Arther continues. "Whole villages packed up and fled the path of your father's armies, abandoning home and field to arrive on the doorstep of Hollow, often with little more than their culture and their lives."

My father's armies. The thought is so alien. I only met Father once, fourteen years ago, just after the demon war, when he came to Hollow to sign the new Pact of the Free Cities. Politics have kept him away ever since.

I was not yet two and don't recall much of it, but I do remember how tall Father was, clad in flowing robes and haloed in a rainbow of color as the gemstones on his crown split the light. When he held me it felt like the safest place in the world. I can't remember what he said; his voice was so deep and soothing I felt it in my bones. I'm told I fell asleep in his arms.

It's difficult to imagine that same man leading a horde of warriors across Thesa, crushing cities and towns to levy men into his demon-killing army, but it isn't in question. Verified historical fact, as Arther would say.

Micha watches Arther impassively as he speaks, her eyes unreadable. She does not correct him or offer defense of our father's actions.

"Another leader would have turned the refugees away," Arther says. "Others *did* turn them away. Fort Angiers closed their city gates. Fort Miln increased the garrison at the crossing to the river Dividing. The Laktonian captains refused to give refugees passage to the city on the lake. Only Duchess Paper offered healing and succor, teaching them to build their own greatwards, interconnected with the keyward of Cutter's Hollow.

"There were sixteen boroughs at the end of the war, but birth rates soared in the years of peace and prosperity that followed. A score of new greatwards have been added since, making Hollow the most populous duchy in Thesa."

I've heard the story before, of course. Tales of Mother's greatness, her bravery, her selflessness in protecting everyone who came to her in search of succor. It's no wonder the people love her. But all I can think of is her disapproving stare, and how hard I have to fight even for small freedoms in half measure. I think of what Perin has hidden beneath the carriage, and wonder if I will have the courage to steal a few days of real freedom.

I let Arther drone on, half listening as I stare out the windows. I've been to many of the inner boroughs alongside Mother as she gave speeches, breaking ground and cutting ribbons at universities, public libraries, and hospits. Now for the first time, I'm traveling into the outer boroughs. By tomorrow I'll be farther from home—farther from Mother—than I have ever been. I take a breath, and already my chest feels lighter.

Our first stop is the market square of New Rizon, where hundreds gather to begin the tour. I move to join Minda and the others, but the boys from the Warders' Academy shy away. The tour has chaperones, but nothing like Captain Wonda who follows a step behind me, looming over everyone in her warded armor.

"Olive," Arther says, "perhaps you can tell the group when the cathedral of New Rizon was built?"

I press my lips, trying to swallow my annoyance. No doubt the minister thinks it grand to have the princess of Hollow as his assistant. Indeed, everyone falls silent to listen. But it's just another way for me to be singled out when all I want is to feel like I belong.

Everyone is waiting. I shake my head to clear it, reciting names and dates drilled into me since I could first read and write. None of them do justice to the building itself, with its massive dome and soaring columns.

As we enter the nave, every neck arches in unison to see the famed painting on the ceiling. Arlen Bales aloft in the night sky, his body alight with the wards tattooed into his flesh, driving the demons from Hollow with fire and lightning.

The cathedral holds a service on that date every year, and Mother always attends, staying long in a seemingly endless receiving line. I've spent countless hours staring at that painting and am no longer awed, but the other tourists gasp at the sight. Some draw wards in the air or whisper prayers. More than a few kneel, and one girl simply bursts into tears. Selen rolls her eyes and I have to keep from smirking.

We spend hours walking around the city center, ending with shopping in the market square. Arther retires and I convince Wonda to walk a few steps back so we can spend time with our classmates. Selen is in fine form, spinning tales and telling jokes. Our laughter has even drawn back some of the boys from the Warders' Academy.

I try to similarly pull ahead of Micha, but she keeps finding some trinket to examine or vendor to talk to that keeps her close. Krasians are famous hagglers, and I don't think I've ever seen Micha pay full price for something. The others watch with awe as she argues vendors into slashing their prices.

All too quickly, the sun sets, and station separates us from our friends. Our classmates go to the common house, while Arther has booked Selen and me into New Rizon's finest inn.

The dinner brought to our rooms is delicious, but out in the square I can hear music and singing and raucous laughter from the common houses, and wish I were there, instead. That just once, I could feel like part of the world and not just an observer.

Selen looks just as trapped. If I hadn't come along with an entourage, she would have found a way to be out there. Instead we play cards, and go to bed still hearing sounds of cheer from the square.

THE TOUR CONTINUES for days. Some villages barely get a mention as we pass them on the road; others have more than we could see in a week, but most are like New Rizon. A few sites of note, then shopping in the market square until Wonda herds us to the inn. As they start to blur together, the size of the group thins. Arther is needed back at the capital, and many of the older tourists return with him. The younger ones have planned their entire summer around the tour, and press on.

At last we reach Pumpforge, one of the border villages where groups are gathering to hike into the borderlands.

The village smells of smoke and rings with the sound of hammering metal. I know the history of the place. Like the Warded Children, the Pumps were another of Mother's experiments during the war. She helped them develop new ways to craft and ward their arms and armor, and now Pump craftsmanship is sought after by Hollowers and Children alike.

But the forges forced them to give up their nomadic ways. The Pumps accepted Mother's rule and the protection of the greatwards, in exchange serving as a link between the duchy proper and their more feral cousins in the borderlands.

The carriage pulls to a stop in the town square, where a giant man is waiting to greet us. His short yellow beard is thick around a strong jaw, his eyes the same icy blue as mine. His arms ripple with muscle under a sleeveless leather vest, and his worn boots and plain breeches belie the Speaker's medallion on his chest, embossed with a hammer striking a speartip atop an anvil.

"Ay, Wonda!"

"Callen!" Wonda leaps down and embraces him, then gives him an affectionate shove. "Good to see you."

"And you." The man's voice seems to vibrate the wood of the carriage as he opens the door. "Ent seen little Olive and Selen since they were . . . " his eyes widen as he sees us, ". . . little."

Wonda laughs. "Ay. Ent that, anymore."

"Welcome to Pumpforge, Princesses." Callen gives a bow.

I have no recollection of meeting this man, but that's no surprise. I've been paraded through Mother's sitting room to let visitors "have a look at me" since I was born. Some are memorable, but even recent ones tend to blur.

But I know the look Cutters get when they consider you family. Speaker Callen's affection is genuine, but it adds one more overprotective set of eyes on us.

"You'll give them the tour?" Wonda asks.

"Ay." Callen flashes us a smile. "Most of the action's in the market square. Town's full to bursting with groups in for the hike, and merchants have come from all over. Caravan from Krasia has everyone in a stir."

"Get merchants from Krasia all the time," Wonda says.

Callen shakes his head. "Not New Krasia. These are in from Desert Spear."

"Tsst!" Micha looks up sharply at the words.

Even Wonda blinks. "Honest word?"

Callen points to a cluster of brightly colored tents in the far corner of the square, a little village amid the usual open stalls of Northern markets.

Desert Spear is home to the so-called lost tribe of Krasia, the Majah. Depending on which history you read, either the Majah deserted my father's army during the demon war and are blood traitors, or the Majah were themselves betrayed by my half brother Asome, and left with honor to avoid civil war.

Regardless, the Majah returned to their ancestral home, the massive walled oasis city of Fort Krasia, known to my father's people as Desert Spear, on the far side of the Krasian desert. That was fifteen summers ago, and no one has heard from them until recently, when they sent a Messenger to Mother's court with a petition to join the Pact of the Free Cities.

"Mother is preparing to host the Majah delegates soon," I say. "Perhaps they are opening the border?"

Micha makes a delicate spitting noise behind her veil. "They are Majah spies."

"Bah." Callen waves a hand. "Ent hurting anyone and we got nothin' to hide. They got good wares to sell, and this is a town that knows its craft."

Callen leans in to Wonda and lowers his voice. I don't have ears like Darin Bales, but they're sharper than most and I catch the words. "You sure Olive can't go on the hike? If Leesha is worried, I can collect a few Forgers and take her myself. Won't be in danger. Ent seen a demon around here in—"

Hope rouses in my breast, but Wonda crushes it. "Mistress says no." There is a finality to her words, like the click of a lock. My hand drifts to my dress, touching the tiny vial secreted in a hidden pocket. I had allowed myself to forget it, but now the feel of the hard glass reawakens the nervous excitement and sick fear at the thought of Selen's plan.

Tomorrow. In just a few hours, I'll be free of Wonda, and Micha, and every other adult Mother has sent to smother me. I'll be with folk who don't know who I am, and regardless of how I am dressed, I'll be able to just be myself for the first time.

If I'm brave enough to do it. Even now, I don't know that I can. I won't have Selen there to goad me into boldness. It will be my choice to use the vial, and I am afraid if I do, Micha and Wonda won't forgive me, and life will never be the same.

PUMPFORGE IS ROUGHER than other villages on the tour. There are no great manses here, and I see little in the way of fashion or luxury. Even Speaker Callen has coal-smudged clothes and dirty fingernails. The women dress much as the men, and all have thick muscles peeking from their shirtsleeves. They look ready to pick up weapons and fight at any moment.

Still, the Forgers are a cheerful lot, with pleasant chatter in the public houses and market square. Traveling merchants drawn to the Solstice Festival have filled the square with a maze of tents to display their wares.

But it is the collection of tents from Desert Spear that draws my gaze and holds it. Micha spoke Krasian to me when I was still in the crib and I've taken Krasian Studies since starting school, but apart from my instructors, a handful of vendors in the capital, and visiting diplomats at court, I have never met any of my people. The Majah are not my tribe, but going into that cluster of tents will be the closest I have ever come to being immersed.

I get the sick feeling in my stomach that comes before a test or one of Mother's lectures. What if my accent is wrong? I've been told blue eyes are rare in Krasia, but I don't know how rare. Will they stand out? Or my skin? I am darker than Hollowers, but lighter than my sister or Favah.

I look down at the rugged but fashionable dress I made to wear for the hike. It was too daring even to show Mother, and scandalously immodest by Krasian standards. Might it cause real offense?

Selen takes my hand, telling me without a word that she understands. "Come on. I'll be right beside you." I squeeze gratefully, and together we move toward the tents.

Micha steps in front of us. "Beware, sister. The Majah cannot be trusted."

"Why?" I ask.

"They are *ginjaz*." Micha makes a dry spitting sound through her veil. "Traitors. The Majah abandoned the armies of the Deliverer at the height of Sharak Ka. They returned to the desert and the old ways, sitting out the war while the other tribes fought and died in glory."

Selen puts her free hand on her hip. "We shouldn't buy their rugs and pottery because they didn't want to die?"

"Cowardice is reason enough," the venom in Micha's voice is surprising, "but the Majah were not afraid to die. It was spite that made them turn their backs on Everam and their brothers in the night."

I have no argument. The histories are kinder to the Majah, but Micha lived through the events, while I only read about them in books. "Mother says we cannot blame a whole people for the decisions of their leaders."

"Perhaps," Micha allows. "But leaders who do not reflect the will of their people do not remain in power. Take my word in this. The Majah are not to be trusted."

Minda and the others have already disappeared into the marketplace. Without letting go of my hand, Selen starts walking. "Don't trust anyone. Ay, got it." I stumble gratefully along after her. Micha's brows tighten, but she keeps silent pace.

The first thing that envelops us is the smell, strange and familiar all at once. Colorful spices are piled high in great baskets. I'm drawn to one, breathing deeply. I turn to Micha. "It smells like your cooking."

"Powdered hava." Micha takes a pinch. "It flavors and preserves meat. It is the center of Krasian cooking." She lifts her veil just enough to sniff at it, then rubs the pinch off her fingers. "But this is not fresh. No doubt they think you greenlanders won't be able to tell."

"Well they did cross the desert with it." If Micha thinks to dissuade me, she is failing. Now that I am here, there is nowhere else I want to be.

A Krasian woman appears, clad in the traditional black robe and veil. Her eyes flick over my clothes, but if she disapproves, she gives no sign.

I'm fluent in modern Krasian, but the woman notes my dark skin and begins speaking quickly in an unfamiliar dialect that is hard to follow at speed. I stand there stunned as she pauses to wait for a reply, trying desperately to formulate a response.

When the silence stretches on too long, Micha steps in. "We were looking at your hava, but it is not fresh."

I know it's rude, but I allow my sister to take my shoulders and lead me away. I keep my distance from the other vendors as we delve deeper into the little bazaar, taking in the sights and smells as I try to get a feel for the language.

The sellers are all women in Krasian blacks. They chatter at every shopper that ventures close, and shout entreaties to those who keep back. Most appear to know only a handful of Thesan words, but they use them aggressively, waving arms for emphasis as they hold up items of interest. "My friends! Come! Come see!"

"This will help you find a husband!" A vendor holds up a colorful silk scarf, and Minda looks up. It's all the opening the woman needs to draw her in.

Drawn to a beautiful vase I enter the largest tent, but this time Micha intercepts the vendor, engaging her with a host of questions before the woman can get to me. Left alone for a moment, I am quick to run hands over the beautiful craft. Machines and mass production have become the fashion in exports from New Krasia, but the items the Majah sell are all handmade—rugs, clothing, pottery, and jewelry with vivid colors and tribal patterns.

There are brilliant bolts of cloth and lamps made of beautifully latticed brass. Cures and curios, furniture and fashion. Copies of the Evejah, the Krasian holy book, along with prayer rugs, candles, and incense. Burning samples fill the air with a heady smoke.

"Ah!" a voice behind me exclaims. "I did not believe it, but it is true! Princess Olive of Hollow, here in my humble bazaar!"

I want to scream. For a few brief moments I was allowed to be myself, but even here, my station demands I be singled out.

But Mother is meeting with the Majah soon. She'll be furious if I am anything but gracious, so I put on my best court smile as I turn to see a small man in garishly colored silks. He is slender, with nothing of a warrior's build. He kneels as my gaze falls on him, putting his hands on the tent floor and touching his forehead between them.

"Rise, please." I try to imitate the Majah accent, but the inflections feel clumsy on my lips.

The man takes his head and hands from the floor and rolls back onto his heels, but he keeps his eyes on my feet as he spreads his arms in greeting. "Welcome, Highness. I am Achman am'Sufatch am'Majah. Your presence honors me beyond my worth."

He does not tell me his father's name, as is the custom in Krasia. That, and his flamboyantly colored silks, tell me much. "You are *khaffit*."

Khaffit were the lowest caste in Krasian society—men unfit for service as *Sharum* warriors. The name was synonymous with coward. But unlike warriors, *khaffit* were allowed to take on other trades, some of them becoming quite wealthy.

"Tsst." Micha's hiss is low, meant for me alone. The sound she makes if I use the wrong fork at dinner. I look at Achman and realize that in stating the obvious, I am being incredibly rude.

"Of course." Achman's smile does not waver. He speaks his native tongue slowly, no doubt for our benefit. "When I saw the carriage marked with your mother's mortar and pestle, I did not dare hope you would grace us with a visit. Come, let me offer you tea and shade."

"We just want to browse," I say carefully.

"Pfagh!" Achman waves a hand at the wares on display as if disgusted at his own stock. "Trinkets for children and *chin*. There is no need for one such as yourself to waste time with trivialities. Sit, sit! Let my wives and daughters bring our finest wares to you."

Chin is Krasian for outsider. Like *khaffit*, it is often derogatory, effectively synonymous with coward. I've never heard Micha use it. She refers to Northerners as greenlanders, instead. I'm not sure if I should be offended on behalf of my mother's people, or flattered that even in Thesan clothes I appear Krasian enough to be accepted as one of their own.

Manners give me no choice but to let the merchant escort us into a canvas-walled back area of the tent. Wonda and Speaker Callen follow us in. They have smiles on their faces, but even the Speaker's eyes are wary. I remember Mother's talk of assassins, but it seems ludicrous that someone would dare strike at me here. What could they gain by harming me?

Inside the accommodations are lavish and rich, with an abundance of silk and color. Achman gestures to a semicircle of thick, velvet pillows. "Will you sit?"

I hesitate, and again Micha steps in, taking a pillow and kneeling gracefully, sitting back on her folded legs. Selen and I mimic her as another woman in black appears. This one has an air of command the others did not. Like Achman, she is short for a Krasian, with a narrow waist but ample curves.

"My *Jiwah Ka*, Fashvah," Achman says, indicating that she is his First Wife, with dominion over the other women in his household. Fashvah bows and says nothing, but I catch her dark eyes watching me from behind her thick black veil.

Fashvah is followed by half a dozen other black-robed women who lay out a silver tea service, dates, nuts, and honeyed cakes. The teapot steams as delicate ceramic cups are set before us, painted in intricate design. Achman does not bother to introduce the other women, and their bulky robes make it difficult to tell which might be wives and which daughters.

Achman takes a pillow across from us. Fashvah kneels between me and her husband, pouring my cup first, then his. He raises his tea, and I mirror him, as I have been taught. In Krasian custom, the host welcomes guests in order of rank, inviting them to speak their names and drink.

"Tsst." Micha raises a finger, stopping Achman before he can speak a toast. "I am Micha vah Ahmann am'Jardir am'Kaji."

Achman is so quick to put down his cup he spills hot tea on his hand. He gasps but does not complain as he puts his hands back on the floor and touches his forehead between them. "Please accept my apologies, Princess. I did not recognize you."

He glances at me, eyes flicking to the cups. His women stand likewise frozen. Micha is older, but the daughter of one of Father's lesser wives, whereas my mother rules these lands. Micha has never put her station above mine before. Instinctively I understand that I could dispute her claim, but there are politics at work I do not fully comprehend.

Achman eyes me, perhaps waiting for me to issue a challenge. When I do not, he nods and Fashvah fills Micha's cup.

"Welcome, Princess of the Kaji." Achman remains supplicant as he raises his refilled cup. "Blessings of Everam upon you."

Micha nods. "And you." She slips the tiny cup behind her veil and tips it back as Achman drinks. She puts the cup down and gives Selen and me a slight nod, her voice too low for any save me to hear. "It is safe to drink, sister."

I blink. Micha usurped my place to taste for poison? Perhaps I should be grateful, but instead I feel even more smothered than I do under Captain Wonda's watchful eye. I barely hear the other toasts as we go through the motions of the tea ceremony.

"This was made by the great smith Ghazin," Achman holds a velvet pillow upon which a curved knife sits, "quenched in the blood of heroes of the Maze."

Handle and sheath are polished silver, etched with intricate wardings and encrusted with rubies and emeralds.

"It's beautiful." I lift the knife reverently and slide the blade free, tilting it to let the wards play across the steel in the candlelight. It is well balanced and sharp, but all the gems and precious metal make it seem more showpiece than weapon.

"It is a *hanzhar*," Achman says, as if reading my mind. "Honed to a razor's edge, but hard as diamond."

Hanzhar are the blades of *dama'ting* priestesses, used not for combat but for surgery, and for the drawing of blood for the dice. It reminds me of Favah.

"I am no *dama'ting*." I slide the blade back into its sheath, flipping it in my fingers to return it hilt-first.

"Tsst," Micha whispers again.

Achman holds up his hands. "I am *khaffit*, Princess, and may not touch such a holy item."

Idiot, I curse myself as the merchant holds out the pillow for me to lay the knife upon.

"It is said your mother casts the dice of foretelling like a *dama'ting*," Achman says. "This might make a worthy gift."

I shake my head, feeling my shoulders tense at the mention of Mother. If Selen and I go through with our plan, no gift will soothe the duchess' anger when I return. "Her Grace is not fond of blades beyond the Gatherer's scalpel."

Achman's smile never wavers as Fashvah takes the blade away. Another woman appears with a jeweled chalice, followed by a series of beautiful rugs woven from fine wool in vibrant tribal patterns. A set of five rings after that, each wrought of silver and delicately warded, connected by fine silver chains to a jeweled bracelet.

I've never seen Selen interested in jewelry before, but she seems transfixed, trying them on and flexing her hand, marveling at the beauty. "How much?" Like mine, her Krasian is careful and succinct.

"Three hundred draki," Achman says. "A beautiful bargain for a beautiful princess."

Micha barks a laugh. "You do nothing to dispel the reputation of

Majah as thieves and cheats, *khaffit*. This is not worth one-fifth the price."

I look to Achman, expecting him to be offended, but instead there is a hint of smile at his lips. What follows is a back-and-forth of shouted Krasian so fast I can barely follow. Selen and I gape as they argue the merits of the piece, then the price in draki, then the exchange rate. Micha calls him a cheat and a thief twice more before grudgingly settling on a value in gold Suns.

Selen happily counts the coins into Achman's palm. Hollow Suns are stamped with Mother's face, and I cannot shake the feeling she is watching, even here.

"Fresh tea for our guests!" The merchant is smiling as he whispers into the ear of one of his daughters, who returns with a light, flexible veil of warded coins, strung with delicate wire.

Achman lifts the item for us to admire. I have never worn a veil, but it is breathtakingly beautiful. He smiles at Micha. "Something else to haggle over, Princess?"

Micha shakes her head, though I've known her long enough to see the interest in her eyes. "It is too immodest."

"For a common *dal'ting*, perhaps." Achman's eyes twinkle. "But worthy of an elder princess of the Kaji at times when it is good to remind others of her station."

"My station in the eyes of Everam is all that matters." Micha dismisses the item with a wave, but her eyes follow it as Achman returns it to the pillow.

Next Fashvah presents a small cylindrical box with a domed top. The box is silver, with a molded circle of defensive wards around its circumference, meeting at a ward circle shaped like a shield with a spear behind it. At the shield's center is a clear gemstone the size of my thumbnail. The negative space around the symbols is painted with brightly colored lacquer.

Achman removes the domed top, revealing two dangling earrings. He holds them up for me to admire. "The purest yellow gold was used for the filigree, and fourteen sequins—a holy number—surround the nine-carat fire opals . . ."

Achman trails off when he sees I am not paying attention, still staring at the open box on the pillow. The little spear behind the shield isn't molded. It's a pin, and there is a hinge on the opposite side. "What is this?"

"A simple trinket box, Your Highness," Achman says. "There is nothing special about it."

"What does it do?" I press.

The merchant shrugs, taking the box and pulling free the little spear. The cylinder opens, and the silver floor falls away. "May I?" He indicates my upper arm.

Micha tenses, but I hold out my arm and allow Achman to close the cuff around my biceps and reinsert the pin. It is snug, but not so tight it restricts me when I flex the muscle. I lift the armlet, marveling at how the colors dance in the light. "I love it. How much?"

"For this?" Achman waves a hand dismissively. "Keep it as my gift to you, Highness."

"Oh, I could never," I say.

"I insist," Achman says.

"No, I must . . . "

"Tsst." Micha's hiss sends a shiver down my spine, and I let the protest die on my lips.

"Thank you." My smile is genuine as I remove the cuff and reassemble the beautiful box.

"It is nothing," Achman says. "I would not have considered it a worthy gift, but if it caught your eye when so many treasures passed without remark, it must be so. May it protect you tomorrow night when you travel beyond the great wards."

The smile fades from my face. "I won't be going on the hike with the others. Mother won't allow it."

Achman nods. "The duchess is wise. Nie's hold may have weakened in your lands, but She is not gone. In Desert Spear, *Sharum* still battle and bleed in the Maze each night."

My eyes widen, and even Micha looks up. "The desert *alagai* were not destroyed by the Deliverer's hand?" She uses the Krasian word for coreling.

"Alas, no." Achman draws a ward in the air. "The *dama* tell us it is because Everam wishes the Majah to remain strong while our greenland cousins grow fat and lax, and perhaps it is so. Others whisper it is the Creator's punishment for our retreat from Sharak Ka."

"*Inevera*," Micha says. The word means "Everam's will," mysterious and unknowable. She could be agreeing with either theory, but considering her attitude toward the Majah tribe, there is little doubt which she believes. Still, there is no satisfaction in her eyes. The news that demons still plague her homeland obviously does not sit well with her. "Perhaps the Shar'Dama Ka will send aid, if a peace can be made."

A hush falls in the tent as she speaks the name. Shar'Dama Ka. Ahmann Jardir, first among the warrior-priests, who sits atop the Skull Throne and commands the greatest army in the world.

My father.

"Perhaps," Achman agrees, but in the silence that follows there is no sense that this is something the Majah desire. Why did they abandon my father and the green lands, returning to the desert fifteen summers ago? Was it cowardice? Spite? Or was there something more?

Tension grows thick in the hot air of the tent. It's too much to bear, and I blurt the first thing I can think of to break it.

"I'll take the earrings." My eyes flick to Micha. "And the veil as well."

6

BOYS

A T EVENING BELL, the merchants close their shops and the Krasians retreat to their colored wagons. Everyone needs their rest, for tomorrow is Solstice, the longest and busiest day of the year. In every city and town across Thesa and Krasia there will be celebrations, but here in Pumpforge, it is even more special.

Tourists gather around the central fountain of the market square, pitching tents and laying out blankets. Groups won't leave for the hike until dawn, but camping in the market square to be ready for an early start has become part of the tradition. Selen is quick to stake a fine spot for her small tent, but she returns soon after.

Flamework lights up the night sky as festival crackers bang and flash on the cobbles between the tents. Jongleurs juggle and play their instruments.

Everyone else is watching the entertainment, but all I can see are the other children as they gather, dance, laugh. Young couples hold hands, snuggled close, and I wonder how it feels to hold someone, or to be held. They seem such simple things, but I ache for them.

"Reckon that's the last of it," Wonda says, as the sky falls dark and the flamework crew begins to pack their implements. "Not as good as the ones your mum used to make, but a good show."

One more thing Mother was perfect at.

"Time to head inside," Wonda says. "Busy day tomorrow. Going to be dancing and games at the Solstice Festival, and Callen's smiths promised a lesson on how to make armor."

I nod, wanting to scream at the words. While my friends meet the Warded Children and see the wild lands beyond the wards, I get to braid flowers in my hair and toss poorly balanced rings at bottles for a chance to win trinkets.

I used to love Solstice Festivals. I would spend months planning my outfit, and count the days until the celebration. Now it feels like a punishment for something I cannot control.

Selen looks excited to go and join the crowd. And why not? I'm the one who's holding her back. She deserves this, and so much more.

"Go," I say. "Add my share of fun to your own."

Selen wraps her arms around me, pulling me close to whisper in my ear. "We'll have it together. I'll be waiting in the woods behind the stable."

My chest tightens, but I nod against her shoulder, too subtly for the others to notice. "It's not fair you get to go." I make the words loud enough for Micha and Wonda to hear.

"I'll tell you all about it in a few days," Selen promises, before dancing off into the crowd.

THE FINEST INN at Pumpforge is not luxurious, but it is spacious, with high ceilings and well-made furniture. We have the entire top floor, including a central dining area. Wonda no doubt thinks it a mercy to keep me from talk of the hike in the common.

It's surprisingly easy to slip the vial from my hidden pocket, counting drops into the pot of strong tea on the tray. Too little, and a big woman like Captain Wonda won't do more than yawn. Too much, and she and Micha won't wake for days. The whole vial and they might not wake at all.

I pick at the food on my plate, but I have no interest in it. My stomach is turning somersaults.

"Ent gonna eat?" Wonda lifts a thick cut of venison on her fork. "Game's fresh out here. Ent like the grain-fed meat at home."

"That makes it better?" I ask.

"Oh, ay." Wonda stuffs the forkful into her mouth, lips smacking with juice as she chews.

Disgusted, I push my plate away. "I've more in common with stock raised in captivity."

"Aw, Olive. It ent like that." Wonda reaches for me.

There is genuine hurt in her eyes, but I don't care. I quickly get to my feet, stepping out of reach. "What's it like, then?"

"Your mum just wants you safe."

I cross my arms. "And the parents of the hundreds of children in the market square don't?"

"'Course they do." Wonda spreads her hands. "It was up to me, I'd take you. Honest word. But it ent."

I stare at Wonda a long time. She means the words, but it makes her no less my goaler. But then her jaw tightens as she swallows a yawn. I never touched the cup of tea I was served, but she and Micha emptied the pot.

"I'll be in my cell." I stomp off to my room, making a show of slamming the door.

Inside I pace, listening to Wonda and Micha talking in low voices. I hear the clatter of plates as the table is cleared and turn down my lamp, letting my eyes adjust to the darkness. I've never needed much light to see—starlight from the window and the lights of other houses are enough. My ears strain, until at last I hear it.

Wonda's snoring.

I slip quietly from the room to find Wonda passed out on the small couch in the common room. The door to Micha's room is closed, with no light coming from beneath.

Holding my breath, I pad across the room. With every floorboard creak I expect Wonda's eyes to snap open, but she doesn't even shift in her sleep as I put an ear to Micha's door.

I close my eyes, focusing on Wonda's snoring and then deliberately tuning it out. There, like a trickle drowned by the roar of a waterfall, my sensitive ears make out the steady sound of Micha's breath.

I return to my room, shutting and locking the door. The window sticks, and for a moment I fear they've nailed it shut. Slowly I increase the pressure, muscles cording. Suddenly it comes loose, opening with a thump.

I freeze, ears straining, but Wonda's snoring continues unabated. I take a deep breath, then throw one leg out the window. A moment later I am perched on the sloping roof of the inn, gently sliding the window shut.

I shiver in excitement as I slide down the roof, catching the awning lip as I go over the edge. My dress billows as I swing to the ground.

My door is locked from the inside, and they will be in no rush to wake me. Even without the potion, they might not realize I'm gone until midmorning. If the tea does its work, I'll have a head start of hours.

And they won't be looking for a boy.

There will be the Core to pay when this is done. Micha and Wonda may never trust me again, and Mother will be a thunderstorm. But for just a few days, I'll have a taste of what it's like to be free.

"How's it feel?" Selen asks as I tighten the last strap of the wooden breastplate. Wooden tassets protect my hips, with vambraces and greaves for my forearms and calves, all of them carved with wards and glazed in hard lacquer. Beneath, I wear a dark coat and sturdy leggings to cushion the plates.

I've taken off the bido, wearing the cotton underclothes Selen says boys favor. I don't ask how she knows. It feels . . . odd to be unstrapped after years of binding myself tight.

"Awkward," I admit. "And lighter than expected. This armor's supposed to protect me?"

"Might not think it's so light after a few days' hike," Selen says. "Wooden armor ent much good against a horse spear or a crank bow, but the wards will turn coreling claws better than steel."

"So they say." I run my fingers doubtfully over the symbols carved into the wood. "When was the last time it was put to the test?"

Selen shrugs. "Ent much chance of it being tested on this trip, either."

She hangs her lantern from a tree branch and holds up a hand mirror as I part my thick black hair in a boy's style, braiding it at the nape of my neck and tucking it inside the breastplate to hide its length. I take my powder kit, darkening my brow and brushing a hint of shadow around my hairless jaw. Then I put on the open-faced wooden helmet and strike a dashing pose. "How do I look?"

"Oh, my." Selen fans herself with the mirror. "You're going to be beating the girls off with your spear."

I open my mouth to snipe in return, but stumble over the retort as Selen steps back and holds up the mirror again. A stranger looks back at me. He has the same shaped face as me, the same sky-blue eyes, but the subtle effect of the hair and makeup is striking. With the armor adding weight and bulk to my frame, I doubt even Mother would recognize me if I walked past her.

And I look . . . good. Handsome and powerful. The kind of boy no one would question on the borough tour. Like I'm about to debut a new dress, I can't wait to see how people react, because it *feels* right.

"My turn!" Selen hands me the mirror and puts on her own helmet. She laughs as she mimics my pose, but the illusion is real. Her broad shoulders carry the breastplate as if it were made for her, and her heavy jaw looks right in the helm.

"If you weren't my aunt," I smile, "I'd hide in a dung stall for a chance to kiss you."

Selen swats at me but I dance away from the blow. "Look a bit like the general, if I'm giving honest word."

Selen smiles. "Mum says he was the handsomest man in Hollow before he lost his hair and added fifty pounds of ale to his belly. Nice to know I have that to look forward to."

I laugh, but Selen continues. "You ent one to tell tales. You look more like some desert prince than your mum." She winks. "Just as well, with the duchess' face on every coin in Hollow."

Mention of the duchess awakens a familiar knot of worry in my stomach. "Let's go before it's too late."

We set a quick pace to the market square, where hundreds of teens have gathered their bedrolls into packs. The sky is turning violet with the coming dawn as youngsters from all over the duchy wait to be assigned guides for the highlight of the borough tour.

Two dozen Warded Children stand by the fountain at the center of the square, holding up hands and shouting for folk to form up into groups of twenty.

Like insects and light, folk are drawn to the Children, but they keep their distance for fear of being burned. The Warded Children are the last remnants of a magic that is passing from the world. Ale stories and tampweed tales of their exploits are spun by every Jongleur in Thesa.

Mother says their powers have diminished since the war, but their very presence remains intimidating. Everyone was said to breathe a sigh of relief when they left Hollow to live in the borderlands. Civilized folk didn't know what to do with them.

The Children embody every freedom I long for, but I do not envy them. I want to join society, not eschew it. Some few wear plain, threadbare robes, but most are clad only in sandals and scraps of ragged cloth that leave little to the imagination. Ward tattoos run up and down their limbs and across their bodies. Their hair is cropped close, often shaved or spiked, with mind wards tattooed on their heads.

Here and there I see bits of armor—greaves and bracers, a small buckler—but nothing close to full protection. Their warded skin is exposed wherever possible. My nostrils flare, catching the stink of sweat and hogroot—an herb known to repel demons.

A handful carry weapons—spears, bows, or knives—but most are unarmed. Few of the Children are even as large as me. It's hard to imagine any of them putting up a fight against an armored soldier—much less a demon—but they move with feral confidence, and folk jump when they bark.

"I don't think that one has anything under his loincloth," a familiar voice says, and there are peals of laughter. I turn to see Minda next to me in the crowd. She catches my eye and smiles, and for a moment, I think we've been caught. Then I note the blush in her pale cheeks, and realize she hasn't recognized me at all. She keeps looking, running a hand along her new silk Krasian scarf, and suddenly it's my face that's coloring. I don't know what shocks me more, the way she's eyeing me, or that I like it.

"Over here." Selen's voice is gruff as she grabs my arm and pulls me through the crowd to where smaller groups from distant villages are banding together. We find some unfamiliar faces gathering by one of the

Children—a tall woman with a pretty face and a long, lithe build. Her blond hair is cropped save in back, where a braid at least three feet long hangs.

She wears the bare minimum of clothing decency requires, and almost every inch of her exposed skin is covered in tattoos. The warding is beautiful, elegant lines sliding under her clothes to make clear even her hidden flesh is inked. I wonder if she bothers with clothes at all, when not in town, and again I feel my face flush.

None of the others seem perturbed at two strangers joining the tour group. Most are staring at our guide with varying degrees of fear, awe, and desire.

As Selen predicted, we're not the only ones with borrowed arms and armor. There are boys in ill-fitting shirts of metal links, leather jerkins studded with steel, and even two suits of warded steel plates. They carry an array of axes and spears, all etched with wards. The worn handles look older than the boys who carry them.

"Ay, look at that one." Selen tilts her head toward a tall boy with a steel helm tucked under one arm. His deep brown eyes match the thick curls of hair cascading over his brow. The steel plates of his armor are too large for his frame, but not by much. A scraggly brown beard clings to his heavy jaw, like the first blades of spring grass. He's beautiful, but my nerve breaks when he looks up. I quickly turn my head before our eyes can meet.

I don't understand what's happening. It isn't as if I haven't taken a shine to people before, but tonight, it's all I seem able to think about.

Most of the girls are unarmored, clad in sensible dresses and boots suited to hiking. They carry bows and small quivers.

Two of them must have relatives who served in Mother's house guard. Their borrowed wooden breastplates are sleeker than those Selen took from her father's armory, with loose pants that flare at the legs before gathering into their boots. Standing still, they have the appearance of dresses, but with greater freedom of movement. I copied the design with a few flourishes for my riding gear. Crank bows are slung from harnesses on their backs with full quivers resting on their hips.

It only takes a moment before Selen and I are noticed. We draw more than a few stares, and I worry again that we've been recognized. Three girls start whispering to one another, their eyes never leaving us. At last, they shove one of the group forward.

"Are you Krasian?" the girl asks as the other two giggle at her back.

I freeze. My mouth opens, but nothing comes out. With every passing moment, I feel more and more exposed.

Selen steps in, smacking me on the back. "Sorry about that. Aman's a bit shy about his desert blood." She bows as smoothly as one of her father's footmen. "I'm Simen. We're from Sweet Succor, north of Cutter's Hollow."

"Lanna." The girl smiles and spreads her skirts as the others gather close. "We're from Apple Hill."

She's pretty, with an upturned nose and round cheeks, brown hair gathered into a braid that rests on her shoulder and hangs down to frame a budding bosom. There's a crank bow peeking from her weathered pack, but she doesn't have the look of a hunter. Quite the opposite. She looks at me the way Minda did, and I feel my heart speed up in response.

As my mind catches up with her words, I breathe out some of my tension. Apple Hill is nearly a week's ride from the capital, and far from Sweet Succor.

"Lotta mudboys born after the war." The beautiful boy whose eyes I couldn't meet steps in front of Lanna.

"Oskar, don't." She puts a hand on his arm, but he yanks it free.

I've heard tales of people with Krasian blood treated poorly in Thesa, but no one has ever dared say a word like *mudboy* in my presence. I stare at him, incredulous, but then he steps in close and by some instinct I mirror him, standing just out of arm's reach. My fist clenches, and this time I meet his eyes with a cold glare.

Oskar is larger than me, but I'm stronger than I look. I visualize Wind Against the Rocks, the *sharukin* that would bring the heel of my palm to his heavy jaw. If he comes at me, I will lay him out on the cobbles.

Selen steps between us, nose-to-nose with Oskar. "Dressing in your da's armor doesn't make you a fighter. You're smart, you'll step back while you can."

Aggression radiates off her like heat, and he takes a step back in surprise. Then he glances at his friends and forces a laugh to cover his fear as he steps back in. "Or what? Mudboy will *sharusahk* me?"

Selen raises a fist, her voice deepened to a growl I hardly recognize. "Ought to be more worried about me."

A few of the other boys, obviously friends of Oskar, gather in close, but whether it's for a view of the brewing fight or a readiness to join in, I can't tell.

These outer-borough boys may be shepherds and farmers, but they have us outnumbered. Selen and I have practiced *sharusahk* forms all our lives, but neither of us has ever really fought anyone. Will our training be enough to stave off a beating? Even if it is, much of *sharusahk* is designed to cripple and kill. There won't be an overnight if we injure one of these boys before we even leave the square.

"Ay! Enough with the rooster strutting!" Our guide claps her hands, and everyone jumps, turning her way. She points a finger at Oskar and he pales visibly. "I know mudboys worth ten of you, apple picker. Leave the pretty one alone or you can stay behind."

Oskar steps back so quickly he stumbles in his heavy armor, and it's only the quick hands of his friends that keep him from falling. He glares at me as they steady him, and I give him a hint of smile.

"Name's Ella Cutter." The Warded Child begins to pace in front of us, as I feel my knotted muscles begin to unclench. "Here to be your guide, not your wet nurse. Anyone doesn't hop when I say jump is going to regret it. Say ay."

"A-ay," everyone stammers.

Ella stomps her foot, and the cobblestone cracks beneath her heel. "Say ay!"

"Ay!" we cry loudly.

Ella gives us a satisfied nod. "Ent ever seen a demon on borough tour, but that don't mean we won't. That happens, you'll need to depend on one another. Gonna pick four leaders. Each will be responsible for four of your group-mates. I ask where any of them are, you'd best have an answer. Anyone in your group has a problem, you solve it, or bring it to me. And Creator help you if your group can't keep pace. Say ay."

"Ay!" everyone shouts in unison.

"Good." Ella points at Selen, first. "You look ready for a fight. Simen is it?" Selen nods, and Ella grunts, pointing to four others in the group. "You four are Simen's now."

Next she points to Lanna. "Taking charge will toughen you up. Can't have boys acting like you're a tackleball to fight over." Lanna spreads her skirts and opens her mouth, but Ella is already turning away to point at Oskar. "Local bully, ay? Might be a little responsibility is what you need." Oskar punches a fist to his chest like a soldier, and Ella snorts, turning to me. "And you, Mudboy. Respect goes a long way with ignorant louts. See if you can earn some."

Again, that awful word, but it's different when Ella says it than Oskar, and she's trusting me to take charge of others. Mother won't even give me charge of myself.

I reach for my skirts to curtsy, realizing too late I have none. By the time I manage a bow, Ella has turned on her heel and started striding for the edge of the cobblestone square. "Right, then! Time to go."

"You heard her!" Selen barks, waving her group along. The rest of us quickly follow.

It's not yet dawn when we step off the last greatward and into the wilds of the borderland. There's no hint of danger, but still a shiver rushes through me. For fifteen summers I've done everything I've been told. Everything Mother ever wanted. Finally, I am doing something for myself.

I want to impress Ella, and for once my training helps. Mother taught me to work a gathering, and I am quick to get to know the members of my group: Gyles, Tam, Boni, and Elexis.

Gyles is shorter than me, with thick brown hair and a charming smile. His armor is worn, with faded wards burned into the leather. Tam is the largest boy on the tour, with thick arms and a barrel chest, but his shirt of metal links is heavy, and he gets out of breath easily. I keep an eye on him to make sure he doesn't slow us down.

Boni and Elexis are the two in the garb of the house guard. They look splendid, but step carefully, as if fearing to return the uniforms soiled. Elexis has her crank bow slung over her shoulder, but Boni has hers in hand.

"Don't keep your bow cranked all day," I tell her. "You'll ruin it."

"What if I need to shoot something?" she asks.

"You're more likely to shoot one of us, carrying a loaded bow," I say. "Better to take a few seconds in the moment than try to shoot with a fouled bow."

"Thank you," Boni says, easing the tension and removing the bolt. She smiles. "If we're attacked, will you protect me, while I crank it?"

I nod, turning away before she can see the surprise on my face. It's amazing, what a few changes to my appearance has done.

We hike for hours, the well-trodden paths near Pumpforge fading into half-overgrown ways, then trails that seem invisible even when you're right on them. Ella sets a hard pace through woods, over rocky rises, and down grassy hills, until I've lost all sense of where we are.

I've gone for walks in Gatherers' Wood, the public park that surrounds Gatherers' University, but I've never seen anything like this. It's like stepping into a landscape painting. I remember the bumpkins gaping at the ceiling of the Cathedral of Rizon, and keep my jaw shut as I take in huge stands of ancient trees, distant mountains, and views that go on for miles without a building in sight.

We break for lunch, but there is no cooking of any sort. Just biscuits, dried fruit, nuts, and tough, smoked meat, washed down with cold water from canteens refilled at passing streams.

My worry that Wonda might wake early and send out search parties fades the farther we go. Dozens of groups set out in different directions this morning, and only Ella seems to know where we are or where we're going.

If anyone expected our guide to teach as she led us into the borderlands, they were mistaken. For the most part, Ella behaves as if we're not there at all, only occasionally barking for stragglers to keep pace, or warning us against loose stones or a boggy patch.

We enter a thickly wooded area in the hills somewhere north of the Laktonian wetlands. Still Ella marches us on, even as the sun dips low in the sky and the floor beneath the forest canopy grows dark. I say nothing, but I stroke the wards on the armlet from the Krasian bazaar, wondering if it could truly protect me if a demon leapt from the shadows beneath the trees.

The sky is purple when we reach a clearing ringed with heavy stones. The clearing is rough and overgrown, but there is a firepit in the center, and room for everyone. The outward faces of the stones are chiseled with wards scraped clear of the moss and lichen that mottles the inner circle.

"Welcome to your new home for the night," Ella says. "Ent any privies, so if you've got to make more than water, suggest you do it before night falls. Simen!"

"Ay!" Selen steps forward.

"Your group can stake spots first," Ella says. "Drop your gear and start collecting firewood."

Selen scans the campsite, quickly settling on the hard-packed dirt near the firepit. "This way. Packs off! You can put out bedrolls and rest when the fire's up!"

"Ay, how come they . . . !" Oskar begins.

"Lanna!" Ella barks. "Your group next." She points a finger. "There's a stream about half a mile that way. Take buckets and bring them back full."

"Ay." Lanna leads her group to the spot on the opposite side of the fire from Selen's, taking buckets hanging from their packs and heading into the woods.

"Aman," Ella says, and it takes a second to realize she's talking to me. "Your group next. Then get to work on the firepit. I want it ready when they come back with kindling."

"Ay," I tell her. The ground behind Selen's group is overgrown and farther from the fire, but the grass is soft as we trample it flat, laying out our things before taking spades to the firepit to clear the ash and shore up the sides. How to build and care for fire was an early lesson in Gatherers' University. There are wooden supports for cookpots and a spit, and we begin cleaning and setting them up.

"What about—?" Oskar cuts off as Ella turns to him.

"You boys been hiking all day in that ridiculous armor." Ella smiles. "Figured you'd want to take a load off. You've got first patrol tonight." She points to the remaining space in the campground. "Bit rocky over there, but you shouldn't notice, wrapped in all that steel."

Ella vanishes, and returns not long after with a deer slung over one shoulder like an impudent toddler. Selen and I watch in morbid fascination as she guts and skins it, but our companions from Apple Hill are unfazed, helping prepare the meat for cooking.

We're tired from the day's hike, but the mood in the camp is festive that evening. None of my worries have materialized, and the smell of cooking venison is heavenly. I feel a giddy excitement as the sun finally dips below the horizon, and I can tell I'm not alone. Selen has her spear ready, body tense like an arrow about to loose. Only Ella seems more interested in dinner as the rest of us watch the edge of the ward circle, half expecting demons to leap out at any moment.

But they don't. There isn't so much as a cry in the distance. I think there is a soft glow to the wards on the stone, but it could just be the flickering firelight.

Ella checks the wards on the weapons and shields of the boys in Oskar's group, spinning them in practiced hands to test weight and balance. She presses the meat of her thumb against Oskar's spearpoint until it draws blood.

She thrusts the weapon back into Oskar's hands. "It'll do." She sketches a rough map of the area in the dirt. "Take your group and start patrolling this route."

Oskar keeps an arched back and a straight face, but he pales a little in the firelight. "Shouldn't we get . . . trainin', or something?"

Ella smiles. "Trainin' you not to be scared of the dark. You see a demon, give a nice shriek, an' I'll come runnin'."

Oskar looks like he might say more, but he glances at the others in his group and swallows it. He takes a torch from his pack, affixing it to a socket on the end of his spear. He touches it to the fire, and it blazes to life. "You heard her, boys. Eyes sharp."

The others produce torches as well. Kenz and Tal hold axes in one hand and torches in the other. Oren holds a torch and a bow, though I don't see how he could use both. Rig, who has the thick arms of a blacksmith, straps his warded hammer to his back, ducking behind a rounded shield. He holds his torch cocked back like a club. All five of them look nervous as they step across the circle of wards and into the naked night.

I feel it, too. For all my scoffing at the chance of seeing a demon when we were safe on the Hollow greatwards, I hold my breath as if expecting corelings to leap out of the shadows to attack them.

But again, nothing happens, and after a few moments, I start to relax. The boys move out beyond the edges of the fire's glow, just bits of floating light in the darkness.

I glance at Ella. She lounges on a rock, seemingly at ease, but the wards tattooed around her eyes glow softly as she tracks Oskar's group through the darkness. Like Mother's spectacles, they grant her wardsight, the ability to see the glow of magic in all living things, illuminating the night with more clarity than brightest day, and letting her peer into the hearts of the unwary. She is letting the boys walk beyond the wards, but not unsupervised. If a coreling was out there, she would see its glow long before it came anywhere near the camp.

She catches me staring, and turns those glowing eyes on me and Selen. Her eyes flick down for a moment, and I feel as exposed as if I were stripped bare. There is a hint of smile on her lips as she turns away, but I cannot fathom its meaning. Like Mother, she has an air of knowing more than she lets on.

A howl cuts through the darkness, and I freeze. It is followed soon after by others, a chorus on the night wind.

"Demons?" Lanna asks.

Ella shakes her head. "Nightwolves. Demons ent the only thing to worry about this far from civilization. Lots of demon carcasses left out in the night during the war. Scavengers fed on them and . . . changed."

"Thought those were just stories," Selen says.

"Demon meat is potent stuff," Ella says. "Addictive. Makes you strong. Feral. Saw a hound grow big as a house after gnawing at the remains of a few battlefields."

"Nightwolves took six of my mam's sheep last winter," one of the girls in Lanna's group, Cayla, agrees. "Saw the prints in the snow myself. Paws bigger than my hand with fingers spread."

More howls in the distance, turning to barks echoing a staccato rhythm through the hills. I fetch my spear from where I left it with my pack. "Now you can load your bows," I tell Boni and Elexis.

"Ent cause for worry." Ella's head is cocked, listening. "They're a long way off. Guessin' they found dinner that's puttin' up a fight."

More howling, cut short by pained yelping. Ella hops down from her rock. She brushes herself off casually, but I see her loosening her knife in its sheath. "Gonna have a quick look. Be back soon."

"Ay, you can't just leave!" Selen calls as Ella crosses the wards. "Who's in charge?"

"You are!" Ella calls back. "Keep patrolling, but stay close to the wards. I'll be back soon." A moment later she is swallowed by the darkness.

The nervous tension returns to the camp, much as it had when Oskar's group started their patrol. Long moments pass without further sounds of nightwolves, and slowly we begin to relax.

There is laughter by the fire, and Cayla produces a fiddle, playing a lively tune. Lanna and some of the other girls begin dancing, skirts twirling as they spin and reel. I ache to join them, but I have no skirts to swish about.

Lanna sees me watching and reaches out a hand. "Dance with us, Aman!"

Why not? Mother's herald Kendall taught me to dance, and it's simple enough to reverse the steps and take the lead. Stepping in time to the music, I catch one girl by the arm, spinning and using her own momentum to lift her momentarily from her feet before bringing her back down in time to meet her next partner. I turn a circuit and link arms with Lanna.

"Didn't expect you to be so light on your feet." Lanna's eyes meet mine, flickering with reflected firelight. The top button of her dress has come undone, but she makes no effort to fix it.

"I'm full of surprises," I say, picking her up to spin. She smells like flowers as I hold her close, then release her, laughing as she reels away to the next partner.

We soon learn Cayla only knows one dancing tune. She plays it twice more before putting the fiddle away, more interested in talking to Gyles. He's woven some tough wildflowers into a garland for her hair.

There is no moon, but the stars are bright and plentiful, much more visible than in the capital where there are lights in every house and street corner. I stand at the edge of the camp, admiring them. The air is crisp and clean with none of the smells of town, and for the first time I can remember, I feel like I can take a full breath.

Selen appears at my side, breathing deeply of the cool night air. "Still having second thoughts?"

I shake my head. "You were right."

Selen gives a snort. "I'm always right."

I want to say more, but Lanna comes over to join us. I point to a line of stars, instead. "There's Kaji's spear. And the lonely nightwolf."

"I don't see a wolf," Lanna says, drawing close. She lays a hand on my arm, and it feels as if all my senses are focused on that one spot.

"I never thought it looked much like a wolf, either," I admit. "Mistress Vika says you have to use your imagination."

"That your village Gatherer?" another girl, Andraya, asks. Her hair is orange, and brown freckles cover her face, running all the way down into the neckline of her dress.

Selen coughs, and I remind myself not to mention the university. "Ay. She has a star chart and likes to teach the children to read the sky."

"What else do you see?" a third girl, Melany, asks.

I look back to the sky, but before I can answer, Oskar appears out of the darkness, pointing upward. "That one is demon's bung."

Andraya and Melany laugh, but Lanna is less impressed. "If you could keep your bung shut, you might learn a thing or two."

"What's to learn?" he asks. "Just use your imagination, ay?" He points to another section of sky where a passing cloud obscures the stars. "That's cow's udder, and over there is Deliverer's turd." More laughter, and even Selen chuckles, running her eyes over him again.

"Shouldn't you be patrolling?" Lanna asks.

"Think we've done our share, while you lot danced and looked at stars," Oskar says. "Why not take your turn?"

I expect Lanna to balk, and open my mouth to volunteer, but she surprises me. "Ay, think you're right. Melany, Andraya, Cayla! Fetch your bows."

She turns to me as the other girls move to comply. "Scary out there. Walk with me?"

"I . . ." My mind races, not sure how to reply. She doesn't look frightened, and something about that scares me. She has more on her mind than demons.

"He'd love to," Selen finishes for me. I stammer something incomprehensible, but Lanna takes Selen's words as an answer and smiles, running off to fetch her bow.

"What are you doing?" I ask.

"Making sure you have a little fun," Selen says. "What's the harm? Now that Oskar's back, I think I might take him for a walk, as well."

"He thinks you're a boy," I remind her.

"Might be that doesn't matter to him. If it does . . . " Selen shrugs. "Maybe I let slip that 'Simen' is really 'Simena,' whose da wouldn't let her go on the borough tour, so she stole his armor and went anyway."

I feel my stomach knotting and don't understand how she can be so calm. "What do I tell Lanna?"

"Who says you need to tell her anything?" Selen asks. "Any fool can see she likes you. Ent like you're getting promised. Just a bit of fun on the borough tour. Go for a walk. See what happens."

I glance around the camp. We're not the only ones. Gyles is kissing Cayla "for luck" before she goes into the night. Rig is putting his big arms to work, helping a perfectly capable Boni crank her bow. Others are talking, laughing, flirting. Why not me?

Lanna returns, and I take a torch, setting it into a socket on my spear. She carries a loaded crank bow, carefully aimed down with the safety engaged. "Shall we?"

I'm afraid and excited as we step together into the naked night, but, like Lanna, it isn't demons on my mind.

WE BEGIN THE patrol as a group, but after several circuits of the camp, Lanna breaks the girls into teams of two and spreads them out, ostensibly to keep watch from all sides. We can still see the campfire, but the figures around it are just silhouettes, too distant to make out.

"We're alone," Lanna says, and something in her voice sends goosebumps running up my arms. I've tried to keep careful watch, scanning the darkness at the end of the torchlight and listening for any sign of disturbance, but my eyes keep flicking back to Lanna. The way her hair bounces around her smooth shoulders. Her round cheeks and large eyes. Her soft lips. The button that's still undone.

I've never given much thought to kissing girls, but I'm thinking about it now. In the same way a change of clothes made girls look at me differently, I'm seeing them in a new way, too. I can feel the kiss coming, like pressure in the air before a storm. My heart is drumming in my chest, a steady thump! Thump! Thump! My face feels flushed and hot.

I look again, and find Lanna looking back with those wide brown eyes. Our gazes meet, and she moistens her lips with her tongue. I feel my mouth water.

Grandmum says the boy should make the first move, but I don't think Selen has ever waited for that. And what of me? I may be dressed as a boy, but I'm not one. I want to reach out—to get on with it because the tension is too much to bear—but what if I'm reading things wrong? What if I am too rough, or not rough enough? Do I open my mouth, or keep it closed?

She takes a step toward me and I step back in surprise. Lanna giggles and steps forward again, backing me into a tree. "Didn't think you'd be shy," she whispers as she sets her crank bow down. "Bet you've kissed plenty of girls back in Sweet Succor."

I squirm against the trunk of the tree, resisting a sudden urge to run. "Not really," I manage. "My . . . mother is very strict."

The answer seems to please Lanna. Her smile widens. "Your mum ent here, is she?"

Mention of Mother does nothing to calm my racing heart, but then Lanna leans in, lips parted slightly, and my resistance breaks. I drop the spear to the ground, torch guttering against the damp soil, and put a hand on her waist, drawing her close like in the paintings of lovers I've seen. My other hand comes up gently to caress her cheek as I lean in and our lips touch.

The kiss is warm and soft and just a little moist, our lips forming a seal that breaks with a soft pop when we finally pull apart. I start to say something, but Lanna isn't interested, leaning in to kiss me back. It's harder than mine, and she presses against me, opening her mouth just a little. I taste her breath and something awakens in me, something primal, unlike anything I've ever felt before. I feel a growl building in the back of my throat, and my whole body thrums with it. It gets louder, vibrating the air around us.

I draw back and open my eyes, seeing Lanna leaning in, eyes still closed, lips puckered, waiting for more. I gulp a breath, but the growling continues, seeming to come from above us. I look up and see branches swaying, but there's no breeze . . .

Then I see it. Eyes black, armor the color of bark, the demon lets go its grip on the trunk and drops down, talons leading.

7

BROKEN TRUST

"Look out!" I shove Lanna harder than intended. She gives a cry, crashing into the ground by the half-smothered torch, bolts flying from her quiver in a clatter.

I'm dead, I think as the demon hits me, claws scrabbling. *I should have listened to Mother. Should have listened to everyone . . .*

But the wards on my breastplate flare to life, and the coreling's claws find no purchase. As its weight bears me to the ground I instinctively revert to Wonda's training, using the demon's momentum to redirect the takedown. We hit the dirt and I use the rebound to roll into a dominant position above the writhing mass of muscle and claws.

The demon isn't much larger than a shepherd's hound, and its long limbs—perfect for leaping from tree to tree—aren't jointed to strike at me while it's prone, but it is not defenseless. Armor, thick and ridged like bark, covers the creature from head to toe.

There are warded gauntlets hanging from my belt, but there's no time to put them on. I ball a bare fist and punch the demon in the head.

It's like punching a tree. Rough scales skin my knuckles and the bones of my hand blaze with pain, but I feel the softer flesh beneath jolt as I strike the wood demon's exoskeleton. I hit it again, and again after that, struggling to keep it pinned.

I glance at Lanna, seeing her frozen with fear right where she struck the ground. "Run! Get help!"

There's no time to see if she complies. The demon twists and avoids my next punch, then snaps its jaws at my arm before I can retract. Rows of razor teeth close on my biceps, but the warded armlet from the Krasian market flares to life. It keeps the demon from biting the arm clean off, but it still gets hold of me in its powerful jaws.

I scream and try to yank free, but it only makes the demon thrash and clamp down harder. I'm thrown from my position and my arm jolts so hard I fear it will be torn from its socket. The demon glares down at me and I know I'm about to die.

Fire scorches my face in a shower of sparks. I look up to see Lanna draw my spear back like a club, hitting the demon again with the torch affixed to the weapon's end. The coreling, unharmed but startled, loosens its grip. I pull my arm free and curl up, kicking the demon in the chest with both feet. It's thrown back and I quickly roll to my feet, snatching the spear from Lanna.

"Go!" I cry, wondering why she doesn't listen, why help hasn't come. It feels like we've been fighting for long minutes, but I realize it's only been seconds. I hear shouting in the darkness, still distant.

Lanna scrambles for her bow, but the bolt has fallen free. She searches blindly in the darkness for one from her emptied quiver. I put up my spear as the wood demon charges back in, but the coreling, faster than I would ever expect for so bulky a creature, pounces before I can bring the point to bear. Again I am knocked onto my back, the spear held horizontally between us.

Like my breastplate, defensive wards that seemed decorative a moment ago blaze to life along the spear shaft. The wood demon fetches up short against it, sparks of magic scorching its armor black.

But the coreling's limbs are long. Its scrabbling hind talons dig into the gaps in the armor covering my thighs. I howl as they pierce flesh.

The demon jerks, the bark across its breast splitting as a speartip, its wards blazing white-hot with magic, bursts from the coreling's chest. Ichor sprays my face, oily and stinking. The creature is yanked away, and I expect to see Ella or even Selen standing over me.

Instead I see a Krasian woman in a black silk robe and pantaloons, the lower half of her face wrapped in a veil of pure white silk. The spear she holds is six feet of clear glass, pointed on both ends. She kicks the demon off the blade, landing it on its back, and spins the weapon deftly before bringing the point down into the coreling's eye. It gives a high-pitched yelp, thrashes as she twists the shaft, then goes limp.

"Tsst!" the woman hisses. "Get up. Put your gauntlets on."

My face goes cold as I recognize the voice. "Micha?"

She kicks me when I do not comply fast enough. "Get up! Apple Hill girl! To us! Now!"

I roll to my feet, staring at the carcass of the wood demon. The ichor that struck my face must have activated the wards on my helmet. I no longer need the torch, seeing everything in perfect clarity despite the darkness. In wardsight all living things—Micha, Lanna, even the trees—give off the soft glow of the magic. It drifts along the ground like a luminescent fog, venting from the Core.

The coreling shines so bright it stings my eyes at first, but as they adjust I see it dimming as ichor bleeds into the dirt.

My mind reels, and not just from the rush of this new spectrum of vision. In the fight I was focused. I expected to lose, but I wasn't afraid. Now, looking at Micha as she stands over the creature, everything that's happened comes crashing in at once.

"You killed it," I say.

"Tsst!" Micha hisses again. "It isn't alone. Stop staring. Gauntlets on. Spear up. Stay alert."

"Micha, I'm sorry—"

Micha lifts her veil and spits, cutting my words short. She turns to look at me, but her eyes are not those of the meek woman who brushes my hair and walks me to class. These eyes are cold, with predatory depth. Terrifying. Who is this person? Was she ever the woman I knew?

"We will settle our differences with the dawn. In the night, we are sisters, always."

Lanna joins us, a fresh bolt loaded onto her bow. "Who are you?"

Micha's voice is flat. "I am Aman's sister, and you will obey me if you wish to live."

Lanna nods dumbly, and Micha turns away. "We have to get back to the others."

Again I hear shouting in the distance, but no longer fighting for my life, I can make out more detail. They aren't the cries of friends coming to help.

Demons are attacking the camp.

THE CAMP IS not far at a run, especially with the night lit up in wardsight, but Lanna remains in the dark, guided only by the light of my torch and the campfire in the distance. She stumbles and I take her arm to steady her.

A booming roar shakes the ground beneath our feet, echoing through the hills. The sound is followed by screaming—in terror or pain I cannot tell.

"Micha!" My cry is tinged with desperation. "Selen is in the camp!"

"Tsst!" The glow of magic around Micha changes color. I can't read auras like Mother, but even I know irritation when I see it. "Be silent!"

We arrive at a scene of utter chaos. One of the great wardstones is shattered, and a ten-foot-tall rock demon stands at the center of the circle. Like the wood demon, the rock has an armored exoskeleton, but instead of rough bark, this one seems carved from the exposed rock face we hiked past earlier in the day, grayish stone sparkling with silicates. Its talons are as long as butcher knives, and its horns could spear a horse. Black eyes the size of my fists reflect the firelight and the pandemonium in the camp.

Smaller corelings race about, savaging the young tourists. Some have found their weapons and are fighting back, but there is blood everywhere, and a number of demons have paused around fallen bodies to feast. Their inhuman shrieks are triumphant as they throw back their heads to swallow great chunks of meat.

Selen is easily spotted, standing shoulder-to-shoulder with Oskar at the center of camp as they face down the rock demon. The beast rakes its huge talons at Selen, but Oskar is quick, throwing his shield up to deflect the blow in a burst of magic. Selen uses the cover to thrust, stabbing her spear at the demon's midsection. Her aim is true and the warded spearhead sends glowing cracks spiderwebbing through a small section of the demon's armored carapace, but she is forced to disengage as the demon swipes a backhand blow at her. It shrieks in pain, but seems more enraged than injured.

Lanna raises her crank bow. Micha turns and throws out a hand to signal her to stop, but whether she was too late or Lanna too frightened to comply, I cannot tell. Lanna pulls the trigger, launching a bolt.

The rock demon is too big to easily miss, but the hit is a glancing one, ricocheting off the demon's thick armor instead of penetrating. The rock turns its great head, noticing us for the first time.

"Fool girl," Micha growls, but she does not hesitate. The element of surprise lost, she ducks her head and charges, faster than I can believe. She is glowing brightly now, cuffs on her wrists and ankles blazing with power.

I know of these from my studies in the Chamber of Shadows. Micha wears *hora* jewelry, demonbones dipped in precious metal and warded, providing a limited well of power the user can draw upon. Such things were common during the demon war, but most have since become inert, unable to recharge without demonic power to Draw upon.

Micha is a blur as she rushes in. The demon roars in challenge, turning a quick circuit to whip its heavy, barbed tail at her. The appendage is bigger than she is, swung with terrifying speed, but Micha never slows, dropping at the last instant to slide beneath it and bury her glass spear in the back of its knee.

The rock demon's roar of pain shakes the ground, knocking human and demon alike from their feet. Micha's spear shines white with power, and I can see it running up her arms, brightening her aura like bellows to a flame. The coreling swipes at her, but Micha does not stay in range. With a twist she detaches half of the double-ended spear, leaving the other half buried in the demon's knee, sending waves of agonizing magic through the beast.

Micha rolls away from the blow, talons plowing the ground like a field for planting. The demon's leg buckles and it falls to one knee.

"Selen!" Micha cries. "Strike now!"

Selen's shocked expression goes slack. "Micha?!"

"Nie's black heart, girl!" Micha barks. "Strike!"

Shaking off her shock, Selen sets her feet and charges in, spear leading. The kneeling demon has brought its chest within reach, and she aims her blow perfectly for the gap between its armored breastplates. The wards on her spear flare as it punches through the armor and into whatever passes for the demon's heart.

The demon shrieks, backhanding Selen. Her armor absorbs the blow, but she is knocked away. Like Micha's, Selen's spear remains embedded in the coreling, shocking it with killing magic. Distracted, the demon tries to claw it free and Oskar seizes his chance, thrusting his own spear up under the demon's chin and into its brain.

The demon jolts and collapses. Oskar leaps back to avoid being crushed by its bulk. He rushes immediately to Selen's side, taking her in his arms like a lover. She's shaking as she gets to her feet, but like Micha, her aura is bright with feedback magic from striking the demon, and she steadies quickly. She puts a boot against the demon's chest and pulls her spear free.

Micha retrieves her weapon as well. It shines with power as she holds it aloft. "To me!" she cries to the other tourists. "Rally to me!" With that, she turns and throws the blazing spear clear across the camp, skewering a hill demon about to ram its curled horns into Cayla as she kneels over Gyles, her dress spattered with his blood.

Of the original twenty, perhaps ten tourists remain upright and able to fight. Micha strides through the group, quickly herding us into a defensive formation, then leads the way as we begin rescuing those survivors too injured or trapped to get to us.

The corelings are on the defensive now, but they do not flee, perhaps sensing the fear and weakness in the group. Long-limbed wood demons with talons like jagged branches and curly-horned hill demons with sharp cloven hooves, black as obsidian. There is a shriek from above and four girls raise crank bows, firing at a circling wind demon. It's impossible to tell which of them strikes true, but while three of the bolts miss, one brings the creature crashing down to the ground.

A hill demon lowers its head and charges me, but this time I am ready, setting my feet and raising my spear. At the last moment I will drop to one knee and drive the point into its chest.

But then a black mist rises from the ground between us, coalescing into Ella Cutter. She shines so bright in wardsight I need to squint to look at her.

"Night!" She lifts a hand and draws a glowing ward in the air. The demon slams into it like a steel wall, then falls away, stunned.

Ella is drawing more wards now, tracing them in silver fire with her fingers, then powering them from her aura like a child might blow a bubble through a ring of soap. The demons still threatening injured tourists are scattered, and then she sets about with killing magics.

Heat wards set wood demons ablaze, and a cutting ward bisects a hill demon, dropping it in two nearly identical halves. Another charges her and Ella catches it by the horns, twisting so hard its neck snaps with an audible crack.

Micha goes on the offensive now, retrieving the other half of her spear and reconnecting the ends. This she spins with terrifying speed and precision, lopping off the leg of a sleek field demon that swipes at her, and opening the throat of a hill demon.

Another hill demon charges at the gathering of tourists at the center of the circle, but Selen, Oskar, and I meet it with a wall of spearpoints, harrying it back until Lanna puts a bolt into its chest. A moment later, Ella slaps it aside with an impact ward.

The remaining demons break, attempting to flee through the gap in the wards, but Ella draws wards in the air, sealing them in with us.

"What is she doing?!" Lanna demands.

Warded Children cannot be trusted, Mother says in my head again. I didn't believe her then. Didn't want to. Now I see how wrong I was.

A hill demon, trapped, puts its horns down and charges Ella. She remains planted, goading it to approach, then at the last moment she sidesteps, seizing it by the horns. I think she is going to break its neck like the other, but then she does something unthinkable.

Hill demons have thick armor plates on their foreheads and snouts, but they are more vulnerable underneath. Ella yanks the creature's head in close, sinking her teeth into its unarmored throat.

She tears away scaled flesh in a spray of putrid ichor, but seems to glory in it, spitting out the tough outer layer and burying her face back into the wound, gnawing demon meat and drinking ichor like wine. Her aura dimmed with each ward she powered, but now it brightens again as she Draws power from the magic-rich repast.

Micha appears at my side. Her spear is at the ready, but it's Ella she is watching, not the demons scrabbling at the wards to escape.

Ella sucks the demon like an orange, then casts the rind aside, pouncing on another coreling scrabbling to fit through a tiny gap in the wards. She takes hold of it from behind, and the wards tattooed on her arms and legs begin to pulse and throb, growing ever brighter. She doesn't even need to bite this one to drain it of magic.

The last coreling left alive in the circle is a wood demon, eight feet tall with long, powerful limbs. It leaps to the attack, but Ella draws a wood ward in the air almost casually, pinning the creature against the outer forbidding of the camp. Magic arcs like lightning along the point of contact, and the demon shrieks in agony.

A large knife appears in Ella's hand and she buries it in the demon's chest, prying apart the armor plates until she can work one hand in, then the other. With a great flex, she cracks open the demon exoskeleton and reaches inside, tearing free its black heart. As the demon falls lifeless to the ground, she holds the prize aloft like she's giving a toast to the crowd.

Then she brings it to her lips, sinking her teeth into the reeking black flesh.

"Beware, sister," Micha whispers. "I do not think she will harm any of us without cause, but remain here, and do nothing to provoke her in this state."

I blink in surprise, but Micha doesn't hesitate, striding toward the Warded Child as she gorges on the demon's heart. She keeps her spear ready as she draws close, feet in fighting stance. Her words sound unnaturally calm. "Well fought, sister."

Ella looks up from her meal in surprise, as if she had forgotten anyone was there. "See you're finally acting yourself again, Micha."

I blink. They know each other? More, this insane, frightening woman seems to know my sister better than me.

"I am always myself, Ella am'Cutter," Micha says calmly.

"You're a lion," Ella tells her, "that squandered fifteen summers pretending to be a mouse."

"Even a lion will sheathe her claws when the hunt is over," Micha responds. "I never killed for the pleasure of it."

Ella scoffs. "Tell me you din't miss this. That you ent thrumming with the rush of it."

"I am not," Micha says.

Ella picks a bit of meat from her teeth and spits black ichor on the ground between them. "Your aura says different."

I glance at Micha's aura, but can make nothing from the colors running through it. Ella's is too bright to make out any color save white. She has become a luminous being, but I feel no safer for it. My hand tightens on my spear as she tears another bite from the heart.

"Where did you go?" Micha asks softly. "These children needed your protection."

"Where were you," Ella retorts, "when your charges snuck out from under Leesha's skirts and crossed the wards? Don't go tellin' tales about how this is my fault." She balls a fist and gets to her feet, ward tattoos glowing fiercely. Her aura becomes a flamework display, hot and violent.

I know Micha sees it as well, but she remains calm, her aura calming even as Ella's blazes. "This is not a matter of blame, sister. We are on the same side, are we not?"

Ella blinks, noticing her extended fist as if for the first time. It seems to require an act of will, but she uncurls her fingers and her glowing wards fade back into normal tattoos. "These weren't the only corelings tonight. Scattered a pack of them hunting nightwolves."

A ripple passes through Micha's aura. "A diversion to draw you away?"

"Thought the same thing," Ella agrees, "but ent seen anythin' like that in . . . "

"Fifteen years," Micha finishes. "You must skate to the capital immediately and inform Mistress Leesha."

Ella shakes her head. "Mrs. Bales will decide what's to be done. But first, I need to hunt the rest of those demons. Meantime, you escort these kids home."

Micha opens her mouth to argue, but Ella fades to mist and is gone.

———

"SELEN, OSKAR, AND Lanna," Micha calls. "Patrol the camp perimeter, but stay inside the wards. The rest of you start making litters for the wounded. It will be a long journey back to Pumpforge with so many to carry."

"What about me?" I ask, as the others hurry to comply.

"You, I am not letting out of my sight," Micha says. "Wash your hands. We have work to do."

I fetch my canteen and a bar of soap, cleaning my filthy, bloody hands. When I return, Micha is kneeling over Tam. He bites on a stick, tears streaming from his eyes, as Micha slowly pushes his intestines back into his abdomen. I retch at the sight, slapping a hand to my mouth.

"Tsst!" Micha hisses. "It is only wind, sister. Bend as the palm and let it blow over you. There is no time for coddling."

I've never seen a palm, but I know the mantra well enough, a Krasian concentration technique I've been taught since birth. I swallow back the vomit in my throat and force myself to look back at the wound with calm detachment. I've trained for this, assisted surgeries in the hospit, but the patients were strangers, and asleep, not sobbing friends staring at their own intestines when they should be dancing and kissing under the stars.

For the remainder of the night I assist as Micha, whom I've never seen bind so much as a paper cut, performs surgery on demon wounds with the skill of an Herb Gatherer. She stitches where she can, and amputates where she cannot, working with the calm of a chef at the carving board. Tears run down my cheeks as I pin her screaming, thrashing patients.

At last the work is done. Six dead and seven wounded, four of them unable to walk. Micha wipes her hands clean. "Rest while you can, little sister. Tomorrow will be a long day."

"We won't make it back to Pumpforge before dusk with four litters to pull," I say.

"No," Micha agrees. The survivors huddle around the firepit, but she walks to the far end of the camp, kneeling beside one of the great wardstones and closing her eyes.

I follow her. "Let me run ahead. I can bring back help."

Micha shakes her head, still facing away from me, eyes closed. Her voice approaches serenity, but I can sense an edge to it. "No. Selen will go."

"I'm faster," I argue. "Stronger. You know I am. I should take the risk."

Micha cracks an eye to look at me. "You *are* the risk."

I know the wise course is to leave her be, but we would not be in this position if I had followed the wise course. There is something festering between us, and it needs to be lanced. "What does that mean?"

"Do you think it coincidence," Micha asks, "that the first tour in over a decade to see a demon is the one you snuck off to join?"

My face goes cold. I shiver, though there is no breeze. "They came . . . because of me?" It makes no sense.

"Of course they came for you!" Micha snaps. "Fifteen years I have protected you, only to have you break my trust and run off into the night, drawing *alagai* like birds to a crust of bread."

The words sting—doubly so because I worry she is right—but the pain does not make me recoil as it should. Not coming from her. "Trust? What trust did we have, 'sister'? Everything I know about you is a lie. Night, are you even really my sister, or is that one more thing I simply took for granted?"

She turns to face me fully now. Rolling back off her knees to squat, coiled like a snake. "I am the second-born daughter of Ahmann Jardir, Shar'Dama Ka and ruler of all Krasia." She rises, taking a step toward me, and I can't help but take one back. "My mother, Thalaja, was a lesser wife, so at nine years old I was taken from my family and given to a merciless drillmaster, sent to live in the underpalace."

She reaches into her robe, pulling free an object she throws at me. Instinctively I catch it. My vial of sleeping potion.

"For a year, Drillmaster Enkido poisoned our food at random to teach us to recognize the taste. If we could guess the poison, we were given the antidote. If we were wrong, or failed to notice at all, we were left to suffer the effects. If we guessed poison and there was none, we were beaten."

She continues to advance, and it's all I can do not to keep backing away. "There were five of us, then. Spear sisters. Now my cousin Ashia wears the white turban of Sharum'ting Ka. My cousin Jarvah is body-guard to the Damajah, herself. My cousins Sikvah and Shanvah died with glory unbound, saving countless lives in Sharak Ka."

I know the names. The *Sharum'ting* were the elite female warriors of Krasia, and their exploits during the demon war are immortalized in his-tories taught throughout the duchy. I hold my ground, but I feel as if I am shrinking as Micha comes to stand nose-to-nose with me.

"And what of my service? My deeds were no less glorious. A demon prince fell to my spear! Yet where my sisters are known throughout the land, I was given a veil and fifteen years of brushing the hair of an un-grateful brat who has no idea how many times death has come for her."

I stumble back at last, reeling at the thought. What was she talking about? What came for me? "Times? This has happened before?"

Micha's eyes flick to the others in the camp. More than one is watch-ing us, even if they cannot hear our words. "We are in the wilds, far from home, sister. We will have a reckoning, you and I, but for now, you will obey."

8

THE FAMILY BUSINESS

"Easy now, Darin," Hary says. "You want to lure him out, not rile him up."

My lips are dry as they dance across the pipes, but I'm too nervous to wet them. I can hear the coreling coming, smell its stink, but even with my night eyes I can't spot it in the thick trees.

Hary Roller sits on a log in the center of the clearing, keeping a steady accompaniment on his cello. The Master Jongleur is calm, confident, but it's all I can do to keep my hands from shaking as I call to a demon with my pipes.

The mournful tune we're playing is a spell, of sorts. Magic responds to emotion, and nothing stirs emotion like music. My playing is a story, telling the demon I am prey, vulnerable, but quick. I tell it to creep quietly close to take me by surprise.

I don't want any of this, if I'm to tell honest word. It should be the militia hunting the demon, or even Mam. Night, this is Bales' land. Why aren't Grandda and my uncles out here with the hands?

But in the Brook, getting rid of lone Wanderers has become just another chore no one else wants to do, like filling the egg basket and milking the cows. My da was famous for killing demons. Everyone expects I will be, too, once I've had a little practice.

"Careful, now." Aunt Selia hovers protectively nearby in full armor, shield in hand and spear at the ready. Her long gray hair is pulled into a tight bun visible at the base of her helmet as she scans the trees around us and the branches above. "Don't see them till they strike, sometimes."

Fear sweat breaks out above my mouth to mock the dryness of my lips. I don't want to be here. I'd rather be playing my pipes down by the swimming hole, or even weeding the fields. Night, I'd rather read a book. Anything but sitting in the dark trying to call a demon.

But this is what folk expect of the Deliverer's son. They know I have a bit of magic, and want me to use it like my da did, keeping folk safe from corelings. But my magic doesn't work like his did, or Mam's. Despite lessons from as far back as I can remember, I'm no great Warder and I don't like to fight. I can't turn into mist, lift a hay wagon over my head. The only thing I've ever really been good at is playing my pipes.

I thought that would be enough to let folk know I wasn't my da, but Mam wasn't satisfied with jaunty tunes. She skated to Hollow and asked Hary Roller, a Master Jongleur, to come all the way to the Brook to teach me to charm corelings.

When your da saves the world, it can cling to you like a skunk's stink.

A rumbling builds in the boughs overhead, resonating with my playing. I stiffen as the wood demon appears, crawling down the trunk of a thick tree like a possum. Its corded arms are long and sinuous, small body armored in the same rough texture and color as the tree bark.

Hary is not impressed. "Lot of work to lure a coreling that's more stump than tree."

"Don't get swollen," Selia warns. "Give it half a chance and even a stump demon's strong enough to rip any of us in two."

She's right. I can see the coreling's magic shining in the night. Sweat forms on my fingers, making them slippery on the pipes, but my wind is steady as I continue to draw the demon closer.

It can no more see me than I could see it a few minutes ago. Around my shoulders is Mam's Cloak of Unsight. Its wards bend the flow of magic around me, making me invisible to demon eyes. Selia and Hary are similarly protected.

But a demon's senses are as keen as mine. It can smell us in the air. Hear our breath, the creak of Selia's armor, Hary's murmured instructions. It knows we're here, somewhere.

Cautiously, it creeps closer. In moments, I will be in range of its talons. I begin thinking less about the pipes and more about the short bow slung across my back. If I took it off my shoulder now, I'd probably have enough time to shoot the demon before it recovered its wits.

Probably.

Aunt Selia raises her spear, armor creaking as she tightens her grip.

"Not yet, Selia. Give the boy time to practice." Hary's playing gets louder, giving lie to his confidence. He's ready to take over the moment I stumble. I sniff the air, catching his worried scent. Night, he *expects* me to stumble.

Nose like a hound, Mam says. Just one on a long list of ways I'm different from other folk. I wonder what it's like for everyone else, unable to smell what the people around them are feeling, where they've been, or what they've been doing.

The way folk tell it, by the time my da was my age, he'd have picked this demon up like a hen that stopped laying and broken its neck. Me, they expect to lose nerve.

I suck in a quick breath and quicken the tempo, instilling in the demon a sense that its prey might flee. It approaches more aggressively now, seeking the source as I stand and walk it around the small clearing until it has its back to Selia and her spear. So fixed on my music, the demon pays her no mind.

With a flourish I stop playing and throw back my cloak. The stump demon's eyes widen and it bares rows of sharp teeth, tamping its muscles to spring.

Selia is quicker, thrusting her spear with two hands into the coreling's back. Wards on the blade flare as it punches through the demon's armor, severing its spine. The demon gives a thrash and falls to the ground, twitching.

"Stupid and reckless boy." Selia pulls her spear free in a spray of ichor. "What if I missed?"

I try not to think about that. "You never miss."

"Everyone misses now and then," Selia says, but I catch a whiff of pleasure on her scent as she kicks the demon onto its back. It stares at her with glossy black eyes. "Ent dead. We leave it be, coreling will heal even a wound like this in a few minutes."

I nod, taking the bow off my shoulder as she prepares a killing blow.

A growl from above checks her. I've got an arrow strung before anyone moves, but the boughs hide the source as the sound echoes from tree to tree. Is it a single demon moving, or . . .

"Ent hunters anymore." Selia buries her spear in the stump demon's eye, twisting to scramble its brains. The wards on the weapon brighten and I can see the power running along the shaft into her hands and up her arms, filling her with strength. She rolls her rounded shield off her shoulder and onto her thick arm. "We're prey."

My hands start to shake, jostling the arrow I have nocked. I take a deep breath and will them into stillness, but I can hear what Hary and Selia cannot.

We're surrounded.

Hary puts bow back to string, and his cello hums to life. The metal spike that grounds the instrument is silver, infused with demonbone and etched with wards of resonance that amplify his playing. It's said Hary Roller can charm a whole copse of wood demons, but before he can build a melody, he's interrupted by a loud crack.

A huge bough drops from the trees above, branches spread wide like a net. He reacts quickly, but while nimble for his years, Hary carries the weight of eighty-three winters, and cellos ent suited to hurry. He stumbles, the instrument flying from his hand as he falls.

I don't have the kind of magic my da had. I can't fly or destroy demons with a wave of my hand. I can't cleanse the land of their taint for a hundred miles in every direction. Mam says it's because I haven't learned to control my magic, but I think it just came differently to me than it did to her and Da. They got their power from warding their flesh and eating demon meat. I was born with mine.

But I'm fast. *Faster than a skittish doe*, Mam says. Hary has just begun his fall when I catch him, hauling him away from the falling bough. We're buffeted by small leaves and branches, but make it out relatively unscathed.

Selia rushes to my side, covering us with her shield. "Get behind me. Cloaks up."

The words are calm. Efficient. There is no fear in her demeanor, but I can smell it in her sudden sweat.

I throw up the hood of my warded cloak and turn to Hary, only to see his cloak hanging in tatters from the fallen branches.

Two wood demons drop from the trees to stand at opposite sides of us. These are much larger than the stump demon that lured us here— eight feet tall, with thick gnarled armor and long, branchlike limbs. They lumber at us like Solstice trees come to life.

Aunt Selia and I put Hary between us. I raise my short bow and fire. The shot sparks as it punches into a woodie's shoulder, but the demon only roars and picks up speed. The other coreling lunges for Selia. Like a thunderbolt, the wards on her shield blaze to life as she catches the blow.

I fire again as the demon moves in on us, but I'm scared, and my sweaty fingers let loose too quickly. The shot flies wide, but the demon, perhaps remembering the sting of the previous one, flinches anyway. It stumbles and for a moment I have a clear shot at its head. I fire, but its horns are a nest of twisted branches that steal the arrow's momentum, catching it fast before it can penetrate the skull.

As I fumble to nock another arrow, the coreling recovers and swipes the bow from my hands, sending it flying across the clearing. I know I should run as it rears back for a killing blow, but Hary is behind me, defenseless.

Or so I think, but then Hary throws a warded knife, embedding it in the wood demon's throat. It stumbles away, choking and clawing at the blade, but the wards on the handle prevent the coreling from pulling it free. I don't think it's a killing blow, but the creature is out of the fight. I unfasten my warded cloak and give it to the old man to replace the one he lost in the boughs.

There are booms and flashes of magic as Selia and the other wood demon exchange blows, but I've seen this before. For a moment or two they will seem evenly matched, and then Selia will figure out its weakness and the fight will end suddenly.

I think we have a chance, until another two wood demons appear at the edge of the clearing. Farther back, I glimpse more in the trees. I'm so fixated, I don't notice the field demon in the branches above me until it drops.

Fieldies are sleek and flexible, built like two-hundred-pound barn cats. They're designed to race across open plain, but they climb nearly as well as wood demons. I look up, seeing little more than a mass of teeth and claws fast approaching.

I shriek and quickstep out of the way. The field demon hits the ground with a bounce, coming right at me.

I'm fast, but not faster than a field demon, and I've never been particularly strong. The demon outweighs me by at least fifty pounds, but I've always been . . . slippery. I can't dissipate into mist like Mam or the Warded Children. I can't melt into the ground like a coreling fleeing the morning sun. But I can relax, squeezing bonelessly into spaces too small for me, like a mouse pressing through a tiny crack under the door. When I do, my skin and clothes turn frictionless, making it near impossible to get a grip on me.

The demon knocks me from my feet, but I melt away from its scrabbling claws, rolling around in the dirt until I am on its back, hooking my legs over its thighs and wrapping my arms around its throat.

Then I pull my other trick, the opposite of going slippery. I suck in, halving the length of my arms as they become dense with compressed mass. The demon is stronger than I am, but I have leverage, and even corelings need breath. It thrashes and makes choked sounds, attempting to dislodge me, but I'm tougher like this, and hang on in sheer terror as it batters me against the ground.

In time I might strangle the demon, but not before the ones coming out of the trees reach us. I'm tough when I suck in, but I don't want to test it against wood demon claws. Hary throws his other knife, but this one skitters off a wood demon's bark without sticking. The demon seems not to notice as it stalks in.

Selia is still locked in combat with the first wood demon. It moves with surprising speed and agility for such a big, stiff brute. She still appears to be in control, but with more approaching, her advantage won't last.

I give up my hold and go slippery again. The demon immediately twists around to bite and claw at me, but I pop from its grasp like a wriggling fish. I land on my feet and dart back to Hary and Selia, pulling the pipes from my belt.

I raise the instrument to my lips just as the wood demon fighting

Selia swipes upward with one log arm, knocking her shield up and baring a seam in her armor joint. One of its long talons flashes and something spatters my face. I touch my hand to it, fingers coming away wet with blood. Selia's shield arm collapses and she staggers, trying to keep her spear up.

"Aunt Selia!" I don't think as I charge in. The demon has its talons raised for a killing blow, but it glances my way at the sound. It catches sight of me, and its focus immediately shifts.

I raise my hand like Mam tried to teach me, taking all my fear and anger and focusing it into my finger as I trace a heat ward in the air, powering it with my own magic. The symbol flares and the demon flinches with a yelp of pain as sparks fly across its chest, but I don't have the power to set the creature ablaze.

The effort leaves me drained, and I stumble to one knee. We're surrounded now, corelings gathering from all sides, and I've only one trick left to play.

I lift the pipes, desperation lending me focus as I recall Hary's lessons and blow a series of rapid notes, high and discordant, that affect the demons like a schoolmam's nails on a chalkboard.

The approaching demons flinch and take a step back. One of their number lies twitching on the ground, an arrow in its shoulder and a knife in its throat. Another growls with pain at the scorch marks on its chest. I weave these threats into my song—if the atonal sounds can even be called that—instilling fear in the corespawn. It's not enough to drive them away completely, but they keep out of reach, hissing and growling as they begin to circle. I can't play forever, and they know it.

I look to Selia, but Hary is already with her. The old man has pulled a hundred colored cloths from his Jongleur's bag of marvels, knotting a tourniquet. His hands and the bright silks are covered in blood, and I wonder if Selia will die. If all of us are going to die.

"Her arm's nearly severed," Hary says. "We need help, boy, and quick. She'll lose the arm either way, but if we don't get to a Gatherer, she'll bleed to death first."

I look around, not knowing how that's possible. Selia can't walk, and neither of us is equipped to carry her. And if I stop playing for even a moment . . .

My hands are slick with sweat and beginning to shake with fear. I can't play much longer in any event. I scan the clearing, spotting Hary's cello, and point to it with the pipes. He nods, pulling my warded cloak close and putting up the hood. So long as he doesn't move too quickly, he'll be invisible to the demons.

Slowly he makes his way to his instrument, avoiding the probing claws of demons that can smell and hear him as they swipe blindly at the air. Sweat drips into my eyes, but I'm afraid to take my hands away from the pipes long enough to brush it away. I feel my heart pounding in my chest as he finds the cello, but fumbles for long moments looking for the bow.

At last he finds it, and I wait long, excruciating moments as he tightens the horsehair and cleans it of debris. The demons hiss as he is forced to throw open the cloak and sit on the fallen bough, putting the instrument between his legs.

I cast a worried glance at Selia. Her eyes are open, but I can see her lifeglow fading. The air is so thick with the smell of her blood, it overpowers everything else.

A discordant twang makes me shudder, and the pipes slip from my lips. I glance back and see Hary frowning as he struggles to fix a broken string. The demons surge forward, but I resume playing and they start circling again, just out of striking distance.

At last Hary sets his bow, and the cello comes to life. "Go, boy."

I drop the pipes to hang from their strap, running as fast as I can. A demon steps into my path, but I go slippery, sliding past quick as a horsefly.

The demons shriek. I hear them give chase, but I don't dare look. It would only slow me when I need to be swift. Grandfather's greatward is barely a mile away. At a full sprint it's barely a minute, but even without looking, I can hear the field demons gaining on me, and don't know if I can make it in time.

I howl, and fear gives me new strength as I put on speed. The night wind is cold on my tears.

At last Grandfather's farmstead comes in sight, the greatward glowing softly in the darkness.

"*Mam!*" The scream, born of terror, rips my throat. "Mam! Help!"

Before I even reach the farm, a mist rises in front of me, coalescing into the shape of Renna Bales, my mother. Her long brown hair is tied in a thick braid, and she wears a simple sleeveless dress of homespun wool. Her tanned skin is unmarked.

Mam's eyes narrow as I pull up short and she takes in the sight of me. I notice for the first time the blood on my hands, and honestly don't know if it's mine. She looks up, seeing the pursuing demons, and her mouth becomes a tight line. Wards appear all over her body, the flowing script glowing beneath her skin.

They're always there, silver ink waiting beneath layers of dermis. Mam can call them with an act of will, but they sometimes glow when her emotions run hot. It's wise to step lightly at times like that.

Mam slips free the large knife she always keeps at her belt. I know it belonged to her father, but not much more. Harl Tanner died before I was born, and no one in the family ever talks about him.

A pair of field demons lead the chase, but Mam's knife seems to cut the air, leaving a trail of silver fire as she carves a field ward. The charging corelings hit it full speed, flattening like sparrows on a window.

Three wood demons bring up the rear, but the heat wards Mam cuts are quick and precise. She doesn't stumble or lose her glow like I did from the drain, but one by one, the demons are immolated in flames. One of them continues its attack, bashing at her with bark arms all ablaze.

Mam dissolves into mist, and the blows pass through her like smoke as she slips past the burning woodies to face a pair of shrieking flame demons bringing up the rear of the attack. They're no bigger than badgers, but their scales are hard as diamond, and their firespit is hot enough to set stone ablaze.

One stops short, hawking a wad of burning phlegm it spits at her. Mam slaps it aside with the flat of her blade, firespit wards on her hand snuffing the flames like a candle. She cuts a cold ward into the air, and steam hisses from the flame demon's body. Then it begins to shriek as hot scales whine and crack under the strain of rapid condensation.

She cuts a tiny impact ward, and the demon shatters like a dropped plate.

The other flamer leaps at Mam, claws leading, but she bats them away and skewers the demon on her knife. It spits fire but she lifts a hand, absorbing the magic. Her wards brighten in waves coming from the knife's hilt as she intensifies the Draw, drinking the coreling's magic like a glass of lemonade on a hot day.

Ent no place in the world as safe as Mam's apron strings. I sob, realizing things are going to be okay.

"Where are the others?" Mam lets the dead demon slide from her knife.

"In the clearing," I choke. "Selia . . . she's hurt!"

"Show me," Mam says. "Hurry now."

I run full speed for the clearing, but Mam paces me easily. When she hears Hary's playing, she effortlessly pulls ahead to enter the clearing first.

Hary's cello is out of tune, and the dirty bow whines on the strings. It gives his music an air of desperation that holds the demons close, even as the harsh sounds keep them at bay. I can see his hand shaking on the strings.

Aunt Selia lies next to him, limp and pale, her breath shallow. The sight crushes me. Her butter cookies are the greatest thing I've ever smelled, and no matter how many times she caught me stealing them, she never stopped setting them on the windowsill.

Now I can smell her dying, and it's my fault. I'm supposed to be the Deliverer's son, but when demons came, all I could do was run.

"That's enough, Hary," Mam says. "Go on and help Darin with Selia."

"Ay." Hary nods, the bow dropping from suddenly nerveless fingers. Hary sees his hands shaking and quickly stuffs them in his armpits, giving Mam a little bow. "Thank you, Mrs. Bales."

I dash to Selia, and panic when I get a clear look. Her eyes are glassy and wet, half open, staring at nothing. Her skin is pale and cold. I focus, filtering the surrounding noise, and find her heartbeat. It's slow. Weak. Fading. "Mam."

"Gonna be all right, Darin." Mam's gaze is locked on the demons shaking off Hary's spell. They pace back and forth, growling as they work themselves up to attack. "Might want to cover your eyes."

A low rumble forms in the back of Mam's throat, and the demons howl in answer to the challenge. They spring forward, and Mam's wards flare. Hary and I have barely a second to close our eyes and throw up an arm before they become blinding.

The demons in front turn to ash as the light strikes them. Those farther back hit the ground on fire. They shriek and roll about, attempting to smother the flames.

There's a crashing above, and I look up to see stunned demons raining down from the boughs. These, Mam sets to with her knife, doing more damage than even their infernal healing powers can recover from.

The sheer number of corelings is terrifying. Finding a single Wanderer near settled land is uncommon. Two or three is rare. But Mam's killed a dozen so far, and still more turn and flee into the woods. This was never some lone Wanderer. This is a pack.

In an eyeblink, Mam crosses the distance to us. "All right, Selia, let's have a look." Her knife is hot with ichor as she cuts away Hary's makeshift bindings.

Bile rises in my throat as I see Selia's arm. The demon's talons cut all the way through the bone, leaving the arm attached by little more than a flap of skin and some muscle. I choke the gorge back down and it roils in my stomach, burning.

"Tk tk tk," Mam clucks as she lifts the arm, fitting the cloven bone back together. "Hold still, now."

Barely awake, Selia ent capable of much else. The wards on Mam's hands brighten; and the muscles, tendons, and arteries of Selia's arm reach out like grasping fingers, finding their severed ends and weaving back together.

In moments the limb is reattached. Mam slides a glowing finger around the wound, erasing even the scar. Color returns to Selia's skin, and something of its old warmth. Her eyes regain lucidity.

"Be bit weak for a few days," Mam says. "And you'll be hungry as the Core."

"Better than having to cut the left sleeves from all my dresses," Selia croaks through dry lips. "Thank you, dear."

"You all right, Darin?" Mam doesn't wait for me to answer. My body itches as she Draws magic through me and Reads the current.

"Just scrapes and scratches," I say, but she already knows. She knows everything, now. How scared I was. How ashamed I am.

I feel tears coming, and I want to run away before they come, but I ent brave enough with the corelings still out there. I try to take a breath, but my chest is too tight. It's all I can do to choke out, "I'm sorry."

"Whatever for?" Hary asks. "We'd both be in a demon's belly if not for you."

"Only because I ran for help," I say.

"Nonsense, my boy," Hary says. "That branch would have crushed me like a mouse in a trap."

Mam lays a hand on my shoulder. "Sure you did all you could."

"Did I?" I pull away, turning to face her. "Tried my bow, but I was too scared to shoot straight. My heat ward was about as useful as a festival cracker. Tried to hold them back with my pipes, but I was so shaky I could barely play." The tears start coming, and there's nothing to do but to let it happen.

"Everyone's lookin' for me to be the Deliverer's son, but there's no tales of Da leaving folk behind to run for help."

"No one expects you to be your da, Darin," Selia says quietly.

"Everyone expects it," I say. "I can smell it on 'em. They're just too sunny to admit it. And all I ever do is disappoint."

"Ent thinking clearly, Darin," Mam says. "Fightin' does that. It's desperate and chaotic and scary as spit. Gotta make it up as you go, and things don't always work like you planned." She reaches out and takes me by the shoulders. "But you kept your head and got everyone back alive. Runnin' to me ent something to be ashamed of. It was smart. Proud of you."

She pulls me into a hug, squeezing out the last of the tears. I take a full breath at last as she turns to Hary. She Reads him same as me, then reaches out a hand. The old Jongleur takes it, and the ambient magic drifting over the ground rushes into him as she pulls him to his feet. The effect is immediate, straightening Hary's back and adding a youthful spring to his step.

"Thank you," he says.

Mam lifts Selia, armor and all, as easily as she would a babe. "Let's get back to the house."

Mam's wards are bright enough to light our way home. The gold-wood fence around the fields and yard sketches the shape of a greatward. Everyone breathes a sigh of relief when we cross into its succor.

Mam turns, eyes scanning the night, searching for something. When she doesn't find it, she exhales slowly, shedding the excess magic she's been holding. Her wards dim and then disappear beneath her flesh, magic pooling at her feet before being sucked into the greatward, strengthening its protection.

"No one leaves the greatward till sunup," Mam says. "Come on inside and I'll put the kettle on."

GRANDDA JEPH ADDED to his farmhouse over the years, and let me have the new attic as my room—as far as possible from the bustling commons two floors below. Still, I can hear every quiet word as adults talk down in the kitchen over tea and Mam's butter cookies, which have never been as good as Selia's.

It feels like trying to recall some terrible dream as I listen to Aunt Selia's account of what happened, focusing mostly on the wood demon she fought.

"Faster'n any woodie had a right to be," Selia says. "Fought smart. Knew how to get around the wards on my shield and armor. And they were waiting for us. It was a bushwhack."

"Could be a mimic riling them up," Mam suggests. "They're cunning, and lesser corelings obey them."

Aunt Selia once told me how she fought a mimic demon before I was born. I had nightmares for a month after. Mimics were shape-shifters. Smarter than other demons, they would learn their victims' names and then take the form of someone they trust, calling for them to step off the safety of the wards.

"Cunning demon wouldn't set a trap next to the rippin' Bales family farm," Selia says. "Plenty of isolated farms with nothing but wardposts around the fields. Why hunt next to the strongest greatward for a hundred miles?"

"A mind, then," Mam allows. "Testing our defenses, or . . . lookin' for something."

"Or some*one*," Selia adds.

"Ay," Mam agrees, but she doesn't elaborate.

She doesn't need to. Mimics can pretend to be someone you know, but minds can take a body over completely, turning folk into puppets. They were the generals of the demon war, at least until my da killed them all.

"You think he's back?" Selia asks quietly. I don't know who they mean, but I can't ask from two floors up, so I listen carefully, hoping for a clue.

"Din't say that," Mam says. "Might just be a juvenile mind that escaped the purge."

"Even a young mind demon ent 'just' anything, Renna," Selia scoffs. "Last one to come to the Brook nearly tore us apart. Town was in flames before it was done, folk turning on their neighbors and thinking it righteous."

Mam makes a spitting sound. "Brook's always had that problem, Selia."

"Can't deny it," Selia said. "Folk gossip and judge and don't always do what's right. But when the night is darkest, we always stand together. If there's a mind looking for you, the Brook—"

"Will be safer with me and Darin far away," Mam cuts in.

9

·

THE BUNKER

I T'S NOT QUITE dawn when there's a knock at the door. I haven't slept at all, and I'm not alone. Hary is dozing in the common, but Selia's been to the kitchen, and the house is filled with the smell of fresh butter cookies.

"Ent a good night for folk to be out and about," Mam says, heading for the door.

I'm out the window and onto the roof before she gets there, peering down to see who it is. I drop down next to Stela Inn just as Mam opens the door.

Like most Warded Children, Stela is covered in tattoos, her hair cropped short and her clothing little more than scraps. "Darin!" She grins when she sees me and tousles my hair. "Must've grown four inches since I saw you last!"

"Stela!" Mam holds out her arms to embrace her. Stela is leader of the Warded Children, but even she answers to Mam. The Children worship Mam, and her affection is real in return.

But then Mam's head tilts. "What's happened?"

"Demons struck a group of children on borough tour tonight," Stela says.

"Night." Mam spits over the porch rail. "Anyone killed?"

"Ay," Stela says. "Ella was lured off before they struck. She cleared the lot when she returned, but several tourists were killed, and others crippled. And that ent all."

"Ay?" Mam asks.

"Princess Olive was in the tour group," Stela says.

I start at the name, and feel a panic rise. It's been years since I last saw Olive, but we've known each other since we were in nappies. If she's hurt . . .

"She all right?" I hear the worry in Mam's voice as well.

"Ay," Stela says. "Micha was there to protect her. Ella left Olive and the others in her care."

Micha? I must have misheard. Hard to picture Olive's meek, veiled nanny being much good against corelings.

"She left?" Anger builds in Mam's normally patient voice. "Demons tried to kill Olive rippin' Paper, and Ella . . . *left?*"

"Told Micha she needed to hunt the remaining corelings," Stela said. "And that you needed to be told."

"Idiot girl!" Mam snaps. "Then why ent she here instead of you?"

"Ella ate demon meat, Mrs. Bales," Stela says. "Hunted for hours after she left Micha. Ent in her right mind. Acting crazy. Violent. You know how it gets. Barely got a rough of the story before she started causin' trouble. Took five of us to haul her into the Bunker."

"Corespawn it." For a moment, the wards beneath Mam's skin start to glow, but then she takes a deep breath and they fade once more. "Too close to dawn to skate back now. Gonna have to wait out the day."

As THE SUN slips below the horizon, Stela fades to mist and disappears. Mam holds out her hand. "Come along, Darin."

She smells angry. Regretful. Impatient. All things I've smelled before—but this is the first time Mam has ever smelled afraid. Stela's news has shaken her even more than the attack by Grandda's farm. She's eager to return to the Children and get to the bottom of things.

Still I hesitate, knowing what's to come.

"Now, Darin." Mam thrusts her hand my way again. This time I take it. I feel her will latch on to me the moment we touch, her magic mingling with mine.

"There you are." Mam's voice is low and soothing. "Mam's got you. Don't be afraid."

Yet I am afraid. I can't mist on my own, and I've never wanted to. Misting killed my da.

But I'm helpless to resist as Mam stretches and hollows my body like she's blowing a soap bubble. I want to scream but I have no voice, pulled thinner and thinner until something inside me bursts and I dissipate with her.

Once when I was little, Mam caught me in a mud puddle. I wouldn't stop splashing, so she dragged me out by the arm.

That's what it feels like now—dragged along like a child as she finds the nearest vent and dives down into it.

It's called skating. Magic vents from the Core to the surface along countless natural paths. The most powerful Warded Children can dissipate and slip into a vent, traveling deep underground to where they intersect with other paths leading to faraway places.

I'm wrenched along like a twig in the brook at spring melt. It's a journey through darkness, but I can "see" with my mind, a blur of roots and soil and stone, water and lichen and burrowing worms. We bounce from vent to vent, crossing hundreds of miles in the time it takes to skip across the stepping-stones of a creek.

It's a dizzying, terrifying experience. The trip only takes seconds, but in the between-state those seconds stretch out like tortured hours. As we go, I can hear it—the call of the Core.

The hot center of the world pulses like a living thing. Composed of the near-infinite power that gives the spark of life to all creatures, the Core is a bright pure light, reaching for me with warmth and welcome.

Da touched it, once. It gave him the strength to save the world, but he never came back.

No one who touches the Core comes back.

Mam has ahold of my essence, but I lock my will on her in return, clinging desperately to keep from being pulled down below.

There is nothing to do but to endure. The journey across Thesa to reach the Warded Children would take a month even on swift horseback. In the immaterial state, it's still twilight when we solidify.

The Children have gathered in numbers I haven't seen in years, filling the camp. Stela's Wardskins, the wildest and most powerful faction, lounge in the shadows like cats, half napping but ready to coil and spring in an instant. Others are gathered in prayer, training, or working around the camp, but all stop what they're doing and come to attention when Mam appears.

I grew up here as much as Tibbet's Brook, these people as familiar as family, but something is different tonight. There is tension in the air, a mix of fear and eagerness that sets me ill at ease.

Brother Franq, the Children's religious leader, is the first to greet us. His brown robes are plain, but the sleeves are rolled up to reveal arms sleeved in ward tattoos.

"Welcome home, Mrs. Bales." Franq bows to Mam, then turns to give me a nod. "Peace find you, Darin. You've grown since I saw you last. Soon the sacrament will be upon you."

I look at my hands, the skin of my palms still unmarked. It is forbidden to tattoo wards on anyone before their sixteenth summer, and next year will be mine.

"Sooner the better with corelings scratching at the wards," Stela says. I wonder how disappointed they'll be—how disappointed everyone will be—when I refuse. Fine the way I am. Don't want my body covered in wards, but the Warded Children are apt to take it personal.

"Enough chatter," Mam says, and everyone falls silent. "Need to see Ella Cutter."

Franq bows again. "Of course, Mrs. Bales. This way."

"I can wait—" I begin.

Mam cuts me off. "Ent gonna coddle you, Darin Bales. World's a dark place sometimes, and there's no hidin' from it. Want you to see up close why it's dangerous to eat demon."

So we go into the Bunker. Dug deep into a hillside, it has three long, narrow corridors, each leading to a cell of poured crete reinforced with steel. Children can't mist through worked stone, and the crete is surrounded on all sides with tons of soil and rock. The doors are warded steel worked with demonbone, thick as my hand. I can feel the wards tugging at my magic as we approach. I could slip through the bars, perhaps—I can slip through most any gap—but the wards might suck the life from me.

"Don't like it in here," I mutter.

"No one does," Mam says. "but it's for folk's own good. Don't get sent to the Bunker unless you're gonna hurt someone—or yourself."

Maybe she's right, but there's no denying what the Bunker is— a goal built to hold Children too strong for normal cells. They say it was a real problem once, but I can't remember the last time it was occupied.

We reach the deepest cell, and Stela opens a viewing panel in the door. Inside is Ella Cutter, whose bawdy jokes make everyone blush, and whose laugh sets them at ease. Ella, the most talented tattooist in Thesa.

Ella, sitting chained to the wall, her hands crusted in her own blood. The scrapes have long since healed, but I can see bloody cracks in the crete walls where she struck them. She looks up and meets my eyes, but I see nothing of the woman I know in that predatory stare.

"Open the door," Mam says.

"Mrs. Bales," Brother Franq warns. "Ella Cutter was one of the first Children. She is strong and dangerous—"

Mam waves him off. "Won't be the first time I needed to take a fool gorged on demon meat and dunk their head in the trough. Open it."

"Ay, Mam," Stela says, pulling the lever that unlatches and opens the door. Even she doesn't want to touch the door itself.

Mam doesn't hesitate, entering the cell and leaving the door open. She approaches Ella directly but unhurriedly. "Evenin', El. How you feelin'?"

Hunched against the wall, Ella lifts her head to meet Mam's eyes. Her ward tattoos glow and pulse with power. "How'd you feel, if you saved a dozen lives and got locked away for it?"

"Ent how I heard it." Mam continues to approach. "Heard you left your post, and a lot of kids died for it. Heard you left Olive Paper out in the naked night because you were drunk on demon ichor."

There is no anger in her voice. No judgment. Just simple fact. Ella bows her head, but I can see her magic gathering. Doubtless Mam sees it, too, but she keeps approaching.

Ella is a blur as she springs, leaping as soon as Mam comes in range of her chains. She bares teeth still stained black with ichor, reaching out with dirty, jagged fingernails.

Mam is ready, catching her by the wrist and pivoting, putting the heel of her hand to Ella's throat. Mam's wards appear on her hands, glowing fiercely. Ella yanks and thrashes about, but Mam holds her steady as a lamb for shearing.

"Kill you! I'll kill you! Kill . . . !" Ella's wards throb, their glow dimming with each pulse even as Mam's brighten. Ella throws a punch, but Mam diverts it, sweeping the younger woman into an embrace, more of her wards flaring as she continues to drain Ella's excess magic.

And then they sink to the cell's smooth crete floor, Mam holding Ella tight as she cries.

"Din't mean it, Mrs. Bales," Ella sobs. "Din't—"

Mam strokes her hair. "Ay, don't give it a thought. You're a good person, Ella Cutter. I was in your shoes more than once."

Ella nods, sniffling, and Mam gives her a moment to compose. "Need you to tell me what you saw. All of it, no matter how unimportant a thing might seem."

"Didn't recognize Princess Olive," Ella says. "Just looked like a boy with a bright aura. I could see her friend was a girl pretending to be a boy, but din't think it was my business. Ent seen Selen Cutter since she was knee-high. Don't know I would have recognized her even if I'd looked closer. Wasn't till Micha showed herself that I put it together, and by then I . . . " She sobs into Mam's breast.

"Weren't yourself," Mam agrees.

"Demons were smart," Ella says. "Killed a pack of nightwolves not far from camp to lure me out for a look, then ambushed me. Thought I was keepin' the fight from the tour group. Din't think they were the target. Thought I was."

"They'd see the lot of us dead if they could," Mam says. "Ent blaming you for being tricked."

"Two groups," Ella notes. "Both actin' smart."

"Three," Mam replies. "At least. One group to bushwhack you, the other to hit the camp . . . and the group that tried to kill Darin last night."

Ella gasps, looking up at me with fear in her eyes. I can see her scan me up and down, making sure I'm all right.

"I'm fine, Ella," I tell her. "Safe and sound."

"Thank the Creator," Ella breathes.

Mam puts her head under Ella's arm, helping the woman to her feet. She wobbles, weak as a kitten, but her scent is relaxed.

"Send scouts," Mam says as she exits the cell. "Groups of three at least. No one goes out alone. Find Olive, see her home safe, and look for other signs."

"Signs of what?" Stela asks.

"Signs he's back," Mam says.

"Who?" I can smell the tension the question brings to the others, but no one answers.

"What will you do?" Brother Franq asks.

Mam sighs. "Gonna need to visit Miss Prissy Perfect."

10

TROUBLE

W E DRAG THE wounded on litters, carrying them over the roughest terrain. Micha sets a brutal pace that I fear will be too much for the weakest of our group, but there is no choice. Selen left hours before dawn, running with full weapons and armor. Even if she encountered no demons, it was twenty miles to Pumpforge along unfamiliar ways with only her helm's wardsight to navigate.

If she made it, help is surely on the way. If not, no pace Micha sets can cover the distance before sunset without abandoning the wounded.

What would Mother do, if faced with such a choice? Abandon her charges to save those she could? Or stay to protect them, with the likeliest outcome their collective destruction?

I don't need to wonder. The history books are filled with the answer. Mother never left her patients.

My resolve tightens, and I nod to myself. Neither will I. If we don't make it back before nightfall and the demons come, they'll need to kill me before they reach the others. The chance to fight and die is more than I deserve. I brought this on everyone. The dead, the wounded, the terrified and grieving, all my fault. Because I was stubborn. Because I thought I knew better than Mother and broke her trust. And Micha's. And Wonda's.

Maybe it's better to die on coreling talons than face them after what I've done.

But it isn't meant to be. We crest a rise and see Captain Wonda and the Hollow Lancers galloping our way, followed by the royal carriage and wagons from Pumpforge. Selen, out of her armor and looking like herself again, rides behind Wonda on her massive Angierian mustang.

The sight of them is such a relief I sob as Lanna and the others give a cheer. She moves to embrace me, but I step away, not wanting to be held. Not deserving it. I poisoned Captain Wonda, and she is going to be furious.

Indeed, we can hear her shouting long before the words are clear, giving orders to her men and urging them to even greater speed.

"Olive!" Wonda cries as they draw close.

"Olive?" Lanna wonders aloud. I look at her a little too sharply, and she tilts her head at me.

I'm saved from that look as Wonda gallops right up to me before reining in. She leaps nimbly from the horse's back and comes at me in a rush. I flinch, expecting a blow and knowing I have it coming.

But Wonda throws her arms around me in a crushing embrace. "Night, Olive, thought we lost you." She shudders, and I realize she's weeping. I didn't think that was possible. "Gonna be all right now, I promise."

The soldiers quickly load the wounded and usher the others into the wagons. Wonda holds the door to Mother's armored carriage, and I have a feeling that, once it closes, I'll never see Lanna and the others again.

I turn and see Lanna has come to the same conclusion. She comes over and I stiffen, but she only smiles. "I kissed Princess Olive? Guess it was my lucky day."

I blink. "You're not upset?"

She surprises me by leaning in and kissing me again. As before, her mouth is soft, but there is a hunger to it. "You saved my life. You can have all the kisses you want."

Wonda coughs, but she averts her gaze, saying nothing. Through the carriage window, Selen looks like she's cheering.

"Take it off," Lanna says.

"What?"

"The helmet," she clarifies. "Take it off."

She deserves that much. I lift the wooden helm, suddenly conscious of my sweat-matted hair and dirty face.

"Not exactly how you imagined the princess of Hollow, is it?" I ask.

Lanna's smile widens. "It's better." She spreads her skirts and dips into a curtsy, then turns and takes her place in the last wagon.

THE DUCHESS RECEIVES us in the small audience hall—the room Mother uses when she wants to privately intimidate visiting dignitaries. The raised dais for her throne means that, sitting or standing, she is always looking down at supplicants. She has her warded spectacles on, and blackout curtains are drawn over the windows. She is Reading my aura even now, and Creator only knows what it is telling her.

She isn't alone on the dais. General Gared stands behind her right hand, arms crossed, his scowl flushed red as he glares at Selen. No matter what trouble she's gotten into, I've never seen the general angry at his daughter, but he is angry now.

I wilt under the scrutiny, missing the anonymity of my wooden helm and armor on the tour, but the price was too high.

"What in the Core were you thinking?!" the duchess demands.

"It was my idea . . . " Selen is ready, as always, to put herself between me and danger. Mother turns a cold glare her way, and I know that this time I cannot allow it.

"No," I blurt before Mother can speak. "Selen aided me, but it was my decision. I was the one who brewed the potion and put it in Wonda and Micha's tea."

Mother's lips draw into a hard line as she returns her glare to me. I shrink back in fear, but then Micha steps forward. She is back in the loose black robes and headwrap I have always known, obscuring the warrior hidden within. She kneels before the dais, placing her hands on the floor, eyes down, much as the *khaffit* in the market.

"The failure was mine, mistress," Micha says. "My spear was lowered to threats from within. I should have noticed the poison in the tea sooner. By the time I did, Wonda vah Flinn had drunk too much."

"But you noticed it before Olive left?" Mother asks.

Micha lowers her head further, touching her forehead to the floor. "Yes, mistress."

"So you *could* have stopped her," Mother snaps. "You *should* have stopped her."

Micha keeps her hands and eyes on the floor. "Princess Olive barred her door from within. I could not prevent her from escaping without breaking my cover."

Cover. The word is a stark reminder that Micha has been lying to me for my entire life. That my gentle nanny was always a living weapon. I knew she was Mother's eyes and ears in my life, but this is something out of an espionage novel.

"I thought it better to follow," Micha continues. "Protect her if needed, let you punish her later if not. There had not been a demon sighting on the tour in a decade. I decided it was best to let the princess . . . assert herself."

Let. My hand curls into a fist. The one small taste of freedom in my life, and it was just another lie. A lie paid for in blood.

If Mother was angry before, it was a gentle rain compared with the storm her face becomes. Her next words are snapped in Krasian, and sharper for it. "It is not for *you* to decide what is best for *my* daughter, Sharum'ting! It is for you to keep your oath and obey."

"Yes, mistress." Micha presses her forehead to the floor. "You may punish me as you see fit."

"I'm not interested in punishment, Micha," Mother snaps. "I'm interested in hearing why it won't happen again, but that is for a later conversation."

Micha shudders ever so slightly, and a bit of sympathy returns. Mother's "conversations" are worse than any punishment.

Micha rolls back to her heels and puts a fist to her heart. "Your will, mistress."

Mother turns her withering gaze back upon me. "But none of this changes the fact that you lied to me, Olive. You poisoned Wonda! Night, you could have killed her if you'd gotten the dosage wrong! And you would have done the same to Micha. You disobeyed a direct command and snuck off, putting your own life in danger."

Every word is a lash that strikes harder because I know they are true. What have these people ever done, save protect me?

"Now six children are dead," Mother continues, "and seven more will carry injuries for the rest of their lives."

I remember every wound as I assisted Micha's healing, every body we had to identify from savaged remains. I think of Gyles and his circlet of flowers. Cayla and her fiddle. Tam, Oren, Boni, Elexis . . . "I'm sorry, I . . ."

"I don't want to hear it!" Mother barks. "Their blood is on your hands, Olive."

It was. Literally, though that isn't how Mother means it with me scrubbed and powdered and back in a dress. She means it's my fault. My fault the demons struck. My fault my friends are dead.

But is it?

Mother is still shouting, but I'm no longer listening. I turn away seeing Micha still kneeling on the floor. Face covered by her veil.

"Olive Paper, you look at me when I—" Mother's shriek cuts off as I turn back to her and stomp my foot down hard, shattering one of the floor tiles.

Silence follows the crash, as Mother and I lock stares. I can feel the tears streaking my makeup, and they just make me angrier. "Yes, I made a bad choice. But maybe I wouldn't have, if you hadn't kept me in a cage and fed me lies."

"Don't be ridiculous," Mother snaps. "All I ever did—"

"Was protect me," I finish. "By putting a killer in my nursery and never telling me. By keeping me from ever seeing the lands and people I am meant to rule. By telling the world a lie and forcing me to live it."

"Ay, what's she talking about?" General Gared asks when, for once, Mother doesn't have a response ready.

"It's a secret," I say. "Mother has them from everyone, it seems."

"*Enough*, Olive." I expect Mother to be angry. Part of me *wants* her to be angry, to force a confrontation. But instead she massages her temple, sounding suddenly tired. "You've made your point. Go to your chambers. You and Selen are confined there until I figure out what to do with you. I'll have meals sent up." She taps her spectacles. "Try to sneak away again, and I'll know."

She'll be using her magic to spy on me, she means. While I am locked away from the world.

Nothing is different. Nothing *will* be different, if I don't force a change.

But suddenly I am tired, too. The nausea is subsiding now that I've vomited my anger up. I don't want to fight anymore.

So I take the offered retreat, turning on my heel and striding out with my head high for once. Selen follows, but Micha remains kneeling on the floor. I catch one last exchange before the doors shut behind us.

"Report, Sharum'ting."

"There can be no doubt, mistress," Micha says. "The *alagai* were hunting Princess Olive."

IT WAS EASY not to think about them, when we were fighting for our lives. When Micha turned my world upside down. When we were marched home to the duchess like criminals to the magistrate. When I could still feel Lanna's kiss on my lips.

But the duchess was right about one thing.

Their blood is on your hands.

After long weeks I am back in my rooms, the only place I've ever felt truly safe. My beautiful creations stand guard around the room, mannequins modeling fashion for various activities. They're meant to remind me that I can be anything, and on most days it works.

Today all I can see are unmoving bodies, strewn around the room. People I had only just begun to think of as friends, torn apart because of me. Because the demons came for me, and the folk of Apple Hill got in the way.

I move to the window, but it is no better. The trees in the garden remind me of wood demons stalking the camp, breaking bones and rending flesh. One lifted Elexis high in the air so all could witness what it did to her.

"Sweep it off!" Selen gives me a shove. "Ent your fault."

The push is enough to send me off the bench if I am not quick. Catching my balance forces my mind back into the moment, and I grasp it like a lifeline, turning to face Selen.

"How is it not my fault?" I demand. "You had permission to go on the tour and I didn't. I went anyway and now people are dead."

"Demonshit," Selen snaps. "Could just be a pack of corelings that found its way from the wilds and saw a target. Might have attacked us anyway."

"Micha said they were hunting me," I say.

Selen shrugs. "Maybe Micha doesn't know everything. Like you said, she ent exactly been honest with us. I don't know who she is, anymore."

"There were dozens of tour groups," I remind her. "Why ours? Why lure Ella away first?"

"It's thin, ay," Selen admits. "But no one knew you were stepping off the ward until the moment it happened, and you covered twenty miles in daylight. If the demons were hunting you, how did they find us so quickly? It's just as likely they were going to attack a tour group this year, one way or another."

The words make sense, but I know them for what they are. An excuse to retreat from blame like I retreated from the audience chamber. To not take responsibility for what happened. I shake my head. "Mother tried to warn me. She shouted it, but I wouldn't listen. If I'd just stayed at the inn—"

"It doesn't ripping matter, Olive!" Selen snaps. "You didn't kill those people. Demons did."

"Because I was stupid enough to step off the greatward," I say, and Selen throws up her hands.

"Stupid is right," a voice cracks behind us. We turn as one to see Grandmum Elona.

"Corespawn it," Selen growls.

"Oh, you'll know what a trip to the Core is like when your father and I are done with you, girl." Elona points to the door. "He's waiting in the Goldwood Room. Run along, now. I'm going to have a word with Olive and join you after the shoutin' dies down."

I've never known Selen to back away from a fight with her mother, but this time she puts her head down and hurries out of the room without a word.

Elona peeks in the hall to make sure she's gone, then closes the door behind her with a cackle. "That girl will glare at me through a whole switching, but tell her Da's disappointed, and she melts like fat on a skillet."

Grandmum has a wide smile as she comes over to join me on the bench.

I blink in surprise. "You're not . . . mad?"

"'Course I ent mad," Grandmum laughs. "Kinda proud, I'm to tell honest word. 'Bout time you two showed some spine. And dressing up as boys to get around your mam!" She slaps her knee. "Expect it was a good look on Selen. Girl never was at home in a dress."

Grandmum shakes her head. "Always expected Selen to be the filly and you to be the stallion, but it turned out the other way round."

"B-but . . . " I'm stunned and strangely proud to have won Grandmum's approval, but it feels undeserved. ". . . I poisoned Wonda."

"Phagh." Elona waves an imaginary smell from the air. "Wonda Cutter needed to be taken down a notch. Strong as a tree, but with a head full of wood. Been entirely too proud of herself since the war, but all she's ever really done is break bones for your mum."

I've never seen Wonda fight outside the practice yard, but I know how loyal she is. If Mother ordered her to break a bone, I have no doubt she would do it and sleep well, never feeling a need to ask why. It's hard to imagine Mother ordering anyone's bones broken, but after learning about Micha, I'm coming to realize I don't know anyone as well as I think.

I cast about for answers to satisfy my own question. "I broke the rules, and now people are dead."

Grandmum reaches out and puts her hand over mine, squeezing gently. "Rules are like the privy, girl. They keep us feeling civilized, but they get too full of shit if you don't empty the pot now and again. The only rules your mum followed in her whole corespawned life were ones she meant to follow anyway. Creator knows I'm no better. Paper women make their own rules."

"Then why did you yell at Selen?" I ask.

"Phagh!" Elona waves again. "She's a Cutter, through and through.

Wouldn't believe she was mine, I hadn't squeezed her out myself. And for once, her doting da really *is* disappointed. I'd be an ill mum if I deprived her of *that* life lesson."

"So I'm not in trouble?" I ask.

Elona's bark of laughter startles me. "'Course you're in trouble! Whole mess of it. Lay odds your mum ent had a real visit to the privy in days. She'll take it out on anyone dumb enough to cross her before her bowels unclench."

She kicks her feet out, making a show of putting her hands behind her head. "Best part is, I don't need to do a corespawned thing. Just sit back and let Gared and Leesha handle all the punishments."

"You're enjoying this," I accuse.

Grandmum shrugs. "Ent my backside. Gettin' in trouble is part of growin' up, girl. But punishments end, and I'll wager your mum will show you a bit more respect on the other side. She's angrier at herself than you right now."

"Impossible," I say. "Mother's always right, isn't she?"

"Not this time," Elona says. "She should have prepared you better and she corespawned knows it. Even I warned her. Gonna enjoy sayin' 'I told you so.' "

"Prepared me for what?" I ask. "Are you saying it's true? The corelings are hunting me? Why?"

"Ent some great mystery, Olive," Grandmum says. "Your parents did as much to hurt the corespawn as anyone alive. Don't need to hunt far for reasons why demons would want to hurt back."

The matter-of-fact way she says it hits hard. "That doesn't make me feel any better."

"I'm supposed to make you feel better?" Grandmum chuckles. "Guess I missed the Messenger on that. I'm not the one to tell you what you *want* to hear. I'm the one you can trust to tell you what you *need* to hear."

She's relaxed and laughing, but still the words send a chill through me. "And what do I need to hear?"

"That the time for secrets is over," Elona says. "Half the duchy saw you running around dressed as a boy, kissing hayseed girls."

"Half the duchy?!" I sputter. "There were barely a dozen—"

"Each of them will tell a dozen more," Elona cuts in, "and those will all be bursting to tell another twelve. Trust me when I tell you, gossip runs faster than a horse at gallop."

"And from that they'll guess Princess Olive has . . . ?" I trail off.

"A pecker?" Elona laughs. "'Course not. But it puts their heads in the right space to hear it, and a couple summers to chew on it before you need to start thinking about getting promised."

I had feared Grandmum would blame me for the ones who died on tour, but this is almost worse. Elona still has her feet up, but I've never felt so afraid.

"I can't do that."

"Ent gonna be easy," Elona says. "Your mum wasn't such a coward, she'd have done it long since. Sorry to say it's on you, now."

"Why?" I demand. "Why's it anyone's business what I've got under my skirt?"

"Because it's a ticking clock," Elona says. "Even if you never sprout a hair on your chin or an apple in your throat, what will you do on your wedding night?"

She's right, of course. Grandmum has a way of knowing what a person is most afraid of and shaking it in their face. I clench my eyes, but it's too late. The tears are already falling.

"Ay, now, don't go ruining your powder." Grandmum is on her feet quick as a cat, whisking a silk kerchief from somewhere in her bodice to dab at the droplets before they can streak my face. "Didn't mean it ill. Just mean you're carrying a weight you don't need. Old hag I worked for used to say, *Let others determine your worth, and you've already lost, because no one wants people worth more than themselves.*"

"Easy for you to say," I tell her.

"Had more than my share of scandals over the years, girl," Elona says. "All us Paper women do. You were a scandal before you were even born. Your mum was courting the prince of Angiers while carrying the Demon of the Desert's baby in her belly. Does it look like it cost her any power when folk found out?"

I shake my head. "I don't care. I'm not you and I'm not Mother. I can't just . . . "

"You're scared. I get it," Grandmum says. "But you need to ask yourself if what you're scared of is worse than what you've already got."

"What do you mean?" I ask.

"That tight bido can't be comfortable, girl," Elona says. "When a scandal's hidden, it eats you from the inside trying to keep it that way. Once it's out, it ent your problem anymore. It's everyone else's."

She presses the kerchief into my hand. "Dry those eyes before they get all puffy."

She turns, gliding for the door. "I've given Selen enough of a head start. Gar should be yellin' by now and I don't want to miss that."

She pauses, looking back. "Don't you go tellin' that girl I'm proud of her."

"Of course, Grandmum." I loop an imaginary button on my lip. Elona winks at me, and is gone, leaving me alone for the first time in weeks.

I go to the door and lock it, then I sink to the floor with my back to it, at last letting all the sadness and anger and pain come rushing out with no thought to my paints and powder.

I I

MICHA'S LESSON

"So she ent mad?" Selen asks again from the bed.

"Said she was proud of us," I say, and I believe it. I don't know how long I cried for, but Grandmum's talk left me feeling better when it was done.

Selen shifts on her stomach, unable to sit or lie on her stripped backside. "Got a funny way of showin' it."

"A sore bottom will soon be the least of your worries, Selen vah Gared." We both look up, startled at Micha's sudden appearance. Where did she come from?

"Need to start barring that door," I mutter.

"No bar can stop me, sister," Micha says.

"What makes you so special?" I ask.

Micha holds out a hand, helping Selen to her feet. "That is what I am here to teach you. Come with me. I have permission to escort you from your chambers."

"I can barely walk," Selen groans.

"Tsst." Micha's hiss is dismissive. "Your honored father did not so much as break the skin. Pain is only wind. Bend and let it pass over you."

I start for the door, but Micha moves deeper into the chambers instead, coming to a wall with a colored mosaic ward circle. Micha presses one of the stones, and it sinks into the pattern with a barely audible click, as she presses another, then a third. No magic here, just hidden mechanics allowing Micha to push the entire wall inward. It swings silently back, revealing a darkened stairway.

Selen gapes. "That's been here this whole time?"

"Of course." I hide my sudden fear, but make no effort to hide the anger in my voice. "Everything else we know is a lie. Why should my own rooms be any different?"

Nevertheless, there is an excited tension in my muscles as we descend the secret stair. A fortress in itself, the underkeep holds stores enough to last months of siege, and protects warded tunnels leading to other parts of the capital, but I don't recognize the section Micha takes us to.

"I grew up in a place much like this." Micha leads us down a dark stone corridor to a heavy goldwood door, reinforced with steel. "It is fitting that I show it to you now."

We enter a large, circular room with a high domed ceiling supported by wooden beams. As Micha closes the door, dim lamps cast flickering light on dozens of weapons hung from the wall. Spears and shields, bows and staves. Scythes, chains, and throwing glass, all artfully arranged. I can smell the oil, see the sharp points and weighted bludgeons, and I know these are no mere decorations. At the center of the room, concentric circles of wards are drawn on the polished wood floor.

There is a resounding thump as Micha drops the bar to the door. Selen was staring with similar wide eyes, but now our attention is drawn back to my sister.

Micha lowers her veil, letting me see her face for the first time since the tour. Her brow is a hard line.

'Course you're in trouble! I remember Grandmum's words and Selen's thrashing. Is it my turn? Mother would never sully her hands with violence, and I can't imagine Wonda doing it. Is Micha here as her hand?

"My spear sisters and I were not allowed to speak in our training room." Micha's hands make an intricate series of gestures to accompany her words. "Master Enkido had no tongue, and spoke only with his fingers. In time, you will learn to speak that way as well. Until then, you will be silent in this place."

Selen and I glance at each other, but Micha claps her hands, startling us. "Do not look at each other when I am talking to you." She holds out a fist, nodding it like a head. "This means yes. Do you understand?"

I raise a fist, nodding it—and my head. Out of the corner of my eye I see Selen do the same.

Micha strides toward me, untying the silk belt of her loose black robe. "You were less than four summers when a Nanji Watcher made it as far as your bedchamber. He was caught by surprise when your nurse-maid fought back, but he was skilled, and still managed to give me this." She tugs back the cloth, baring a breast to show me a raised scar running across her ribs. "I was forced to kill him before he could be put to the question. To this day, we are not sure who sent him."

I blink, not knowing what to say. Watchers were legendary warriors, trained in stealth and special weapons, spies and assassins. If one was in my room . . . I shiver in fear.

Micha holds my gaze for a long breath, then steps away to slip off her sandals and lay them by the door. Her silk robe falls quickly once she drops it from her shoulders. It thumps as it hits the floor, no doubt weighted with the armored plates Krasian warriors secrete in their battle robes. Without its formless bulk, my sister is lithe and muscular, a grace-ful dancer with an acrobat's build.

Micha unties her headwrap, spooling the black silk onto her hand with a swift, practiced motion. She ties off the roll and lays it in a cubby on the wall. She folds the robe in quick, efficient motions that muffle any sound of the plates, tying it with her belt to lay in the cubby.

Micha is beautiful, her black hair long and thick—the kind that draws appreciative looks from all sides—but I've never seen her wear it down. No sooner does she shake it free than she begins dividing and braiding. "Remove your dresses."

Selen and I do not look at each other as we comply, undressing and slipping into tan *sharusahk* practice robes folded with the same ritual precision in wall cubbies on our side of the room. Wordlessly, we begin braiding our hair as well.

Micha wears only her bido—a long length of black silk wrapped in a precise pattern over and through her legs—and a similar binding for her breasts. My eyes drift to the textured burn on her toned left leg. It is faded, but does not look like it will ever heal completely.

I remember the night she got it. I was seven, and woke in the middle of the night to a room full of smoke. I sat there, frozen, terrified, not knowing what to do. Then Micha burst in, robe torn and smoldering, covered in soot and ash. She scooped me up like a toddler and went to Selen next, effortlessly carrying us down to the safety of the underkeep while the house guard pumped water through the windows. "The fire . . . " I am so caught in the memory I forget my promise not to speak.

"Was not caused by a maid knocking over a lamp," Micha growls. "Perhaps realizing they could not get close, the next Watcher decided to simply set fire to an entire wing of your mother's keep. I captured him, but he poisoned himself rather than be put to the question."

The cold tone makes me fear the lengths my sister might go to for answers. Who is this woman? Did I take her so for granted that I never knew her at all?

Micha strides to the center of the practice circle. My horror grows with each scar I glimpse on her skin—each no doubt with its own story. How many times has Micha saved my life while I flitted about sewing silks and lace, or fretted over Herb Lore?

Micha kneels, back rigidly straight, head high, meeting my eyes. "I was born Micha vah Ahmann am'Jardir am'Kaji, *Sharum'ting* spear sister. When news reached Krasia of your birth, the Damajah sent me to Hollow to be your guardian and teach you to defend yourself." Micha leans forward, placing her hands on the floor, and drops her eyes. "I have failed in both regards. For that I apologize. Your mother did not trust me at first, and preferred Captain Wonda to instruct you."

"Why didn't she trust you?" I see now that I owe my sister more respect than I have given, but the question is too important to keep silent. I have to know.

Micha rolls back to sit on her ankles, lifting her head and meeting my eyes once more. "She believed I was the Damajah's creature."

"Were you?" I ask.

Micha nodded. "Of course. But I made an oath to your mother, and I have kept it ever since."

"Do you miss your home?" Selen asks.

"Once, but no longer. When I married Kendall, I became Hollow tribe. I am Micha am'Hollow, now, and I would not wish to return to Krasia. Wives without a husband to give them children are not looked upon well there."

"What about your family?" I ask.

Micha shrugs. "My mother is the least of Father's many wives. She is a glorified servant in the palace, and it pains me to see it so. Father taught my brothers to fight and to ride, but had little time for his daughters. He didn't even question it when I went into training and did not see him for years."

Micha flows smoothly back to her feet. "And now it is your turn, sister. None can deny that Wonda vah Flinn is a great warrior, but she held you in your birthing blood, and could not bring herself to impose the discipline a true warrior needs."

Micha assumes a *sharusahk* stance. "But now the enemy has touched you, and found you wanting." She points to Selen, then a spot outside the ring. "Kneel and be silent."

Selen does as she's told, kneeling as Micha beckons me with a curled finger.

I am wary as I move to face her, taking a *sharusahk* pose of my own. Words slip from my lips before I can catch them. "Micha, I'm sorry."

"You will be," Micha promises. "And you will remember the lesson."

I've practiced *sharusahk* for as long as I can remember. It is required learning at Gatherers' University, a slow series of movements that can become deadly when applied with knowledge, force, and will. Many of the women who practice the art do not even see it as a weapon. It is a time of peaceful meditation, separate from the conflicts of the day.

Micha prefers a more practical approach. She starts slowly, with grabs and punches she knows I can block or avoid. I am not naïve enough to counter these probing blows. She will seize the limb if I do, turning the strength of my attack into the force that takes me down.

Every time I avoid a blow, the next comes faster. I parry a punch, and another follows so quickly I barely catch it on my folded arm. The muscle absorbs the impact, but the blow stings and I realize Micha isn't pulling her punches. If I hadn't blocked in time, she might have broken my jaw.

I recover, but not fast enough to avoid her push-kick. Her heel connects solidly with my midsection, blowing the breath from my lungs and folding me in half as I'm knocked to the hardwood floor.

Selen or Wonda would step back after such a blow, giving me a chance to recover and consider my mistake. Not Micha.

"Your mother could have united the Free Cities of Thesa and become queen. She gave up a throne to protect you!" I barely roll aside in time to avoid a stomp of her heel that would have cracked ribs.

The words hit just as hard. Could it be true? Did Mother give up rule to protect me? Why?

"Wonda vah Flinn could have been a general in the greatest army the world has ever seen!" Micha kicks down again. I catch it on my forearms and push back, but she's ready, and pulls away before I can throw her off balance.

"And me," Micha growls as I take the opportunity to scramble to my feet, fists up to cover my head. "My name struck from the histories, my deeds forgotten, all to protect you!" She comes in fast, jabbing stiffened fingers into my ribs. A punch I might have shrugged off, but her fingers thrust into a convergence point, sending a shock of muscle-seizing pain convulsing through me.

Dama'ting Favah taught me there are convergence points on every living thing. Places where their energy flows connect. Increasing or decreasing pressure on those convergences can cause disruptions that ripple through the entire body.

But we studied them for healing, not to strike. I am horrified at the idea. Such blows could cripple, or even kill.

When the fight began, I was resigned. I deserved it. But this . . . how *dare* she? I am her sister, the princess of Hollow, not some enemy assassin.

I bull forward, trying to force Micha back, but she stops me short with a stiffened arm and then drives the heel of her hand into the convergence point on my forehead. "And you don't even care!"

I've never been purposely hit so hard. The impact resounds in my head, light blossoming across my eyes like festival flamework. I hit the floor hard, trying not to black out.

"Get up," Micha growls. "Dodges and parries are less important than learning to recover when struck."

My vision spins and I struggle to find a focal point in the featureless room. At last I find Selen, fists clenched as she kneels outside the circle. She looks ready to leap in to defend me, but we both know that would be a mistake. She might last a few moments longer than I, but in the end, we'd both be bloody on the floor.

"Get up." Micha delivers a short, stabbing kick that makes my stomach seize. I taste vomit in my mouth, and swallow it back down. "One day I will not be there to protect you, sister. Will you lie down and die?"

The derision in her voice strikes harder than her kicks and punches. What was I apologizing for? Not knowing secrets she made enormous effort to keep from me? Wanting a life of my own?

Already I can feel my face swelling, and wonder what it's going to look like later. Paints and powders might cover a bruise, but they won't cover this. What will people say?

I grit my teeth and push off the floor. Micha sweeps my legs from under me before I can set my feet. Her open-handed blow doubles the impact as I strike the floor again.

"Human or *alagai*, assassins will come for you again." Micha stands over me. "When they do, you must be prepared."

She kicks me in the side, knocking spittle from my mouth as I'm flipped onto my stomach. "And that only comes from experience."

She takes my wrist from behind, torquing it back as she puts a foot on my spine, pinning me in place. Pain screams up my arm, and I know she can break it with little effort. I struggle, though it is futile to resist such leverage.

And yet . . . I do. I pull in an angry breath, and new strength floods my limbs. Against all reason I twist onto my back, yanking Micha down to my level. The left hook I throw is close and awkward, but it connects solidly.

For once, Micha is caught by surprise and knocked away. I roll to my feet and set my stance as realization comes to me.

I'm stronger than she is.

Micha recovers quickly, and a smile, low and dangerous, crosses her face. "There it is. Show me, Princess." She sweeps back in, kicking and punching, throwing elbows and knees, always ready to catch my return blows and use them against me.

I know I should be afraid, but I am too angry to care. For once I don't pull my punches, moving with more strength and speed than I've ever dared reveal in the practice yard. Micha snatches at the blows, but they are too fast, my guard too tight. I catch or dodge more of her blows than not, and barely feel those that get through. Micha's face is expressionless, but there is a tightness around her eyes, a bead of sweat on her normally impeccable brow. She's barely in time to parry my next punch, and for a moment, there's an opening.

My kick is a perfect pivot onto the ball of my left foot, right shin flying for Micha's temple with everything I have. I know even before it connects that the fight is over, and somehow, against all odds, I have won. If Micha wants respect, she'll have to give it in return.

But at the last moment, Micha drops beneath the kick, catching the limb. I realize as she uses my own force to throw me to the ground that the opening, her vulnerability, was all a ruse.

She punches raised knuckles into my shoulder joint and my arm goes numb. Another blow to my hip and my leg buckles, dropping me to one knee as I struggle to rise. I lash out and strike her across the face with an open blow from my other hand, but she locks on to the wrist before I can retract it, twisting my arm in ways nature never intended. She rolls and puts a knee into my throat, scowling as she increases the pressure.

I realize how arrogant I have been, even after seeing Micha fight against the demons. I might force a bead of sweat, but she was always going to win this fight.

"The *sharusahk* my master learned from the *dama'ting* is called Precise Strike," Micha says quietly. "Your mother forbade me from teaching it, for it uses the healer's art to harm."

Darkness creeps in at the edges of my vision, and my sudden unnatural strength withers like an unwatered vine. I can't breathe, and my face swells until it feels ready to burst. I kick my feet helplessly, pulling at the knee in my throat with fingers fast going numb.

"But the female fighting forms are powerful, Princess. I will attempt to teach them in our sessions here, though you and Selen have ever been . . . blunter instruments."

Passing out, I slap her knee in submission, but Micha does not relent. "Know that I do this with love, sister."

"Enough!" I hear Selen shout. "You've made your point!"

Micha releases me. I fall limply to the wooden floor as the blackness closes in.

"At last you find your voice, Selen vah Gared," Micha congratulates from far away. "You want to protect your niece? Come show me your mettle."

As my eyes slip closed, I see Selen's feet as she steps into the ring.

I BLINK, AND open my eyes to find Selen lying next to me. She looks so peaceful I would think her asleep if not for her blackening eyes and fat, bloodied lip. My own eye is so swollen I can barely open it.

Micha kneels next to us, eyes closed, breathing slow and even. "You wake quickly," she says without so much as cracking an eye. "You are strong, sister. You will be a formidable weapon when I am through with you."

The compliment makes me prouder than I will admit, but it does not cool my anger. "I don't want to be a weapon."

Micha shrugs. "Neither did I, but it was *inevera*."

Her eyes open now, and she meets my gaze. "You and Selen conspired to poison me. I could claim blood debt, but we have shed demon ichor together in *alagai'sharak*. I am your *ajin'pan*, now. Your blood sister. If we were not as siblings before, let us be so now. I will coddle you no longer."

She holds an open hand to me, and I look at it, incredulous. "You beat me unconscious and expect me to take your hand?"

"I offer you a warrior's trust," Micha says, "if you have the courage to accept it." She snorts. "But if you think me cruel, wait until you see what your mother has planned."

12

BLOOD TIES

I STARE IN THE mirror, studying the bruises on my face. Time and ice have brought the swelling down, but the skin is still puffy and purple. It stings every time I blink and the eye won't stop tearing, which doesn't bode well for concealer.

But the alternative is walking around Mother's keep looking like a tavern brawler. Selen seems not to mind, wearing her bruises with pride. For me, they are a reminder of my shame. I take a pad and load it with powder, wincing as I touch it to my face.

"Tsk. Micha wasn't gentle, was she?"

I look up to see Mother standing in the doorway. She closes the door behind her and glides over to the vanity. "Let me have a look."

I stiffen, but offer no resistance as the duchess takes my chin in a firm hand, tilting my head into the light to better examine the damage.

"It looks worse than it is," she says at last. "The way you heal, it should be gone in a day."

"Lucky me," I mutter.

"You are lucky," Mother says. "Lucky to be alive after that stunt you pulled."

"So you sent Micha to beat me for it, and call it training?" The words are bitter on my tongue. I know they are not fair, but neither was the position Mother put me in.

"This is why I wouldn't let Micha train you in the first place. I thought Wonda could do as good a job without . . . " Mother flicks her hand at the bruise. "But you're right."

I purse my lips, sensing a trap. "Right about what?"

Mother sits back, blowing a tense breath out her nose. "I've sheltered you. Kept you a child for too long. It was selfish of me, and now you're not ready."

The words are more conciliatory than I expect, but still vague. "Ready for *what?*"

Mother walks around the room, running her fingers over the dresses on stands. She lingers by the bed, picking up a cloth doll from Father that has slept with me for as long as I can remember. It was in his image once, though many mendings have lessened the likeness.

"When you were still in my belly," Mother says, "I was summoned to Angiers. One night on the road, I was lured from the wards by a mimic demon that took the form of a friend, calling my name."

A chill runs through me, the flesh of my arms pimpling as she goes on.

"I was alone in the dark. Separated from my protectors. By the time I realized what had happened, I was surrounded."

Mother leans in closer. "They knew me, Olive. They were hunting *me*. By name. And it worked."

I have to swallow a lump in my throat to speak. "What happened?"

"I took out my *hora* wand and I fought as the corelings struck." Mother clutches the doll, her blue eyes going distant as the sky on a cloudless day. "As I drew wards to defend myself, I could feel the magic flowing through me. Flowing through *you*."

Mother's eyes glitter, and I realize they are welling with tears. "You kicked and thrashed in my belly. I didn't know what the power was doing to you. I was afraid I was killing you." She has the doll in a stranglehold now. "But what could I do? Stop fighting? Let the demons have us both? So I kept on, and prayed to the Creator you would be all right. I swore if you were, I would never so stupidly endanger you again."

She turns and meets my eyes. "*That* was why I didn't want you on the borough tour, Olive. I should have told you, and I'm sorry."

"It's all right." I am not sure it is, but I'll say anything to ease the tension. Seeing Mother angry is terrifying. Seeing her in tears is more than my nerves can handle.

Mother suddenly realizes she is clutching the doll and lets it go, surreptitiously wiping tears as she turns her back to return it to my pillow.

" 'Is that why I'm . . . the way I am?" I ask.

"I suspect it's why you're strong," Mother says. "Why you heal faster than other folk. Not just because of that time, but all the times I used magic during the war, starting on the night you were conceived."

Eyes dried, Mother turns to me again, opening her arms. We embrace, and I feel truly safe for the first time in weeks.

"I won't keep secrets from you any longer, Olive," she whispers. "If you're determined to be an adult, I will try to treat you like one, and prepare you properly."

The words do not comfort me. I am not even sure they were meant to.

"STAND UP STRAIGHT," the duchess says. "Don't smile, but don't scowl, either. If it's a small group, make eye contact with the speakers, but then meet the eye of each in turn, continually, as you reply. If it is a larger group, look just over their heads, and it will seem you are making eye contact with all of them at once."

Mother has a thousand rules like these. A constant litany as I follow her through halls and stand a step back from her right hand through countless meetings.

It makes me restless at court, shifting uncomfortably in stylish court gowns I would have been thrilled for an excuse to wear not long ago.

When Mother said she meant to prepare me, I thought it would be secrets of magic, or unspoken tales of the demon war like the one she told in my chambers. Thus far, it has been simply to become the duchess' shadow, listening to an endless parade of petitioners in open court, and the small councils where the decisions are actually made.

I know more than I ever wanted about trade disputes and border patrols and which barons are late with their taxes, but nothing about the demons Mother believes are hunting me.

When I am not at her side, private tutors continue my lessons in the keep so I am always at Mother's disposal. The calls to stand in her receiving rooms are never-ending.

Worse in some ways is the change in how I am treated. Servants I used to fear might catch me running in the halls or spilling on the rug now bow and scrape, whispering fearfully after I pass. Ministers and counselors and royals who command vast powers in Hollow are suddenly falling silent when I speak, and refusing to admit I am wrong, even when I myself realize I am.

Micha was right that I would favor her lessons over Mother's. Our daily sessions in the underkeep are now something I look forward to, if only because being punched and kicked and choked unconscious is preferable to sitting through a meeting of the sanitation council.

Selen, too, has thrown herself into the training. After just a few days with Micha, both of us have advanced enough to see how utterly unprepared we were to face corelings on the borough tour.

Mother is right about one thing. I will not be unprepared again.

"Tsst!" MICHA HISSES as she plaits my hair. "Hold still."

The words are familiar, but the woman saying them no longer is. I'm stronger than Micha, but except for that first fight, I haven't been able to land a serious blow on her in the last two days of secret training, even as my body has become a mass of contusions.

She's left my face alone since that first time, at least. The bruise faded quickly as Mother said it would. I can find no sign of it in the mirror as Grandmum works her magic with the powder kit.

"Today you meet the emissaries of the Majah tribe," Micha says. "To them you represent not just Hollow, but Father and the Kaji tribe. You must look perfect. You must be perfect. And you—"

"—must not trust anything they say," I finish. Micha has repeated that advice a thousand times.

"Do not make light of this, sister," Micha says. "I do not know their intentions, but they will not be honorable."

"How can you know that?" I ask. "We don't even know why, after all this time, they've opened the border."

"They've opened nothing," Micha says. "No Messenger or merchant entering the desert has returned in fifteen years."

"But they are sending their own," I note. "Achman—"

"Is a spy," Micha cuts in.

"You would know, I suppose." I try to keep the bite from my tone, but the words are lash enough.

"I do," Micha agrees. "And if you did more with your eyes than paint the lashes, you would know it, too. Achman was not in Pumpforge by accident, sister, and everyone in that caravan spoke Thesan, no matter what they pretended. Likely they trained for years before this mission."

"What mission?" Selen stands a few feet away, practicing her *sharusahk* forms. "To sell us trinkets in some far-flung borough?" Not subjected to the time at court, she's used the hours of house arrest to hone her skills, and it pays dividends every time my back hits the practice floor.

Micha glances at her. "Your stance is too wide." She turns back to her work with a shrug. "Who can say what the Majah want? But wisdom dictates they send spies across their border to ensure we have not laid a trap for their emissaries."

"Mother would never—" I start.

"Don't be so sure." This time it's Grandmum who cuts in. "Your mum was a hostage once, herself. Sometimes that's how things go."

"All the more reason she wouldn't do it to anyone else," I say.

"It is unfortunate," Micha says, "but often necessary to ensure enemies and rivals keep to their honor. The Majah are not without hostages of their own. They took Father's Majah wife Belina and our brother Iraven with them into the desert all those years ago, to dissuade Father from knocking down their walls when he returned from the abyss."

"Ahmann Jardir let the Majah keep his wife and son?" Selen gapes. "Thought your da was the most powerful man in the world."

"Even the Shar'Dama Ka's power has limits," Micha replies. "Desert Spear was given to the Majah in good faith, and Belina and Iraven are of that tribe. Honor demands he forbear."

She finishes with my hair, as Grandmum puts the finishing touches on my face and removes the cloth protecting my gown.

"Micha." We look up to see Mother has appeared. I wonder if there is some magic in how she keeps entering without making a sound.

"Yes, mistress?" Micha responds.

"The Majah emissaries have arrived," Mother says. "I believe you know them."

One of Micha's eyebrows rises. "Oh?"

"Dama'ting Belina and your half brother Iraven." Suddenly, Mother has my full attention.

"Impossible," Micha says. "They are hostages."

"Fifteen years ago, perhaps," Mother says, "but they are here, now. What can you tell me about them?"

"Be on guard, mistress," Micha says. "Belina was the most powerful seer of Father's *dama'ting* wives, second only to the Damajah, herself. She will have made foretellings on this meeting to seek advantage, and may have other magics about her. It would be wise for you to meet in sunlight to neutralize her powers."

Mother nods. "And Prince Iraven?"

For once, I am excited for a meeting. No doubt the subject matter will remain dull—trade routes or tariffs or something equally tedious—but one of the negotiators will be my brother. Father has fifteen wives and over seventy children, but Micha is the only one of my siblings I have ever met.

"I have seen him fight, mistress," Micha says. "Majah *sharusahk* is legendary, and my brother is a master. Few of our brothers could match his glory on the battlefield. Even disarmed, he is dangerous. Keep Wonda vah Flinn at your side, and post extra guards at the door. If you wish, I—"

"Thank you, Micha," Mother cuts in, "but this is a delicate negotiation. I don't pretend to understand all the politics of your people, but I know enough to see that your presence would be a . . . complication."

Micha bows. "Of course, mistress. But—"

Mother holds up a hand. "I, too, have cast the bones for this meeting. The Majah will ask for something we do not expect, something precious, but I do not anticipate violence."

Micha seems mollified at that, but still she looks wary as she escorts us to the council room, eyeing the Majah bodyguards that wait outside with Mother's house guard.

"Greet them warmly," Mother reminds me, "but you are not to speak during the negotiations. You're here to learn."

"Yes, Mother," I say.

Mother's herald, Kendall Demonsong, is waiting within with the ambassadors as we enter. She wears a fine blouse and breeches in a Jongleur's patchwork of colors, with a few buttons of the top undone. While normal in Hollow, the low décolletage would offend our Majah guests, if not for the scarred lines of demon claws across her breast. Such scars are revered in Krasia, something Kendall, Micha's wife, knows well.

Kendall executes a sharp bow. "Your Grace, may I present Dama'ting Belina and her son, Prince Iraven asu Ahmann am'Jardir am'Majah."

Iraven looks to be in his early thirties, tall and handsome in *Sharum* blacks under an elaborate breastplate of warded glass. He is sleeveless— thick arms corded with muscle and crisscrossed scars.

Belina waits for the door to close, then, among only women and family, she unveils to show a lovely face with the ageless quality of a *hora* magic user—too mature to be young, too smooth-skinned to be old. Krasians tend to be tall, but Belina is shy of five feet, and curvy. Not threatening of stature, but there is something intimidating in her dark eyes.

"Welcome to Hollow, Belina vah Ahmann, Iraven asu Ahmann." Mother's face is porcelain as she steps forward, Kendall passing her a ceremonial chalice. "Share water from our table, and be at peace."

It is a Krasian custom Mother researched carefully, an oath of peace placed upon one of the most sacred things to the desert people—water.

"I accept your water, Leesha vah Erny, Duchess of Hollow," Belina says, taking the chalice and drinking. "There is peace between Hollow and the Majah."

Iraven drinks next, then Mother turns to me. "May I present my daughter, Olive vah Ahmann am'Paper am'Hollow."

"Am . . . Paper?" Iraven asks.

Mother fixes him with the *look*. "I declined your father's invitation to become his *sixteenth* wife, Prince Iraven. Princess Olive is mine."

Mine. The word squeezes me, suffocating. Is that what I am to her, to all of these people? A possession?

"Let us sit," Mother moves to the head of the council table, indicating the seat at her right hand to me, then the one at her left to Belina. Iraven sits beside his mother, then Kendall next to me. Used to kneeling or reclining on pillows, the Krasians sit rigidly in their chairs, taking no support from the backs or arms.

"Tea?" Mother asks.

"Please," Belina says, and I rise from my seat, reaching for the steaming pot on the service at the center of the table.

Another ritual, like the one in Achman's tent. I pour for Mother first, then Belina. The two of them drink, then I pour for Iraven, followed by Kendall. The four of them drink. Only then do I pour my own cup and sit.

"She pours well," Belina notes.

I should. Mother has been teaching me since I was old enough to hold a toy cup. I still might bungle brewing a cure, but I've been able to pour one-handed without spilling a drop since I was six.

Mother smiles. "Tea politics are not so different in the North from those of Krasia, but we're not here to discuss my daughter."

Belina's face reveals so little she might as well be veiled. "We're here to discuss terms for inclusion of Desert Spear in your Pact of Free Cities."

"We would be most pleased to have you," Mother says. "Your husband sent Messengers to Desert Spear to invite your emissaries to attend the signing. I am told they never returned."

She leaves the question unspoken, but Belina answers it anyway. "The Messengers are unharmed, but after we were betrayed, Damaji Aleveran in his wisdom declared the border closed."

"Those men must be returned, unharmed as you say, before any agreement can be ratified," the duchess says. "The pact holds all its signatories to the same peace. Your blood feud with the Kaji must be set aside."

"Peace," Belina agrees. "But peace is not friendship. Peace is not enriching those who have wronged you. Forgoing blood does not mean forgiveness."

The duchess sits back, considering the words. "If you have no wish to move forward in friendship, why sign the pact?"

"Because betrayal by Everam's Bounty does not mean we wish to be cut off from the other Free Cities," Iraven says. "Because the desert is harsh, and fighting *alagai'sharak* in the Maze is costly."

The duchess looks at the prince in surprise. "*Alagai'sharak?* The demon war is ended, Prince Iraven."

"For you greenlanders, perhaps," Iraven says. "But the magic that purged the *alagai* from your lands did not reach across the desert wastes."

"Perhaps not," Mother allows, "but the Maze was designed for warriors without magic to fight back against the corelings. Armed with warded weapons, you should have swept your lands clean by now."

Iraven nods. "For a time, we thought we had. There were harsh battles on our return, but Everam was with us and we were victorious. We lived in relative peace and prosperity for nearly a decade. But the desert is vast, and now the *alagai* have returned in numbers. Without minds to lead them, the sand demons have . . . evolved. They have become cannier, banding together into far-ranging storms that can number in the thousands. If a sand demon storm comes across a village with a gap in its wards, however small, they will find it. Even Desert Spear must raise the defense when one blows our way."

"The corelings are a plague on all that lives," Mother says. "If you require military aid, Hollow—"

"We do not," Belina cuts in. "Forgive me for speaking bluntly, Duchess, but there is always a hidden price to such aid. We will accept no foreign warriors in our lands, and would treat their presence as an act of war."

"Are not all men brothers in the night?" Mother says, paraphrasing from the Evejah, the Krasian holy book that defines them as a people. Unity against demonkind is the defining tenet of the Evejan peoples.

"They are," Belina agrees. "But unlike *alagai*, soldiers do not disappear when day breaks. Brothers can become enemies as easily as they can lower their night veils."

"Then what is it you do want?" the duchess asks.

"Trade routes," Belina says. "Laktonian ships to transport our goods without passing through the territories of New Krasia. Access to Northern markets to buy and sell."

"If what you need is Laktonian ships, why come to me?" the duchess asks. "Why not make contact with the Laktonians?"

"We have." The derision in Belina's tone never reaches her face. "They have no love for Krasia, but it is their largest trading partner, and has an army on their border. They won't risk helping us without the protection of the pact, and everyone knows the North will agree to whatever Duchess Paper decides."

Mother chuckles. "Would that it were so. Still, if what you say is true, I see no reason to oppose adding the Majah to the pact."

"You question our honesty," Belina notes.

Behind Mother, Wonda tenses. Iraven's eyes fix on her. I remember Micha's warning. *Majah sharusahk is legendary, and my brother is a master.*

Kendall's hand slips below the table, no doubt to finger one of the throwing knives I've seen her use to entertain a crowd. She can put one into a gourd atop an assistant's head without cleaving so much as a hair.

But Belina only nods. "You are wise to do so, daughter of Erny. As wisdom dictates we must question yours. The pact must be sealed in blood."

"Blood?" Mother asks. At her back, Wonda has not relaxed.

"Damaji Aleveran, leader of the Majah, has a grandson, Chadan," Belina says. "He has seventeen years, and soon will earn his blacks. We are here to negotiate Princess Olive's hand for him."

I gasp, and Mother's eyes flick to me in irritation. I drop my gaze to the table, trying to center myself. Surprise, anger, fear, and confusion churn to a boil in my stomach as I realize that, like the demons, the appearance of the Majah isn't random.

They've come for *me.*

"That will not be necessary," Mother says after a long silence. "There are other ways to build trust."

"Your forgiveness, Duchess," Belina says, "but there is nothing so binding as blood. It is a good match. Chadan is handsome, heir to an ancient family with abundant wealth and thousands of warriors at their command. Princess Olive would be Chadan's First Wife, with dominion over his household, and her children will one day rule Krasia."

Mother waves a hand at the papers on the table, outlining trade routes and tax proposals. "Was this all a ruse to give Aleveran's issue a claim to the throne of New Krasia?"

"Nonsense," Belina says. "If that was our wish, we would have gone to my husband directly. He would marry his heir, Prince Kaji, to a Majah princess in an instant, if he thought it would reunify the tribes. This is a union between Majah and Hollow."

I clench my fists under the table, as they continue to speak as if I am not in the room. As if I have no say in who I will marry, and why.

Mother frowns. "None of the other cities sealed the pact with blood."

Belina arches an eyebrow. "Did you not, Leesha vah Erny? Hollow would be under Krasia's sandal much as the southland, had you not bedded my husband."

"Ay, you can't talk to her like that!" I snap, drawing Belina and Iraven's eyes to me, even as Wonda reaches for her bow.

The duchess raises a finger at me without looking. I can always tell when Mother is angry, and right now she is furious. "Be silent, Olive."

"The girl pours well, but she is spoiled and willful," Belina notes, sounding like Micha noting flaws in an item before haggling the price. "She has not yet learned her place. Perhaps it would be best to send her away for the negotiations."

I want to punch Belina in her ageless face, but I know it will likely end with Wonda or my brother on the floor, and blood feud with the Majah. I grind my teeth, making no effort to remove myself.

"There aren't going to be any negotiations," Mother says. "I think you have misunderstood Hollow's role in these talks, Dama'ting, so please allow me to make one thing perfectly clear. I will not marry my daughter to settle her father's disputes. There is nothing to discuss or debate. No argument to make or dower great enough. Olive will marry—or not—at her own liberty."

I want to laugh. *Liberty?* From the woman who just told me to be silent? The woman who not long ago was speaking of the army of prospective suitors awaiting permission to approach? I may be safe from this match, but liberty is one thing I will never have.

"The *alagai hora* demand it," Belina says. "If Olive Paper does not join her blood with Majah, Desert Spear will fall."

The words fall heavily upon me. What does that mean? The dice do not lie, but neither is their truth ever completely clear. Will people die if I don't go?

You must not trust anything they say. I hear Micha's voice in my head as clearly as if she were beside me. It is sin for a *dama'ting* to bear false witness against the dice, but that doesn't mean it's never been done.

Mother is unmoved. "If that is so, it will be because you are too stubborn and mistrustful to accept aid offered in good faith.

"Let us adjourn for the day." Mother rises smoothly from her seat, open hands spread with palms showing. "We have assigned your delegation a walled manse for the duration of your stay. There are stables and yard for your wagons and animals, and rooms for you and your staff. Take time to consider—"

"There is nothing to consider, daughter of Erny," Belina says. "The Evejah teaches us there is no trust without ties of blood. Are you certain you will not entertain the match?"

Mother raises her chin. "Not for an instant."

"Then there is no point in continuing these negotiations." Belina rises, as well. "We apologize for wasting your time. Tomorrow, we return to Desert Spear."

"You can't be serious," Mother says.

Now it is Belina who lifts her chin as she draws her veil back over her face. "As serious as a storm."

Indeed, despite Mother's increasingly generous entreaties, the Krasians begin packing immediately, and the next morning they are gone.

13

OLD PLAYMATES

I'M THE FIRST to look up as one of Mam's scouts mists into the Warded Children's camp. There's a hissing noise when they rise out of the ground and begin reassembling themselves. Others can't hear it, but I can.

It's been a week since the attack. Scouts come and go every night, tracking coreling movements and carrying messages to and from the duchess of Hollow. Mam and Leesha were closer when I was little. We spent summers in Cutter's Hollow and winters in Everam's Bounty, the capital of New Krasia, and everyone got on. But then Mam and Leesha had that stupid fight, and we ent been back since.

I'd just as soon not hear the worrying reports, but sometimes my ears are a curse. Mam will barely let me out of her sight, and even when they whisper I catch every word.

Something is building, and the reaction among the Children is a restless eagerness. They polish weapons and touch up tattoos, pacing the camp like demons at the wards.

But I can smell their fear, and their hunger. Ella isn't the only Child with a latent addiction to the rush of power that comes from eating demon meat.

The mist takes the shape of Stela Inn. "She's ready to receive you."

Unnerved, I feel my bladder straining, and step from the camp to find a private spot to relieve myself. As I do, a figure breaks from the crowd, following a few paces back. Ella Cutter.

I try to ignore her, but it's no use. I won't be able to go with her watching.

"Night, Ella," I call over my shoulder, "can I make water by myself?"

Ella puts her hands on her hips. "Changed your wet nappies, Darin Bales, and held you steady while you aimed at the privy. Why so shy now?"

"Already got a shadow," I say. "Don't see why I need another."

"Your mam just wants you safe," Ella says. "Somethin's in the air, Darin. Don't pretend ya can't smell it."

"Ay," I say. "But I ent some city boy never seen a demon. Been goin' out in the naked night my whole life. Give slack on the leash so I can step behind a rippin' bush."

Ella twists her lip, fighting a smile as she turns her back and allows me to take a few steps away to untie my pants.

Mam is waiting as I come back into the camp. She holds a hand out to me. "Come along, Darin."

I swallow my fear and nod, holding my breath as I take her hand. For a moment her magic joins with mine, filling me with love and warmth and fierce protection.

And then she rips me apart.

I wonder if this is what Da felt when he died. Just the sense of being pulled until I can no longer hold on to my sense of self and blow away like a handful of ash on the wind.

But I don't have to hold on.

Mam's got you, Darin. I feel the words more than hear them. And she does. I can feel her will controlling our dissolution, as smooth and effortless as whisking eggs in a bowl. Then it's the frying pan.

Mam finds a magic vent—a natural pathway for magic to seep up to the surface from the Core—and we flush down it like a drainpipe into the dark below, following a vast network of vents at the speed of thought.

We come closer to the Core, but not close. The power at the center of the world is still an immensely distant thing. But here, without sunlight to burn the magic away, everything is saturated with it, humming the call of the Core. A sound resonating in my mind, so beautiful it is nearly impossible to resist. All I want to do is get closer, to snuggle up to it like a fireplace on a cold night.

But get too close, and you get burned. Like Da.

I never met him, but I've got a picture in my mind. He looks something like Grandda and something like his paintings and statues, and nothing at all like me. I think of him diving into the Core, like a wooden doll thrown on the fire. I see him burning, and I scream.

And then I'm solid again, materializing in Duchess Paper's private office.

It's a small, intimate space, but I'm still screaming. I try to stop but it needs to run its course until the need for air forces my body to pause long enough to suck in a breath.

I feel everyone's eyes on me, but worse is what I feel through the bond with Mam.

Pity. Shame.

I pull my hand away and turn my back on the reception, sleeving my tears away before I turn to face everyone.

Their eyes are all down, politely giving me time to compose myself. But I can smell their pity, their embarrassment at having been forced to witness my humiliation. Part of me wishes I had answered the Core's call. Gone down and burned away, just like Da. The song is so beautiful. It can't feel worse than this.

Olive and Selen look at me with the eyes of strangers. I pull in a deep breath and straighten as quick as I can, but the damage is done.

How many times has Mam misted me here, to Aunt Leesha's office? Never made a fool of myself before. But now, when we ent been here five summers, this is how I make my entrance.

Selen and Olive and I used to play Wanderers and Regulars in this very room, hiding in the folds of the banner behind the duchess' desk, or somewhere within the wall of heavy curtains. Nothing has changed.

Duchess Leesha and General Gared stand at the center of the room to greet us, but I barely see them, my eyes drawn to the princesses. Selen and Olive were my first friends, and if I'm honest, I never really made others, because who could compare? Who else in all the world understood me?

But the children I recall bear little resemblance to the women I see. They were always taller than me, but everyone said that would change in a few years. It hasn't.

Olive was always a little vain, obsessed with fancy clothes and hair, but she's mastered the spell since I've been gone. She's everything boys look for in a pretty girl.

But she doesn't smell like Olive anymore. Even from across the room I can smell the wax and dust and colorful herbs in the paint and powder on her face. The scents mix with her perfume into a vapor that burns my nostrils. If I focus on it too long, it will give me a headache that will last for days.

Her gown is pristine, trimmed with lace and wards stitched in silver thread. Thick muscled arms strain her sleeves. A circlet of gold holds back long, lustrous black hair, oiled with essence of flowers.

I am suddenly aware of my own shabby appearance, barefoot in a plain tan shirt and overalls rolled to my shins. Fine for Tibbet's Brook, where everyone's got dirt under their fingernails. Clean even, for the Warded Children, most of whom go weeks or months without a bath.

But here in the royal keep, I look like a hound that chased a cat through the mud. Mam ent much better in her homespun work dress, but she and Aunt Leesha don't much like each other, and she's always taken pleasure in tweaking the duchess' nose.

I glance at Selen, grown much as Olive. Taller and broader, her pale brown hair is woven in a simple braid and her gown is of coarser cloth, but still finer by far than anything in Tibbet's Brook. Her face is blushed from fresh scrubbing, but I smell a remnant of wax. She'd been painted for this meeting, and purposely washed it off.

I smile without meaning to. Selen's mouth quirks in return and she throws me a secret wink that hits me like a punch in the chest. Selen Cutter never needed paints or powders to hit me.

I wink back, and just like that, everything is all right.

General Cutter is the first to break the peace, having decided he's waited long enough to pretend my little display never happened. "Darin! Come give your uncle Gared a hug!"

He lunges forward and tries to sweep his arms around me, like he did when I was five. Like then, I let myself go slippery, sliding out of his grasp.

I don't like being touched.

I remember shrieking with laughter as we played that game. The general is laughing right now. But I'm not five anymore, and I wish he'd just stop.

The duchess clucks. "Do I need to chase you for a hug, Darin Bales?"

She spreads her arms. Mam stiffens, but I know better than to slip this one, and I don't mind hugging Aunt Leesha. The duchess' heartbeat is strong and steady, and she doesn't paint herself like Olive. Aunt Leesha's hands smell of soap, but I catch a hint of fresh soil on her fingers. She's been to the garden recently. Deep pockets in her dress are stuffed with dried herbs, enough to produce any number of remedies on the spot. Her hands are gentle, but they are not soft. They squeeze tight and I feel safe.

I smell Mam's irritation as the embrace lingers. I think Aunt Leesha feels it, too, and we both let go and take a step back.

Aunt Leesha reaches out, brushing back the tangle of brown locks that normally hide my eyes. "My how you've grown. Starting to look a bit like your father."

I know not to argue, but the idea is ridiculous. In paintings, Da is seven feet tall and covered in muscle. Mam says that's all nonsense, but I find it hard to imagine he looked much like me. I'm not particularly tall, or strong. Ent even got a spot of whiskers on my chin. If I'm to give honest word, I'm not much to look at. I toss my head just a little to shake the hair back across my eyes.

"Leesha." Mam steps forward, already smelling of irritation. She gives a nod of respect.

"Renna." The duchess bows to her in turn. Her tone is respectful. Even intimate. But it isn't loving.

"Ay, Renna!" General Cutter booms, giving her the hug meant for me. He lifts her feet from the floor and spins about.

"Gared Cutter, you put me down!" Mam cries, but she's laughing as well, and hugs him tight when he sets her on the floor. "Missed you, too, Gar. How's Emelia?"

The general looks like he swallowed a peach pit at the mention of his wife. "Same as ever."

Mam laughs. "That bad, ay?"

"Olive," Duchess Leesha says. "It's been a few years since Darin visited. Why don't you and Selen show him around while Mrs. Bales and I have tea?"

Olive flashes me a bright smile, but I catch irritation in her scent. I can't blame her. I'd rather stay and listen in on the adults than walk around the keep with her watching me to make sure I don't touch or sit on anything for fear I'll dirty it.

Before anyone else moves, Selen sweeps over and holds out an arm, amusement in her eyes and scent alike. "Come on, Dar. Let's go play Wanderers and Regulars."

I take her arm without hesitation. I'd go anywhere, if it was with Selen Cutter.

AUNT LEESHA'S KEEP is beautiful in wardsight. Most places have ambient magic drifting along the ground like fireflies, waiting for emotion or force of will to Draw it. Even well-warded places always have a bit floating around, like dust in a sunbeam.

But Aunt Leesha's keep is . . . spotless. My eyes run along the wards trimming the walls, lintels, and jambs as Selen leads us down into the underkeep. The symbols shine like lectric bulbs to guide our way—not a speck of energy wasted in the air.

More than that, the wards . . . talk to one another. Power runs along the grid like raindrops down a window, gathering excess magic and allocating it around the keep as the duchess wills. When I had ten summers, it felt like the safest place in the world.

But that was five summers ago. Now the halls run with ghosts. Olive, Selen, and I, hiding, hunting, and chasing one another through these same corridors, laughing all the while.

But now we're acting like strangers. "Aren't we a little old for Wanderers and Regulars?" I ask as we reach an empty landing.

Selen snorts, dropping my arm and rounding on me. She puffs a breath to blow the hair from my eyes. "Demons attacked you, too?"

I blink. "Ay."

"Were you hurt?" The irritation is gone from Olive's scent, replaced by concern.

Suddenly the years melt away, and I realize I've been a fool.

"Just scrapes and bruises," I say. "Was trying to lure a demon out of the trees with my pipes, so Aunt Selia could kill it."

"You figured it out?" Selen asks. "You can use those pipes for more than giving us something to dance to?"

"Darin, that's incredible," Olive says.

Both of them smell . . . proud. Olive and Selen were always the brave ones. I'm faster, but somehow I was always chasing after them. They look at me with new respect, no doubt imagining me in some heroic stand against the demons with my music, like Hary Roller. They don't know how I failed, again and again, nearly getting everyone killed.

It would be easy not to tell them. No one's going to say different. Just a bit of glory, to wash away some of my humiliation in the duchess' office.

But it ent honest. "Ay, when it's one coreling and I've got Aunt Selia standing over me to keep me safe and Hary at the ready to take over if I slip up. But when it was a copse of wood demons trying to kill us, all I could do was run for help."

"It wasn't much different for us," Olive says. "I would have died before I even got my spear up, if not for Micha."

A chill runs down my spine as I remember the attack on Olive was occurring at almost exactly the same time, hundreds of miles distant. It can't be coincidence.

"Micha?" Her words finally catch up to my racing mind. "What did Nanny Micha do?"

"Oh, they didn't tell you, either?" Olive leans in. "*Nanny* Micha is . . ."

"Tsst!" a voice hisses, making me jump. "There is little point in keeping to the shadows, sister, if you are going to blurt my secrets aloud in an open hall."

Instinctively I go slippery as a Krasian warrior slides out of a dark alcove. She is slender and light-footed, but no one's ever gotten so close without me sensing it. Some sort of powder masks her scent. She is of a size with Nanny Micha, but her heartbeat, stance, movements, even her aura, are all different. How can it be the same woman?

But it is. "Hiding from you was always a challenge, son of Arlen." Micha's voice is as kind as I remember. "Come."

She leads us down the corridors to a heavy stone door that opens to a circular practice room. I see wards of silence on the frame as she closes the door behind us. No sound will escape this chamber.

"Welcome back, Darin asu Arlen am'Bales am'Brook," Micha says. "Long have I waited to see the Par'chin's son reach manhood."

Chin is an insult in Krasian. It technically means "outsider"—someone lacking Krasian blood—but in practice it is synonymous with weakling and coward. My father was the first *chin* in centuries to live and fight among the Krasians, earning him the singular title of Par'chin, or "brave outsider."

Asu means "son." Asu Arlen, the Par'chin's son. Micha was always kind to me, but just like every other adult, she doesn't see *me*, just my da's child.

Selen puts her back against mine, measuring my height against hers. She's head and neck taller than me, with Olive not much shorter. "Think he's a few summers short of manhood, Micha."

"A warrior is more than his stature," Micha says. "The *sharusahk* of the Warded Children is revered even among heroes."

The words are respectful, but there is something in Micha's scent. A challenge.

I shrug. "Never liked fighting."

"Neither did Princess Olive, yet fighting has found you both. It would please me to see what training you have. Will you spar?"

"Against you?" The last thing I expected from this visit was for Olive's nanny to challenge me to a fight. I don't think I could ever hit her, and I don't think I'd stand much chance even if I tried.

Micha bows. "It would be an honor, but I meant against one of my students." She smiles. "If your pride can handle sparring with your friends?"

The scent of challenge is clear now. She thinks either of the girls can put me on my back, and looking at them I'm not certain she's wrong. Olive and Selen both return the look, eyes suddenly predatory. They know it, too.

Since we arrived, I've been on my back foot. From the moment I materialized, screaming and crying, to admitting I ran from the demons on Solstice. Olive and Selen will always be my friends, but if I don't catch myself soon, things ent ever going to be the same between us.

I take off the satchel and pipes, setting them safely in a cubby on the wall. "Think my pride can manage."

"Turn your back and close your eyes," Olive orders. "Count to a hundred." I do, and hear the rustling of cloth behind me. I breathe steadily, trying not to imagine the two princesses undressing.

"One hundred." I turn at last and see Olive and Selen waiting in the ring in *sharusahk* robes. I move to face them, bowing.

"The challenge was mine, son of Arlen," Micha says. "Honor grants you the choice of opponent."

Olive and Selen stand cross-armed, reeking of confidence. And why not? Their biceps are thicker than my thighs.

But there's really only one choice, if I want everyone's respect. "Olive."

"First pin wins." Micha gestures and Olive steps forward, a comfortable smile on her face.

"I'll go easy on you," she promises.

"Really think you're gonna win this?" I ask.

Olive throws a laugh. "No offense, Dar, but you don't have a chance."

"Willing to bet on it?" I ask.

"We'll double your money," Selen sneers from outside the circle.

"Ent got any money." I smile. "How about, if Olive can pin me, I'll let you dress me in fancy silk breeches and a velvet coat, like when we were kids."

Olive's eyes glitter at the words. "I have a lace cravat that will look just precious, once we dump a bucket of water over you and drag a comb through that thicket on your head."

Micha hangs back, smelling amused, content to let this play out.

"But if you tap out before a pin," I tell Olive, "you can't powder your face for a fortnight."

Selen laughs. "Now it's interesting!"

I spare her a glance. "And *you* can't wash your powder off."

"Core with that," Selen says. "I ent even fighting."

"Double my money, you promised," I remind her.

Selen puts her hands on her hips. "Fine. Ent like we're gonna have to pay."

Olive claps in delight, then turns and eyes me like a barn cat that's found a mouse.

"Begin." Olive lunges before the word is fully out of Micha's mouth.

"Tsst!" Micha hisses. "I did not—"

Neither of us are paying attention. Olive is quick, but not quick enough. She'd have caught a normal opponent, but to me she moves like she's thigh-deep in water. It's simple to step aside and dance away as she is forced to take a step in the wrong direction to arrest her momentum.

She comes at me more cautiously now, and I know I won't fool her again. She starts to circle, winding closer with each pass. I can see by the set of her feet and her fists that she knows what she's doing.

Mam tried to teach me to fight. Selia and Grandda, too. But I never liked it, and was as apt to disappear as show up for lessons. I've always been better at running away than fighting.

Olive fakes a lunge. When I sidestep, she uses her momentum to spin into a kick so smooth and fast it nearly connects.

She's limber, the kick high as a dancer's, but that works to her disadvantage as I duck under and give her thigh a shove as it passes, throwing her off balance. I put one hand on the floor, scissoring my legs to take her support leg out from under her.

I rush in to put her in a headlock as she falls, but Olive recovers faster than I expect, twisting on the floor to throw a punch.

I exhale and go slippery. Olive's fist slides off my jaw without impact, but it's too close for comfort. I skitter back to recover as she kicks her feet into the air, then snaps them back down hard enough to whip herself upright.

"Almost had you," she says, and I know she's right. If not for my powers, the fight would likely have ended there.

But Olive has powers, too. I've never seen an aura like hers, and she's always been stronger'n anyone has a right to be. That's why it had to be her.

She comes in punching and kicking. I slip around the blows, but

Olive isn't just strong, she's fast, and knows how to position me from one strike to the next. It's all I can do to keep ahead of her, mostly by giving ground. She smiles, taking my retreat as a sign of her dominance.

She may well be right. I try not to think about that as I pick my moment and rush in. Faster than she can follow, I slip around Olive's guard, grabbing her arm. I twist, positioning my legs to break her balance as I pivot into a throw.

Only Olive doesn't move. I strain, but her muscles are like iron. Too late I realize the trap. Before I can exhale and slip away, she punches me in the chest.

It's like being kicked by a horse. I'm thrown from my feet and hit the floor hard, skidding dangerously close to the circle's edge. If I cross the line, I forfeit the match.

She rushes in, and it's all I can do just to keep from being pinned. Olive, heavier, stronger, and nearly as fast, has the advantage at wrestling.

I turn slippery, popping from her grasp like a snap pea from its pod, but I'm starting to reckon I was overconfident, challenging Olive ripping Paper to a fight. I can only imagine what foppish ensemble they'll dress me in if I lose.

I give up offense entirely, making her chase me around the ring as I slip her punches and attempts to grapple. I don't tire as easily as most folk.

Yet Olive keeps pace. Her heart and lungs pump faster, but she is not out of breath. "You're not getting away that easily, Dar."

I nod and turn to face her. She throws a punch and I slap it aside, coming in fast. I deliver a hook to her ribs with all the strength I have, but if Olive so much as feels the blow, it doesn't show. In return I get an open palm to the temple that sends me sprawling.

Olive pounces, grabbing my wrists, but I go slippery, sliding from her grip. I grab the back of her robe, wriggling around to get behind her. She tries to keep hold of me, but it's like trying to catch a greased piglet at a Solstice Festival.

Once I'm on her back she pushes off hard and flips over backward, slamming me into the hardwood floor. It knocks the breath from me, but doesn't stop me from snaking an arm around her throat. I wrap my legs around her, digging my heels into her hips. Then I suck in, and shrink.

Olive pulls at my arm around her throat, and her strength is enormous. I could never match her muscle for muscle, but when I suck in, I become denser. Olive might as well be pulling against steel cables.

She gives up, instead driving her elbows into my ribs. I can't go slippery, but it doesn't matter. The smaller I get, the tougher and more numb I become. I barely feel the blows even as the impacts rack her with pain, like driving her elbows into a goldwood tree.

Still Olive struggles, first managing to get to her knees, then to stand up fully, even as I ride on her back. I see her look toward the wall. "Step out of the ring to ram me against the wall and you forfeit," I remind her.

She lets out a grunt and throws herself backward again, but the impact does more damage to the floorboards than it does to me. She starts to go limp, but I can hear her heartbeat and am not fooled. I wait as she tries to gather her strength in hope I will loosen my grasp. It is only as her heart truly begins to slow that she taps my thigh.

"Tsst!" I release Olive immediately at Micha's hiss. I exhale and go slippery again, sliding away to put some distance between us.

For the first time, Micha gives me a warrior's bow. "I underestimated you, son of Arlen."

I shrug. "Just magic tricks."

"Cheating, you mean." Olive's voice is hoarse.

I turn to her, thankful for the locks of hair that fall across my eyes, saving me from having to meet her glare. "Wasn't the only one usin' magic in that fight, Olive Paper, and you know it."

Olive keeps the scowl on her face, but she knows better than to argue.

"Fights are not won by magic alone," Micha says, as much to Olive as me. "Both of you did well."

"This mean I need to go ask Tarisa to make me up, again?" Selen asks as Olive sits at the vanity in their chambers, scrubbing the powder from her face.

"Just a dumb bet," I say. "You don't have to . . . "

"The Core we don't," Olive says. "I'll paint her myself. We sure as the sun would have dressed you up if you'd lost."

The brave words are belied by her scent. Olive hates being seen without her smelly paints, powders, and perfumes, though for the life of me, I can't understand why.

Micha is back in her shapeless robes. I remember Olive's nanny chasing us all over the keep, trying to keep us out of trouble. Who better, to be a hidden bodyguard? I'm tracking her all the time, now, but even in plain sight, Micha has a way of fading into the background so well it makes my usual lurking seem downright social.

Olive drags Selen to the vanity, grinning. Selen huffs, but her scent is amused.

"Just because you lost doesn't mean you can't have a bath and clean clothes, Darin," Olive notes as she begins powdering Selen's face with a soft brush.

"Had a bath two days ago," I say. "Clean clothes, too. Soap stink only just wore off."

I'm not exactly giving honest word. Truer is, I'd love a soak in hot water and a set of clothes fresh off the line, but I like tweaking their noses more. The years melt away, and things are back the way they used to be.

I reach into my satchel for the pipes as Olive works. I'm still taut with adrenaline after the fighting, but as I begin to play, I fall into the music and my tension eases.

"Ay, Darin," Selen says. "When did you get so good at that?"

I have to suppress a stupid smile at the compliment. I shrug instead, continuing to play. Then something unexpected happens.

Micha begins to sing.

At first it is a wordless harmony, weaving itself in and out of my tune. But her voice rises in power and soon she is leading me, singing boldly in Krasian. I speak the language, but the intonations are different in song. Her words are hard to follow as I struggle to keep pace with her shifts and changes. Sweat gathers on my upper lip as I slide my wind from pipe to pipe, taking quick breaths between notes.

When Micha finally ends the song, Olive and Selen burst into applause, the powder kit forgotten.

"Who taught you the *Song of Waning*?" Micha asks.

The song was another relic of the war. The first written music to charm demons. "It was the first thing I started practicing when Mam brought Hary Roller in to coach me."

Micha nods knowingly. "The honor of Master Roller is boundless. My *jiwah*, Kendall, was also an apprentice of his. Armies of demons danced to his music in the war."

"He saved everyone's lives back on Solstice," I say. "But I din't see much dancing. It was all we could do just to keep from being cored."

"Apologies. I meant no disrespect." Micha bows, dropping her eyes to the carpet. "We were all . . . taken unawares on Solstice. But we are all siblings in the night, and together, we can prevail."

14

BONES

SELEN AND I barely resemble the girls we were the last time we saw him, but Darin is still just Darin, a few inches taller. The sometimes annoying little brother we love to bully, but would die to protect.

Except Selen casts a nervous glace at Darin, slouching against a wall with his pipes. He tosses the hair that's always covering his eyes, and she jerks her gaze away, blushing before I even touch her with the brush.

She sighs. "Bet's a bet."

"You got the better end of it," I say.

"Like night I did." Selen looks like she's sucked a lemon. "You're still the pretty one, even with your face scrubbed and mine painted up like some Angierian debutante."

Again she glances at Darin. She knows he can hear every word we're saying with those bat ears of his, but he was never one for banter. Like old times, he just follows us around, keeping his distance unless we corner him. He'll talk when he's got something worth saying, but he prefers to let his pipes speak for him.

Darin isn't handsome like Perin. He isn't tall and beautiful, with muscular arms and a booming voice like Oskar. Darin Bales is shy and quiet where the young men who tend to catch Selen's notice are loud and boisterous. His face is round and soft-cheeked, when I know she prefers a square jaw.

Yet Selen's eyes keep drifting to him in the mirror as I work, watching Darin's puckered lips kiss each mouthpiece in its turn as they dance across his pipes.

I can't imagine shining on Darin Bales, yet I can't help but feel a bit of jealousy at the attention Selen gives him. After all, Darin Bales was the first boy Selen ever played kissy with. It was years ago—all of us children, another of our ridiculous bets.

Both of them made faces after, and no one's mentioned it since. Still, the three of us had always been inseparable, and something changed that day. I don't know if it was them or me, but it . . . *itched* that the two of them shared something so intimate without me.

I followed Darin around for a week after, hoping for a chance to kiss him, if only to correct the imbalance. He was oblivious, of course. Grandmum says boys always are, when you're the one chasing them.

Summer ended, and like every year, Darin went back to Tibbet's Brook to help with reaping. Mrs. Bales and Darin came to Hollow every spring after sowing, and stayed until reap. I vowed to settle things the next year.

But they didn't come back the next year. Or the year after. Or since. Court gossips say Mother and Mrs. Bales had an argument about Darin's da, but no one really knows for sure.

After five years, I've lost all desire to kiss Darin, and I know it's foolish to be jealous of Selen's attention. But I see him glance back at Selen when she isn't looking, and I worry one of them is going to end up with a broken heart.

EVEN AT NIGHT, the thick velvet curtains are drawn in Mother's library, blocking the faint starlight from tainting her spells. Mother and Mrs. Bales are sipping tea and talking pleasantly when we arrive, but I know the look of women feigning friendship to hide their dislike of each other.

It isn't hard to imagine why. Mother and Arlen Bales played a bit of kissy of their own before he married Mrs. Bales. No one did wrong, but I'm starting to wonder if kissing is worth all the trouble it brings.

But that can't be the whole story. After coming every summer for ten years, something must have happened to make them stop. Something that took a demon attack to overcome.

"Olive." Mrs. Bales gets to her feet. "Aren't you pretty as a sunrise."

If anyone else had said that while my face was scrubbed clean I would have argued, but I doubt Mrs. Bales has ever so much as painted her lips or put on anything that wasn't homespun. Her long hair is in a simple braid, tied on itself. Yet still she carries herself like a queen, and gets treated like one. I forgot how much I crave her approval.

"Aunt Ren." I reach out and she takes me into her arms. "I missed you."

"Missed you, too, girl," Mrs. Bales says. "Your da sends his love, as well."

I pull back to look at her. "You've seen my da?"

"Darin and I skate down there some winters," Mrs. Bales says. "Still warm in Krasia during the cold months. Been a while, but your da asks about you every time."

The words hit me harder than the compliment.

Mother clears her throat. She is holding a pair of polished goldwood boxes. One she hands to Selen, and the other to me. I open it to find a midnight-blue hooded cloak, much like the one Mother wears. A cloak worthy of royalty, embroidered along the seams and back with hundreds of silver wards, stitched in Mother's flawless hand. I throw it around my shoulders and it drifts about like a breeze, then settles to cover me almost completely.

Selen finds a similar cloak in her box, green and brown with wards embroidered in thread of gold. "Night, this must have taken forever to make."

"I've had time," Mother says. "I knew this day was coming. I just thought it was a bit further off."

"Din't make one for Darin?" I ask.

"Darin has one, already," Mother says. "The one I made for his father."

"Been to the Core and back," Mrs. Bales says. "Kept me safe in the dark below."

"Keep them close, as night falls," Mother says.

"Even in places you think safe," Mrs. Bales adds.

I am out of patience for meaningless platitudes that tell us nothing. "Safe from what, precisely?"

"Maybe nothing," Mrs. Bales says.

I look to Mother, reminding her with my eyes of her promise. Mother purses her lips. "The crown prince of the demon hive. The Krasians call him Alagai Ka."

"Hah!" Selen says. "Now I know you're spinning ale stories."

"Anyone with half a brain knows not to take Tender's tales on their face," Mrs. Bales agrees. "But Alagai Ka is real. I helped your das capture him to lead us down into the demon hive."

My chest tightens, and it's hard to breathe. I know the story as well as any, but every version I've read ends the same way. "Wasn't he destroyed in the Deliverer's purge?"

Mrs. Bales shrugs. "Probably."

"Probably?!" I can barely form the word. Is everything I think I know about the war a lie?

"Things got sticky when we reached the hive," Mrs. Bales says. "Demon broke his chains and found a chance to cut and run."

"Darin's father killed every demon for more than a hundred miles in every direction," Mother says. "We hoped he was caught in the purge along with the others."

"And might be he was," Mrs. Bales says. "Or run off for good, hiding at the edge of the world with his little stump tail between his legs."

"The dice are unclear on this," Mother says. "To them all mind demons are Alagai Ka. But something has taken control of the remaining corelings, and it knows who you are." She looks to me and Darin and Selen. "All of you. It lacks only opportunity to strike, and we must keep it that way until it can be found and eliminated."

My anger is doused by cold fear. Can I never leave the greatward again?

Mrs. Bales puts her hands on her hips. "It's a mistake, not bringin' Olive's da into this."

Mother shakes her head. "If we use magic to communicate over the miles, there's a chance the mind might intercept it."

Mrs. Bales rolls her eyes but doesn't argue. "Then I'll just skate down there and tell him to come. He can travel almost as fast as me."

Again, Mother shakes her head. "Inevera will never allow it. She . . . doesn't trust us together."

"Ay, hear that can happen when you stick a woman's husband behind her back," Mrs. Bales says. "Want them both in any event."

Unbelievably, Mother accepts the barb. "I don't trust her any more than she does me." She removes the dice from the pouch at her waist and moves to her casting table, goldwood coated with pristine white felt, edges raised to prevent dice from rolling off. "I can cast as well as Inevera."

Mrs. Bales snorts. "Ay, well. Let's be on with it, then."

Mother's dice look nothing like Favah's. The art of foretelling requires seven *alagai hora*, dice carved out of demonbones, each with a different shape and number of sides. Wards carved onto every face focus their power and tell a tale of what might be, for those trained to see it. I've never had the gift—much to Favah's sorrow—but Mother is famed for hers.

Dama'ting Favah's dice are black demonbone, smooth as polished obsidian, while the duchess has coated hers in priceless electrum, the only metal that can hold and conduct Core magic without loss. They glitter like silver in one of her hands. Instead of a *hanzhar*, she holds a surgical lance in the other.

"Olive, let's start with you."

I sigh, holding out my arm. Mother has the process down to a ritual. She disinfects the pad of my left index finger, then uses the lance to pierce a tiny scar, the precise place she's taken blood from countless times over the years.

"Five . . . six . . . seven." She squeezes a single drop of blood onto each of the dice, then puts pressure on the wound until it closes. It heals in moments, but the scar is always itchy. The duchess says it's my imagination.

She puts her hands together, dice clattering as she gently shakes them to distribute the blood.

I've never seen the duchess pray. Even at cathedral services, she does no more than bow her head respectfully. *A ruler must act in the interest of her people*, she taught, *not in what she imagines is the interest of the divine.* But in the ritual of the dice, even Mother acknowledges a higher power.

"Creator, giver of light and life, I seek knowledge of my child, Olive Paper of Hollow, whose father is Ahmann Jardir of Krasia. What is the source of the attack on Olive's life last new moon?"

As she speaks, the dice begin to glow, brighter and brighter until they shine through her fingers. She casts them down and there is a flash as the tumbling bones are pulled out of their natural trajectories by the wards of prophecy. They roll to a stop, throbbing softly with dim light, and everyone holds their breath.

At least at first.

Darin, Selen, and Mrs. Bales lean in, but I can tell the collection of symbols means little to them. After Mother studies the throw in silence for long moments, the tension wanes and they withdraw.

Darin flits across the room, scampering like a squirrel to perch atop a high shelf of books. He seems far away, but I know he can see, hear, and smell better from that distance than most folks can up close.

Selen drifts away next, helping herself to a cup of tea and a biscuit before sitting on a divan and putting her feet on the table. Normally, Mother would snap at her for that, but the duchess is so focused on the dice, she doesn't even notice.

Mrs. Bales stares at the dice long and hard, trying to pierce their mysteries. At last she huffs and moves away. She walks along a bookcase, running a finger along the spines before selecting a volume. She sits right there on the floor, curling her legs under as she begins to read in wardlight.

"What do you see, Olive?" Mother asks quietly.

My stomach clenches as I look at the dice. I recognize all the symbols, but I feel just as lost as I did trying to predict the weather with Favah. Every symbol has multiple meanings, interpreted from context, direction, and proximity to the others. Even after years of training, I've never understood how anyone makes sense of it.

Mother points to where a die with a rock ward and a die with a wind ward have fallen beside each other. "This grouping was one of the first

I ever threw, when Favah began instructing me. I was so sure I knew what it meant, and Favah called me an arrogant, idiot girl."

"Were you right?" I ask.

Mother shrugs. "I was lucky. The future is a story, and there are many ways to tell the same story. It might not mean now what it meant then."

"What was that?" I'm unused to the sound of humility in the duchess' voice, and I'm not sure I care for it. If she's not sure, then what chance have I?

"Rock and wind wards intersecting can mean a mountain." Mother traces invisible lines where the ward edges of the dice would meet, then gestures back to the die showing the rock ward. "But the rock ward is upside down. What do you think that means?"

"Inversion often means opposition," I recite from the text.

"And what is the opposite of mountain?" Mother asks.

I hesitate. The duchess loves to ask questions like this one, treating my answer like some invisible exam. I hate it even as my stomach burns with the need to win her approval.

But what is the opposite of mountain? A lake? The sea? The sky?

I look at Mother's face, silently testing each against her serene façade. If I think out loud, she will critique each guess, but however patient she appears, every question required to circle to the right answer will be held against me in the duchess' esteem.

I close my eyes, imagining a mountain. I'd never seen one until the borough tour, but I remember them now, standing proudly along the horizon. I think of their shape, how they displace the air around them. I try to imagine the opposite of that, but there is only air, filling the space that was once occupied by the mountain.

Could that be it? An upside-down rock ward and a wind ward cancel each other?

Again I look at Mother, testing the answer against her. The duchess loves trick questions that require a bold answer, but she also loves questions that are deceptively simple, masked in complexity. Creator help me, if I guess something bold and wrong. I think back to her exact words.

The rock ward is upside down. Invert a mountain, and you don't get empty air, you get displaced soil.

"Valley," I blurt, before I can overthink it.

Mother turns back to the dice, but there is a faint hint of upward curl at the very edge of her lips. Mother is stingy with praise. When I was younger, these little successes would ease the burning in my stomach, at least for a while, but now I know better. This was only the beginning.

Mother grills me for hours, as Darin and Mrs. Bales silently eavesdrop. Selen, at least, has given me a bit of privacy by falling asleep on the divan. The questions are endless, some simple, some difficult, and some deceptive. This is how Mother teaches. Not with lectures or books, just a slow interrogation with bits of knowledge dropped like breadcrumbs along the way.

Mother leads me about the bookcases, pulling tomes of foretelling off the shelves and piling them in my arms. I consult passages as she directs, reading silently even as Mother recites them from memory. Then back to the dice for more questions, altering the meanings we first divined based on the passages I've read.

Next she takes me to the stand on the great rug in the center of the library, woven into a perfect map of the known world, a globe cut and flattened like an orange peel. We stand between the mountains of Miln and the shores of the Krasian Sea, but there are whole continents beyond, marked only with their names from the old world—before the corelings returned. That was hundreds of years ago. Who can say what's there, now?

Such places could have been destroyed in the Return, or turned into something entirely other than what they were in the old world, much like Hollow and the Krasian empire. Or they could be exactly the same, unthreatened by a demon hive even as our lands descended into chaos.

Mother paces the rug carefully, counting out calculations I deduced after ninety minutes of hard questioning. There was no hint of smile on Mother's face then.

I've grown increasingly nauseous as it has dragged on, and I fear I will sick up if things continue much longer without a break.

"*A mimic demon hungers beneath a city in an eastern mountain valley.*" Mother speaks the words with finality. "Here." She waves a foot vaguely over a valley in the eastern mountains, covering an area that might be hundreds of square miles. It was the country of Rusk, once upon a time, and there was more than one city—and Creator knew how many villages—in the area indicated.

The book she was reading thumps to the floor as Mrs. Bales dissipates into smoke, flowing across the room to rematerialize right between us on the floor. I hop back with a gasp.

"Mimics are like sheepdogs." Mrs. Bales sounds skeptical. "They keep the other corelings in line, but they ent exactly known as great thinkers."

"Prince Iraven said the demons in the desert have evolved," Mother says. "Mimics follow victims, learning their names, then taking the form of someone trusted to call out and lure them from the wards. They may not be master tacticians, but they are cunning."

Mrs. Bales nods. "Ay, and maybe the minds kept them dumb. Don't want the sheepdogs startin' to think for themselves."

"But if this one's been on its own for fifteen years . . . " Mother says.

"Then maybe it ent him," Mrs. Bales says. "Just a wasp nest we need to smoke out of the barn."

I should be relieved to have the focus off me, but I feel even sicker. "Then why would it be after me?"

Mrs. Bales shrugs. "Any mimic demon that survived the purge would remember your mam and me. If they smelled our blood on you—"

"At the same time?" I hate to pick holes in an answer I like, but the puzzle doesn't fit. "The tour was hundreds of miles from this valley. Tibbet's Brook is hundreds beyond that."

"Mimics can dissipate, same as me," Mrs. Bales says. "They can cross a thousand miles like skippin' over a puddle."

Mrs. Bales looks at me a long moment, then turns back to Mother. "Girl's got a point, though. Need a big rippin' evolution to go from learning to say someone's name to coordinating attacks all over Thesa."

A little bit of my tension eases. The need to impress Mrs. Bales is almost as strong as the need to impress Mother.

"Agreed." The duchess turns to eye Darin, still perched atop the bookshelf, watching and listening to every word. "We need to know more."

15

THE FATHER

A UNT LEESHA IS confident in her wards, and she ought to be. What Olive calls wardsight is just . . . sight for me. Always has been. I can see the way Aunt Leesha's wardnet wraps around her library like a blanket, a glowing web impenetrable to corelings.

Her sound wards, too, form a bubble around the rooms. Normally I could listen in on the servants in the pantry two floors below without cocking my head. Now there's absolute silence beyond the wardnet. I might find it peaceful, but the unnatural nature of the quiet is disconcerting. Less like silence than a kind of deafness. There could be demons at the doors and I'd never hear them coming.

The windows have no bars. The warded glass in the panes is stronger than steel. Even a crank bow bolt wouldn't cause so much as a scratch. Secure in her keep, Leesha has left one of them open two inches to allow in the fresh air.

I'm thinking about that window as Aunt Leesha suddenly turns to meet my gaze. Two inches is big as a wagon track when I've gone slippery. I could cross the room before she realizes I've moved and be out that window without slowing. The guards on the grounds might as well be hip-deep in water, for all their chance of running me down.

I don't want to know what the dice have to say about me. I just want to play my pipes by the swimming hole.

Mam looks at me, and I know she sees the fear in my aura. "Gonna be all right, Darin. Won't hurt."

Ent worried about hurt. I let out a breath, going slippery as I hop down from the shelf. Aunt Leesha's library has a two-story ceiling. It's a fifteen-foot drop from my perch, but I'm lighter when I go slippery, falling slower and with less force. Olive gives me a sympathetic look as I touch down and approach the casting table. Selen, thank the Creator, is still fast asleep. The steady rhythm of her breathing calms me as I hold out my arm.

Aunt Leesha is nothing like the Herb Gatherer back in the Brook. Coline Trigg never stops talking—asking after folk, sending regards, and spreading gossip. Go to her with anything short of a broken bone and half your treatment will be a lecture on how you're not taking good care, and the other half will be drinking some awful-smelling tea. Coline's scent fluctuates with her mood as the conversation wanders.

Aunt Leesha's scent seldom changes. She always smells . . . focused. She looks at a problem, plans a solution, and then acts with quick precision to carry it out. Her normally gentle hands are firm as she lances my finger and guides it over the pyramid die, squeezing out the first drop.

Looking close, I see my aura well and stretch with the droplet. Even outside my body, the blood is a part of me.

But then the droplet falls, and a tiny piece of my aura snaps off with it. The glowing droplet strikes the electrum die and the wards pulse as they drink the light of my aura, absorbing everything there is to know about me. Maybe things I don't even know, myself.

The square die next, and on five more times, until all seven dice have attuned to me. Before the eighth drop begins to well, Aunt Leesha presses her thumb hard against the spot, closing the wound. "Keep pressure on that." The words are precise. Economical. Inviting no discussion. Her mind is already on the dice.

I like that about her. Why talk when there's music to make?

Olive steps close. She doesn't say anything or take her eyes off the dice, but she slips her hand into mine, and I suddenly realize how scared I am. I've learned to tune out the sound of my own heart, but it is beating so fast it's like a drumming in my head.

I feel like I'm falling, and I hold on to what I can. I squeeze Olive's hand and focus again on Selen's steady, peaceful breath. I force myself to match her, chest expanding and contracting in sync with hers. Slowly, I begin to calm, heart slowing back to its normal rhythm.

"Creator, giver of light and life, I seek knowledge of Darin Bales, son of Arlen and Renna, of Tibbet's Brook. What is the source of the attack on his life last new moon?"

The dice glow increasingly bright as Aunt Leesha shakes, then flash like lightning as she casts them across the table. I hear seven tiny *wumps!* of air as they pull up unnaturally short.

The duchess becomes a statue as she concentrates. Even her scent goes flat as she works to coax meaning from the dice the way I coax music from my pipes.

There's a sudden flare in her aura, but I can't tell what it means. Auras are more complicated than scents. I've never been able to read auras like that.

Mam can, though. "What? What did you see?"

"Be silent." Aunt Leesha raises a finger without so much as turning.

Mam doesn't like that. She mists across the room, materializing between the duchess and the table, inches from Aunt Leesha's face. "Tell me again not to ask about my boy."

The duchess jumps back with a yelp, hand darting to her *hora* wand, but it's a bad idea and she knows it. In all the years we've been coming to Hollow, this is the first time I've ever smelled Aunt Leesha frightened. She opens her mouth, but Mam cuts her off.

"Been real patient tonight, Leesha, but ent got three hours to sit around while you walk Olive through a puzzle you've already solved. Something out there took a shot at my boy, and I want to know what. Tell. Me. What. You. Saw."

Anger slips into Aunt Leesha's scent, now. I don't expect she's used to being bullied by anyone. She grips her wand tightly, and I can sense the massive charge of the item.

Mam tucks her thumbs into the belt of her dress. There is nothing threatening in the move itself, but it draws the duchess' eyes to the heavy knife that hangs there in easy reach. Aunt Leesha is still afraid, but the focus is back, and I half expect her to pull the wand from her belt and attempt to draw a ward before Mam can take it from her. I wouldn't give it good odds.

Aunt Leesha seems to come to the same conclusion. She straightens, face going serene as she lets go of the wand and deliberately moves her hand away. "I'm sorry, Renna. I was caught up in the dice and forgot who I was talking to."

"Don't need an apology," Mam says. "Just what you saw."

"I expected more about the mimic, or this hidden city in the eastern mountains," Aunt Leesha says, "but it was something else entirely."

"You're saying the attacks ent related?" Mam sounds doubtful.

"Don't be ridiculous," Aunt Leesha says. "I don't think it's a coincidence any more than you. I just haven't proved it."

"Still hedging," Mam says, "tellin' me what the dice don't say, instead of what they do." It ent often Mam needs to ask for something a third time, and when she does, it means the end of her patience.

But Aunt Leesha is on firmer ground, now. "I'll tell you when I've had another look to make sure, Renna Bales, and not a moment before. I won't give out irresponsible answers because you're too impatient to let me check the math."

Mam takes a deep breath. "Ay, fair." She crosses her arms, but steps aside to grant access to the table.

Aunt Leesha returns her attention to the dice, and after a few moments, her scent is flat, again. She stares for a long time before speaking. "*The father waits below in darkness for his progeny to return.*"

My hand starts to shake, slipping from Olive's. I clench my fist to keep the convulsion from spreading.

"Da."

ARLEN BALES, MY da, died to save the world.

I don't believe everything the Tenders say about him, but I believe Mam, and she was there to see it.

But Da didn't die like other folks. He breathed out too far, like me when I go slippery, or Mam dissipating. The more you exhale, the harder it gets to suck back in and pull yourself together, until finally, you can't. It's killed more than a few Warded Children over the years, a constant reminder of the danger.

It's why I get so scared when Mam makes me dissipate with her. I can hear the call of the Core, feel its Draw. Breathe out too much and it will pull me in like smoke through a fan.

Mam says it was a peaceful way to go. "A drop of rain becoming part of the bubbling brook."

That part, I don't believe. Mam can't know what it's like to die. No one can. But I know one thing. The Core isn't soothing and cool like a bubbling brook. It is heat and fire and we are only coals. If I was to guess, I'd say being sucked in is like being burned alive. I picture Da that way sometimes, frozen in time without a throat to scream his pain.

"You think it's my da?"

"That sent demons up out of the Core to find you?" Mam spits on the floor. "Only thing your da ever did with demons was kill them."

"Except the one time he kept one alive and used it to lead the way into the hive," the duchess notes. Mam glares at her, but Aunt Leesha only shrugs. Every Jongleur in Thesa sings about that story.

"Da died on the same spot I was born." My throat is suddenly dry. "In the darkness of the demon hive. What if he's . . . trapped there? What if he's callin' me, and the demons just intercepted the message?"

"If your da was trapped, I would've found him," Mam says. "Don't think I didn't look."

I steel myself. "If Da—"

"Your da is gone." Mam's voice is calm, but her aura is a vortex of emotions, too complex to read. "Ent no coming back from where he went. Creator willing, we'll join him there when our time comes."

She means the words as comfort, but they are anything but. "What if it just took him some time to suck back in? What if he's stuck, and needs us to come and rescue him?" My voice cracks and I barely manage to finish the thought before I start to cry.

I hate crying. I hate it. I hate when others do it, and I hate it the most when I do. It's like my body is betraying me.

I don't know if it is the words or the tears, but Mam's scent fills with feelings of anguish and regret. I smell the tears even before they well in her eyes. "Promised your da I wouldn't try to do that, Darin. Not while I've got you to look after."

I find my voice at the words. "And if you din't?"

"Then I would have gone with him," Mam says without hesitation. "But don't fool yourself. Just be another raindrop in the brook. Ent no rescue from that."

"But——" I press.

"Alagai Ka," Aunt Leesha cuts in, "is also known as the Father of Demons. That was his hive, and his circles of power were never found. Perhaps he has returned to his seat, and is calling the remaining demons back to rebuild. Perhaps Darin's connection to the place makes him some kind of threat."

"Took a couple 'perhapses' to get there, Leesha," Mam says. "But we'll never know, because we ent goin' anywhere near the place. His da gave his life so Darin and I could get out of there alive once. Won't risk it again."

"Agreed," the duchess says. "We don't have enough information to act on this yet."

"So we follow Olive's lead and see where they connect," Mam says. "I can mist over to that mountain valley. If there's a city there, it shouldn't take me long to find it."

"Absolutely not," Aunt Leesha says. "It's too dangerous to go alone. Even for you."

"Ent one of your subjects, Leesha," Mam notes. "You don't get to tell me what to do."

Aunt Leesha's jaw tightens. "Perhaps, but I can tell you not to be a fool. Even if it's just a mimic, why face it alone?"

That gets Mam's back up. She doesn't care for being called a fool.

And I can't stand it anymore.

"Wasn't done talking!" I shout.

"Whazzat?" Selen jerks upright on the couch.

Everyone's looking at me, now. I swallow and force myself to breathe. "Can't just . . . do that!" I wave my hand, a meaningless gesture, but it feels right. "Can't just tell me somethin' like that and just turn and change the rippin' subject!"

Mam smells hurt, but she doesn't care for being shouted at, either. "Talk about this later, Darin. Honest word. But right now your elders are talking."

There is a rush of anger in Olive's scent, and she takes a protective step in front of me. "Our *elders* are acting like ripping children if they can't spare a moment of bickering for someone in pain!"

Both women are flabbergasted at the outburst, and while they stand frozen, Selen steps next to me, taking my arm. "Let's go, Dar. Let the children bicker."

The words are sharp, and the princesses smell ready to fight, but Mam and the duchess don't protest as they escort me away. Truer is, I can smell their relief.

"Fine," Mam tells Aunt Leesha. "I'll take a few of the Children with me."

"And me," Aunt Leesha says.

Mam shakes her head. "Taking you means carriages and horses and wagons . . . "

"Just as well," Aunt Leesha says. "I will be bringing along a sizable force of Cutters and they will need to be fed and supplied."

"Adding weeks to something we can do in a day," Mam says.

"Renna." Aunt Leesha lets the mask on her face fall away. "Something tried to kill our children. Better a thousand warriors too many, than one too few."

Then the library doors shut behind us, and the wards of silence sever us from the conversation.

16

GENERAL CUTTER

THE DUCHESS' SERVANTS are up hours before dawn, readying for the day as their employers continue their slumber, blissfully unaware.

To me, it's a racket to wake the dead. The clatter of silverware and porcelain are thunder in my skull. I can smell every rasher of bacon, boiled oat, and morning privy visit. Hear their coughs and quiet conversations. The endless splashing of water as basins and pitchers are filled and pots set over the fire.

I'd be glad of the unnatural silence of the duchess' library now, or even Grandda's corespawned rooster crowing. Sunrise in Hollow is even worse than in Tibbet's Brook.

I flee to the still-quiet courtyard, comforted by the cloak of darkness, but I can feel the weight in the sky as dawn approaches. I flit through the yard unnoticed by the guards, just a shadow in the darkness. I find a familiar spot and scale the western watchtower.

I've always been a good climber, but in darkness I can cheat a bit. Same way I get slippery, I can turn sticky when I want, misting just enough to slide the skin of my fingers and toes into cracks and fissures too small for most folk to see, then expanding to fill them.

I climb like a spider above the guards' post to a small archery nook with shuttered views of the road and yard, just large enough for a single shooter. From the inside, it can only be accessed by a narrow, winding stair. It's the shadiest spot in the yard, and no one ever goes there. Used to come here all the time, when I was little.

I nestle into the darkness, closing my eyes and focusing on the quiet conversation of the guards below to help tune out the keep's rising bustle.

"You ent heard where they're headed?" one says. He's older, and I can hear his stomach rumbling as the end of his shift approaches. He smells of alcohol, but he isn't drunk. He chews sourleaf in an attempt to mask it on his breath.

"No one knows," his relief officer says. She's younger, freshly fed, and clean. "Wherever they're goin', one thing's for sure. Either the duchess expects to find a fight, or she's lookin' to start one."

I don't have to wonder what they're talking about. The preparations have been underway for a week.

Soon enough, the yard comes to life as well. Animals are led out and hitched, and the wagons loaded the night before ready themselves to leave.

I can smell the chemicals and acrid scent of the three carts of flame-work, another dozen laden with supplies. Two carts from the Warders' Guild, and another of Jongleurs. And that's not to mention all the men and women to cook meals, wash laundry, and otherwise facilitate for the convoy. Inside the carts, cooks are already peeling potatoes and chopping vegetables for a lunch stop that is hours away. I can feel the onion fumes on my eyes.

Five hundred mounted Hollow Lancers atop giant Angierian mustangs come up the road like a rockslide, so loud I need to stick fingers in my ears to blunt the worst of it. They muster at the gate in polished wooden armor, long spears upright like a forest in miniature. Even from atop the wall I can hear their words to one another, but the topic is the same. All they know is they are headed into the borderlands to hunt demons. Some are veterans from the demon war, but others came of age long after and have never faced corelings in battle. The elders have a lot of advice, but as I learned for myself, little of it is useful without the perspective only a charging demon can give.

Mam's been skating back and forth for a week, readying the Children to join Hollow's forces at the edge of the borderlands.

Aunt Leesha wasn't exaggerating when she said she was taking no chances.

"Spend a lot of time up here for a boy with two pretty princesses to keep him company." Mam's head appears in the window.

I'm not surprised. Mam can't dissipate with the sun up. She avoided the steps and climbed the wall quietly enough, but I could smell her coming.

"Nice shady spot," I say. "Got a view of everything. Ent quiet, but ent usually bothered here."

"That what I am to you?" Mam slips her legs over the sill and sits in the window, uncaring of the thirty-foot drop at her back. "Or can I set a bit? Keep you company?"

"Worried I'll stow away in one of the carriages?" I ask.

"Should I be?" Mam replies.

"No," I say. "Ent interested in goin' to pick a fight with a mimic demon."

Mam's nose is as sharp as mine, even when she can't see my aura. She knows I mean it. "Then what?"

I shrug. "Just feel so helpless setting here, and I can't help but wonder . . ."

I trail off, but not quickly enough. "Already know what you mean, Darin," Mam says. "Might as well just say it."

My voice hardens. "If you're going in the wrong direction. Don't want to go down to the old hive any more than you, but if there's a chance Da is . . . stuck there—"

"He ent," Mam says. "He was, I'd already be down there, no matter what the rippin' dice say. Your da was still alive," she lifts her left hand, running a thumb over the wards of her wedding band, "I'd know."

I want to believe her. I know I should. I don't doubt that Mam would do anything to bring back Da—short of putting me at risk—but there's a place where the two overlap, and that makes it hard to trust.

"Would you really have gone into the Core with him, if not for me?" I ask.

"Would have gone anywhere to be with your da," Mam says. "Loved Arlen Bales like crops love rain. Din't think I could live without him."

She lays a hand on my shoulder. "But then I met you, and realized I had more to live for than I thought."

My throat tightens, but I force the words out, anyway. "What if he needs us?"

Mam squeezes, trying to massage some of the tension away, but I'm wound like a clock spring. "Then he'll need a better Messenger than a couple demon attacks and some old coreling bones."

She's right. She's got to be. I ent ready to live in a world where Mam could be wrong, and there's no way for me to find my way down to that place without her. I nod, wiping a tear from my eye with the cuff of my shirt.

"Ent gonna be gone long," Mam says. "Really is just a mimic, Miss Prissy Perfect and I should be able to handle it without much fuss and be back in a few weeks."

"And if it's more?" I ask.

Mam shrugs. "Goin' in heavy. There's a fight, it won't end well for the demons."

"I don't want to stay here," I say. "Can't you skate me home to the Brook before you go?"

"You're *askin'* to skate?" Mam's eyes narrow. "Olive and Selen treating you so bad?"

I shake my head. "They're fine. Just don't fit in, here."

"Ay, get that," Mam says. "But demons got too close to your grandda's farm for my liking. Until this business is settled, Hollow's the safest place. Your uncle Gared will take good care of you, and maybe you and Selen will get a chance to sneak another kiss."

I look up at her, unable to hide my shock, and she throws me a wink. "Thought I didn't know about that? You two behave."

I feel my face heat, and Mam laughs, hugging me tight and kissing the curly hair atop my head. "Love you, Darin Bales."

"Love you, Mam."

SELEN AND OLIVE find me atop the parapet wall as I watch the carts and horses recede in the distance from the shadows of my warded cloak's hood. A week since the bet, Olive is painting her face again, but the smells of her various perfumes are preferable to the slowly fading stench of the convoy.

"Ready to head over to Da's manse?" Selen asks. "I can ask the porters to pack your one dirty shirt and overalls."

"Don't bother," Olive says. "The staff gave up trying to wash them and just set them aflame."

"I was wondering what that stink was!" Selen cries. Both girls squeal with laughter, and I wonder how long it would take me to get back to Tibbet's Brook if I set off at a run. The trip takes a Messenger on horseback two weeks, but I reckon I could beat that.

I don't know if the servants burned my clothes, but the moment I stepped into a tub, they made off with them, leaving behind a robe and some underclothes to wear as the duchess' tailors ambushed me. Ran their tapes so far up my leg I thought they were going to wipe my bottom.

I try to stuff my hands in my pockets, but for some reason, my new pants don't have any. The ones on my jacket are too small to put anything of use in. "Feel like I'm the one lost a bet. Got suede and velvet for every occasion now, and not a thing that's comfortable."

"Creator be praised," Selen says. "You'll need your fanciest for Sixthday supper tonight with the general." Selen's casual accent switches to the stuffy Angierian court speech Hary puts on when he wants to sound officious. "The baroness requires formal dress at the Sixthday table. Seating is promptly at six, do not be late. Supper shall continue until the general and the baroness get too drunk to be civil."

"Ay!" I put up my hands as Olive laughs. "Never agreed to that."

"Ent got a choice," Selen says. "Don't like it any more than you, but Da's been looking forward to this all week. Won't kill you to eat with us on Sixthdays. It's not like Emelia wants me around more than that, anyway."

"You and your stepmam still don't get on?" I ask.

"Get on with the living embodiment of the scandal that soured her marriage before it even began?" Selen asks. "She hates Sixthday dinner even more than I do."

Selen lays a hand on my shoulder. Even through my suede jacket and silk shirt I can feel its warmth. "Hoping you'll sit between us and turn slippery."

"She doesn't like me, either," I say.

"Ay, but scratching at you is asking for a visit from Mrs. Bales, and even the baroness ent stupid enough to tempt that." She squeezes my shoulder and looks me in the eyes. "Please?"

My knees weaken, but I make my voice gruff. "Ay, fine."

Selen lets out a squeal and hugs me. "Apologies now for my brothers."

In truth, I can handle the baroness and Selen's half brothers just fine. It's Uncle Gared that makes me uncomfortable. I hate it when Da's old friends want a look at me. Always searching for something exceptional— something of the great man they knew—in his only son. I can smell their disappointment when they can't find anything.

"Can we get off this wall, now?" Olive asks. "The wind is ruining my hair."

We walk down to the yard and back into the residence, where I split off to gather the few things left in my room to bring to General Cutter's manse. They wait till I turn a corner down the hall, but I can still hear the girls talking.

"You've got a dinner date with Darin Baaaaales—!" Olive's sing-song voice is cut off by the sound of Selen shoving her.

"Oh, ay," Selen says. "Real romantic. Da getting drunk while Emelia and her mother snipe at us and my brothers bark and pee the carpet."

Olive laughs. "No way you can get out of it?"

"It's all Da's been talking about," Selen says. "The general swears Arlen Bales was the Deliverer, and to him that makes Darin half Deliverer, too. Be good for Da to see he's just some dirty bumpkin."

Mam says my special senses are a gift, but there are times when I truly hate them.

"Night," Selen declares when I open the door.

Took me an hour to make sense of all the buckles, laces, buttons, knots, and cuffs of the dinner clothes the servants laid out, but it's worth it to see her breath catch.

"You weren't spinning stories about the tailors," Selen says. "They cleaned you up good."

I smile with more teeth than strictly necessary. "Wouldn't want your da to look at me and think I'm just some dirty bumpkin."

"Heard all that, did you?" I feel the flush as Selen's face heats. She's ashamed, at least.

I want to stay mad, but she ent making it easy. Used to seeing Selen in leggings or a wide-skirted court dress. Now she's clad in a dark blue velvet gown that accents her height and muscular frame. It hugs tight around her ribs, leaving her broad shoulders bare. Her arms are thicker than mine. She's even let Olive paint her lips and pin her hair, though the bet's long over. She's beautiful.

Try as I might, I can't stop thinking about the last summer I spent in Hollow. Folk gossiped that I kissed her, but truer was Selen did the kissing and I just melted in her arms. Every time I see her, I wonder if she's going to do it again.

"Hear everything," I say. "There's seven servants bustling around the supper table downstairs. Two are out of breath. One maid's tryin' to hide a sniffle. Butler has a loose heel on his shoe that clacks when he walks."

"So no one's got any privacy, that it?" Selen asks. "Better not have gas on the privy! Darin's always listening."

"Ent like I got a choice!" I'm irritated at her attempt to turn it back on me. "Sometimes I can filter out all the sounds and smells, sometimes I can't. And why should I have to? So folk can insult me when I'm not around?"

Selen crosses her thick arms. "Would have said those exact words to your face, Darin Bales, and you know it."

"That supposed to make it better?" I scoff. "Never say things like that to you."

"That's because you ent got a sense of humor." Selen winks.

"Don't forget who wagered you into having to paint your face," I say. "And don't fool yourself. Master Hary says, '*Mean's an easy shortcut to a laugh, but it ent comedy.*'"

"Fun, though." Selen's mouth quirks in a smile that threatens to make me forget why I was angry. "Don't be mad, Darin. Three of us have been throwing shadow at each other since we were in nappies. Ent the time to get all sensitive."

She senses my weakness, threading her arm through mine. I try to pull away, but it's a token effort, and she knows it.

"You just want me as a shield against your stepmam."

"Ay." Selen starts guiding me down the hall to the stair. "But it ent like you've got anything better to do."

SELEN'S THREE BROTHERS are loitering outside the dining room like a cluster of goldwood trees.

I've got two summers on the oldest, Steave Cutter, but he's been a head taller than me since we were out of nappies. At thirteen he's closing on six feet with no sign of stopping. I could still look down at Gared Young on my last visit, but he has inches on me now. Even Flinn, six summers behind, can look me straight in the eye.

"Ay, would you look at that." Steave looks me up and down as Selen and I join them. "You get shorter, Bales?"

He stinks of challenge. Every time I visit Hollow, Steave tries to pick a fight. Sometimes it's words and sometimes it's physical, but he's always trying to get a rise out of me so he can establish dominance in front of his brothers. More than once when we were kids, I had to put him on the floor. Now, after putting on five summers and thirty pounds of muscle, he looks eager to make up the loss.

It's all so . . . primitive. Boring. Fighting Uncle Gared's boys ent worth the hassle. Easier to just let Steave look big in front of his brothers.

I smile as they cluster in like a pack of nightwolves. "Never seem to get as much rain and sunshine as you Cutters. All shot up, ent you?"

Selen steps in front of me. Her scent is sharp with anger, but her words are almost singsong. "Steave's just sour that his sister beat the snot out of him in the practice yard the other day."

"You cheated," Steave growls, but a current of fear has slipped into his challenge scent.

Selen gives a derisive snort. "Ay, that's why you ent won a round against me your whole life."

Gared Young and Flinn snicker at that, and the moment defuses. If the Cutter boys are nightwolves, Selen has always been their alpha.

"Look pretty tonight, sis." Steave changes tactics, and I can smell Selen's irritation. She doesn't like being dressed up any more than I do, and Steave knows it. She looks ready to put him down right in the hall before Sixthday dinner. He takes a step back as she advances, and she pulls up short with a laugh. Flinn and Gared Young laugh along, but Steave smells angry, and it's building. He's about to do something stupid to save face.

"Darin!" Uncle Gared booms from down the hall, breaking the tension. More than seven feet tall, he towers over everyone, including his children, but out of the wooden armor he wears almost everywhere, Gared Cutter looks older than I remember. His coat buttons strain against a rounded belly, and there are thick jowls beneath his graying beard.

"Creator, it's good to have you under my roof again!" I suck in a bit as the general claps me on the shoulder. It's all that keeps him from knocking me over. "See you're catchin' up with the boys?"

"Ay, sir," I say. "Thank you for offering succor while Mam is away."

"Least I could do," he says. "And never mind all that 'sir' business. Used to call me Uncle Gar when you were still a sapling. Know we ent blood, but you're as good as. Ever tell you about the time your mum carried me on her back out of a demon ambush?"

"Only every time you see him." Selen stands on tiptoes to kiss her father on the cheek.

"It's a good story," he says.

"Ay," I agree, "but the way Mam tells it, Halfgrip saved you both, that day."

Rojer Inn, the famous Jongleur known as Halfgrip, has always been a hero of mine. He was the first person in thousands of years to charm corelings with his music, a skill that saved countless lives during the war, even after his death.

"Honest word." Gared smells sad, and proud. "Don't think any of us would have survived that attack otherwise. Hear you're a bit of a demon charmer yourself with those pipes."

My mind flashes back to the attack, my sweaty fingers slipping on the reeds, unable to hold the corelings back. "Nothing as special as that, si . . . Uncle Gar."

"Indeed," a woman's voice says. "It would take a swollen head for a boy to claim he's the next fiddle wizard." I look up and see Lady Lacquer, Selen's step-grandmother, enter the room, Baroness Emelia close behind.

"Welcome, Darin." The baroness' words and smile are warm, but her scent is derisive as she takes my arms and kisses the air to either side of my face. Her eyes flick over Selen like a pile of dung she needs to step around. "Selen. Your face looks lovely. You should powder it more often."

"Baroness. Lady Lacquer." Selen's curtsy is perfect as a dancer's, but if her scent was irritated before, it's inflamed now. Like Steave, the baroness knows she's struck a nerve, and smells of smug satisfaction.

The baroness turns to regard the general. "Husband. You look ready to pop your buttons. Shall I have the tailors let your coat out . . . again?"

Uncle Gared doesn't growl, precisely, but I feel the low rumble inside him, even if the others don't. His face reddens, just slightly, but he ignores the question. "All here, so let's sit. For some reason, I'm suddenly thirsty."

Indeed, the servants have already poured for the adults. A massive wooden mug, crackling with foaming ale, sits by Uncle Gared's place at the table's head. Waiting in Baroness Emelia's place at the foot, as far from her husband as possible, is a large wineglass overfilled with a red so deep its scent is like sandpaper in my sinuses.

We circle the table, Steave, Gared Young, and Flinn crowding on one side, with Selen, myself, and Lady Lacquer on the other.

"Sit," the general commands, and a servant slides my chair forward until the edge touches the backs of my knees. I drop down into it, wondering why they think we need help to sit down.

The baroness reaches for her napkin, opening it with a snap and laying it across her lap. The rest of us follow along.

Dinner starts off well enough. There are a few fancy Angierian dishes for the baroness and her mother. These the chefs introduce personally, listing every ingredient, though I hardly see why. The flavors of the food are drowned in sauces and seasoning.

The general and his children favor simpler dishes, meat still moist in its own juices and plain grilled vegetables. While the baroness and her mother debate which slice of cheese will best complement a particular bread, the rest of us are holding bones in sticky fingers, rending the meat with our teeth as we laugh at Uncle Gared's stories.

"Buried my axe in the wood demon's behind, but it gets stuck, and the woodie jerks it out of my hands, knocking me sprawling!" Uncle Gared waves his third mug, splashing a bit of ale. "The thing starts beating me with its great club arms!" He pounds his fist on the table, then the mug with another splash, then his fist again. "But I can still see my axe, hanging between its legs like a rippin' tail!"

I laugh so hard I nearly choke on my water. All the children are howling.

"So I take the hits, bide my time, then reach right between the demon's legs!" Uncle Gared sweeps an arm out, splashing yet more ale, and one of the brass buttons on his jacket pops free with an audible rip, bouncing and rolling along the table toward the baroness.

Steave points, and he and his brothers howl anew. Even Uncle Gared starts to laugh, until Baroness Emelia gives an audible sniff. "I told you your clothes need letting out. If you're determined to keep getting fatter, you might need a new wardrobe entirely."

"Just a rippin' button." This time Uncle Gared really does growl, irritated at having his story derailed right at the climax.

"Ripping is right," Lady Lacquer says, and both women titter.

"What was it Duchess Araine told you at your Bachelor's Ball?" Emelia asks. "*No one respects a fat man on a throne?*"

Steave breaks the tension before she can retort. "I want to hear about the Warded Children!" I look up to see him staring right at me, and wonder if he's smarter than he lets on, deflecting attention from his father. "You live with them, ay, Darin?"

"Some of the time." I don't trust Steave. He might protect his da, but he's always poking at me.

"It true they ward their peckers?" Steave asks, sending Gared Young and Flinn into peals of laughter.

Uncle Gared swats Steave on the back of his head. I don't think it was meant to cause real harm, but he's a big man, and Steave is knocked face-first into the table with an audible thump. He looks up at his father, more betrayed than hurt, and the general balls a fist in response. "Serves ya right! Show some corespawned respect!"

Steave immediately bows his head. "Ay, sir. Sorry, sir."

"Sorry about that, Darin," Uncle Gared says. "Thought my boys'd have more sense, but I guess they need it beat into them."

"It's nothing." I look at Steave with a grin. "Only knew one man who warded his pecker. Folk said he put impact wards around the tip."

The Cutter boys look awestruck at my words, and even Uncle Gared gapes. "Did that . . . work?"

"Search my pockets," I tell him. "Wasn't able to find anyone willing to try it out. Ella says all it's good for now is drilling holes in trees."

The general roars with laughter, pounding the table. His boys follow along, as much to please their father as at the joke.

"Steave, go sit with your sister a spell," Uncle Gared says. "Darin, come sit by me."

Everyone stops laughing at that. Emelia stiffens, and even Selen sucks in a breath. Steave complies, glaring daggers at me as we switch places.

Uncle Gared seems not to notice, leaning in and fixing me with that probing stare I've come to hate. Trying desperately to see something of Arlen Bales in me. But whatever it is he's looking for isn't there. Maybe my da was something special, but I ent.

At last the general grunts and leans back. "Remind me more o' Rojer than your da, I'm to give honest word."

I don't know how to answer that, looking back uncomfortably until Selen clears her throat.

"Met one of the Warded Children on the borough tour," she notes.

"You mean when you stole armor from your father's soldiers and snuck off, putting your and Princess Olive's lives at risk?" The baroness holds out her empty glass, and a servant is quick to refill it.

"Ay, that." Selen's eyes flick to her father, but when he raises no protest, she continues on. "Saw her fight a coreling barehanded."

She has her brothers' full attention now, and takes her time reeling them in.

"Did you really see a demon?" Flinn's eyes are wide.

"Saw a lot more than one," Selen says. "Whole camp was overrun."

"What were they like?" Gared Young is no less entranced than his younger brother.

"Tough," Selen says. "Bashed one with my shield, hard as can be, and barely fazed it."

"Did you kill any?" Arlen asks.

Selen shrugs. "Got in a few hits, but they heal fast. Stabbed a rock demon in the chest, after . . . " she smells suddenly unsure, no doubt realizing she was about to mention Micha, ". . . someone took it in the knee. Wasn't alone, though. Took more than a few spears to put it down for good."

"Ent an easy thing to do, standing toe-to-talon with a rockie." The general's voice is gruff, but he smells of pride.

"Don't encourage her foolishness, Gared," the baroness snips.

"Ent encouragin'!" Uncle Gared holds up his hands. "Girl knows how I feel about what she done. Just sayin' it's tricky, puttin' your spear between a rock's armor plates."

"I'm sure she did no such thing," Lady Lacquer says. "These children likely saw one demon and are spinning it into the Battle of Cutter's Hollow. There aren't enough corelings left to cause that kind of trouble."

For once, I'm the one who wants to fight. This spoiled old woman's probably never seen a demon in her life, but she's calling Selen a liar? I open my mouth to retort but Selen beats me to it.

"Tell that to the parents of the kids who were cored."

"Plenty of demons left off the greatwards," I add before the other end of the table can volley. "Da . . . " My throat goes suddenly tight. "When he . . . " An image flashes in my mind, Da trapped burning in the Core, screaming my name.

Everyone is looking at me. How long since I trailed off? I force out the rest of my thought. "It was just the ones laying siege on the cities that were destroyed."

"Boy's right, Mum," Uncle Gared's tone is respectful, but firm. "This is not a subject for debate. Lotta witnesses giving the same story you just heard from Selen." He takes the heavy serving spoon to scoop potatoes onto his plate. "Leesha wouldn't have gone to investigate if it wern't serious."

"Weren't serious," Emelia says.

"Ay?" Gared pauses mid-scoop.

"Weren't, not wern't," she says. "If things were truly dire, you'd think Duchess Leesha would have sent her . . . best general." The pause isn't long, but we all feel it. "Instead you'll be sitting for her at court. What will people say when they hear the Baron of Cutter's Hollow still speaking like some backwoods bumpkin?"

I feel the flush of heat as the general's face reddens. His scent is angry—dangerously so, though the baroness looks anything but frightened.

"They'll say I was the first to answer the Deliverer's call," Uncle Gared says. "Say I stood in the Corelings' Graveyard when the Hollow lost its feet. Say I held back a horde at the Dividing." He clutches the heavy silver serving spoon in his fist. "Say I got to be baron with blood and ichor and my own corespawned hands, not by talkin' like rippin' city folk!" His thumb bends the thick metal spoon like it was nothing.

That gets his attention. He stares down at the spoon, breathing deeply. He tries to bend it back to its original shape, but the implement is hopelessly mangled.

Turning his attention back to the potatoes, he starts furiously scooping food onto his plate with it anyway.

I feel terrible for him—for all of them really. This isn't what family is supposed to be. But there is an uneasy silence at the table now, and everyone seems to prefer it that way. I focus on my own potatoes instead.

"LIKE THAT EVERY time?" I ask as Selen walks me back to my room.

"Same scene every Sixthday," Selen says. "Da and Emelia cut at each other until one of them, usually Da, starts shouting and breaks something. All the while, my brothers drool and chase attention like a pack of hounds."

"Why does she hate him so much?" I ask.

"Because he didn't have to claim me," Selen says. "I was the duchess' sister, and Elona's still married to Leesha's da. He could have just let it be, but he didn't. I don't think she'll ever forgive that."

"No wonder you live in the duchess' keep," I say.

"Da wants me here full-time," Selen says, "but every time I stay more than a few days, Emelia gets jealous he's paying attention to me instead of the boys. Does her best to make my life a misery, so I keep away."

We reach the door to my room, but Selen makes no move to continue on as I stop. She's looking at me in that way she has, and I wonder if she's going to kiss me, again. Is it wrong to be excited she might? I need to force my frozen lungs to breathe.

"Olive would throw a fit, she saw us like this." Selen's scent is . . . predatory.

"Like what?" I'm barely listening, just staring into her eyes like a mouse before a snake.

"Alone in a dim hallway, dressed in our Sixthday best." I tense as Selen squeezes my arm, grateful she can't smell my fear.

"Why should Olive care?" I ask.

I tense as Selen leans close, dropping her voice to a whisper. "Emelia's not the only one who gets jealous."

"Of me or you?" I drop my voice to match, though we're alone in the hall.

Selen's eyebrows knit and her mouth puckers. "Now that you mention it, maybe a bit of both. She wouldn't talk to me for a week after we kissed."

"What?" I squeak. "Why would she do that? Olive doesn't shine on me."

"For a boy who can count heartbeats two floors down, you don't catch much," Selen says. "Everything the three of us did back then, we did together. But that was something she wasn't part of."

"She din't stop talking to me," I say.

"'Course not, dummy," Selen snaps. "She was trying to get you alone."

Now I'm completely lost. "Why?"

Selen steps closer. I can feel her warmth in the air between us. "To get her kiss, so it'd all be even again."

She lays a hand on my chest, looking at me with a mischievous smile. "Who knows what she'd do now?"

She leans in, and I close my eyes. I feel her breath as she puts her lips to my ear. "So we'd best behave . . . "

Her hand lifts from my chest, and I feel her step away. I open my eyes, and she flashes me a bright smile. ". . . at least for tonight." She winks and turns to walk swiftly down the hall.

"Good night, Darin."

I watch until she turns the corner, then rush into my room and put my back to the door as I wait for my breathing to return to normal.

I realize I forgot to say good night in return.

17

TAKEN

MOTHER'S KEEP IS eerily quiet without her.

I've always known that most of the people in the keep on any given day were there to be close to the duchess, but it's unnerving to see it in practice. Doors I am accustomed to seeing open, day or night, now stand closed. Offices that reliably had a light under the door until late in the evening, now dark. The chandeliers are still lit, but without the other lights they cast deep shadows as we walk through abandoned halls.

This has never happened before. Mother will sometimes spend a night or two in another borough, but Mother hasn't left the greatward since the day I was born. That she is willing to do so now worries me, no matter how many soldiers and Warded Children she takes with her.

What would happen if she did not return? Would the army of clerks and courtiers return, looking to me for instructions and wages? Or will they stay away, leaving me in an empty keep until I appoint ministers of my own?

That's assuming power falls to me. As likely Baron Cutter would step in as regent until I'm older. Creator love Uncle Gared, but he can't even manage his own house. The general would just sit on the throne and delegate everything to Minister Arther.

That wouldn't be so bad. It would give me space to fall apart.

"Do you think she's safe?" I ask Micha.

"Your mother is . . . formidable," Micha says, "and her warriors are the finest north of Krasia. We have both witnessed what the Warded Children are capable of, and their power is but a dim reflection of Renna am'Bales. There is always risk in confronting the *alagai*, but I have difficulty imagining a threat they cannot overcome. *Inevera*, they will return triumphant."

I know she means to comfort me, but the words that stand out are the qualifiers. *There is always risk. I have difficulty imagining. Inevera.*

The last one sets me on edge most of all. *Inevera* literally means "Everam willing," words meant to remind people that all things, great and small, are subject to the Creator's whim.

But if the Creator is all-powerful, why are there demons at all? Why is there suffering? And if he isn't . . .

My throat catches and my legs turn to water. I cover my mouth as I sob, hurrying to one of the velvet benches in the empty hall. I sit, pulling out a kerchief to dab at my eyes.

"Tsst!" Micha snatches the kerchief away. She unstoppers a tiny glass bottle with an extended lip, honed sharp. Skillfully, she uses the lip to scrape the tears streaking my face into the bottle. She moves higher then, catching the next tear right as it leaves my eye, and all those to follow. When I am done, the bottle is full, with scant room even for the stopper.

"In the lands about Desert Spear, water is worth more than gold," Micha says. "There is no greater way to honor a loved one than a sacrifice of that which is most precious."

She holds the bottle up to the light, so I can see the liquid collected within. "There is power in this, sister. It will keep you bound to your mother until she returns."

I nod, sniffling. "Honor or no, I'm glad Darin wasn't here for that. He's got his own mum to worry about. Doesn't need to see me blubbering over mine."

I know the words are a lie even as I speak them. I might not have noticed how quiet things were, if not for the absence of Selen and Darin. The past week felt like old times, the three of us together again.

I wonder if he's worried, too, or if he and Selen are kissing in some darkened servants' alcove. I wish that thought didn't bother me.

It's not just the fear that they'll break up our easy trio. It's that I can't have the same. It's been weeks but I can't stop hearing Elona's voice in my head.

The time for secrets is over.

"Grandmum says I should tell everyone," I say.

"Tell everyone what?" Micha asks.

"That I'm not like other girls," I say.

Micha's eyes are carefully neutral. "What do you think?"

I sniff, eyes and nose still wet. "I think I'm scared, but maybe it's because I know she's right."

"Is she?" Micha asks.

"She said it's a ticking clock," I say. "Unless I want my husband to unwrap my bido on my wedding night and find a pecker bigger than his."

Beside me, Micha stiffens, sniffing the air. Her hand grips my arm, squeezing painfully as she stands, pulling me up with her.

"What is it?"

Micha touches the choker at her throat and I see its wards come to life. Her next words echo, trapped in a bubble of sound.

"Lean close to me and walk. Continue to appear distraught. We must attempt to reach the hidden stair in your chambers." She sets a pace designed to move at speed without looking hurried.

I feel an adrenaline surge of power in my muscles, but play along, pulling another kerchief to sniffle into and hide my lips as we speak in Micha's bubble. "What did you smell?"

"Alomom powder," Micha says. "Krasian Watchers use it to hide the scent of their sweat. They have attempted to encircle us while you were weeping."

"You know all that from a whiff of powder?" I ask.

"From the scent, and from what my spear sisters and I would do, if we were sent to assassinate a princess." Micha's cold words are a terrifying reminder of who my sister really is. If she is this tense, then things are already dire.

Micha slows as we approach the stairs up to my chambers. She cocks her head, pulling us up short. "We're surrounded. Find a weapon."

I glance back at the darkened door of Mother's first minister. "Lord Arther has a spear mounted above his desk."

"Swiftly," Micha says, still guiding my arm as we walk to Arther's office. "Watchers do not fight like other warriors. They are quick and will attempt to dazzle you with theatrics to hide their true attacks. Do not be fooled. If they throw a handful of powder at you, shut your eyes tight and hold your breath for as long as you can. Find a damp cloth to filter it. Spit on your kerchief if you need to."

It's all I can do to keep my hands from shaking at the casual way Micha describes the men coming to kill us. Arther's office door is locked, but over the years Selen and I have learned how to slip almost every door in the keep. Lord Arther's has a loose jamb. A little pressure in the right place and a heavy shoulder are enough to pop it open.

I breathe a sigh of relief when I see the short fencing spear still hanging above the first minister's desk. I rush over and snatch it from the wall, but the weapon, barely more than half as long as the spear I carried on the borough tour, feels clumsy in my hands. Stabbing at corelings with a long infantry spear is one thing. Facing off against a trained spear fencer is another. There were no lessons in spearwork at Gatherers' University, and Micha has refused to teach weapons until I master hand-to-hand.

"You take it." I push the weapon at Micha.

"I have other weapons." Micha reaches into her robe, pulling out a palm-sized triangle of sharpened glass. "Use the spear defensively. If it becomes a burden, fight with your hands."

"Surrender, instead," a voice says in Krasian, though I cannot place the accent through the muffle of a night veil. "You will not be harmed."

A man appears from the shadows deep in the room. Was he waiting for us? How did he know? I'm relieved to see he carries no spear, just a six-foot wooden ladder, banded with warded steel. It looks awkward—more tool than weapon.

A window slides open and another Watcher enters, pulling his ladder in after him. Micha and I back slowly toward the door to the hall, but it opens and a third warrior enters. All are clad in black *Sharum* robes and sandals wrapped in black silk. Their black turbans and veils hide all but their eyes, darkened with kohl.

"Nanji." Micha lifts her veil to spit on the floor. "Former Watcher tribe of the Majah. They swore fealty to the Skull Throne when the Majah abandoned the Deliverer's army and returned to the desert."

"Your Nanji half brother swore fealty to the Skull Throne," the Watcher corrects. "After he murdered our *Damaji* and stole the black turban."

"And so you serve the Majah, still," Micha says.

The Watcher does not reply, nudging his ladder in our direction. "Surrender. I will not offer it a third time."

He's arrogant. He doesn't expect a pair of spoiled princesses to put up a fight. "There are only three of them," I whisper. "We can win this."

"Perhaps." Micha appraises the men coldly.

There is no warning as they attack. All three men charge at once, swinging ladders off their shoulders. Micha flicks a throwing glass at one, but he puts his ladder into a spin and there is a thunk as the glass embeds harmlessly in the wood.

Another ladder cuts between us and I instinctively dodge aside, realizing too late the intent to split us apart.

"Hold nothing back!" Micha cries as two of the Watchers begin circling her, ladders whirling to box her in.

I focus instead on the one closing on me, the Watcher who offered us a chance to surrender. He swings his ladder and I nimbly slip to the side, feet light and balanced beneath my wide skirts. I attempt to counter but he reverses too fast for me to follow, rolling the ladder across his shoulders to come at me from the other direction. I raise Arther's spear in time to block, but contact is jarring, the thick ladder knocking me back a step.

Before I can recover, the ladder spins again, coming in at a third angle. I move to block, but I am not quick enough, and it clubs me full across the face.

There's an explosion of sound and light inside my head like a round of Mother's festival flamework. My ears are ringing as I hit the floor, breath knocked from my lungs. I taste blood, and feel loose teeth as I grind them together.

Get up. Micha is embroiled in her own fight, but I hear her lesson in my head. *Dodges and parries are less important than learning to recover when struck.*

The Watcher thrusts his ladder down, meaning to pin me between the side rails and put the lowest rung into my throat. I roll aside just in time, kicking at his legs. He skitters out of reach, giving me a second to spring back to my feet.

He moves back in immediately, but this time I refuse to give ground, stepping in with quick thrusts of my spear. These he parries, but the ladder is less suited to defending against such a light weapon. I wait until it is out of alignment and lunge, meaning to drive the point through the man's chest.

The Watcher rolls aside, and as my spear thrusts between the rungs of his ladder I realize he drew me in purposely. With a twist he catches my weapon fast, and I am not quick enough to let go. I'm yanked forward into a kick that hits me in the chest like a woodcutter's sledge.

There is a shriek of pain across my back as I slam into the edge of Arther's heavy goldwood desk. For a moment my whole body goes numb, but I grit my teeth, hands groping at the desk, hoping to find a letter opener. A bottle of ink. Anything I can throw or use as a weapon. But the first minister is fastidious, leaving no clutter in an office closed for the night. I grab the blotter, flinging it at the Watcher as he closes back in. It buys me a second to shove off the desk, just in time to avoid another blow from the ladder.

I assume a *sharusahk* stance, probing with kicks and punches, watching the way the Watcher spins his ladder to parry them. There are only so many ways to keep the ladder in motion in such a cramped space, and the next time it comes along a predictable path, I reach out to take hold of a rung, meaning to pull the Watcher into a kick of my own.

Instead, the ladder reverses direction mid-swing. I follow it with my gaze, turning my head right into a fistful of thrown dust. I snap my eyes shut, but they're already burning. I choke, trying not to inhale as my lungs seize.

The blows come quickly. A swing of the ladder to the head that opens my mouth in a reflexive gasp. The dust in the air is dissipating, but it's enough to set me coughing even as the ladder comes up into my stomach, blowing the breath back out and doubling me over. Another cracks across my already sore back, and I slam hard into the floor.

The Watcher drives his knees into my shoulder blades, pinning me. He puts my head between the rungs of his ladder and pulls. I arch my back but pinned I can't stop him from choking me with the sidebar.

I pull helplessly against the ladder, but the Watcher has all the leverage, and even with my strength I can't loosen the hold. I open my stinging eyes and see Micha fighting hard against her two foes.

The glass knives are almost invisible in her fast hands. Her fingers are slipped into protective holes on the handles, raised knuckles of warded glass adding power to her punches.

But where one Nanji ladder fighter was overwhelming to me, it is terrifying to watch two of them working in unison. With their greater reach, even Micha is not quick enough to strike at them effectively. She parries and dodges most of the blows, but a few glance off her, keeping her on the defensive. Jewelry pulses with magic about her body, making her faster, stronger, but the Watchers seem similarly equipped, negating the advantage.

One of the spinning ladders hooks Micha's ankle and she stumbles right into a swing from the other warrior. It looks like a telling blow, but then Micha twists out of the way and I realize she guided the men on purpose. She grabs a ladder rung and pulls, straightening the warrior's arm as she delivers a quick punch to his elbow with her glass knuckles.

With an audible pop, the joint hyperextends through the ladder rungs, and the Watcher, silent until now, lets out a grunt of pain.

"Your sister fights well, for a woman," the Watcher holding me says. "Had you been her equal, you might have had a chance."

Micha whirls from the crippling blow to catch the other Watcher's swinging ladder in a cross of her knives. She heaves upward and delivers a push-kick that knocks the man back. She lunges, knife poised to end the threat, but she stumbles, a knife buried in the back of her knee.

Incredibly, the man she crippled is back in the fight. One arm hangs limp, but the other holds a collapsible baton that cracks across the back of my sister's headscarf. The Watcher kicks her feet from under her and scissors his legs around her throat, squeezing.

Micha stabs at him, but the other Watcher has recovered and pins her arms with his ladder, holding it in place with his knees to free his hands for pummeling.

Micha continues to struggle for a time, but her movements grow slower and weaker with each passing moment. I wonder if they mean to kill her.

I pull at the rung choking me enough to croak, "Stop."

"Surrender was offered and refused," the Watcher tells me.

"Please," I gasp.

The pressure eases just a bit. "What will you do to save your sister?"

I look to the other men, still pinning and beating Micha, though her body lies limp, convulsing only with the impact of each blow. "Anything," I whisper.

The man pinning me gives a hiss, and the others cease their attack, drawing back. If Micha was faking, now would be the time for her to strike. When she doesn't, I fear the worst. The men pull stout cords from their belts, binding her arms and legs.

I feel a loop of cord around my own legs and don't resist as it pulls tight. When the knots are finished, I flex experimentally. The cord is tough, wrapped many times, and tight. I don't think I can break it.

"I want—"

My words are cut off as the Watcher slams my head into the floor. "This is not a negotiation, girl. Obey, or we will kill your sister here and now."

One of the Watchers takes a knife from his belt, holding it to Micha's throat, while the other binds his injured arm. I am hauled up and sat at Lord Arther's desk, a parchment placed in front of me. Somehow, it is written in my own hand, an apology and weak explanation as to why I feel the need to disobey Mother's command and follow her into the mountains. They must have gotten hold of some letters of mine, because even the phrasing is my own.

"Sign," the Watcher hisses, pushing a pen into my hands.

I glance again at Micha, blade to her throat, and comply.

The moment I'm done, the pen is snatched away. My arms are pulled roughly behind me and bound tight. A rag is shoved in my mouth, and another tied around my head to hold it in place. The cloth is soaked in some chemical, fumy and disorienting. They pull a hood over my head, and everything goes dark.

I FEEL DIZZY and nauseous as my arms are looped through the rungs and bound tight to the Watcher's ladder. He hooks my legs and binds my ankles to a lower rung, then hefts the whole thing onto his shoulders, still managing to move at speed as he hauls me out Arther's office window.

I feel the wind blowing against me as the Watcher climbs to the roof. I am bound too tight to struggle, but even so I tense, afraid to make a move that might throw the man off balance and plummet us to our deaths on the cobbles below.

I bounce to the smooth beat of the Watcher's footfalls as he runs along the rooftops, but I hear nothing, not even the wind. We are behind a veil of silence much like the one cast by Micha's choker.

I'm desperate to know what happened to her. Do the other men run beside us in their own envelopes of silence? Did they take Micha with them? Is she still alive?

I feel the Watcher drop low and twist, and suddenly I am falling. It stops abruptly, then his feet kick off hard and we drop again until the Watcher catches something on the adjacent wall, again arresting our fall before he drops the remaining way to the ground.

Years of sneaking around the rooftops with Darin and Selen is enough for me to guess where we are—the thirty-foot drop into Mother's garden. The adjacent walls are close enough for one to leap from sill to sill on the way down, but only Darin was mad enough to try it. Selen and I regretted the bet the moment he agreed, watching white-knuckled from the roof until he was safely down.

The Watcher does it with me strung to a ladder on his back.

We land lightly on soft soil. During the day, the garden is heavily patrolled. Mother starts and ends every day there, meeting with aides and ministers as she plants, harvests, weeds, and prunes. At night the place stands empty.

The garden has a number of secret exits. I smell roses, and I realize the Watchers have found the one that leads to the stables.

I'm set down and my back fetches up against what can only be the keep's east wall. The hood loosens, and I slowly nudge my chin along the cobbles, trying to work it free. To what end, I don't know. I'm still dizzy from the fumes, in no position to fight.

The Watcher doesn't seem to notice, unbinding me from the ladder with quick efficiency and carrying it away. Free of the restriction I curl up, catching the edge of the hood with my teeth. I fling my head back. The sudden motion makes bile rise in my throat, but the hood flies high enough for me to see. I swallow sour vomit as I look around.

Micha lies next to me in the shadow of the wall. She is similarly bound and hooded. I can hear her breath, weak and fluttering. I wonder if they intend to keep her alive, or if they are just removing a body to delay questions. If I ran off, Micha would surely follow.

I rub my face against the cobbles, working free the gag as the three Watchers gather at the wall, marrying the ends of their six-foot ladders together. The result is still short of the thirty-foot wall, but they seem unconcerned, bracing it as one of the men nimbly runs up, standing balanced against the wall on the top rung.

A second Watcher follows, clambering over his fellow like another set of ladder rungs to stand on the first one's shoulders. At last, the leader returns to us, tugging the hood back over my face. "Do that again and I will put out your sister's eyes."

He picks me up, easily slinging me over his shoulders. He runs up the ladders and scrambles over his accomplices. I am thankful for the hood as he leaps from the last man's shoulders, flying just high enough to catch the wall's lip.

I thought myself numb, but a chill of fear finds me as we swing for a moment in empty air before he pulls us up and lays me on the walltop. "What did you do to the guards?"

"Less than they deserve for being so lax," the man murmurs. "They were half drunk even before we drugged their goblets. They will wake with headaches before their shifts end, and never dare admit the lapse when put to the question. And if they are discovered in a drugged sleep?" He chuckles. "Is not Princess Olive known for such tactics?

"It will be as if my brothers and I were never here."

BOUND TO THE ladder across the Watcher's back, I feel the breeze on my clothes. The vibration as his legs propel us down the streets of the capital. The arrest as he pulls to a stop here and there, no doubt to evade discovery. But I hear nothing.

After a time, we pause and the ladder is taken off his shoulder and lashed to a horse. The drugs finally take hold, and I am thankful as I lose consciousness amid the jolting of the horse's gallop.

I wake as the animal dances to a halt. The pounding in my head suggests I was out for some time, but it's not yet dawn. I am untied from the ladder, but my bound limbs are numb. I fall, shaking and sick, like a shot deer that hasn't yet had the sense to die.

A pair of strong arms catch me, and I am carried several steps to a wooden stair. The doorway is small, and the wood floor creaks under our weight. A wagon?

"You have done well, brothers." The voice is not that of the Watcher who captured me. Even muffled by the hood, it is familiar.

"Glory to Majah," the Watcher says.

"Glory to Nanji." My hood is snatched away and my half brother Iraven meets my eyes. "Apologies, little sister. We are all caught in *inevera*."

I try to spit in his face, but Iraven is quick. He backhands me so hard the spittle is knocked from my mouth to spatter across my cheek. He grabs my chin, forcing me to look at him again. "If you are wise, you will not try such foolishness with the *dama'ting*."

"Enough, my son," Belina says from across the compartment where she kneels with the Watcher who captured me at her left hand.

"Of course, Mother." Iraven bows and retreats to kneel at his mother's right.

"You have done well, Kai Tomoka," Belina tells the Watcher.

"The *dama'ting* honors me." Tomoka bows, putting his hands on the floor and lowering his face to them, but his hard eyes never leave mine.

Iraven raps his knuckles against the wall, and the wagon lurches into motion. I glance around, but Micha is nowhere to be seen.

"Wh . . . " With the last of my spittle gone, the word chokes off before I get far. My throat feels like a thornbush as I clear it and draw new breath. "Where is my sister?"

"Safe," Belina inclines her head, "so long as you remain compliant."

Compliant? Who in the Core does she think she is? "When my mother hears—"

"We will be half a world away," Belina cuts in. "The duchess of Hollow's reach is great, but even she does not have the strength to cross the sands and challenge Desert Spear."

"I wouldn't be so sure," I growl. "But if not her, my father surely does."

"Indeed," Belina nods. "But I know my husband better than you, girl. The betrayal of the Majah eats at him even now. He will not bring an army to our gates over you. I have foreseen it."

She rises, coming over to me. "You should be proud. Your marriage will restore peace between the tribes, and see your brother raised to First Warrior of Desert Spear."

"Proud to be taken a slave?" I ask.

"Tsst." Belina hisses gently. "Marriage is hardly that. Your betrothed is heir to the throne of Desert Spear. As his *Jiwah Ka* you will live in wealth and luxury."

"As a prisoner," I say.

"We are all prisoners," Belina says. "Only in Heaven are we truly free. It is up to you if you wish to be captive in luxury, or bound on the floor."

I bite my lip, considering. I'm in no condition to attempt escape, and that's not likely to improve if I remain bound. "Luxury."

"Wise," Belina congratulates me. She slides her *hanzhar* from its sheath at her belt, severing the cord binding my arms and legs. Immediately I retreat until I fetch up against the back of the wagon, rubbing my limbs to restore my circulation.

Belina does not pursue, opening a cloth holding my possessions. Rings and bracelets and jeweled earrings. "Baubles," she sneers. "Not a *hora* stone among them. No wonder Kai Tomoka and his men took you so easily." She grunts as she finds the tear bottle. "Whose tears are these?"

"My aunt Selen's," I lie. I know enough of *hora* magic to know tears are second only to blood as a component for spells and foretelling. Belina eyes me doubtfully, but she doesn't press.

Instead she runs a finger over the armlet I bought from Achman. She pulls free the little spear, opening the hinge. "I'm so pleased you were drawn to this. The dice were unclear if you would choose the box, the earrings, or the *hanzhar*."

I go cold at the words. Micha was right. The Majah in the market-place at Pumpforge were spies. No doubt I am in one of their wagons right now.

I meet Belina's eyes again, and this time I recognize her. "Fashvah." Achman's *Jiwah Ka*. I am such a fool.

Belina nods. "Hold her."

As one, Iraven and Tomoka move forward, grabbing my limbs and pinning me as Belina closes the armlet around my biceps again. She sets the little spear back in place, and presses her thumb into the sharp tip. Blood wells for a moment, and then is sucked away. The clear gemstone turns red.

As soon as it is done, the three of them retreat, kneeling at the far end of the wagon like Tenders at prayer.

"That is a blood lock," Belina says. "Now that it's sealed, only my blood can open it."

She reaches into her *hora* pouch, producing a tiny replica of the warded band, complete with the spear, shield, and stone. She squeezes the ring in her fingers, and my armlet responds, constricting to dig deep into my biceps. I scream at the intense shock of pain, but then the *dama'ting* eases off the pressure.

"The armlet will lead me to you no matter where you run," Belina whispers, "and if you disobey . . . "

She squeezes the tiny band again, and the armlet shrinks so tight I fear my arm will break. I collapse on the floor, twitching and howling, and the longer it goes on, the more I fear she means to cripple me, here and now.

"Please!" I scream. "Please stop!" A sob escapes my lips. "Oh, Creator, please!"

At last Belina relents. I remain on the floor, shuddering with fear and pain. She kneels beside me, taking my arm and gently massaging the muscles to restore circulation even as she works her fingers against convergence points to numb the pain.

I stare at her, and she turns to meet my eyes. "Do we understand each other, Princess?"

I nod, numbly.

"Good." Belina retreats again. "I trust you will not require additional reminders as we take you to your future husband."

Kai Tomoka clears his throat, a sound so quiet one might miss it if one wasn't paying attention, but Belina turns to him immediately.

Tomoka puts his hands on the floor and bows again, still staring at me. "*Dama'ting*, there is something my men overheard . . . "

For a moment I don't understand, but then I remember my last words to Micha before she caught their scent.

Belina leans for Tomoka to whisper in her ear. She keeps the famed *dama'ting* serenity, but her reaction is immediate, touching a gem on the circlet of warded coins about her brow.

I see the wards activate, giving her sight much like Mother's spectacles. I shift uncomfortably as her eyes flick down for just a moment. "Tsst."

"Mother?" Iraven asks. "What is it?"

"Inevera was right to fear the daughter of Erny," Belina whispers. "Ahmann's greenland *heasah*, the duchess of Hollow, has been hiding a prince."

18

THE HIDDEN PRINCE

OR A MOMENT, sheer, naked terror takes hold and I freeze. Mother always told me that if the Krasians believed I was male, they would kill me before I could attempt to lay claim to the Skull Throne—as if I would ever want it. It's the reason Mother kept the truth of my body secret, why I've always been too afraid to tell anyone.

But they don't kill me.

Even now, I can tell they don't truly understand. I fear Belina will probe deeper and learn the truth, but the *dama'ting* averts her eyes the moment she sees the outline of my body in my aura. Just as Mother said, the moment I fail to fall into one box, they place me in the other without question.

Iraven watches me with martial tension now, as if expecting attack. "Apologies, little brother. We did not know." Even his tone is more respectful than before. It makes me want to scream.

"I'm no use to you as a bride," I say carefully. "No one has died. If you let us go now and return to the desert, it will be impractical for either of my parents to pursue."

Iraven shakes his head. "I am afraid it has come too far for that."

"The dice demanded you, Prince Olive," Belina says, and her tone, too, has shifted. "Female or not, Krasia needs your blood if it is to survive."

The words send a chill down my spine, but I am careful to keep my face neutral.

"Do not fear, brother," Iraven says. "This is the sound of glory calling. Your mother's ruse has heaped great indignity upon you, but it is not too late. We can yet make you a man."

The words hit harder than I expect. Make me a man? Can they really know what that means? Can anyone?

I've read the Krasian holy book, the Evejah. A book Mother says was penned by strong men, building into their scripture the subjugation of women and the weak.

And yet, the Tenders' Canon, celebrated in every cathedral in Hollow, is little better. The blow is softer, but the dogma much the same. A woman's place is home with the children, and the man's to protect and lead.

Like sheep, Mother would say. She's worked to change things since taking the throne, appointing women to positions of real power and opening Gatherers' University, but I am living proof that she still sees a gender line. I had more freedom in one night as Aman than fifteen years as Princess Olive.

Even captive here, I have a taste of it now, and there is a part of me that wants more. That wants to be appreciated. Respected. Like Iraven.

Like a man.

KAI TOMOKA IS dismissed, and Iraven returns to his horse as Belina's carriage breaks away from the main caravan with an escort of mounted warriors.

I'm given tan pants and robe, along with a loose scarf to protect my face and hair from sun and sand—traditional clothes for a child in the Krasian desert. They give me bido cloth as well, but I dare not unweave my own, and Belina says nothing as I decline to remove it while I change.

I am not bound, or kept from the windows, but as we race east along empty, forgotten roads, the trees are a blur and I quickly lose track of the forks and turns. I can see wards glowing on the horses' hooves, making their strides tireless and impossibly fast.

The unnatural speed slows at sunrise, but there is no rest. We press on at a mortal—but no less frantic—pace, and by twilight come to the shore of the great lake. A landing boat awaits us on the beach, its mother ship a dark silhouette out on the water.

I cast about for Micha as we leave the carriage and animals behind to board the ship, but there is no sign of her.

There are wards along the planks and keel of the boat, but still I shudder as we push off. We are far from Mother's greatwards. It is said the lake is so deep, water demons do not need to return to the Core to flee the sun, only sink below the light. I watch the water, waiting for a horned tentacle to rise from the lake and wrap itself around the bow.

"You are wise to fear the demons beneath the waves," Iraven says. "On land they are formidable, but we have ground to stand on, air to breathe as we fight. In the dark water, there is only cold and blackness."

I am led to a small cabin on the ship, still unbound, but with a pair of guards posted at the door. I remember how easily the Watcher defeated me. I do not think I would last even that long against two armed and armored *Sharum*, and even if I could, it isn't as if swimming is an option.

We sail for two days, skirting shipping and patrol routes as we head south. Whenever the winds weaken, oarsmen bend their backs to keep up the pace until we reach the southern shore where a camp awaits with fresh animals and supply.

We move more slowly during the increasingly hot days, resting frequently, but at night the animals race across the desert on warded feet that eat the miles. The magic Belina is expending is enormous.

I've studied *hora* magic my entire life, but demonbones have become increasingly rare in Hollow since the Deliverer's purge and the building of the greatwards. Belina is draining a king's hoard of their power to spirit me away before anyone can figure out what's happened.

In my heart, I expected to be rescued by now. For General Cutter to appear with a cavalry of Hollow Lancers to take me home.

The maps in Mother's study say it can take a month for a Messenger to travel from Hollow to Desert Spear, but in less than a week, we crest a rise and I see it in the distance, great spires topping a massive wall of warded sandstone.

Fort Krasia, the Desert Spear.

Rescue isn't coming.

19

—·—

MYSTERY

LIKE MY OTHER senses, touch is overly sensitive for me. I usually sleep atop the bedding, because the rough sheets in Tibbet's Brook feel like sandpaper scraping my skin.

The sheets in Baron Cutter's manse are fine silk, the mattress feathered, and I feel like I'm lying on a cloud.

But I can't sleep. All I can think about is Selen.

I toss and turn, wondering if she'd wanted me to lean in. To let go. To admit to her—to myself—what I wanted.

Her scent confused me. It always does. A mix of desire and amusement, like a cat batting around a trapped mouse while deciding if it's hungry.

And what did she mean about Olive? It made no sense. Olive Paper is like the sun. Beautiful to look on, dangerous to stare at, and utterly out of reach. I can't imagine a world where she'd want to kiss me, or where I'd even want her to. Be like kissing my sister.

I don't *think* I can sleep, but then I wake with a start and realize I must have drifted off. Someone is pounding on my door.

"Darin Bales, get up this instant!" Selen is shouting.

I'm moving before I realize it, vaulting out of bed and running a hand through my hair. I grab my shirt, throwing it over my head as I reach for the door, wondering what I've done wrong.

Selen looks stricken, but it's her scent that jolts me, a sour stink of fear so intense it wafts from her like a skunk's spray.

"What's happened?" I reach for her arm, no hesitation now as I squeeze. Tears well in her eyes and she throws her arms around me.

"Olive and Micha are missing."

I keep my arms around her as I pull back to meet her eyes. "How? When? We just saw them . . ."

Selen puts her hands against my chest and gently pushes me away. "Don't know. Messenger just arrived from the duchess' keep. Da's on his way over. Says if we're coming, it needs to be now."

In the time it takes Selen to draw her next breath, I rush across the room to snatch up my satchel and return to the door, pushing into the hall. "Let's go."

"Don't you need your boots?" Selen asks.

I shake my head. "All they do is slow me down."

Lord Arther,

Before Mother left, I borrowed her alagai hora for a casting of my own.

The dice tell me I need to be with her—that she needs me— and I cannot ignore it.

I know you—everyone—would try to stop me, and so I must go alone. I am sorry for the trouble this will cause.

With regret,
Olive Paper

LORD ARTHER, FIRST Minister of Hollow, is a former cavalryman. He remains fit for the saddle, but his demeanor is more boring than threatening, despite the military decorations hanging below his spear on the wall behind his desk. I can smell fresh oil on the blade.

The minister's usually dull eyes are sharp as he watches us read Olive's letter, his breathing is slow and steady, and he stinks of suspicion. General Gared, who already read it, looks down at us with similarly mistrustful eyes.

I ignore them, bringing the letter to my nose for a sniff. Olive's scent still clings to the paper. I can smell the precise spots where her fingers touched. The ink of the signature is fresher than the rest, but folk often read a letter over a few times before signing.

"This is Olive's handwriting," Arther says. It's not a question. I glance at his desk and see sheets written in similar hand, used for comparison.

"Ay," Selen agrees, "but it doesn't make sense. Olive can't predict her next trip to the privy with the dice, much less convince herself to run off. And when does Leesha ever put her dice down long enough to borrow?"

Arther manages to keep his voice calm, but there is tension in his muscles, and impatience in his scent. "Selen, if you know anything . . . if you helped her . . . "

"Didn't." Selen shoves the paper back at him. "And Olive didn't write this."

Arther is unconvinced. "Some of the wall guards were drugged with a sleeping draft much like the one Captain Wonda described."

Selen shakes her head. "No corespawned way Olive would run off without telling me."

"In that, we agree," Arther says carefully. "Finding Princess Olive is paramount. If you can help, you won't be punished . . . "

"Ay, don't say that," General Gared growls. "I find out you helped her run off, gonna be the Core to pay."

Selen's scent is fearful at the words, hurt, but her sudden anger overpowers the other smells. "I didn't ripping help her, and she didn't run off! She ent like that."

"Not like that?!" the general roars. "Two of ya pulled this same rippin' trick not three weeks ago!"

"Ay," Selen agrees. "Together! Night, it was my idea! This is different. Olive isn't impulsive."

The general frowns. "Get that you're trying to take the switch for your friend, Sel, but I ent such a fool as to fall for it twice." He turns to Arther. "Micha's gone, too. Means she's already on the trail. She'll keep Olive out of trouble while we send some Cutters to fetch her home."

I catch a faint whiff of blood in the air. Could be anything. Folk bleed all the time for all sorts of reasons, but there's call to be suspicious. The others are too busy arguing to notice me slip away. I pad softly around the room, sniffing.

There's a strange odor—something I've never smelled before. It's strongest on one section of carpet, and I squat down to run my fingers over the heavy pile. They come away gritty with a faint powder that seems to absorb and mute other scents.

At a glance the carpet appears clean, but as I brush my hand through the wool, there is a faint stain of red below the surface. I pinch it and sniff my fingers. Definitely blood.

Now that I have the scent and a starting point, it's easy enough to follow. The floor's been wiped clean, but while that might fool the others, it's another sign to me. Would Arther pause to have his office cleaned, his spear polished with fresh oil, if the first thing he found on his desk in the morning was Olive's note?

The trail leads to the window and I open it, throwing a leg over the sill.

"Ay, Darin!" the general shouts. "What in the Core ya think yur doin'?"

I ignore him, slipping out of the window and catching the lintel to pull myself up. Talk is meaningless. I have the spoor. I follow the faint trail to the roof, then along the sloping tiles to the familiar eaves above the duchess' gardens.

I am stronger in the shadowy nook, leaping down to the windowsill across the way like I did to win a bet, years ago. I jump back to bounce off my momentum on the first wall before sucking in for the final drop. A shock runs up my legs at the impact, but my bones are harder when I suck in, my skin like leather. I'm unhurt as I begin searching for the trail.

Olive might be strong enough to make that descent, but I can't imagine her attempting it. Selen is right. Olive isn't that impulsive. She might have used a rope, but if so, there is no sign.

I pick up the smell of blood, faint amid the fragrant herbs, and follow it through the garden. Here and there I find bruises on grass or plants that would have been imperceptible to others, patterns where soil has been swept and smoothed to hide passage. I find a hidden exit in the rosebushes and track the blood smell to the stables. If Olive was attempting to go after her mother, it follows she would need a horse.

Stablehands stare at me as I sniff around the stalls, but even the wood reeks of urine and droppings and dried mud. I lose the scent entirely, forced to exit the stables and circle outward hoping to pick it back up.

I'm about to give up when I find the spoor again, on the ground near the keep wall. I can smell Olive's perfume clearly. She was not the one bleeding. Someone was with her. A Krasian. Micha? Did they rest here briefly, or hide to avoid detection?

After that, the trail vanishes. Either they mounted—and there is no sign they did—or they scaled the wall. I climb to the top, but it is windy, and if there was a trail, it's blown away.

SELEN GLARES AT me as I return to Lord Arther's office, this time through the door. I tell them what I found, but all three remain skeptical.

"Ya followed her . . . scent?" the general asks dubiously. "Like a hound?"

"Straight up a wall, along a roof, and back down through an herb garden?" Arther adds. "Impossible."

I walk over to the minister, pointedly inhaling through my nose. "You ent had breakfast yet."

Arther frowns. "That doesn't prove—"

"You brushed your teeth with minted paste when you woke," I cut in, "but it doesn't change your breath as much as you think. You had pheasant last night, with herb-crusted potatoes and . . . leek soup. There was blackberry jelly for the pheasant on the table, but you didn't use any."

Arther's face has gone slack. "How can you . . . "

I point to his wrist. "Must've got a bit on the cuff of your jacket when you reached across the table."

Arther lifts his sleeve, eyes widening as he notices the stain. He purses his lips. "This proves nothing if the two of you are protecting Olive. I know the three of you well enough to trust that if she asked you to hold her secrets, you would."

"Corespawn it," Selen growls. "Something's happened to her, and you've got your head too far up—"

"Ay, that's enough!" the general barks. "Ent got anything useful to share, you can keep quiet." Selen looks as if she's been slapped as he turns to the first minister. "No one saw 'em leave, so Darin's story is as good as anything. Doesn't change what we need to do. I'll gather some Cutters and go after them."

"I want to come," Selen says, but her father's scoff denies her without a word.

I step forward. "I can track—"

"You can stay put, is what you can do," the general tells me. "Promised your mam I'd keep you safe. Bad enough Olive's missin'. Won't add you to the tally."

Selen balls a fist, her scent fierce and angry. Before she can open her mouth, I lay a hand over her fist, squeezing gently. "Ay, all right."

Selen whirls on me, but I only squeeze tighter. "We're just worried about Olive, is all. Won't get underfoot."

The general blinks. "Never had an argument with your da go so easy."

I shrug, pretending the words don't sting. "Ay, well. Ent my da."

"Why did you give in?" Selen demands the moment we're alone in the underkeep. Her scent is sharp, angry, and I don't understand why.

"Because we don't need a thousand Cutters trampling the trail," I say. "We need to follow it now, while it's still fresh."

Confusion mixes with the anger smell. "I thought you lost it."

I shrug. "Lost it on top of the wall. Reckon I can pick it back up on the other side, if I head out now. Can you steal some food from the pantry and meet me outside the wall?"

Selen stares for a moment, then throws her arms around me, crushing so tight I instinctively start to turn slippery.

"No you don't." Selen hugs tighter, keeping me from melting in her arms. "Thank you, Darin. You didn't have to—"

"'Course I did." Now I do melt, slipping away to solidify two steps back. "Ent a coward, no matter what folk say. Olive needs us."

Selen puts up her hands. "You're right. I'm sorry."

The words, her doubt, still stings. But now ent the time to debate it. "Outside the wall. Quick as a rabbit."

"Ay," Selen nods. "Get some other things, too. Clothes. Matches. A tent."

"Don't weigh us down," I say. "This is a race, and they've got the lead. Food, your cloak, and a spear."

SELEN MEETS ME outside the walls, dressed much as the stories of her adventure with Olive describe, in a borrowed wooden helm and cuirass, carved with wards and the crossed axe and machete of Baron Cutter's house.

The armor is lacquered and polished smooth, still smelling of whatever soldier wore it last. A round shield is strapped to her back, along with a short, warded spear. I can smell bread and meat and cheese in her pack, and gold in her purse.

She walks my way casually, amusement in her scent. She thinks I won't recognize her.

"Took you long enough," I say when she draws close.

"Corespawn it, Darin," Selen growls, pulling off the helm. "Needed a disguise to slip away. Picked the smelliest breastplate I could find, and walked right past Da's guards. How'd you know it was me?"

I shrug. "Way you walk. Your eyes. Beat of your heart. And I can still smell you under all the sweat."

Selen blinks. "Ent sure how to take that, Darin."

"Like flowers in an outhouse," I say.

Selen rolls her eyes. "I guess that means you're up to this."

I nod. "Found something."

"I did, too." Selen reaches into her pack, producing Olive's warded cloak. "Ent a chance in the Core Olive ran off after her mum without this."

I take her along the wall to a place where some low trees give cover to a spot not far from where I lost the trail on the wall above. "Horses were waiting here last night."

Selen looks around, brow tightening.

"Droppings have been cleaned," I say. "Hoofprints brushed away. But I can smell them."

She looks at me, doubt leaking into her scent. "If you say so."

"There were four of them," I say.

"So Olive wasn't alone," Selen says. "You're saying someone took her."

I don't like guesses. They feel like a promise you ent sure you can keep. I prefer to trust my senses. "Saying there were four horses here, and they all rode off with Olive and Micha."

"Can you follow them through town?" Selen asks.

I blow out a breath, thinking of the thousand ways to lose a trail in a busy town with cobbled streets. A thousand stinks cover those stones, no matter how often it rains. I honestly don't think I can do it. But if Olive's in trouble, she's depending on us.

So I look at Selen, and make a promise I ent sure I can keep.

"Yes."

20

AURAS

S OME OF MY worry proves unfounded. The trail doesn't pass
through Corelings' Graveyard, the market district, or any of a
dozen other parts of Cutter's Hollow where shops, animals, carts,
and foot traffic would bury the scent.

Ent all good news. Outside the keep walls, our quarry abandons
stealth for speed. I follow the horses easily as they bypass the busy streets
of the capital and take the fastest route out of town.

The sky is darkening by the time we reach the open road, and the
horses' strides increase as they are given their head. Too fast for me to
catch with Selen in tow.

I swallow, knowing she won't like what I say next. "You need to go
back."

"The Core, we do." Selen's voice is low, dangerous. I can smell the
embers of her anger, waiting for my next words to fan them into flame.

"Not we," I say. "You."

Selen crosses her arms, waiting for me to say more.

I'm not good at talking. At telling folk what they want to hear, or
convincing them to do what I want. And night, I don't even want this.
Might have told Selen I'm not a coward, but that don't make it true.
Scared to go on without her. Folk tough enough to catch Olive and
Micha ent trouble I want to take on alone.

But facts are facts. As Selen eyes me, I walk back a few steps to stand in a set of hoofprints. I jump the short distance to the next set. "Walk."

I stride forward to another set, but this time I have to leap far to reach the next set. "Gallop. They're moving too fast. The trail will go cold before we find where it leads."

Selen uncrosses her arms, and for a moment I am hopeful, but she puts them on her hips, which is worse. "So I need to go back, but not you? Telling me you can outrun a horse?"

I look up at the sky. "Once it's dark, ay. Can sprint faster than any stallion."

"Gonna sprint for six hours?" Selen asks.

I shake my head. "But they can't gallop forever, and I don't get tired at night. Need to catch sight of them before they get to a crossroad big enough to muddy the tracks, or we might as well just throw dice on which way they went."

"If they're following Leesha and your mam, they're headed east," Selen says.

"Ay, but we don't know they are," I say. "If that letter's fake like you say, why tell us where they were really headed?"

Selen shifts for a moment, but I can smell the stubborn on her. She's not going to give in. "If someone really did kidnap Olive and Micha right under our noses, then they're dangerous, Darin. I can't let you go alone. We follow the trail as far as we can, then make a best guess."

My teeth grind, in part because I know she's right. I should just go. Even if she tried to follow, Selen could never keep up. But I don't think she'd turn back, and she would certainly never forgive me.

Twilight fades as I consider how to convince her. With the darkness comes magic, leaching up from the Core through invisible vents all around us. In the boroughs of Hollow, this power is absorbed by the greatwards, but here it's like a soft glowing fog, wafting about the road. It moves not with the breeze but with a life of its own, pooling around trees and our feet, attracted to life. Wardposts along the road Draw some of the power, slowly flickering to life. So, too, do the wards on Selen's armor, and that gives me a thought.

"Bit of a magic trick we could try," I say. "Risky, though."

Selen looks at me, her scent becoming hopeful. "I trust you."

"Don't know if you should," I admit. "Ent good at this sort of thing. Might get both of us hurt. Mam would kill me for even suggestin' it."

"Olive's getting farther away while we argue," Selen says. "Whatever the risk, it's worth it."

I don't want to take chances with Selen, but she's right. If I go alone, I'll just find a way to muck things up.

"Warned you." I close my eyes and hold out my hand. Selen doesn't hesitate to reach back, her strong fingers lacing through mine and squeezing tight.

With our hands touching, I can feel Selen's aura the same way I feel the warmth of her skin, the beat of her pulse. I reach out with my will, pulling gently, like the suction of a kiss. She inhales sharply as our auras touch.

Aura is like a reflection, Mam used to say. *Magic hides from the sunlight inside us, but at night it's too much to contain. Learn to Read them, you can sense everything a body is feeling, even things they want to keep hidden.*

But the only aura I've ever touched is Mam's, and she knows how to keep hers in check. I felt her love, her protectiveness, but the rest, the dark parts, shame and pain and sorrow, were only shadows drifting just out of reach.

Selen's aura is nothing like Mam's. There are no deep shadows, just the brightness of youth and curiosity with a surface tension of worry and hard determination. I know without question she means to find Olive or die trying. I was right to think she would never turn back.

The rush of feelings is so strong I open my eyes, aching to see the source, and find her staring back at me, sympathy in her eyes that echoes in her aura. "You don't have to feel so lonely, Darin. Olive and I tease, but if it was you missing, you can bet the manse she'd be out here with me right now."

The words hit me like a mallet to the chest, expressing something I've never dared even speak aloud. I don't know what to say, so I say nothing. I don't have to. Selen feels my reply, and squeezes my hand in response.

"Ready?" I ask.

A bit of the confidence in Selen's aura wavers. "Are we going to . . . disappear like you and your mam?"

I shake my head. "Can't do that on my own, and wouldn't risk it, even if I could. That's how my da died."

More sympathy pours through the bond, and Selen squeezes again. "What, then?"

I've never been a natural with magic. The power responds to emotions, and I've too much fear and anxiety pushing it away. I have nothing close to the skill or power of the Warded Children, but even I can Draw a little power when I'm calm. It's easier when there isn't an angry demon charging your way.

I reach out with my will, my own aura, down through Selen's body to pull at the ambient magic pooling at her feet. Like sucking on a straw, I Draw the magic into Selen, watching her aura and the wards on her armor brighten in response.

"Tingles," she gasps. Her warm fingers quiver in mine, but she does not pull away. I keep Drawing until the excess begins to flow into me, and it's my turn to gasp.

Pull a bit of magic through them and into yourself, you can Know a body better than they know themselves, Mam once said. *Everything they are, everything they could be. What they fear and want and aspire to.*

I feel it, a level of intimacy that transcends the feeling of our auras touching. I see a flash of her mother screaming at her, another of her stepmother's cold anger and disdain. The constant battle for dominance with her half brothers, the need for her father's approval. It feels invasive, like reading her diary, but I've never done this before, and don't know how to make it stop.

I could focus in deeper. A part of me wants to, even though I know it's wrong. I want to understand the game Selen was playing the other night, leaning in as if to kiss me, then walking away.

The thought alone triggers a probe, and suddenly I see Selen dressed in wooden armor just like she is now, kissing a tall, handsome boy outside at night. I recoil and there's another flash—Selen in a beautiful dress, kissing a boy in her father's stables. Then I *am* her. I can feel the stableboy's tongue probing my mouth, even as my own probes his.

Again I try to pull back, but the images keep coming, boys and girls, so many of them I lose track. I thought our kiss meant something. Held it in a secret place in my heart those long years when Mam and Aunt Leesha weren't speaking. Ent kissed anyone else since.

But now it just feels like a game she likes to play, making folk breathless and then walking away.

I shudder, and Selen tightens her grip. "You all right, Darin?"

I realize she doesn't know. I'm rooting through her mind like a sundry drawer, but this deeper connection is one-way—me pulling through her. I feel my cheeks heat and am filled with shame. Ent my business who Selen Cutter kisses, or why.

The wards on her armor glow brighter now, but I can feel the resistance as the magic passes through her body. Olive and I were shaped by Core magic in the womb, our bodies made to accept it, to channel it, to hold it like a cellar holds cool air against the noon sun.

Selen isn't like that—her blood can't absorb the power. I feel it trying to flow into her wards, into me, back down into the ground. I have to actively prevent its escape as I stop the Draw, like covering the tip of a straw with my tongue to keep it full without drinking.

Immediately, the influx of images and emotions stops. I breathe deeply in relief, searching for my calm. Olive is out there somewhere, probably in danger, drawing farther away with every moment, and I'm distracted by kissing.

Selen's aura, beautiful before, shines now. She takes a breath, flexing her arms and legs. "I feel like I did when my spear struck the demon. Some of its magic ran up the wards on the shaft and hit me like a lectric shock. Felt like I slept for a month, then dumped the whole sugar bowl into a pot of coffee and drank it all down."

"Sounds about right from what I've heard," I say.

"Is . . . " Selen's grip on my hand shifts as I feel her will tugging at my aura, ". . . is this what you feel like all the time?"

I suck in a little, resisting her probe, too ashamed she might know what I was thinking. "I guess."

"Always knew there was magic about you," Selen says, "but this . . . " She holds up her free hand, curling it into a fist. "I don't think I've ever felt so alive."

"Ent all sunshine," I say. "Magic comes with its own problems. Even if this trick doesn't kill us, we might end up wishin' it did."

"Best get running, then." I can feel Selen flexing her feet, readying herself.

"If I let go, the power will flow back out of you," I warn.

Selen smiles, her fingers tightening around mine. "Then you'd best not let go."

Unbidden, one of the images comes to mind, Selen with her arms around a boy who's everything I'm not—taller than her, broad and handsome. I feel like a child compared to him.

I look away, breathing to calm myself. Got work to be done. We run, and holding the power, Selen's long legs match my speed. Tireless, we keep the pace for over an hour, miles bleeding away under the blur of our feet.

We encounter no demons, but nevertheless I feel exposed. Warded cloaks don't mean spit at this speed. Past the road's wardposts, the lands are open to the naked night. Corelings could come right up to the curb. If the demons really are hunting me, I'm not hard to find.

I have to keep a gentle pull on the magic through our clasped hands. It took little effort at first, but like keeping a muscle tensed, it becomes increasingly painful. My fingernails get hot, my eyes and mouth dry out. My muscles start to burn.

These are signs Mam has talked about my whole life. Ent safe to use magic for too long, or pull too much. Magic is limitless, but the mortal body is not.

Da learned that the hard way.

But Olive needs us. I focus on Selen's hand in mine and keep running. Occasionally she squeezes, and I shiver with pleasure, despite the growing pain.

The trail leads east, much as Mam and the duchess were said to have been heading, though it takes roads less traveled than the duchess' escort of wagons and mounted soldiers requires.

The spoor grows warmer for a time, but time is working against us. I can feel the weight of dawn approaching. We can't keep this trick up much longer.

Selen knows it, too. The longer we maintain the link, the more we can sense what the other is thinking, feeling. We are unified in our desire to run until the sun burns the magic away.

But then we come to a crossroads, ringed with massive wardposts. A great many tracks intersect here—wagon grooves, horses, footprints. We'll need to investigate to see which way our quarry went, if we even can.

As one, we pull to a stop and reluctantly release our handhold.

"Whoo!" Selen stumbles as the power leaves her. I try to catch her, but my legs buckle, and I miss, falling to my knees. My mouth is dry paste, sinuses raw, eyes burning. Every breath feels like fire.

"Darin, are youuu . . . " Selen begins, but then she collapses. Her aura is dimmer than any I've ever seen. I look at my own hands and see them similarly dark. We Drew too much, ran too long, and when the magic drained away, there was nothing left.

I can hear Mam in my head. *Ought to slap the fool out of you, boy, pullin' a stunt like that!*

Mam never raised her hand to me once, but this once, she'd be right to. If Selen dies, I have no one to blame but myself.

I crawl to her, every movement an act of sheer will upon a body that no longer wishes to obey. My senses are dulled by the parch in my nose and throat, the ringing in my ears, the burning pain along my skin.

Selen's breathing is shallow, her heartbeat rapid but weak. Her skin is cold. I fumble with my waterskin, spilling not a little as I put it to her lips. She swallows, but her eyes remain closed, her body limp.

I'm not much better off. Dawn will come at any moment. Already I feel its heat on my skin. Even at full strength, I hate the sun. Depleted as I am, I worry it might kill me.

But Selen needs me, so I risk making things worse by taking her hand again and attempting to Draw just a bit of power—just enough to get us to a safe spot to sleep the day away.

A sliver of fire cuts over the horizon, blinding and burning. Even as I reach for the magic pooled around us, the power evaporates.

My every instinct is to flee as the blaze grows, bathing everything in flames. It stings my skin and fills my lungs with fire. It will kill me if I don't find cover, and running away's what I'm best at.

Instead I throw up my hood and turn my back to the dawn as inch by inch, I drag Selen out of the road, taking succor in the shadow of one of the great wardposts that ring the crossroads.

I get her to drink more, then finish what's left in the skin. My throat is raw like I'd tipped back a boiling kettle. I put our backs to the wardpost and nestle next to Selen, throwing my cloak over us. I give myself permission to close my eyes for just a moment.

Darin!

The voice comes to me from far off in the distance.

Darin!

I try to lift my head, but it's like I'm deep underwater, crushed by the weight of the air around me.

"Darin!"

It's closer now, a wind that tosses me about like a leaf.

"Darin, corespawn it!"

I open my eyes to see Selen in the flickering haze above me, and I wonder if I'm dreaming. Her face looks desperate, but I can't find her scent. She reaches for me, but I feel nothing save the wind. She's shouting, but I hear it distantly, like the dinner bell from down the road. I reach for her, but my hand slides away.

From far below, I feel a pull.

Panic grips me as I realize I've gone slippery in my sleep for the first time since I was a kid. I suck in, feeling myself solidify. Selen snaps into focus, and I'm jolted about like a doll in a dog's teeth as her shaking hands find purchase at last.

I gasp a breath, tearing from her grasp and stumbling back on hands and feet. Selen lets go immediately, raising her hands. "It's okay, Dar. Ent gonna hurt you."

"What happened?" I croak.

"Slept the day away." Selen holds out her waterskin. "Both of us. I only came to a few minutes ago. Went to check on you, and found you all slippery."

Shame hits me, almost more than I can bear. Last thing I want is for Selen to see how little control I have. How recklessly I put her in danger. She's got every right to be mad.

But she doesn't smell mad. My sinuses are still raw and dry, but I know *angry Selen* smell as well as I know anything, and she isn't. She's concerned. "Didn't know you did that when you slept."

"Ay, well," I say. "You're lucky I didn't wet the bedding." Honest word, it might have been less humiliating.

Selen doesn't laugh. "Didn't know the dawn hurts you, either. Didn't know a lot of things I know now." She puts a hand on my face. "Worried about you."

Worried? She'd be terrified if she knew the truth. Da lost cohesion and was sucked down into the Core, never to be seen again. It takes an act of will to stop my hands from shaking at the thought. "We overdid it last night."

"You think?" The sarcasm in Selen's voice makes me flinch, but she drops her hand from my face to squeeze my arm. "Ent blaming you, Darin. You warned me, and we had call to be desperate. Still do. We're no closer to finding Olive."

The name is a reminder of why we're here, and I cling to it as I force myself to roll onto my feet and stand. Every muscle aches and it still burns to breathe, but after I get my balance, each step is easier than the one before it. Magic wisps and whorls around the ground in the darkness, and I realize my body must have instinctively Drawn some to restore itself after the sun set. That's what caused me to go slippery. Has to be.

Selen pulls bread from her pack, and jars of honey and nuts. We sit for a cold meal, and I feel stronger with every bite. When we're done, we walk into the crossroads.

The food, water, and rest have helped restore my senses. I crouch to examine each of the intersecting paths, noting tracks and sniffing the ground. There were a lot of carts and animals here recently, with trails in every direction.

"Well?" Selen asks, when I am on my third way around.

I circle the crossroads a fourth time, walking a bit down each path, searching. If someone kidnapped Olive, they knew how to cover their tracks. With trails everywhere, there's no reason to pick one over another.

"Core if I know." I throw up my hands. "Whole caravan's been through here recently, and seems to have scattered. Olive could have gone down any one of these paths."

Selen's aura, still dim, pales in fear. "What do we do?"

My teeth grind as I give the answer neither of us wants. "We take the coreling by the horns and go find Mam and Duchess Leesha."

WITH THE TRAIL gone cold and both of us still weak, I don't dare pull more magic to speed our passage, but having a clear destination simplifies things. On foot we won't catch up to the duchess' mounted forces, but they were headed to the Warded Children's camp, and I know those lands well. I take us off road whenever possible to shave time off the journey, and we move mostly late in the day and at night when I am strongest and Selen's armor pulls a bit of a charge from ambient magic. We keep our cloaks pulled close, but there is no sign of demons.

It's over a week before the territory gets familiar. Selen's food is long gone, and we've been managing on what I can catch or forage. It's enough, but neither of us has had a full belly in days. At last, I see a ruin of the old world, a once great keep, its walls long shattered, and know where we are.

"Another few hours," I say, "and we'll reach the place Mam was waiting with the Children to meet the duchess. Either they'll be there, or we'll find folk who know where they've gone."

"Do you really think Leesha's dice can find Olive?" Selen asks.

I shrug. "Don't know. Mam says the dice are never wrong, but they don't always say what you think they say. But if it works, Mam can skate to Olive in the time it takes to count our fingers."

Selen nods, but I smell doubt. I can't blame her for it, but there's nothing to be done save press on.

Long before we reach the camp, I know something's wrong. There's an acrid stench on the wind, ash and charred flesh, that leaves me feeling nauseous and afraid. I pick up the pace.

"Ay, slow down," Selen says. "Can't keep up with you when we're not holding hands."

I slow my pace until she can catch up, but every muscle in my body twitches, wanting to sprint ahead. Instead, I grit my teeth and move at the limit of Selen's endurance. It feels like a turtle's pace.

Before long, Selen's nostrils flare as well. "What's that smell?"

"Death," I say as we come through a stand of trees to arrive at the Warded Children's camp.

Or what's left of it.

The tents are all burnt away, and the ground is littered with charred bodies. Many are demon remains—corpses that caught flame when sunlight struck them the next morning. It's a sign my people fought back, and I cling to it like a lifeline as we walk in horror through the camp, seeing half-eaten remains of folk I've known all my life, and corpses so blackened and burnt they are beyond recognition.

I feel sick from the sights and smells, but the pain and sorrow is muted by my rising panic as we search for survivors.

"Mam!" I cry, hoping against hope she is nearby, and well. It's almost unthinkable that a demon could ever catch or kill her, but little of the last few weeks was thinkable a month ago.

Selen cups her hands to her mouth "Leesha!"

The remains of the duchess' soldiers lie here, as well. Horses torn down by tooth and talon, shattered carts and supply immolated by firespit. There's a crater where the flamework cart exploded. Spears lie scattered on the ground, many jutting from dirt or demon ashes, along with shields and wooden armor; breastplates lie cracked like nut shells, the meat within consumed. Demonshit is scattered about, some with human bones sticking from the stinking piles.

"Anyone!" I shout. "It's Darin Bales!"

There's no response. I feel wetness on my face and realize I've been weeping. When I try to wipe the tears away, my shaking hands leave ashy smears on my face.

"Darin," Selen says gently. I turn to see her holding a familiar object, and my silent weeping becomes a sob.

Mam's knife.

I drop to my knees, and Selen rushes to me, saying nothing as she takes me in her arms. No doubt she has friends among the soldiers as well, men and women from her father's own house, but she puts it aside, holding me as I fall to pieces.

———

WE SEARCH FOR days, finding no sign of any survivors, or further proof of Mam or Leesha's fate. Mam always seemed closer to the Creator than a mortal woman. Even now it's hard to believe she was killed when she could have misted away. But Mam ent one to run when folk need her help. That's my way. And even if she did, ent ever seen her without her knife. She would have come back for it.

We do what we can for the dead, but there are too many to bury and most of the bodies are burnt anyway. When the dead demons caught fire in the sun, the flames quickly spread through the camp. Everything that remains is covered in greasy ash and char.

At night we take shelter in the Bunker. Its wards are still intact, the heavy doors strong. It doesn't feel safe, though. It feels like what it is—a prison.

"We need to get back to Hollow," Selen says on the fourth night. "My father needs to hear about this."

I shake my head. "Nothin' against your da, but you see how Hollow Soldiers fared against whatever did this. Uncle Gared ent a match for anything that could take out Leesha, Mam, and the Children."

"What are we supposed to do?" Selen asks. "Head off into the mountains looking for some ancient lost city?"

"'Course not," I say. "Be like lookin' through a pasture for a particular blade of grass, and we ent up to a fight like this, either."

Selen puts her hands on her hips. She's been weeping when she thinks I don't see, and her patience is at an end. "Then what?"

"Way I see it, we only got one choice," I say.

"And that is?" Selen asks.

"We go to Krasia and see my bloodfather."

Selen gapes at me. "You mean . . . ?"

"The man who delivered me, not ten feet from where my da died," I say. "Olive's da. Ahmann Jardir."

21

FORT KRASIA

I LEARNED IN KRASIAN Studies that the underground river that feeds
the city's oasis runs deep below the sands, but occasionally bubbles close enough to the surface to create pockets of life out in the
waste.

Wars had been fought over those little strips of land, and the winners
built great *csars*—walled towns to guard against rivals and *alagai* alike.
Seven of them—one for each pillar of Heaven.

We've passed three of them, so far. From the carriage window I see
nothing but broken walls and ruined towns. There is a look of history to
them, but these are not ancient remains, worn down by years of wind
and sand. The stone from the shattered wall is still discolored. Blackened stalks cling to the ground in the burnt fields.

The damage is fresh.

"What happened?" I haven't spoken to my captors in days, but I
have to know.

"Storms of sand *alagai*," Belina says. "Thousands, descending like
locusts and overwhelming the wards."

I shake my head in disbelief. "How can there be so many?"

"The sands were always rife with them," Belina says. "Too far from
whatever magic your father and the Par'chin worked to purge the green
lands of *alagai*. But they were scattered by Krasia's full might during the

war. A nuisance to the *csars* at first—packs of three or four, or the occasional storm numbering in the dozens."

She looks sadly at the gaping hole in the *csar* wall. "But the storms swept the desert, picking up stray packs and merging other storms. Dozens became hundreds. And hundreds, thousands."

I remember the pack of demons attacking the tour group. The bodies and rent limbs flash across my mind's eye. The screams.

Their coreling savagery made them seem more numerous, but in truth, had there even been a dozen? The thought of thousands of demons pouring through the walls of an entire village is horrifying, like something from the war.

"The dice did not warn you?" I ask. "Aren't you a famed seer?"

Belina gives a gentle shrug, ignoring the barb in my tone. "Everam speaks to me when He wishes to. We sent warning to a few *csars* in time to flee to Desert Spear, but Majah are stubborn and mistrustful by nature. They thought it was a trick to take their fortresses and refused to leave."

I swallow with a throat gone suddenly dry. "There are no *csars* left?"

The silk of her veil billows as Belina shakes her head. "What remains of Majah succors in Desert Spear, now. Fortunately, the city that once housed a dozen tribes is more than enough to support one."

"How many of you are left?" I wonder, not expecting an answer.

But Belina seems to have nothing to hide. "Not twenty thousand Majah remain, many of them born after the return, too young to fight or marry."

The number is devastating. One of the largest tribes in Krasia, reduced to a shadow of its former strength.

"Perhaps twice that number in thralls," Belina adds, as if it is of little consequence.

Thralls. The word grates at me. Slaves, she means. When my father conquered southern Thesa, he divided the lands among the twelve tribes. Each tribe's *Damaji* took control of the individual localities, imposing taxes and levying men for the war. The Thesans outnumbered them more than two to one, but they were mostly farming towns, with no trained fighters to match the elite Krasian military.

When the Majah abandoned the war effort and returned to Desert Spear, they took everything, including the locals, with them as spoils of war. A permanent underclass upon which to rebuild their city. Mother was planning to insist on returning some of them to their families in the North as part of any trade agreement.

I sit back, remembering why I chose not to speak, and we ride in silence for a time. Then the city comes into view again, this time up close, and for a moment, I forget my fear and anger, caught up in the wonder of a sight no Northerner has laid eyes upon in my lifetime.

Thesans refer to Desert Spear as Fort Krasia, but *fort* fails to do justice to the massive city, its walls stretching as far as the eye can see in both directions. I have to crane my head to see the banners atop the watchtowers, flying the Spear of Majah. Beyond the walls, great spires reach into the sky, minarets for the *dama* to sing the call to prayer at dawn, and the call to battle at dusk. The white sandstone catches the sun, like towers of gold.

Desert Spear is breathtakingly beautiful. A legend come to life.

We approach one of the city's side gates. The windows of the *dama'ting* carriage are silvered so the guards cannot see inside, but there is no mistaking Prince Iraven or his elite guard. One of the watchmen falls to his knees while the other scurries to open the gate.

The archway looms over us, tall enough for a rock demon to enter unbent. The wall is thick, layer upon layer of stone carved deep with powerful wardings. It takes minutes to pass through the tunnel at a walk, and the walls are lined with slots for spears and arrows all the way to a second gate. This is a gate, but it is also a trap.

The light at the end of the tunnel is so bright it stings my eyes. I squint as it grows larger, opening up to the famed Great Bazaar, a labyrinth of tents and carts and ramshackle adobe buildings that stretches as far as the eye can see, selling anything and everything.

The vast majority of vendors and customers are women. All are veiled and covered, but some wear black, and others, robes of dark, muted green. It is immediately clear that the women in black are giving orders and haggling, while those in green are doing the majority of the physical labor.

Chin thralls.

I listen to chatter, sifting words from the general din. Most of the chatter is in the Majah dialect, but I hear Thesan, as well.

I draw a bit of strength from the familiar sounds. I look out again at the vastness of the tents. It would be hard to find anyone in that maze, much less one who spoke both languages and could pass as a girl one day and a boy the next.

Surely there is resentment among the *chin*. Could that and my mother's name find me shelter among them?

I am still unbound, the doors unlocked. Out in the desert, I had nowhere to run. Is it any better here? With enough of a head start, it should be easy to lose pursuit. None in our escort, even Iraven, can run as long or as fast in daylight as I can. But just because I speak their language doesn't mean I know anything about these people.

Still, I tense, eyeing Belina in my peripheral vision as I watch the streets, waiting for my moment—a clear path into the maze of tents. I don't know what I will do if it comes.

But then the guardhouse opens and an entire unit of warriors surrounds us to reinforce our escort as we enter the city. If the sight of the prince wasn't enough to clear the path, their cracking whips and shouted commands see it done.

I sink back into my seat, deflated.

"We are not fools, Prince Olive," Belina says quietly.

We pass through the market tents into districts with sturdier structures, then grander buildings still as they approach the oasis at the city's center. The water is circled by grand domed palaces, each with walls of their own.

"Where are you taking me?" I ask.

Belina looks at me like a puzzle she has yet to solve. It would be easier to play coy with my usual defenses. Paints and powder for my face, colorful silk dresses and dyed leather shoes to catch the eye and breath. They were my armor, reminding folk of my position and keeping them at a distance.

Now that armor is stripped away. My hair is tied back from a face scrubbed clean, tan robes rough against my skin. My sandals are little more than braided cord over slips of wood.

"You will be taken directly to the *Damaji*," Belina says. "It will be Aleveran who will judge you and decide your fate."

I don't argue. What would be the point? I cannot stop them from dragging me before their leader, but I'll be corespawned before I let him, or Belina, or even my own mother "decide" my fate ever again.

I get enough of that at home.

I can feel the armlet hugging my biceps. A welcome presence once, it carries new weight, laden with invisible chains that bind me to the *dama'ting's* will.

For now.

Belina may think me broken, but I've had time during our journey to collect myself, and I have a little fight left in me. They need something from me, or they wouldn't have risked open war with the North. Whatever it is the *Damaji* wants, he'll need to give something in return.

THE CARRIAGE STOPS and I step out into blazing sunlight, beating down with an almost physical weight. The air is thick with dust, and I put the veil over my face without thinking.

"Tsst!" Belina's hiss is nearly identical to Micha's. "Men do not veil inside the city walls during the day."

I look around. The women are all veiled, but the men are not. Krasian warriors wear veils at night to hide their identities, that personal feuds be put aside when they must stand as brothers against the *alagai*. *Grant no trust to the man who remains veiled in the day*, the Evejah said, *for hiding his identity gives freedom to act dishonorably without retribution.*

It seems a poor reason to force their men to breathe dust all day, but I lower the cloth, taking shallow breaths. Our *Sharum* escort forms up around us, a wall of armored warriors to discourage prying eyes as we are led forward. I look up and reflexively gasp, choking on the dusty air.

Belina nods approvingly at the awe on my face. "Sharik Hora, the temple of heroes' bones. No doubt you've heard of it?"

I nod numbly. The temple is known throughout the world. I always knew it was large, but my imagination never did it justice. I'd pictured a single-domed, sandstone structure, dull and colorless.

Sharik Hora is anything but. Smooth wide steps climb to a series of broad plazas, leading inexorably higher to a domed temple with soaring minarets that seem to touch the sky. Built to honor the Creator, the pointed arches of its doors and windows are covered by intricate mosaics, scintillating with bright color and precious metal.

I had thought the Cathedral of the Deliverer in Hollow, which fills an entire city block, was grand. It pales in comparison with the mammoth complex before me. I turn my head this way and that, but it never seems to end. A city in itself, the clerical district has its own walls, sprawling over a vast area, and even many of its smaller domes are larger than Mother's entire keep.

But the most eerie part is how empty it all seems. This city was built to hold millions. This temple was built to seat more souls at a single service than the Majah and all their slaves combined.

But the streets are empty, as are the steps and plazas. The only people in sight are my escort and the white-sleeved temple guards, rigid and unmoving as stone statues. The Cathedral of the Deliverer is a fraction the size, but it is always bustling with people—worshippers, Tenders, acolytes, and clerks.

Sharik Hora is all the more daunting for its emptiness. I can feel the weight of centuries upon the place, and see it in places along walls and roofs where collections of the ever-blowing dust and sand have hardened into stone of their own.

The central doors to the temple grow ever larger as we ascend. The pointed arch soars overhead, as if meant to grant access to a race of giants. A pair of fifteen-foot-tall rock demons could walk abreast through the passage with room to spare, were it not for the beautiful wardwork around the frame. Some of the powerful sigils are cut into the stone and painted, others formed by countless tiles of semiprecious stone set in gold.

"Enter humbly, son of Ahmann," Belina says. "This is Everam's home, but also a place of honor for countless warriors who have gone to the Creator defending us from the *alagai*."

As we pass through vaulted archways three stories high, I see what she means. It is one thing to read about Sharik Hora—another to see it up close. The name literally translates to "heroes' bones," and indeed, everything inside the temple is made from dried and polished human bones, worn smooth by the passage of time untold.

Multicolored light floods the temple from enormous windows of intricate stained glass, illuminating walls armored in countless bones. They frame alcoves and paintings, form the bars that hold tapestries and the sconces for lamps. Tables and chairs stand on human legs, holding bowls and chalices made from hollowed craniums. Chandeliers snake out from central mountings on reticulated spines, ending in skulls that stare with sunken eyeholes. I imagine those eyes glowing with oil light at night and suppress a shudder.

Everything is heavy with history in a way I have never known. Hollow is large and powerful, but also new. Few structures are much older than I am, and not a one has seen a century pass. But along the walls of Sharik Hora the bones change color in subtle layers like sediment. They have been laid, generation after generation, since before the calendar of my mother's people even begins.

I am given little time to stare, escorted directly to the great hall. Pews built from polished femurs provide seating for thousands around the altar, upon which sits the fabled Skull Throne.

Not the original, of course. My father brought that with him twenty years ago when he led his people north to conquer the green lands. This throne is new—the skulls white and fresh in contrast with the yellowed bones all around us, or the ancient brown of the seven steps that lead to the dais upon which it sits.

For some reason, those stark white skulls bring home the reality of Sharik Hora more than all the rest. Not long ago, those were living, breathing warriors. Brave warriors, fallen in battle, who did not have their bodies returned to their families or properly burned. Instead, they were beheaded, eyes gouged out, brains scrambled and pulled through the nostrils, flesh boiled away.

All to make a chair.

No doubt the warriors thought it a great honor, but I choke back bile in my throat as I raise my gaze to look upon the man who sits on that throne.

Damaji Aleveran's cold eyes are set deep behind bushy eyebrows and a beard that climbs high on his cheeks and falls nearly to his waist.

His hair is as starkly white as his robes, contrasted only by his dark skin and the black cloth of his turban. His clothes look to be wool—not silk, as the wealthy Krasians I have known prefer. His sandals are as plain as mine.

There is a jewel at the center of Aleveran's headpiece, but he wears no other adornment. No rings on his fingers or ears, though surely a man of such status could have warded jewelry infused with *hora* to grant him powers beyond those of other men. Mother is covered in the stuff.

I take in the others in the room. All are austere, but I'm no stranger to court. These people may not be my own, but I can read their status as easily as one of Lord Arther's rosters.

The *Damaji* leads the men of the tribe, but leadership of the women falls to the *Damaji'ting*. The Majah tribe's is the famed Chavis, whom even Favah spoke of with respect. She stands two steps down from the throne in white robes with a black headscarf and veil. Her only visible jewelry is the netting of warded gold coins that rests over her head like a crown, but there are slight impressions in the cloth of her robe. A man might not notice, but I know what it looks like when a woman wears jewelry beneath her clothes.

At the *Damaji'ting's* belt are a curved *hanzhar*, two black velvet *hora* pouches, and an electrum wand. The smaller pouch no doubt holds her dice, but the other, larger pouch and the wand are ready for more versatile spells. With them, she is more dangerous than the spear-wielding guards that surround me, but this is not the source of her imposing presence.

Chavis is old. I can see it in the skin around her eyes—the only visible bit of flesh—but she does not appear weak or bowed with age. This is a woman who has seen rivals rise and fall. She was forced to abdicate when my father rose to the Skull Throne and made Belina *Damaji'ting* of Majah. Old even then, Chavis bided her time, and was ready to take power back when the Majah broke from my father's empire.

At the base of the seven steps to the throne are two venerable groups. To the *Damaji's* right are the white-robed council of *dama*. Six men, each with a brightly colored gemstone on his white turban, and a silver ring in his right ear. They lean on flexible whip staves banded with silver, and barbed alagai tails hang at their belts next to warded knuckle silvers with contoured finger loops. *Shar'dama*. Fighting priests. Their black beards are streaked with gray, or perhaps it is the other way around.

Across the aisle to the throne's left are six veiled *dama'ting*, each with a silver netting of coins atop her white headscarf. Like their leader, they too wear jewelry beneath their robes. *Hanzhar* and velvet *hora* pouches hang from their belts. The eyes behind their veils seem ageless.

Aleveran alone is unarmed and unadorned, and this speaks to his might more than any display of strength. His power here is almost absolute.

Almost.

Iraven and Belina flank me, striding to the center of a mosaic ward circle laid on the floor before the altar of bones. My brother thumps his spear, and he and Belina kneel. He lays his spear flat as they both put hands on the floor and press their foreheads between them.

"Tsst!" Belina glances at me, seeing I do not kneel.

But why should I? This is not my *Damaji*, not my temple, not a priest of my Creator. This is my captor's stronghold, nothing more.

I feel strong for a moment as everyone in the room gapes at me, but then Iraven snatches up his spear and whirls it faster than I can follow, striking the back of my knees. My tiny bit of power is stolen as my legs fold and I fall, knees slamming into the hard stone. I'm forced to put my hands on the floor to keep from smashing my face.

"So this is the hidden prince," Aleveran says. "Insolent. He knows nothing of our ways."

Belina hisses again as I raise my eyes, but I ignore her. She's no longer the power in the room. "Why should I kneel before a man who sent Watchers into sovereign lands to kidnap me like they were . . . " I struggle to remember the proper Krasian term, ". . . stealing a well?"

I hear the whoosh of air as Iraven draws back his spear for another blow. I brace myself, but Aleveran checks him simply by raising a finger.

"Arrogant and willful, too," the *Damaji* notes. "It is good to see something of a prince's pride in the boy forced to wear women's clothing, but even a prince must learn pridefulness before his betters comes at a cost."

He lowers his finger, and the shaft of my brother's spear cracks like a whip across my back. "Stop this," Iraven whispers as pain lances across my body.

Perhaps he thinks the words will make me submit, but they have the opposite effect. He speaks as if he cares, even as his is the arm that strikes me. The lie of it enrages me, but I do not let it show. Not here, not now. There will be time later to cry in pain. For now, resistance is the only power I have, and I must hold it until I have what I need.

I raise my eyes again.

"Stubborn," Chavis observes. Aleveran nods, and my brother's next blow slams me into the floor. I turn my face aside just in time to spare my teeth and nose from breaking.

"Do not." Iraven warns as I put my hands under me to push back up. I ignore him, and my brother lifts his spear again.

"Enough." Aleveran holds up a hand. "You have proven your loyalty, Prince Iraven, and you will have that which was promised. Attend me."

A chill runs through the fire across my back as Iraven walks to the base of the Skull Throne and kneels, laying his spear at his side.

Chavis produces a white turban with a jewel at its center. I can see the point of the warded glass helm it contains glittering at the top. Iraven removes his black turban and bows as she places it atop his head.

"Rise, Sharum Ka." Aleveran does not shout, but the acoustics of the room make the words bounce to every corner.

I see an apology in Iraven's eyes as he turns to face me, but it is meaningless. His actions speak louder than any look. He's no brother of mine. He traded my life for his own ambition.

"And you, *nie'Damaji'ting*." Chavis reaches into a pocket of her robe, drawing out a black silk veil. "Unless the dice call another, you have earned back the succession, on my natural death."

Natural. The word seems a warning. Nevertheless, Belina leaves my side to ascend three steps. Only Chavis and Aleveran see her face as the *Damaji'ting* removes her white veil and replaces it with black, marking her as Chavis' heir.

"As for you, son of Ahmann." Aleveran turns his cold eyes back to me. "You seem determined to speak out of turn, so let us speak. You may think us cruel, but it is nothing compared to what your own mother has done. Leesha vah Erny am'Paper am'Hollow has shamed you beyond measure with her deception."

"Perhaps she simply sought to keep me from being kidnapped by honorless rivals who wish to make a political tool of me," I say.

There are sharp intakes of breath at that. Iraven tightens his grip on his spear, but none dare interrupt when the *Damaji* is speaking.

"Honorless was robbing you of your birthright," Aleveran says. "Honorless was stealing your manhood and making you into some sort of . . . " he waves a hand in disgust, ". . . *push'ting.*"

Push'ting. The closest translation is "false woman," but there are layers to the word I don't entirely understand. I know from my studies that Krasians don't forbid folk from lying with others of their own sex—like many of the Tenders of the Creator do in the North—but a man so devoted to loving men that he refuses to father children is considered beneath contempt in Krasia. Their endless war against demonkind cost too many lives, and their numbers are dwindling.

"You are young, yet," Aleveran goes on. "You cannot be expected to understand the damage your mother has done. Everam willing, there is time to undo what she has wrought and teach you to be a man."

"Oh, I'd love to learn," I say. "Does being a man mean attacking unarmed women two-to-one like your Nanji?"

"To win!" Aleveran barks. "To see what must be done and achieve victory, no matter the cost."

"And the dice say your victory requires me," I say. "*If Olive Paper does not join her blood with Majah, Desert Spear will fall,* Belina told Mother."

For an instant, Chavis' eyes flick to Belina in irritation. I suppress a smile despite the pain that still lances across me. She wasn't supposed to show those cards.

"Dice are fickle things," Chavis returns her full attention to me, "and there is more than one way to read a throw. 'Join' made the most sense when we thought you a princess; as a prince, it could be interpreted more . . . literally." She strokes the handle of her *hanzhar*, and I do not miss the gesture.

"I want to see my sister," I say.

"You are in no position to make demands," Aleveran says.

Slowly, painfully, I get to my feet, never breaking eye contact. "I think I am, Damaji. If my blood is all you need, take it and have done. But I, too, studied in the Chamber of Shadows."

"Tsst," the women in the room hiss almost in unison, including Chavis herself. No doubt they are scandalized at the notion of a boy learning the *dama'ting's* art.

"Perhaps, Damaji, your priestesses have not told you that there must be consent, with blood magic."

"For the dice, perhaps," Chavis says. "This could mean something else, entirely."

I keep my eyes on Aleveran. "Are you willing to gamble Majah's future on 'perhaps'? Whatever your prophecy demands, your chances are better if I do it willingly, and that I will never do if I am not allowed to speak to my sister and have continued assurance she is alive and well."

Aleveran leans back in his chair, steepling his wrinkled fingers. "And if she is not? If she fell with honor defending her brother?"

I cross my arms. "Then everything I have been told about the honorless Majah is true, and the abyss can take you, for all I care."

Finally, a twitch of emotion on his face, suppressed almost instantly. I'm playing a dangerous game, but I'm not bluffing. If they killed Micha, I'll be corespawned before I lift a finger on their behalf.

"No doubt you are used to being treated as a princess," the *Damaji* says at last. "Men fear to strike the insolent mouth of a princess." He leans forward in his throne, and I tense as if he could reach me from across the room. "But you are no princess."

He lifts a finger of each hand, and two *Sharum* guards rush in, grabbing my arms. I pull hard and one of the men, unprepared for my strength, is thrown to the floor. The other, off balance, is easily pulled in as I punch him in the stomach.

My hand strikes armor plating, and I bite down to keep from crying out as guards swarm from both sides, looping cords around my wrists and pulling them tight, denying me leverage as my legs are kicked out from behind me and my knees slam back into the stone with a sharp, jagged pain.

"Your pride and vanity must be stripped away, like those womanly locks," Aleveran says. He nods to one of the guards, who produces a knife and takes a fistful of my hair. I grind my teeth, thrashing, but I cannot stop him from cutting it away.

It's like losing a limb. My hair has always been a part of my identity, and I can feel each strand as the blade cleaves them away. It will take years to grow back.

The guard casts the hair to the floor and keeps to his work until the tiles around me are littered with black locks, and only a jagged patchwork of stubble remains.

"Sharum Ka," Aleveran says. "Teach your brother the price of insolence before the Skull Throne."

Iraven nods, his mouth a grim line as he hands his spear to a guard, accepting an alagai tail from one of the *dama*. His eyes are hard as he strides toward me. "I warned you."

"You sold your own blood for a white turban. I hope it buries you under its weight." I try to spit in his face, but I've never spat at anyone before, and don't use enough force. The spittle falls short, and my mouth is too dry from the dusty air to produce more.

Iraven scowls, uncoiling the whip with a crack that echoes in the great domed chamber. The braided leather narrows to three thin tips, each with a bit of sharpened metal in the weave.

Iraven strides behind me, and I shudder and tense. *Fear and pain are only wind*, Micha taught. *Find your center and bend as the palm, letting them blow over you.*

But as the first lash tears through the thin tan shirt, my limbs turn to water, and my center—whatever that truly means—is lost. I cry out despite my determination not to.

Again the alagai tail strikes, and again I scream. Over and over it comes, until my shirt is a tattered ruin and my entire back feels like an open wound. Iraven gives me a moment to breathe between each lash, but it is not a mercy. It simply ensures the pain of each strike is endured fully before covering it with the next.

I hang limply from the cords now, weeping openly. Without the men holding the ends, I would have long ago collapsed. I look up between blows, seeing Aleveran through eyes blurred with tears. He does not smile, but there is satisfaction on his face.

He notices my gaze. "You see you are no princess here, Olive asu

Ahmann. You are not even a prince, just the bastard of a *chin heasah*. You will do as you are bid."

He waits, as if expecting a reply, and Iraven waits as well. My brother is no hero, but even he does not wish to lash me to death.

My limbs feel like gelatin that has not set. My back is aflame, and every muscle in my body screams in agony from clenching against each blow. I cannot fight. Cannot stand. Even the act of raising my head takes reserves of strength I didn't know I had.

"I . . . " My voice is a croak, words cut short as a throat screamed raw and dry seizes up. There's blood in my mouth—I don't know where from—and I swish it about to lubricate my tongue before choking it down to unstick my throat.

"I . . . " The words hurt so much, but I suck in a breath and force them out. "I want to see my sister."

Aleveran's eyes widen, and there are murmurs among the councils of clerics.

"Sister, please." There is pleading in Iraven's tone now. Desperation. It gives me strength.

I spit blood onto the floor. "This . . . is the only . . . blood . . . you'll have."

"Damaji." There is a tremor in Iraven's voice. Perhaps it is the beginning of a spine, but it is too little, too late. If Aleveran commands him to keep lashing until I am dead, my brother is too far gone to deny him.

Aleveran regards me for a long time, his bushy brows furrowed. At last he relaxes and sits back, swishing a hand through the air. "I would be a fool to kill a brave and promising young warrior, however insolent, over a boon that costs me nothing." He points a finger at me. "But take care, boy. Everam's patience is infinite, but the Skull Throne's is not."

The guards ease the cords that bind me, and I collapse to my hands and knees on the floor before the elders of the tribe. All thoughts of pride, of appearances, are gone. I weep in pain and terror, tasting blood and tears and the snot running from my nose. The Majah elders look on impassively. If there is any sympathy in them, they are not willing to show it in front of the *Damaji*.

22

NEVER STOP FIGHTING

Eventually I regain control. When Iraven staggered his blows, it made each strike individual, layering in fresh pain before I could grow accustomed to the old. But now the pain is a constant, and eventually I can bend as Micha taught, letting it wash over me.

My sobs ease and I bring my breath into a steady rhythm, bending more easily with each moment. I remain on my knees because it is the easiest on my battered body, and not out of fear of Aleveran.

That's what I tell myself, anyway.

Iraven pushes a water bottle in front of me and I slap it away, regretting the move even as it happens. My throat is dry as the cracked clay flats of the desert. Who do I help, by refusing water? Certainly not myself.

Whether he can sense my internal debate, or is simply eaten by guilt, Iraven caps the bottle and sets it on the floor next to me. I watch it with the side of my eye, trying not to stare, wondering how long my stubborn pride will keep me from picking it up.

A door on the *dama'ting* side of the altar opens and my heart leaps, pain forgotten at the sight of my sister. Micha's head is bowed in submission, and manacles around her wrists and ankles are bound with thick chain to a central ring. The chains are so short she cannot raise her hands without kneeling, or move at anything close to a full stride.

But she is alive, and appears well. No doubt Belina had her treated the night we were captured and simply kept us apart for the journey to Desert Spear.

Micha is escorted to the floor by a pair of *Sharum'ting*—female warriors like herself. Common enough in modern Krasia—my father gave able-bodied women and *khaffit* who joined his forces the same rights as his other warriors. But it was said the Majah went back to the old ways when they returned to the desert, forbidding the spear to all but the warrior caste.

It was posited at Gatherers' University that these rights would be the first things eliminated upon the Majah secession, but Mother never believed it. "Rights given are not easily stripped away," she said.

It seems there is some truth to the words as I eye the hard women of Micha's escort. They are not lax, watching my sister as if she might break her chains and become a rock demon at any moment. Each has a short, stabbing spear in one hand, another strapped to her back with a rounded shield.

Micha gasps when she sees me, moving toward me as fast as her chains will allow. It is a snail's pace that seems to take an eternity. I wobble on my knees, wondering if I can keep from passing out long enough to speak to her.

At last she makes it across the floor, dropping to her knees and flinging her arms around my neck, careful not to touch the raised and bloody welts left by the alagai tail. She sobs, pulling our foreheads together. Tears run down her nose to touch mine, and suddenly we are both weeping.

"Are you all right?" I whisper, not knowing how long we have. "Have they . . . "

"Belina healed me . . . each time," Micha says quietly.

"Each time?" I ask.

"Each time I tried to escape," Micha says. "I killed two guards on the boat and nearly made it to your cabin before they caught me."

She says it so matter-of-factly. Of course she tried to escape. But not me. Perhaps my will is more broken than I think.

"What about you?" Micha asks. "Your back . . . "

"I had to know you were alive," I say. "I told them I would not help them without proof that you are well."

"You took the alagai tail . . . for me?" Micha's voice is an uncustomary squeak.

"You killed two guards for me." I take her face in my hands, feeling the wet of her tears soaking through her veil. "We're sisters."

"They will treat you as my brother." Micha pulls me close to breathe her next words into my ear. "And you must let them. War is deception. Become what they expect, so they remain ignorant of who you truly are. Hide your strength and bide your time."

"Bide it for what?" I whisper. Does she have a plan?

"You see now your sister is alive and well." Aleveran's words pierce the bubble around us, and suddenly I remember we are before the throne, surrounded by the court. "We have not harmed her, despite the Majah blood she has shed. Micha vah Ahmann fought with honor, and deserves honor in return. Even a lesser daughter of Ahmann Jardir is a valuable bride, though her work with the spear has stolen her most fertile years."

As I stare at Aleveran, a fantasy plays across my mind—charging up the steps to put my hands around the old man's throat. Micha only passed her thirtieth summer last year. Grandmum was nearly fifty when she had Selen.

"On the first morning of Waning each month, your sister will be brought before you to assure you she is well," Aleveran says. "In return, you will go to *sharaj* and obey the drillmasters in all things. If you do not . . ."

The two female *Sharum*, so still I had forgotten they were even there, spring into action. Their hands flick back, drawing their second spears. In the blink of an eye there are four spearpoints aimed at Micha, targeting heart, throat, spine, and liver. Any of the four would kill her, but my sister looks unperturbed.

I meet Aleveran's gaze and widen my eyes like Grandmum taught me, sticking my lower lip out just a hint. *Looking scared is enough for most men, but if that don't work, most find tears unbearable.*

Elona taught me to weep on command, but the real tears streaking my cheeks are enough. I look as I imagine Aleveran wants me to—deathly afraid and willing to promise anything. "I understand."

At a wave from Chavis, the *Sharum'ting* lower their weapons, each sheathing one to free a hand.

"In *sharaj*, fight," Micha whispers as they reach for her arms. "It is the only thing men respect." The guards pull her to her feet, but she keeps talking. "The first day, fight. Every day, fight. When you lose, fight. When you win, fight." The guards yank her away so hard she stumbles on her chain. They pause while she regains her balance, and Micha meets my eyes one last time.

"Never stop fighting."

23

·

CHADAN

I sit back on my heels, shaking, as they drag Micha away. Pain, exhaustion, and anguish all work together to push me over, and soon they will have their victory.

Never stop fighting.

I don't know if I have the strength, the courage, to do as Micha asks. There is a difference between choosing the right moment to be stubborn, and committing to a life without fear.

But still I strain, refusing to collapse in front of the court. Relief floods me as Aleveran adjourns, but no one rushes to leave. Chavis ascends to the throne, leaning in to confer with the *Damaji*. On both sides of the aisle, clerical councils put their heads together.

I remember similar informal sessions in Mother's court, councilors taking the time together to confer on the news of the day and prepare strategies. Today there is much to discuss. Iraven was sent to capture a princess, and has returned with a prince, no doubt casting all their plans and schemes into disarray.

But for every minute they linger, a part of me dies. Soon there will be nothing left, and I fear I will die here on my knees.

"That was very stupid, brother." Iraven drops to squat beside me, whispering. "Aleveran might have killed you."

I shake my head, surprised at how light it feels with my hair cut away. The sensation of sweat cooling off the top of my head is strange and unpleasant. "No—"

I choke on a throat gone sticky and rough. Iraven brings the water bottle to my lips, and this time I am not too proud to drink. I pull so hard I cough the first swallow back up. After that I drink more slowly until the passage reopens and something of my voice returns.

"No," I say again. "*You* might have killed me. You, Iraven asu Ahmann am'Jardir am'Majah, would have beaten your own brother to death for your *Damaji's* favor."

"Do not presume to know me, brother." Iraven's whisper turns harsh. "You have no idea what we face. I serve the Majah, not my own ambition."

I force a laugh I don't feel—the snort of derision I've seen Grandmum wield like a lash. "Keep telling yourself that tampweed tale."

A vein pulses on Iraven's jaw, and I think he might strike me. I hope he does. I'm in such pain I will hardly feel it, but the loss of control will weaken him in the eyes of the tribe's elders.

Iraven understands that, too. His breathing becomes slow and even, and the vein disappears. "*Hannu Pash* will be good for you, brother. The *sharaj* will beat the insolent tongue from you better than I ever could. Now get up."

He slides an arm under mine and attempts to haul me to my feet. My legs feel like ice that has just begun to form. I fear they will shatter if I put my full weight on them. I am disgusted with myself as I cling to Iraven's steady arm, desperately needing its support.

"I can't walk." I grimace at the whimper in my voice.

"You have to," Iraven says. "When you were my sister, I could carry you. Now you are my brother, and in Krasia, warriors walk before the Skull Throne."

"I'm not a warrior," I say.

Iraven looks at me as if I am a fool. "It is preferable to the alternative, I assure you."

I glance around. Everyone, from the *dama* and *dama'ting* of the council to the servants and guards, casts glances my way as they go about their business, watching while pretending not to watch. I don't know a lot about Majah customs, but I understand palace gossip. All of them are hungry for tales of the *push'ting* prince to bring back to their personal fiefdoms.

So I grit my teeth and stumble along, step by agonizing step, until we reach Belina, waiting by an exit door on the *dama'ting* side of the altar. I stumble through into a private corridor, and as the door shuts behind us, Iraven sweeps me up into his arms. "You bore that well, brother."

The compliment should sicken me, but I'm too relieved to be off my feet. I melt, feeling consciousness slipping away.

"Take him to the Chambers of Healing," Belina says.

That wakes me. Sharik Hora is famed for its warrior bones, its mammoth size and architecture, its vast libraries of ancient texts, dating as far back as the first demon war, three thousand years ago. But no place was spoken of in Gatherers' University with as much awe and wonder as the Dama'ting Chambers of Healing. Our Krasian instructors would invoke the legendary place like it was the final authority in medicine.

Even in my haze, I cannot help but take in what I can. This part of the temple is not covered in bones, the magnificent halls warded with intricate mosaics, brightly woven carpets, rich tapestries, and paintings so vivid it feels they might come to life. *Sharum'ting* guards are posted in the halls, and everything smells of dried herbs and old books.

It reminds me of Mother's office, and that frightens me most of all.

I am taken into a private chamber with a table for medical procedures and an array of bottles, jars, and surgical implements. Iraven lays me facedown on the table as Belina begins filling a mortar with various herbs and oils.

"It is forbidden to cast healing spells on wounds from the alagai tail," Belina says, grinding the mix into paste with a stone pestle. "Remember that, the next time you choose to speak out of turn and make demands of the *Damaji*."

She strips away my shredded shirt, methodically cleaning and inspecting my lacerated back. There is a needle and thread on her tray, but the wounds are too shallow to stitch. Instead she spreads the paste over my back. It is pungent and stings at first, but the feeling soon fades into comfortable numbness as the herbs do their work.

"Rest now while you can," Belina says. "The *Damaji* wants you in *sharaj* before the day is out."

"I will take him myself," Iraven says.

"Best bark quickly, when master says speak," I say.

"Tsst!" Belina slaps me across the back, and I gasp in pain. "Silly, stupid boy. You understand nothing of what your brother has sacrificed to regain what was taken from him."

"He has sacrificed *me*," I reply. "What else is there to understand? To replace what was taken from him, he has robbed its measure from me." I turn to stare at Iraven. "You owe me a blood debt, brother. One day I will collect, if our father doesn't call it due, first."

"When he learns of your mother's deception, his anger will be for her, not us," Belina says.

He already knows. I think the words rather than speak them, for they come too close to my secret. "You know him better than I," I say instead. "What will he do, if he learns I am prisoner to the tribe who deserted Sharak Ka in humanity's hour of need?"

Belina looks at me with sad eyes. "His first wish will be to send an army to crush us, even if thousands die on both sides of Desert Spear's walls. That is what a blood debt means, little greenland prince. Are you prepared for it to be paid in innocent blood?"

I look away, unable to meet her gaze any longer. Belina is right. I don't understand. Not truly. And I am so tired. "Then why tempt it?"

"Because we have nothing to lose," Belina says. "The storms continue to build. They will consume us as surely if we do nothing."

I'M ON MY feet just a few hours later, but already I feel stronger. I heal faster than other folk, especially when I sleep. The wounds on my back have already closed, but it is a tentative thing. Even a gentle stretch in the wrong direction could reopen them.

Iraven is talking about something as he leads me through the training grounds. I'm barely listening. He never shuts up.

"Once, there were twelve great pavilions," Iraven says. "A *sharaj* for every tribe in Krasia."

The yard is massive, enough for every man, woman, and child in the city to march and practice formations, but much of it is dusty and unused. Instead of twelve pavilions, I see four, each surrounded by a cluster of low, clay buildings.

"Now the *sharaji* are divided by blood," Iraven continues. "Full blood for the sons of pure-blooded Majah warrior families. Half blood for the sons of *dal'Sharum* and *chin* women. Coward's blood for the sons of *khaffit*, and green blood for the sons of *chin* fathers."

The sky is awash with color as Iraven leads me through the grounds to the largest pavilion. As we pass, warriors take note of his white turban and bow, punching fists to their chests. One goes even further, dropping to one knee. The red veil of a drillmaster is loose around his throat. "First Warrior. News spread quickly of your rise. It is good to see you in the white turban at last."

"Rise, my friend," Iraven reaches out a hand and the drillmaster takes it, allowing himself to be pulled to his feet.

"You honor us with your presence," the drillmaster says. "The class is ready for your inspection." He gestures to a line of skinny boys, many of them clad in nothing but tan bidos and wooden sandals. Some of them are breathing hard and sweating. The dust has not yet settled at their feet. They must have assembled in a hurry when the pavilion guards spotted Iraven's approach.

"That is not necessary, Chikga." Iraven gives the boys a dismissive wave of his hand. "I am only here to deliver Prince Olive into your hands."

"The *push'ting* prince?" Chikga laughs. "His mother is a greenland *heasah*. Send him to the half-bloods." Some of the boys snicker, and I feel my flesh crawl. What is he delivering me to? What is my life about to become?

Iraven isn't laughing. His face darkens, and the drillmaster takes immediate note. "Tsst!"

The hiss is enough to silence the boys. Some look at the drillmaster with open fear, others with respect, but none dare question him.

"Olive is the son of Ahmann Jardir, Chikga, and he is my brother." Iraven's words are quiet, but weighted with menace. "Can the other pavilions train him as well as yours?"

Chikga swallows any retort, taking a step back and punching a fist to his chest. "Of course not, Sharum Ka. *Inevera*, it will be done."

Iraven turns to look at me. He doesn't shout, but he raises his voice enough that even the students can hear. "Do not expect any special treatment beyond that, brother. Life in the green lands has no doubt made you soft. The coming days will be difficult, but they will harden you." He steps close, lowering his voice so only I can hear. "And if you wish to see your sister again next Waning, you had best obey the drill-master's every command."

With that, he turns and walks off. Already an entourage of *kai'Sharum* and drillmasters is waiting, doubtless to congratulate him on being raised to First Warrior, and escort him to his new palace.

"Quit staring, boy." Drillmaster Chikga slaps the back of my head. With my hair shorn away, the blow sounds with a sharp crack. "Strip down and join the others in line."

"Strip?" I immediately regret the question as the drillmaster scowls.

"Bidos and sandals only, *nie'Sharum*," he sneers. "Boys must earn their robes."

I grit my teeth as the other students snigger, but the sounds choke off as I turn my back and pull off my shirt, revealing the lines Iraven's whip left across my back, crusted with blood and Belina's healing paste.

Even Chikga blows out a breath at the sight. "Tougher than you look, I'll give you that."

I am thankful the sight keeps their attention from my front. For now, my chest remains as flat as the other boys, but even Mother could only guess if it would remain that way, or if I would soon be lacing myself into a bodice like her and Grandmum. What will happen if my breasts start to show before I'm allowed to wear more than just a bido?

"What's this?" The drillmaster slaps the armlet around my biceps. "It's a pretty bauble—my daughter has one just like it—but we wear no trinkets here."

More laughter from the other boys, but I pay it no mind. Chikga is the power here. "It was put there by nie'Damaji'ting Belina to ensure my obedience. If you can break her wardings and remove it, I would be most grateful."

The drillmaster's dark skin pales a little at the name, and he shakes his head. "I am not fool enough to interfere with *dama'ting* scheming. Keep your pretty jewelry."

I step into the line, and see the boys smirking. "I like it." One of them nods at the armlet. "Makes you look like a princess."

I clench my fist and anger makes me forget my fear. The *Damaji* may have *Sharum* to enforce his will, but I'll be corespawned before I let some skinny boy bully me. Breaking his nose would clear away that sneer. If I was half myself, I'd do it.

But I am barely a shadow. Every muscle still sore and weak, I'm lucky to be on my feet at all. I'm not ready to pick a fight. I breathe deeply, and let my fingers uncurl.

The other students burst out laughing, and even Chikga joins in the mirth. He laughs as he walks up to the boy who spoke. "Well done, Thivan. You've just volunteered to teach 'Princess' Olive the basics of the *sharaj*. If I find her uninformed, the punishment will be shared by you both."

Thivan's mirth vanishes as the other boys keep chortling. He glares at me as if it's my fault he's a coreling's ass.

"Fall out," Chikga barks.

"THIS IS WHERE we sleep." Thivan's voice is cold as he gestures to a large room with a stone floor. There are no beds, no furnishings at all, just a few dusty blankets—far fewer than there are students.

A chill of fear runs through me. The thought of sleeping on a stone floor with the other boys, cold and uncovered, frightens me more than Iraven's whip, but I say nothing. What could I say? It is not as if I could convince Thivan to conjure me a bed from thin air, or expect sympathy from a boy who seems to resent my very existence.

Thivan is shorter than me, and perhaps a year or two younger. He is thin as a reed, just wiry muscle, skin, and bone. His head is shaved smooth, whereas mine still has jagged patches of hair clinging to it. It's worse than being naked in some ways, to look so ragged even compared with the other boys.

Like all the full-blood *nie'Sharum*, Thivan's skin is darker than mine. In Hollow, my skin marked me as an outsider. Even though my rank and privilege forced others to accept me, I was often jealous of Selen and the other girls who could so effortlessly *belong*. I used to dream of visiting Krasia and experiencing what it was like to be among others who looked like me.

But it is not to be. Here, I stand out for my lightness, and lack rank or privilege to armor me. I wish Iraven had put me in the half-blood *sharaj*, though it is doubtless just as dismal. Perhaps there I might fit in.

"Gruel is served twice a day—after morning *sharusahk*, and at sunset," Thivan says. "There's never enough, so those at the end of the line go hungry. If you are wise, you will not let that happen. Even a single missed meal can weaken you enough for others to take advantage."

I realize I must have missed supper, though "gruel" hardly sounds appetizing. My stomach aches, but I ignore it. Admitting to hunger will be a sign of weakness. "What happens to the ones who don't eat?"

Thivan looks at me as he would an idiot. "When a *nie'Sharum* drops from hunger, they are cast out as *khaffit*. After that, who cares? Begging in the street for scraps, if they're lucky."

"*Princess* Olive cares, because she will be joining them soon," a sly voice says behind me. I turn to see a group of smirking *nie'Sharum* led by a boy perhaps a year or two older than me. Unlike the others—thin and stringy—this one is muscled and broad-shouldered, moving with an easy grace. His shaved head gleams like dark polished wood, and his square jaw makes him look older than his fellows, handsome and ready to leave *sharaj* a man.

"The Nie Ka," Thivan advises.

The term translates "first of nothing," an honorific for the leader of a class of *nie'Sharum*. My father was Nie Ka in his day. It means this boy stands at the front of the food lines, and is likely the most dangerous fighter here.

The Nie Ka moves in close, looking me up and down, lip curled in exaggerated disgust. "The *push'ting* prince, raised as a woman. Tell me, did they teach you pillow dancing and how to paint your face?"

The other boys hoot and howl. Some pretend to lunge forward in hope of making me flinch. I can tell the feints by the set of their feet, and don't react. They won't attack without approval from the Nie Ka.

Night. Is this what passes for banter in the desert? It makes Oskar seem witty by comparison.

Ignoring the others, I return the Nie Ka's appraisal with an unimpressed look of my own. "We don't pillow dance in the North, but I can paint your face, if you wish. It might make you less ugly."

"Ugly is a fine trait in a *Sharum*," the Nie Ka says. "You, on the other hand, are too pretty to be a boy. We'll have to do something about that."

"And who are you," I ask, "to worry so over my looks?"

"I am Chadan asu Maroch asu Aleveran," the boy says proudly, "Nie Ka of the full-blood *sharaj*."

My face goes cold. The *Damaji's* grandson. The one Belina kidnapped me to marry.

"To think Grandfather wanted me to have you as my *Jiwah Ka*!" Chadan laughs, and the boys around him all join in. "A pathetic *push'ting* in silk veils." He spits on the floor at my feet.

In sharaj, fight, Micha said. *The first day, fight.* The advice frightened me, but Chadan is making it easy.

"Hah!" I channel Grandmum Elona's derisive bark. "As if there was any hope some backwoods princeling from a tribe of cowards was good enough for the princess of Hollow. Your grandfather needed to kidnap me for you to even have a chance."

He snarls, and I see the blow before it comes. His fist strikes the place my face had been a second before, but I've already slid to the side, catching the arm before he can retract it. I use his own energy against him, pulling Chadan off balance and throwing him across the floor. He lands hard on his stomach, breath wuffing from his lungs, and I hope I haven't hurt him too badly. They'll never let me see my sister again if I cripple the *Damaji's* grandson.

Chadan's entourage gapes for a moment, but then their fists ball and one gives a shout, lunging for me. I set my feet, ready to meet him head-on. I may not be able to take them all, but I can teach them I am not some . . .

"Wait!" Chadan pushes himself up, kicking his feet under him. "He's mine."

I turn to face him, careful not to put my back to the others. "I don't want to hurt you."

There is blood on his teeth as Chadan smiles. "It's too late for that, you greenblood rat, because I am most certainly going to hurt you."

He stalks in, hands at the ready, and I am careful not to underestimate him. The Majah are famed for their *sharusahk*, and no doubt the grandson of their leader has been training harder and longer than I.

But even without magic, I'm stronger than I look, and trained by two legendary warriors.

I manage to parry or sidestep Chadan's blows, but his defenses are in place, and my return strikes are similarly evaded, keeping me from bringing my full strength to bear.

No matter. He will tire before me, and with my strength I only need to land a single blow to turn the battle. Pain lances across my back as I move and strike. I can feel the wounds reopening, seeping blood, but it's more irritant than inhibitor.

We circle for a few more moments, and then I see an opening when Chadan blocks a blow he could have evaded. His blocking arm snaps out for a quick return blow and I sidestep, reaching for it.

But this time, Chadan isn't where I expect. I catch only air as he grabs my wrist and twists, pulling my arm straight and locking the elbow joint. The limb screams with pain as he follows through, using the power of my own attack against me. I have no choice but to assist his throw, leaping in the direction he pulls to prevent the built-up energy from breaking my arm.

I hit the stone floor hard. The breath is knocked from me, but I remember Micha's lesson and do not linger, rolling quickly back to my feet.

"We're even, greenblood." Chadan allows me to collect myself, but I can see in his eyes the fight isn't over. "Let us see what Hollow men are made of."

With that he comes back in, and his blows seem to have tripled in speed. I catch the first two, but the third hits me square in the mouth, and I taste blood as my head rocks back. Before I can recover, he lands two more jolting blows to my body, then hooks one of my flailing arms into another throw, slamming me painfully to the stone once again.

Chadan could have put me in a submission hold and ended the fight, but it's clear he wants this to last. I see now that I was lucky with that first throw, catching him by surprise. He has my measure now, and we both know I am not his equal. He fights with the grace of a cleric and the ferocity of a warrior.

Again he comes at me, and I keep my guard in close, refusing to offer any energy he can turn against me, or limbs to force into submission. I stay on my toes, hoping to evade with minimal contact until he begins to tire. I slip his first punch, rolling under the second. I step back from the third and realize my mistake too late as he spins like a dancer, kicking me in the face.

The sound is deafening, and I feel like I was hit by a club. I reel backward, struggling to think, unable to keep my balance.

Again, Chadan does not immediately pursue, allowing me time to recover when he could have forced a submission and finished the fight. I shake my head, trying to clear my vision and the ringing in my ears. My back feels like a roaring fire, and every one of Chadan's previous blows throbs with pain. I realize how precise the blows were, each striking a convergence point that leaves my joints weak and my muscles feeling like gelatin.

Micha's Precise Strike school of *sharusahk* targets the places in the body where convergences of energy are focused, but it seems the Majah have their own version.

War is deception, Micha said. *Hide your strength and bide your time.*

I give in to the pain and weakness, letting my guard slouch just a little. I gasp for air, groaning my pain, then grit my teeth and roar like a demon, springing forward.

Chadan takes the invitation to grapple, just as I'd hoped. I can't beat him in an open fight, but in a grapple, muscle against muscle, I have an advantage greater than skill.

He gets behind me as we strike the floor, snatching my right arm to twist into submission. I contort, making sure his back is flat on the floor. Just before my elbow locks, I flex with all my strength, halting his momentum and reversing the pull. Before he can let go, I yank him up and see his eyes widen with disbelief just before I hook my left fist into his chest with everything I have.

Chadan slams hard into the floor, his shaved head cracking against the stone with a sound that echoes through the chamber. It is so violent

I recoil, afraid I've killed him. It's a relief when his eyes open and he quickly rolls back to his feet.

Another mistake. Chadan might have settled for humiliating me before, but now his eyes have the primal fury of the demons that attacked the borough tour. I don't think he'll hesitate to kill, as I did.

We come together for another pass, and this time Chadan knows better than to grapple. He takes his time, hitting me again and again, each blow targeted for maximum pain and disorientation. I lose track of how many times he hits me, jolted by every blow.

Eventually, he tires of the game. A push-kick drives me into the crowd of jeering *nie'Sharum*.

"Give the *push'ting* prince a proper welcome."

Never stop fighting.

I flatten the nose of the first boy who comes at me, but there are too many, all rushing in at once with kicks and punches. I black an eye here and punch a stomach there, but there is little I can do to stop the blows. Before long I curl up in a fetal position, just trying to protect my head as the onslaught continues.

"Enough," Chadan says, and immediately the others cease their attack, leaving me a weeping, shuddering ball as they go to claim spaces on the floor to sleep.

24

TIKKA

I WAKE SHIVERING ON the floor, still lying in the place I fell.

They didn't kill me.

I suppose it's a victory of sorts. It was the first day, and I fought, as Micha bade. I will live to see the second.

I imagine it will be very much like the first.

It's hard to focus on that distant worry, though, when the cold is here, now. I always imagined the desert to be eternally hot, but learned on the journey that the night quickly grows chill when the sun sets and the heat leaches away.

The floor of the *sharaj* is cut below ground level to offer a cooler space during the day, but in the night . . . I understand now how coveted the scarce blankets I saw on the floor must be.

I open my eyes, but it takes some time to adjust to the dim moonlight. I can make out Chadan in the spot closest to where I lay. He is the only one who sleeps alone, wrapped in two blankets.

Others huddle in groups of three and four beneath the remaining blankets, and the remainder sleep skin-to-skin in shifting piles, pooling their body heat.

Slowly, painfully, I roll to my knees. I'm cold, but I don't dare join one of the piles, even those with younger students. Instead I crawl until I can put my back to a wall, hugging my legs close.

I catch bits of sleep, but there is no way to tell if they are seconds, minutes, or hours. Again and again I am awakened by pain and discomfort. Each time I jolt, looking around frantically to ensure I am not threatened, then allow exhaustion to pull me back down.

The call to prayer cuts through the haze, a high-pitched song that is both beautiful and jarring, designed to pull worshippers from the clutches of sleep to give praise to Everam.

The *nie'Sharum* all rise and begin to file out of the room, beginning with Chadan, then the older, stronger boys who shared blankets, and finally the younger, weaker ones who slept in sweaty piles.

"Come, greenblood," Thivan says. "You will be on time for prayers or Chikga will have both our hides."

I follow the other boys into a training yard where the drillmasters are already kneeling. Their bodies are at rest, but their eyes watch as the boys file into the yard and kneel in neat rows. The strongest are in the front, the weakest in back. I kneel next to Thivan, close to the center.

When the last boy has taken his place, the drillmasters begin making their obeisance. Facing toward Anoch Sun, the ancient city of the Deliverer, they press foreheads to the ground, whispering prayers.

I know the words from Krasian Studies, but the prayers mean little to me. Mother gave clerics a place in her court, but she was not a practitioner. *There is power in faith, and we must show it respect,* Mother used to say, *but a leader cannot be ruled by holy men, or depend on the divine to build bridges and collect the trash.*

I've always felt the same, never believing there was some cosmic Will watching over the world. I haven't said a serious prayer since I was a young child. But here, under the watchful eyes of the drillmasters, I do not want to call any more attention to myself than I already have. What difference does it make if I speak the words to a Creator who does not exist?

"Everam, giver of life and light, grant me strength . . . "

When prayers are over, the drillmasters rise and begin leading morning *sharusahk*. The poses are different from the low, graceful ones I am familiar with. These are fast and violent, kicks and punches more suited to fighting other humans than demons.

Thivan scowls, but after a glance at Chikga, he comes over to me.

"Like this." He assumes a pose, correcting my stance, then takes me through the rest of the forms of the *sharukin*, kicking my feet and pulling my arms into the proper positions.

"He even fights like a woman," one of the boys says, and others snicker until the drillmaster looks their way.

As we practice, I begin to see the power in the simple moves. They lack the precision of the styles I've studied, using weight and brute force over finesse. Given warning and room to maneuver, a *dama'ting* could kill even a drillmaster in single combat, but a dozen *Sharum* charging down a narrow hall would mow down a like number of *dama'ting* like wheat before the scythe.

So I listen and I learn, throwing myself into the practice. Why shouldn't I learn to kick and punch like *Sharum*? It will be easier to blend in if I can fight like a "man."

When the exercise is over, Thivan leads me to where an old woman, face and head wrapped in a black *dal'ting* scarf, stands over a great pot, spooning a brown slop into bowls. Like the blankets, the pot looks too small to feed us all.

"That's our Tikka." Thivan nods at the old woman. "She does the cooking and distributes clean bidos once a week. Do not offend her, or you will regret it."

I haven't the slightest idea what would offend a woman like that, but I have a more pressing question.

"Why isn't there enough food?" Fort Krasia's walls surround a great oasis, with fertile land and abundant fruit trees. Perhaps it was not enough when the city's population was teeming, but for just the Majah there seems no reason why any should go hungry.

"Because the drillmasters want us strong," Thivan says. "They want us to fight, to lie, cheat, and steal when we must. They want us to do whatever it takes to survive, because it will prepare us to fight twice as hard to survive the night."

I'm sickened by the idea. The drillmasters torture these boys to turn them into weapons against the demons. Is this what was done to Micha? To my father?

Thivan moves to the center of the line, meeting eyes with another boy, who steps back to make room without challenging him. I try to follow, but the boy quickly closes the gap, shoving me away. "Back of the line, *push'ting!*"

I look to Thivan, but he only laughs. "The drillmaster said to show you our ways, not fight your battles. Accept Parkot's challenge, or go to the back of the line."

I look back to Parkot, his hands and feet set in an unfamiliar stance. He is thin like the others, but his place in line says he is fed and rested, while my stomach roils with hunger and my body is a mass of bruises. I can feel the scabbing on my back, thin and stiff, and know that if I exert myself, it will tear once more.

But a glance at the back of the line offers no comfort. The boys there are pale things, ashen skin lighter than my own pulled tight over visible bones. They stare at me with sunken eyes, and I know that giving in will mean becoming one of them.

On the other end of the line, Chadan already has his bowl, but he watches me with interest.

Fight, Micha whispers. *Every day, fight.*

I turn to meet Parkot's eyes. "Step ba—"

I don't even finish speaking before Parkot leaps forward, leading with a flurry of punches.

Remembering Chadan's deadly mix of strikes, throws, and submission holds, I keep my guard up, evading blows while I take Parkot's measure. He's aggressive, looking to power through a fight on pure ferocity.

A novice fights their opponent, Micha taught, *but a master lets their opponent fight themselves*. Parkot is wasting energy trying to bring the fight to a quick end. I catch his arm on the next pass, twisting to use the force of his swing against him. He hits the dusty ground hard, and his shoulder comes free of its socket with an audible pop.

Parkot screams, writhing in the dust and clutching his unnaturally twisted arm. The boys behind him in line recoil in horror, while those in front snigger. My face goes cold. I hadn't meant to dislocate his shoulder.

Chikga appears, and the *nie'Sharum* immediately straighten. I slip into Parkot's spot in line, hoping to draw less attention. Parkot is still writhing and moaning as the drillmaster drops to one knee to examine him.

"Everam's balls, quit whining." Chikga begins his examination by cuffing Parkot in the face. "Embrace the pain and be silent, or I will show you real pain."

Parkot's face reddens and his jaw clenches, biting back his moans as Chikga lifts his twisted arm. He puts a knee into Parkot's chest to keep him immobilized as he works the shoulder back into its socket.

There is another pop, and the arm locks in place. Parkot thrashes once, then goes limp, passed out from pain. Chikga shakes his head and spits in the dust as he gets to his feet. "He'll have a sore arm when he wakes," he says to no one in particular, "but it will obey him."

His eyes scan the line of boys, coming to rest on me. He notes my place in line, and that Parkot collapsed just a few feet from where I stand. I tense, expecting some sort of punishment, but Chikga says nothing. He turns away and returns to the company of the other drillmasters, who are partaking of a much more appetizing morning repast.

My reward for almost crippling a boy I just met is a ladle of thick brown gruel in my bowl. It smells rank. Even so, I meet Tikka's gaze. "Thank you."

Tikka's eyes narrow in suspicion. She raises her ladle threateningly. "You're not getting more, new boy. Go eat while it's warm."

"Yes, Tikka," I nod, but it's hard to contain my surprise.

Tikka returns to her work, and I realize every bowl has a little less than the one before. Chadan and his entourage received full bowls at the front of the line. Farther down the line, mine is barely half full. What will be left for the ones at the back?

"That was well done," Thivan says as we look for a place to sit and eat. "What a laugh, to see Parkot put down like a dog."

I'm barely listening, watching the bowls empty as the line dwindles. The second-to-last boy barely has the bottom of his bowl coated, but he immediately puts his face into it, licking up every bit of moisture.

Tikka flicks her ladle into the last boy's bowl, but only a single drop strikes the clay.

"Please, Tikka," the boy begs.

"The pot is empty," Tikka says.

"Please," the boy says again. "Just let me lick the ladle. Anything."

He reaches for the ladle's handle, but Tikka wields it deftly, spinning it out of reach and using it to crack the boy on the wrist. He cries out in pain, snatching the hand back. "You want to eat?" Tikka snaps. "Don't wait at the back of the line."

Thivan and the others laugh as the boy walks away dejected. I feel ill at the sight of his ribs, visible through thin skin stretched tight over bone. I realize I recognize him from last night. He kicked me in my own ribs just a few hours ago.

Yet looking at him now, I can't help but feel pity. He must have been desperate to gain some level of status before hunger caused him to be cast out. What happened to me isn't his fault.

I step into his path and the boy comes up short, fear in his eyes. "What is your name?"

"Faseek," the boy says.

"Take my gruel, Faseek." I push the clay bowl into his hands. "I'm not hungry."

Faseek gapes at me for a moment, then bobs his head. "Thank you."

"That was stupid," Thivan sneers as Faseek runs off with his prize. "Now you're going to go hungry."

I turn to him. "No, I'm not, Thivan. You're going to give me your bowl."

He freezes, and I smile, nodding at Parkot, still passed out on the ground. "Unless you want to end up next to Parkot?"

"BOY, COME WITH me." Tikka does not slow as she passes by.

I throw back the remaining gruel and hand the empty bowl to Thivan. One of his eyes is fast swelling. He glares at me with the other, but now he knows better than to show his teeth.

Tikka is a Krasian term of affection for grandmothers. I don't fully understand her place in *sharaj*, but until I do, it seems wise to obey as if she were a drillmaster. I hop to my feet and fall into step behind her. She takes me to a stone alcove where a bowl of steaming water sits beside a cake of soap, some folded cloth, and a razor.

"Sit," Tikka points to a mat on the floor. I do, and she sits upon a bench behind me, throwing a cloth over my shoulders.

Tikka massages warm soap onto my scalp through the patchwork of hair, and it feels heavenly. I tense as she lifts the razor, drawing a sharp breath as the cold metal scrapes along my skin.

I'm horrified at the sensation. I've always been so proud of my hair. Black and thick, it shone like the polished obsidian of a rock demon's armor. So dark it gave life to even the simplest ornaments. And long enough to reach my waist braided.

Now it's all gone, the last wisps falling in sudsy clots onto the cloth. The sensation of her fingers running over the skin around my skull is alien—pleasurable and discomfiting at the same time. I turn my head and lean over, looking at my reflection in the water bowl.

A stranger looks back at me. Their eyes are familiar, but without hair, my whole face looks different, especially now when it is puffed and bruised. I don't know who I am anymore, but Princess Olive is gone.

Tikka gives me a moment to stare, then pulls my head back so she can continue her work. "Every boy stares the first time. You'll get used to it."

"I don't suppose I have a choice," I say.

Tikka snorts. "You should be higher in line."

I look over my shoulder. "Why do you say that?"

Tikka's hands are surprisingly strong as she twists my head to face front. "I've been watching boys fight in the gruel line longer than you've been alive, boy. I know when someone's holding back."

"I don't want to hurt anyone," I say. "I could have crippled Parkot."

"Phagh, he would have done as much to you." She scrapes another patch of hair, flicking it off the razor and onto the cloth. "You should be behind Chadan in line, with a full bowl every meal."

"Why not in front of him?" I ask.

"Tsst," Tikka says. "You are not ready for that, and you'll find no allies against him. Your family name is feared among the Majah, but it is not loved as his."

"He made all this clear to me last night." The words come through gritted teeth.

"That is good," Tikka says. "Now that the other boys know he is your better, Chadan has no need to bully you, and he does not enjoy it as some others do. He won't lift a finger if you challenge anyone below him. So long as you defer to him, you will not go hungry."

Don't offend her, Thivan warned, but I have no idea what offends a woman who will let children go hungry in front of her. I've heard tales of beggars, but they always seemed distant things. After guiding her people through the privations of war, Mother would sell her own crown before she allowed an empty belly in Hollow.

Fight, Micha whispers, and my next words come in a rush. "Why must anyone go hungry?"

"It's a mercy." Tikka's hands continue their steady work. "Some boys do not have the hearts of warriors. They are safer as *khaffit* than in a demon's belly."

"How can they learn their hearts," I ask, "if the smallest and weakest are never allowed to grow strong?"

"Heart doesn't keep *alagai* talons at bay," Tikka says. "I've watched a lot of boys walk into the Maze over the years. Some come back blooded, as men. Others, usually the smallest and the weakest, don't come back at all."

"And if they die begging on the street, instead?" I ask.

"*Inevera*," Tikka says, but I see in her eyes it isn't so simple.

"You could fill every bowl equally if you wanted," I say.

"If I wished to turn the drillmasters' eyes off the boys and onto me." Tikka's voice is sharp. "Boys in the gruel line may fear me, but I assure you Chikga does not."

I am an idiot, blaming an old woman for not standing up to the drillmasters when I myself fear to. "Of course you are correct, Tikka," I say. "I apologize."

Tikka snorts again. "You're really not like the other boys." She takes up the cloth to wipe away the remaining suds and shorn hair. "I remember our short years in the green lands. For a moment, we all wondered what a generation raised in plenty could have made of us."

"Am I a disappointment?" I ask, surprised to discover I care what she will say.

Tikka shakes her head. "I wish all our children could live so. But you will need to harden yourself, if you are to survive here."

25

GRUEL

"WE'RE ALLOWED A quarter turn at the privy pits before training." Thivan's tone is more respectful now. I suppose a
black eye will do that. I expected him to begin avoiding
me, but apparently the drillmaster's order still carries weight.

The privy pits aren't anything close to private, just a foul trench to
stand or squat over. Many of the boys are doing just that, bidos around
their ankles as they hug their knees and strain.

"Keep your guard near the pits," Thivan warns. "Sometimes the
other drillmasters will send their *nie'Sharum* on a raid during privy
time."

"A raid?" I ask. "What could they possibly steal?"

"Glory!" Thivan laughs. "Come back with a rival's bido, it's a shame
his brothers will never let him forget. Kick one into the pits and you
become a legend."

I struggle to keep my face calm. "You kick each other into the privy
pits for fun? Do you have any idea how sick that could make someone?"

Thivan shrugs. "The weak are not meant for the Maze. The *alagai*
will not warn us before they strike. Drillmaster Chikga says we must
always be ready. If a boy is caught unprepared at the pits . . . *inevera.*"

Everam's will. That boys are taken and put in this place. Beaten and starved and exposed to sickness, all to test their manhood against some impossible scale.

Nevertheless, I take the advice, stepping away from Thivan and the others to find an open space over the pit. I hold my breath against the stench.

The idea of exposing myself to anyone was a nightmare not long ago, but the other boys do it without a thought, some of them talking amiably as they make water. I don't want to draw attention, so I lower my bido and take myself in hand.

No one even looks my way, but still it takes a while to go. My muscles are tense, ready to fight anyone who comes within striking distance, but the act requires I relax.

I manage at last, but I'm thankful the missed dinner and sparse breakfast don't leave me with an urge to do more. I'm not ready to remove my bido entirely and risk someone seeing more than I wish.

His own business tended, Thivan is waiting for me a safe distance from the pits. My nose curls at the stench, and I can no longer hold back the question that's been on my mind since I arrived.

"Are there baths?"

Thivan snorts. "Are we women? Go to the sweat room if you need to scrape yourself off."

I don't know what a sweat room is, but I don't care for the sound of it. I'm about to ask more when the drillmaster's horn summons us to the training grounds. I look around as the boys line up, finding a noticeable absence. "Where is Chadan?"

"Training with his father and the *nie'dama*," Thivan says. "He will be a *kai* when raised to the black."

I understand then why Chadan is so much better than the others, why he was able to turn my strength against me. The *dama* have long maintained control over the *Sharum* by withholding the secrets of their most powerful *sharukin*. If Chadan is training with the *dama*, he is far more dangerous than I thought.

The rest of us are split into pairs to practice the forms from morning *sharusahk* against a live opponent. I am paired with one of the lesser of the dozen or so boys in Chadan's entourage. Menin is tall, and stands high enough in the gruel line to maintain a thick build. His head is shaved like the other boys', but a carpet of hair is already spreading across his chest, limbs, and back. Unwashed like all the boys, he smells terrible, the thick curls of his body hair holding the scent of his sweat and musk.

"I bet you looked pretty as a girl," Menin growls as he takes a stance opposing me and waits for Chikga to signal us to begin.

I take a stance that mirrors his. "Better than looking like a hairy dog's arse."

Menin scowls, and I hope I have read him well as the drillmaster shouts for us to begin.

My lessons from Micha were rooted in *dama'ting sharusahk*—quick, elegant, and precise. Skilled in healing and medicine, the priestesses put their focus on *where* to strike, choosing convergence points where a properly struck blow can stun, cripple, or kill. Their target chosen, the *dama'ting* guide their opponents into position to make those points vulnerable.

For practitioners with a high level of skill, the *dama'ting* style gives distinct advantages, but the application is so complex it is little more than a dance for novices.

Wonda's lessons were always more practical, a cold application of force and leverage targeting whatever one's opponent leaves unguarded until there is an opening to grapple and force a submission.

The style the drillmasters teach in *sharaj* is philosophically akin to Wonda's, but far more aggressive. Menin keeps his defenses tight, offering little free energy even as his fists move at a blur to probe my upper defenses. His stomping advance keeps him in perfect balance as he searches for openings in my lower guard for a kick or trip.

Lighter and faster, I avoid his blows with minimal contact, but my own punches are blocked with wrists and forearms that instantly turn into return strikes. Menin blends defenses with counters so smoothly it seems like he never stops attacking. Parkot's rapid punches in the gruel line make more sense now, but where Parkot had only fury, Menin has control and is more deadly by far.

But after my years of rivalry with Selen—tall, quick, and clever—Menin's moves soon become predictable. Twice, he tries to stomp on my thigh, just above the knee, to force a hyperextension. The third time I offer the target, then take hold of his leg as he raises it for the kick. I lock the joint, bend my knees and twist with my full weight, forcing him to throw himself off balance to keep me from breaking the captured limb. He hits the dust hard, but I keep hold of the leg, twisting steadily until he cries out and slaps the ground in submission.

"On your feet!" Chikga was watching the match with interest, and kicks Menin hard in the stomach when he does not rise quickly enough. "A dozen laps around the training grounds for losing to a half-blood *push'ting*!"

None of the lesser boys will face me after that, so I watch the older boys spar. They are faster, more creative, and dangerous. The strongest after Chadan is Gorvan, a particularly vicious brute. More than once, Gorvan leaves an opponent bloody, or maintains a hold after they tap out, simply out of sheer enjoyment of dominance. He was the first to strike last night when Chadan threw me to the other boys. Gorvan kept laughing as he hit me again and again.

"Weapons!" Chikga calls when sparring is over. "I want a spear and shield in every hand!"

I go to the racks, stocked with wooden practice weapons. The round shields are unwarded, thicker and heavier than those the *Sharum* use. The spears are lengths of stiff but flexible rattan, their points blunted for use in the practice yard.

I reach for one, but am shoved aside so violently I stumble. Something hooks my ankle, and I crash into the dusty ground.

"That one is mine, *push'ting*." Gorvan takes the spear and looms over me, waiting to see what I will do.

Everyone else is waiting, as well. Chadan has returned to join the others for weapons work, and it seems the entire *sharaj* is holding their breath. With Menin's defeat I can enter the gruel line far ahead of Thivan, but still well behind Gorvan. This fight could determine much, come supper. Even Chikga is watching, though he feigns disinterest.

But whatever Micha's advice, I have no intention of fighting for its own sake. I do not know if I would be victorious against Gorvan, and there is nothing to gain by fighting over a cheap practice spear. Instead I get up, dust myself off, choose another spear, and move to join the other boys lining in formation.

Gorvan laughs, spitting in my direction, and Chikga shakes his head. I can sense his disappointment, but it means nothing to me. Chikga can make us sparring partners if he truly wants us to fight.

"Honor!" the drillmaster shouts as he strides in front of us. "Glory! These are not just empty words. They speak of a life lived in Everam's light, a life without fear! A life where your brothers know they can count on you, and you know you can count on them! What will you do when you face the *alagai*? The weakest sand demon is stronger than any warrior. Will you stand beside one who runs from every challenge?"

Chikga looks at me as he speaks, but I keep my eyes forward, refusing to give him the satisfaction of a reaction.

Weapons work is harder. I realize now how sheltered I've been. Mother never wanted a warrior's life for me or anyone at Gatherers' University. Self-defense class was just that. Wonda's lessons were always empty hand, and though I looked longingly at the weapons in Micha's training room, she said I was not ready for them.

Again, I feel a wave of anger at Mother and her dice. In protecting me, she put me in the same box she warned against, and left me ill prepared.

My head turns from side to side, watching the other boys as I struggle to learn the spear and shield *sharukin*. The movements look so simple and fluid, but they are awkward in application.

Keeping step when marching in formation is easier—just another form of dancing—but the subtle differences of footwork and positioning between Shield Walls and Push Guards elude me.

By the time we're finished, my arms feel like lead and my ears are ringing from the sound of Chikga's shouting. I'm grateful when we're given a respite for prayers and supper, but the sight of the gruel line offers no comfort.

My own meal is all but assured. I could take Menin's place in line, but the older boy glowers at me, eager for a rematch. It would mean a fuller bowl, but a few extra mouthfuls of gruel hardly seem worth it. I step in front of Thivan, instead.

"What are you doing?" Thivan asks. "Menin will think you are afraid of him."

Indeed, the older boy laughs and spits in my direction. The move is echoed by the others at the head of the line. They take their full bowls from Tikka and stand about, watching with amusement the struggles at the back of the line.

The morning meal hasn't restored Faseek's body, but it has brought back something of his spirit. Konin, the next boy in line, proves no match for him, much to the delight of the onlookers. They cheer the victory, but I know it is meaningless. A boy that age can no more survive on the few drops in the second-to-last bowl than he can on an empty one.

The stronger boys know it, too. "Dye your bidos now and have done!" Gorvan calls. In Krasia, only *khaffit* wear colored clothing in public. The boys behind Gorvan laugh as if this was some great witticism.

Tikka tsks when I come up to her, shaking her head as she hands me a half-full bowl. I immediately bring it to my lips, swallowing it in one great gulp, then stride over to where Chadan and his entourage have gathered.

The boys eye me warily, but none offer challenge when they see where I am headed. I walk right up to Gorvan, nodding at his full bowl. "One meal and Faseek has a victory. Let's see how well he and Konin do after they share your bowl tonight."

Gorvan looks at me, incredulous, then starts to snarl. Before he can react, I grab his bowl with my left hand. He instinctively pulls back, but he's not prepared for my strength. I don't budge, and for just a second, he is off balance. It's all the time I need. I punch him hard in the nose, hearing the crunch as it flattens beneath my fist. Blood spurts and he loses his grip on the bowl, stumbling a few steps before falling onto his backside, stunned.

My eyes flick to the others, but none seems willing to defend Gorvan. I turn to Chadan, but as Tikka said, challenges filter up the line, not down. He has nothing to gain by fighting me a second time. His mouth quirks in what might be a suppressed smile as he gives me a slight nod.

Gorvan remains on the ground, holding his nose. He does not whine or moan, but neither does he appear to be gathering himself to attack. A lesser fighter might try to reclaim something of their pride with a wild lunge, but Gorvan is skilled enough not to challenge me with stars dancing in his eyes. I turn my back on him and walk toward the end of the line.

Gorvan's nose blood spatters my knuckles, and a few drops float atop the gruel. Konin does not seem to mind, taking the bowl eagerly. Faseek, who fought so hard for a symbolic serving, looks on hungrily, no doubt wishing he hadn't bothered.

I fix Konin with a stare, and he immediately drops his eyes. "Pour half in Faseek's bowl."

"Yes, Prince Olive." Konin nods and complies without hesitation. Half a bowl is still more than either boy could hope to win on his own. I flick my eyes to the drillmasters. All of them are watching, but none, not even Chikga, gets involved.

WE RETURN TO the barracks, and I remember last night's bitter cold. I don't want that again, but there aren't a lot of options. I eye the sparse blankets and the boys that huddle under them. I might manage to take one, but it would mean fighting two or even three of the stronger boys at once. Even if I won, how well would I sleep in a room with them looking for vengeance? The rest of the *nie'Sharum* sleep in huddles, but none appear welcoming. I've made a lot of enemies since arriving, but no friends.

There is a rumble of whispered conversation throughout the room, and I turn to see Gorvan return from the *dama'ting* pavilion with two black eyes and his nose splinted. He stares at me with open hatred, but he doesn't approach. I wonder if I will wake tonight with him choking me. My strength will mean little if he has leverage, and though I managed to take him unawares, I know Gorvan's skill. He would give me trouble in a fair fight, and won't be satisfied with breaking my nose if he gains the upper hand.

I search the walls for a defensible space to curl up through the chill of the night, but the best ones are taken. I will fight to avoid starving, but not for a wall corner that makes it slightly harder to surround me while I sleep.

"Prince Olive?" I turn to see Faseek standing before me. He wrings his hands but manages to meet my eyes. "The night will grow cold. You can sleep with us, if you wish."

He gestures to a group of boys, Konin among them. All have the hollow look of the underfed—those at the very back of the line. Yet last night, all of them managed a kick while I was on the floor. Now they are offering me a place to sleep?

"You can put your back to the wall," Faseek says. "We won't be much help if Gorvan or the others come for you, but you'll have warning, at least."

Mother was always a pacifist. *Kindness and diplomacy solve more problems than spears*, she was fond of saying. I'm not naïve enough to trust these boys fully, but they seem sincere, and my options are few. "Thank you."

It's strange, lying in the huddle. I've never slept with anyone, much less half a dozen boys in loincloths, stinking of dirt and sweat. Still, I don't smell much better, and as the heat leaches from the ground, the warmth is welcome. I start with my back to the wall, but as the night grows cold, I squirm deeper into the pile, basking in the shared heat of their skin.

Sleep comes and goes. I worry about Micha. About what Selen and Darin must be thinking after finding my note. No doubt the general sent Messengers to Mother. Is she building an army to come fetch me even now? There will be blood if she does. How many lives is my freedom worth?

I hear something in the middle of the night, coming out of sleep with sudden tension. I'm wondering how quickly I can extract myself from the pile and get to my feet when I realize it is the sound of two boys in our huddle kissing.

None of the other boys reacts, so I don't, either. I strain my eyes and ears, searching for another threat. There doesn't seem to be one, though as I sift through the sounds of snoring and shifting bodies, I realize other boys in the room are similarly entangled. It seems some share more than warmth at night.

I can't blame them. There is little enough comfort to be found in this corespawned place for those at the back of the line. Let them take what they can.

———

I WAKE A few more times, but when morning comes, I feel refreshed. Already the scabs across my back are beginning to flake away, the bruises fading.

Prayers and *sharusahk* proceed much as they did the day before. My poses are better today, but I am still adapting to the change in style and know I stand out to drillmaster and student alike. The sooner I blend in with the other boys while doing the forms, the better.

In the breakfast line I swallow my half bowl quickly, then approach Gorvan again. Yesterday I won by surprise, but that won't be enough today. I need to beat him fairly, or his threat will continue.

Splinted nose or not, Gorvan looks more than ready to fight, but instead of swallowing his bowl or putting it aside, he makes a point of holding it out and tipping it over, spilling the gruel onto the ground.

"The dust can have my gruel, half-blood, before I give it to boys destined to be *khaffit*."

"Tsst!" Tikka hisses at the sight of wasted food, and Chikga gets to his feet, eyes alight with fury. I don't give them time to step in, my slow approach becoming a rush.

Gorvan is ready for me this time, and I haven't underestimated his skill. He sidesteps my rush and comes at me from offline. I'm ready for it and roll beneath his punch, throwing a knee at his stomach.

Gorvan blocks it with a raised calf, then hits me in the chin with an open-hand blow that makes me bite my tongue. Blood wells in my mouth as I stumble back, and Gorvan presses the advantage, coming in fast with a drumroll of punches, individually too fast to follow. It's all I can do to keep my arms up, catching most on my biceps and shoulders. One strikes me in the ribs, blowing the breath from me, and two more rapid fists hook into the opening before I can react.

Gorvan thinks he has me now, but his confidence lets him remain close a second too long. I manage to grab his neck and pull him into a clinch. He mirrors the hold, driving his forehead into mine, but I accept the blow to find secure footing. It's muscle against muscle now, and though Gorvan is heavier, I am stronger. He strains, trying to twist me to the ground, and I see fear in his eyes when he cannot.

With a growl, I kick him in the knee, bending it against the joint. The limb buckles and I twist, picking Gorvan bodily off the ground and slamming him down onto his back. I keep hold of his arm, twisting it behind him.

"You are beaten." Blood drips from my mouth as I growl the words. "Submit or I will break your arm."

"Nie take me before I submit to a greenblood *push'ting*." Gorvan forces the words through gritted teeth.

I twist harder, and Gorvan gives an involuntary cry of pain. "Submit," I say again, "while some dignity remains to you."

These last words seem to get through where the others didn't. Gorvan slaps his hand on the ground for all to see. Immediately I release him, getting quickly to my feet. I turn to Montidahr, the next in line after Gorvan. "Give Konin and Faseek your bowl."

Montidahr stares at me for a long moment, holding his bowl in one hand and flexing his fist in the other. His eyes flick to Gorvan on the ground, and when they come back to my face, I bare my teeth, ready to make an example of him if I have to.

Montidahr sees it in my face and he lets out a breath, seeming to deflate. He nods and walks to the end of the line, pouring out his bowl into those of the lesser boys.

I expect the submission to make me feel relieved, but anger and adrenaline are still boiling inside me, screaming for release. I can't keep doing this every day.

"No one goes hungry!" I shout, casting my eyes over the rest of the boys in line. "The drillmasters speak of honor, but they look away as we prey on the weak. They want us to lie, to cheat and steal and bully, because they think it will make us strong. But there is no strength in letting our brothers starve while those in front eat more than they need! By hoarding for ourselves, we weaken the whole. If some lack the strength for a warrior's life, let it be seen in training, not at meals."

The difference in reactions is pronounced. The stronger boys scowl, while the weaker nod their heads. I cast my eyes up and down the line, muscles still tense and ready for a challenge. When there is none from the lesser boys, including Gorvan who has managed to find his feet, I turn to Chadan. The prince only smirks at me. I can't force him to give up his bowl, and he knows it. Tikka's gaze is carefully neutral. She gives a nod so slight I wonder if I've imagined it.

Last I turn to Chikga. The hulking drillmaster glowers at me, and I am not fool enough to think I am a match for him. He stalks toward me like the Watchers who attacked Mother's keep. It's all I can do not to shrink back.

Fight, Micha whispers. *It is the only thing men respect.*

I ready myself, hoping I can earn a bit of respect before he puts me down, but before he reaches me, the drillmaster whirls and catches Gorvan by the arm, flipping him over to land face-first in the puddle of gruel he poured into the dust.

"We don't waste food, dog," Chikga snarls. "Eat."

THE SECOND DAY is much like the first. I let the stronger boys have their breakfast, conserving my strength for dinner.

The drillmasters do not seek to punish my words, but they are not forgiving of my missed steps and lack of weapon skills. More than once I am sent running around the grounds or given some menial task to build strength while I reflect on my failures, but in truth I prefer the sharp words and penitence labor to Mother's method of disappointed stares and tedious lectures.

Suppertime comes, and again I am leaden and exhausted. My tongue is swollen and tender where I bit into it, and for once I am glad not to have a meal I need to chew. I move toward the spot behind Chadan, and no one, even Gorvan, challenges me. The prince eyes me, searching for a threat.

Fight.

I may be tired, but I'm stronger now than I was that first night. If I challenge Chadan and win, I will have undisputed control of the gruel line, but if I fail . . .

I'm not afraid of him, but neither do I have delusions of being his better. If I manage a victory, it will be hard fought and in doubt until one of us submits.

Doing nothing has its own disadvantages. If I don't challenge him, the others will take it as weakness.

Your family is not loved here, Tikka said. Even victory could cost me. How would Majah drillmasters react if a Kaji prince defeated the heir to the Majah Skull Throne? How would the *Damaji* react, if I took place ahead of his grandson?

Chadan watches me with calm confidence. He's ready to fight, but not eager for it. I don't think it's fear—quite the contrary, his eyes seem to see through me, exposing all my doubts. Chadan knows he has every advantage.

In the end, I keep my hands at my sides and don't meet his eyes as I step into the line. Chadan smiles, knowing it for a victory. "What will you do, now that you have a full bowl of your own?"

"Share it," I say without hesitation. "No one goes hungry."

There is scuffling farther back in the line, and we turn as one to see Faseek rolling on the ground with Levan, a larger boy who usually stands three spaces higher in line than Faseek. Levan is pummeling Faseek and before I realize it, I am moving their way.

Chadan puts a hand on my arm, holding me back. "You do Faseek no honor by helping. He has the hold. Watch."

I look again, and see he is right. Levan's blows are ones of desperation, growing weaker as Faseek accepts the punches to keep pressure on the larger boy's throat, cutting off the flow of blood to his brain.

It isn't long before the hold begins to tell. Levan's face turns purple. He raises a hand for one last, halfhearted punch, then thinks better of it and weakly slaps Faseek's arm to signal his submission. Faseek releases him, taking Levan's place in line as the larger boy lies gasping in the dust.

Tikka bangs her ladle against the pot impatiently, and Chadan starts. He takes one last look at Faseek and Levan, then steps up to the pot. "Half a bowl today, Tikka."

Tikka ignores him, ladling his bowl to the brim. "The serve is the serve, boy. Pour your share into one of the other bowls if you want to be noble."

"Of course, Tikka." Chadan executes a respectful bow and takes a second bowl. He pours half his serve into it and walks over to Levan, squatting to set the bowl beside him. When he stands, he eyes the rest of the line. "Anyone who touches Levan's bowl will answer to me." He turns to me and winks. "No one goes hungry."

26

—◆—

WEAPONS

I KEEP MY LEGS closed as Thivan runs the scraper over my back in the sweat room. The lighting is dim and I don't think any of these boys have ever seen a woman without clothes, but nevertheless, I am anxious they will notice I am different, and word will spread.

A week ago, my flow came. I'd lost track of the calendar, and could feel myself bleeding into my white bido. Luckily, I was sparring with Gorvan, who was looking for a chance to reclaim his pride. His nose had barely started to heal when I hit him there a second time, bloodying my fist. As he hit the ground, I made a show of wiping it on my bido.

Tikka tsked when she saw the bloody cloth, and sent me to take a fresh one. I stole another, tearing it into strips I could wad to absorb the blood until my flow stopped. It was a close call, not the first and not the last. They come every time I let down my guard.

What would happen if Belina or Chavis or Damaji Aleveran found out the truth? The scriptures of the Holy Evejah lay out the many rights accorded to men, and the far fewer accorded to women. They dictate as well the division of labor between the sexes, and there women receive the greater share of the burden, freeing men to pursue the spear.

Occasionally there is mention of *push'ting*, a word that refers to either gender. Sometimes the book condemns *push'ting* as men and women so committed to lying with their own sex that they refuse to procreate. Other *push'ting* tales are whimsical stories of men living as women, or women putting on a man's armor and becoming warriors.

But there is no tale or scripture about one like me, in the Evejah or the Tenders' Canon. Mother found mention of intersex children in musty Gatherers' journals and medical texts from the old world, but it took her some time to find Herb Gatherers in her correspondence with personal experience.

None of the cases sounded quite like mine—the scales between sexes so evenly balanced. I never had health concerns, and Mother is convinced I can procreate as either gender. There is no precedent for that in Mother's journals.

Are there intersex among the Majah? It's likely, but no doubt they have as much incentive as I did to stay hidden. Each tribe interprets the sacred texts differently. Who knows how the Majah would see me? The uncertainty invites me to imagine the worst, and I have always had an active imagination. Even in Hollow, I never believed I could be accepted, no matter what Grandmum said.

Konin ladles water on the hot stones in the center of the chamber, and I breathe deeply as the soothing hiss fills the sweat room with steam.

It isn't the same as a bath. I miss long hot soaks that leave my fingers and toes wrinkled, scented soaps, and brushes to cleanse and exfoliate my skin. I miss Micha's singing as she lathers my hair.

But neither is the sweat room as unpleasant as I'd feared. In the dry heat of Krasia, it feels luxurious to fill the very air with moisture, letting it seep all the way to my bones. Sweat loosens the dust and grime of the day much as soap does, and the scraper massages tired muscles as it scours the filth away.

And there is peace here. The yard and barracks are full of chatter and struggles for dominance, but the sweat room is a place of quiet. Those who speak do so in low voices, and only as necessary. Chadan and several of the other boys practice their meditation here.

The *nie'Sharum* are seldom without their bidos, but in the sweat room they are shameless about their nudity. I try not to let my eyes linger, but much as they have not seen women unclad, the sight of naked young men is new to me, and not displeasing. I can imagine all the things

Selen would say if she were here. Our training is hard, and the *nie'Sharum* are . . . fit.

Even Konin and Faseek have put on weight in the weeks since we began sharing food. They were close to being cast out when I first saw them, but now they are thriving. There is still scuffling for position in line, with the stronger boys getting a larger serve, but even those at the end receive half a bowl. Faseek has fought his way up the line, receiving a nearly full serving, but he does not hesitate to share when it's his turn. Konin is farther back, but no longer at the end of the line.

As in the barracks at night, some of the boys are intimate in the sweat room. They steal kisses and caresses as they scrape one another clean, but even the drillmasters do not stare or call them out. There is more to being *push'ting* than a few kisses, it seems.

"Enough," Chikga calls from the corner of the room where he sits cross-legged in meditation, naked save for a cloth laid across his lap. Thick curls of hair cover a body made entirely of scars and muscle. "Waning comes in two days, and you will be sent home to your fathers, that they might inspect you before going into the darkest nights. So tomorrow, we have prepared a test for you to prove yourselves. Rest while you can."

It is not yet dark as we emerge from the sweat room, but the warm air feels cool on my damp skin. Hot as it is in the yard, the sweat room is hotter.

"Share our blanket," Montidahr offers as he and Menin settle down to sleep. It is a generous offer, but not too generous. They know I could take it from them if I wished. I was a match for either of them when I arrived, and my skills have only increased in the weeks since. I've sparred with all my classmates in the yard, learning their tricks and tells. All save Chadan, who continues his private training with the *dama*.

"You honor me," I say, "but the warmth of the others is enough." I'm surprised to discover I mean the words. Faseek and the younger boys have become fiercely loyal since I helped them find a fair portion of gruel. I've grown accustomed to their comforting heat enveloping me in the night. So much that I wonder if I could rest at all if I were alone on the floor, blanket or no. My feathered bed in Cutter's Hollow, big enough to sleep half a dozen *nie'Sharum*, is a fading memory.

———

AFTER BREAKFAST, WE are led to one of the low adobe buildings in the training grounds, where Master Amaj waits. Each drillmaster has a specialty, and we've visited each in turn, learning different weapons and techniques.

"Fists may serve you in the gruel line, but hitting an *alagai* with your bare hand can have a heavy price." Drillmaster Amaj removes the clawed metal cap at the end of his muscular right arm. His wrist ends in a mass of scars, faded with age. "You must learn to find other weapons. Rekaj, step forward."

Rekaj is the weakest of the full-bloods, standing at the back of the gruel line at most meals. He isn't a coward, but he lacks aggression, more likely to defend than commit to an attack. I've seen it cost him again and again. Everyone is fed now, but none are fool enough to think the drillmasters won't still make the weakest boys *khaffit*. I wonder how long he has left to prove himself.

"The test is simple." Amaj gestures to the darkened doorway of the training building. "Enter, find weapons, defend yourself, and make your way to the exit." He points to another doorway at the far end of the building.

"Simple," Thivan scoffs. "The drillmasters love nothing more than to send boys home bandaged and bruised, so our fathers know they are making men of us."

Rekaj seems equally skeptical, but he does not hesitate, descending the steps and entering warily, already with his fists raised in a guard position.

For a few moments, there is silence. The *nie'Sharum* all hold their breath, waiting, until there is a crash, and Rekaj cries out. I tense, wanting to go to him, but I am not so stupid as to interfere with the test. Soon after, Rekaj is thrown back out the door he entered, and the boys around me jeer and laugh.

Drillmaster Amaj walks over and hauls Rekaj to his feet. There is blood on his face, one eye swelling, and welts are forming on his arms and body.

"Konin!" Amaj calls. "Enter!"

Konin freezes, and I can see fresh sweat break out on his shaved head. I lay a hand on his arm. "You can do this."

He nods, but his shoulders slump as he walks to the doorway, a boy on his way to punishment, not a test. And indeed, in less time than it took with Rekaj, he is cast out clutching a leg that is already turning purple.

"He'll be at the back of the line again tonight!" Gorvan laughs, and others join him, though many of them have worried looks of their own. What is inside that building?

And so it goes, each student called in turn. Some last longer than others, with sounds echoing from deep in the building, but none of them make it to the far door. All are cast out the way they came in, bloody and bruised.

With every failure, the jeering of the boys who have yet to enter grows louder, a sign of their own increasing tension. The boys who have been tested are kept separate, but they, too, shout and hoot as each new boy is cast out. Perhaps it isn't cruelty, as I once thought. If everyone fails, it is merely a rite of passage.

By the time Gorvan is cast out, his face purpling with bruises, my stomach is in a knot. I remind myself that it is day—that whatever's inside that building is human and not coreling—but it does nothing to alleviate the tension in my muscles.

"Princess Olive!" Amaj mocks, pointing to me.

I swallow the lump in my throat and march forward. Aleveran promised I could see Micha on Waning. Whatever's in that building stands between me and my sister, and I won't hide from it.

"Olive!" Faseek calls, and the other boys I sleep with take up the cry.

"Olive. Olive. Olive." The chanting does nothing to calm my nerves as I approach the door.

"Enter, find weapons, defend yourself, and make your way to the exit." Amaj sneers as I pass him. Chikga has eased his harassment of me as my skills have improved, but the other drillmasters have not.

Dim light filters through the half-drawn window curtains of the building as I enter, illuminating a room with little feature. A waist-high rectangular wooden table sits in the middle with wooden benches on all sides, two long and two short. The floor is hard clay. There is nothing resembling a weapon—or a threat—in the first room, so I move to the far doorway, presumably leading to a hall.

Before I am halfway across the room, two figures emerge from the shadows of the doorway. They are clad in gray robes, veiled and turbaned, and they are not as large as the warriors I have seen drilling in the grounds. Older students from another *sharaj*, perhaps. Each carries a sturdy baton.

I see now what the drillmaster meant. If we want weapons, we will have to take them.

The first assailant swings his baton at me, but I leap to the side, putting one foot on a bench and kicking off to add power as I punch him in the head.

My fist cracks against a helm wrapped beneath his turban, and I cry out in pain. I stumble as I land, cradling the hand, and the other attacker strikes me across the back with his baton.

I roll with the blow, tumbling out of reach as I flex my fingers. My hand does not appear to be broken, but it was a near thing. My fingers scream with pain, but they obey me as the two come at me again.

I catch one by the wrist, twisting to yank him into the path of the other, fumbling his attack. I grab the baton with my other hand and bend my knees, twisting into a throw that will send the attacker hard into the ground, leaving his weapon in my hand.

The throw is perfect, but instead of yanking his weapon away, I am the one pulled off balance. I realize too late the baton is lashed to his hand to prevent students from taking it.

Find weapons.

I cast around the room helplessly. The curtains are held by a thin rod. If I could get to it, I might use it as a weapon, but what good would it do against armored foes?

I manage a forearm block as the other student attacks again, and the blow nearly breaks my arm. I kick out to drive him back and create space, but like my hand, my foot strikes armor beneath his robe.

I'm limping as he stumbles back, but like my hand, my foot continues to obey, albeit painfully. The student gives a grunt of pain as he strikes the table, and then I begin to understand.

I snatch one of the smaller benches, lifting it like a shield as I rush the first attacker, who is getting to his feet. I drive him into the adobe wall, blowing the breath from him, then pivot just in time to catch the other baton on the bench. I kick the student's knee and as he stumbles I charge him with the bench as well, throwing my full weight down on him as he begins to fall.

The floor and bench are harder than my hands and feet, and I feel the breath blow out of the student as we land. The wood of the bench cracks, but it's still enough to deflect the other baton as I roll away from the grounded student in time to meet his fellow.

His baton strikes are rapid now, jarring my arms and numbing my hands as he tries to knock the bench from my hands. I give ground, but the odds grow worse as the other student gets to his feet, moving to flank me.

As he comes in close, I shove the first attacker back, then throw the bench at the second. He is unprepared for the move, and cannot deflect it fully. Before either can recover, I tear one of the curtains from the wall and wrap it around the first student's head, twisting and pulling tight as I roll around, yanking him from his feet and smashing his back into the corner of the heavy table. I punch him twice in his covered face for good measure, then leap the table just in time to avoid the other student's baton.

The first attacker does not rise as the other and I circle. I snatch the bench off the floor, holding it before me like a shield.

"Half-blood scum," the student growls, and charges in. I lift the bench, but he delivers a powerful kick, shattering the cracked wood and splitting the bench in two. The blow is blunted by the time his foot hits my chest, sparing me a broken sternum, but I am sent stumbling backward as he presses the attack.

I still hold a crossed pair of bench legs in each hand, now attached to jagged boards of wood. Instinctively, I bring them together, my opponent's helmeted head in between. The blow stuns him, and I drop the bench legs, tackling him about the midsection. I lift him clear off his feet and throw him through the doorway I entered. Outside, I hear the *nie'Sharum* shouting at the sight, and the sound gives me new strength.

I grab the other short bench and run the other way, through the door at the far end of the room. As expected, it opens into a long hallway.

There are doorways on either side, but I am focused on the light at the far end.

The exit.

I sprint down the hall, but am not caught unaware when another baton-wielding student emerges from one of the darkened doorways. I shift direction mid-run, putting my shoulder to the bench and smashing him into the doorframe. He grunts and falls back into the room, and I waste no time to see if he recovers, turning and resuming my mad dash for the end of the hall.

Another figure appears and I throw the bench at his legs, tripping him long enough to deliver a kick to his face and run past. A third appears, and a fourth silhouette steps in front of the exit, but I've already seen my next weapon. A small, unassuming table stands against one of the hallway walls. I veer to the opposite wall just as I come in range of the student's baton, then duck his swing and cut back the other way, leaping atop the table as his baton strikes the hard clay wall, sending a shock up his arm.

He whirls and tries to sweep my legs with the baton, but I jump over the wild swing, hooking his weapon arm as he retracts it. I throw myself into a somersault off the table, and the student has no choice but to throw himself head over heels to keep me from breaking his shoulder. I deliver an open-hand blow to his unprotected throat, leaving him gasping on the floor, then upend the table and break off two of the sturdy legs before I approach the final opponent between me and the exit.

If he's concerned that I have two weapons to his one, he doesn't show it. He works his baton masterfully, parrying blows from both the table legs, but as I watch him fight, I begin to see the drawbacks of a weapon lashed to one's hand. He can't adjust his grip, or move it with the fluidity that I can. On the third pass, I lock his weapon in a clinch with one of mine and turn a half circuit, swinging the other one in an arc that comes up right between his legs.

It's hard to armor the groin and maintain mobility. The table leg connects solidly and the student cries out, crumpling up to protect himself . . . too late. I kick off one wall, driving him hard into the other, then barrel out the exit into the sunlight.

The *nie'Sharum* cheer, and I've never felt so alive.

———

A MOMENT LATER, three of the gray-robed *nie'Sharum* fighters charge out the doorway behind me. I'm breathing hard, too tired to put up much resistance, but Drillmaster Amaj holds up his claw hand, stopping them. "Go. Reset. Replace the injured."

The students are unaccustomed to losing. They growl and glare at me, but they comply, disappearing back into the building.

"Well done." The drillmaster's tone is grudging, but respectful. "I can't remember the last time a student so young passed the test. No gruel tonight. You'll have meat and couscous."

My mouth waters at the words. It's a wonder that such a simple reward could have that effect. I want to refuse, to make some show of solidarity with the other students, but I can see how it stings the drillmaster to offer it, so I bow instead, hiding my delight. "Thank you, Drillmaster."

"Chadan!" Amaj says. "Let us see if you can do as well as the half-blood."

I catch Chadan's eye as he walks past, winking. He smiles in return, eyes twinkling. "You were slow."

Indeed, Chadan enters, and there are crashes and shouts from his assailants. I made it through with a mass of welts and contusions, but when the Majah prince exits the far end of the building—in half the time it took me—there isn't a mark on him.

The *nie'Sharum* cheered me, but they lose all control at this, stomping their feet and filling the air with an enormous cacophony. "Nie Ka! Nie Ka! Nie Ka!"

27

———— · ————

WANING

I DON'T THINK I'VE ever felt so full as I do after the meal of meat and couscous. I curl contentedly into the pile of *nie'Sharum* and fall deeply asleep.

Dawn's light is just beginning to filter through the windows of the clay building when I am awakened by a nudging foot. It's gentle, nothing like the swift kick Drillmaster Chikga is fond of giving when he wishes to wake a sleeping boy.

I look up to see Chadan standing over me. The light is at his back, haloing his handsome face as he tosses a folded set of light gray robes to me. "Come. It is the first day of Waning, and I am to escort you to the palace."

The other *nie'Sharum* continue their slumber as I pull on the robes with as much modesty as I can manage. After weeks in nothing but a bido and sandals, I thought my modesty was gone, yet dressing in front of someone still feels . . . intimate. I eye Chadan warily as I get to my feet.

"You don't trust me?" he asks.

"Should I?" I ask. "It wasn't long ago that you and your friends beat me in this very place."

Chadan shrugs as if this is nothing of note. "It was your first night in *sharaj*. Everyone is tested their first night."

I turn to meet his eye. "Were you, *Prince* Chadan?"

Chadan smiles. "The Nie Ka came for me, yes. He spent a week in the *dama'ting* pavilion, and six more before his casts were removed. No *nie'Sharum* has dared challenge me since . . . save you."

"It's nice to know I'm special," I say.

"You're special in many ways," he says. "And they're not my friends."

Despite my mistrust, the unexpected praise pleases me so much it takes a moment for my mind to catch up with what was said after. "Who aren't?"

He nods to the boys sleeping in blankets. "Gorvan. Montidahr. Menin." He sweeps a hand over the entire sleeping class. "All of them, really. They obey me, but . . . " He chuckles. "They're more your friends than mine."

"Whose fault is that?" I follow as Chadan strides toward the door. "The seeds of friendship cannot grow, if you do not plant them."

"One day we will be men, and I will lead them in *alagai'sharak*," Chadan says. "Some, I may order to their deaths. Others, I may have to kill myself, if they break and run from the enemy. Father says it is best not to befriend such men."

"And me?" Chadan and I have stood next to each other at every meal for a month, but seldom spoken. He's kept out of my way, and I, his. I don't know anything about him, including how he feels about me.

He shrugs. "Grandfather told me Princess Olive was to be my bride—something I wanted no more than you, I assure you. But then they returned with a prince, a son of Ahmann Jardir, and Father warned you might try to supplant me."

I snort. The very idea is ridiculous. "I have no interest in being Nie Ka."

"Perhaps," Chadan says. "But neither do you lack ambition. You give orders and expect the others to follow you, title or no. Father says you challenged the *Damaji*, himself."

"He's not my *Damaji*," I say. "He's my goaler."

"He's my grandfather," Chadan says. "Who saved our people from serving a corrupt regime when your brother murdered Damaji Aleverak in his attempted coup."

"Before I was even born," I note. "In another country where I have dozens of brothers I've never met. Does a blood debt carry so far?"

Chadan shrugs. "If Everam wills us to be enemies, it will be so. Until then . . . "

"We are who we choose to be," I say.

He grunts. "It's not like anyone else in *sharaj* will ever understand us."

"Us?" I ask.

"Princes," he says.

"Ah," I say. "Someone who understands the horrors of palace life."

"You mean to say you were never punished because the servants discovered something you'd carefully hidden while 'cleaning' your chambers?"

"Night, that's my whole life," I say.

Chadan smiles. "Perhaps we are not so different, after all."

We fall into silence as we cross the training grounds and exit to the narrow streets of the city proper. The training grounds guards say nothing as we pass, simply nodding at the young prince.

"No one's worried I'll try to escape?" I ask.

"Run if you wish." Chadan shrugs. "It's not my job to stop you." He nods at my armlet. "How far do you think you'll get, before the *dama'ting's* trinket brings you to heel?"

I can't argue. If Micha has an escape plan, it had best involve keeping both my arms.

The city is just coming to life, preparing to celebrate the first day of Waning, when the moon is new and the demons will be their strongest. In Krasia, Wanings are sacred days of peace, when families come together, debts are paid, and transgressions forgiven.

The air is full of the smells of cooking food—hava spice most of all, mixed with meats and vegetables; fried dough, yogurts and sour cheeses. Black-robed women are filling the streets, some shopping for the day and others pushing carts to hawk flowers or fresh bread.

The workers are mostly pale-skinned greenlanders, the conquered "thralls" of the Majah tribe. I imagine they once felt as I do—kidnapped and trapped with an endless desert between them and their homes—but after fifteen summers, they seem to have assimilated.

They wear muted colors and keep scarves around their shoulders, but I see women with bare faces and uncovered—if bound—hair. They call out their wares in a perfect Majah dialect, but speak Thesan to one another. My heart aches to hear the familiar sounds, and for a moment I allow myself to wonder about home.

Mother must have returned by now. She would be tearing the duchy apart looking for me, if the dice have not already pointed her here. Belina is right that it would be difficult to move an army all the way here from Hollow, but Mother is stubborn. She won't just let me go.

I shake the thoughts away. There's no point guessing what she might or might not do. I turn my attention back to the present.

The *chin* street vendors take one glance at our dark skin and gray robes, and make way as we pass. Even *nie'Sharum* are several castes above them, destined to become part of the ruling class.

Indeed, we soon reach the gates of the Holy City with their white-sleeved guards, the Arms of Everam. Even the Holy City is massive—large enough to house the Majah tribe in its entirety, thralls and all. Yet most of the buildings we pass are deserted, and many are in ill repair. Desert Spear was built to give home to millions, and the Majah are but a tiny fraction of that. Everywhere there are signs of a glory long gone.

Even the lesser palaces of Krasia dwarf the manses of Hollow, with high warded walls, mushroom-domed roofs, and minarets that serve as both guard towers and places for dama to sing the call to prayer. But the *dama* will not allow commoners to live in palaces, so they stand with gates open, yards deserted and covered in dust, like corpses that no one had time to burn.

Sharik Hora is not in disrepair, however. As we draw close to its great dome and soaring minarets, I see fresh paints and mosaic, with Arms of Everam patrolling the walls. They call out at the sight of Chadan and rush to open the gates.

Inside the walls are lush gardens rich with fruiting trees and manicured grass, tinkling fountains surrounded by statues of heroes and leaders past. The whole of Gatherers' University and the Cathedral of Hollow could fit within these walls, with room to spare.

"You . . . live here?" I think of the scant blanket Chadan wraps around himself on the cold floor of *sharaj*.

He shrugs. "I did. Now I live in *sharaj*, the same as you. Father says it is good not to become attached to material things."

"Easy to say, when surrounded in such wealth," I note. Chadan glances my way, but he says nothing.

In gray *nie'sharum* robes, I am not considered a man, and am thus allowed into the private gardens of the palace harem. Micha is my sister, and there is no dishonor in my seeing her here.

Unlike the gritty dust outside in the city, the gardens are lush and green, filled with tinkling fountains and awash in colorful blooms. It is more visual than utilitarian, but still it reminds me of Mother's private gardens in Hollow, and I feel a pang of homesickness.

The women are in their finest robes, hurrying to and fro with food and gifts to greet husbands, sons, and fathers visiting for Waning. There are joyful cries as families are reunited, and the sounds of singing and prayer. I realize how little I know about my Krasian heritage, and feel sadness for something I never realized I was missing.

When I finally come to the place where my sister awaits, I almost don't recognize her. I am unprepared to find her clad in light, flowing silks of emerald green, her wrists and ankles jingling with jewelry. There is a lattice of gold coins over her headscarf, a necklace around her throat, and her fingers glitter with rings.

I am drab and colorless by comparison. Once it would have made me jealous, but the Olive who enjoyed such finery feels like a different person entirely, much as this new Micha does.

"Sister," I breathe. "You look—"

"Like a *heasah* pillow dancer," she cuts in.

"—beautiful," I finish, and she snorts.

"Not beautiful enough for them to find me a suitor after I broke the last one's arm."

I smile in spite of myself. "What did he do?"

Micha shrugs. "He was Majah. And I am already wed, though even my people do not consider marriage to a woman to be an impediment to finding a proper *jiwan* to 'bless us with children.'"

She leaves out that the Tenders in Thesa are little better, though

Mother keeps a tight rein on their power in Hollow. Even so, goodwives gossip and men leer when she and Kendall show affection in public.

"Let us not waste what time we have on such things," Micha says. Tell me of *sharaj*. You have done well."

I glance at the yellowed bruises all over my body. I am a fast healer, but even I can't recover from a baton beating overnight. "What makes you say that?"

"They whisper of you in the harem," Micha says. "The greenland prince who will not suffer his brothers to go hungry."

"They're not my brothers," I say.

"They are not," Micha agrees. "But that is not how the palace women see it. They expected you to be weak. Effeminate. The *push'ting* prince raised in greenland gowns. Instead you dominate, as I knew you would. I am so proud of you, sister."

Sister. How long has it been, since someone has referred to me as female without mockery? It's a reminder of who I was, as is Micha, even in her pillow silks.

But I'm not sure that is who I am anymore, either.

"Every matchmaker in the city is looking to sell you a bride, once you take the black," Micha says.

"Sell?" The idea of treating women like property makes me no less angry as a "male" than it did when Belina came to Hollow to bargain for me.

Micha shrugs. "Krasians value women differently, but it is not so different in Hollow. Krasian women do the majority of the work, so men can fight. They bear their children, and raise them. Women are valuable, so a father must be compensated when a man takes one of his daughters as *jiwah*."

"And the woman?" I ask. "What does she get?"

"A good husband, who will give her comfort and strong children, if she is lucky," Micha says.

"And if she is not?" I ask.

"Then she must endure," Micha says. "Luck is a rarity."

"I don't want that," I say. "Not to be a man's possession, nor to own a woman."

"I thought your mother's ways decadent, when I was first sent to the

North." Micha drops her eyes. "Now, I must admit that if my duties were relieved, I would wish to stay in Hollow, and not just for Kendall." She shakes her head, and for the first time, her voice cracks. "She must be so worried, if she even holds out hope I am still alive."

She produces a tear bottle, and I take it, collecting my sister's tears for her lost wife. As I lean close, I whisper in her ear. "We have to escape."

"It will be difficult." Micha lifts the cuffs of her flowing pants, revealing a pair of warded anklets, not unlike my armlet. They are beautiful, but I see the familiar metal fang and red stone of a blood lock. "Belina has seen to it that if I try to escape again, I will not get far."

"So we are trapped?" I ask.

Micha shakes her head. "It is only a matter of time before Belina drops her guard and I free myself. One way or another, I will bring her blood with me when I come for you."

The image of Belina flat on her back with a bloody nose, knocked cold by Micha's Precise Strike is not a displeasing one. But the *dama'ting* invented Micha's fighting art, and she may not be so easy a target. "And then?"

"Our escape will begin here, in Sharik Hora," Micha whispers. "My spear sisters and I were raised in the catacombs beneath the temple of Heroes' Bones, and guarded the Damajah as she walked its halls. There are secret passages even Belina will not know, and the magic in its walls will shield us from her dice."

"So we spend the rest of our lives hiding behind the bones of the dead?" I ask.

"Only until we can gather supplies to cross the desert," Micha says. "There are tunnels beneath the temple that can take us into the city unseen. Aleveran lacks the warriors to guard every inch of the city walls. We can find a place to climb and disappear into the sands."

"And the sand demons?" I ask.

Micha shrugs. "First we have to make it that far."

It's a thin plan, but it is all we have, and I cling to it. "What can I do?"

"Nothing," Micha says, "save what you are doing. Endure. Fight. Win glory. The more you appear to be one of them, the less you resist, the more lax their guard will grow and the better our chances when the time comes to escape."

I nod. "I will make you proud."

"Oh, sister," Micha takes me into her arms, "you already have."

The words, the gesture, are meant to offer strength, but instead they sap the strength from me. My resolve melts away, and Micha holds me close as I shudder, close to tears. But then I feel my sister stiffen, and turn to see Chadan waiting. Like me, he is still in his bido, and thus allowed in the harem, but still he keeps his back turned out of respect.

"We must go," he says.

"I've only just gotten here," I protest. "I was promised—"

"You were promised proof your sister was alive and well," Chadan says, "and you have had that. I do not wish this interruption any more than you, but we are needed atop the walls tonight.

"There is a storm coming."

28

WALLTOPS

THE HORN OF Sharak sounds again from the minarets of the Palace of the Sharum Ka. The drillmasters stand grim-faced as *nie'Sharum* classes muster outside the famed Maze of Krasia— the killing ground where my father's people have fought demonkind for centuries. I've read about the place in histories, but never laid eyes on its carefully crafted terrain.

"Some of you," Drillmaster Chikga nods at Chadan and a few of the older boys, "have seen storms before. Others have not. They are rare, thank Everam, but the *dama'ting* predict a great one is coming tonight, and the *alagai hora* are never wrong.

"It is Waning, when the moon is dark and the *alagai* can bring their strongest forces to bear. It is said that on Waning, Alagai Ka walks the surface of Ala, guiding his infernal forces personally. We must be vigilant, and prepared."

He taps the top of the helm jutting from his turban, etched with mind demon wards. Each of the *nie'Sharum*, myself included, has similar wards drawn on our shaved heads with blackstem, a paste that stains the skin. The wards will remain for a week or more before fading. More than time enough to get us through the new moon. In addition, there are wards around our eyes that will charge slowly with ambient magic once the sun sets, granting us wardsight in the darkness.

I don't know if we need the mind wards. It is said Arlen Bales killed all the mind demons, but it's not something I'd risk my life on. I think of Mother's argument with Mrs. Bales. Could the Father of Demons truly be out there, hunting me and Darin?

Iraven seemed not to think so. I remember his words from our first meeting. *Without minds to lead them, the sand demons have become . . . cannier. They've formed into far-ranging storms that can number in the thousands.*

Just a handful of demons were enough to destroy the borough tour camp and overcome a fit, if inexperienced, fighting force. What could a storm of thousands of them accomplish? Could even the fabled walls of Desert Spear stem such a flow?

"But you have drilled for this!" Chikga shouts. "You have practiced and studied until your very nature is attuned to Sharak. Remember your training, and you will live to see the dawn."

The drillmaster paces back and forth, meeting the eyes of each boy in turn, searching for a sign of cowardice, a sign that we will break before the coming storm. I meet his gaze with a hard one of my own. I may not know storms or the Maze, but I have seen up close what a demon attack can do. Whatever my feelings about Aleveran, this city is full of innocents.

"Remember the rules," Chikga growls. "*Nie'Sharum* do not fight. *Nie'Sharum* do not set foot on the Maze floor. You are here to scout, ferry supplies, and relay messages. You will follow the chain of command, and obey instantly when a *Sharum* gives you orders. Do you understand?"

"Yes, Drillmaster!" we all shout.

"Again!" Chikga barks. "Everam is listening!"

"YES, DRILLMASTER!" we boom.

"Good," Chikga says. "Because if any of you disobey, if you break the rules, or worse, run, I'll kill you myself."

I glance around, and see the other drillmasters are giving similar speeches to their classes. All of them seem agitated. More than one slips a small bottle of couzi from their robe turning away to throw back a mouthful of the strong spirit.

Alcohol is a violation of Evejan law, but knowing what they face, I cannot blame the men for wanting a sip of courage.

———

THE STARS ARE brighter in Desert Spear than they are in Hollow. "Light pollution" Mother called it. The glow of the greatward and abundance of lectric lights in the capital canceling out the light from above.

There is no light pollution here. Constellations I've only read about are visible to the naked eye, and as my sight adjusts, I find they are enough for me to see where the sky ends and the sand dunes begin. My stomach clenches as I trace their shapes with my eyes, searching for sign of the enemy.

It comes slowly, and not as the individual cries and dark, loping shapes I remember from the borough tour. It is a droning buzz, like a swarm of flies, rising in pitch until it is a whine that grates on my nerves like nails on slate. It is a cloud of dust, rolling over the dunes like a wind-borne fog.

The Watchers set great wardlights shining out into the sands, and we watch in silent tension as, slowly but inexorably, the sands begin to churn with demons. Most are no larger than dogs, but they are all sharp edges. Thousands of hard scales like jagged glass, matching the color of the desert sands. If not for their movements and the spotlights, they would be all but invisible.

"There must be hundreds of them." Gorvan is no coward, but he looks ready to flee, and I can't blame him.

"Quiet," Chikga snaps. "This is only the first wave. We must deal with them swiftly, before their fellows arrive."

Iraven is not far from us, standing on the battlements above the gate. I cannot deny he looks dashing in his white turban and *Sharum* blacks, an inspiration to all who see him. The spear and shield slung across his back are infused with *hora*, their wards glowing even now, pregnant with power.

Iraven signals one of his lieutenants, who puts a horn to his lips and blows a series of notes. Immediately, the great gears of the portcullis begin to screech and turn as the gate is raised. The sand demons waste no time, racing through the opening into the Maze.

A handful of warriors stand ready to greet them, vastly outnumbered. As the corelings come howling toward them I clench my fists in fear. "What are they doing?"

"Baiting them," Chadan says. "Baiters lure the *alagai* into ambushes and traps to thin their numbers and separate them from their brethren. It is the most dangerous task in the Maze. Their glory is boundless."

Indeed, the Baiters shout and clash their spears against their shields, raising a cacophony to draw the demons' attention, waiting long moments before they turn and race deeper into the Maze as the sand demons give chase.

When enough corelings have entered, Iraven signals the horn player again. The chains are freed and gravity pulls the heavy portcullis down with tremendous speed and power. The wards on its spiked bottom flash as they strike the demons still pressuring to get inside, cutting more than a few of them in half. These scrabble forward on their front claws, shrieking and slavering, seemingly unaware they are dying.

The sand demons racing after the Baiters are faster on open ground, but the twists, turns, and obstacles of the Maze slow them. From atop the walls I can see how the Maze was built on ancient ruins, territory ceded to the night when the corelings first returned. Many of the old walls and buildings still stand, used along with new construction to hinder pursuit and funnel the enemy into ambush points.

"Oot!" a Baiter cries as he races full tilt around a corner into a dead end, a pack of sand demons on his heels. He moves with practiced ease into a warded alcove as the demons roar in after him. They scrabble ineffectually as the wards around the alcove spark and flare, turning their claws. Warriors charge from ambush pockets to either side, skewering them on warded spears.

I clench a fist at the sight as if the victory is my own. In a way it is. There is no tribe here, no blood debts. Veiled, we are only men, standing against the *alagai*. A win for them is a win for us all.

Other traps are similarly sprung. One Baiter quicksteps over a narrow path and the sand demons charging after him collapse dusty tarps covering demon pits to either side. The corelings shriek as they fall, some impaled on the warded stakes at the bottom, and others stymied by the circle of power that let them enter, but won't let them leave. They will be trapped until the sun rises to burn them away.

Two of the demons make it across the same pathway the Baiter used.

One is quickly dropped by the short bow of a Watcher atop the walls. The other is netted by an ambush team and speared.

The wards along the warriors' weapons flare as they puncture the demon's armor, and I see a bit of the power pulse up their arms, giving them added strength and vitality. I remember the rush of it from the night of the borough tour. Part of me has craved that feeling ever since.

All around are similar ambushes. One Baiter, chased by a lone demon, turns and sets his feet, bashing the creature with his shield. The wards flare, driving the demon into the Maze wall where wards cut into the stone shock through its body like lightning. It drops, stunned, and the warrior drives his spear through its skull.

"You see?" Drillmaster Amaj says. "Fight when you must, but let the terrain fight for you when you can."

The sand demons are nimble, their claws finding easy purchase on the sandstone walls. Some of them climb, attempting to get above their prey, but wardings run along the walls at regular intervals, and they find themselves suddenly thrown to the ground, vulnerable.

More Baiters lead large packs still deeper into the Maze, where ambush teams lie in wait, and dead ends are shaped into wards so powerful any demon touching them might as well step into sunlight.

With the first wave under control, Iraven signals his hornblower again, and the portcullis is raised. Demons pour through the gates, but as I look back to the dunes beyond the city walls, the sight makes me fear I will foul my bido. The cloud of dust on the horizon has only grown. If it was hundreds before, it is thousands now.

Iraven sees it, too. "A short raising only," he tells Chikga. "We'll thin their numbers as much as we can, but I want the portcullis down and the gates sealed before the storm arrives in full. It will be missile fire after that."

"Your will, Sharum Ka." Chikga punches a fist to his chest and turns to Chadan. "Nie Ka, assist the scorpion and sling teams in loading."

Chadan punches a fist to his chest and begins shouting orders, breaking the *nie'Sharum* into small teams to assist individual machines. The scorpions are gigantic crank bows, powered by heavy springs. They throw spears the size of small trees. It normally takes two boys to haul one of the giant stingers, but I easily heft one over my shoulder, leaving Thivan empty-handed. He runs instead to carry the baskets of small warded stones, dumping them into sling buckets big enough to bathe in. The sling teams will be able to launch deadly swarms of stones into the coming storm.

A shriek from above turns our eyes skyward as a flight of wind demons swoops down on the city. In their hind talons each carries a large chunk of masonry, and I feel I might sick up at the sight.

"They're attacking with the broken walls of the *csars*." Iraven draws a ward in the air, and the rest of us quickly follow suit. Individually, wind demons cannot carry enough mass to damage the walls, but there are hundreds of them, and should the corelings fly just above the ward-net, they could rain them down on the warriors in the Maze.

Iraven turns to the hornblower. "Tell the men to take cover."

The order is quickly relayed, and the warriors in the Maze scramble into shelters as the scorpion teams turn their massive bows skyward, waiting for the demons to come into range. The catapult teams race to make adjustments, but the great machines, aimed at the mass of demons before the gates, are slow to reposition.

The demons, however, do not fly out over the Maze. Instead they pull up short, releasing their projectiles into the mass of corelings crowding the open gate. The scorpions fire into the mass, dropping some of the demons from the sky, but it makes little difference as their stones fall like rain in the open ground before the gates.

It seems mad, but then the sands explode as snub-nosed clay demons burst from the ground. They swarm the stones like ants, using their armored faceplates to push them into the breach.

"What are they doing?" I ask aloud.

"I don't . . ." Chikga gasps. "Everam's beard! They're going to hold open the gate!"

"Close the portcullis!" Iraven cries. "Now!"

The hornblower raises his instrument to his lips, but before he can sound the notes, one of the flying demons lets loose a thunderous cry, and a bolt of lightning flies from its beak, blasting the hornblower off the wall. He lands on the Maze floor, scorched and smoking.

"Nie's black heart!" Drillmaster Amaj is moving for the stair even as the rest of us dive for cover. He leaps over the wall, dropping to the first landing and racing into the gatehouse.

A few moments later, the portcullis drops, but the damage has been done. The clay demons have piled enough stones in place that the gate cannot close fully, and corelings continue to pour through the gap. On the horizon, two massive shapes appear.

Rock demons.

For a moment, Iraven stands frozen.

"Sharum Ka?" Chikga prods.

Iraven shakes himself, then rolls his shield down onto his arm even as he reaches over his shoulder for his spear. He raises the weapon, pointing. "Scorpions! Target the rock demons! Do not let them get close enough to raise the portcullis further! Sling teams! Scatter the demons making for the gates!"

He turns, eyes falling on Chadan. "Nie Ka. Send your *nie'Sharum* to inform the warriors in the Maze to break position and muster in the fourth layer. Call out clear paths to avoid the *alagai* until we can regroup. They are not to engage. Drillmasters, you're with me."

"What is the plan?" Amaj asks.

A chill runs through me as I follow Iraven's gaze down to the corelings flooding into the Maze. "We're going to retake the gate and seal it."

CHADAN BREAKS THE *nie'Sharum* into pairs, sending them scattered in every direction, racing along the walltops to call Iraven's orders down to the warriors. As I wait to be assigned, I watch my brother ready his personal guard to march to what is most likely their doom.

Iraven kidnapped me. Sold me for the white turban in some Majah power struggle I barely understand. I thought him a coward. I thought he didn't value life as I do. But there is no hesitation, no cowardice, as he throws down his life for his people.

"Men of Majah!" Prince Iraven clashes his spear against his shield. "The Father of Demons comes for your mothers! He comes for your sisters and wives and children! What path must he take?"

The *Sharum* clatter their spears and shout in reply. "The path of spears!"

"Everam is watching!" Iraven barks. "Make Him proud!" He charges for the gatehouse stair. His men give a shout and follow, all of them ready to die for Desert Spear and its people.

Perhaps that is what being a man means to them. And if so, I was wrong to sneer. It is a trait worth emulating. Mother commands the Hollow Soldiers, but she does not lead from the front. She protects Hollow with plots and magic, not blood and bone.

"Olive." I look back to see Chadan waiting. The rest of the *nie'Sharum* are gone. "You're with me."

I shake off my surprise. "Wouldn't it make sense—?"

"To pair you with a weaker boy?" Chadan finishes. "No. The weakest go to inner layers, where the Maze is still clear. The *Sharum* stationed there will begin immediate retreat, and use their hornblowers to amplify the command. We are princes, and the strongest among them. It is our duty to go where the fighting is thickest."

The attack on the borough tour flashes before my eyes again. The screams. The blood. The seemingly endless hours after, spent tending the wounded.

"I'm afraid," I admit.

Chadan lays a hand on my shoulder. "So am I. But we are still going." I nod, and we run.

As we feared, the outermost layers are sorely pressed. The fighting is everywhere, tight formations broken into chaotic bubbles of individual combat. There is no retreat for these men. They are scattered with the enemy all around them, but still they fight. If Iraven can close the gate, some of them might survive. If he cannot . . .

"The *alagai* have wedged the gate!" Chadan calls to a team of eight warriors lying in wait in an ambush pocket. "The outer layers are overrun! Fall back to the fourth layer and join the formations waiting on the Sharum Ka's signal!"

The men start to leave cover to comply, but then their Baiter runs around the corner crying "Oot! Oot!"

With quick precision, the warriors retreat to their warded ambush pocket, invisible to the dozen or more corelings that come howling after the fleeing warrior.

The Baiter, oblivious to the battle raging in his wake, keeps his focus, running swiftly across the seven-inch path between two large demon pits, camouflaged with heavy, sand-covered tarps.

We've practiced the Push Guard drill countless times in *sharaj*. Coming out of the narrow tunnel into the wider ambush pit, the demons will spread out in an attempt to surround the warrior. Unable to distinguish the pits, they will collapse the tarps, falling onto a bed of warded spears.

The Push Guard lock shields and lower their spears. Before the trap is sprung, they are already moving from the ambush pocket, beginning a charge that will drive any demons that manage to pull up in time into the pit with the others.

One lucky demon follows the Baiter closely enough to find the secure path, and I get my first close look at a sand demon. The size of a large hound, its yellow scales glitter like broken glass, with jagged spikes protecting the joints and a sharp ridge along its back. Its horns are low and curve backward, offering no resistance to its sleek four-legged lope. Its talons leave great grooves in the hard clay of the path.

But even as that one races ahead, the others pull up well short of the pits, suddenly turning on the advancing Push Guard.

"What?" Chadan breathes.

"How could they know?" I ask.

"They couldn't," he says, but somehow, they did. Suddenly, the guard is outnumbered two to one, with the trap unsprung. The small team is designed to ram stray demons into the pits, not fight directly against long odds.

The sudden shouts of the men cause the Baiter to look back over his shoulder before he makes it to his warded escape pocket. He stumbles at the sight, and it's all the sand demon needs to close the gap and leap, catching him in the leg with a hooked talon that severs an artery with almost surgical precision. Blood spurts from the wound and the warrior gives a cry as the leg collapses. He gets his shield up, knocking the demon away, and hurls his spear, taking the coreling in the side.

The demon drops, but the damage is done. The warrior tries to rise, but he is losing blood too quickly, and his fellows cannot get to him. Already two of the Push Guard are being torn apart. Two more are bleeding freely, and the others are hard-pressed. The demons have cut them off from the safety of the ambush pocket.

"Retreat!" the Baiter cries. "Find reinforcements! My soul is ready for the lonely path!"

I watch, incredulous, as the remaining guard lock shields and throw back one last press, then turn and flee. "Your glory this night will not be forgotten, brother!" one of them cries.

The demons follow, pouring from the ambush pocket, but the warriors know the terrain better, slipping into warded buildings to access tunnels beneath the walls.

I look back to the Baiter, clutching at his wound in an attempt to stem the flow of blood pooling around him. The sand demon he dropped whines, scrabbling with its paws at the spear embedded in its side until the weapon is knocked free. I know from experience that the coreling is already healing. Given time, demons can recover from almost any wound that does not sever a body part or kill them outright.

I turn to Chadan. "We have to help him!"

"No!" the Nie Ka orders. "We're unarmed, and it is forbidden for *nie'Sharum* to set foot in the Maze."

He's right. We're wearing only bidos and sandals, and without warded weapons, the strongest blows momentarily stun a coreling at best. If we go down there, we'll be lucky to come out alive.

The demon gets shakily to its feet. The warrior, focused on crawling toward the warded alcove he meant to shelter in, seems unaware of the threat. He's lost so much blood it's hard to believe he's conscious at all, but still he struggles.

Never stop fighting.

"To the Core with what's forbidden," I growl, hoping the words will strike to the heart of him. "Are we men, or not?"

Then I leap from the wall.

29

MEN

THE MAZE WALLS are twenty feet tall. Too high for others to jump, perhaps, but I'm not like other people. The impact shocks up my legs as I hit the sandstone floor of the Maze, but I embrace the pain and absorb it, rolling away as much of the energy as I can.

"Olive!" Chadan shouts as I come back to my feet, running to the fallen warrior.

"Begone," the Baiter croaks. "My soul is . . . "

"Quiet." I grab his night veil and pull it away, twisting the cloth as I tie it tightly around his leg to stem the blood flow. The wound is severe, but I know the surgeons at Gatherers' University could save the leg. No doubt the *dama'ting* can as well, if the man lives long enough to see them.

I keep an eye on the demon as I work. It breathes in a wet wheeze, but each stumbling step in our direction is steadier than the last. I reach for the warrior's shield as a rope drops from above, and Chadan rappels down to land lightly beside us.

"You're going to get us killed," he says, but he takes up the shield, positioning himself between us and the demon.

Demons can smell blood from great distance, Chikga taught, *and will always go for the wounded first.*

I eye the spear lying just a few yards away, and take a sliding step along the wall toward it. "It will come for the Baiter. If you can hold it back for one pass, I can retrieve the spear."

Chadan nods. "Be swift."

The scent of blood is overpowering, even to me. The demon's eyes are fixed on the Baiter as it tamps down, hindquarters wriggling in preparation to leap. Drool dripping from its jaws, the coreling ignores me completely as I take a second slow step toward the spear, and a third.

But then the demon sniffs the air and turns its head, meeting my eyes with something frighteningly akin to recognition. The sick feeling in my stomach returns as the coreling shifts targets from the bleeding warrior to me.

"Olive!" Chadan cries as it shrieks and charges, but I barely hear him, setting my feet and focusing on the sand demon as it leaps at me, claws leading.

Let the terrain fight for you, Drillmaster Amaj taught. I grab the demon's lead paw at the wrist and pivot, using the creature's momentum to drive it into one of the lectric wards chiseled into the sandstone wall. Power shocks through the demon and into me as well.

My limbs twitch and lock, no longer obeying my commands. I stumble and land on my backside as the stunned demon drops to the Maze floor, shaking itself vigorously as its internal magic works to heal this new injury.

I struggle to rise as well, but the demon recovers first, leaping to bury its long, hooked foretalons in my flesh.

But Chadan is there, interposing himself and catching the demon on the shield. He puts his shoulder into it, driving the coreling back into the lectric wards.

This time I am ready as it drops away stunned, catching the thrashing creature and ignoring the scales and flailing talons that cut into my flesh. With a great heave I lift it over my head and I charge a few steps, throwing it into the center of the tarp covering one of the demon pits.

The heavy cloth collapses, revealing wards designed to allow corespawn to pass in, but not back out. The sand demon disappears with a muffled shriek and a cloud of dust, hopelessly tangled as it hits the floor of the pit twenty feet below.

I glance at the lacerations the demon gave me, but none of them are serious. I hurry to the injured Baiter. He has lost consciousness, but his heart is still beating. Chadan gapes as I lift him up, armor and all, and sling him across my shoulders, but he says nothing. He puts the *Sharum's* spear through the loops of his shield and wears them on his back like a warrior as he scurries up the rope to help from the top as I climb with a man on my back.

OTHER *NIE'SHARUM*, RETURNING from their missions, have gathered as I make the walltop. Too stunned to help, they stare with wide eyes as I lay the warrior down and tend his wound while Chadan pulls up the remaining rope.

Baiters, prone to injury and often needing to take cover alone while their compatriots ambush the demons at their heels, keep basic medical supplies in their belt pouches. In this man's case, just forceps, some couzi, a needle and thread. I cleanse the wound as best I can, tying off the severed artery and veins in a manner I hope a more skilled healer can repair.

"What did you do?" Thivan asks Chadan. "It is forbidden . . . "

"You saw nothing!" Chadan barks, and the other boys take a step back at the ferocity of it.

Gorvan slaps Thivan on the back of his head. "What did you see?"

Thivan drops to his knees, hands on the walltop. "I saw nothing, Nie Ka."

The other boys all bow, nodding vigorously. "We saw nothing."

Chadan nods as if he expected nothing less. "Gorvan, report."

Gorvan looks down at the ambush pocket we've just climbed out of. "It wasn't just here, Nie Ka. Traps all over the outer layers lie unsprung. The *alagai* seemed to know they were there, and the hidden warriors. Fighting has been fierce."

He's here. The Krasians speak of the Father of Demons like a metaphorical being, but this is too much to ignore. Corelings are powerful, but the brightest aren't known to be much smarter than an average hound. Certainly not enough to suddenly turn traps that have worked for hundreds of years on their builders.

And that sand demon knew me.

"Thivan," Chadan says. "Rise and report."

"The majority of our forces evacuated in time, Nie Ka." Thivan bows one last time before taking his hands off the ground and rising. "They are mustering behind the wall of the fourth layer, and will be ready when the Sharum Ka retakes the gate."

If he retakes it. I curse myself for the doubt, but it remains.

"Return to the outer wall and assist the sling and scorpion teams," Chadan orders. "Olive and I will bring this warrior to the *dama'ting*. Gorvan is Nie Ka until we return."

Chadan and I carry the injured Baiter along the walltops and down to the *dama'ting* pavilion just outside the Maze. Already it is filling with wounded, and I am surprised to see Belina herself leading the healers. She notices me, eyebrows lifting to disappear into her headscarf.

"What happened?" she demands.

I open my mouth, but Chadan speaks first. "This warrior was separated from his unit and injured. We threw him a rope and he managed to tie it around himself before passing out. We hauled him to the walltop and carried him here."

Belina looks skeptically at him for a moment, her eyes flicking to the lacerations on my flesh. Both of us are covered in the warrior's blood, our white bidos soaked red, and I hope my blood will be taken for his.

"Were you wounded?" Belina asks.

"It is nothing, *dama'ting*," Chadan says. "Shrapnel from a shattered stone dropped by a wind demon."

Belina stares a moment longer, then grunts, turning her attention to the Baiter's wound. "Whose work is this?"

"Mine," I say, before Chadan can speak again. "I used his veil as a tourniquet and tied off the femoral artery and veins as best I could, but he has lost a great deal of blood."

Belina blinks as some of the other *dama'ting* look up at my words. "Where did you learn this?"

"Gatherers' University in Hollow," I say. "I studied under Headmistress Darsy and Dama'ting Favah before I was . . . brought here."

"Favah," I hear one of the other priestesses breathe, and they begin whispering to one another. It seems even here, half a world away among the tribe of her enemies, my ancient teacher has a reputation.

Belina eyes me, and nods. "Favah has taught you well. You saved this man's leg, and probably his life." Like Mother's rare praise, I am surprised and disgusted at how Belina's words please me. "Go now, return to your duty. The night will be long, still."

"YOU LIED TO Belina." I'm careful not to meet Chadan's eyes as we head back to the Maze. I can tell he's angry, even if he's careful not to let it show. I just don't understand why.

"A second sin to cover the first," Chadan says. "Twice, tonight, I've had to save you from yourself."

"That warrior would be dead otherwise," I say. "You said yourself it was our duty to go where the fighting was thickest. To what end, if not to help?"

"You may not believe in Everam, but I do," Chadan says. "The Evejah forbids the unblooded to set foot in the Maze."

"Then why did you follow?" I demand. "You were willing to let the warrior die. Why break the law for me?"

Chadan spreads his hands. "Because we're brothers."

"No, we're not!" I snap. "This is *your* home. The *nie'Sharum* are *your* brothers. I was kidnapped and dragged here against my will to be your ripping bride. I'm not one of you. Not Majah or Evejan, and I don't need to follow your rules."

"Then why did you leap into the Maze to save a Majah warrior?" Chadan demands. "If we're your goalers, why risk yourself for one of us?"

"Because I'll be corespawned before I stand by and let a demon eat someone when I could stop it." The last words come out in a growl. I feel my heart pounding, my anger building. I meet Chadan's eyes now, and wonder if the time has come to challenge him once and for all.

He sees the challenge in my eyes, but raises his hands, palms open. "And that's why I followed. Brother or no, your honor was boundless, Olive asu Ahmann am'Paper am'Hollow. What kind of man would I be if I let you face the *alagai* alone?"

The words break through my anger. I see in his eyes he means them. That sand demon nearly killed me. Chadan saved my life in the Maze, then lied to save it again. Why am I arguing with him?

"Rules are like a privy, my Tikka says," I tell him. "They keep us feeling civilized, but they get too full of shit if you don't empty the pot now and again."

Chadan laughs, and something of the tension between us eases. "Just how strong are you?"

I'm not expecting the question, and it cuts too close to my other secrets. Micha warned me of this. "I don't know. How strong are you?"

Chadan stops walking, and I am forced to stop and look at him. "I'm not a fool, son of Ahmann. Your father is Shar'Dama Ka, and your strength is . . . inhuman. I felt it the first time we fought. You leap off twenty-foot walls and throw sand demons like children."

I shrug. "I don't know if it was my father or my mother. She used *hora* magic while I was in her womb. Perhaps too much. I've always been stronger than the other children, but not as strong as a demon. It was thrashing so hard, I don't think I could have held on if there hadn't been a pit to throw it in."

Chadan resumes walking, long fast strides meant to return us quickly to the wall. "A useful trait for a warrior."

I hurry to match his pace. "I don't think it's much different from the charge warriors get when they spear a demon and absorb some of its magic."

I feel his eyes upon me again, but I keep my gaze ahead. As we reach the wall, we hear the horns signaling Iraven has retaken the gate, and both of us break into a run.

The remainder of the night is spent running the walltops, calling out positions to warriors on the ground, delivering fresh spears and shields, evacuating wounded, and helping the fire teams reload.

Wind demons attempt to take out the artillery with more dropped stones, but the fire teams have their measure now, slings filling the air with warded stones that punch through wings and crush the demons' hollow bones, when the scorpions don't simply blast them from the sky. The lone lightning demon does not appear again.

Whatever my feelings about Iraven, I cannot deny he is a good leader to his men. He leads the most dangerous charges personally, his armor spattered with demon ichor.

They sweep layer after layer of the Maze until every demon is dead or trapped in a pit to await the sun. The sands beyond the city still swarm with demons when the sky begins to purple, then they dissipate, slipping back down into the Core before the light can burn them away.

"They'll be back tomorrow night," Drillmaster Chikga says.

Iraven nods. "But we won't be fooled this time."

30

GREENBLOODS

I SMELL THE COOKPOTS as we return to the barracks at dawn, but it isn't gruel Tikka has over the fires. I inhale, and my dry mouth begins to water.

"You did the work of men last night," Chikga says, "and so you will eat like men. Soft couscous, piled with vegetables and spiced meat dripping with fat, as much as you can eat."

There is a moment of stunned hesitation, and then we are all hurrying to take a bowl, with the swiftest feet determining order, rather than rank. For perhaps the first time in his life, Faseek eats first.

"There will be no family visits today," Chikga announces. "It will be back to the walltops tonight. For now, eat and sleep. Those who wish a few hours of liberty can leave the grounds this afternoon."

Tikka fills my bowl, thrusting a pair of eating sticks to stand upright in the couscous. The sticks remind me of home, of Krasian Studies and Micha's cooking. I pick them up expertly, taking a precise portion of couscous and bringing it to my mouth without spilling a grain.

The flavor is like nothing I've ever tasted. Perhaps the weeks of gruel play a part, but the food seems to come alive in my mouth, salt and fat and filling starch, rich with hava. I take a bit of meat, lifting it to take a delicate bite.

"You won't do your princess reputation any good eating like that,"

Chadan says, coming to join me. I look around and see he's right. The other boys hold the tilted bowls right to their lips, using the sticks to simply shovel the food into their mouths.

Chadan smiles, deftly spinning the sticks in his hand before lifting his own bowl to his lips and using them like a blunt instrument. I'm so hungry I don't argue, joining the others in savaging the meal.

Gorvan is the first to finish his bowl. The burly boy could break Tikka in half, but he approaches her as warily as he would a sand demon. We all watch, half expecting such largesse to be snatched away, but when Tikka wordlessly refills his bowl, a second line quickly forms.

We retreat inside as the sun begins to heat the yard. My mind is still racing with the events of the previous night. The air is already warming as I lie on the stone floor. I think sleep will be difficult to find, but I am so tired, and my belly so blessedly full, that it comes as soon as I rest my head on my arms.

In my dreams, I again see the sand demon turn its head to stare at me in recognition. This time I flee, racing along the walltops, but the coreling gives chase, calling my name.

I WAKE WITH a start, bathed in sweat, and see that I am not alone. Thivan thrashes in his sleep, groaning as if in some illusory pain. Konin sits hugging his knees and staring at nothing, mind trapped in some horror of its own conjuring.

All around the room, there are others in a similar state. We are all of us haunted by what we saw in the Maze. The drillmasters spoke at length of the infinite glory of *alagai'sharak*, but they never did justice to its horror.

I glance around for Chadan, but he is nowhere to be found. The ban on family Waning visits obviously does not apply to the *Damaji's* grandson.

But I am Nie Domin, the second of none. If the Nie Ka isn't here, it is my responsibility to lead the *sharaj* until he returns. I want to offer the boys comfort, but I am in sore need of it myself. I have no words to soothe their fears and pain.

The best leader leads by example, Mother used to say, as often to coerce me into eating my vegetables at state dinners as to advise on governance. Still, as with many of Mother's irritating lessons, I look back and realize she was right.

I glance at the windows. It feels like I slept only minutes, but the angle of the light tells me it is midday. I inhale, and the scent of fresh, hava spiced meat is on the air. My stomach grumbles in response.

I look at the other *nie'Sharum*, clinging to restless sleep, pacing, staring into space, and clap my hands as loud as I can, sending a resounding *crack* through the room. Boys start awake, or snap their heads around and crouch as if under attack.

"Lunch is hot," I say loudly. "Tikka will be unforgiving if we let it go cold. First come, first served, and every bowl will be full."

That shines a light through the bars of whatever mental prisons they were building. I crack my hands a second time to break them free. "Now."

I turn and start walking as the others scramble to line up behind me. Moments later, we are back in the sun, and Tikka's great cauldron has everyone's attention, keeping their minds in the present.

Again we eat quickly, as if expecting the food to be snatched away. The speed causes belching, and before long the boys make foul contest of it, roaring with laughter as they see who can sustain the longest, or bring forth the most noxious smell. Princess Olive would have been horrified, but I find myself laughing along.

"Some of us are going into the city," Faseek says over his bowl. "You should come."

I can hardly believe it, but Chigka and the other drillmasters are at the gate, handing each boy a few draki as we leave the training grounds. "For food," he growls. "You don't want to be hungry tonight. Don't waste it on *heasah*, and anyone caught with couzi will be whipped and have the spirits poured on their bloody back."

Gorvan rubs the draki in his palm together. "Hardly enough for either, unless we want to share a greenblood *push'ting*." The other boys laugh, paying Chikga's threat no mind, but I remember my own whipping all too well, and the sting of Belina's disinfectant.

Still, while I have little interest in couzi or . . . *heasah*, my ears perk up. "*Push'ting?*"

Gorvan laughs. "Of course Princess Olive would take note at that!"

The others join his mirth, but it dies down as my eyes narrow. "Have any of you even met a *push'ting*?" I ask.

Most drop their eyes at that, but Gorvan is still smiling. "My father says every brothel has *push'ting*, for those with tight purse strings."

There is laughter again, but I have their measure, now. Boys are all for raucous talk, but they are parroting their elders rather than speaking from experience or malice. I don't want to see a brothel, but it might be worth it for the chance to learn more. I have questions about myself that perhaps *push'ting* are better suited to answer.

I'm quickly taken in by the sights and sounds of the city. Desert Spear is vast, with buildings dating back hundreds or even thousands of years. Some are grand palaces, but many of the low, sturdy buildings the commoners live in carry as much age and history.

I wonder if my father roamed these same streets, wearing away with his sandals the same smooth, ancient stones that I tread upon. I wonder if my father's father walked past this building or that, or his father before him, and on through the centuries. For a moment I touch something bigger than myself, and feel a connection to this place, a world away from home.

"Mangoes!" a voice calls. "Mangoes and prickle pears!"

I pull up short at the sound of the Northern tongue, turning to see a Thesan woman, her skin deeply tanned, but still pale compared with mine, which has darkened in the sun to something close to that of my full-blood compatriots. She has a scarf over her hair, but her face is uncovered, and there is a bit of faded color in her threadbare robe.

She sees me looking and takes a small prickle pear from her cart, deftly shaving away the spiked skin of the fruit with a heavy knife. "Taste one free, young warrior," she says in thickly accented Krasian. "Six for a draki. You won't find a better bargain anywhere in the city."

"The greenbloods grunt like pigs," Gorvan says, and Thivan snorts.

"You sound piggish yourself," I say, moving to take the fruit the woman holds out to me. I've never tasted prickle pear, and its juicy flesh is cool and sweet in my mouth. I eat it more quickly than I intend, and hand over one of my coins for more.

"Are you honestly going to spend your money on fruit?" Montidahr is incredulous.

"Hoping to find some toothless gray *chin* woman who will lie with you for your three draki, Montidahr?" Gorvan laughs. "Even *push'ting heasah* have higher standards."

Gorvan isn't my friend, but he is loyal. As third in line, he takes it on himself to enforce Chadan's and my commands, and is quick to chastise any who do not show us proper respect. I let the other boys enjoy a laugh at Montidahr's expense before I put an end to it.

"Quiet, all of you," I keep my voice pleasant, "it's not as if Gorvan has touched a woman since they pulled him from his mother." Even Gorvan laughs at that, and they take a few steps back, talking while I turn my attention back to the vendor.

"Where are you from?" I ask in the Northern tongue.

The woman looks startled, but then she seems to notice my blue eyes, and her eyes flick over my skin, noting its shade. "I was born in Edon's Vineyard, south of Fort Rizon, before the demon of the desert came and gave us to the Majah. Are you half-blood? What are you doing with this lot?"

The demon of the desert. The schoolbooks say that is what the Northerners called my father when he came forth from the desert to conquer southern Thesa, but no one has ever dared speak it to my face. "I was born in Hollow, just after the war. I have only recently come to Fort Krasia."

"Honest word? Have they opened the borders at last?"

There is such desperate hope in her eyes that I wince, knowing I must quash it. "They have not. I am a . . . special case."

"No matter." The woman whisks her hand, as if brushing away hope is commonplace for her. "Can you tell me any news? Is Leesha Paper still Mistress of Hollow County?"

Now it is my turn to be startled, hearing my mother's name a thousand miles from home. "Leesha Paper is duchess of Hollow, yes."

"Duchess!" The woman claps her hands in delight. "My cousin fled to the Hollow when the Krasians came. She begged me to come, but my mother was too old for the journey. Now . . . " She waves a hand at her cart. "Mother died crossing the desert instead, and I live here."

"I'm sorry," I say, knowing the words are insufficient.

Again she brushes the pain away. "It was a long time ago. I've made my peace with it. What of Rizon? Did you pass through my home on your way here?"

I shake my head. "We sailed across the great lake instead, but by all accounts, my . . . " I nearly choke on the word *father*, covering it with a cough.

"Here." The woman hands me a cup, filling it with a splash of water from a jug on her cart.

I take it gratefully, drinking. "Ahmann Jardir has proved a better leader than folk feared. Everam's Bounty has been prosperous and at peace since the war."

"At peace with all save the Majah, since he has no doubt given our homes away." The woman makes a spitting sound, but wastes no moisture in the dry air.

I cannot blame her. The walk through the city has shown me much. The greenland thralls brought back with the Majah have formed a huge underclass in Desert Spear. They and even their half-blood children have limited rights, many living in deeper squalor than this fruit seller, when they aren't owned outright by Krasian masters. The owned often live in greater luxury, but I know well that luxury is not the same as liberty.

Mother and the histories say that Father's conquest was to levy forces in time to fight the demon war, and that he stopped his advance when it ended, but can even that excuse what was done to these people? What would have been done to me, if I had humbler parentage? Krasians speak of blood debts that span generations, but if that is true, my debt is vast.

"Olive, can we move on while you grunt at the greenblood?" Gorvan calls. "The day is wasting."

The woman tilts her head at me. "Olive? Like the Princess of Hollow County?"

"I have to go," I say quickly, pressing a second coin into the woman's hand. Before she can react, I hurry after the others.

"Did you just pay two draki for a handful of pears?" Thivan is incredulous.

"Does that mean you don't want one?" I reply.

WE WANDER THE city for hours, but Gorvan and Montidahr never find *heasah* of any sort, or couzi for that matter. As the sun begins its descent, they grudgingly spend their coins on spiced meat skewers and fruit nectars on our way back to the training grounds.

Chadan is there, looking freshly bathed and fed. The rest of us had a few minutes in the sweat room and a fresh bido from Tikka, but more than anything, I long for a proper bath.

I catch Chadan looking at me when he thinks my attention is elsewhere, but he drops his eyes whenever I turn to face him. I wonder if Belina believed his story, and if he's been questioned further, but it doesn't matter. It's clear the rules don't apply equally to everyone in Krasia. Aleveran isn't going to punish his own grandson, and so long as he believes he needs me for something, he isn't going to punish me any more than he has to.

By sunset we are atop the walls again, each carrying a waterskin for thirsty warriors in the Maze as we haul sling stones and scorpion bolts within earshot of the Sharum Ka. Chikga's *nie'Sharum* support my brother directly, as much, I think, for Chadan's benefit as my own. The Sharum Ka cannot show favoritism openly, but he can keep us close.

Iraven catches my eye and gestures for me to come to him. I obey instinctively, though the sight of him brings with it an ugly churn of emotion.

I want to hate my brother. Part of me still does. But even I was inspired by his courage in the night. Wherever the fighting was thickest as they retook the Maze, Iraven was there. He is the best fighter I have ever seen—graceful, quick, and precise like Micha, but with another hundred pounds of muscle and far greater reach. My threat of a blood debt against him was foolish posturing. Even after weeks of near-constant training, Iraven could kill me in three strokes.

I keep my eyes on the wall, saying nothing as I approach. Iraven does not take his attention from the sands beyond the gates as he hands me a satchel. "Mother wanted you to have this."

I take the soft leather bag, understanding its purpose before I even open it. Favah had one just like it, back at Gatherers' University. I open it to find herbs, a small mortar and pestle, tongs, and other healing implements. I turn it over to reveal the hidden sheath built into the back of the bag, containing a curved *hanzhar* dagger.

And not just any *hanzhar*. A thin scrap of brown leather covers the jeweled hilt, but I recognize it all the same as I half draw the blade. It is the very knife Belina tried to sell me all those months ago in Achman's bazaar. No doubt this one has magic the *dama'ting* can turn against me as well, but I cannot deny I feel safer with a warded blade.

In both our cultures, words and a show of gratitude are expected upon receiving such a valuable gift, but I offer no thanks. My forgiveness won't be bought so cheaply. "Healing will be easier with this."

"Healing is a woman's art," Iraven says.

"I was raised a woman," I say.

He turns to look at me. "And what are you now?"

I meet his gaze. "Your prisoner."

Iraven points to the Maze floor where a familiar Baiter stands, restored by *dama'ting* demonbone magic. "A prisoner would not leap down into the Maze to save a warrior from an enemy tribe."

I don't ask how he knows. "The Evejah says all men are brothers in the night."

"So you are a man," Iraven notes.

"Are women not all sisters in the night?" I ask. "Are we not all siblings? Women sacrifice no less than men when the demons come."

"You are a woman, then?"

I thrust the blade back into its sheath, irritated at his parsing of words. "Your mind is too small to understand what I am, brother." The words are dangerously close to my secret, but in my anger I don't care. My grip on the hilt of the *hanzhar* is so tight I feel the gemstones cutting through the leather.

Drillmaster Chikga approaches before Iraven can reply. My brother turns his eyes back to the sands, careful not to be seen giving me too much attention. "Return to your post."

I bow and sling the satchel's strap over my head, resuming my work.

———

THE CORELINGS RISE in numbers as the sun's last light slips away, but not as great as I remember.

Drillmaster Chikga seems to agree. "There are less of them. Perhaps the storm is passing."

"Perhaps," Iraven echoes, but he sounds unconvinced. Laborers have spent the day hauling away the stones the demons brought, but we all know how quickly they can be replaced. "Raise the portcullis for a few minutes only."

Iraven's new hornblower gives the command, and again the great gears turn, letting a wave of demons through before dropping the heavy gate back down, crushing any corelings unfortunate enough to be under the arch.

The Baiters whoop and clash their shields, leading the demons as they did the night before, but there is an edge to everyone's nerves tonight. Hidden in ambush pockets and gatehouses throughout the Maze, more than triple the number of *Sharum* lie in wait. If there is another trick tonight, Iraven means to be ready for it.

But he isn't. None of us are, as horns begin blowing from another part of the city.

The greenblood quarter.

"THEY'VE BREACHED THE wall," Iraven says, listening to the pattern of the horns.

"Is that even possible?" Drillmaster Amaj asks. "No demon has entered the city in three thousand years."

Iraven ignores him. "Sound the alarms. Every citizen to the undercity."

"With respect, Sharum Ka," Chikga interjects, "the undercity hasn't been used in twenty years. The palaces and full-blood districts will have maintained their entrances, but the *chin* . . . "

"Won't even know where theirs are." Iraven is already moving. "Chikga, you and your students are with me. Amaj, you have the gate. Signal Kai Unden that the Maze is his until I return. Keep the portcullis closed and kill the *alagai* inside as quickly as possible. We may need reinforcements."

"Where are we going?" Chikga's tone makes it clear he already knows, and does not approve.

"To get the *chin* to the undercity." Iraven turns to Konin. "The *chi'Sharum* know the district best and are better prepared to lead the evacuation. Find their *kai* and have him send his men ahead while we muster a force of *dal'Sharum* to seal the breach."

Konin punches a fist to his chest and runs off. Thivan and Rekaj are similarly sent to alert the *kai* of the elite units Iraven wants at his back.

Chikga frowns. "The *alagai* may be trying to take our attention from the gate. How many warriors can we spare to defend the *chin* quarter?"

Unspoken is the sentiment many of the *Sharum* seem to share. No *chin* is worth a full-blood warrior's life.

Iraven moves faster than I would have believed possible, punching Chikga in the face and dropping him to the walltop. "We are one people in the night, Drillmaster. I will not leave anyone, from the *Damaji* himself to the lowest *chin* beggar, to the *alagai*. Suggest otherwise, say anything other than 'your will, Sharum Ka,' and I will throw you from this wall."

"Your will, Sharum Ka," Chikga groans. "I meant no offense."

My brother casts his gaze around at the other warriors staring at the scene. "That goes for all of you."

As one, man and boy alike punch fists to their chests. "Your will, Sharum Ka!"

Iraven's eyes turn to me. I grit my teeth, but he's right, and everyone is watching. I put my fist to my chest. "Your will, brother."

"Nie Ka." Iraven turns to Chadan. "You will command the *nie'Sharum* of all four *sharaj*—full-blood, half, *khaffit*, and *chin*. Assist in the evacuation of the greenbloods and escort them to the undercity while the *chi'Sharum* hold the *alagai* at bay. Go to the armory first for shields."

"Why not spears?" Gorvan dares ask.

Chikga cuffs him on the back of the head. "So you're not tempted to do something foolish, boy."

Iraven nods. "You're not here to fight. When the last of the *chin* make it to the undercity, you're to lock yourselves in with them until dawn."

———

WE RUN ALONG the wall to the *chin* quarter, where the source of the breach is obvious. Cracked and upended paving stones lie in scattered ruin around a mound of soil like a gigantic molehill. The corelings managed somehow to tunnel beneath the wall and find a gap in the wards. It shouldn't be possible. The walls of Desert Spear are legendary, and the guile and forethought to plan such an attack should be beyond demon ken.

Yet sand and clay demons are pouring through the breach. They were contained last night—the Maze was built to offer *Sharum* every advantage—but now they are on the open streets of the city, in the poorest district where wardings are meager at best.

The *chi'Sharum*, warriors levied from the Thesan thralls of the Majah tribe, outnumber the *dal'Sharum*. They have inferior training and equipment, but despite the bragging of the full-bloods, they are a formidable force, motivated as much by the need to protect their families as a sense of duty. They have locked shields across the narrow streets, creating bottlenecks that drive the demons away from the fleeing Thesans.

"They should be killing, not holding the *alagai* at bay," Chikga growls, but he is careful not to make it seem a criticism of the Sharum Ka, who watches impassively. If the goal is to protect life, the *chi'Sharum* are taking the wisest course, deflecting the enemy until their families can reach safety.

We descend from the wall via a guard tower to a plaza where Iraven's warriors are already mustering. The demons haven't gotten this far yet, but it won't be long if they are not contained.

Pit Warders, the elite *dal'Sharum* who maintain the wards in the Maze, have already prepared a solution in the form of a cartload of wardposts.

"Sharum Ka." Their *kai* steps forward. "We can form a ward circle around the breach, but we will need to contain the *alagai* long enough to set and align the posts."

"How long?" Iraven asks.

"If the plaza was clear? Perhaps ten minutes," the *kai* says. "In this chaos?" He shrugs.

"What will stop them from tunneling somewhere else?" Chikga asks.

"There are wards built into the foundations of the city," the *kai* says. "I do not think this was spontaneous or luck. It would have taken the *alagai* some time to dig this tunnel without anyone noticing."

"Waning," Iraven says. "A demon prince is directing them."

The minds are all dead. I want to believe it. I *need* to believe it. But the way that demon looked at me . . .

I get that feeling in my stomach like I might be sick, and breathe in rhythm as the drillmasters taught us, embracing the feeling rather than fighting it, then blowing it out with my breath.

For the first time, I wish for my mother's warded cloak, left in my chambers a thousand miles away. I want to run away, to hide in the undercity. I will draw corelings like flies if they see me, putting everyone in danger.

Iraven is shouting orders, readying his men with talk of Everam and glory. Would he listen if I went to him now? I don't think so. Certainly Chikga would not.

I heft the shield. Large and heavy, made of wood with a warded sheet of steel hammered and riveted to its convex surface, it is proof against any coreling blow. The circle of wards around the rim is large enough to stand on, offering an area of protection just large enough to create a forbidding around a single warrior.

"Keep low," I whisper to myself. "Do your job and get to the undercity."

"What was that?" Chadan asks—the first words he's spoken to me since breakfast.

I shake the fear away, meeting his eyes. "Nothing, Nie Ka."

He eyes me a moment, then nods, shouting orders much like Iraven. Chadan has trained all his life for this, and it shows. As the *dal'Sharum* make for the breach, we cut through the warded doorways of buildings to get behind the *chi'Sharum* lines.

The streets are in chaos. Some of the *chin* have lanterns, and there are a few lamps burning in the streets, but they do little to abate the darkness. Folk stumble half blind, some carrying children or pulling them by the hand. Others struggle to assist the elderly and infirm. Just a few blocks away, wardlight flashes like lightning as warriors shout and demons shriek, adding terror to the frantic evacuation.

We *nie'Sharum* have wards of sight painted around our eyes, powered by the ambient magic in the air. Instead of light, we see the world illuminated by the spectrum of magic—the ambient power all around us, the wards that gather it, and the auras of living things. It is more powerful than normal vision, but the extra input takes time to grow accustomed to.

A woman rushing with a babe in her arms shoulders past a gray-bearded man, knocking him to the paving stones. She runs on, oblivious, but Chadan points. "Thivan. Help him. The rest of you, make sure these buildings are empty and lead the people to the undercity entrance!"

As Chikga warned, several of the undercity entrances are no longer usable, rusted or collapsed after twenty years of neglect. The nearest working one is a mile away. Not far for a swift-footed *nie'Sharum*, but for folk fumbling in dim lamplight through the dark, slowed by children, old, and infirm, it is a considerable distance.

Here and there, *chi'Sharum* deserters escort their families. The wards on the helms under their dark green turbans allow them to see in wardsight, and they search the darkness, looking for threats. They eye us warily, knowing there will be a heavy price if they live to see the dawn and we report them for breaking ranks. But they are armed and armored and we are not. If Chadan were to challenge them now, it would not end well for us.

To his credit, Chadan is more focused on getting folk to safety. A young boy rides his back like a camel as he guides a woman and her elderly mother through the darkness, calling commands all the while.

A scrabbling sound is the only warning as a sand demon drops on a woman carrying two children. Her sharp cry is quickly silenced by its talons and razor teeth. Her aura, bright a moment ago, snuffs like a candle before my eyes.

I spare a glance upward, and terror grips me. "They're on the rooftops!"

The buildings are crawling with sand and clay demons, climbing the façades like spiders and running along the roofs. Unable to get past the warriors locking shields across the streets, they went up the walls instead. Here and there, defensive wards flash, but even these are old and poorly maintained. There hasn't been a demon in the city in centuries.

A clay demon drops onto Chadan, but he is ready, raising his shield over both himself and the boy on his back. The wards flash as the demon scrabbles for purchase. Chadan sets the boy down lightly, then puts his shoulder into a shield rush that drives the coreling into a warded doorway. Caught between two wardnets, power shocks through the creature and it drops to the ground, stunned.

"Take who you can and run!" Chadan cries as the coreling shakes itself off, struggling to regain its feet.

It's a practical decision. The kind of command Prince Chadan was trained for—the kind that decides lives. For, of course, "who you can" means those with a chance of outrunning the demons.

The two children the slaughtered woman was carrying shriek and dart after the crowd, but the sand demon, jaws still wet with the mother's blood, tamps down to go after them. It is met instead with a pair of *chi'Sharum*. The warriors come at it from two sides, batting its swiping paws aside with shields as they stab with their long spears.

The demon is quickly dispatched, but while their attention is fixed on it, more drop from above. One sinks its teeth into a warrior's neck and hot blood, bright with his lifelight, spurts like a fountain from the wound.

Unable to bring his spear to bear, the warrior drops it, fumbling for the knife on his belt even as his life bleeds away. I can see his aura dimming like a lamp being turned down. The blade is still half in its sheath as he drops to his knees. The demon kicks its hind legs, shredding the warrior's robe until his armor plates fall away and it reaches the vulnerable flesh beneath.

The other warrior gets his shield up in time to deflect an attack from above, but the demon lands on its paws a few feet away. It is joined by another as they come at him from opposite sides, hunting in concert.

More demons are landing in the street, and I know it's only a matter of time before they spot me. I should run, but I stand transfixed by the scene.

A cry catches my attention, and I see the fruit seller from earlier in the day, her robes lifted above bare legs as she runs from a clay demon. Surprisingly quick on its stubby legs, the coreling can see in the darkness, while she is half blind. It gains rapidly.

31

ALAGAI'SHARAK

I'M MOVING BEFORE I realize what I'm doing, reflex taking the conscious decision from me. The fallen warrior is still thrashing under the sand demon's teeth and claws as I scoop up his dropped spear and throw. The piercing wards on its tip punch through the clay demon's armor, and it collapses, the weapon deeply embedded in its carapace. The fruit seller runs on, oblivious to what happened behind her.

The sand demon looks up from the *chi'Sharum's* bloody body, but I rush it with my shield, pinning it as I draw my *hanzhar*. Again and again I stab, the cutting wards on the blade sucking at the demon's magic to power the attack. A bit of that energy runs tingling up my arms, and I feel a rush of strength and vitality. My forearm is a blur spraying hot ichor across my chest as I cut new wounds faster than the demon can heal.

The other warrior is fighting for his life as I pounce on one of the sand demons circling him. Gone are the careful forms we learned in *sharaj*. With magic pumping hot in my veins, my attack is pure animal fury. I yank on one of its horns with my shield hand, the curved *hanzhar* a talon I rake across the coreling's exposed throat.

I keep pulling as ichor pours from the wound and the creature thrashes, choking on it. The hesitation costs me as demons drop from the walls all around me, circling in with low growls. They swarm the warrior I tried to save, pulling him down like a pack of dogs.

If there was any doubt left about the demons' purpose, it is gone, now. They've stopped feeding, stopped chasing the fleeing civilians. They are fixated on one thing, and one thing only.

Me.

I'm dead. The thought breaks me out of the berserk rage that had overcome me. Perhaps I deserve it. The warriors dead in the Maze last night, everyone slaughtered tonight, all of it is my fault. Just as with my friends on the borough tour. Whatever Fort Krasia is facing, they're facing because of me.

But with the guilt comes anger. Anger at the demons. Anger at being born different, at having enemies before I emerged from between my mother's legs. I bang the hilt of the knife on my shield like a Baiter in the Maze. "Come on, then! If I'm going to die, I'm taking some of you with me!"

The demons shriek in response, and one launches itself at me, racing with blinding speed. I set my feet, ready to catch it with my shield and put my knife between its eyes.

I never get the chance. A spear punches into the demon's side, dropping it hard to the cobblestone street. I look up and see Chadan rushing in after it, plowing through the demons with the forbidding of his shield.

He is point in an inverted V of screaming *nie'Sharum,* charging in formation with shields locked. Faseek and Gorvan, Thivan and Konin, Montidahr, Rekaj, Menin, and dozens I don't even recognize. Students of all bloods and classes, violating the drillmasters' orders to come to my aid. Some carry knives and spears scavenged from fallen warriors, but many have only their shields and their courage.

I swallow the lump in my throat and pin the fallen sand demon with one sandal as I tear the spear from its body. Chadan takes the spear from the remains of the warrior behind me, and Gorvan takes his knife. Faseek takes the knife the dying *chi'Sharum* never managed to finish drawing. We form a circle, eyes outward as the demon horde continues to grow.

"Everam is watching!" Chadan shouts. "Make Him proud, warriors of Majah!"

THE CORELINGS CHARGE, but we lock shields, bracing as they slam into the forbiddance, then shoving forward to reflect the attack at them, throwing the demons back. Those with weapons strike during the press, sending a number of the demons stumbling away shrieking and dripping ichor.

The wounds begin to close as soon as our weapons pull free of their flesh, but some of my brothers get their first taste of demon feedback magic. I see it crackle through their auras like lightning.

"Find weapons!" I shout as the demons regroup. Most of us lock shields again, but a few of the boys scatter, searching the terrain and the bodies of the fallen for anything they can use.

Menin finds a wheelbarrow, smashing the edge of his shield through the thick wooden handles to produce a pair of clubs. One of the greenblood *nie'Sharum* finds a rusty awl and takes the clubs, cutting crude bludgeoning wards onto the jagged ends.

"Will that work?" Parkot asks, taking a club.

"We'll know soon enough." Menin swings the other back and forth, trying to get a feel for its balance.

Again the demons charge, jaws slavering as they lunge at me. They are not so far gone that they ignore the other enemies, but the press is tightest around me.

"Courage, brother." Chadan stands shoulder-to-shoulder with me, and we move together like dancers, lifting the foe with our shields and stabbing underneath with our spears. Sand demon armor is weakest about the abdomen, and our spearheads punch through their hearts in almost identical blows, casting them back into the press thrashing in their death throes.

Menin swings his club, and the wards cut into it flare, bashing a clay demon's head down onto the cobbles. The blow isn't enough to do more than stun the heavily armored creature, but Parkot hits it next and the impact wards on his club send the creature tumbling head over heels away from them.

Armed with only a knife, Faseek doesn't have the reach of a spear or club, but each time his blade drinks of a demon's magic, the small, swift boy grows faster—fiercer. He severs a sand demon's paw, then blinds a clay demon with a quick slash across its eyes. The coreling falls back, shrieking, and Gorvan, who has lashed his knife to the end of a sturdy awning pole, impales it with the makeshift spear.

Not all my brothers fare so well. Rekaj managed to secure a fallen warrior's spear, but his conservative way of fighting—leaning heavily on defense while he awaits the perfect opening to attack—costs him when a sand demon stands on its hind legs, swatting at his shield instead of charging fully. He catches the first two blows, but is hesitant to retaliate. A lash of the demon's tail sweeps his legs, and before he can recover, it tears out his throat.

Konin, who warmed me at night and mumbled prayers in his sleep, gets his shield in place to stop the head-slam of a clay demon, but he isn't strong enough to absorb the impact, and is knocked onto his back. He kicks at the demon's armored snout—the last thing he should have done. He does more damage to his heel than the coreling, and it responds by biting off his foot.

Faseek gives a cry and tackles the demon away from his friend, stabbing it repeatedly as they tumble across the cobbles. I can already see it will be too late for Konin, whose aura is dimming rapidly as he screams and clutches the spurting stump of his leg.

I want to help, but there is little I can do. Chadan and I fight back-to-back now against three demons, barely holding our own.

Armed with only a shield, Thivan charges in, knocking one of the demons into another. Chadan takes the opportunity to stab into the tangle, and one of the sand demons does not rise.

The other springs at Thivan, catching the edge of his shield with a hooked talon and pulling it aside. I throw my spear, taking the demon down before it can kill my brother, but it leaves me with only the *hanzhar* on my belt as the third sand demon comes at me.

Like the one that attacked Rekaj, the demon is smart enough not to throw itself at my shield. It stands and bats with its powerful paws instead. The blows are almost too fast to follow, and I block as much on instinct as intent. I'm ready for the swipe of its tail, hopping back, but I lose my footing, slipping on the bloody cobbles.

My shield is out of alignment as the demon leaps, but as I land on my back I curl a leg and kick out, holding the demon at bay for a moment as it scrabbles at the edge of my shield. I fumble blindly, hand at last closing about the hilt of the *hanzhar* strapped to my healing satchel. I pull it free and slash along the demon's belly, opening it up like dissecting a frog in Gatherers' University. It thrashes for a moment before Chadan and Thivan skewer it with their spears.

There is a moment to draw breath, and I glance around. A dozen *nie'Sharum* lie still and cold in the street, but so do as many demons. Those of us that remain have auras bright with strength and seething with anger. Blood and ichor spatters all of our skin, and almost everyone has a weapon of some kind, dripping ichor.

I walk to Konin's body, dropping to one knee as I reach out a shaking hand to close his wide, staring eyes. I draw a ward in the air above him. "Everam guide you on the lonely path, brother."

I stand, looking down at him. If I hadn't interceded, if I hadn't broken the rules of *sharaj*, he and Faseek would have been cast from the training grounds weeks ago. They would be *khaffit*, but Konin would be alive. All the fallen would be alive, if not for me.

Did the Majah read the prophecy wrong? What if I am not their savior, but their doom?

Chadan steps close, laying a hand on my shoulder. "It isn't your fault, brother. This was the *alagai's* doing, not yours. Konin died with glory on *alagai* talons because of you. His bones will be taken to Sharik Hora, interred with honor among our ancestors."

The words are more comforting than I expect, but I know Konin and Rekaj are only the beginning. "This isn't over."

"No," Chadan agrees, setting his feet and putting up his shield. "*Nie'Sharum*, to me!"

My brothers and I form around the Nie Ka and begin a steady advance down the street, picking up stragglers and growing in strength as we go. We follow the shrieks of demons that have gone in search of easier prey and find *alagai* and greenbloods both. The *chin* come out of hiding as we drive back the demons, falling behind our line as we continue the press for the entrance to the undercity.

There are dozens of them cowering behind us as we make it to the gate and find a scowling Drillmaster Chikga waiting.

32

—•—

TWO PRINCES

W E HOLD A collective breath as Drillmaster Chikga eyes us. In taking arms and engaging in *alagai'sharak*, we violated his orders, and a direct order from the Sharum Ka. Worse, we did it to defend greenbloods, whom the drillmaster considers less than human.

But it was me who started it. Me who turned to fight when Chadan told us to run. Me who pulled my brothers back into the fight to save my life.

It's my fault that Konin and Rekaj have gone down the lonely path to Everam's judgment, along with others whose names I never even knew.

My fault the storm came at all.

I swallow the lump in my throat and lift my foot. I will step forward and take the blame for my brothers. Let them cast me out of *sharaj*. They would be better off without me. All of Desert Spear would be better off if I were far from this place.

But before I take that step, Chikga bangs his spear on his shield, making all of us jump. "I see you, warriors of Majah! Everam sees you!"

I don't know how to respond. My heart is pounding, blood rushing with a heady mix of magic and adrenaline. Ready to run or fight, I'm unprepared for praise.

"Nie Ka!" Chikga shouts.

Chadan steps forward. Chikga lifts his spear vertically and punches the fist holding it to his chest. "You have done honor to your tribe and *sharaj* by blooding your brothers this night." We gape as he drops to one knee. "You may not take the black until the *dama'ting* foretells your death, but in my eyes, it is already done, my prince. You are *ajin'pel*, blooded to many. It is my honor to serve."

Chadan blinks, then gives his head a tiny shake, stepping forward to lay his ichor-covered spear on the drillmaster's shoulder with the same royal grace and poise Mother and Minister Arther spent so many hours drilling into me. "Rise, Chikga asu Rabban am'Darid am'Majah. The blood on our spears belongs as much to you as any. Every drillmaster is *ajin'pel*. Our honor is yours."

Chikga rises, and I am stunned to see moisture in his eyes. I did not think him capable of such emotion.

"The Sharum Ka has the breach contained," Chikga says, "but there are *alagai* still inside the city walls. He has sent warriors to hunt them, but will take no more chances with your lives. His orders are for you and your brothers to go into the undercity with the *chin* to rest and tend your wounds in safety until sunrise."

THE UNDERCITY OF Fort Krasia is nearly as ancient as the city above, and even more impressive. There is nothing to compare in Thesa, putting even the great Cathedral of the Deliverer in Hollow to shame. Its beauty and the grandeur of the long-dead artisans of ancient Krasia take my breath away.

Low tunnels connect soaring caverns containing everything a people could need. There are homes and wellhouses. Houses of worship, markets, *sharaj*, smithies, and pens for livestock.

Wardpillars—great obelisks cut deeply with defensive wards—line the streets and anchor the squares. Demons cannot rise through cut stone, so the streets are cobbled, the colors of the stones and mortar creating great mosaic circles of protection. Wards are chiseled into the tunnel walls. Even if by some catastrophe demons broke in, they would have to fight the wards for every inch.

The undercity was meant as a last retreat if Desert Spear ever fell to the corelings. For centuries, before Darin's father found the lost fighting wards, the women, children, and *khaffit* of old Krasia would hide in the undercity each night while the *Sharum* fought *alagai'sharak* with nothing more than plain spears.

But after the fighting wards were found and Krasia regained its strength, such precaution was no longer needed. The undercity, particularly in the poorer districts, fell into disrepair. Some of the tunnels have partially collapsed, and more than a few of the buildings look unsafe to enter. Everything is covered in a fine coating of sediment.

But the wardpillars remain, and the great mosaics. Greenlanders hurry to and fro, cleaning off the wards to strengthen the protections.

A building has been set aside for a *nie'Sharum* billet. The *chin* we escorted here step cautiously around us, but they do not forget our sacrifice for their safety. Some of the women fetch water and cloth, returning to clean the blood and ichor from my brothers. The boys look stiff and uncomfortable under their ministrations—unused to the touch of a woman who is not Tikka or their mother.

I reach for my healing satchel. The feedback magic warriors absorb speeds healing—closing superficial cuts and abrasions, turning serious contusions into little more than bruises—but the magic will not clear shrapnel from a wound, or set broken bones.

"The pain is less," Montidahr says as I examine his broken arm.

I nod. "It has already begun healing, but crooked. If you want to keep full use of it, I will need to break it again and set it properly."

Montidahr pales, and a sheen of sweat breaks out across his shaved head, but he does not argue. "Do it."

The satchel contains a bite rod, thick leather sewn over a wooden dowel. I put it in his mouth, pressing his tongue back so he does not bite through it or shatter teeth when his jaw clenches from pain. "Hold him."

Gorvan pins Montidahr's legs and Chadan sits on his chest, pressing his shoulders down. "Cast your thoughts back to the pain of the breaking, brother," the Nie Ka says. "Hold that feeling in your mind's embrace, and breathe."

I hold up his arm, letting him take a few steady breaths as I plan my move. The bone has only just begun to knit, and with my strength it's like snapping a twig to break it again. Montidahr grunts and his muscles seize, but Chadan and Gorvan keep him still. His teeth sink into the leather and tears run down his eyes, but it only takes a few moments more to reset the bone and splint it. I use a length of clean bido cloth to bind the splint in place.

I move between half-bloods and greenbloods and the sons of *khaffit* with no regard for caste, focusing on the most serious cases first. I pull broken claws and demon teeth from wounds, cleansing them with herbs to kill the infection corelings carry. There are more bones and dislocations to set, the oozing stump of a wrist to cauterize, and other injuries. Years of needlepoint has given me a swift and precise stitching hand. Wounds close to tight, even seams under my ministrations.

Princess Olive of Hollow would have been sickened by the blood and pus and filth. More than a few of the wounded have vomited, and many faces are stretched into a brutal mask of pain.

But they are my brothers now, and I feel none of the churning in my gut that I felt assisting Micha, after the massacre of the borough tour. They need me, and I am there for them.

There are a handful of injuries beyond my skills—wounds magic has closed that show signs of internal bleeding beneath, and a broken horn embedded so deeply in a boy's side I fear to remove it. All seem stable enough, and I say a silent prayer to Everam that they survive long enough for the *dama'ting* to see to them.

Chadan shadows me throughout, helping when he can, offering words of encouragement when he cannot. His very presence soothes many of the *nie'Sharum*, who look at him with worship in their eyes.

"That's the last of them." I snip the final thread. My herb pouch is depleted, and we had to get creative in finding linen for bandages, but everyone has been seen to.

"We owe you a debt," Chadan says.

He means the words kindly, but they sting nonetheless. Every one of these injuries sits on my conscience twice over, once for drawing the demons here, and once for forcing my brothers to come to my rescue.

I turn from him wordlessly, retreating to a private space with a bucket of fresh water and the last bit of clean cloth in the building to tend myself.

Chadan follows. "Let me help you." He reaches for the cloth, and grimaces. I notice how pale he's become, and immediately move to examine him. The blood and ichor streaking his flesh make it difficult to see, so I run my hands over his muscles, searching. I find it under his armpit, something hard beneath his flesh that moves as I prod it with my fingers, drawing a gasp of pain from the young prince.

"Why didn't you say something?" I ask.

"It is nothing," Chadan said. "Our brothers needed you more."

I press my thumb against the mass, and he grimaces again. "This isn't nothing, Nie Ka." I take the cloth and clean the area, finding the red scar of a wound, already healed over with magic. I reach into my pouch for the bite rod, its leather pocked and torn from repeated use.

Chadan raises a hand to forestall me, his breathing becoming slow and even. "I do not need it. I will embrace the pain."

"You'd better." I lift the *hanzhar*. "It will be dangerous if you move."

To his credit, Chadan's breathing remains deep and steady. He does not wince as my blade cuts through layers of muscle until it strikes the hard bit. A thin hiss escapes his lips as I slip in the tongs, drawing out a broken piece of demon talon and holding it up for him to see. "Demon wounds infect, Highness. This might have killed you."

I half expect him to argue as other, brasher boys might, professing his strength and fortitude, but that is not the prince of Majah's way. He accepts the chastening with a bow of his head. "Thank you, brother."

As gently as I can, I cleanse the wound and pull the flesh back together with neat, even stitches. Then I take the cloth and cleanse the filth from him, searching for other injuries. All of us have them, but I find nothing else serious—most of it already healing on its own. His skin is warm under my hands, and he sighs.

Chadan reaches out, our fingers touching lightly as he takes the cloth from me. Wordlessly he rinses the blood and grime from it, squeezing the water out. Then he begins to clean me as I did him, running the cloth over my flesh with one hand, and following it with the other as he probes for injuries. I tense, but I do not stop him. His hands are firm, but gentle.

"I saw you take a lash of a sand demon's tail right here," he squeezes my side, "but there isn't even a mark."

"The magic must have healed it," I say.

"Was it magic that let you fight me nearly to a standstill your first night in *sharaj*, even after grandfather had you whipped?"

I shrug. "I've always been a quick healer."

"The honor should have been yours," he says.

"Eh?"

"*Ajin'pel*, blooded to many," Chadan says. "It should have been you. I ordered our brothers to flee. It was you who chose to fight."

I shake my head. "You had the responsibility of command. Our brothers, the *chin*, their lives were in your hands. You made the right decision. What I did was . . . selfish."

"Damn me to the abyss, if it was." Chadan spits on the floor. It is the first time I've seen him spit since the night we met.

"You came back for me," I remind him.

"Faseek was already turning to help you when I realized what was happening," Chadan says. "He worships you."

"But the others wouldn't have, if you hadn't turned as well."

"Perhaps." Chadan seems unconvinced. "But if I walked the path of honor, it is only because you showed it to me, just like you did last night in the Maze. The victory, the blooding, it is all because of you."

"Victory?" I ask. "What victory? How many of our brothers died in that running battle? How many *chin* did we fail to save? It would have been better if you had abandoned me."

"Nonsense," Chadan snaps. "Why would you say such a thing?"

I meet his eyes, unsure even now if I can trust him, but the need to tell *someone* is unbearable.

"The demons knew me."

Chadan blinks. Whatever he was expecting me to say, this wasn't it. "What?"

"This happened before. In Hollow." I tell him the story of the borough tour, leaving out only a few details, and relay what happened in the Maze last night.

"You were already blooded?" he breathes, turning to stare into the darkness. "No wonder you could not stand by. No wonder you did not fear to tread the Maze."

"That isn't what I'm saying," I grab his face and turn him back to me. "The demons are hunting me."

I can see in his eyes he doesn't believe it. "Why?"

I shrug. "Because of my father? Or perhaps my mother. Or both. I don't know. All I know is the moment they saw me, the demons . . . fixated."

"Of course," Chadan said. "The *alagai* crave nothing more than our deaths. That does not mean they recognized you."

It's different, but I don't know how to convince him of that. "Then why the storm?" I ask. "Demons aren't much smarter than dogs. Why do they suddenly have the intelligence to hold open the gate? To penetrate the wall? Iraven said it himself. They have a mind, and it is hunting *me*."

"Even if that were true, it changes nothing," Chadan says. "If the Father of Demons wants you, it is our duty as Evejans, as *Sharum*, to deny him."

"At what cost?" I ask. "So long as I am in Desert Spear, everyone is in danger."

"So you say," Chadan agrees, "but there is no proof. And I for one feel safer with you . . . close."

We're silent a moment, staring at each other. I struggle to find words to convince him.

"I'm sorry Grandfather brought you here," Chadan says. "It was wrong of him, just as it was wrong to take the greenbloods across the waste to Desert Spear. None of you belong here."

"He brought me here for *you*," I say.

"That is what he claims," Chadan admits. "But Grandfather has his own reasons for what he does—reasons of politics and prophecy. It was never something I wanted. I would have been as unwilling as you on our wedding night, had you been a girl."

I twist my lips into a mocking pout. "A princess of Hollow isn't good enough for you?"

Chadan shakes his head. He is very close. I can feel the warmth of his breath. "I would not have wanted to marry any princess."

Suddenly, I understand, and lean closer still. "What about a prince?"

Chadan does not reply.

He kisses me, instead.

33

DEATH FORETOLD

I WAKE, FEELING THE heat of the boy nestled behind me, and for a moment I think it must be Konin, who often snuggled close in the chill of night.

Then I remember Konin is dead. I am not in the *sharaj* barracks, sleeping in a pile with my brothers. The darkness around me is not the cloak of night, it is the eternal gloom of the undercity. There is no way to know if it is still dark outside, or if we slept through the morning bell.

Chadan shifts in his slumber, and suddenly everything comes back in a flood. All we did was kiss and hold each other, but it feels like the whole world has shifted.

I've tried not to think too much about Selen these last weeks— thoughts of home only made things worse, made my situation unbearable. Only by living in the present could I keep from falling into despair.

But now . . . I smile in spite of myself. I've finally got a kissing story she can't beat, and she's not around to share it with.

The thought brings back memories of Lanna and the borough tour. I've kissed all of two people in my life, and both tales include a demon attack.

Beyond that, there weren't a lot of similarities between Lanna and Chadan. With Lanna, I had been the pursuer, though she was willing prey. Chadan was the one to initiate our kiss—leaving me to wonder how long he had been wanting to do it.

But where Lanna kissed aggressively, opening her mouth, pressing against my body, Chadan was tentative, his kisses small and light, fingers gentle on my face. It didn't seem like he had any more experience than me. And why should he?

Chadan deliberately kept himself apart from other boys, knowing he might be forced to order any of them to their deaths. Knowing he would one day have to marry a princess his grandfather selected, whether he wanted it or not. This might be the first time he allowed himself a moment of vulnerability.

I twist around, kissing his sleeping forehead. He opens his eyes, and I am unable to stop myself from breaking into a smile as they meet mine.

He reaches out, a slow, sleepy gesture as he gently strokes my cheek with the back of his hand. "Is it morning?"

"I don't—" My words are cut off by the sudden sound coming from the doorway to the common area where our *nie'Sharum* brothers are sleeping. I hear their low murmurs, and above them a high sharp voice that sends a shiver down my spine.

"Where are they?" Belina demands.

"WHERE ARE WE going?" I ask as we walk at the head of columns of marching *nie'Sharum*. Already we have passed through several gates, walking long distances in tunnels barely high enough to stand upright.

I know my questions irk Belina, but I feel the weight of all that stone above our heads, straining, wanting to fill the void of the tunnel. Irking the woman who kidnapped me is a welcome distraction.

"To the undertemple of Sharik Hora." Belina does not so much as glance my way.

"All the way from the *chin* quarter?" I've read about the undercity, but never truly understood the enormity of it. We're traversing many miles without ever going aboveground.

"All roads in Desert Spear lead to Sharik Hora, Prince Olive." Belina looks over her shoulder at me. "For Everam is omnipresent in our lives." As she turns back, I see her eyes flick to Chadan, just for an instant.

I wonder if she suspects what happened between us. Like Mother with her spectacles, Belina sees in wardsight, and trained for years in the art of reading auras.

But Chadan has fallen into his breathing trance, and his aura is tranquil. I finally understand why my old teacher Favah was so frustrated by my dislike of meditation. It's like Grandmum's advice about the powder kit. *There's power in controlling what folk see when they look at you.*

I try to lose myself in my breath, clawing at memories of Favah's teaching. I manage to inhale and exhale in the proper rhythm, but as always, I struggle to clear my mind. Even as my body relaxes, my thoughts continue to race.

Something strange is happening to the magic around us. With their wards of sight, even the untrained eyes of my spear brothers can see it.

In wardsight, raw magic radiating from the Core looks like a softly illuminated fog, colorless and drifting. When that formless power encounters the fangs of a ward, the fog is sucked into the symbol like a bellows, and the ward begins to glow in various colors, depending on how it shapes the magic.

As we approach the Holy Undercity, the fog of ambient magic remains, formless and drifting, but the white light becomes peppered with gold, like flakes of dust in a sunbeam. They multiply and spread like tea in water, coalescing into clouds that grow so large they meld together until we ourselves are inside the cloud. Everything around us glows with golden light now.

But it isn't just the way the magic *looks* that shifts. I feel a growing sense of warmth and protection with every step forward and know instinctively that this place is anathema to demonkind. Corespawn could as easily walk into a sunbeam as approach the Holy Undercity.

We round a bend in the tunnel and encounter the first gate. For a moment, the light is blinding. When my eyes adjust, I see a wall of human bones—the source of the golden light—blazing like a bonfire in the tunnel.

The wall is set with an archway built entirely of human skulls. Empty eye sockets gape at us as we approach a gate constructed with arm and leg bones for bars. A plaque above is formed by shoulder blades, its ancient inscription glittering like a shower of sparks against the flames as a log collapses in the fireplace.

The plaque bears the spear and drum crest Baiters often paint in the center of their shields, and reads simply:

FIRST TO GREET DEATH
FIRST TO ENTER HEAVEN

The gate is unlocked and unguarded. What would be the point? If a corespawn could reach this far, its power has already failed. Belina opens it as casually as a shutter.

As I pass beneath the empty eye sockets of ancient heroes, I nevertheless feel watched. I see names cut into the bones, glowing in glory for all eternity.

As we exit the gate the tunnel ends in a deep crevasse. A bridge made of glowing human bone spans the gap, casting light into the void below. The pit is so deep I cannot see the bottom. CAMEL UNIT, a shoulder blade plaque proclaims. OUR DEEDS BORE THE WEIGHT OF EMPIRE. The names and deeds of this famed *dal'Sharum* unit are recorded on more of the bone plaques as we cross.

At the far end of the Camel Bridge is the massive cavern where the Holy City sits, blazing like gold in the sun and casting a forbidding that spans miles. Mother's greatwards accomplish these same ends, but they are cold things, like Mother herself.

This is *sacred* ground, and it is the most beautiful thing I have ever seen.

"How is this possible?" I breathe.

Belina spares me a glance. "This, child, is what happens to the bones of warriors whose souls enter Heaven."

I WALK IN stunned silence the rest of the way to the undertemple, struggling to process Belina's words, even as the great temple doors close behind us.

A glance around shows the other students looking as awestruck as I feel. In my head I know it is a tactic. An orchestrated revelation of the power of a warrior's sacrifice right before we are asked to pledge our lives to the First War.

But my heart cannot deny the power around us. What sacrifice could be more honorable than giving one's life to keep others safe?

Belina turns to face the columns of *nie'Sharum*. "It will take some time to cast the *alagai hora* for all of you. Those of you in need of healing will be tended before your foretellings."

White-robed *nie'dama'ting* step forward, sorting the students into groups and assigning them numbers, but there is no line for Chadan and me.

Chavis is waiting in the outer hall, and for a moment, there is a spike of fear in Chadan's placid aura. It subsides quickly, but Chadan looks like he's walking to a whipping as the ancient *Damaji'ting* escorts him away.

"Come, boy." Belina takes my arm gently, but the move draws my attention to the blood-locked armlet—a reminder that she is in control here. I imagine lunging at her, trying to pierce her skin with the tiny spear that holds the armlet together. Just a drop, and the blood lock would be open.

But then what? Where would I go? How far could I get before being run down and shackled again, or worse?

We come to a private chamber, and Belina kneels, spreading her pristine white casting cloth on the floor. "Kneel, boy."

Cautiously I kneel opposite her as Belina draws her *hanzhar*. "Hold out your arm."

I hesitate. Belina made it sound like a command, but I know from Favah's teaching that blood must be surrendered willingly or unknowingly for a casting to work. To take it by force is forbidden. It is a violation that colors the blood's magic, fouling the cast.

There are loopholes, of course. Belina might find and collect my blood from the streets of the *chin* quarter, if she could distinguish it from the rest. If she knew the truth about me, she could even use one of the wads of stolen bido cloth I bleed into each month, if I was not careful to throw them in the fire when no one is looking. But here and now, if I refuse, Belina cannot insist.

That seems reason enough to deny her. I don't know this woman. It may be she is as honorable as her son, putting the greater good above all. Or she might only serve herself. Either way, I know Belina will never consider my interests. Only my value.

Yet I cannot stop thinking about the glow of heroes' bones. About the thought of Konin and Rekaj and the others added to this place. A monument to fallen *nie'Sharum*, glowing gold. How many generations of my forefathers are interred here, sacrificed before their time so others could live their full allotted span?

Maybe Chadan is right. Maybe it is *inevera* that a part of me should long to be part of this place. But I will not give her what she wants without a bargain. "Why should I?"

Belina looks at me as if I am a fool. "You cannot take the black until I cast the dice."

"This is not my home," I say. "You are not my people. Why should I surrender my fate to you for some meaningless title?"

"Meaningless?!" Belina's aura flashes hot. Like me, she has a temper even meditation cannot fully control. "You look at the bones of the warriors who guard this place, and think it meaningless?"

It's like she read my thoughts. Like Mother sometimes seemed to do. Now she's trying to use them against me. It only strengthens my resolve to resist. "You forget I was tutored by Dama'ting Favah. I know your tricks and dissembling. It doesn't take a title to die fighting on *alagai* talons, and that is all the Evejah requires. The title, the black veil, the casting, they are tools to manipulate men. The sacrifice of *Sharum* is not meaningless, but neither is it reason to surrender my blood to you."

"You would prefer to remain *nie'Sharum* forever?" Belina asks. "Kept in your bido as all your brothers are raised to the black? Training alone in the yard until a new crop of boys arrives, and another after that, ever younger, even as the years wither you away?"

I smile. "We both know that fate doesn't fit your plans for me."

"We have no plans for you," Belina says. "All our plans were made for *Princess* Olive." She holds up the dice. "Now, young prince, we need a new plan."

"How did you get the first?" I ask.

"You were such an active child." Belina smiles. "Our Watchers did not have to wait long for you to have a scrape in the yard. They stole into your chambers for the bandages, but only one escaped alive. Someone—your sister, presumably—found and killed the other."

"Should I have sympathy for a man who breaks into my home to steal my fate?" I ask. "If I failed to have a scrape, I assume they would have arranged one?"

Belina sits back on her ankles. "Of course."

I break out in gooseflesh, thinking of a lifetime oblivious to danger, of taking Micha for granted even as she put herself between me and every possible threat.

I pull my thoughts back to the present. "Casting me as male will show a different fate? How can fate be changed so easily if it is *inevera*— part of the Creator's design before our very birth?"

"Everam created infinite worlds, child," Belina says patiently. "Each like our own, but for the choices we make. The dice can guide our choices, showing us a glimpse of the futures most likely to occur, but Everam does not lift every foot and script every word of our lives. In the end, our fate is the shape we make it."

It makes sense. The dice are vague by design, giving hint to a portion of infinite possibility. A list of variables, some more likely than others, that a skilled seer can build into a story of what might be.

What did it matter, if Belina saw my fate? Despite her crimes against me, I do not think her evil. Despite Chadan's doubts, I know what I saw in the corelings' eyes. They knew me. They hunted *me*. The storms will keep coming, so long as I remain in Fort Krasia. The dice might be the only way to prove it before the city is overrun. What is my privacy, against the lives of thousands?

And perhaps I can glean something, too. I've never been good at reading the dice, but neither am I entirely unschooled. I know more than Belina is likely to suspect.

I take on Mother's regal tone. "Tell me what the first prophecy said."

"It is forbidden—" Belina begins.

I cut her off with a snort, folding my arms and sitting back. "We both know that's a lie *dama'ting* tell men. Nothing forbids you from sharing a prophecy."

"Perhaps," Belina agrees, "but that does not make it wise."

"Tell me the prophecy, swear by your hope of Heaven that it is complete and true, and I will give you seven drops of blood for this casting."

Belina is moving before I finish, putting her hands on the cloth and pressing her forehead between them. "By Everam and my hope of Heaven these are the precise words Damaji'ting Chavis divined:

"The storms will end when the heir of Hollow joins blood with the Majah, and the princess stands in the eye."

I wait a long moment, wondering if I can trust her, wondering if she has omitted something, or twisted a phrase, but the more I think of it, the more I believe her.

"Perhaps I do not stand in the eye," I say. "Perhaps I *am* the eye."

"Eh?" Belina's eyes narrow.

I tell her everything I told Chadan. What happened in the Maze, and in the streets of the greenblood quarter. I tell her of the attack on the borough tour, and my belief the demons are hunting me.

"Nonsense," Belina scoffs. "You are a child. What would the Father of Demons want with you?"

"Let us ask." I take the *hanzhar* from my healing pouch, putting the point to the pad of my left index finger. The skin breaks effortlessly, and a drop of blood wells.

Belina does not hesitate, pulling out her *hora* pouch and shaking the seven demonbone dice into her hand. They are black, like polished obsidian, but in wardsight they shine bright with power. Not the pure gold of *Sharum* bones, but something more primal, held in tight check by the wards cut into their faces.

She holds them out and I stretch my finger over them, letting a single drop fall on each die. Belina closes her hand, rolling the dice together to distribute the blood. "Everam, giver of life and light, your children need answers. Tell me the fate of Prince Olive asu Ahmann am'Paper am'Hollow."

As she speaks, the wards on the dice brighten, throbbing with power. She throws, and there is a flash as the magic chooses their arrangement. Whatever my reservations about the dice, the throws are never random, and never the same twice, unless the question is repeated verbatim.

Both of us stare at the throw, eyes scanning the wards and where they fell in relation to one another. I wish I had my textbook, however vexing it might be.

"Tsst." Belina's veil billows slightly with her quiet hiss. I tilt my head, trying to make some sense of what I see. There is *domin*—the symbol for two—a warrior symbol, and a clerical one.

"I don't understand." I don't want to reveal that I can read the dice at all, but I need to know. "Am I the warrior or the cleric?"

Belina points a long nail at the *domin* symbol. "You are divided. Your mother chose to raise you as some kind of greenland *dama'ting*, but if you walk the path of the warrior, you will be a great one."

"And if I walk the other?" I ask.

Belina's eyes narrow behind her veil. "Your father, too, was called to *alagai'sharak* before his time. The Damajah sent him to Sharik Hora to train with the *nie'dama* before he was allowed to take the black."

"Like Chadan does?" I ask.

Belina nods. "Your Nie Ka has been training to be a *kai* since he took his first steps."

"Is that what will happen to me?" I ask.

"There is no time," Belina sweeps her hand over symbols for air, sand, and lightning, swirling around the warrior and cleric symbols at the center of the cast. "A storm is coming." She points to the mind ward at the top of the pattern, and my stomach sinks. "I fear you may be correct. A prince of the abyss hunts you."

I AM STILL reeling from the reading—all my fears come true—when Belina escorts me to court. Chadan is kneeling in front of the seven steps leading to the Skull Throne. His grandfather sits atop the dais, leaning to hear Chavis' soft-spoken counsel. At the base of the dais, Iraven in his white turban stands at the center between the councils of *dama* and *dama'ting*. White-sleeved Arms of Everam guard the exits.

"Wait here," Belina says, leaving me at Chadan's side to ascend the steps. The conversation pauses as she bends to whisper her own foretelling in the *Damaji's* other ear. Aleveran eyes us both as Chavis and Belina raise their gazes and begin conversing directly.

At last, the *Damaji* raises a hand, silencing them. "Enough debate. The dice have spoken."

I look at him, wondering if he will let me go so easily. If the Father of Demons is hunting me, the only hope Fort Krasia has is to send me away.

My eyes flick to Chadan, and I feel my skin heat at the sight of him. I want to reach out, to take his hand, to let him know it is fate pulling us apart, and not my desire. But there is nothing I can do with so many eyes upon us.

"Chadan asu Maroch." Chadan puts his hands on the floor, pressing his forehead between them. "Nie Ka. *Ajin'pel.* You have served your brothers and your city with honor and distinction. For the glory you have won in the night, you will be raised to the black, and wear the white veil of *kai'Sharum.* No doubt many, if not all, of your *nie'Sharum* brothers will be raised before the day is out. They will be yours to command."

It is a great honor. With four full classes of *nie'Sharum*, Chadan will command one of the largest units in the Maze, with warriors of all castes. Our brothers may lack experience, but their youth may prove an advantage in learning to fight as one.

Chadan rolls up to sit on his ankles, back rigidly straight. "The honor belongs to all my brothers, Grandfather. *Inevera*, I will be worthy of them."

"Of that, I have no doubt," the *Damaji* says. "Olive asu Ahmann."

All eyes turn to me. I know I should put my hands on the floor and make obeisance, but even now, I cannot. Not to this man, who took me from my home. Not before these people, who watched me lashed in this very place just weeks ago. I look up, meeting the *Damaji's* eyes, instead.

"Still insolent," Chavis mouths quietly to Aleveran.

"You, too, have proven your valor in battle," the *Damaji* says, "and it has not gone unnoticed that your . . . *dama'ting* training has saved the lives and limbs of many of Majah's warriors. You shall also wear a white veil with your blacks, as Chadan's second."

The words fall like a death sentence. He is not sending me away. How many will suffer for that decision, tonight, and in every new moon to come?

But one word keeps repeating itself in my head.

Second. Domin.

Two *kai'Sharum,* warriors trained by clerics. I remember the prophecy Belina spoke, and my stomach drops. She misunderstood it, all those years ago, when she thought me a woman. It was "princes," not "princess."

Princes, in the eye of the storm.

34

—◆—

THE TWINS

I STARE AT THE knife in my hands, watching the wards pulse and
glow. Mam says there's no demonbone inside, but it holds power
the same way *hora* weapons do.

Magic's like a thing alive, Darin, Mam used to say. *Ent got a will of its
own, so it's drawn to emotions like a moth to light.*

There's a lot of emotion imprinted on Mam's knife. More than other
weapons that saw heavy use in the war. Its mystery is deeper—darker—
than just killing demons. Its aura is . . . hungry.

Folk in Tibbet's Brook always kept their manners when Mam was
about, but I could smell their fear. There's a story there, and the knife is
part of it.

I rub its bone handle, worn smooth from decades of use. I could
Read the knife—pulling magic through the blade and into myself in an
attempt to unlock its secrets—but it feels like a violation of Mam's privacy.

She's dead, I remind myself. *Ent got a need for privacy anymore.*

But I don't want to believe it. Reading the knife would be admitting
she's gone forever. Ent ready for that.

My fingers drift along the blade and the cutting wards throb, pulling
at my aura even as they sharpen the blade, eager to bite into my flesh.

"Darin."

Selen's voice startles me out of my trance and I sit up straight, suddenly realizing how light the sky has become.

"Sun's comin' up," Selen says. "We should head out before someone realizes we're sleeping in their hayloft."

Sleeping. I want to laugh. Don't think I've had more than an hour a night since we found the remains of the Warded Children. Since we found Mam's knife.

Selen cried herself to sleep for the first few nights, but now she's more focused on finding Olive than mourning her sister. I wish I had her strength of will, but I can't stop staring at the knife, feeling lost, like I'm drowning, like Da must have felt when he was pulled down into the Core.

The father waits in darkness . . .

I suppress a shiver, sliding Mam's knife back into the sheath I've made, uncured leather looped through my belt. My hand drifts to it instinctively now, assuring myself it's still there a dozen times a day.

It's taken longer than expected to make the journey. A well-provisioned Messenger on horseback can make it from Cutter's Hollow to Everam's Bounty in two weeks. On foot it's taken thrice that, but I don't dare use magic to speed our feet again, not unless all the Core is at our heels. We were lucky to survive it the once.

Selen had some money when we started out, but it quickly dwindled, then vanished entirely. We've had to stop periodically to hunt, find shelter from the weather, and do odd jobs for food and lodging. We've kept the hoods of our warded cloaks up in the night, but there's been no sign of demons.

"They've got a pile of logs in back," Selen notes. "Might give us breakfast if I chop them."

"Where did a princess learn to cord wood?" I ask.

"Still a Cutter." Selen smells indignant. "Da taught me to swing an axe as soon as I could lift one."

We climb down from the hayloft and back to the road while it's still dark, finding a shady spot to clean up and handle our necessaries while I acclimate to the dawn. I can hear folk rousing at the farm, and once they're up and out in the yard, Selen and I appear on the road, making no effort to hide our approach.

Banner in the yard tells me the owner of this property is a warrior of the Mehnding, the second largest tribe in New Krasia. The next thing I notice is the casual dress. The women working the fields and yard wear scarves in their hair, but they don't cover everything, and vary in color. Their faces are bare. Their dresses are conservative, but no more so than women wear back in the Brook. Certainly ent the wrist-to-ankle black robes Nanny Micha used to wear. I wonder if she's all right.

The women look up as we approach, eyes flicking first to the bow slung over my shoulder, and then to Selen's leggings and bare arms, but they make no comment.

"Is there work we might do in exchange for some food?" My Krasian is out of practice, but I can make conversation when I need to.

Soon Selen is swinging an axe and I am at the archery range, having tea and making awkward small talk with the warrior who owns the farm and his sons while we take turns shooting. I'm good at shooting things that aren't rushing to kill me. Ent an eye sharper than mine, and I can sense even the slightest breeze. I hold my own against the sons, and think to let the father win to spare his honor, but he is everything Mehnding archery masters are said to be. With every bull's-eye we take a stride back, until we're just firing into the sky to arc the shots. Still he hits center target every time.

"Ay, why didn't they put you to work, too?" Selen asks when we're back on our way, bellies full and with a sack of vegetables in her pack.

"They saw my bow," I tell her. "The Mehnding are the far-reaching tribe. Missile experts. They assumed I was a warrior. It would be dishonorable to make me work for a meal."

"They didn't see the spear and shield on my back?" Selen asks.

"Obviously you're carrying them for me." I wink and dodge her swat in response, but the irritation in her scent is real.

The food is gone two days later, as the capital city of Everam's Bounty comes into view. We're tired, hungry, and both of us have smelled better. We haven't spoken more than necessary in days.

"This had better be worth it," Selen mutters.

"Only hope we've got," I say. "Olive's da, my bloodfather, is married to Inevera, the only seer more famous than Aunt Leesha."

Selen doesn't reply, and I catch pain and sadness in her scent. Both of us are struggling.

Like Hollow, Everam's Bounty is protected from demons, but the Krasians use massive stone obelisks graven with wards rather than shape their streets and fields to the twisting demands of the symbols. The giant pillars reach out from the city like the spokes of a wheel, protecting countless acres of rich farmland.

It is harvesttime, and the fields bustle with workers, but as with the other farms we've visited, adherence to the strict dress Krasians once uniformly embraced has fallen off. Occasionally there is a woman in full blacks and veil, but most look little different from Thesan women with kerchiefs in their hair. All look well fed and often there is laughter while they work. The land is prosperous, and all share in it.

The prosperity works against us as we enter the city proper. Here there are more men in *Sharum* blacks and women in veils, the materials pressed and clean, but it seems more a fashion choice than law. Selen and I look like beggars by contrast, and the locals shy away from us, hands on their purses.

There are bakeries and sweet shops that smell so good my mouth fills with water, and plentiful bookshops devoted to religion and the sciences. Clothing shops do brisk custom, and there are theaters and museums. Folk laugh at outdoor restaurants as street entertainers play for coin, and even these look askance at us.

The ever-present obelisks are at almost every intersection, often at the center of water fountains, or sitting atop intricately designed pedestals.

The guards to the walled inner city shift their spears, eyes narrowing as we approach. A few that were previously milling about drift toward the gate, watching us.

"Sure this is a good idea?" Selen asks.

I smile. Ent often I get to impress Selen Cutter. "Ay. Watch this."

A hulking warrior appears with the red veil of a drillmaster around his throat. I walk right up to him, ignoring his threatening glare. With a smile I give a polite bow. "I am Darin asu'Arlen am'Bales am'Brook. It is urgent I speak to my bloodfather, Ahmann asu Hoshkamin am'Jardir, the Shar'Dama Ka."

The drillmaster's eyes widen, and several of the guards stare with mouths open. For a moment that seems to stretch on into minutes, no one says anything. Then the drillmaster turns to the nearest warrior and gives him a shove. "Stop gawking and deliver the message, fool." He turns to the others. "Open the gate and prepare a palanquin!"

THE PALANQUIN BOBS slightly with the steps of the men carrying the poles, but sunk into the silk feather pillows, I hardly notice. There is a jug of cold water, warm couscous with spiced meat and vegetables, dried fruits and nuts, and an incense burner, no doubt more for the benefit of others than ourselves. The incense threatens to give me a headache, but this deep in a crowded city, I am glad for its dulling of my senses.

Selen and I eat hungrily as we watch the inner city go by through curtains of impossibly thin translucent silk.

"Night," Selen says through a mouth full of food. "You call me princess, but I ent ever had a pack of soldiers fall over themselves to put a silk pillow under my bum. Why didn't you do this a week ago?"

She's got a right to know, though I don't like talking about it. "Most everyone in Thesa thinks my da is the Deliverer, and my bloodfather is half demon," I say. "Here, it's the reverse. And if my da is half demon to them . . ."

"You are, too," Selen finishes.

"Ay," I say. "Mam always said religion makes folks unpredictable. That we couldn't trust folk we didn't know. But here in the capital, no one hinders the Jardir family."

"And you count as family?" Selen asks.

"Ahmann Jardir delivered me," I say, feeling my throat tighten. "The son of his fallen best friend, in the deep dark below the world. Mam says his hands were still wet with Da's blood when he smacked out my first cry. That means something in Krasia."

"Think that would mean something anywhere." Selen lays a gentle hand on my arm.

"Last time we visited, I think I was forty-third in line for the throne," I note.

Selen pulls back suddenly, glaring at me. Her scent is unreadable.

"What?" I ask.

"Darin Bales," she swats me on the arm, "are you telling me that for all these years you've been making fun at me and Olive, you've been a ripping *prince?*"

I roll my eyes. "Barely. If the forty-three ahead of me died, they'd add a forty-fourth before letting a *chin* take the throne."

"Still counts," Selen says. "Wait till I tell Olive. She is going to spit!"

THE PALANQUIN PAUSES at the palace steps for a while as messengers run back and forth. They don't disturb us, and by the time we are moving again, Selen is asleep on the pillows, and my eyes have grown heavy as well. It's been a long time since I relaxed on a pillow with a full stomach in a safe place.

The bearers carry us away from the main entrance to the family wing. There are more guards, but they have been alerted and let us pass without delay. Then the palanquin tilts as they carry it up the broad steps.

Selen is jolted awake. "Ay, they don't need to carry us up the ripping steps."

"Believe me when I say it ent worth arguing," I tell her. "They take it as an insult to their hospitality if visiting royals have to climb a step on their own."

"Where are they taking us?" Selen asks.

"They're delaying," I say. "If they were prepared, we'd start in the throne room. Reckon our showing up unexpected turned everyone's day upside down. Mam used to love this game."

I think of how Mam used to chuckle to herself, seeing everyone scramble when we skated in unannounced and showed up at the gate. The servants and Damajah always smelled of irritation, but the pleasure in Jardir's scent at seeing us overpowered everything. The memory makes my heart ache, and my hand drifts of its own accord to grip the handle of Mam's knife.

"Olive's da is King of Everything here," I go on. "Might be lounging in a silk sleepshirt in his library reading a book, or he might be on the other side of the duchy blessing crops and kissing babies. No telling how long it will take before he's ready to see us."

The palanquin is set down, and the curtains are pulled back to reveal the twins have come to greet us. "In the meantime, they stall us with family."

"Oh, cousin," Rojvah pouts, "but of course we had to come! Who else would have the nerve to tell you that you smell like a goat, and need a bath and fresh clothes before you track dust through the sacred halls?" Arick snickers at that, and I press my lips together to keep my own smile from breaking out.

It will only make things worse if I encourage her.

Rojvah and Arick have the same father—the famous Rojer Halfgrip, first Jongleur to learn to charm demons with his music. Like my da, Halfgrip died during the war, but he's always been a hero to me.

Despite being born to different mothers, Mam always called Rojvah and Arick the twins. Both have cinnamon hair—darker than their da's fabled flame red, but a coveted rarity in Krasia. Their skin is lighter than Olive's, though nothing like the pale white shown in portraits of Rojer Halfgrip. In the North it might pass for too much time in the sun, but here in the palace surrounded by full-blood Krasians, it's enough to draw notice.

But the twins attract attention in any event. They say Rojvah's grandmother Damajah Inevera is the most beautiful woman in Krasia, and I ent one to argue. At fourteen, all can see Rojvah is following in her footsteps. A pouch of unfinished demonbones hangs from her waist, but she looks decidedly uncomfortable in the white silk robe and headscarf of a Krasian priestess-in-training.

And Arick . . . I hear Selen's breath catch as she looks at him, and the scent she gives off makes jealousy surge in my chest.

Arick asu Rojer am'Inn am'Kaji wears brightly colored robes and carries a fine instrument case on his back. He's played the kamanj his entire life, but he's more warrior than Jongleur—tall, with bunched muscle and nothing of a tumbler's agility. His heavy jaw frames a face that looks sculpted from marble. He has Krasian features, but his skin is light as any in the North, and his hair is more orange than the rusty red that crops up here and there in Krasia.

He puts his hand out to shake in the Northern fashion. I take it, knowing what is coming next. Arick clutches my hand tight, pulling me in close as his left fist balls and throws a hook at my shoulder.

The punch is playful, but as with Selen's brothers, it is also an attempt at dominance in front of the women. I'm ready for the blow, turning my hand slippery just long enough to slide from his grasp. I duck the fist and take a quick step back out of range as Arick stumbles and loses a bit of dignity. I could hit back, but to what end? It would only escalate things, and I doubt he'd even feel it.

Arick barks a laugh. "One day, am'Bales!"

"You'll need to move faster than a snail on crutches." I smile despite the tiresome game. I've missed my cousins, and we've never been more in need of friendly faces.

Rojvah opens her arms to embrace me, but then sniffs and draws back, holding her nose. "You may have a proper greeting when you've had a bath."

"Stink clings to him even when he's good and scrubbed," Selen says. "Honest word, we've tried."

Rojvah titters and Arick throws his head back to laugh, as if it's better to stink of perfume than accept your own scent. I sweep an arm toward Selen. "Selen vah Gared am'Cutter am'Hollow, meet the twins, Rojvah and Arick—"

"The children of Rojer Halfgrip," Selen cuts in. Rojvah smiles at that, but her brother's face darkens.

"Welcome," Rojvah gives a shallow bow. "It is good to know our father's name is still known in the North."

"Known," Selen snorts. "Man's practically a saint."

"Your father is renowned in the warrior halls of Krasia." Arick's bow is much lower than his sister's, meeting Selen's eyes boldly. "It is said none can match him in a feat of strength."

A nice word about her da will always set Selen smiling, but this time it bothers me. I don't like her smiling at Arick like that, and I definitely don't like the way he's looking at her. Again, the images flash in my mind from when our auras touched. I'm not the only boy Selen's kissed. Not by a far sight. Got no right to be jealous.

But I am, and need a deep breath to calm myself. Rojvah tilts her head, eyes flicking to Selen and back to me. She moves forward, her playful reluctance gone as she takes my arm. "Come, let us see to your comforts."

Rojvah takes off her headscarf the moment the servants close the door behind us, shaking out waves of cinnamon hair. Known her all my life, but still I can't help staring. Rojvah's always been pretty as a sunset. I catch a whiff of annoyance from Selen, and for once the smell pleases me.

Rojvah turns to a mirror, examining her hair. "Another few moments and that dreadful scarf would have flattened it for the rest of the day."

She turns to Selen. "Can you manage a bath without servants?" She gestures with her hand to a screen at the far side of the room. There is moisture in the air, and I can smell the soap. Even I am eager for a scrub.

"Ay, think I can manage." Selen is already moving for the screen.

"Thanks be to Everam," Rojvah says. "The servants will all tsst to Mother if I so much as unbind my hair in front of the son of Arlen, since we're intended."

Selen stops short. "Ay, what?"

"Marriage broker nonsense," I say quickly. Rojvah's scent is playful, but I'm afraid her games will get me in more trouble than I want. "I'm on some list with a hundred other eligible bachelors, but until Rojvah gets promised to someone else we're considered courting."

"Indeed it is nonsense," Rojvah agrees, but the hand she lays on my arm implies otherwise. "Darin is practically my brother, and indeed low on the list." She gives my arm a squeeze. "But fear not, cousin. *Inevera*, one day you will find a bride with . . . exotic taste."

"Ay, what's that supposed to mean?" I demand.

Rojvah doesn't reply. She pulls away, gesturing to Selen. "Come, I'll see you to the bath while I change into something with a bit more color."

She glides across the room and slips behind the screen as Selen scowls at her back. She throws an annoyed glance my way before following.

I turn to Arick, who has picked up Selen's spear and shield and set his feet in a fighting stance. He spins the weapon through a series of *sharukin*, testing its reach and balance. Then he taps his finger on the point, a gentle touch that nonetheless draws a drop of blood.

"Fine weapon," he grunts. "A bit long and heavy for you, I think."

"It's Selen's," I tell him.

Arick's eyebrows leap into his orange hair as he turns to look at the silhouettes of the women in the screen. "She is *Sharum'ting*?"

"Stabbed a rock demon in the heart," I say.

Arick gives a low whistle and it's my turn to be annoyed. "Now, *that's* a woman." He lays down the spear and takes up my bow, stringing it in a quick and easy motion. "You prefer to kill from afar, like some Mehnding gray?"

The words are derisive. The Krasian army would have collapsed long ago without Mehnding bows and war machines, but other warriors call them "gray robes," because they're smart enough not to fight demons in close when they don't have to.

"Prefer not to kill at all." I pat the pipes hanging at my hip. "Had my way, I'd just play my pipes."

Arick shakes his head. "Would that we could trade lives, cousin. I am forbidden to fight."

"Still?" I ask. "That can't be right."

"This is my weapon, so they say." Arick slaps his kamanj case in disgust. "I come from an unbroken line of warriors dating back centuries. My mother wore *Sharum* black and led thousands of warriors on the walls of Docktown, holding back an *alagai* horde even as I rode in her womb. My grandfather was bodyguard to Shar'Dama Ka himself."

He looks down at his multicolored robes and makes a spitting noise. "Instead I am denied the spear and forced to dress like some *chin* jester to honor my father, who died in shame in some greenland prison."

Rojvah steps from around the screen. Her face is serene, but even from across the room I can smell her anger. "Shame? Our father died taking a spear meant for my mother, and his music turned the tide in countless battles of Sharak Ka. His glory was boundless. But Arick would rather idolize his Baba Hasik, who died a castrated traitor, than wear a colored robe in his father's honor."

Arick bares his teeth at his sister, but she stares him down. Rojvah's mother is more royal than Arick's, and Rojvah is inviolate in her clerical white. Still, the sudden anger I smell on Arick puts me on edge.

"Pine for the spear if you wish, brother, but speak no lies about Father." Rojvah moves to a wardrobe near the bath, selecting an armful of dresses and retreating back to the screen.

"Why not just tell Jardir you want to be a warrior?" I keep my voice flat, acting like Arick doesn't smell like he's about to flip the table.

Arick laughs, his anger stink dissipating with a smell of resignation. "As if my wishes matter, when I have so famous a father."

I blow out a breath. "Know what that feels like. Ent exactly a *par'chin* myself. Boys got carry their das' weight along with their own."

"Guess it's good I ent a boy," Selen says, emerging from behind the screen in a beautiful blue dress, cut in the Angierian style. "My da's carrying three hundred pounds just in his belly."

Rojvah laughs at the joke, but Arick and I just stare at Selen, whom I've seldom seen wear anything so . . . feminine.

"All she's got are white robes and frilly debutante gowns." Selen flicks her hand over the dress, annoyed.

"You look great," I say.

Selen catches me staring and balls a fist. "Now ent a good time to add a punch line, Darin."

"You and Olive are the ones who throw shadow at folk about their clothes," I say.

"Ay, fair," Selen allows. I can tell she feels Olive's absence even more keenly. It's like a part of us is missing.

"I don't know what you're complaining about," Rojvah huffs. "Our ambassador in the North sends me all the latest fashions."

The words draw my eyes as Rojvah steps back behind the screen. No doubt she thinks the watercolored paper shows only silhouettes, but unlike the others, I can see through it quite clearly. She unfastens something, and her robes seem to blow away like smoke.

I feel a rush of blood color my cheeks, and turn away a bit too quickly. Selen's eyes flick to the screen, then back to me, and she scowls.

Rojvah emerges in an emerald-green dress with a lace bodice and ruffled straps. Her flowing skirts flare to show off her calves as she spins. "What do you think?"

Selen catches me staring and I can smell her irritation. "Ruffles are a bit last season."

Rojvah deflates at the words, and Selen's scent changes from annoyance to satisfaction.

"It's not as if anyone other than you will ever see me in it," Rojvah laments. "Women are beginning to wear color throughout Everam's Bounty, and I'm forever trapped in white."

She gives a sad shake of her head. "You boys bemoan the weight of your fathers, but the burden is no less for women. Mother is *Damaji'ting* of the Kaji and I am her only daughter. I was destined for the white before I was even born."

Selen looks a little abashed. "Seen paintings of your grandmother wearing colors. Won't you be Damajah one day?"

Rojvah laughs, a sound like a tinkling fountain. "There is only one Damajah. It is not a title that can be passed. It will die with my grandmother, until the dice call another. The last was three thousand years ago, and it may be so again." She shrugs. "I do not covet the Pillow Throne in any event."

"Be glad of that, cousin," a voice says from the door. "The throne has a weight greater than fathers and mothers combined."

We turn to see Crown Prince Kaji, the Deliverer's eldest grandson, and first in line for the Skull Throne of New Krasia. A year older than me, Kaji is tall, slender, and graceful, like some majestic bird. Already he wears the white robe and jeweled turban of a full *dama*, but at his belt are warded silver knuckles and an alagai tail, the signs of a warrior-priest.

Selen straightens at the sight of him.

"Selen vah Gared, meet Dama Kaji." I lean close to her, but do not drop my voice. "Kaji is King-of-Everything-in-training."

"Ah, got it," Selen says, as Rojvah puts a hand to her mouth to cover a smile.

Kaji is composed as always as he comes forward. I've never been able to read his scent, so I can't tell if my casual introduction annoys him. He is unflappable.

But that doesn't mean I stop trying. Too many people bow and scrape to Kaji, day and night. Ent good for him. I'm one of the few who can get away with giving him a poke now and again.

"We've met before, daughter of Gared," Kaji says with a formal bow. "You were still in your mother's arms, but I remember." He looks around. "This is the first time in fifteen years we've all been together. If Olive were here, the reunion would be complete."

The words are spoken casually, but I feel his eyes on us, searching for information the mention of Olive might shake free.

Selen doesn't take the bait, spreading her skirts in a perfect, if out-of-character, curtsy. "Good to see you again, Prince Kaji."

"I've come from Grandfather," Kaji says when nothing else is forthcoming. "Shar'Dama Ka is preparing and will see you as soon as he is able."

"*Preparing* means his wife won't let him say hello until she casts her dice on it," I tell Selen.

"Of course," Rojvah agrees, still admiring herself in a mirror. "You show up out of nowhere looking like a beggar and traveling alone with the daughter of Hollow's greatest general? Of course Tikka won't let him see you without a casting."

"Sounds like she's the King of Everything, then," Selen observes, and everyone, even Kaji, has a laugh at that.

"So why *are* you here?" Rojvah asks. "It must be quite the tale. Did your parents not approve the match?"

"Ay, what?" It takes me a moment to realize what she's asking. Then suddenly my face flushes hot. "Night, you think we're here to elope?!"

"Pfagh!" Disgust fills Selen's scent and expression. More than necessary, you ask me. "Be like marrying my brother!"

The words wrap around me, like a curtain blocking out the light. But they are . . . freeing, too. Now that I know what I am to her, I understand what she must be to me. For once, I don't have to guess, to overthink every word and scent.

"I meant no offense," Rojvah says. "It seemed a logical assumption. You both coming of age, after all, and why else would you arrive alone?"

This is the real reason they have stayed with us. I spent more than a few winters here, but Kaji spent most of his time with his tutors, Rojvah was bossy, and Arick was always looking for a fight. I was never as close to my Krasian cousins as I was to Selen and Olive.

Anything they learn will go straight to Jardir and Inevera to help them prepare for our audience. Normally, that would be fine, but with Leesha and Olive both missing, Hollow is vulnerable. It isn't something I want getting around. "I'm here to tell it to Bloodfather, and none other."

"Nonsense, cousin," Arick says. "You are family. Your enemies are our enemies."

"My brother is a little too eager to have his first enemy," Rojvah says. "But he isn't wrong, cousin."

I'm a little ashamed when I realize they mean the words. There is no lie in their scents. "Thanks." I shuffle, unable to meet their eyes. "But I ent sure myself who my enemies are, and some of the secrets I'm keeping ent mine. I've a right to seek my bloodfather's advice before any other."

"Of course, cousin." Kaji bows, already turning to go. "I will inform Grandfather. An escort will take you to him at nightfall."

35

BLOODFATHER

Once they realize they're not getting anything from us, Kaji leaves to report back to my bloodfather while the twins push me into the bath.

The water is hot, and I shiver with pleasure as I step in, letting it envelop me. Ent normally a person who likes to be squeezed, but there is something . . . uniform about the way a tub of hot water holds you, like a warm hug from someone you love. I breathe deeply as I lean back, inviting it to soak in.

No sooner do I close my eyes than I hear Rojvah reach around the privacy screen to steal my clothes.

Annoying, but it ent surprising. The once-fine breeches, shirt, and coat Aunt Leesha's tailors made for me are torn, worn, and filthy. Court folk always do this. Olive and Selen were no better. Seeing you in worn clothes makes royals itch in all their silk and frippery, especially when you've got a famous da.

"Where you goin' with those?" I call, already knowing the answer.

"They smell like a dead animal," Rojvah says. "I'll give them to the servants to wash." There's a click of the door, and I can smell the serving woman waiting outside.

"The cloaks are to be treated as holy raiment," Rojvah whispers. "Burn the rest."

"Your will," the woman replies, and I hear the door click closed again.

"I can hear you," I say loudly.

Again, that musical laugh. "I've seen the cleaning women work miracles, cousin, but they are not the Creator Himself. No amount of scrubbing will make those rags worthy to clean your feet, Darin asu Par'chin. You and Princess Selen should be clad in the raiments of royalty, not beggar's robes."

No doubt she searched the clothes on the way, but there's nothing to find. I love the twins like cousins, but ent such a fool that I trust them. I put everything of value, including Mam's knife, in the satchel with my pipes before undressing, and that rests beside me on the edge of the tub.

Rojvah steps away into the wardrobe chamber, and I hear the whisking hiss of silk sliding against silk.

I've worked up a lather a few moments later when she returns, coming around the screen, bold as a hound. She laughs her tinkling laugh as I splash and scramble to cover myself. "You needn't be ashamed, cousin. I have a brother, after all."

"Ay, that's enough of that," Selen comes around the screen as well, but she keeps her back to me, blocking Rojvah's line of sight. She smells protective.

"Fine," Rojvah huffs, averting her gaze as she holds out a neatly folded pile of clothes.

Most able-bodied Krasian men are *Sharum* caste, and wear black robes. Some few are *dama*, and wear white. The weaklings, *khaffit*, wear tan like children.

I have not had *Hannu Pash*, the Krasian coming-of-age trial that determines caste. In the eyes of people of the Evejan faith, I am still a child. By custom, I should be dressed in tan robes, if of fine quality.

But the rules are different for the children of Krasia's rulers. Princes and princesses before the trial wear colors so bright they hurt my eyes.

Rojvah holds out a pumpkin-orange silk robe with white wardwork stitched along the breast, hem, and sleeves. Bright blue silk pants with legs wide enough to fit my entire body into, tapering down to narrow cuffs. Thin orange silk slippers with pointed toes. If clothes could shout, these would be screaming.

"I'm not wearing that," I say.

"Do not complain to me," Rojvah says. "They are Arick's robes."

"From when I was twelve," Arick notes.

"Well he certainly won't fit what you're wearing now," Rojvah says, as if Arick's bright motley robes would be preferable.

"I'm not wearing that," I say again.

"I don't blame you," Arick agrees. "Better a bido than a woman's pillow silks."

"Ent walking around in just a nappy, either," I growl. "Get me something else, or tell my bloodfather I cannot meet him because you had the servants burn my clothes."

Rojvah half turns her head my way, a smile pulling at her lips. "You're welcome to go through Arick's wardrobe yourself, Darin asu Arlen, but I assure you all his clothes are like this."

"Welcome to my personal abyss," Arick says.

"Let's see." Selen bulls Rojvah back around the screen, and I hear them in the wardrobe rummaging about. They don't speak. Both of them know I can hear anything they say.

"Still ent gonna like it," Selen says when they return, "but at least you'll be all one color instead of looking like a rainbow's sick-up."

"Why didn't you tell them why we've come?" Selen asks that evening, when Arick and Rojvah finally take their leave. "Thought you said the twins were family."

"You tell all your secrets to your brothers?" I ask.

Selen scratches her neck. "Ay, fair point."

"Arick and Rojvah are family," I say, "but they're not going to lie to their grandparents. Anything we told them has already been passed on to Jardir and Inevera. Even now, there are servants in the walls, listening in."

Selen sits up. "Ay, really?"

I raise my voice. "THEY ENT AS QUIET AS THEY THINK." I hear some fumbling in the walls at that, and chuckle to myself.

Selen moves from her chair to the divan where I sit, scooching me to the side with her hips to sit next to me and lean close to whisper. "Still, doesn't answer the question. Ent we here to ask for help?"

"Ay," I tell her, "and when I see my bloodfather, we'll tell him everything. Hollow and Krasia might have peace, but they ent exactly friends and this ent some show for palace gossip. Less people know what happened, the better."

I hear the sound of crutches in the hall and cross the room, opening the door before the man on the other side has a chance to knock. He's a familiar sight, a man in brightly colored robes and turban. Just visible at the hems is a bit of silk underclothing in *khaffit* tan. He is adorned with rings and necklaces and earrings. Gold glitters in his mouth where some teeth are missing. Even standing still, he needs the support of two crutches, carved in the shape of camelbacks, with armpit cushions between the humps.

"Son of Arlen, welcome to Krasia!" the man calls.

"Abban!" I'm genuinely happy to see my father's old friend. Abban may call me son of Arlen, but he's the only one of Da's friends who sees me for who I am, instead of looking for something of Da in me. Every time Mam and I visited over the years, Abban would greet me with gifts and stories of my father—not as the Deliverer, but before all that, when he was just a young, reckless Messenger.

I love Abban, but he's Bloodfather's spy, too. Perhaps him most of all.

"By Everam, it is good to see you, son of Arlen." Abban bows as deep as his crutches will allow. "I trust you and your family are well?"

"Funny you should ask that," I say, changing the topic before he can probe further. "It seems a certain Krasian merchant owes us a horse."

Abban is surprisingly graceful on his crutches as he takes a step back and puts a hand on his heart. "Surely you cannot mean to suggest that merchant is me? I have ever been your father's true friend and never cheated him or left my debts unpaid."

"Never *succeeded* in cheating him, you mean," I say.

Abban spreads his hands, smiling. "All is fair at the haggling table, my friend. Your father always understood that."

I nod. "But it seems he left a horse in your keeping the night he was cast out of Krasia and left to die on the sands."

"I had nothing to do with that," Abban says. "But yes, he left his courser, Nighteye, in my keeping. When the Par'chin did not return, we thought him dead, and with no one to claim the animal, it became mine by right of possession."

"But he wasn't dead," I say.

"It was years before I learned that," Abban notes.

I shrug. "Horses live a long time."

"I don't have it anymore," Abban says.

"I'll accept a replacement," I say. "And not some pack animal. A sturdy Messenger horse."

I can smell the mix of emotions at war in the man. He wants to haggle. Relishes the idea, in fact. But there is guilt in his scent as well. He knows I'm right, and that it is the least he can do.

At last, Abban holds up his hands. "Who am I, to argue with the son of the Par'chin? The debt will be repaid before you leave."

Selen crosses the room, and Abban bows again. "Everam's blessings upon you, Your Royal Highness, Selen vah Gared am'Cutter am'Hollow. I know your father well, and always judged him a fair and honorable man. If there is anything that can be done to make your first visit to Krasia more comfortable, Princess, do not hesitate to ask."

Abban escorts us from our chambers to court, talking all the while. He moves easily on his crutches, keeping something close to what most folks would think a comfortable pace. To me it feels like we're wading through molasses, but I keep my manners and match him. The *khaffit* merchant keeps his chatter amiable, but again and again his probing questions come uncomfortably close to topics I want to discuss with him least of all.

WHITE-SLEEVED GUARDS OPEN the doors to a throne room empty save for my bloodfather, Ahmann Jardir the Shar'Dama Ka, and his First Wife, Damajah Inevera. They bar Abban from entering, closing the doors behind Selen and me.

I hate the throne room. I have to blink and squint, lifting a hand to blot out the worst of it as I try to adjust.

Shining gold, sparkling jewels, vivid silk tapestries, mosaics of semiprecious stone, and windows of stained glass make it like looking in a kaleidoscope even without wardsight. Add in the magic, and it's like standing in the center of a festival flamework display. It's more than I can process, hurting my eyes and making me feel sick and dizzy.

The Skull Throne stands atop a dais of seven steps, a seat built from the heads of Krasia's ancient leaders, topped with the severed head of a mind demon. The bones are coated in priceless, magic-conductive electrum. The seat throbs with power, mixing faith protections with raw Core magic. Anyone sitting on it would radiate strength like a god. Across its arms lies the Spear of Kaji, the strongest weapon ever made. It throbs with power like something alive.

Next to it on the top of the dais is the Pillow Throne, a canopied bed of silk cushions that shines with almost as much magic as the Skull Throne itself.

There are other magics about the room; wardwork that seems decorative provides powerful protections, as do the ever-present heroes' bones. Wards of silence surround us, much as in Aunt Leesha's office.

But none of the room's raw power matches what radiates from the couple who wait for us at the base of the steps. Ahmann Jardir doesn't dress fancy. Just simple warrior blacks beneath an outer robe and turban of stark white. He's tall as a Cutter, thick with muscle, but no Cutter keeps their beard so impeccably trimmed and oiled.

My bloodfather has close to sixty summers, but like many who use magic, he remains physically in his prime. I wonder if that's my fate, too—still looking like I have thirty summers on my hundredth born day.

But while his clothes are plain, the crown atop my bloodfather's head is not. Seven points of shining electrum rise from his turban, each affixed with a different gemstone the size of a chestnut. The gems catch the lamplight, splitting it into a full spectrum of color, even as the crown's magic does the same in wardsight.

Like my mam's, Bloodfather's skin is warded. Hers are inked into her flesh, but his are raised scars, painstakingly cut. They pump magic through him like a pulse.

Beside him is Inevera, his *Jiwah Ka* or First Wife. The Damajah can steal the breath from anyone, the most beautiful woman I've ever seen.

Her purple headwrap and veil are transparent, showing every twist of her full lips and delicate nose. Her long black hair is oiled and bound in gold, and her gossamer purple robes are just opaque enough for decency in layers. They flow around her like smoke, leading the eye to search fruitlessly for gaps in coverage that always seem just a slight draft away. She is older than my bloodfather, but ageless like him.

The wand at the Damajah's belt is as powerful as Aunt Leesha's, and her many rings, bracelets, necklaces, earrings, and headpiece all shine with demonbone magic, glittering about her like stars.

"Darin!" Jardir's voice is warm as he holds his arms open.

"Bloodfather." I embrace him gratefully, feeling safe for the first time in months. The sensation makes me choke, and it's only sheer force of will that keeps me from weeping into his shoulder. Suddenly I am so tired.

I ease back before I lose what remains of my dignity. Jardir lets me go, turning to give Selen a shallow bow. "Welcome, Selen vah Gared am'Cutter am'Hollow. Your father is one of the greatest warriors I have ever met. I am honored to call him friend. He will no doubt be overjoyed to hear you are well."

Selen hesitates at the mention of her father, but recovers, dipping into a curtsy. "You honor me, Shar'Dama Ka."

The Damajah sweeps forward, her diaphanous robes swirling around her as if they have life of their own. "Welcome, Darin asu Arlen am'Bales am'Brook, the light born in darkness." She nods at me, and I suppress a shudder as I return the gesture. I've always been uneasy around the Damajah. Somethin' . . . hungry about her, and I feel like the meal.

"And to you, Selen vah Elona," Inevera continues. "Your father's strength is legend, but your mother is no less formidable."

"Ay, that's honest word." Selen curtsies, but she, too, smells wary. Ent just me Inevera unnerves.

"It has been too long since you and your mother last visited," Jardir says. "It is good to see you grown into a man."

Standing before him in silk robes of cobalt blue, embroidered with wardwork in silver thread and pants that taper wide as a ball gown, I hardly feel like a grown man. "Ay, maybe not quite there yet."

"A man is more than his stature," Jardir says. "Your father was never the largest warrior, nor the strongest. His *sharusahk* was not the best, nor was he the quickest, or the smartest. But again and again, death came for the Par'chin, and again and again he cast it back. I was honored to be his *ajin'pal*. His brother in day and night."

He lays his hands on my shoulders the way Grandda does when he's got something heavy to say. "I know I am not your true sire, Darin Bales, but if ever you need a boon so great that only a son might ask it of his father, you may ask it of me. Lands. Titles. Riches. Matchmakers and dower to find you wives to give you children. All this I owe the son of Arlen, and more beside."

"Don't need any land or riches," I tell Jardir.

My bloodfather nods. "And yet here you are, arriving on my doorstep unannounced and on foot, dressed in rags, alone save for the daughter of Gared."

"Don't tell me you think we're here to elope, too," I say.

"It was Rojvah's guess, but as good as any," Inevera says. "You had opportunity with your mothers away hunting the demons that attacked the princesses on Solstice."

"Without so much as consulting me." Jardir's fist clenches at his side, and I catch a whiff of his anger before he suppresses it.

"Dice didn't tell you?" I try to keep bitterness from my tone, but ent sure I succeed. Wouldn't be in this fix if not for the ripping dice. All the corespawned things do is turn lives upside down.

"The dice have ever been . . . elusive where you were concerned, Darin Bales." Something about Inevera's words makes me profoundly uneasy. "At least, without your blood to focus the casting."

The Damajah's face is serene, her breathing deep and even. She does a good job of masking her natural scent in perfume, making it hard to sniff out what she's feeling. Even her aura is placid. But her eyes and easy grace are . . . predatory. She will ask for that blood when she hears our tale. Mam always said the blood was all Inevera really cared about, and I should never give her any, but corespawn me, this time I ent got much choice.

"Enough games." Jardir's voice deepens, like Mam getting ready to drag me from a puddle. "If it is not to marry the daughter of Gared, why are you here?"

"Demons didn't just attack Olive and Selen on Solstice," I say. "Hit me in the Brook, too."

"On the same night?" Jardir asks.

"Same hour," I say.

"Tsst!" Inevera hisses. "How could they not inform us of such a portent?"

"Mam wanted to, but Aunt Leesha wasn't . . . comfortable reaching out." My eyes flick to the Damajah, but she says nothing. "They cast the dice, and think they found some kind of nest."

Again Bloodfather's aura turns briefly stormy, then blows away. I can smell his fear, and concern, even if his words try to hide them. "Nevertheless, I am certain they are well. Leesha Paper is even more formidable than her mother, and Renna am'Bales put a spear in a demon queen's eye."

"Thought so, too, till we found this." I reach into my robe, producing Mam's knife.

"Tsst!" Inevera hisses.

Jardir's eyes widen, and this time when his aura turns stormy, it does not calm. "Where did you find that?"

"In a field of blood and burning bodies," I say. "Hundreds of Wooden Soldiers and Warded Children. No sign of survivors. Looked like they were bushwhacked."

I have never seen my bloodfather angry, but he is angry now. He lifts an arm and the Spear of Kaji flies from the dais to his hand, the wards along its length burning with power.

"When?" Jardir demands.

"Two moons ago," I say.

Inevera lays a hand on Jardir's wrist, just above the hand that holds the spear. "Peace, husband. If it has been so long, we must learn all we can before taking action."

Jardir grimaces, but he nods, breathing away his fear and anger as I relate the attack near my grandda's farm, and Selen retells what happened on the borough tour. Their faces are calm, but even the Damajah's aura begins to boil at having been kept in the dark about the danger to Olive and me.

"Aunt Leesha's bones pointed to a city in the eastern mountains," I say. "She left with five hundred Hollow Lancers, Mam, and all the Warded Children."

"Such a force should have been a match for any demon ambush," Jardir says.

"The prophecy," Inevera presses. "Do you recall Leesha vah Elona's precise words?"

Inevera turns to me, and I shift uncomfortably. Even Mam never trusted the Damajah fully, but we need help, and they're the only ones who can give it to us.

"*A mimic demon hungers beneath a city in an eastern mountain valley*," I say. "She showed us an area that was once part of the country of Rusk. I can mark it on a map."

"Immediately," Jardir says. "But still, that does not explain why you, Darin asu Arlen am'Bales am'Brook, are here in Krasia. I will not ask a third time."

"Olive is missing, too," Selen says. "We think she was kidnapped the night after Leesha and Mrs. Bales left Hollow."

"Kidnapped?" Jardir asks. "By whom?"

"We don't know for sure, but I have a suspicion," Selen says. "It happened not long after your wife tried to buy Olive."

Jardir turns to Inevera, but the Damajah is aghast. "I did no such thing!"

"Your other wife," Selen says. "Belina."

Both eyes snap back to Selen. "Belina was in Hollow?" Inevera's voice is low and dangerous. This time, it is *her* aura that will not calm.

"Belina and Iraven came to negotiate joining the Pact of Free Cities," Selen said. "Wanted to seal the deal with a wedding. Olive and prince . . . Chad."

"Chadan asu Maroch," Inevera advises. "Aleverak's great-grandson. Barely out of swaddling when the Majah returned to Desert Spear." She snorts in derision. "Belina came with a purse full of sand and tried to bargain for the sun."

"Leesha saw it that way, too," Selen says. "Shut it down so hard they left town the next day."

"They could have left spies behind," Jardir says.

I shake my head. "Whoever took Olive was Krasian, but I don't think they were Majah."

Everyone gives me the look of confusion I've seen so many times.

"I smelled it in Lord Arther's room, where we found Olive's note. Krasians. Thought it was Micha at the time, but it was too spread out, and there were male scents."

Selen looks at me. "You can smell what country folk are from?"

"Country?" I huff. "I can smell what part of town they're from."

"You can . . . smell tribe?" Jardir asks.

"Ay," I say. "Ent hard. Northerners might think all your food's alike, but each tribe has its differences, and it changes how they smell. Never smelled Majah before they came to Hollow, but they were just leaving when we arrived, and their scent was all over the keep. Spice mixed with a dust that just smelled . . . dead."

"Desert dust," Jardir says.

I nod. "Whoever kidnapped Olive didn't smell like that."

"Spies use alomom powder to hide their scents," Inevera says.

Something clicks into place. That dust that deadened the scents in Arther's office. Now that I have a name for it, I can filter it in the future. Still, I shake my head. "Powder didn't hide as much as they think. Whoever they were, they didn't smell like Majah."

"Watchers, then," Jardir says. "Not the Krevakh, surely. It would have to be the Nanji. Their tribe served the Majah for centuries. The blood debts run deep."

Again, I relate everything I can recall, as my bloodfather listens impassively.

"You did the right thing, coming to me, Darin," he says at last.

He turns to Selen. "As for you, Selen vah Gared, it is time we called your father."

36

THE CORE TO PAY

"Because you wouldn't listen!" Selen shouts. "Olive was kidnapped and you wouldn't even listen. What were we supposed to do?"

"Sure as the Core wern't supposed to run off to rippin' Krasia!" the general's voice roars back through the resonance stone at the center of the Damajah's casting chamber. It glowed brightly with magic when contact began, but already it is dimming. The power needed to communicate over such distance is enormous.

"Got no one but yourself to blame if I din't trust you!" the general goes on. That one strikes home. I can smell Selen's sudden shame.

But it ent fair. I take a step forward, even though he is hundreds of miles away. "What about me, Uncle Gared?"

"Ay, what's that, Darin?" he says.

I make my voice innocent as one of Aunt Selia's butter cookies. "What did I do, to earn your mistrust?"

The general isn't having it, but he stops yelling, and that's a start. "You're a good boy, Darin, but those girls've always had you wrapped around their fingers. Ent your fault."

I swallow a lump of fear and press. "Is. I wasn't going to let Olive's trail go cold because you wouldn't listen. Asked Selen to steal some food and a spear to come with me."

"And what did that get you?" Uncle Gared demands. "Ent found Olive any more than we did, and you took a forest full of stupid chances along the way. Lucky you din't end up like . . . "

He trails off, unwilling to finish the sentence.

"Indeed, where has any of this deception gotten us?" Jardir demands. "The adults of Hollow were no less foolish than its children. I should have been informed before your forces left, and shouldn't have to hear of their destruction from a child, moons after the fact."

"I had my orders to keep it quiet, from Leesha herself," the general says.

"And who gives orders in Hollow now, with your duchess and her heir both missing?" the Damajah asks.

"Me, for now," Gared concedes. "But if Olive ent back here soon, it's going to end up being Elona, and ent a soul in the world wants that."

Selen draws a ward in the air in front of her. "Creator forbid."

"All the more reason you should have trusted me," Jardir says.

"Ay, don't act like you don't know why that is," Gared says. "Can't throw a rock in Hollow without hittin' someone whose home you took."

"Those who fled our advance are welcome to return, son of Steave," Jardir says tightly, but I can tell he ent used to being spoken to like this.

"Oh, ay?" the general presses. "Gonna give them their land back? Unkill their sons?"

"Enough," Jardir growls. "Whatever disputes our people have in the day is irrelevant. These are blood matters. Leesha am'Paper and Renna am'Bales are as sisters to me. I would never have allowed harm to come to them. And by Everam, when my *daughter* disappeared, honor demanded I be informed, as I have informed you when I found yours shivering in my doorstep."

"Wasn't shivering," Selen notes, but a *tsst!* from Inevera quiets her.

"Ay, fair and true," the general concedes at last. "But when Leesha didn't come back . . . "

"You thought it might have been me who stole her away?" Jardir asks.

"Thought crossed my mind," Uncle Gared admits. "Sorry about that. But now that we know you din't, it narrows the list."

"We have yet to cast the dice," Jardir says, "but we are not without suspicion."

"The Majah," Uncle Gared guesses. "Leesha was spittin' fire after they tried to bid on Olive like a horse."

"There is no shame in bargaining properly over a match," the Damajah says, "but the Majah were flies attempting to haggle a spider."

"We will seek Leesha and Darin's mother first," Jardir says, "while we investigate the Majah."

"Got men searching those hills now," the general says.

"Either they will find nothing," Bloodfather says, "or they will die. Anything powerful enough to defeat my intended's forces will make short work of your scouts."

"Maybe," Gared agrees, "but I can't just sit on my hands about it, either."

"Of course not," Jardir says. "You are a man of honor, and will do what must be done. When the dice are cast, I can fly to the scene and investigate properly."

"So you'll let us know what the dice tell you?" Gared asks.

"Tsst!" Inevera's hiss cuts off Jardir's response. "The mysteries of the *alagai hora* are not to be bandied about."

Jardir nods. "We will conduct our investigations, and inform you when we find something."

"Ent gonna be good enough." Some of the boom returns to the general's voice. "I'm sending an escort for Selen and Darin, now. Be there in a fortnight, and I want them packed up and ready to go."

My bloodfather's nostrils flare, but he keeps his temper in check. "The pact is clear, and you will have them. I forgive your rudeness and disrespect for suggesting it might be otherwise. I know you are a man of honor, and this is a father's fear affecting your manners."

"Got that right," Gared says. "And if there ent news of Olive when I get there, we're gonna see if that sand fort you're all so proud of can stand when a hundred thousand Cutters come to knock it down."

"I will not allow a force that size to pass through Krasian lands," Jardir says. "We will consider it an act of war."

The general growls. "Then we'll go around."

"That will add weeks to your journey," Jardir says. "If attempting to move so many men across the sands doesn't kill you, you will break against Desert Spear's walls like waves against a cliff."

"I won't abandon Princess Olive," the general says, and I catch a whiff of pride from Selen at the words.

"She may be your princess," Jardir says, "but she is my daughter. I will see to her safety. If we discover she is with the Majah, we will . . . ask them to return her."

Gared snorts. "And if they say no?"

"Then you may accompany me when I knock down their walls and take her," Jardir says.

"Tsst!" Inevera removes one of the wardstones on the resonance table, breaking the connection. She and Jardir glare at each other but say nothing more.

I STARE AT the *hanzhar* on Inevera's belt as she kneels before her white casting cloth. Long as Mam's knife, the curved dagger is hot with magic. *Hanzhar* are reputed to be sharp as razors. I wonder if I will even feel it slicing my flesh as she draws blood for the dice.

But the Damajah never reaches for the blade, instead producing a surgical needle, tubing, and several stoppered vials—enough for multiple castings.

I shift uneasily. Mam warned me never to do this. *Your aunt Leesha's bad enough, but I know where her head is at. Ent a body that knows what's in Inevera's head 'cept Inevera.*

"Hold out your arm." The Damajah does not look at me, seemingly focused on the tubing she will tie around my arm, but it's an act. I can smell her hunger.

I hesitate. Been around enough magic users to know the power of blood. Even one vial would allow Inevera to target any number of spells at me, some up close and others at a distance. More, they allow her dice to look into my past and present to predict my future. Who I am. Where I come from. Who I am meant to be. What I am meant to do.

How I will die.

Does anyone have a right to know secrets like that?

I steal a glance at her, thankful for the curls of hair over my eyes that keep us from locking stares. She waits patiently, seeing my indecision.

"I cannot take the blood from you, son of Arlen," she says quietly. "You must give it willingly for the prophecy to be strong. Your blood is something I have desired for many years, though your mother would not allow it since . . . "

"Since what?" I ask when she trails off.

"Since she had you in her belly," Jardir finishes. "She gave one vial, asking if you would survive the journey below."

"What . . . " I swallow. "What did the dice say?"

Inevera flicks an annoyed glance at her husband before answering. *"He will be born in darkness."*

I shiver, even as I realize she has only told me part of the prophecy. The part that has already come to pass, as Jardir delivered me in the bowels of the demon hive. What is the rest? What doesn't she want me to know?

I take a deep breath. It doesn't matter. All that matters is Mam and Aunt Leesha and Olive.

"Three vials," I say. "To be used to find Mam and Aunt Leesha and Olive, and no other reason."

The Damajah's eyes narrow. "Powerful forces are at work here, son of Arlen. It may require more to glean what we need."

I nod. "You can have three. You need more, you can ask me then."

I see her lips tighten through the gossamer silks of her veil, but she nods. "Done."

The last thing I want to do is push the Damajah too far, but I imagine what Mam would say. "Swear it."

Even through all the perfume, I can smell Inevera's indignation at the challenge to her integrity, but she does not hesitate. "I swear by Everam and my hope of Heaven, I will take three vials and no more, to be used exclusively in search of your mother and Leesha and Olive am'Paper."

I nod and hold out my arm.

AUNT LEESHA CAST the bones once, poring over the throw for hours. The Damajah is quicker, using the other vials to ask follow-up questions, whispered with wards of silence around her and my bloodfather preventing even me from hearing her prayers. She faces away so I cannot read her lips, and her scent tells me nothing.

I've paced the room more times than I can count when I notice Selen lounging on a bench. "How can you be so calm?"

Selen shrugs. "I grew up watching Leesha waste countless hours staring at dice. Got bored of it a long time ago. Either they'll find something, or they won't. Ent a thing we can do about it." She lets out a deflating breath. "The way things look, we won't even get to see this through."

She's right about that. The price of asking Bloodfather's help was our liberty. Now that they have us, neither my bloodfather nor the general is likely to let us out of their sight again.

"Ent about us," I say. "Now that Bloodfather's involved, it'll get sorted quick. You'll see." Selen nods, and I wish I had half the confidence I'm pretending.

At last, Jardir and Inevera rise and come over to us.

"I do not believe your mother is dead, Darin am'Bales," the Damajah says. "The death of one so powerful leaves an imprint, and the *alagai hora* have found none such."

She says nothing of what she did see in the dice, only what she did not. "Then where is she?"

"The results are . . . inconclusive," Inevera says.

"We will find her," Jardir assures me. "We will find them both."

"And now for Olive." The Damajah takes her needle again, this time blooding both Selen and Jardir, mixing the blood of father and aunt into a passable substitute for Olive's.

"Do you have a personal item of Olive's to focus the throw?" Inevera asks.

Selen produces Olive's warded cloak, folded safe in her pack these many weeks. "Will this do?"

Inevera nods, returning to her silenced circle and spreading the cloak out like a casting cloth. The dice flash as she throws, and she stares at them a long time.

I watch my bloodfather's lips as he speaks in the ring of silence, reading them as easily as a book. "What do you see, *jiwah?*"

Inevera turns to look at him. Reckon she trusts the layers of her veils to cover her lips, but I squint and peer through. "She is in the one place you cannot go, husband."

Jardir's brow furrows. "There is nowhere I cannot go to reach Olive Paper."

Inevera gives a sad shake of her head, veils wafting after. "The prophecy stands. Now that the gates of Desert Spear have closed behind the Majah, they will not open again for you without bloodshed."

"If the Majah kidnapped my daughter," Jardir growls, "then bloodshed they shall have."

"It will wash away all hope of a reunified Krasia in your lifetime," Inevera says. "They have our *Jiwah Sen* Belina. Your son Iraven. Why is this different?"

"You know what Olive is," Jardir says. "You saw it yourself in the bones."

"No. I do not," Inevera tells him, "and neither do you. We know what she *might* be. Either Everam wills it so, or He does not."

"You said the same about me," Jardir says.

"Indeed," Inevera says, "and the account has yet to be audited in full."

What might she be? It's pointless to ask. I know they won't tell me. It will only inform them that I can read lips through a veil.

Jardir's knuckles press pale against his skin as he grips his spear. "Iraven and Belina are of Majah, and chose to remain with their people. Olive is not and did not. Aleveran cannot be allowed to hold her."

Again the Damajah shakes her head. "If you go, you will make matters worse."

"A worry for when I have found her mother," Jardir growls. He turns on a heel. "Darin, attend me."

I follow him out of the casting chamber to another room off the main court: his private study and map room. Books and scrolls line the walls, with great tables for research. He selects maps of the eastern mountains, laying them out for me to look over. I show him where we found the remains of the expedition, and the large area Aunt Leesha indicated where the city might be.

"Husband." Inevera appears at the door.

"Enough bones and cryptic words," Jardir says, striding from the chamber onto an open-air balcony. "I will seek my blood sister and my intended. While I am gone, you are to divine a way to return Olive to us, or I will visit the Majah next, and the dice be damned."

He grips his spear in both hands then, and it begins to glow brighter and brighter. Then he holds it in the air and it pulls him aloft. Up off the balcony he rises, then he twists in midair and flies off into the night.

The Damajah doesn't shout. She doesn't tsst. Nothing breaks the perfect serenity on her face.

But she smells furious.

37

SPEAR & OLIVE

"OLIVE, LOOK OUT!" Chadan cries.

The demon leaps at me from above as we pass an abandoned clay dwelling. It moves so fast I barely see more than tooth and talon and razor scales. I pivot, bringing my shield into position. My spear drops low, ready to stab up beneath once the *alagai* fetches against the wards.

I needn't have bothered. Faseek, Thivan, and Parkot close ranks around me before the demon even gets close, overlapping their shields in a clover lock. The demon is only four feet from snout to tail, but sand demons are heavier than they look. Two hundred pounds of tooth and claw and cabled muscle slams against the shields, but the wards flare, absorbing the impact. My brothers are braced against the rebound, and the formation holds.

Like synchronized dancers, we break apart as Gorvan steps up and thrusts his spear, skewering the demon through its poorly armored belly as it hangs in midair. Gorvan falls back, guiding with his spear as gravity does the work of throwing the *alagai* into the kill zone at the center of our unit formation. No sooner has the demon struck the ground than it is pierced by half a dozen spears.

Still the pinned creature thrashes. I spin my weapon across my shoulders and bring it down hard enough to behead the demon with the broad blade of my spearhead.

"Are there more?" I look to Chadan, but our Ka isn't watching. He's kept his eyes forward, trusting in his warriors to neutralize the threat as Watchers report in.

"This neighborhood is crawling with them." Chadan's voice is tight. "An entire pack of sand demons broke off chase from the Baiters of Kai Fiza's Viper Unit. A dozen at least."

"And the Sharum Ka sends us to clean it up," Gorvan spits. "While the pampered Vipers sip couzi, safe in their warded ambush pocket."

Chadan whirls on him so quickly the larger boy stumbles back. "The Sharum Ka sent his best men!" He clashes his spear against his shield.

That's my cue. "Let the other *kai* cower in their hiding places while we rob them of glory! Do we fear a pack of," I pause to spit, "*sand* demons?"

Our warriors clash their spears against their shields in response. "No, my princes!"

The men have good reason to be afraid. I feel it, too. But there's nothing to be done but embrace the feeling and let it go.

Some parts of the Maze are carefully crafted to bestow every advantage on *Sharum* holding the ground, but most parts are like this one, flattened neighborhoods our ancestors ceded to the *alagai* in their retreat after the Return. Abandoned homes, schools, temples. Public fountains and marketplaces. Like a layer of Nie's abyss, the terrain is a reminder of our fate, should we falter before the *alagai*.

Over the years the *Sharum* scavenged some buildings for material to reinforce others, providing layers of protection for warriors as they advance from the safety of the inner city, or draw the demons into traps with a choreographed retreat. The walls here are unwarded, encouraging the predatory instincts of the *alagai* as they chase warriors to ambush points.

But that works against us when the demons break off pursuit. With ample cover, the *alagai* make full use of their natural advantages. Sand demon talons are hard as steel, and they can cling to walls and ceilings as easily as flat ground. Worse, they hunt cooperatively. Those we see are dangerous enough, but it's the unseen ones that keep my stomach in a twist. Given a moment's surprise, a sand demon can take down a strong warrior before he can bring his weapon to bear.

But neither are the *alagai* prepared for my brothers and me. Comprised of an entire crop of *nie'Sharum* from every blood and caste, we are the largest unit in the Maze. The oldest of us are younger than any other warrior in Krasia, the youngest not yet at their full strength, yet we top the kill counts night after night.

I was scared of the Maze, at first. Scared of getting hurt, or scarred, or dying. But more and more, I hunger for it during the day. Here, with Chadan, surrounded by my brothers as death comes for us, is where I feel most alive.

I break the warriors into shield teams to search the buildings as others keep watch on the streets. Chadan's scouts come and go as he directs the overall operation.

We corner a pair of demons in back of one of the cramped buildings, but as we press the attack, two more drop down from a hidden ledge.

They're getting smarter.

Faseek shield-bashes one of the demons in midair, knocking it prone for Thivan and Parkot to stab. Levan is not so quick, and the other demon lands on his shoulders, driving him to his knees with the impact.

I am closest, but I can't risk hitting Levan with a spear thrust, and a shield rush won't knock it away before it can rip out his unarmored throat.

Instead I drop my spear and shield, reaching out to grab the demon's ridged tail.

Like a thousand shards of glass, the demon's scales shred the thick leather of my gloves as its tail writhes in my grip, but I am able to yank it off Levan in time.

The sand demon falls backward toward me. I let go of the tail and snatch one of its wrists, snaking the other hand under its armpit for a hold behind its head. I drop to my back, hooking my ankles around its powerful thighs.

The *alagai* is stronger than me, but I am not afraid. I have leverage and physics on my side, redirecting its limbs to keep the demon off its feet. It throws its head back, nearly managing to gore my face with its horns, but then my brothers are there.

Menin and Parkot still carry the clubs they used that first night we fought, though with stronger wardings. They use them now to batter and stun the demon while Faseek and Thivan produce heavy cleavers that look more suited to a butcher shop than a warrior's kit. They hack the demon to pieces with the warded blades, showering me in black ichor that sizzles against my armor's wards.

We continue our steady press, clearing buildings and exterminating demons as we sweep the neighborhood. Faseek chops the horns from every demon we kill—fourteen sand demons in total—before we pronounce the neighborhood clear.

"The Princes Unit returns," Kai Fiza calls as we join the warriors mustering for count before dawn.

Fiza pronounces it *princess* and I bristle, knowing it is as an insult directed at me. I've heard other *Sharum* using it. There are sniggers from the crowd.

Fiza is larger than me, but past his prime. As a fellow *kai*, there is nothing stopping me from blacking his eye. I take a step forward.

"Peace, brother." Chadan's gentle hand on my arm is all it takes to calm my raging heart. Inner peace radiates from my *ajin'pal*, and when I am with him, sometimes I can find just a little of it.

"I am glad to see you well, Kai Fiza!" Chadan calls. "I feared you might have injured your backside, sitting while we cleared the *alagai* your Baiters lost."

Many of the mustered warriors laugh at that, and it is the Viper Unit's turn to bristle. Kai Fiza looks ready to retort when Chadan lifts a finger.

On cue, Faseek takes the sack off his shoulder and drops it to the ground, spilling sand demon horns into the dust. The sight quiets whatever Fiza was about to say, and even the other *kai* stare jealously at the pile.

"Well done, my precocious warriors," Iraven calls, striding over with his hands spread. "What you lack in years, you make up in ferocity."

A niggle of irritation returns at the sight of my brother. Iraven's bravery is undeniable, but the band around my arm is a constant reminder that I cannot trust him. His words sound like praise, but there is condescension in them, as well.

But there is no condescension from Iraven's tally man, who counts the horns, making a note in his ledger. Our purses will be full this week.

"Any losses?" Iraven asks.

"None," Chadan says proudly. We haven't lost a warrior in the weeks since Waning, though we have been in the thick of battle almost every night. We still train with Chikga during the day, and keep the youngest from the front lines, but all have shed blood and ichor in the Maze.

There is good cheer as we return to the pavilions for meat and couscous. "Join us in the harem, brothers!" Gorvan calls, his arms already around the necks of Menin and Parkot. "Let the *Jiwah'Sharum* soothe the aches from your body!"

My face heats and I look away as Gorvan laughs, half dragging the others along with him. When we've been seen and congratulated our brothers, Chadan and I steal away to the sweat room.

It has become a ritual now, wearing only towels as we scrape the sweat from each other, seeking out the many scrapes and bruises of a night's battle and lovingly tending them.

Tales of the demon war lionize elders who put down canes and picked up weapons when all seemed lost. Magic shaved whole summers off their bodies, slowly nudging them toward their physical primes.

But the changes magic wrought upon those who lifted a warded spear or axe before their full growth were no less pronounced.

Feedback magic has wrought changes on all my spear brothers in the weeks since we entered the Maze, but I am most intimate with the changes upon Chadan. He is taller and heavier with muscle, voice deepened and a beard beginning to shadow his cheeks.

I, too, have put on inches and pounds of muscle, but my voice— never high to begin with—hasn't changed significantly. Neither has more hair sprouted on my face than the occasional stray Grandmum Elona used to mercilessly pluck.

My breast has broadened, but not the heavy swell of Mother or Grandmum. Nothing that would show through *Sharum* robes, much less armor. Here in the sweat room my reflection simply seems thick with muscle from the front, but in profile I have a more feminine shape. Chadan has never commented on it, but I've taken to wearing my towel higher to flatten my shadow.

With magic augmenting our healing, even Chadan's wounds are all closed. Scabs slough away as I run the sweat scraper over his shoulder, revealing pink lines of flesh on his brown skin. Soon even those will darken to his natural color.

"You need better armor," I note. "They found the seam between the plates in your robe."

Chadan leans back into the brush. "Father has already commissioned something 'worthy of the heir of Majah.' "

Now that he has earned the white veil, Chadan has come back into the family wealth he was denied while in *nie'Sharum* robes. I can see how it discomfits him after so long in the austerity of *sharaj*. His response has been generosity, using his personal funds to outfit our warriors with fine spears, shields, and armor plates of light, indestructible warded glass tucked into the pockets of their robes.

Despite the new equipment, many—like Menin and Parkot—still carry as well the crude weapons they made themselves that first night, tucked away like my *hanzhar* for use if they are ever separated from their spears.

I shudder, remembering how just a few short hours ago I dropped my spear and shield, wrestling a sand demon with my bare hands. In the heat of battle, I hadn't given it a second thought, but now it feels so reckless. A move born of desperation.

"The *alagai* are getting smarter," I say.

Chadan nods. "Dodging the Baiters. Choosing favorable terrain. Luring us into a building where their clutchmates lay in wait. There are similar reports from all over the Maze."

He shakes his head. "I should not have shamed Kai Fiza and the Vipers. We may need their loyalty one day."

"They insulted us first." The vehemence in my tone surprises even me. Battle magic doesn't just make you strong. It heightens emotions, anger chief among them. I regulate my breath, calming myself.

"The Vipers are an ambush unit," Chadan says, "and good at what they do. But they are used to preparing every inch of their terrain, knowing where the enemy will be, and where they can retreat to. They would have been torn apart hunting sand demons through abandoned buildings. Fiza knows this. His jeering was just a weak attempt to salve his pride."

He shakes his head. "I must rise above such things, if I mean to lead. Your brother may have given us the Viper's glory, but we did not need to take their honor, as well. I fear Iraven is deliberately sowing dissent between us and the other units."

I hadn't thought of that. "To what end?"

Chadan purses his lips and does not reply. I put down the scraper and knead his shoulders with my hands, working the knots from his muscles with strong fingers. "My brother kidnapped me from my home and sold me to your father. I have no love for him, but why would he want to turn the other warriors against us?"

"Think on it," Chadan says. "My grandfather will sit the Skull Throne for another decade, at least. If he lives as long as his predecessor, it could be three times that. And my father is still young. I will never be *Damaji* while he lives. To prevent me from becoming a rival, they made me take the black, with the intent of making me Sharum Ka."

At last, I understand. "But then the storms worsened, and a Sharum Ka was needed while you were still in your bido."

Chadan nods. "Prince Iraven was already a man, the most famous *kai* in the Maze, and ambitious. Your father still has loyalists among the Majah. Those who feel shame for deserting the Deliverer's army on the eve of Sharak Ka. They count many warriors among their number, and follow the son of Jardir. When the *alagai* returned in force, Grandfather gave him more and more dangerous tasks, hoping to see him fail and his threat be removed."

"But he never failed," I say.

Chadan nods. "Iraven's loyalists and seer mother keep him safe. And now that he has the power, he's doing to us what my grandfather did to him. We will be sent into the thick of every battle until we are dead, or our glory outweighs his."

"That's insane." Even as I say the word, I realize it isn't the one I'm looking for. "Monstrous. And to what end? I'm no threat to him. I wouldn't even be here if not for him."

"Dama'ting Belina's dice produced a convenient prophecy that allowed Iraven to trade his sister for the white turban," Chadan says.

"But I wasn't a sister," I say, feeling that awful twisting in my gut.

"A daughter of Ahmann Jardir is a limited threat. A son, however . . ."

"No one wanted that," I say.

Chadan shrugs, smiling in a way he would never dare in front of the other warriors. "I don't mind."

I stare, smiling like an idiot until he clears his throat. "Even if you were no threat to Iraven, certainly I am. If I prove myself in the Maze, I will be seen as his natural successor for the white turban. So long as Jardir loyalists control the warriors of the tribe, Grandfather is not fully in control."

"Perhaps that's a good thing," I say. "A balance of power does more to keep the peace than men's honor."

"I assure you, I want the white turban no more than you," Chadan says. "But if I am forced to choose between glory in the Maze and dying for your brother's convenience, I will choose glory."

"From your lips to Everam's ears," I say.

We leave the private sweat lodge and go into Chadan's pavilion. It's not just the men who benefit from our Ka's new wealth. His pavilion is lavish, with fresh towels and robes of black silk waiting for us. We spend our days luxuriating, eating fresh fruit and a rich variety of savories that seem all the more decadent after months of nothing but gruel, couscous, and spiced meat.

The air in the *Sharum* pavilion is hot and thick, a rank mix of spiced sweat and couzi breath, coupled with the ever-present nostril-burning stink of vomit from overindulgent warriors trying to forget the Maze. The air in Chadan's pavilion is cool, lightly scented with incense and bowls of dried flowers.

Instead of scooping cups from a communal bucket, we drink cool water from crystal glasses with speared olives floating atop them to add flavor. A chilled pitcher collects moisture on a tray, with servants waiting to refill it.

It feels so decadent, but I can't deny I love it. Longed for it. I was raised in a place like this, and unlike pampered Princess Olive, I have earned the luxury, trading blood for ichor in *alagai'sharak*. Why shouldn't I wear silk during the day, when each night might be my last?

"There is glory yet to come, for the Princess Unit," I say. Outside this chamber, the name is an insult, but between us, it is a private joke, warm and intimate as a caress.

"*Inevera*." Chadan touches his water with a fingertip, letting a single drop fall to the carpet. The ritual sacrifice of something so precious is meant to fend off the misfortune that befalls those who are prideful before Everam.

"The Vipers have snakes painted on their shields," I note, "and sewn as patches on their robes. Our men wear only their house emblems, if they even have one." Chadan's armor, robe, and shield are adorned with the lone spear of the Majah tribe. My own are blank.

"You are a son of Ahmann Jardir," Chadan says. "You have every right to bear House Jardir's sigil."

I shake my head. I could draw the spear, cloak, and crown of Father's house sigil with my eyes closed, but I have never felt a part of it. "I don't even know him, Chadan, or him me. I am not Olive am'Jardir. I am Olive Paper."

"Then your mother's sigil," Chadan suggests.

"My mother's sigil is a mortar and pestle surrounded by herbs," I say. "It doesn't precisely fill enemy hearts with fear."

"Most established units have their own emblem," Chadan muses. "It gives the men pride. Perhaps it's time we made our own."

My nose crinkles as he falls into my trap. "I already have."

I tug at my collar, folding back the lapel of my robe to show the icon I embroidered onto the silk. I worried my hands had lost their touch, but making clothes was my first love, and my needlework is nimble as ever.

Chadan leans in for a closer look. The sigil I've made resembles the Spear of Majah, but driven through an olive, much like the ones flavoring our drinks.

"Not the most fearsome sigil," I acknowledge, "but better than a mortar and pestle."

Chadan shakes his head. "It's perfect."

I fold back my lapel to hide the patch again, giving the spot a soft pat.

"I keep it close to my heart." I don't bother to retighten my robe as I lean in close. "I made one for you . . . if you want."

Chadan touches my face gently, but the world falls away until all I can feel are his fingers. "I would wear it with pride."

I reach into my satchel, producing a patch and a needle with fine thread. Gently, I fold back his robe, baring a bit of his chest as I measure the length of his lapel to position the patch properly. I take the needle to stitch it in place when Chadan lays a hand over mine. "No."

I look at him, confused for a moment, then increasingly stung as the word hangs in the air.

Chadan pushes it aside with a kiss. We share them frequently now, when alone in his pavilion. His lips linger on mine until the tension leaves me. Gorvan and the others might need to prove themselves men in the harem, but Chadan and I are in no hurry to move on to other things when sharing warmth and kisses still feels stolen and triumphant.

"Some things we have to hide," Chadan whispers, taking the patch from me, "but not our brotherhood." He lets his lapel fall back into place and lays the spear and olive directly on the front of his robe, over his heart like other *Sharum* units.

"Sew it here."

I lift the needle, but my hand is shaking. Wearing the patch openly credits us both with leadership of the Princes Unit, something the other *kai* have refused to acknowledge. But more, it declares our partnership.

For once, I don't have to hide. I may still wear a shackle, but I have never felt so free.

38

BROTHER

I LOOK UP AS Chadan enters the pavilion, and in that moment's distraction, the needle slides clear through the meat of my thumb.

"Night!" I hiss. It doesn't hurt . . . yet. Just a sensation of wrongness, an alien presence in my flesh. I haven't stuck myself in years.

"Why are you still doing that?" Chadan asks.

"Everyone wants a spear and olive patch, now." I pull the needle free, put pressure on the wound. *That* hurts, but it closes quickly. There are thimbles in the sewing kit, but Mother always disdained them.

Sometimes the best cure is a callus, she would say. I've gained many, these past months, but it seems I've lost some, as well.

"Montidahr has a surprisingly steady hand at painting shields," I say, "but he can no more meet the demand than I can."

"No." Chadan comes to sit beside me. "Why are *you*, Prince Olive asu'Ahmann, sewing? Get a woman to do it."

I blink at him. "Eh?"

Chadan shakes his head. "You are a *kai'Sharum*! This is beneath you. And Montidahr, for that matter. Give Tikka a handful of draki. She'll go to the bazaar and have a women's circle sew and paint more in one night than you could in a year—and come back with change."

Relief floods through me. Designing and making patches for Chadan and myself was intimate and pleasurable. Sewing more than a hundred of them is tedium, and not a good use of my time, especially today.

It is the first day of Waning.

"You will have to cut short your visit with your sister," Chadan says. "Grandfather has bade the Sharum Ka to convene a final war council this afternoon, and we are commanded to attend."

It is a tremendous honor. Not every *kai* attends war council. But like Iraven, our glory in the Maze speaks for itself. Everyone in that room will be my enemy, but that makes earning a place there all the more satisfying. No matter what our disputes in the day, none of us wants demons in the city again.

"The preparations are complete," Chadan says. "Every district in the city has active evacuation routes now, and everyone is expected belowground before sunset. Only the *Sharum* will be in the city tonight."

"We've done what we can," I agree, but a cold knot of fear twists my stomach. I know he feels it, too. If there truly is a mind demon out there, we have no way to guess what fresh torment the abyss will spit forth when the sun sets.

"Best not to dwell on it," he tells me. "Waning is about enjoying our loved ones, not worrying over sunset."

I lay my hand over his. "You're right. It is."

Now that I have taken the veil, the Krasians consider me a man. I am barred from the harem, and must meet Micha in the public gardens instead. Chadan walks with me as I go seeking her through the maze of hedges on the outskirts of the garden of Sharik Hora.

The same architects that built the killing Maze that protects our city also designed this tribute to life, a labyrinth of green that creates countless secluded bowers around fountains, statues, and grand perennials. It's one of the most beautiful places I've ever been, and Chadan laughs whenever I stop to smell a flower.

Again, I think of Mother, and how she seemed to devote more of her attention to her garden than to me. I didn't appreciate growing up in those gardens until I spent a few months in the sand.

A voice cuts through the bushes and I recognize my sister, but not her girlish laughter. I pick up speed, following the sounds until we round a last hedge and see her.

My sister is veiled and scarved in silk *dal'ting* blacks, looking more like the woman I have always known than the painted beauty in colored pillow silk I saw on my last visit.

But a man stands with her amid the blooms. Our eyes widen as we recognize Kai Fiza. Micha is facing away from us, but Fiza sees our approach. A hint of smile plays at his lips as he leans in, murmuring something close to Micha's ear.

My sister shrieks with laughter in response, and I know something is wrong. I've never heard her laugh like that in my entire life. She lays a hand on his chest for support, letting it linger.

"The abyss has frozen," I whisper.

"Nonsense," Chadan says. "This is natural as the rain, if every bit as rare. It is good."

"Good?" Micha is already married, and to a woman. I've never known her to have the slightest interest in men, and she hates the Majah. None of this makes sense.

"Children will settle her," Chadan says. I look at him, incredulous, but he only smiles, oblivious to his condescension. "And if she stays, I'm in less danger of losing you."

I am not sure if I want to kiss him or punch him, but I can do neither with Fiza watching. There is no shame in men showing love for one another, but a relationship between Chadan and me would be more than just gossip about *push'ting* princes.

Worse, Chadan brings up questions I am not prepared to think about. I have no intention of spending the rest of my life in Krasia, but the thought of leaving Chadan is difficult to reconcile. As always, I shove the thought aside to worry over another day.

Kai Fiza gives a fine bracelet to Micha, and she literally hops with excitement as he slips it on and they both admire it.

With a bow, Fiza takes his leave, walking past us to exit the bowers. "My princess."

"Breathe," Chadan whispers as I clench a fist. "I will see you at the war council." Then he, too, is gone.

"Sister." Micha glides over to me. The word sounds strange after so much time surrounded by my spear brothers. "Black suits you." She touches my face, brushing her hand up under my turban to run her fingers through the soft carpet of black atop my head. "Your hair is already coming back." Her hand falls to the white silk fallen loose around my neck. "And a *kai's* veil. I am so proud of you."

Her fingers drop lower, gliding gently over the spear and olive patch, and I take a step back. "Enough demonshit, Micha," I snap. "What in the Core did I just see? Kai Fiza?!"

"Tsst!" Micha hisses. "Keep your voice down and embrace me, you fool girl."

The sudden return to the sister I know takes away my discomfort, if not my confusion. I take her in my arms, squeezing gratefully. She smells as she always has, but something about the embrace feels different. Suddenly, it dawns on me. Every hug, since I was in swaddling, was Micha holding me. Now I am holding her, and it feels alien, like the needle in my flesh. I break the embrace.

"They guarded me too closely when I resisted," Micha says. "But in the end, even the *dama'ting* see what they want to see. The Majah believe they returned to the desert before their women could be 'corrupted' by Northern heresies. To them, even a *Sharum'ting* is just another witless girl at heart, handed a spear when what she truly wants is a husband whose glory exceeds her own."

I snort. "You won't find that in Kai Fiza. His men are skilled at attacking demons from behind, but they fold like paper when the *alagai* turn and fight."

Micha cocks her head at me. "You even sound like them. It's an impressive illusion."

"It's not an illusion," I say.

Once again she tilts her head, studying me. "Perhaps not, but neither is it the whole of you, sister."

Again, that word. Perhaps the most alien of all.

"Today, we escape." Micha speaks so quietly it takes a moment for the words to register.

I start when my mind catches up. "What?!"

"Tsst!" Micha hisses again. "Listen closely. The morning of each Waning, Prince Iraven meets with his mother for precisely two hours, ending at highsun. After that, she retreats into her Chamber of Shadows until the war council."

"So?" I ask.

"The water Belina finds waiting for her will be drugged," Micha says. "As will the cloth I slip over her mouth. It is death to kill or even strike a *dama'ting*, but putting one to sleep . . . " She shrugs. "A superficial cut behind the shoulder blade will be enough to fill a tear bottle with blood without her ever noticing. Enough to open the blood locks and set us free."

My hand drifts over to the armlet. I'm so used to it now, it feels like a part of me. More than once, its wards have turned the teeth of an *alagai*.

"Just after highsun, meet me by the statue of Inevera in the lower hall. There is a *Sharum'ting* tunnel there that will get us into the undercity. The Holy Undercity is designed to keep demons out, not people in. We slip out into one of the outer districts by nightfall, and blend in until I . . . " she holds up the gold bracelet Kai Fiza gave her, ". . . can sell the generous gifts of my suitors and use the funds to purchase supplies for a trek through the desert."

My mind reels. Leave? Today? Before the Majah and their Thesan thralls shelter in the undercity? Before my spear brothers muster and hold their breath, waiting for an attack that is sure to come? Before I can see Chadan again? I can't desert them all, in their hour of need.

An hour ago I thought escape all but impossible. A distant worry. Micha makes it sound so plausible I'm forced to make a decision here and now. "No."

"They will expect us to head for the Oasis of Dawn," Micha goes on, "but we will . . . eh?"

"We're not heading anywhere," I say. "I'm not ready to leave."

"You're not rea—" Micha cuts herself off. "Tsst! Silly, stupid girl! You would sell yourself to the Majah for a white veil and spear? At least Iraven took a throne in exchange for his honor."

"I'm not the one giggling like an idiot at every man that gives me a bracelet," I growl. "Tonight is Waning. The *alagai* nearly took the city last month. Am I to abandon my brothers?"

"This is not your fight," Micha says. "The Majah chose to abandon the Deliverer's army in Sharak Ka, and this is their punishment."

She's wrong. I feel it deep in my bones. "It's all our fight. You said yourself the demons are hunting me."

Micha nods. "And the Majah brought their attention here by stealing you from the safety of your mother's greatwards."

"What difference does that make, with the sun about to set?" I demand. "Isn't that the first law of our people? All men are brothers in the night."

Micha shakes her head. "We are not men, sister."

But Micha doesn't understand. I'm still in a box to her. Selen was the only person who ever came close to getting it, and she's a thousand miles away, safe in Hollow.

"How do you know what I am?" I ask. "How does anyone, when I don't even know, myself?"

Micha reaches out, taking my hand. "Sister, please. This is what *sharaj* does. It breaks you and rebuilds you in the image the drillmasters desire. You mustn't lose yourself."

She still doesn't get it. "I'm not losing anything. If anything, I'm finally finding myself. Without you reporting my every move to Mother. Without Grandmum dressing me like a doll, painting my face and calling it armor. Without Mother forcing me to become an herb gathering witch, no matter what I want. While *alagai* gathered, I was left on a pedestal. Why? Because Mother flipped a klat and decided I was a girl?"

"Tsst!" Micha hisses. "Do not speak of your mother so disrespectfully. You have no idea what she's done for you. The dice . . . "

She trails off without saying more, and the omission angers me most of all. Even now, she keeps secrets, nudging me toward some future Mother finds favorable. I see Mother's condescending face illuminated in the glow of her *alagai hora* and I want to scream.

"Always the dice." The words come out in a growl. "No more lies, you swore to me, sister, but you hold Mother's secrets, still."

Micha tries to meet my stare, but she cannot hold it long, and drops her eyes. "Of course you are correct, sister, but it is not just your mother's secret. When you were born, Duchess Paper cast the dice in your birthing blood, but Damaji'ting Amanvah, our eldest sister, attended her and confirmed the throw. The Damajah herself studied their findings. All of them agreed."

"Agreed. To. What." I bite off each word, their taste foul in my mouth.

Micha falls into her breath, and her voice goes cold. "That too many of the futures where you presented male were . . . short."

"Short?" I ask. "What does that mean?"

"It means you died before reaching adulthood," Micha says. "They concluded your chances of surviving childhood were higher as a girl."

"My . . . chances of survival?" I can't believe what I'm hearing. My whole identity, my entire upbringing, was a hedged bet? "What do my chances of survival have to do with who I am?"

"We are what life makes us, sister," Micha says.

Again that word, like a needle stuck through the heart of me.

"Brother!" I snap, and it feels right.

Micha is taken aback for a moment, but she takes a deep breath and immediately her tension eases. She nods. "Brother. Forgive me if it takes some getting used to."

I'm so ready for a fight it takes a moment for the concession to sink in.

"It changes nothing about our situation," Micha says. "We are prisoners of the Majah, and have a moral right to escape."

"We're not prisoners of the Majah," I say, "we're prisoners of the dice."

"All things serve Everam's will," Micha says.

The words only anger me further. I've seen no evidence Everam—or the Creator for that matter—even exist, much less speak to folk through dice of demonbone. The foretellings may come to pass, but there is nothing holy about the *alagai hora*. Just *dama'ting* ambition.

"Did you know the Watcher who gave you the scar in my nursery wasn't trying to kill me?" I ask. "He was after blood for a foretelling."

Micha's face hardens. "That is little better. Do not weep for his death. Chavis and Belina have no right to steal blood without consent."

"How is that different from casting in my birthing blood?" I ask. "I didn't consent to that, either."

Micha looks aghast. "Because one was done by your enemies, and one by your *mother*."

There's a sour taste in my mouth. Have Mother's foretellings served me better? "It doesn't matter if what Belina saw was true. The Majah are losing ground to the *alagai*, and without me, it will only worsen."

"You cannot possibly know that," Micha says. "If you leave Desert Spear, the demons may turn their attention elsewhere."

I shake my head, reciting Belina's prophecy:

"The storms will end when the heir of Hollow joins blood with the Majah, and the princess stands in the eye."

"That could mean many things," Micha says.

I nod. "Even Belina did not fully understand, because she and Chavis believed me a girl when they cast the dice."

"Why does that matter?" Micha asks.

"It's not 'princess,' it's *princes*," I say. "Chadan and I command the Princes Unit, and it is Waning. I am meant to be here, sister. If such a thing exists, it is *inevera*."

"Princes." Micha lifts her jaw like she finally understands. "So this is about Chadan."

I glare at her. "What about him?"

"Harem gossip has the two of you inseparable." She pokes a finger into the spear and olive patch on my breast. "Is that what this means? Has he put his spear into you?"

I smack her hand away. "Of course not! How dare you!" I raise a hand as if to strike her, and she eyes it with a single raised brow. Even now, after months of training and fighting in the Maze, I do not know if I am anything close to a match for my sister. I lower my hand, but it does little to defuse my sudden anger.

"He is Majah," Micha says. "He cannot be trusted."

"Nor can your judgment," I snap, "when you lay it equally upon thirty thousand people, to justify walking away when they have demons at the walls. Chadan is my *ajin'pal*. I trust him with my life."

"What am I, then?" Micha demands. "Did we not bleed together in the night, months before your Majah rebirth? Have you forgotten that you would be dead on *alagai* talons if not for me?"

"No," I say. "But I might not have been in danger in the first place if you hadn't lied to me for my entire life. If you'd prepared me for the night as you were bade. Instead I was sent to Herb Lore and given a sewing kit."

I straighten my back. "You and Mother were so fixated on protecting me, you never gave me the means to protect myself. The Majah have."

"They care nothing for you," Micha says.

"They came back for me!" I snap. "Chadan came back. Last Waning, the demons recognized me. They came for me as one—every demon on the streets. But Chadan . . . "

Micha tilts her head. "You love him."

"What? Don't be ridiculous."

"What is ridiculous?" Micha asks. "I have seen Prince Chadan. He is Majah, but there is no denying he is beautiful. I hope he is who you think he is. I hope he is *what* you think he is. But in the end, the Majah will do what is best for the Majah. You are still a prisoner here. We both are."

"I was," I say. "But no longer. I will not abandon my spear brother as storms gather. I have seen Majah honor, and it is not what you told me. Why should I believe you now?"

Micha shrugs. "If you think me wrong, ask Belina to unlock your armlet."

I scowl. She's right, of course, but deliberately missing the point.

It's not yet highsun. I am allowed hours yet with my sister, but I've had enough for one day. I turn to go.

Micha lays a hand on my arm. "Olive."

"If you want to go home, sister, then go." I pull myself free and start walking. "I don't need you to rescue me anymore."

For three nights, we patrol the walls and city, ready for the storm, but all is quiet this Waning. Not even the night's usual scattering of demons to lure into the Maze.

The idle time is not what I need. I would rather be holding back the jaws and talons of a pack of demons than wallowing in my own anguish. I cannot turn my back on my spear brothers, on Chadan, but is turning my back on Micha any better? Regardless of how I feel about her secrets, I cannot deny she has devoted her life to protecting me, and in return I am leaving her stranded. I know her well enough to understand she will never leave without me.

"What is it?" Chadan asks for the thousandth time. He knows something is bothering me, but he cannot discern what.

I deflect the question. "Where are they?"

Chadan casts his gaze out into the night and sighs. "Perhaps the storm is passed. Perhaps we broke them when their assault failed last month."

I can see in his eyes he doesn't believe that any more than I do. There is no fighting in the city, yet I feel no safer. Something is still in the air, a tension I cannot name, infecting everyone. The entire unit shifts its feet uneasily.

This isn't safety. It is the silence before the strike.

39

·

A SILK PRISON

Y ELATION AT seeing my bloodfather fly off to search for Mam and Aunt Leesha dampens quickly when I realize he's left us alone with the Damajah, and she is not pleased. Selen senses it, too. She smells like a trapped hare.

Inevera touches one of the charms on her bracelet, activating a ward. A moment later, the doors open and a pair of her eunuch servants appear. The men are thick with muscle, clad in loose black pants and black vests. The golden bands around their wrists and ankles are meant to symbolize subservience, but they glow with magic, empowering the men to enforce her will.

Rojvah once told me the *dama'ting* cut the tongues from their eunuchs, but I couldn't tell if she was serious or just telling ale stories. All I know is I've never heard one speak, and I hear everything.

"Escort the children to the family residence to await the girl's father and his honor guard."

The children. I ent one for long goodbyes, but the coldness of her dismissal is striking now that Jardir is gone. She doesn't even look at us.

I glance at Selen and am relieved to see her tip her head toward the door. We count our blessings and hustle out of the room quick as dignity allows.

———

THE TWINS ARE waiting when we return to our chambers.

Rojvah strides up to me, smelling so angry I instinctively turn slippery before I even see the slap, too quick to dodge.

"Ay!" Selen barks.

Rojvah ignores her. The blow slides off my slippery cheek, but she keeps advancing. I stumble back until I sense the wall behind me. Slippery and quick, I could still escape, but Selen is moving our way, and it won't end well if I give her a clear path.

I flinch as Rojvah raises her arms, but then she throws them around me, and pulls me into an embrace. "Tsst, Darin! Why didn't you tell us about your mother?!"

Night. How did she find out already? "Might as well have, since nobody in this palace can keep a rippin' secret."

"Do not be a fool," Rojvah snaps. "Grandmother spoke the news into my earring because I have a right to know. We are family."

She means it. She smells protective, like Selen whenever anyone other than her or Olive tries to bully me. I've never smelled that on Rojvah, and instinctively I go solid, returning the embrace. "I'm to tell honest word, I always got the impression you and Arick didn't like me."

"Of course we don't like you," Arick says. "You're family."

Rojvah laughs, Selen snorts, and for once even I get the joke. All my cousins on Grandda's farm, I don't much like any of them, and the feeling's mutual. But if someone hurt one of them, or the twins . . .

My throat tightens. "You're right. I should have told you. I'm sorry."

"We forgive you." Rojvah gives me a last squeeze before letting go. "Family does that, too. And do not fear. Grandmother told us so that we could provide for you in your time of need. No one else knows."

Arick looms at her shoulder. There is no scent of challenge on him now, only sadness. "It will be all right. The Shar'Dama Ka will find them."

I want to believe it, but remembering the field of dead where we found Mam's knife, it's hard to hold on to hope.

The quarters we've been given are fancy, full of silk and velvet and servants to cater to our needs, but even with their wards of silence and alomom powder, I can sense the Damajah's eunuch guards outside the doors. They'll call it protection, but we all know they're to keep us from goin' anywhere before Uncle Gared comes to fetch us. Ent the Bunker, but even a silk prison is a prison.

And what of Olive? Is she truly captive in Desert Spear, across countless miles of sunburnt waste? Once Uncle Gared gets here, we may never find out.

I'M SOUND ASLEEP when the world fills with fire. Stinging light blazes through my eyelids, and my skin feels like someone emptied a boiling kettle on me. I shriek, curling up with my arms over my head as I reach out with my other senses. A rustle of heavy cloth. Slippered feet. Familiar scents. The serving women have come with breakfast and drawn the morning curtains.

"Ay, what in the Core's the matter with you?!" Selen barks.

"Apologies, Highness," one of the women says. "We only thought to—"

"Shut the damn curtain!" I hear the rush of air as Selen throws a pillow clear across the room to thump against the cloth beside the woman. "Can't you see it's hurting him?!"

"Of course, Highness." Curtains rustle and the light recedes as the women hurry to comply.

"What kind of man is hurt by the sun?" one of them whispers, thinking her voice too low to hear.

"They say Shar'Dama Ka's greenland bloodson was born in the abyss," the other whispers back. "He has *alagai* blood."

"Everam preserve us."

I'm not surprised. I heard a palace servant call me "*alagai* blood" once before. Asked Mam about it, and she dragged me back to the Brook that same day. Ent been back since. I hoped the rumors had died away, but in my heart I knew better.

The light winks out, and it's like cool water on my skin. I crack my eyes open just as the women pass my bed of pillows. They draw wards in the air as they pass.

"Ay, you've got cheek!" Selen sounds more like Elona berating a servant than herself. She leaps from her own bed of pillows, shouting curses at the women's backs as they scurry out the door.

As soon as it closes she comes over to sit beside me, but she knows me well enough not to touch. "You all right, Darin?"

"Ay." I groan, but already I'm cooling off, eyes readjusting. "Just surprised, is all."

"Don't pay those women any mind, Darin. They don't know you like we do."

"Who's we?" I ask. "Mam and Leesha are gone, Jardir with them. For all we know, Olive's on the other side of the desert. Ent no one else who knows me."

Slowly, she slides her hand over mine. Not grabbing. Not squeezing. Just a gentle, soothing weight, like a warm blanket.

"Why does it burn?" she asks quietly.

If anyone else had asked, I would have gotten defensive, but she has that protective smell, and I know I can trust her.

I shrug. "Reckon it's my demon blood."

"That ent funny, Darin," she says. "Dangerous, having folk spread a lie like that."

"Ent a lie," I say. "Mam and Da both ate demon meat. It's why they had powers other folk din't. Gatherers say you are what you eat."

"Folk in Hollow ate a lot of rabbit stew during the war," Selen says. "Mum and Da love the stuff, but I never touch it. You reckon that makes me part bunny?"

"Always thought you had long ears," I say.

Selen smiles. "And a nose that twitches when someone avoids a question."

"Whatever the reason," I allow, "magic clings to the air around me like a stink. Sunlight burns magic away. When the light hits me too sudden, it feels like I'm on fire. If I keep to the shadows and let it burn off gradually, it doesn't hurt as much."

"As much?" Selen asks.

I shrug again. "Used to it."

Selen squeezes my hand once and gets to her feet. "That mean it's all right if I crack the drapes enough so I don't trip and break my neck?"

She's exaggerating, but not by much. The palace curtains are thick, blotting out light almost entirely to aid with *hora* magic. It's why I was so deep asleep I didn't feel the dawn coming.

"Ay, go ahead." I squint my eyes and put up a hand as she sends a sliver of hot sunlight slicing across the room.

There is a knock at the door soon after, and we open it to find Rojvah, Arick, and Abban. The *khaffit* merchant pushes a cart of food with his ample belly as he walks on his crutches. When the twins make no effort to help him, I hurry over, taking the cart from him.

"I am afraid Princess Selen scared away your servants before they could lay breakfast," Abban says.

Rojvah's tinkling laugh is triumphant. "It seems you're a princess after all, Selen vah Gared. We were starting to wonder."

Selen doesn't rise to the bait, but I can smell her irritation.

"Who can blame them for opening the curtains?" Arick asks. "It's dark enough for an *alagai* in here."

"Darin Bales, born in darkness," Rojvah echoes the Damajah's greeting. Together with Arick's demon talk, it puts me on edge. I can never tell when my Krasian cousins are teasing or serious.

Steeling myself, I find a steady breath as I walk to the curtains and draw them open myself, pretending it doesn't feel like leaping into a boiling tub as I fill the room with sunlight. I turn and let the fire lance across my back, holding up my arms to stand in the light in front of everyone.

Abban coughs gently. "I bring you these, as well." He holds out a tied bundle of black silk.

"Warrior blacks?" I've been itching to get out of Arick's garish robes, but I don't understand.

Neither does Arick. I can smell his jealousy. "Why does *he* get blacks?"

"He's right," I say, before his jealousy can spark into anger. "I've never killed a demon."

"Shot one, though," Selen puts in, ignoring my irritated stare. "Wrestled one to the ground to keep it from eating your friend."

"Whatever your exploits in the night," Abban says, "my master deemed them enough to award you these, and his word is law."

"He isn't even Krasian," Arick complains. "The robes should be green, at least."

"Perhaps," Abban agrees. "When next you see him, explain to the Shar'Dama Ka why the Par'chin's son is unworthy of black robes, and when he is convinced by your wisdom, I will happily procure robes of whatever color desired."

Arick pales. Abban's words are pleasant, but his rebuke is not. Abban is *khaffit*—the lowest caste in Krasian society—but he is also rich beyond measure, and when he speaks, it is with my bloodfather's voice. Arick may be half Krasian, but he's even further from the throne than I am.

I smell my cousin's shame and humiliation, and can't help but empathize. Arick and I were never friends—not really. Just kids of an age thrown together while our parents had a visit. But I remember his joke about family, and how we don't have to like each other to be on the same side.

They won't let Arick take the black because his da was a famous Jongleur. Why shouldn't he be jealous that I get a set just because my da killed a lot of demons?

"No," I say. "Arick's right. Don't want those any more than this." I lift my foot, showing off a bright orange slipper. "I want a proper set of Northern clothes. Denim britches, a green shirt, and a soft brown leather jacket with button cuffs."

Something about the request turns Arick's scent angry, and while the patient smile never leaves Abban's face, there is surprise in his scent. "When next you see him, explain to Shar'Dama Ka—"

"Cut the demonshit, Abban," I say. "My parents never dressed Krasian, and I'm not going to, either. Either you get me clothes to replace the ones you all burned, or the next time you see my bloodfather, *you* can explain to *him* why I'm walkin' around in a bido."

Abban eyes me, trying to see if I'm bluffing, but I ent. Mam says Krasians like to play games without telling you the rules. *Got to put your foot down sometimes, to keep from getting sucked in.*

After a moment, Abban spreads his crutches and bows. "Very well. I will have clothes made for you in the Northern style."

Selen quietly clears her throat. "For Selen, as well," I say.

"Of course," Abban says. "But it will take some time."

I hold up my palms. "We got nowhere to be."

Abban bows again. "Apologies, son of Arlen, but I am afraid you do. After you have broken fast, I am to bring you to the Damajah."

Selen perks up at that. "Is there news of Leesha and Mrs. Bales?"

Abban shakes his head. "Not that I am aware of. The Damajah has more questions."

ABBAN HAS SERVANTS rush to the bazaar, reappearing within the hour with a variety of Northern clothing for me to choose from while they take measurements for a custom set. The britches are a bit stiff, but they'll wear in, and the shirt is something like the Seventhday best folk wear back in the Brook. I feel closer to regular than I have in months.

Yet Arick's angry scent burns my nostrils, laced with jealousy, shame, and resentment. But at whom? I keep looking his way, hoping to catch his eye, but he keeps his head down, giving me no chance.

Rojvah drifts over, her scent full of curiosity rather than its typical amusement. "You really don't understand, do you?" Her voice is less than a whisper, barely a breath at all, but it's clear to me.

"Understand what?" I whisper. "Why your brother's cross with me even after I took his side?"

"He did not want you to take his side," Rojvah breathes.

"Don't make sense," I whisper. "Said himself we were family, and family sticks up for each other."

"Sometimes," Rojvah agrees. "And sometimes we respect each other enough to let them fail with dignity."

"What does that even mean?" I ask.

Rojvah shakes her head like I'm the class dunce. "By standing up to Abban where he could not, you only shamed him further. Then you likened *Sharum* blacks to the filth-covered sole of your foot. There can be no greater insult to a warrior."

"I . . . " I pull back, nonplussed. "What?"

No mistaking her scent, now. She thinks I'm an idiot. "You said you didn't want *Sharum* blacks any more than 'this' and pointed to your foot. Men have been killed for less."

Horror comes over me as I recall the gesture. "Night! I only meant the color! Black, green, orange—they all feel like pretending to be something I'm not."

Rojvah throws back her head and laughs, making everyone look up, even Arick. She lays a sympathetic hand on my shoulder. "Oh, cousin. You have so much to learn."

Rojvah doesn't say anything to Arick for me, but when Abban appears with an escort of eunuchs to bring us to the Damajah, the twins join us.

They walk us not to court, but to the Damajah's wing of the palace, and then down into her underpalace, cut deep into the hill upon which the palace stands. The walls throb with magic as we descend below natural light, and I feel wisps of it clinging to me as we pass, restoring the powers that dawn burned away.

We descend even further, leaving rich palace halls for tunnels of solid stone, cut deep into bedrock and carved with powerful wardings. The air is cold, stale, and stinks of unwashed bodies and despair.

It smells like the Bunker.

Indeed, we find the Damajah waiting in a goal cell where four Krasian men kneel with black hoods over their faces, bound wrist-to-ankle. I look at her curiously.

"Go on." Inevera whisks a hand at the men. "Smell them."

I shift uncomfortably, eyeing the door. I don't like being in a cell, especially in a place designed to keep folk like me from getting away, but I know what she's playing at, and my curiosity overcomes my anxious nature. I walk over to the men, sniffing the air.

It's been a long time since I found the spoor in Lord Arther's office. It was weak even then, partially absorbed by the alomom powder, but there is a faint aroma of alomom on these men even now. I inhale deeper, sifting for scent markers of diet or habit. Their food is blander than the other tribes, no doubt to mask their scent further, but that is telling in its own way. In this hot dungeon, they cannot help but sweat, and that tells me all I need.

"It's them," I say.

Selen looks ready to shout, but Inevera raises a hand to stop her. "Are you certain, son of Arlen?"

I nod, and Inevera flicks a finger. A eunuch kicks one of the men onto the floor in front of us. "This is Kai Tomoka, of the Nanji. Their tribe of Watchers once served the Majah, but pledged to your bloodfather when the Majah fled Sharak Ka to return to the sands. But it seems Nanji honor is thin."

The eunuch produces an alagai tail, the harsh barbed whip used in Krasian punishment. A single stroke opens a line on the man's back, and I smell fresh blood, but even as he screams, there is a mocking laugh in his throat.

"I will go to Everam pure of spirit!" he claims. "It was not only the Majah who were betrayed on the Night of Hora!"

The Night of Hora was the infamous coup of Jardir's son Asome, who had his twelve *dama* brothers, one from each tribe, murder their *Damaji* to cement his rise to power. Only the Majah brother failed.

Inevera flicks a finger again, and the eunuch resumes lashing Tomoka with the alagai tail until the laughter is beaten from him. I flinch with each strike, backing away as the room fills with a nauseating stench of sweat and blood.

The others don't seem to mind. Inevera observes with a serene indifference that Rojvah does a fair job emulating. Abban studies his nails even as the *kai's* screams ring so loud I fear my eardrums will burst. Selen and Arick watch like hawks. If eyes were a lash, they would be doing the whipping themselves.

At last the Damajah signals the eunuch to stop. Tomoka lies shivering on the ground, still bound wrist-to-ankle. Blood covers his back and dribbles from his lips as he coughs out a breath.

"I am going to ask you some questions, Tomoka," Inevera says quietly. "I will know if you lie, and all Nanji will suffer."

For long moments, the man gasps for breath, then, in a hoarse wheeze, he speaks. "I would never lie to the Damajah." Near as I can tell, he means it.

"Where is Princess Olive?" Inevera asks.

"Beyond your reach in Desert Spear," Tomoka says. "Shar'Dama Ka's Second Wife had *dama'ting* magic to spirit Olive across the sands. No doubt they have been there for months."

"Why?" Inevera's voice remains placid, but she smells furious.

"The dice say Olive must shed blood for Majah, if Desert Spear is to survive," Tomoka says.

"Belina told you this?" Inevera asks. "Were those her exact words?"

Tomoka nods.

"And you believed her?"

Something about the bruised and bloody Watcher chuckling sets my nerves on edge. "I am *Sharum*, Damajah. I have learned not to question the *dama'ting* when they speak of dice."

"Not a complete fool, then," Inevera says. "And Micha?"

"She fought with surprising skill," Tomoka says. "It took two Watchers to subdue her, and not without wounds of their own."

"So she is alive?" Inevera asks.

Tomoka nods. "She proved a valuable incentive for Olive's behavior."

"The Majah are without honor," Arick growls. "This cannot stand."

"That is not for you to decide." As if remembering we are still present, Inevera tilts her head in our direction. Her eunuchs move in immediately, ushering us out of the cold stone Nanji cell and escorting us back to our warm silk one.

SEEMS LIKE EVERY time I settle into an evening bath, someone steals my clothes. Only this time I ent bothered, because the new ones are made to order . . . sort of. Abban's seamstresses have given the garments a distinctly Krasian flair—loose limbs tapering to tight button cuffs and a matching scarf to keep out dust and sand.

They used sturdy Northern denim for the britches like I asked, but unlike the stiff pair from the bazaar, this cloth is already massaged to softness. The silk shirt and bido are a gentle breeze across my skin. The jacket is a brown so dark it is nearly black. It has no collar to put up against the sun, but it buttons tight, and the silk scarf is long enough to cover my head and face if I wish.

But even with the trappings of Northern style, these are clearly a warrior's garments. They are sturdy and light, meant for protection and ease of movement. Pockets in the lining of the jacket and britches are meant for armor plates, but I reckon I can find other uses for them.

"I take it the son of Arlen is pleased?" Abban asks with an exaggerated bow as I come around the screen.

"Love 'em," I say.

Selen smells equally pleased in her new leggings and coat. No doubt some of the Krasians will be scandalized, but Selen has a better claim to warrior garb than I do, and it seems the Damajah respects that. She's already experimenting with the armor plates.

"The young master will be pleased to know that I have also procured him a horse," Abban says. "A light Angierian courser like your father's, barely more than a colt and stronger than a camel. You will look regal as you accompany your escort back to Hollow."

Don't much care for the sound of that, or of seeing Uncle Gared. Going home feels like giving up. What home do I have anyway, without Mam? The Warded Children are gone. The Brook is too small and isolated, but Hollow with all its crowds and noise is worse, and it would be no better here in Krasia. Long as I was with Mam, they were all just places to visit and set awhile. Now I'm going to need to pick one.

It's been over a week, with no word from Jardir and no sign of Inevera. They let us stroll around the family wing and the palace grounds with our eunuch escort, but no farther. Our every need is taken care of instantly, except the need for more information, or freedom.

"What does everyone think?" I ask, giving a turn in my new clothes.

"Gonna leave a lot of doe-eyed girls sighing as you ride by," Selen says. It's a tampweed tale, but I feel my face color anyway.

"You look well enough for a *chin* peasant." Rojvah brings me back to the ground. "But a man's clothing should shout. These are barely a whisper."

I look down at the muted colors, unlike the stark black or white of most Krasian clothes, or the flamboyant colors of children and *khaffit*. "Like it that way."

Arick doesn't smell as angry as he did a few days ago, but neither does he answer. He comes every day with Rojvah to join us for meals and walks in the gardens, but he gives all his attention to Selen and his sister.

"Appreciate you making our captivity more pleasant," I tell Rojvah, "but you don't have to spend all your time here, if you don't want to."

Rojvah laughs. "Is that what you think, cousin? That we visit your silk prison during the day and leave at night?" She shakes her head. "It is you who are visiting ours. In a few days, you will be gone, and the *dama'ting* will drag me back down to the Chamber of Shadows to continue my studies."

"Ent fair, for you or Arick." I poke a finger into a large pocket in my jacket, meant to hold the armor plate that protects my heart. I think of Olive, locked in a tower somewhere. "Or for any of us."

After Abban leaves, Selen paces our chambers like she's about to give a speech before a crowd. "How long you think this is going to take? The general's going to be here in a few days, and Olive's da still ent back."

"Already taken too long," I say. "Doubt it took two hours for Bloodfather to fly to the mountains. If there was a city there, he'd spot it faster'n a hound sniffs out a rabbit hole in the barley field."

"Perhaps Grandfather found this city, but it was only the beginning of the trail," Rojvah says.

"Or perhaps he found something you did not on the battlefield, and is investigating," Arick says.

"For goin' on ten days without sendin' word?" It doesn't feel right.

"You're worried they got him, too." Selen's flat tone tells me I'm not the only one thinking it.

"Ridiculous," Arick says. "Ahmann Jardir is Shar'Dama Ka. He carries the Crown and Spear of Kaji. No *alagai* can stand against him."

The words are like a cold blade in my heart, and it's a conscious effort to hold back tears. "That's what I used to think about Mam. But it looks like the corelings knew she was coming. What if they were expecting Jardir, too?"

"How's that possible?" Selen asks.

"Core if I know," I say. But with every day that passes, it seems more and more like the only answer that makes sense.

"All we can do is wait, and pray," Rojvah says.

"Sit on our arses, you mean," Selen growls, "while Olive, the ripping duchess of Hollow, is held prisoner."

"The Damajah has foreseen the gates of Desert Spear will not open without bloodshed," Rojvah says.

"If that is what the gates require," Arick says, "then we should drown them in treacherous Majah blood."

"Ay, maybe," Selen says. "But maybe we could just throw a rope over the wall, if we weren't locked up."

Arick snorts, but Selen has a point. I've got a knack for squeezing into places other folk don't fit.

"Only locked up as long as we want to be," I say.

"Ay, maybe you are," Selen says, "but I can't slip through the crack under the door, or jump out a window without breaking my neck."

It's the moment on the road all over again. Could I have caught Olive's kidnappers if I'd left Selen behind and run on my own? What would I have done if I had?

"But every day we wait is a day they're trying to force some Majah prince on Olive," Selen says.

She's right. I spring to my feet. We've waited enough.

"Where are you going?" Rojvah asks as I climb the wall to a high window, opening it to the cool night air.

"To see your Tikka and get some corespawned answers."

Rojvah laughs. "You will not make it to the first hall before her guards surround you?"

"The eunuchs?" I sniff. "They won't even see me."

"I would not be so certain of that," Rojvah says, "but the eunuchs are servants, not guards. Those you see only when they strike."

DAMAJAH

IT'S EASY TO slip by the eunuchs and servants on my way to the Damajah's chambers. When I'm slippery, I get fuzzy around the edges.
Hard to notice. Hard to remember. I move so quick and quiet, it's
easy to dismiss me as a wisp of smoke or trick of light. I'm light as a
feather, and can jump like a stone skipped across the water.

I don't know precisely where I'm going. I've never been in the Damajah's private wing of the palace, and it is enormous. But I know what
Inevera smells like, and it ent alomom powder. Her fragrance drifts
along currents in the air, and I follow it like a burbling stream.

I hear a powerful pair of heartbeats ahead, and breathe in, smelling
oil, metal, and the dye used to keep warrior blacks from fading. These
must be the guards Rojvah warned about.

My sensitive fingers slip into invisible fissures in the walls, turning
sticky as I climb to the ceiling and scurry along like a spider, passing unnoticed over two gold-cuffed eunuchs, armed and armored, with the
white sleeves of holy guard.

I drop behind them, silent as a shadow. There's a gap at the base of
the door they guard, and I squeeze through it like dough under a rolling
pin.

I circumvent a tighter door by slipping out a window and climbing
along the wall, to one past the barrier. After that it gets harder. The

doors are sealed with magic that binds their seams, and the windows are all shut.

I'm getting close.

Twice I wait long minutes for someone to pass through a portal, breezing through before it swings shut. Official business in the palace concluded at sunset, but it is early enough that servants are still bustling about.

The third time I get tired of waiting, and examine the lock on a door. I've seen from the other portals that unlocking the door will disable the wards long enough to pass. I slide a slippery finger into the keyhole, probing for tumblers. I remember the pattern, and take out my picks.

Hary Roller was teaching me more about being a Jongleur than just piping. There were juggling lessons, stories and jokes to memorize, pratfalls and tumbling to practice.

And there was picking locks.

Some nights, the biggest show is after the curtain falls, he liked to say.

I pop the lock and quickly slip through, finding at last the Holy Residence—where Damajah keeps her personal chambers.

Here the gates are sealed tight, great golden doors covered in wards and throbbing with magic. I feel the symbols tugging at my power like the door to the Bunker. Ent gonna squeeze through that.

I search for a locking mechanism, but there ent one to be found. If it's held fast by magic, I haven't much hope of opening it. I decide to slip into the shadows and wait for someone to pass, but before I can move, I'm startled by the sudden click of a latch. I leap for the ceiling and stick there as the doors swing silently open, but the warrior on the other side easily finds me in the shadows.

"You were not invited here, Darin asu Arlen." I freeze as I recognize that stern, motherly tone. Kaji's mother—Ashia—remembered from summers long past. The Sharum'ting Ka.

Ashia wears a helm wrapped in a white turban, and a white veil over her mouth and nose; the rest of her is clad in *Sharum* blacks. Two short, close-combat spears cross her back in easy reach, along with a rounded shield, all of indestructible warded glass.

I was always a little bit afraid of Kaji's mam, and that ent changed with time. Micha hid what she was, but Ashia's legend was too great to hide. There are songs about how she went into battle with infant Kaji strapped to her breast, a story often called for in taverns and around hearths even in Thesa. Hary Roller made me memorize it.

But then I realize there's more to fear than Kaji's mam. Shadows detach from the hallway at my back, *Sharum'ting* materializing to surround me, spears pointed at my heart. Thought I was good at sneakin', but it seems I'm still in the little kids' classroom.

They link shields as they approach, spears long enough to strike up at me from the floor. I get so scared I go slippery on instinct, losing my grip on the ceiling and tumbling down. I twist in midair, managing to land on my feet, but it's a clumsy move and leaves me vulnerable.

But the warriors don't press the advantage and Ashia doesn't reach for her spear. There's no need. Slippery or not, I can't get past the wall of spears around me without being spitted like a pig. My heart is beating like a cornered rabbit's, making my whole body feel like it's shaking.

"How long?" I ask as Ashia stalks in.

She pauses. "What?"

"How long have they been following me?" I say.

Ashia's eyes crinkle behind her veil, and I smell her amusement. "Since you left your quarters, young prince."

Much as I hate to admit it, Rojvah was right. "Guarding or spying?"

Again, amusement. "Both, of course. It is unwise to come unsummoned to the Holy Residence, son of Par'chin. Even for you."

"Need answers," I say.

"Are they worth your life?"

"Don't think so," I reply, "but seein' as Olive may die without them, ent got much choice but to take the risk."

"The Damajah is aware of the danger to Olive Paper," Ashia says. "If there is anything to be done—"

"Ent good enough," I cut in, surprising her. Ashia ent accustomed to being interrupted. The look she gives makes me feel like I'm five summers old and in for a trip to the woodshed. "And it ent just Olive in trouble."

Ashia tilts her head at me.

"Tracked the Majah myself until they hid the trail," I say, loud enough for all to hear. "They had Nanny Micha slung over a horse alongside Olive."

The *Sharum'ting* say nothing, but their breathing changes, and their collective smell becomes a mix of worry, doubt, and slowly rising anger. Micha was one of their own.

"Damajah didn't tell you that part, did she?" I ask.

Ashia's scent changes to one of challenge, and I realize I've made another mistake. Thought mentioning Micha would get sympathy, but like with Arick, I've misunderstood how the Krasians look at the world.

There is a hiss as Ashia's short spears come out of their harnesses. With a quick twist she marries the ends of them together into a weapon taller than she is, with a foot of sharpened glass at either end. There is a glow of magic about her. She'll be as fast as I am, and going slippery won't stop those blades from cleaving me in two.

"What the Damajah tells us is what we are meant to know," the Sharum'ting Ka says in a low, dangerous voice. "Our lives are hers. Micha vah Ahmann understands this, even if you do not. Micha is a *kai'Sharum'ting* of Everam's spear sisters. Her glorious deeds have already assured her place in Heaven. Either she is working even now to free Olive, or she has died honorably in the attempt."

Mam told me never to get on my knees in Krasia, but I do it now, placing my hands on the floor. "Sorry. Mam always said my nose gets me into trouble. Din't mean any offense."

"Even as a child you never wanted trouble," Ashia says, "but you were always finding it."

"Still need to see your boss," I say.

Ashia steps aside, opening a path into the Holy Residence. "You are fortunate, then, son of Arlen. She has been expecting you."

"You MUST BE very brave, or very foolish, coming in here uninvited, son of Arlen." The Damajah kneels facing away from me, staring at the pattern of the dice on the cloth before her.

It's so portrait-perfect I know it's a pose, meant to put a scare into me. Creator knows, any other time, it might have worked, but I'm getting tired of Krasian head games.

"Ay, well." I stick my hands in my pockets. "Mam always says my da had more sack than sense. Might be we've got something in common after all."

"That is a common trait in men who die young." Inevera's words wipe the smile from my face. "And in great men. Which will you be?"

"You're the one who sees the future," I say.

"I knew you would come," Inevera's voice is distant as she gazes at the dice, her silk veils illuminated in their soft glow, "though in truth I expected it to be sooner."

Everyone, it seems, expects me to be braver than I am. "Sorry to disappoint."

The Damajah shrugs. "That is not a bad thing. It shows you are not arrogant or unduly impulsive, regardless of how much . . . sack you carry."

"Did the dice tell you that, when you cast in my mother's blood?" I'm supposed to be here for Olive, but there are things I need to understand about myself, as well, and Inevera may be the only person left alive who can help.

"They told me you would be born in darkness," she says again.

"Ay, but that ent all," I say.

"It is dangerous to have knowledge of one's own future," the Damajah whispers. "The burden can lead to choices we might not otherwise make, choices that can have . . . consequences."

"I'm already burdened," I say. "It wasn't just Olive Leesha cast for, that night."

The Damajah whirls so suddenly I leap backward, going slippery. Frictionless, my feet slide back as if I were on polished ice.

"There was another prophecy, and you kept it from me?!" The wand comes off her belt, and with a flick, she activates wards all around the room. Like Aunt Leesha's, they will keep sound from escaping, but I can see that's not all. They keep *me* from escaping, as well.

I take a deep breath, solidifying. I'm in her place of power, and the Damajah knows magic a lot better than me. Nothing to gain trying to run, or fight. "You kept something from me, so we're even."

She raises the *hora* wand, its wards burning with an angry light. "Even?! My husband is missing! I haven't heard from him since . . . "

"Since when?" I ask when she trails off.

The Damajah shakes her head. "Nothing more for you, son of Arlen. Tell me what you know, or I will throw you in a cell even you cannot escape."

I shake my head, planting my feet and crossing my arms. "Your husband is missing, ay. So is my mam. And Aunt Leesha and Olive Paper. But what I know ent got anything to do with where they went. Aunt Leesha said so. It's my prophecy, and it makes no sense. But maybe, combined with yours . . . "

The Damajah looks at me a long time, but her *hora* wand slowly dims. At last she returns it to her belt. "Come kneel with me, son of Arlen."

She returns to her casting cloth, gathering her scattered dice with a practiced sweep of her hand. I kneel across from her, amazed at the change in her aura. A moment ago, she was furious. More than willing to hurt me. Now she is calm as still water.

"You may not like what you hear," she says softly.

I shrug. "Don't like much of anything these days, but things keep happening all the same."

She closes her eyes, her voice taking on that distant quality it had when she was staring at the dice.

"*A boy of limitless potential, and a future of despair.*" I shudder at the Damajah's whisper. "*He will be born in darkness, and will carry it inside him.*"

The words are recited like an ancient cradle rhyme, something replayed in her mind countless times over the last fifteen summers, hoping to glean . . . what?

"What does it mean?" I ask. "Darkness inside me? A future of despair?"

"The darkness could mean the magic you carry within you," the Damajah says. "Power born in darkness like you, that cannot withstand the light."

I think of the pain of sunrise. Of my "*alagai* blood."

"Despair might mean the burden of growing up without a father," the Damajah says.

"And my 'limitless potential'?" I ask.

Inevera shrugs. "All potential is limitless. It may be the prophecy has already come to pass, but prophecies are tricky things, and there is always a deeper meaning. Whatever is coming, you have a part to play, I think."

She returns the *alagai hora* to a pouch at her waist, and I relax a little. "I have kept my side of our bargain, son of Arlen. Now tell me what the Mistress of Hollow saw in her dice."

I close my eyes. Like Inevera, the words come easily, replayed a thousand times in my mind since that night in Aunt Leesha's study. They have haunted me.

"*The father waits below in darkness for his progeny to return.*"

The Damajah's eyes narrow as they meet mine. I shake my head slightly to let my hair fall over my eyes, but she keeps staring, seeing right through. "You think this is about the Par'chin."

"What else could it be?" I ask. "My blood, my father. It means he might still be down there, stuck like a cork in a jug."

"Perhaps," Inevera says. "But it is not that simple. Alagai Ka is the Father of Demons. Ahmann is your bloodfather. You and Olive are both his children, in a sense."

"Hadn't thought of that," I admit.

"Why should you?" Inevera asks. "You have no skill at prophecy. Even Leesha Paper came to the practice late in life. But she was too prideful and you too stubborn to share with me."

"Ent bein' stubborn," I say. "It's personal. It's about my da. I feel it in my bones."

"Prophecy is like that," Inevera says. "It is tempting to let our feelings guide us, to let emotion read the dice instead of logic. That is why the dice are so dangerous in untrained hands. We will always see what we want to see, if we let ourselves."

"Wanting something doesn't make it wrong," I say.

"But it is illogical." The Damajah points to a hearth against the wall, burning with crackling orange flame. "The abyss is not a bottle. It is a fire. The flames that heat Ala from within even as the sun does without." There is a pop as fire licks a pocket of moisture, and sparks fly from the wood.

"The sparks are brighter than the flame," she whispers, "if only for a moment. So it was with your father. His flare cleansed the *alagai* from our lands, but it consumed him."

"But the energy ent gone," I say. "Spark turns to heat."

"And with his heat, Arlen asu Jeph burned the *alagai* from our cities," the Damajah says, "and in so doing, sent his spirit on the lonely path to be judged by Everam. Your father awaits you, I have no doubt, but it is in Heaven, not Ala."

"How can you possibly know that?" Mam always said, once a Tender starts telling you what happens when you die, it's time to stop listening, because they're just spinning tampweed tales.

"Some things," the Damajah says, "must be taken on faith. I too know what it is like to have your parents taken from you, but do not let your desire to have them return color a prophecy you do not understand."

"Do you understand it?" I ask.

There is a ripple in the Damajah's aura. I imagine she's not used to people asking her such blunt questions.

"Ay, thought not," I say. "Guess we're both letting faith get in the way."

"Tsst," the Damajah hisses, and I know I've struck a nerve. It's a mad game, antagonizing her like this, but when adults won't take you seriously, sometimes it's the only tool left in the shed.

"The dice are not a map to follow," Inevera says, "or an equation to solve. It can take months or years to find meaning in a throw. Many are not understood fully until after they come to pass."

"Don't have months," I say. "Can't just sit here waiting for Uncle Gared."

"My honored husband said as much." The Damajah's tone is careful and measured. "Now he has disappeared. I will not let you or Princess Selen risk yourselves further. You will return to Hollow and its greatwards until we can learn more."

"Even if it takes months," I say. "Or years."

"I see we understand each other," Inevera says.

"This ent the first time my bloodfather's disappeared," I say. "Last time, he came back with me."

"Indeed," the Damajah agrees. "I have learned not to underestimate my husband, but you are not him, Darin Bales. Nor are you your father."

She's got the right of that, but it still cuts to hear. "Ay. Know that. But maybe I can do something they can't."

"And what is that?" The Damajah smells amused.

"The dice told you that if Bloodfather returns to Desert Spear, he would make things worse."

"How do you know that?" she asks.

"Ears like a bat, Mam says."

"The Majah are numerous," Inevera says. "Their city lies across an unforgiving terrain, fortified around the only arable land for many miles. Thousands will die if we try to force their gates open. No one, not even Olive Paper, is worth such a price. If she is there, it is Everam's will, we must trust in Everam to bring her through."

If a drawn curtain brings pain enough for me to scream, what would a week or more be like under the desert sun? Yet still, against my better judgment, the words come to my lips. "What if someone else went?"

The Damajah snorts. "You? What makes you think you can succeed where the Shar'Dama Ka could not?"

I smile. "Limitless potential?"

That gets a full laugh from her, something I wouldn't have thought possible. Her scent is absolutely delighted, and I use it as an opening to press the case.

"Bloodfather is bound by treaties, but I ent. Maybe it would start a ruckus if he went down there, but if I'm caught . . . " I lift my empty hands, palms out. "Just another *chin* to them, ent I?"

"Do not underestimate the Majah," Inevera says. "You *will* be caught."

I shrug. "Don't matter. Ent a cell that can hold me."

The Damajah raises an eyebrow. "Try to leave this room, son of Arlen."

I glance again at the wards surrounding us. "Ay, but you know me," I concede. "Majah left before I was ever born. Don't reckon they'll go to all the trouble of warding up an airtight cell on account of one scruffy greenblood."

"Indeed, it is easy to underestimate you," Inevera says. "But like your father, you are more than you appear. Rojvah tells me you have a gift."

"Ay?" The mention of Da distracts me, and it takes a moment for the Damajah's last words to register.

She reaches out a hand. "Your pipes."

My hand drops protectively over the satchel I always carry. I'd sooner let the Damajah hold Mam's knife, but we both know the statement was a request, and here in her place of power, a request is a command. I reach inside, clutching the instrument for a long moment before handing it to her.

The Damajah takes the pipes respectfully, closing her eyes and gliding her fingertips lightly over the wood, feeling its energy. Then she opens her eyes, studying the pipes with night eyes. Like taking a breath, she pulls a wisp of magic through them and into herself, Reading it, like Mam taught me.

"You cut the wood yourself," she whispers. "Wove your own cord. Boiled your own glue. There is power in that, Darin Bales."

"Ay, well . . . " My fingers itch to snatch the instrument back. It's mine, and I've never liked folk touching it, not even Hary. I could take it before she even knew I'd moved, but I reckon I'd come to regret it.

"Why don't you use *hora* to enhance the pipes' resonance," she asks, "as other *alagai* charmers do?"

" 'Cause I never wanted to be a demon charmer," I say.

"You will have to be, if you wish to make it to Desert Spear alive," the Damajah says. Then, as if she had known all along, she reaches into her *hora* pouch, producing what looks like a warded silver shell on a delicate chain.

The shell hums with power, evidence of a sliver of demonbone within. Inevera skillfully threads the chain through the cord that binds the reeds together, letting it hang like a tassel.

I know what she's doing, and she's right. Hary would never have held off the corelings back home if his cello hadn't been similarly enchanted.

But then she lays out a brush and a bowl of pure black paint.

"Ay!" I reach out as she raises the brush.

"Tsst." The hiss makes me jump, pulling back my hand instinctively.

Before I recover, she begins her work, painting wards along the reeds. The symbols are beautiful, but still it feels like a violation, like she's tattooing my arm without permission. With every stroke of the brush my muscles get tenser, until it feels like I'm vibrating.

Before I know it, she's done. "The shell will resonate and multiply the sound of your playing," the Damajah says. "By placing your fingers on the wards along the reeds, you can control how many multiples it will take to fill a space."

Seems a complicated way to say the wards make it louder, but I bow as she returns the pipes, just happy to have them back in my hands. It's an incredible gift, but Mam always says magic has a price, and I expect I'll be paying it soon enough. "Thank you."

"General Cutter rides hard for Everam's Bounty," Inevera says. "He will be here in three days to collect you and his daughter."

Sooner than we thought. Too soon.

"Then I'll leave before he gets here," I say.

"The pact demands that I keep you and the daughter of Gared safe," Inevera says. "If you try to leave the palace, the guards will stop you."

"If your guards can stop us," I say, "we ent much good to Olive."

The Damajah does not reply, but there is amusement mixed in with the scent of her perfume, and that is all the answer I need.

"Uncle Gared will be steamed," I warn.

The Damajah whisks a hand dismissively through the air. "He is only a man, and out of his depth. A few wails and false tears, and he'll ride out from Everam's Bounty believing you've run off again, and leave me blameless."

"Won't be lyin'," I say. "But he'll come after us."

"Alas," Inevera says. "The pact gives us the right to deny armed men passage through our lands, and with Ahmann gone, I may be *helpless* to stop my generals from enforcing it."

I smile. Helpless, this woman ent, but Krasians like their head games.

41

———•———

DUSK RUNNER

I PINCH A FEW things on my way back. Nothing irreplaceable or sentimental, but the palace is full of fancy baubles just lying about, and we'll need money for supplies on the road south. Even if we had time to pack, getting Selen out of the palace will be tricky enough without having to ruck too much gear.

"Took you long enough," Selen says as I slip through the cracked window into our chambers.

"Where are Rojvah and Arick?" I ask as I drop down beside her, listening carefully. The twins are gone, and even the spies in the walls have pulled stakes for the night. We're alone.

"They got tired of watching me pace around the room and went off to bed," Selen says. "Which is just as well, since I was getting close to punching Rojvah in the mouth just to wipe off that smug smile."

I'm flattered. Usually it's me losing sleep to worry. Selen can doze through most anything. "Should've slept while you had the chance. We're leaving. Now."

Selen doesn't argue, or ask questions. She simply nods, fetching our weathered packs, already stuffed with clothing. I can hear the clink of our warded glass armor plates weighing the bottoms. "Refilled our canteens, but there ent much in the way of food. Just some nuts and dried fruit I pocketed when no one was looking."

I realize she's been planning this all along. Probably since the moment her da said he was coming to get us. Seems like everyone expected me to find my stones sooner.

"That's all right." I reach into the many pockets of my jacket and pants, producing a small jade vase, a marble statuette, a silver tray, and a pair of golden candlesticks.

"You little thief!" Selen's smile drives off a bit of my embarrassment, but the relief is short-lived. We have work to do.

I retrieve my bow and quiver while Selen harnesses her spear and slings her shield over her.

"Best to leave the wooden armor behind," I say. "Carrying too much to be very sneaky, already."

"Won't miss it," Selen says.

"Ay?" I'm a little surprised. "You took care of that armor like it was your own babe on the road."

"Da taught us early to take care of armor," Selen says. "*Anythin' you bet your life on is worth a polish every night.* But that ripping thing was hot as the Core, and clunky. Shaped for a man. Krasian armor is downright comfortable by comparison—stronger, lighter, and flexible so you can move."

"Ay, fair," I concede. I love my Krasian silk, but I don't expect I'll ever use the armor plates. Warded glass won't turn slippery when I do, and I feel ill at the thought of all those plates shifting and squeezing against my skin.

"How do we get past the guards outside the door?" Selen asks.

"Same way I did," I say.

Selen glances at the window. "You gonna carry me up there?"

I'd love to say yes. It's what the hero should say, ay? It's what Da would do, or Olive. I don't like touching most folk, but I wouldn't mind if it was Selen.

It's a nice little fantasy, but I ent that strong, and I know it. Selen alone outweighs me, not to mention all our gear.

There's a silk pull rope in our chambers to summon servants. I climb the wall and use Mam's knife to slice it right where it meets the ceiling, dropping it to Selen. "Tie this around your waist."

"Ent gonna be long enough," she warns.

"Don't need it too long," I say. "Got something else in mind."

"DARIN BALES," SELEN growls into the wind as we step onto the ward-work ledge outside our window. "If we die, I'm going to kill you."

I laugh. "Just like walking a log."

"Log ent three inches wide," Selen says. "That's a stick."

Anything wide enough for a cat is a country stroll for me, but I know other folks ent the same way.

Selen looks nervously at the drop—more than six stories down into a garden full of stone paths that would dash us both apart. "You sure this is going to work?"

"Ent gonna let you fall," I say, pressing slippery fingers into the cracks of the wall, then turning sticky. "Honest word."

She nods, taking up the slack of the rope that ties us together. She pulls hard against my makeshift harness before testing her weight to the rope, but I suck in, almost becoming part of the wall. The rope is secure.

She rappels down to a ward, carved in relief on the palace wall, with ridges just wide enough for her hands and feet to catch a brief hold. The moment she's secure, I skitter down the wall after her.

"Night that's unsettling," Selen says.

"Demon blood has advantages," I say, but then Selen's foot slips, and she drops before I can secure myself again. I'm pulled free save for one sticky hand, and my arm screams as the rope goes taut with our collective weight.

To her credit, Selen doesn't cry out, but I can't keep from groaning in pain. It feels like the flesh of my hand will tear off, or my arm pull from its socket. I hang on desperately until the swinging of the rope eases enough for me to latch on with my other hand and feet.

"Put your feet on the wall," I say, trying to keep the strain from my voice. "Gonna walk us down."

I keep three limbs locked to the wall at all times as I steadily climb down, sucking in to keep from doing myself serious harm as we make our way to the garden. At last, Selen touches down and I drop the last ten feet.

"Well done," a silky voice says, "but if you'd asked us, we could have just taken you out the royal passage."

I've got Mam's knife in hand before the voice registers. I look up and see Rojvah and Arick approaching from a hidden bower, their scents masked by the flowers. Rojvah wears a warded shawl around her shoulders, much like Mam's Cloak of Unsight. Even to me, she looks blurry, like I must appear to folk when I'm slippery.

Arick has abandoned his multicolored silk for *Sharum* blacks. I can hear plates of warded glass shifting between the layers. He carries a spear and shield, and looks every inch the *dal'Sharum* warrior, save for the kamanj slung over his back.

"What are you doing?" I hiss, worried we will be overheard. White-sleeved guards patrol the grounds, and they are not known for laxity.

"Making sure you don't die in the desert," Arick says.

"You can't stop us." Selen pops the button on the spear harness on her back, loosening the weapon. "We're going."

"You misunderstand," Rojvah says.

"Olive Paper is family," Arick says. "We will no more abandon her to Majah scum than you."

A lump forms in my throat at the words. For all my doubts about where I stand with my Krasian cousins, here they are, ready to step into harm's way for us.

But it ent right. Much as I want company on this trip, it's selfish to put them at risk. "No."

"Do not mistake us, cousin," Rojvah says. "We are not asking permission. You know nothing of the desert waste, and though you speak our language, you will be out of your depth when you reach Desert Spear."

"Hate to say it, but they've got a point," Selen says.

They do, but I'm not ready to concede just yet. "You ent been to the desert any more'n us."

"It's in our blood," Arick says.

"Always comes back to blood," I say. "Green blood, desert blood, *alagai* blood. None of it means a corespawned thing to me."

"Be that as it may," Rojvah says, "the waste shaped our people. For three thousand years, the tribes of Krasia called it our home. It darkened our skin and dictated our clothes and cooking. Every sacred scripture, every song we sing, every cautionary tale we tell children, all take place in the Krasian desert."

"We were learning to survive the sands and flats before we learned to roll over," Arick says.

I can't argue that, so I don't. "Say you're right. Even if this works, you'll be in for a world of trouble when you get back."

Arick shrugs. "The path to glory is full of danger, and victors are seldom punished for disobedience."

"You are not victors, yet," a deeper voice intones. I turn in surprise to see Kaji, shocked that he was able to sneak up on me. No one's ever gotten the drop on me before tonight, and now it's happening at every turn. Maybe I ent as sneaky as I think.

"Back inside, all of you, and this will be forgotten," Kaji says. "Force me to call the guard, and you will face punishment for disobedience without the shield of glory."

"Olive Paper is your blood, too," Selen says. "If you don't have the stones to go after her, then someone needs to."

The words, spoken by a woman, no less, are a challenge to the ego that would set most Krasian men into a fit, but Kaji's always been unflappable. Never could get a read on him like I can other folk.

"Olive vah Ahmann is not forgotten." Kaji's voice is soothing. Calm. "The Majah will be dealt with for this offense."

"Majah went back to the desert because your da murdered their *Damaji*," I remind him. "They hit back, now you hit them and they swear revenge. On and on and on. When does it end?"

"Never," Rojvah says. "The Kaji and the Majah have been in blood feud through the rise and fall of the old world, and since the Return. Only when my grandfather united the tribes did they hold a fragile peace."

"Bring an army to their doorstep, you'll have another three thousand years of blood," I say, "and it still ent guaranteed to get Olive back."

"You think you can?" Kaji sounds unconvinced.

"Won't start a war, we fail," I say.

"But you'll put more of my family at risk," Kaji says.

"I ent your family," Selen says.

"Ay," I add, "and tell me I can't stand by Olive, then I ent, either."

Kaji scowls, but he sweeps a hand out into the night. "Go, then. But my cousins stay here."

Arick steps forward, gesturing to his black robe. "Look at me."

"You look like a *Sharum*, cousin," Kaji says, "but you are not one. The blacks are for men who have killed *alagai*."

"How can I kill one, if you will not let me serve?" Arick demands.

"That was not my decision," Kaji says. "I spoke to Grandfather on your behalf, but his decision is law."

"Grandfather is gone, Kaji." The pleading in Arick's voice makes me uncomfortable, like I'm listening in to something private. "You sit the throne, at least for now. Your decision is law. You can let me be the person we both know I am, not the fraud Grandfather demands."

"You're no fraud, cousin," Kaji says. "Your father's magic—"

"Has far better practitioners than me, and we both know it," Arick cuts in. "I need this, cousin. Better I die on *alagai* talons, than live my life as the court fool."

Kaji remains calm, like he was floating on his back in a summer pond. But he has no quick reply, and that's a rarity.

He turns, meeting Rojvah's eyes. She touches a choker at her throat. "In the desert, we can all be who we wish to be."

At last Kaji gives a short nod. "Everam's blessings upon you." He turns, heading into the shadows of the wall. "I saw nothing."

I'd expected a similarly unpleasant climb of the palace wall, but Arick and Rojvah scoff, taking us through a hidden tunnel reserved for the royal family.

We exit into a plaza down the street from the palace, ringed with giant warded obelisks. In the shadow of the post across from us, four horses nicker softly. They're hidden from sight, but I can smell the oiled leather saddlebags and the supplies within.

A familiar shape emerges, holding the reins of a powerful young courser, laden with provisions.

"Abban." I can't believe it. Did everyone but me know we were leaving tonight?

"I owed you a horse, son of Arlen, and by Everam, I am a man who pays his debts."

"And the other horses?" I ask. "All that tack?"

"Prince Arick and Princess Rojvah have their own animals, and full coffers to pay for provisions." Abban smiles. "You, of course, will have to pay for Princess Selen's horse, and the other supplies."

I frown. I read Da's journals about haggling, but there's no haggle for empty pockets. "How much?"

Abban produces a small writing slate, running down the list with his pencil. "I'd say one small jade vase, one marble statuette, one silver tray, and a pair of golden candlesticks."

I laugh, pulling the items from my pockets. Damajah's funnier than I gave her credit for. I hand them over and go to the beautiful young colt. Grandda had horses on the farm, but I've always spooked them for some reason. I know my way around tack and care, but ent spent much time in the saddle.

I reckon this one's about my age in horse summers, lean and long-legged, but still with a bit of growing to do. His coat is so brown it's almost black, and there are wards cut into his hooves, painted silver. He looks moody, uncomfortable with the bridle, but I can smell he ent scared.

"Is the son of Arlen pleased?" Abban asks. "May I mark my debt to your family paid in full?"

"Ay," I say, taking an apple from my pack. "He's perfect. What's his name?"

"Whatever you wish it to be," Abban replies.

I hold out the apple slowly, letting him sniff at it and me. When he takes it I reach out and touch him. He digs at the ground with his hooves, hungry to run.

"Easy, boy," I take gentle hold of the bridle. Da's old messenger horse was named Dawn Runner, because Da was always running to make it to sunrise. But I ent my da.

"Gonna call you Dusk Runner."

42

DUST

"Everam's Watch guards the desert road," Rojvah says. "It is the last village before we cross into the waste."

"Read about it in Da's old Messenger journals," I say. "Called Lookout Hill, back then. On a clear day you can see miles into the desert from the hilltop."

"Oh, I'd like to see that," Selen says.

"We'll camp there tonight," I say, "even if it costs a few hours."

"That will not be possible," Rojvah says.

"Why not?" I ask, but before she answers, we round a bend and I see the town in the distance. To the others it's still a speck on the horizon, but to my eyes it's just up the road.

One of Da's better journal illustrations was an idyllic watercolor of Lookout Hill. I used to stare at it for hours—a lonely watchtower atop a proud hill with a small town at its base, overlooking a line of wayposts shrinking and fading into the endless sandy flats of the waste until they touched the pink-and-blue horizon of a setting sun. The colors were so vivid, I felt like I'd been there myself. I'd been hoping that seeing that tower in real life would make me feel a little closer to him.

But Da made that painting before the Krasians came. The lonely watchtower is gone, replaced by a walled fort that dominates the entire hilltop, flying the scorpion banner of the Mehnding tribe.

The fort's thick walls are lined with crenellations for archers, rock slingers, and scorpions—gigantic crank bows that fire stingers three times the size of a *Sharum* spear. Five tall watchtowers look out over the town below, standing silent guardian over the wayposts disappearing into the waste.

"They gonna let us pass without a problem?" I ask.

"The Mehnding guard against enemies from the waste, not fools walking into it," Rojvah says. "In any event, they will not hinder emissaries traveling under the royal seal."

I look over at her. "Since when do we have a royal seal?"

Rojvah shrugs. A hint of smile quirks her lips, and beneath the jasmine perfume she smells of satisfaction. "I had Arick bat his eyes at one of the palace clerks and ask after her mother. I had all the time in the world to borrow the seal and return it."

"The woman talked for hours," Arick growls, and Selen barks a laugh.

Rojvah takes the lead when we reach the town. She gives a false name and produces the writ from the throne empowering her and her entourage—a *Sharum* bodyguard and two *chin* servants—to cross the desert and treat with the Majah.

I can tell Selen chafes at the servant's role, but I'm happy to keep my head down and my mouth shut. We don't linger, setting immediately through the gate and onto the desert road, even as evening approaches. The wayposts—great stone obelisks, cut deep with wards—grant islands of succor, even as they lead the way through a featureless land.

"They're watching us," I say as we make camp at the first waypost. Looking back at the towers, I can see the guards spying on us with their distance lenses.

"It is their duty to watch over the desert road," Arick says.

"Ent the eyes on this side we've got to worry over," Selen says.

"Indeed," Rojvah says. "The Majah will have *csars* on the road to the city, and towers that can see far."

"How do we avoid being seen?" I ask.

"We don't, unless we leave the road, and we would be fools to do that. We have the seal of Royal Messengers. Let them see us coming, and take us right to the *Damaji*."

"Ay," Selen says, "except every Messenger that's gone into the desert for the last fifteen summers ent been seen again."

"It is a crime against Everam to harm a Messenger," Rojvah says. "No doubt they are safe in a silk prison."

"Like your grandmum kept us," I note.

Rojvah smiles. "And we see how well that held you."

WITH NO THICK Krasian curtains to block the light, I wake well before dawn, feeling the sun's approach like a weight on my chest.

It unsettles folk to see me at my normal speed, but the others are still asleep, so there's no need to act slow. The animals startle, suddenly discovering food in front of them. I saddle Dusk Runner, stowing my pack and sleeping roll while he's still eating. I lead him to the western side of the obelisk, where we will be in shadow for sunrise.

Among the supplies Abban provided for the desert crossing are canopies for our saddles—stout canvas on simple poles to grant shade to horse and rider, both. I set mine up and take care of my necessaries, climbing into the saddle before the others begin to stir.

Feel like I'm a blob of butter, waiting for the skillet to heat. Slowly, the sun crests the horizon, flooding the flat plain with light. It feels like fire, closing in from all sides.

I don't mind heat, or cold for that matter. I love feeling the change of seasons on my skin. But winter or summer, I burn quickly in bright sun. A shine that might turn other folk a little pink leaves me red and blistered. Even the scant bit of light that penetrates the shade and my clothes is enough to itch.

The loose Krasian clothes makes sense now—allowing bodies to breathe while shielding skin from the beating sun. I button up my jacket and wind the scarf over my face and head, leaving only a thin eye slit. I put on my gloves and I strap into the saddle, dozing away the early hours as Dusk Runner follows the other horses across flatlands of clay, cracked by the baking sun. The cracked flats go as far as the eye can see, like a flagstone path to infinity. My compass and the sun might point us in the right direction, but without the wayposts, we'd quickly lose the path and risk wandering in the desert until our stores ran out.

"Thought the desert was supposed to be sand," Selen grumbles after a long day of trudging.

Rojvah snorts. "Did you expect a perfect line where the lush grasses of the green lands turn suddenly to grit?"

She's trying to get a rise out of Selen, and I can smell it working. "We're in a dried-up lake bed," I cut in before Selen can retort. "Should get to the other side tomorrow. That's when you'll start findin' sand in your shoes."

Rojvah looks at me in surprise. "How do you know so much?"

"Da made the Messenger run from Fort Rizon to Fort Krasia for years," I say. "Crossed the desert more than a dozen times, and wrote about it in his journals. Read those books over and over, tryin' to know him better."

Selen loosens her scarf to wipe sweat from her brow. "What's there to say, apart from *It's hot and everything's dead?*"

"Everythin' ent dead." I take a deep breath, letting the silk filter out the clouds of clay dust in the air. "There's life here. I can smell it. Sleepin' like a bear in winter, but it's there, waiting for the rain to come and wake it up, if only for a while."

"*Alagai* blood," Arick mutters under his breath, too low for the others to hear.

"What's that, Arick?" I ask cheerfully, turning all eyes his way.

Arick smiles at me. "Just clearing my throat, cousin."

Selen and Rojvah ride with their canopies up, but Arick leaves his stowed, even as the sun beats down on his head. His skin isn't as vulnerable as mine, but he is pale by Krasian standards, and likely no friend to the sun. He has wrapped himself carefully in his *Sharum* blacks, but he doesn't seem uncomfortable. He smells . . . proud.

"Don't know how you can wear black in this sun," Selen says. "Doesn't it just absorb the heat?"

"I've dreamed of wearing the black for my entire life," Arick says. "I was in my mother's belly when she defended the walls of Everam's Reservoir from the *alagai*. There wasn't a boy my age who could stand against me in the practice yard, but one by one, they were all called to *sharaj* while I was left behind."

He spreads his arms, lifting his face to the sun. "Now at last I am free to be who I really am, and no sun is going to make me hide, or drive me back into a jester's robes."

WE MAKE CAMP under another of the ancient obelisks. Da's journals say the wayposts project a forbidding twenty paces in every direction, enough to shelter a small caravan.

The horses are hobbled and blinded. The saddle canopies, drawn with great wards of unsight, have been raised to hide them from above. The Mehnding lands were hunted clean of demons, but almost two days into the waste, we've crossed from their protection.

At dusk the heat leaches from the ground and dissipates, leaving a cold that bites like a winter night. I don't mind the chill, because it brings power. My night eyes come to life as magic seeps up from the ground to drift along the flats like a low rolling fog.

Drawn to the wards, the magic flows through us on its way to the waypost. The others barely notice, but for me it's like jumping into the swimming hole on a hot day. Power clings to me, like coming out wet.

I reach out with my expanding senses, but even with night eyes and bat ears, the demons get uncomfortably close before I spot them. Corelings have brighter auras than surface creatures, but they've evolved to mask it by adapting to the terrain they hunt.

Swamp and bog demons hide underwater and in trees. Wind demons keep to the clouds. Wood demons have armor so thick the outer layers are hardened and magic-dead, masking the strength within.

Clay demons remind me of the turtles Mam taught me to catch by the brook. Tough, muscular bodies encased in a hard shell the exact color of the flats all around us, thick and magic-dead.

Drawn to the light of our fire, they stalk in on short, thick limbs, slow and silent, but Da wrote they can be terrible fast when they charge—butting their blunt, armored heads hard enough to shatter stone. They don't have teeth precisely, just a sharp beak of armor to crush and sever chunks to swallow whole. Their retractable claws can tunnel through most anything, including steel armor plate.

I pull Mam's Cloak of Unsight closer around me as they take their time, circling the camp to view it from all sides before closing in. I string my bow and take an arrow from my quiver, but I don't know what good it will do. The demons' shells are blunt and smooth, giving no magic to power the piercing wards on the arrowheads. Anything other than a direct hit will just skitter off, and even a perfect shot might shatter against the shell.

Selen sees me nock the arrow and comes over. She has her armor plates in, but they don't seem to hinder her easy grace. Even her helmet is unobtrusive, hidden beneath the scarf covering her head, save for the warded rim that grants her wardsight. Her Cloak of Unsight is draped around her, wards glowing softly as they shield her from the demon eyes.

She scans the night, smelling of frustration. "You see something?"

"Four of them," I say, "circling in close."

Everyone looks, but I can tell none of them see. The demons are in no hurry, and the wait is agonizing before at last Arick points at one of them. "There."

He steps forward for a closer look.

"Stay close to the waypost, brother," Rojvah says. Even her white robes have started to orange at the hems from the clay dust, but the shawl she's placed over her shoulders is stark white, stitched in silver thread with wards of unsight much like those on our cloaks. Like Selen and I, she is invisible to demons.

Arick is not.

"The protection extends twenty paces." Arick takes nineteen precise paces forward, peering into the night for a better look at the foe. His shield is at the ready, and he grips the spear so tightly I can hear his muscles creak. He smells of adrenaline, excitement, and hunger.

"Nothin' to gain, picking a fight tonight, Arick," I say before he does something wood-headed.

"You said yourself there are only four of them." Arick flexes his arms and shoulders, limbering his muscles. "We could kill them and have done."

"Have you lost your mind?" Selen asks. "Fifty miles from the nearest earshot, and you want to fight corelings when you don't have to?"

"My brother has not learned to fear the *alagai*," Rojvah says. "Too many tales of glory, too little experience."

Arick rolls his eyes. "My sister speaks as if she's ever seen more than an *alagai's* boiled bones."

"Ent wrong, though," I say. "One thing to stare down a demon over the wards, or watch one dance to your tune. Seein' one cripple your friend and come racing at you with bloody talons is somethin' different."

As if on cue, the demon Arick was eyeing suddenly charges. It does not look agile, but even I am shocked by its speed as it lowers its blunt armored head and horns, smashing heavily against the forbidding.

Silver light flashes just before the demon smashes into Arick, the light bowing in midair stopping the charge and throwing the demon back.

Arick, for all his courage and hunger to prove himself, is caught off guard at the sudden assault. He gives a cry and stumbles back just as the wards activate, thrown off balance as the anticipated blow never comes. He lands on his backside, spear and shield clattering, but no one laughs.

Another clay demon strikes the wards even as the first shakes itself off and rolls back to its feet. Growling, it digs claws into the clay, readying for another charge. The horses whinny in fear, pulling at the stakes, drawing the cries of yet more demons in the distance.

"Standing there without a cloak, you're callin' 'em like a bell at suppertime," I tell Arick as he gets to his feet, murder in his eyes.

"Arick asu Sikvah!" Rojvah snaps, and the mention of his mother gets her brother's attention. "A *Sharum's* duty is to defend their people, not to seek battle for the sake of foolish pride and lust for ichor. We have a week at least left in the crossing. Will you leave us to attempt it without our strongest fighter?"

"You assume I will die, sister," Arick growls.

"I assume you will act with discipline," Rojvah retorts, "not shame your mother by throwing yourself at *alagai* talons the first chance you get."

Arick scowls, but he breathes away his anger and returns to the obelisk, setting down his spear and shield. He opens his kamanj case and rosins the bow, bracing the instrument's spiked end on a thick leather band that wraps around his thigh.

The bow seems flimsy and delicate in his big hands. His meaty fingers are less nimble than mine, but they move with workmanlike competence over the strings as he plays his father Rojer Halfgrip's most famous composition, the *Song of Waning*.

Don't know what I expected, but Arick's playing is short of it. He gets all the notes right, but Hary Roller could play circles around him. Night, I've heard backyard jug bands in Tibbet's Brook play with more spirit.

Still, the defensive field Arick weaves around us is undeniable. The clay demons cease trying to batter through the wards and back away. There's a cry from above and a great flap of leathern wings as a silently circling wind demon flies off in search of other prey.

"How come you don't have a warded cloak?" Selen asks.

"He does." Rojvah crosses her arms. "A cloak with a legend all its own. But he refuses to wear it."

"Halfgrip's motley cloak," I breathe. Arick's da is a bit of a hero to me. He saved almost as many lives as mine, but he did it without fighting anyone. Just his fiddle and his magic cloak.

"If you love it so much, you wear it," Arick growls. "I'd as soon wear your white *dama'ting* shawl."

Rojvah remains outwardly calm, but her scent is angry, now. "Would that I could, brother. This trip frees you to dress as you please, but I can hardly slip unnoticed into Majah lands in the clothing I favor. They would stone me for a *heasah*."

"The Majah will treat a greenland Jongleur with no more respect than a *heasah*," Arick says. "At least you *like* to perform. Come, sing so I can put this cursed instrument down."

Rojvah still smells of irritation, but she kneels beside her brother and lowers her veil. She begins to hum, building tension in the air, before vocalizing a series of notes that weave into Arick's melody, at first matching him, then, as Rojvah touches the choker at her throat, overwhelming the kamanj.

And then she begins to sing.

If Arick was a workman, his sister is an artisan. Rojvah effortlessly delivers a song with passion and power that her brother could never have mustered, laying a musical spell over the camp that has a noticeable effect. Arick drove the demons back, but they drifted at the edge of the music, auras still predatory, waiting for the protection to wane.

Rojvah's music calms the demons' auras, and they lose interest, taking no more notice of us than they would if we all wore Cloaks of Unsight.

Arick doesn't waste time, taking bow from string and tucking his kamanj back into its case. He smells of shame, anger, and jealousy all at once. It's clear he wants no part of whatever his sister is building.

But I do. Her song calls to me, thrumming in my blood, resonating in my bones. I wonder if this is how the corelings felt when her spell fell over them.

I reach for my pipes, not knowing if I am out of line as I fumble them to my lips. Doesn't matter. Couldn't stop myself if I wanted. Something primal compels me to join the song.

Rojvah nods as I blow the first notes, weaving my piping around her voice. She begins to test me, changing key and altering the pace, but following her is effortless, like following her scent through the hedge maze in the Krasian palace gardens when we were kids. I want to laugh at the joy of it.

Rojvah turns her attention back to the demons, taking the song up an octave, and then another, her voice going higher than any voice has a right to. I don't even have to look at the demons to know the effect she is creating. I feel it in my stones.

The demons shriek and run for their lives. The four I originally spotted, and three more out on the flats that had been slowly inching our way. Their fear is so all-encompassing, it may be miles before they stop running, and they will be reluctant to return.

Rojvah turns my way, and I see her smile as she tests my limits, taking the song to new and difficult places, just to see if I can follow. She's better than me—far better—but I refuse to fall behind, going wherever her voice leads.

"Ay, enough with the racket," Selen says after what could have been hours, or mere minutes.

Rojvah and I both break off, turning to her in surprise. I can smell her irritation, sharp and hot, but I don't know the cause.

"Demons are gone," Selen says. "Ent any point in playing all night. Going to need our rest come morning."

"What if they come back?" I ask.

Selen reaches into her pack, pulling out Olive's Cloak of Unsight. Unlike the famed multicolored cloak of Rojer Halfgrip, this one is midnight blue—almost black—and its wards look like silver fire.

She goes to Arick. "This belongs to Olive, but I don't think she'd mind you using it until we can return it to her."

Arick reaches out, and their hands touch for a little too long as he takes the cloak from her. "You honor me, Selen vah Gared. One day I will give you a gift of equal value in return."

"You already have," Selen says, "coming along with us." They stare at each other a while longer, then she turns away, shivering as she slips into her bedroll, draping her own cloak over her.

The mood shattered, I drop my pipes, letting them hang from their strap. "Din't know you could do that," I tell Rojvah. "You make my pipes sound like a dented bugle."

"Nonsense," Rojvah says, but she smiles again. "My brother resents our father's legacy, but I do not. Rojer asu Jessum was bound in greater glory than the warriors Arick idolizes. Even Arick's mother was known more for her song than her work with the spear."

"Then why don't you be the Jongleur, and let Arick wear the black?" I ask quietly. Arick and Selen are both in their bedrolls, but I can hear their hearts and breath. Both are awake and listening.

"Because Arick is the *son*." Rojvah's hiss is low and venomous. "And I am my mother's heir, set to one day succeed her as *Damaji'ting* of the Kaji tribe."

"Doesn't sound so bad," I say.

Rojvah surprises me by spitting in the dust. She turns away, looking out over the empty orange flats. "I would have been a great Jongleur. Like my father the royal herald, I could be the voice of the Shar'dama Ka and Damajah in foreign lands. A diva, stylish in my colored gowns, voice known far and wide, with lovers in every court."

She looks down at her white robes. "Instead, I am given plain white, and told my body belongs to Everam."

43

SANDSTORM

THE CLAY FLATS give way to sand, our tracks slowly swept away by a seemingly endless wind that blows the grit into great mounds that stretch out over the horizon. The silk veil filters out most of the particles, but not their taste. My mouth is pasty with it.

The wayposts become inconsistent as we enter the dunes, some standing as tall and clear as when they were built, thousands of years ago. Others are half buried in the sand.

It's been fifteen years since anyone has made this crossing and told the tale. Fifteen years of wind and sand. I'm scared some might be missing entirely, swallowed by the dunes.

We find another half-buried post before nightfall. We make camp around its base, still offering some protection, though nothing like the twenty paces full pillars offer.

We lay portable ward circles around the animals and our bedrolls for added security, but the wind worries me. Sand blows across the ward-plates, threatening to weaken the protections. We take turns on watch, sweeping the wards clean regularly until dawn, but the demons are few this far from civilization.

We continue two more days, but as the third night approaches, we find ourselves without a waypost at all, just a wooden pole in the sand where the pillar lay buried, with an arrow pointing the way.

To make matters worse, a powerful wind kicks up, blowing sand and grit everywhere. We pace the perimeter of our portable warding circle, but the plates are being covered faster than we can sweep them clean. We try to make music, but Rojvah's throat is dry, her voice muffled by her veil. I'm forced to lower my veil entirely to play the pipes, inhaling grit every time I take a breath. Sand gets in the strings and bow of Arick's kamanj. He continues to play, but it fouls what sound isn't drowned by the howl of the wind.

Even the protection of our cloaks starts to weaken as blowing sand collects on the threads, making the wards fuzzy and ineffective.

And amid the howling wind and our shouts to one another, I hear sand demon cries.

My hand goes instinctively for my bow, but I know it's pointless. My hands already shake when I'm aiming at something tryin' to kill me, and I ent a good enough shot to account for wind like this.

I grip the bone handle of Mam's knife, instead, as I search the blowing sands. Da wrote that sand demons look so much like the dunes, they're near impossible to see in normal vision. I can see their auras with my night eyes, but they've adapted to use the blowing sand to their advantage. The swirling particles in the air reflect the glow, making the shapes vague and diffuse. It's impossible to tell how many there are, or how close.

Suddenly, the wardnet around us flashes to life, revealing dangerously large gaps in the web where sand has marred the wards.

Selen screams, and I turn to see her stumble back, spear knocked from her grasp by the swipe of a clawed arm as a sand demon attempts to force its way through a hole in the wards in front of her.

In a flash the bow is off my shoulder. I nock and loose, but as I feared, the wind throws off my aim and the missile flies wide, nearly hitting one of the horses.

"Selen!" I cry, pulling Mam's knife and running her way.

I needn't have bothered.

Selen balls a fist and swings, her punch striking the demon like a thunderstick. There's a flash on impact, and the demon is knocked back. I don't understand how it's possible until I see the jewelry on her spear hand—a set of five silver rings, warded and connected by fine silver chains to a jeweled bracelet around her wrist.

Already the demon is shaking off even this, tamping down for an-other leap. Before it can strike, Selen sweeps clean the weakened ward-plates. When the demon leaps, it flattens against a solid wardnet and is thrown back.

But more sand's flying through the air, and the circle is far from se-cure. Arick stubbornly keeps playing as Selen once again takes up her spear, eyes searching for the next breach.

When another demon finds a gap in the wards, Selen is there to meet it head-on, driving her warded spear down its throat. The wards glow fiercely, and her aura brightens as feedback magic runs up her arm.

"To the abyss with it!" Arick drops his kamanj and picks up his spear and shield as another demon starts probing the wards. He doesn't wait for the coreling to find a gap, stabbing it in the shoulder and collapsing it to the ground. Magic rushes into him, and he gives a primal roar that carries on the wind.

The next few hours are chaos. Arick and Selen do the fighting, lop-ing about the camp to throw back sand demons seeking gaps in the net. Selen is quiet, focused, but Arick's laughter seems amplified by the din, as frightening as the cries of the demons.

I want to help Arick and Selen, but there ent much I can do, save get in their way. A demon pierces the wardnet near Rojvah, and I race to her instead, interposing myself with Mam's knife held high, as if I know how to use it in a fight. Still, the coreling must sense the weapon's power, because it pulls up warily, hissing like a cat as it displays razor-sharp claws and teeth.

As with the others, Rojvah doesn't need my help. "Step aside, cousin." She reaches into her *hora* pouch, drawing out a demon tooth the size of my middle finger, tiny wards etched into its surface. She points it at the sand demon, sliding a finger to cover some wards and reveal others.

A bolt of lightning leaps from the tooth, striking the demon in the chest and hurling it back into the swirling sands.

It's a tough tea to swallow, but I focus instead on the one thing I can do, moving around the camp's perimeter at speed, using a small brush to clear off the wardplates. It helps, but the task seems endless as the wind continues to howl and more and more demons are drawn to the storm.

Sand demons don't come much bigger than hounds, but I'd rather fight a pack of rabid dogs than a single one of the fast, vicious creatures. With every blow he strikes, Arick's aura grows brighter, and his aggression grows. Ent long before he looks a bit rabid, himself. He stabs a sand demon, and when it does not rise, he turns to see Selen in a fighting stance, spear and shield at the ready to meet the charge of another of the small, muscular beasts.

Arick leaps into the demon's path, shoving Selen aside. Where she waited patiently with her shield up, he abandons defense in favor of a devastating thrust of his spear that punches through the demon's armor and into its chest.

"Ay, what was that?!" Selen cries. Arick ignores her, shouting something incoherent as he stabs the creature again and again, the wards on his spear hot with magic.

All of us stay out of Arick's way after that. He rushes around the circle, whirling his spear through the air to stab demon after demon. The look in his eyes reminds me of Ella Cutter when the Children locked her in the Bunker.

The wind dies down after a time and the attacks taper off, but Arick continues to pace the perimeter of the circle like an animal, growling incoherent words to himself.

"He's rattlin' my nerves." Selen's aura is hot with stolen magic, too, and I can smell her anger. "Can't stop thinking about how he *shoved* me." The word comes out in a growl as she tightens her grip on her spear, and I see where this is going.

"I'll go talk to him," I say, before things can escalate.

"It should be me," Rojvah says. "I can get through to him."

"Ay, maybe," I say. "But he's magic-drunk. Seen it before. Get far enough gone, you can't tell friend from foe."

"My brother would never hurt me," Rojvah says, but there is doubt in her scent.

"Just let me feel him out," I say. "Ent much good in a fight, but I'm great at slippin' punches."

But I don't go slippery as I approach Arick. Instinctively I suck in, making my flesh tougher, my bones harder. The effect shrinks me a bit. Might make Arick feel less threatened, or it might make him feel like a cat spotting a barn mouse.

"You were right, Arick," I say at his back. As he turns, I hold my empty hands palms up. "No one can deny you the black, now."

Arick stares like he doesn't know me, breathing great gulps of cold night air through his veil.

"All friends here, ay?" I continue to approach, hands out wide. His breathing steadies and I start to relax, but then I take one step too many and enter into his striking zone.

Arick gives a shout, slashing with the wide blade at the end of his spear. He's fast, but I'm ready, turning slippery as I quickstep out of reach. Arick spins the spear this way and that to stab and club at me, growling all the while. Powered by feedback magic and adrenaline, he's got speed to rival mine, and I reckon he's strong enough to arm-wrestle Olive Paper. A single one of his blows could take off my head.

But I'm not looking to fight back. So long as I stay slippery and focus only on defense, Arick can't do more than strike a glancing blow that slides right off me. He swings again and again, but I give him no magic to feed off, and slowly his frantic pace begins to drain away some of the excess energy.

It's wearing on me, too. It's been a long night, and I'm not sure which of us will tire first. "This ent you, Arick," I huff, barely rolling around a thrust of his spear in time. "It's the magic talking."

"Embrace the feeling, brother," Rojvah calls, "and let it pass over you."

"Or have the stones to pick on someone your own size." Selen steps forward, spear and shield at the ready.

"Ent helpin', Sel," I say.

Arick responds to this new threat with a growl, turning to face Selen. There's a hint of smile on her face as she sets her feet to meet him. Has everyone gone crazy?

Before Arick can move Selen's way, Rojvah steps in front of him, slapping him hard across the face.

It's a terrible insult to slap a Krasian man. More oft than not a precursor to a duel that will claim at least one life before satisfaction. Shocked, Arick stumbles back, shaking his head.

Selen steps in front of me, spear up. "Stay behind me, Dar." I drop a hand to Mam's knife, and even Rojvah has a demonbone in her hand.

Arick squeezes his eyes shut for a long moment, then opens them, something of his sanity restored as he sees the three of us staring at him.

"Fight's over, Arick," I say. "We won."

He stares at me a moment, then throws back his head and laughs, thrusting his spear in the air.

No one sleeps. Arick and Selen keep watch, as much over each other as the sands. Both remain awash in power, and jittery. Arick still hasn't spoken. Selen seems to have a better lid on it, but I wouldn't want to get in an argument with her now.

Rojvah looks exhausted, her white robes crusted with dust. With Arick out of sorts, I can tell she doesn't know who to trust. I want to help her, but with dawn approaching, I've got problems of my own.

With no obelisk shadow to shelter in, I set up Dusk Runner's canopy and strap myself into the saddle, carefully covering every inch of myself and putting my cloak's hood up for good measure. I look at my friends sadly. They have no idea what's about to happen, but maybe that's for the best.

Shaded and layered, sunrise is bright and hot, the light making my skin itch, but I've gotten used to the feeling.

Arick and Selen are not so fortunate. Selen yelps first, as the demon ichor staining her spear and shield and armor smokes and then sparks into flame. She drops her arms and beats at the flame, even as Arick bellows and begins a similar dance.

Then the sunlight hits them more fully, burning away the excess magic radiating from their auras, and they scream.

It doesn't last long. The worst of it never does, especially when you're caught in the light. Just a hot flash of pain that leaves you breathless and shaking in its wake. Selen and Arick quiet after a bit, and then it's like all our strings are cut.

I half doze, listening as the others follow my example. They cover their skin and stiffly feed and water their mounts from our lightening supply. While the horses eat, they saddle them and raise the canopies.

I hear sighs of relief as they climb into the saddles, but no one makes any effort to move. I allow myself to drift off completely.

———

"Ay, Darin." Selen shakes me awake.

The light is blinding as I open my eyes, and I hiss, holding up a hand to block the worst of it.

"It was a lot worse at sunrise," Selen says. "Is that what it's like for you every morning?"

I shrug. "Get used to it."

"I don't think I could ever get used to being on fire," Selen says.

"Ay," I agree, "but you make a fuss and folk start whispering you've got demon blood."

"Folk are always whispering," Selen says. "It's up to you whether to listen."

As if it's so easy to shut out whispers when you can hear a butterfly flapping its wings. I glance at the noon sun overhead. "Lost the mornin', I guess."

"Lost more than that," Selen says. "Can't spot the next waypost."

That sits me up straight. I look back to the signpost, but it's bent over in the sand, arrow knocked askew. Can't tell which way it was pointing. The entire landscape looks different after last night's storm.

Panic knots my muscles, but I try not to show it. The desert road doesn't run a straight line. If we stray too far off course, we could lose it forever. Without the wayposts to guide us, we could miss Fort Krasia by a hundred miles and never know it.

I cover up as best I can and climb the tallest dune, using my compass and the sun to aid me as I search the sands for the desert road. I can see for miles, but there is no sign of the next post.

One look at my face as I come back down tells the others all they need to know. "Anyone remember which way the sign was pointing?"

"That way," Selen points. "Near where we dug the firepit."

I squint away the sunlight as I peer in that direction. "Sure about that?"

Selen blows out a breath. "Mostly. I think."

"Are we to trust our lives to 'mostly'?" Rojvah asks.

"You could throw your dice, if you had any," Selen grunts. Rojvah glares at her, but Selen is not easily intimidated. "Don't see you offering better."

I wish I had something to add, but between the weather and the demons, we're all turned around. Arick produces his map, though it doesn't tell us much without the posts to mark the land. Most of it's blank, with vague markings where ancient ruins are supposedly buried.

"Krasia's to the southeast," I say. "Closer to the mountains that feed the oasis." I check my compass, and Selen's guess is as good as any.

"Can't stay here," I say. "So either we turn back—"

"No," Selen cuts in.

I nod. "Then *mostly's* all we got."

"The compass and a fuzzy memory may be more precise than wild guesses," Rojvah says, "but they could still lead us far enough from our goal to miss it entirely in the sands. We don't have supplies to wander the desert until fortune finds our way."

"Go back, if you're scared," Selen says. "But I didn't come all this way to turn around because the wind blew a sign over."

"Need to get moving so we don't lose the day," I say. "Want to get as far as we can from here. Corelings always rise in the same area they left to flee the sun. Reckon there'll be a whole mess of 'em come nightfall."

"What say you, brother?" Rojvah looks to Arick, but her brother is staring into the distance, his face euphoric. I'm not even sure he's listening until he whispers a reply.

"Let them come."

44

OASIS OF DAWN

WE COVER A fair distance from the camp, but it's not enough. The corelings will rise at dusk and follow our trail, moving far faster than we can over the sands. We've bought ourselves a few hours, at best.

"Should have seen three wayposts by now," I say.

"Which means either they all got buried," Selen begins, "or—"

"We're off course." Arick is studying his map. "We should have passed a spring an hour ago."

Travelers depend on the springs along the desert road to sustain them on the crossing. Life clings to those little patches of land surrounding small seepage pools, easily waded across, but more valuable than gold. We packed water, but all of us are consuming more than expected, the animals included. We can afford to miss this spring, but not all of them. And without the wayposts to guide us . . .

"Might as well set camp now," I say. "No point pushing on till we know where we are. Maybe the stars can tell us more than a compass and a map."

The night is clear, and the moon a thinning crescent. With no city lights and greatwards to blot them, countless stars light up the sky. All the groupings from astronomy maps, speckled with stars only my eyes can see, invisible even to the astronomers of the old world with great distance lenses or my friends with their warded sight.

Still, Rojvah is the first to speak, lifting a finger to point at a cluster of stars. "We are too far east."

"Ay." Selen's scent is less sure as she stares up at the sky. "But there's no way to tell how many wayposts have been buried in sandstorms over the last fifteen years. We could cross the desert road a dozen times and never know it."

"She's right." Arick rolls his map and puts it back in the tube. "And without the springs, we don't have enough water to wander for long."

"Then we don't make for the road," I say.

Everyone looks at me, and it takes me a moment to realize they don't understand. "Da says there's only one place to head, if you're lost in the waste."

"The oasis." Rojvah turns her eyes back to the sky even as Arick reopens his map tube.

"Oasis?" Selen asks.

"The Oasis of Dawn," Arick says, "has greeted every traveler through the waste since the desert road was blazed. *Inevera*, we will have water enough to reach it."

"Da wrote a lot about the oasis," I say, trying to keep the eagerness from my voice. "Might encounter other folk there, and sometimes animals come to drink. There's shelter, fruit trees, even a fishing hole."

"Ay, I'm sold," Selen says. "How do we find it?"

It takes a while to figure. The Krasians have different names for the constellations than the ones Da used, but eventually, we work it out. Between the map, the compass, and the stars, we hazard a reasonably educated guess.

"How educated?" Selen hasn't been able to help, and it's made her prickly.

"Reckon I can smell a big pool like that for miles," I say. "Even if we're off a little, we'll come close enough for me to sniff it out."

Selen seems satisfied with that reply, but Rojvah clearly is not. "Even if you are correct, it will take three days to reach the oasis. Do we have water enough?"

"Barely," Arick says. "We will need to conserve without lessening our pace."

"Not dyin's a good motivator," I say. "Can't afford to dally in any event, 'less we want to get caught outside the walls at new moon."

That sobers everyone. Selen goes to her bedroll. "Best we get some rest before the demons catch up."

"I'll take first watch." Arick finishes polishing his spear and shield, rising to hold them like lovers. I've no doubt he'll take the second watch, too. And the third. As long as it takes to find another chance to drive his warded spear into a demon, tasting its magic.

"We've got hard level ground tonight," I tell him, "and not a lot of wind. The circle will hold. Might be smart to clean the grit from your kamanj. We're safer using music, and fighting as a last resort."

Arick laughs. "I threw my kamanj into the sand before we left camp this morning, son of Arlen!" He points with his spear back the way we've come. "Half a day's walk that way."

"Everam's beard, you are a fool." Rojvah spits in the dust.

"Fool was father's job," Arick says. "I know what I am, now."

I don't want to get involved. Night, I wish I could mist into the ground like a demon to flee the building conflict. But from the looks they're givin' each other and the way they smell, this is gonna escalate if I don't say something. "Ay, it's all sunny," I cut in before Rojvah spits a venomous reply. "I'll play, instead."

Arick shrugs. "Do as you wish."

There is no concession in his scent, but there's no point arguing. I run a finger over the *hora* coin the Damajah affixed to my pipes, wondering if I can keep the demons too far away for him to pick a fight.

I move to my own bedroll, hoping to catch a bit of rest before the demons catch up. I pass Selen, propped up on one arm staring at Arick.

"You be careful around that one," she whispers. "Reminds me of Ella Cutter, when she got drunk on demon ichor."

"Ay." I squat beside her. "Saw her too. But this ent that."

"You sure?" Selen asks. "I felt it, too. Never felt so good in my life. Wasn't like the fight on the borough tour."

"Reckon your wooden armor took most of the charge," I say. "Mam says it was designed that way, to help Hollow Soldiers keep control. This time it went right into you."

"Ay, maybe," Selen agrees.

"But it ent magic that's got Arick and Rojvah ready to boil over," I say. "This scrap's been building for years. Best we stay out of it as much as we can."

"Ay." Selen snorts a laugh. "Creator knows, I want to punch my wood-brained brothers often enough."

Rojvah puts her head down. She's better at faking sleep than Selen, but not enough to fool me. She's wide awake and watching us through slitted eyes, but she's too far off to hear our low voices.

"Who taught you to read the stars?" Selen asks.

"Da kept the charts, but Mam taught me to read 'em," I say. "Figuring out where you are by the stars is extra important when you can skate a thousand miles in a heartbeat but can't see where you're going."

"Why don't you?" Selen asks.

I'm confused. "Why don't I what?"

"Just skate to Krasia," Selen asks. "I've seen you do it."

I shake my head. "You saw Mam drag me. Ent the same thing."

"Why not?" Selen asks.

He will be born in darkness, the Damajah said, *and will carry it inside him.*

"Magic burns off with the sun," I tell her, "so surface life never adapted to it. But corelings live in magic like fish live in water. Their bodies absorb and hold it like coals buried in ash. So when Mam and my da . . . " I get queasy at the thought, "*ate* demons, it . . . changed them."

Selen nods. "Gave them powers."

"I guess," I say. "I've never eaten demon. Whatever seed of magic they passed to me is only a fraction of that."

"Little seeds can grow into big trees, Darin," Selen says.

The words remind me of the hidden part of the Damajah's foretelling—the part I wish I could make myself forget.

A boy of limitless potential, and a future of despair.

Does that mean I'm going to fail no matter what I do? Not every seed gets to be a tree. And if I don't, who I got to blame but myself?

"Hey." Selen lays a hand on my foot. The pressure through the soft leather of my boot is gentle, but it's enough to pull me back. "Where did you go?"

I shake my head. "Just thinkin'." It ent that I don't trust her, but I'm comin' to see why folk keep prophecies a secret. Makes you second-guess everything.

I go back to the original question. "Wouldn't skate to Krasia even if I could. Hate it."

She tilts her head at me. "That why you were screaming when you and your mam skated in that last time?"

The memory of that humiliating moment is burned into my mind, always ready to fill me with fresh shame. It's no wonder Selen doesn't want to kiss me anymore, but that ent her problem, it's mine.

Always a struggle getting folk to understand my troubles, but maybe this one I can explain. "Think the sun hurt when it burned off your magic this morning? Try having every bit of you pulled apart until you burst into mist and are sucked down into a twister during a lightning storm."

Selen squeezes her hand on my foot. "How do you keep from just . . . blowing away?"

"Mam says it's will, but Core if I could ever understand it," I admit. "And even will's got its limits. That's how my da died. Stretched so far he couldn't pull himself back together."

Selen puts a hand over her mouth. "Oh, Darin, I'm so sorry."

She rises to embrace me, but I'm barely holding together, and that would put it over the edge. I back away, just enough for her to get the message. She nods, sitting on her bedroll and patting a spot next to her.

I take the offered seat. "Know going after Olive ent a game and I don't wanna seem selfish, but this trip . . . seein' places Da wrote about, it's been like gettin' to know him a bit."

"Nothing selfish about wanting to know your da better," Selen says.

"Guess not," I say. "Da called the Oasis of Dawn the most beautiful place in the world. Said it saved his life more than once."

"It's nice that you can read your da's journals," Selen says. "See who he really was. The general's got his tales, but I've heard them get bigger every year. Who knows where the truth ends and the ale story begins?"

"You could just ask him." The words come out harder than I intend. Selen is trying to understand, but she doesn't—not really. "Give anything to be able to go up to my da and ask him a question, even if all I got was an ale story."

"Sorry." Selen keeps her eyes forward, staring in the same direction as me, but she reaches out a hand, laying it over mine. "What would you ask him, if you could?"

I hesitate. The answer's personal, but it ent a prophecy. Who in the world can I trust, if not Selen Cutter? "Why he left us, I guess."

Selen is quiet a long time. "Saving the world ent some small thing, Darin."

"Know that," I say, "but whenever I imagine meeting him, it's the first thing I ask."

"And the second?" Selen asks.

"Just . . . " If the first one was personal, this is being caught naked on a cold day. ". . . what he thinks of me." I choke, and suddenly my eyes are blurry. I squeeze them shut to force the water out, feeling tears run down my cheeks. "Not much, I expect."

I feel Selen's arms close around me, and this time I don't have the will to resist. "That's tampweed talk, Darin Bales. You're smart and brave and make beautiful music. You'd do anything to help your friends. What da wouldn't be proud of all that?"

I sob, and Selen pulls me close, squeezing me tight as I weep into her shoulder for just a few moments. I feel ashamed when it's done, turning away to dab my eyes with my scarf.

Across the fire I see Rojvah watching, and the feeling worsens. Creator only knows what she's thinkin'. Krasian women take tears seriously. Got whole rituals about it.

But the men ent supposed to cry.

Protected by a ring of massive wardstones, the Oasis of Dawn is an island of perfection in the waste, fed by an underground river that passes close to the surface. Sand and hard clay give way suddenly to verdant grasses, shaded by fruiting trees and bushes growing in clusters with medicinal herbs—some natural and some cultivated over time for utility and beauty. The crystal water in the deep pool is clean to drink, and large enough for an entire caravan of people and animals to wade in and quench their thirst along with the local fauna.

———

THAT'S WHAT DA'S journal said, at least. It ent what we find.

The warded obelisks are fully revealed and easily spotted, but inside their succor the fruiting trees and bushes have all been cut, the remains torn up root and stump to leave puddles amid soil packed hard as a wagon rut. The pool is drained down to a murky and brackish pond at the center of a wide, muddy depression buzzing with insects. I could smell its stink a mile out.

Patches of coarse vegetation cling stubbornly to the land, but ent nothing close to "verdant."

"Sixty thousand of us crossed the desert to the green lands," Rojvah says. "When the Majah returned with their *chin* thralls, it was nearly as many. Everam never meant this place to support such numbers."

"Sucked the orange dry." I feel sick inside. "Turned the most beautiful place in the world into a warded mud puddle." How many times had I dreamed of this place, poring over Da's description and illustrations? Is there anything in the world left I can share with him?

"Bah," Arick says. "Everam wills as Everam will." The words are the first he's spoken since the night before, and don't sound like him at all. "The Creator placed the oasis here to aid his grand army in their path north to Sharak Sun and eternal glory."

Sharak Sun. The Daylight War of prophecy, where my bloodfather's army sacked and annexed southern Thesa, levying the people of Fort Rizon and Lakton into his demon-killing army. I ball a fist. "Nothin' glorious about what your people did in Sharak Sun, Arick."

"The histories agree the green lands were too soft," Rojvah says. "The dukes bickered and fought among themselves, hiding from the *alagai* like cowards. It was only my grandfather's coming that hardened them in time."

"Demonshit." Selen spits in the dust. "Darin's da and Hollow were already starting to fight back against the demons before all the murder and theft you hide in 'grandfather's coming.'"

The words don't seem to bother Rojvah. If anything, she smells satisfied. "A brushfire when you needed an inferno."

I smell Selen taking the bait before she opens her mouth. We're all tired, hungry, and thirsty. Worried.

I try to imagine sixty thousand people, but it's too big a number. Folk carrying their lives on their backs or in carts, holding children and helping elderly. Pack animals, livestock, hounds. All of them tired, all of them hungry, all of them thirsty. Worried about survival, not some pretty garden. Worried about freezing if they don't find something to burn.

Ent right the most beautiful place in the world had to pay the price, but I can't bring myself to blame folk in need.

Selen is shouting now, and Arick is shouting back. Rojvah lets her brother carry the bulk of the argument while throwing in quiet darts to needle Selen, who looks ready to throttle them both.

"Ay, what does it matter, who was right?" I snap, and everyone turns my way. "War was over before any of us learned to crawl, and nothin's gonna bring the folk we lost to it back. Got more important worries right now."

"Honest word." Selen seems to deflate. "We got enough water to make it to Fort Krasia?"

Arick shakes his head. "Desert Spear is three days away, at least. Four if we're dehydrated. We don't have enough to last another day."

Rojvah looks to the murky, fetid pool. "Perhaps we can filter the water with silk and boil it."

"Ay, maybe." I inhale deeply through my nose, catching another scent hidden beneath the stink. "But I want a closer look."

I remember roughly Da's map of the oasis, but apart from the obelisks, all the landmarks are gone. It gives me a rough idea of where to look, but that's all I need to sniff out the ancient stair, cut first into the trampled soil and baked clay, and then into harder material as it leads down, down. Long before we get close, I can hear the rush of the river— smell the fresh water—but I say nothing until the others sense it, too. I can smell their relief as Selen gives a cheer, taking the last steps two at a time in her hurry to drink and fill her waterskins.

The others follow, even Rojvah sacrificing a bit of dignity to lift the hem of her robe and hurry down to the water. I climb back up the stairs instead, slowly counting. My tension grows until I reach the step Da wrote about and run my hand over a certain dry stone. The clay mortar crumbles around it, and I pull the stone free, revealing a small, dry compartment. My throat tightens and my hands shake as I reach inside, pull-ing out a carefully folded mass of knotted rope.

Da's fishing net.

I have to keep my hands from shaking as I hold it, taking it in with every sense at once. The texture of the rope fibers. The creak as I tug and test their strength.

I inhale, tasting his scent, preserved in the dry heat. I know it well. I used to play in Da's old rummage trunks just to sit in that smell.

Da made it with his own hands. Wove every lattice. Tied every knot. The feelings are so intense I feel myself going slippery to escape them. I have to suck in before the net slips from my fingers.

The father waits below . . .

The similarity to Aunt Leesha's prophecy is hard to shake. I wish to share something with my da, and here I find his old net hidden below-ground, waiting for me. But it's got to be a coincidence. If this is the prophecy made true, the Creator's got a strange sense of humor.

I take it in a little longer, then head back down to the river.

"Who's hungry for fish?"

THREE DAYS LATER, bellies full and throats still moist, we reach Fort Kra-sia, the Desert Spear. The city walls tower over the landscape, its great gates big enough for three rock demons to walk abreast.

We pass two ruined *csars* on the way, the char still pungent. The sights are an unnerving reminder that the corelings are up to something, and we'll reach the city just hours before the first night of new moon.

"Nearly three months now, since Olive was taken," Selen says. "Think she's all right?"

"Reckon she's in a silk prison full of servants and pretty clothes, just like we were," I say.

"She'd have loved that," Selen says, "if they hadn't kidnapped her and dragged her a thousand miles from home. You think they tried to marry her to that prince?"

I shrug. "If they did, reckon he's got two broken arms by now."

Selen laughs, but she still smells sad and afraid. And why not? I feel it, too. I want to reach out, to touch her arm the way she did when I

needed comfort, but I hesitate. I'm not used to touching anyone. If anything, they touch me.

And then the moment is gone.

"Reckon I can scale that wall without a problem," I say. "Maybe
open one of those side gates."

"Unless the guards are utter fools, they have already spotted us,"
Rojvah says. "With the *csars* destroyed, any travelers on this road will
stand out like wayposts."

"Night," I say. "Now what do we do?"

"We don't *do* anything, son of Arlen," Rojvah says, "save ride to the
gate, show the royal seal, and demand an audience with the *Damaji*. Did
you think to sneak over the wall and into the palace?"

I blink. That's exactly what I thought, and now I look like an idiot.
Even Selen has a hand over her face, shaking her head quietly.

"You passed the Damajah's test," Rojvah says, "but not even you
could manage that."

"Test?" I ask.

"Of course." Rojvah's smile is patient. "Though it took longer than
she expected for you to lose patience and offer to steal away and rescue
Olive."

"But . . . " I fumble for words, not entirely knowing what it is I'm
feeling. "Why? Why not just ask me?"

Rojvah is still looking at me like I am a fool. "So that when your
uncle reaches the city, or Grandfather returns, she can swear she had
nothing to do with it."

"Corespawned witch," Selen growls. "We lost a week and more sitting on pillows!"

"We left when we were meant to leave," Rojvah says. "It is *inevera*."

I wonder if there were other throws of the dice at work. Arick's fate,
or Rojvah's to inform the Damajah's decision. "That mean this is gonna
work?"

Rojvah shrugs. "It means we succeed in more futures than her other
options."

"Well that ent exactly comforting," Selen says.

"The Majah are honorless," Arick says. "The last thing we want to
be is comfortable."

45

VANITY

I STAND AT THE flap of Chadan's pavilion, watching with pride as our brothers polish weapons and paint sight wards around their eyes as they prepare for muster.

My prince was right about Tikka and women's work. In the past weeks, every warrior in the Princes Unit has gotten patches and a painted shield emblazoned with the spear and olive. We have banners now, stamps to mark equipment, and new pavilion canvas. Some of the *chi'Sharum* even got tattoos, though permanently marking flesh with ink is forbidden by the Evejah.

Our warriors strut like court dandies, proudly displaying their new gear. Older *Sharum* shake their heads and snigger, but every one of them wishes for a fraction of the glory we claim each night.

These last weeks have been some of the happiest of my life. Whether fighting *alagai* in the Maze or sharing kisses in the cool comfort of Chadan's pavilion, I've been able to forget the world I left behind and just live in the now.

"What do you think?"

I turn at the sound of Chadan's voice, sucking a breath at the sight of him.

The cost of equipping all the *Sharum* with steel is prohibitive, so apart from the mind-warded steel helms they wear beneath their turbans, our men are armored simply in tough layered robes with pockets for armor plates to cover their most vulnerable areas. The plates are simple fired clay that shatters on impact, distributing the force of a blow. Cheap, light, and easy to replace, they allow warriors to stay fast and mobile with some measure of protection.

But Chadan is the prince of Majah, and on his raising to the veil, his father commissioned a suit worthy of the *Damaji's* grandson. For weeks he's been attending fittings with the women of the famed Tazhan clan, the most sought-after armorers in Desert Spear. Their secret techniques are passed from mother to daughter, and for each son, the mother crafts a suit of armor, protecting him with the work of her own loving hand in the night. Their men make up one of the fiercest units in the Maze, all but invulnerable in their Tazhan steel.

My prince is clad in a suit of black steel scales with golden wardwork around each plate. He spreads his arms and tries to take a step my way, only to be yanked back by a pair of Tazhan armorers attempting to complete his final fitting.

Recheda, *Jiwah Ka* of the Tazhan clan, covers her face in our presence, but I can tell from the lines around her eyes that she is older than Grandmum. Her callused hands are thick and strong from countless hours at the anvil.

"Hold still." The Tazhan matriarch does not speak to Chadan as a prince. Her tone is sharp as any impatient Tikka's, and Chadan responds immediately, standing up straight and becoming motionless as a statue as the women complete their work.

Recheda places a snug helm on Chadan's head, with intricate wardwork in golden filigree for protection and wardsight.

"Is it heavy?" I ask. The wooden breastplates Selen stole were light, but steel . . .

"It's actually not bad." Chadan flexes his arm, and I'm amazed at how the scales ripple with the movement, giving him impressive range and fluidity.

"It looks like . . . " I glance at the armorer.

"Demon scales," the woman agrees. "My great-grandmother invented the *alagai*-scale technique, to turn Nie's own dark machinations against Her. The women of my family have preserved and guarded it ever since. Each scale is individually warded, overlapping protection even if scales are damaged or lost. They allow ease of movement, and distribute force to absorb impacts."

She tightens a last strap and steps back. Chadan begins a series of *sharukin*, flowing through the poses with little restriction.

"When the wards are charged, the metal will store power for them to focus," the armorer says. "You will be stronger in the suit than out of it."

Chadan looks at me and winks. "Perhaps even as strong as you."

"As if you need it, my prince," I say. "You beat me even without that advantage."

"You weren't exactly at your best that night," Chadan says. "You've come a long way since then."

The words are true, but I've seen the Majah prince fight. If we faced each other again today, I have little doubt the outcome would be the same.

"All that's left is your sigil." Recheda holds up a box of polished goldwood. Expensive in the North, and priceless here. She opens it to reveal a large pin of polished brass, depicting the Spear of Majah.

The symbol is already emblazoned on his shield, cloak, and helm, but the sigil one wears over one's heart has special meaning.

"Thank you," Chadan bows respectfully, "but I have my own." He reaches into his belt and produces another brass pin, nearly identical to the one Recheda holds, save for the olive it pierces.

I feel my chest tighten, a mix of pride and love, but also a tinge of worry.

"Tsst." Recheda confirms my fear. "A lesser *Sharum* might abandon his house sigil for the greater glory of his unit, but you are Chadan, son of Maroch, prince of Majah. You must carry your house's honor in the Maze."

"And so I do." Chadan taps the Majah spear on his shield with a steel-scaled toe. "But if I seek the white turban, I must earn glory beyond family."

"Tsst," Recheda says again. "Nothing is beyond family, young prince."

"Indeed," Chadan agrees. "And I am *ajin'pal*, bound with blood to all my spear brothers. I carry their honor, as well."

Recheda does not protest further, but I can sense her unease. Normally the armorer would secure the sigil in place, but she makes no effort to assist Chadan.

I step close, touching his arm. "Perhaps she's right."

"No," Chadan says. "Keeping distance from the *Sharum* that they might more dispassionately spend their lives is the *dama* way. I am *Sharum*, one with my brothers."

He says brothers, but it's my eyes he looks into, and the truth is unspoken between us, overwhelming my uneasiness.

Chadan turns to Recheda, his bow deep and long, showing great respect. "Thank you, Tikka. Know that when I fight tonight, and every night to come, I will add to the already boundless Tazhan honor." He punches a fist to his chest, a warrior's gesture that sends a ripple through the scales.

Recheda seems mollified at that. "Of that I have no doubt, young prince."

They leave soon after, and Chadan hands me the sigil. "Will you help me? It is difficult to affix while I am wearing it."

I smile at the obvious lie. He wants me to do it. And I want it as well. I lay a gentle hand over his heart as I secure the spear and olive. He lays his own hand over mine, and as I look up, our lips meet.

"I love you," I whisper. I didn't know it myself until I spoke the words, but now I feel the truth of it in my bones.

Chadan stiffens at the words, and my heart stops until he wraps his arms around me, holding me tight. For a moment I luxuriate in the embrace, but then I feel him shake, ever so slightly. I feel wetness on my shoulder, and realize he is weeping. Serene, unflappable Chadan, who controls his emotions better than anyone I have ever known.

"What is it?" I don't let go, but I pull my head back enough to look at him.

"We live on borrowed time." He looks up and his eyes are wet, making it even more real.

I shake my head. "With *alagai*-scale armor and my spear at your back, you will be invincible in the Maze. If you die on *alagai* talons, it will be at a time of your choosing, not Nie's."

Chadan shakes his head. "I am not talking about the Maze."

I reach out a gentle hand, feeling the cool wetness on his cheek. "Then what?"

"This." Chadan pulls me tighter. "Us. My grandfather will not allow it forever. We must make the most of every moment."

"Why?" I ask. "Many warriors are pillow friends. There is no dishonor in it."

"They are not the *Damaji's* heir," Chadan says. "I have many sisters, but no brothers. My family fears I will fail to father sons if I am devoted to you, and they are not wrong. I'm not interested in women enough to do . . . that."

But then it hits me. The reason I am here. I can shed blood for the Majah in the Maze, but also secure their line. For the first time in my life, I feel a sense of . . . *inevera*.

"You don't have to be." I take his hands, and the words come out of me in a rush. "I can have children."

Chadan shakes his head. "It is not enough. They must bear my blood."

He doesn't understand. There is still time to keep my secret, but I realize I don't want it anymore. Perhaps I never did.

Again Belina's words of prophecy echo in my mind. *The storms will end when the heir of Hollow joins blood with the Majah, and the princes stand in the eye.*

I squeeze his hands again. "There's a reason I was raised a woman. It is because I am one."

"Impossible," Chadan looks at me incredulously. "The *dama'ting* saw your . . . Everam's beard, in the sweat room, even *I* have seen . . . "

I nod. "But none of you looked closer."

Chadan cocks his head curiously. "Closer?"

"I have a woman's parts as well as a man's," I tell him.

"How is that possible?" Chadan does not argue, but I see the confusion on his face. I have earned his trust, but this taxes even the bond between us.

"I was meant to be twins," I tell him, "but some trick of Mother's magic . . . joined us."

He stares at me a moment, brows in a tight furrow as he struggles to process the concept. I am excited and terrified in equal measure, but he has not pulled his hands from mine, so I hold my breath, giving him time.

"You are saying you can bear children?" Chadan asks at last.

"Mother believes so," I tell him, "and she is the most famed Gatherer in Thesa."

Chadan pulls away at last, but it is only to gesticulate in a most un-Chadan fashion. "This changes everything! This—" He stops suddenly, sitting on a bone bench, deflated.

"What is it?" I ask.

"You're offering everything I want," Chadan says. "Anyone who has read a djinn tale knows such dreams come at a price, if they come at all."

I put a hand on his shoulder. "I am no djinn, my prince. I am flesh and blood, like you. There is no hidden price."

Chadan lays his hand over mine, squeezing even as he sighs. "I may not be the one to pay it. My people came back to Desert Spear to return to the old ways. Women are not allowed to take up the spear or fight in the Maze."

That stops me. "What of the *Sharum'ting*?"

"Most were stripped of arms and returned to their families," Chadan says. "The best were kept by the *dama'ting* as bodyguards and harem sentries. When age forces them to lay down their spears, there will be no more."

I purse my lips. I've seen Micha and Selen fight. The very idea that women be forced to disarm offends me. The idea that *I* might be forced to disarm . . .

"I am not just a woman," I say. "I am a man, as well. I won't give up my spear."

Chadan nods. "I would not want you to, but I don't know if Grandfather can accept you as both. I'm still trying to understand it fully, myself."

"We don't need to tell him now," I say. "If we are on borrowed time, let us borrow as much as we can to prepare. We're young, still."

"Everam willing, let it be so," Chadan says. "But will there be a later? Are you not still honor-bound to escape?"

The words remind me of Micha, held against her will in the very harem I would refuse for myself. I wonder if Chadan would flee north with us, but I have already lain so much on his shoulders, and in my heart I know he will not desert his people in their time of need.

My hesitation says everything, and Chadan takes a step back, nodding as the customary detachment returns to his demeanor.

"DEATH STALKS THE Maze!" Chadan is majestic in his new armor as he paces before the assembled men, and they stare at him with a respect bordering on awe.

I feel it, too.

"Close your eyes, and imagine it!" Chadan shouts. "The *alagai* that gets past your guard, its teeth sinking into your soft throat. Claws piercing organs and talons rending the flesh from your bones. Imagine your death, and embrace it."

The men close their eyes as bade, and I stand at their backs, giving them time to visualize an honorable death. Then I take a step forward and shout, "We are the *Sharum* of Desert Spear! What is our fate?"

"To spend our lives on *alagai* talons!" the men thunder in reply, a mantra that has led *Sharum* into battle for three thousand years.

Chadan and I have given this speech every night since we were raised to the veil. The drillmasters taught us one version, but it is the task of every unit leader to make it their own. My prince paces in front of the men and I walk among them as we honor those martyred before us, and prepare our spirits for the inevitability of our own deaths.

"Nie is not like the enemies of the day!" Chadan calls. "She does not fight for land or resources. She does not come to steal our wells or our wives."

"What does she come for?" I am closer to him as I shout, inspecting the men as I approach Chadan at the head of the assembly.

"She comes to exterminate us!" He booms his reply for all to hear. "She comes to undo Creation and return us to the Void! Nie cannot be reasoned with!"

I clatter my spear against my shield, and the sound echoes through the training grounds as a hundred brothers follow my lead.

"Nie cannot be placated or satiated!" Chadan shouts, and twice more

I lead a clash of spears. "Nie can only be fought!" This time I raise my spear into the air and roar, echoed by two hundred of my brothers. A sound that reaches all the way to the Heavens.

Chadan raises his spear to match us. "I will spend my life on *alagai* talons! But I will not spend it cheaply!"

"Prince Chadan's a miser!" I shout. "Should we help him haggle?"

"Haggle!" the men clash their spears again. "Haggle! Haggle!" Then they roar with laughter, though they've surely heard that joke every night for two moons.

Waning approaches, and the *alagai* are restless in the Maze. Even without a mind to guide them, they move with more intelligence than we've come to expect, avoiding traps and ignoring Baiters, leaving teams of *Sharum* hiding uselessly in ambush pockets while the *alagai* strike elsewhere.

But even the clever demons are unprepared for the Princes Unit. Chadan fights with a new, aggressive confidence, wading into the thickest battles, all but invulnerable in his new armor as he hacks and impales any demon that comes within reach. Soon the *alagai* part around him in search of other prey.

They find me, instead. I might not have new *alagai*-scale armor, but this past month has honed my strength and my skill to new sharpness. I feel more powerful than ever, even before my spear tastes ichor, sending an invigorating shock of magic up my arms.

Like they did in the food line, the men compete for a taste of the demon magic, rushing to attack the *alagai* that slip around me, and to finish off demons Chadan and I leave injured in our wake, lest their preternatural healing put them back in the fight.

Our brothers are all bigger and stronger than they were two months ago. Many in our unit should be summers away from full growth, but the magic has aged them beyond their years.

We studied the phenomenon at Gatherers' University—how feedback magic makes a body trend toward its physical prime. But it's one thing to read about it, and another to feel it in my own body. I feel a sudden empathy for Ella Cutter, for the . . . *lust* she felt as she tore demons apart with her teeth.

My brothers are ferocious, and word has spread of our exploits.

Warriors respect us now, in and out of the Maze. Even units loyal to the Sharum Ka are forced to resentfully give us our due, for none can deny our glory is boundless.

THE MEN ARE singing as we return to the training grounds just before dawn, Chadan and I loudest of all. All of us are covered in demon ichor, and still pent with excess magic. Not a man lost—not so much as injured—in our unit. Tomorrow is Waning, and we will go to our families with pride.

But Chadan's family is already waiting. His father Maroch stands in our pavilion, pulling the two of us up short. The joy I felt a moment ago vanishes, crushed by sudden anxiety.

"Father." Chadan's mirth has disappeared as well. He is cool as he dips into a bow. "I did not expect you."

"Indeed." Maroch is a tall man, powerfully built, with a prominent forehead and thick brows leading into a blunt nose hanging over a beard just beginning to gray at the roots. He moves with grace for one so big, but that is to be expected in a *sharusahk* grandmaster. Maroch instructs Chadan personally, and to hear my prince tell it, he is not yet close to a match for his father.

We stood our ground against the *alagai* not long before, but Chadan and I both shrink back as Dama Maroch comes to loom over us. "So it is true." He flicks a finger against the sigil over Chadan's heart. "You have turned your back on your own family, for," his eyes flick to me with disgust, "your men."

"It was my idea," I blurt. "I was the one—"

"No." Chadan holds up a hand and I trail off in surprise. "It was my decision, and I will not forsake it."

"You will," Maroch growls. "The *Damaji* has summoned you."

Chadan does not argue, dropping his gaze and heading for the tent flap at a gesture from his father.

Maroch turns to me. "You have been summoned as well, half-blood. The *Damaji* wishes you to see and hear the price of your insolence."

———

"Vain, stupid boy," Aleveran growls from on high as Chadan kneels with his hands on the floor before the dais of the Skull Throne.

It's a closed court, just members of the royal family and their personal guards, along with Damaji'ting Chavis and her loyalists. Iraven is conspicuously absent, but Belina stands a step behind Chavis, her eyes inscrutable.

I worry that standing next to Chadan on his knees will make matters worse, but I will not kneel before my kidnappers, even now. For the moment, no one comments on my continued defiance. All eyes are on Chadan.

"The Spear of Majah has been our family seal for thousands of years," Aleveran says. "And you replace it with this . . . perversion?"

I can hear the grind of my own teeth at the words. I glance up at Aleveran, measuring the distance between us, and picture myself bounding up the seven steps to the top of the dais and putting out the *Damaji's* teeth. Aleveran is a famed *sharusahk* grandmaster, but he is old . . .

I force myself to breathe, long and even. Even I am not that stupid.

"Grandfather, every unit has . . . " Chadan begins, but the *Damaji* smacks the throne, cutting him short.

"Do not make excuses, boy. You are not here to plead your case, you are here to listen. Waning is almost upon us, and the Seers foretell a dark one. You should be focused on the Maze, not prideful preening as you flaunt your *push'ting* relationship with Prince Olive."

My nostrils flare as I draw another deep breath. Chadan glances at me, pleading with fearful eyes for me to keep silent. He's right. Now is not the time. I chew my lips to keep them closed.

"That relationship ends now," Aleveran growls. "Stand."

Chadan gets to his feet, and Maroch tears the spear and olive from his chest, dropping it to the floor and stomping on it. Then he strips the *alagai*-scale suit from his son as Chadan stands there limply, face a mask of shame.

Maroch carries the armor to the foot of his father's throne, laying it at the base of the seven steps. "You will have your armor back tonight," Aleveran says, "when the armorers have melted down your ridiculous emblem and permanently affixed a proper crest."

Anger flares hot in my breast and I ball a fist as Aleveran turns his attention to me. "Still insolent." The *Damaji* raises a finger. "Belina."

Belina's eyes betray her irritation, but she does not hesitate, producing the small replica of my arm cuff and squeezing.

I bite my lip, but the pain is so intense it does little to stifle my scream as I collapse, clutching my arm.

"Olive!" Chadan rushes toward me, but he is intercepted by a pair of guards.

At least, they try to intercept him. Chadan catches the first by his wrist and the front of his robe, pivoting to turn the force of the warrior's charge into a throw that sends him sailing through the air.

Chadan does not pause, slipping under the reach of the second warrior and catching his arm. He seems only to tap the man's elbow, but everyone in the room hears the sound of his arm breaking.

Then he is holding me in his arms, pulling helplessly at the cuff. When he sees it is futile, he turns to his grandfather. "Stop this! Please!"

Aleveran's expression does not change, but he lowers his finger, and Belina releases the cuff. I gasp a breath, looking down to see the flesh of my throbbing arm turning an ugly purple around the armlet.

"Have we not kept our bargain?" Aleveran asks. "Your sister is safe, and you have been given power and privilege beyond anything in your homeland. Yet still you seek to defy us."

Pain lances through my entire body, but I struggle to my feet. "How have I defied you, Damaji?" I ask as respectfully as I can manage. "By fighting in the Maze each night to defend your city? By wearing a variation of your own sigil, though you remain my goalers? By showing affection and loyalty to your grandson?"

"You may dress as a man, son of Ahmann, but you have a woman's wiles about you still, and I will not see you corrupt my grandson with them."

He turns back to Chadan. "I've given you too much liberty, and too little responsibility. Effective immediately, you will move into the Majah Palace. There are barracks in the outer walls for your warriors, drillmasters, and . . . " he looks pointedly at me, ". . . subordinate *kai*."

Desert Spear is full of empty palaces, but to be given one entirely is a huge boon. In the eyes of the warriors and citizens, Prince Chadan has been paid a great honor for his glory.

But I see it for what it is. A reminder to him, to the men—and to me, most of all—that Chadan is above us. That we are not his family, as he proclaimed last night. He will live alone in the palace with an army of servants and not a single confidant, while the rest of us reside in the walls like rodents.

More, we will be under the *Damaji's* eye, for doubtless the palace is already stocked with family staff loyal not to the prince, but to Aleveran. Every coming and going between the palace and the barracks will be noted and reported.

My stomach ties itself in knots. Will Chadan and I ever be alone again? Am I losing him?

The *Damaji's* next words are answer enough. "I've arranged a suitable *Jiwah Ka* for you. You will be wed as soon as the arrangements can be made."

Chadan swallows. "Who?"

His grandfather dismisses the question with a flick of his fingers. "It does not matter. She is suitable."

Chadan stares at the floor. "Yes, Grandfather." I wish he'd press the question, though I do not know the point. No bride will please a *push'ting*. I think how I could as easily have been that bride, and I want to scream.

A RUNNER COMES to whisper in the *Damaji's* ear, and we are dismissed. I should be livid as we walk from the throne room, but I feel broken, perhaps even more than my last visit, when Iraven had to carry me from my whipping. The doors close behind us, and for a moment, walking down the hall, Chadan and I are alone. Perhaps for the last time.

For his part, Chadan seems equally shattered. Usually his walk is a powerful stride toward a chosen location, but he seems to drift aimlessly.

I know we may not be able to speak in confidence again for some time, but I find I have nothing to say to my prince, and looking at him causes only pain. I turn down the hall to the gardens.

"Olive?" Even Chadan's voice is weak. "Where are you going?"

"To see my sister." I don't turn. I can't bear to look at him for fear my resolve will break and I will start weeping here in the hall.

"It was foolish of me to wear our symbol on my armor," Chadan says. "Recheda warned me. *You* warned me. But I was so . . . "

"It's not your fault." I turn at last. "I was glad you did." Immediately, tears well in my eyes, and a tiny sob escapes my lips.

If we were alone, he would have gone to me, taken me in his arms, soothed the tears away. But the guards outside the throne room can still see us, even if we are out of earshot. Chadan stands frozen, and though I know it would only make things worse, I cannot help but hate his cowardice. "It was always borrowed time, Olive."

I nod, and begin to turn away once more. Micha, at least, might still hold me, though I have treated her horribly.

But before I can go, a commotion in the hall draws our attention. I look up to see a group of Arms of Everam hauling Selen Cutter and Darin Bales, hands bound, to the throne room.

46

PRINCE OLIVE

PANIC FILLS ME, and I grab Chadan, pulling him into the side hall.
"Olive, what is it?" I hear the question distantly, too occupied to reply. I don't know why my friends are here, but I'm suddenly terrified they will see me like this—dressed like a man and standing
among my kidnappers as if I were one of them.

Peeking around the corner, I take a closer look. Selen and Darin look
tired and dusty, but uninjured. What must they have gone through, to
come this far? Were they kidnapped as I was, or—perhaps worse—did
they follow me all this way?

Their clothes are strange, a mix of Northern styles with a Krasian
cut and *Sharum* flair. Darin looks downright fashionable, though the ensemble would be more at home in my father's modern Krasia than the
austere Majah of Desert Spear. I can see the armor plates in Selen's fighting garb, and she looks ready to pick up a spear and join my brothers in
the Maze.

So stunned by the appearance of Selen and Darin, I almost miss the
other captives. A large and thickly muscled man in *Sharum* blacks walks
with his head down, purple bruises forming on a face pale even for a
half-blood. Red hair is not unknown among the Majah, but nothing
close to the orange flames of this warrior's curls.

His *Sharum* escort gives him a shove, and I see the man's eye is swelling behind his veil. My eyes flick to the other guards, and see several with bruises. It seems the warrior gave as good as he was given.

At the front of the group walks a beautiful young woman in clerical white. Her hair is wrapped, but she does not wear the veil. A *nie'dama'ting*. Unlike the others, even the Arms of Everam are reluctant to put hands on her, and her hands remain unbound. She glides across the floor with her head held high, as if she were in charge, and not being escorted alongside companions in chains.

I tug my turban low as they draw even with the hall, fluffing the loose white veil around my neck so that my chin and lower lip fall into it. I look like a common *kai*, but Darin has other senses. Can he smell me?

Perhaps not. I've always worn perfume around him, and even my sweat smells different after months of Krasian spices.

"Greenlanders?" Chadan casts a questioning glance my way as he moves beside me to look. "Do you know them?"

Darin turns his head and I duck out of sight, holding up a closed fist. Chadan falls quiet at the sign, a common signal for silence when tracking *alagai* in the Maze.

The guards usher them into the throne room without delay. I wait until my friends are inside, then move quickly to join the cluster of guards following them in.

"What are you doing?" Chadan hisses, grabbing my arm. "We were not summoned."

I twist, thrusting two stiffened fingers at the pressure point in his arm that will force open his grip, but as always, Chadan is too fast, blocking the blow. I settle for brute strength instead, tearing my arm free.

"What's gotten into you?" He hurries after me, but keeps his hands to himself.

I turn to look at him at last. "I am getting into that council, so either come with me or stand frozen while someone else makes decisions. It's what you're best at."

Chadan stares at me like I am a stranger, and perhaps I am. Our problems seem so petty with my friends in danger. Aleveran may have broken me, but I will burn this palace down if he tries to hurt my friends.

———

WE SLIP IN unnoticed, all eyes are on the prisoners standing before the throne. The full court has hastily assembled, the council of *dama* and *dama'ting* alike, along with Iraven in his white turban. Belina glances up, catching sight of me, but her gaze does not linger. She says nothing as we blend in with the other warriors, shouldering our way forward in the *kai* way, daring the lesser *Sharum* to stop us. It's terribly rude, but effective.

"What is the meaning of this?" Damaji Aleveran glares down at my friends, imposing from atop the seven steps.

The *kai* leading the guards prostrates himself before the throne. "These greenblood spies tried to infiltrate the city, Damaji."

Selen rolls her eyes. "Sneaky as Watchers, walking right up to the gate like that." Her Krasian is fluent, but after months of immersion, her accent is thick to my ears, her diction slow.

The guard holding her kicks Selen behind the knees, dropping her to the hard stone floor much as they did me, those months ago. Instinctively, I reach over my shoulder for my spear, but I am not allowed arms in the *Damaji's* presence.

I take a step forward, and Chadan catches my arm again, this time pinching tight. "Do not be a fool!" His whisper is harsh.

He's right. I know it. But I feel the blood pumping behind my eyes, making my vision narrow like it does when I pick targets in the Maze. I need the pinch of his strong fingers to keep me from doing something that might get my friends killed.

The *kai* yanks the scarf from Selen's head, revealing her long hair and feminine features. "A woman, Damaji. She carried a warrior's spear and shield."

Aleveran sneers. "Even with their lands at peace, our Northern brethren continue their perversion of the Evejah's proscriptions for women."

"That is not all," the *kai* says as one of the prisoners I don't recognize is hauled forward. He is so big that even with a guard holding each arm, they struggle to restrain him. It takes a third to force him to his knees. "This one wears *Sharum* black, though his pale skin and flaming hair scream his *chin* blood." He puts his spear under the giant's chin, lifting to display an innocent, freckled face that does not seem to belong atop such a powerful physique. He looks younger than me. For all his size, he is like my spear brothers—a boy who should still be in *sharaj*, thrust into the role of a man.

"Who are you, to masquerade in the black of true men?" the *Damaji* demands.

The young man forces his chin down to meet the *Damaji's* eye. "I am Arick asu Rojer am'Inn am'Kaji."

Murmurs flow through the court. Even the Majah have heard of Rojer Halfgrip, the famed fiddle wizard who ensorcelled countless demons with his music. His portrait hangs in Mother's keep, and more than once, I've found Mother weeping there. He was like a brother to her, and his son . . .

Cousin Arick? He was an infant the one time we met, but I've corresponded for years with his sister . . . My eyes flick to the young *nie'dama'ting*, and a heavy dread settles into the pit of my stomach.

Aleveran is unimpressed. "Being the son of a *chin khaffit* does not qualify you for the black, boy."

"My mother was Sharum'ting Ka Sikvah vah Hasik am'Jardir am'Kaji," Arick says. "My grandfather was bodyguard to Shar'Dama Ka himself."

Aleveran dismisses the claim with a wave. "I knew your grandfather, boy. He was a great warrior, as a dog might be a great warrior. But like many dogs, his aggression outgrew his usefulness, so he was gelded and cast out in shame. You have no claim to a man's robes." He raises a finger to the guards. "Strip the black from him."

Arick screams and throws off the warriors holding him, but half a dozen more swoop in, holding him as the *kai* cuts away his blacks.

I can hear a whine in my head, and realize I am grinding my teeth. There is a dampness on my palms, and I glance down to see my fists clenched so tight my nails have drawn blood.

"Release my brother." Rojvah takes a step toward the guards when they do not unhand Arick quickly enough. "We come as emissaries under the seal of Shar'Dama Ka. You dishonor this holy place with your inhospitality."

At first the guards look ready to pacify her, as well, but then they glance at her white robes and think better of it. The Evejah states it is death to strike a woman in white. The guards hesitate, glancing up to the throne.

Rojvah is the daughter of my half sister Amanvah, technically my niece, but we have always called each other cousin in our letters—hers in Thesan and mine in Krasian—as we practiced our language by writing poetry and discussing fashion. I remember laughing until my face hurt over our attempts to one-up to each other with stories of Grandmum Elona and Tikka Kajivah.

Now I really am picking targets, plotting a course of broken bones through the guards to reach my family. Arick and Selen still look ready to fight, and my *hanzhar* can slice their bonds in a single stroke. No doubt Darin can slip his anytime he wants.

Still, the odds are against us in a room filled with *sharusahk* masters and *dama'ting* sorceresses. Where could we run, in any event?

Chavis leans over, whispering in Aleveran's ear. He grunts and nods. "The novice whites of the Kaji betrayers mean nothing here, girl. The guards do not risk Heaven if they strike you. You would be wise to show respect if you do not wish them torn from you before the court like your brother's blacks."

"Ent us, bein' uncivil." Darin's Krasian is surprisingly good, though his Brook accent is as thick as it is when he speaks Thesan.

For some reason, hearing Darin's voice makes it all too real. Nothing can hold Darin Bales if he doesn't want it to. If he's here, this wasn't a kidnapping. They're here for *me*.

I swallow the sudden lump in my throat as all eyes turn to Darin. He shrinks a little, like he does when he's toughening his body against a blow.

"And you are?" Aleveran asks.

"Darin asu Arlen am'Bales am'Brook."

Again, chatter runs through the court. The Krasians returned to the desert before Darin was born, but his father is as famous as mine.

"Here as Messengers, like Rojvah says," Darin continues. Aleveran and Chavis still consult in whispered tones, but if I know Darin, he can hear every word. "Lots of ale stories about honorless Majah in the North, but never paid 'em any mind till now. Countess Leesha accepted your delegation with respect. You ent good enough to do the same?"

Aleveran flicks a finger for the guards to release Arick. They give him a last shove, then quickly leap back before he can recover. He gets to his feet, taking great breaths to calm himself as he stands seething in only a blue bido.

The *Damaji* sits back against the Skull Throne, feigning ease when the tension in the room says anything but. "Speak, then, son of Par'chin. Why have you come?"

"Lookin' for Princess Olive of Hollow." I'd already deduced it, but hearing the words out loud still shakes me, like seeing a torch stuck into a funeral pyre.

"Why would you look here?" Aleveran asks.

"Watchers who kidnapped her weren't as sneaky as they thought," Darin says bluntly.

The *Damaji* gives him a tight smile. "Nevertheless, *Princess* Olive is not here."

Chadan's hand finds mine, and it's like fingers on the taut string of a bow. He squeezes, warning me not to speak. Even knowing full well the danger, I need the reminder. It will only get worse if I reveal myself. If I remain silent, perhaps the *Damaji* will let them go.

Darin's nostrils flare, and I wonder if he can smell the lie on Aleveran. "Damajah's bones say she is. Only a matter of time before her da comes to look for himself, and his army won't be as easy to bully as four teenagers. Givin' you a chance to stop a war."

Aleveran steeples his fingers. "And so you have, son of Par'chin, by delivering more of his family to hostage. Even so, the Shar'Dama Ka will no more find the missing princess than you."

"Liar," Selen growls. "Where is Olive?"

One of the Arms of Everam raises his spear to beat the insolence from her. I know from experience how the Majah treat those who dare speak bluntly to their *Damaji*.

I am moving before I realize it, leaping out to catch the shaft of the descending spear. I pull it into a circle that misses the target and follow through. As expected, the guard refuses to let go and is yanked along with the weapon, flipping over to slam into the floor.

I plant a foot on him and pull, but still he holds tightly to the weapon.

I give a hard twist, popping his white-sleeved arm from its shoulder socket. He screams as I tear the spear from his grasp.

Other guards move in to protect their brother, but I have a weapon now, and am ready to use it. They won't find me as helpless as they did my first time in this place.

"Stop!" Aleveran booms, before the guards can attack.

Selen looks at me as the warriors put up their weapons. "Olive?!"

"You shouldn't have come here, Sel," I say. "You need to go."

"Would that it were so simple," Aleveran says. "But now they have seen you."

"You gave me no choice," I growl. "But there is still time." I play the one card I have left. "Let them leave in peace, and I will stay willingly, even if my father comes to demand my release."

"Olive, no!" Selen cries, but it's too late.

"Done," Aleveran says, and the word closes around me like a blood lock. This was what he wanted all along. I want to renege, out of spite if nothing else, but the *Damaji* holds my friends' lives in his hands now, like he did my sister's before. What can I do, save give him what he wants?

"What have you done?" Rojvah asks.

"Saved all your lives," I say, though I know that is only the point of the spear I have driven through my life. I force myself to remain in the moment.

"Waning will soon be upon us," Aleveran says. "Prove your loyalty, and I will set them free."

"They will not be harmed in any way," I tell him, "or our pact means nothing."

"Agreed," Aleveran says, as the Arms of Everam haul my friends away.

I'm not even allowed to speak with them.

47

LOYALTIES

CHADAN IS KEPT behind as I am escorted from Sharik Hora by six white-sleeved holy warriors. They fall back as I leave the temple grounds, but continue to follow until I exit the Holy City entirely.

I've given him everything he wants, given my own life away, but still Damaji Aleveran doesn't trust me.

I force a breath into a chest tight with anxiety, swallowing the urge to sick up from helpless anger.

But who am I angry at? Everyone acts from love. Aleveran, for the love of his people, puts their welfare before his own honor, or my life. Darin, Selen, and the twins risked their lives out of love to find me and bring me home. Even Mother, who kept me in safe succor like a bird in a cage, acted out of love.

All of them moved like game pieces at the behest of the demon dice. Is that where my anger should go? Throws of the *alagai hora* have shaped every moment of my life, even before I was born. But the dice only offer predictions based on probability, like the little women who come to Mother with their ledgers, predicting births and harvests and taxes years in advance.

The very act of looking into the future threatens to change it, Favah used to say.

The bones are not truth tellers. They didn't know who I was or what I would want. Such things are irrelevant. They simply calculated better odds if I was raised as the princess of Hollow.

Micha was right when she said I was losing myself. I'm not Princess Olive anymore. I cannot go back to that life—hiding who I was, what I could do, struggling to be perfect enough to satisfy an insatiable mother.

But neither is Prince Olive the perfect fit I once thought he was, and there is no denying his life expectancy is far shorter than his sister's would have been.

What point is there, being angry at a handful of dice? They are not truth tellers, but neither are they liars.

I tell myself the blame lies with the *alagai*, whose hunt for me has left countless dead in its wake. But demons are nameless, faceless. They try to kill me, but it was not their decisions that pulled out the stitches of my life to leave me exposed.

In my heart, I know the truth. I'm not angry at the Majah, or my friends, not at my mother or the demons or the dice.

I am angry at myself, because I am a fool.

Chadan loves me. I am sure of it. He doesn't care that I am intersex, or that *chin* blood runs in my veins, only who I am. He accepts *me*.

But I see now the rest of the Majah will not. *The world will try to fit you into one of two boxes*, Mother said. Even if Aleveran allowed me to be with his grandson, would it be as I am, or would the *privilege* of bearing Chadan's children see me forced back into the harem? Would they try to take my rights, earned with blood and ichor in the Maze, to hide me behind a veil?

I shake my head. Now that I have earned the spear, I won't give it up—ever. Mother fought off an ambush by a mimic demon and its horde while I was in her belly. I won't be told I am less than her because Aleveran has forced his people to step backward in history.

My prince is the most skilled fighter I have ever seen, but he was willing to let the Baiter in the Maze die rather than break tradition. To let the *alagai* have the folk in the greenblood quarter, rather than defy orders. Is he strong enough to stand up to his father, his grandfather—the whole tribe—to fight for what we might have?

It frightens me that I have to think about the answer. That I doubt my *ajin'pal*. But all I can think of is his silence and downcast eyes as his father had the armorers strip him of the symbol of our union. As he was informed they had chosen him a bride.

But Selen, Darin, and the twins—they came for me. I feel an ache in my throat at the thought. They followed me all the way from Hollow, across hundreds of miles of demon-infested land and an unforgiving desert. I want to be angry at them for their foolishness, but would I have done any less?

I think of Micha, and my stupid, hurtful words the last time we spoke. *Oh sister, I am so sorry.*

I RETURN TO the training grounds to find an empty field where the spear and olive pavilions once stood. An older dal'ting woman in black robes waits there, rising at my approach. She does not make obeisance on the dusty ground, but her bow is deep and long.

"Prince Olive," she says when she rises. "I am Madana, head of the women of the Majah Palace. I am here to escort you to your new quarters."

There is much about Krasia I struggle with, but palace servants I understand. Mother's head maid is one of most powerful women in Thesa. Madana may have bowed low for me, but I would be wise not to cross her. I follow as she escorts me to our new barracks, built into the outer walls of Chadan's new palace.

Banners fly atop the turrets, signifying Chadan is in residence, but the busy courtyard that stands between the barracks and the palace itself might as well be a moat full of water demons. It will not be easy to cross without word getting back to the *Damaji*.

I don't much wish to see my prince in any event, and the feeling appears mutual. Tomorrow is Waning—we should be making plans and drilling the men, but there are no messages waiting as Gorvan lets me pass into the barracks.

"The men billet on the first floor," Madana says. "Meals are served below in the hall beside the harem."

I raise an eyebrow. "We have our own harem?"

"Of course," she says, misunderstanding my interest. "You and your warriors need a place to rest and eat and relax after fighting in the Maze. To drink cool water and have your pains massaged away. Without wives of your own, the *Jiwah'Sharum* are there to see to your needs. If you wish, I can . . . "

I shake my head. "I do not require *heasah*."

Madana's eyes bulge. *"Jiwah'Sharum* are NOT *heasah*!"

Her shout startles me, and I react on instinct, taking a quick step back and assuming a *sharusahk* stance.

Madana notes the move, and her air of control evaporates. She might have dominion over the *dal'ting* servants, but I am a man, and a prince of the Kaji. She falls to her knees, pressing her forehead to the floor. "Mercy, Prince Olive!"

Mercy? Just what does she think I'm going to do to her? She's shaking with fear.

"Rise, Tikka," I say, hoping the term of endearment will put her at ease. "It is I who should apologize. I meant no offense."

Madana eases back onto her heels. She looks scandalized as I offer a hand, but she takes it and lets me pull her to her feet.

She withdraws her hand quickly from mine. "It is easy to forget you are new to many of our ways, Prince Olive. I will remind the servants of this, so you are not . . . startled again."

"You can start by telling me how I gave offense," I say.

"*Heasah* are transactional," Madana says. "Lending their bodies for a handful of draki or a jug of water, taking herbs to prevent the seeds of their unions from taking root." She looks ready to spit, even in her veil.

"*Jiwah'Sharum* are sister-wives, your spear brothers our husbands. It is a position of honor and respect. You protect and provide, and we give comfort and care, carrying the children of the glorious Princes Unit into the next generation."

"I understand," I say, though I am not sure I do. I've only kissed two people, but both times, it was freely given, not a sacred duty or paid service. My brothers speak often of the incense-filled pillow chambers of the *Jiwah'Sharum*, but I have never dared follow them there.

"Your chamber is located above, down the hall from the drillmasters." Madana leads me to a private room. The space is not mean, and is comfortably furnished with all my possessions—many of them the lavish gifts of a doting prince—already stowed or on display. Still, compared with the luxury of Chadan's private pavilion, it is small and unimpressive. I had bigger closets in Hollow.

I ignore the dinner bell as I pace the room. Night falls, but there is no Horn of Sharak to call us to muster. Other units have been assigned to guard the Maze to keep the Princes Unit fresh for Waning, and I am glad of it. I no more want to face my spear brothers than I do Chadan.

My mind keeps going back to Selen, Darin, and the twins. Here, in Krasia! It seems like a dream. I love them for their tenacity, but the timing is terrible. If new moon brings a storm, they are targets, too. I'm thankful at least that they are being held in the Holy City, shielded by the powerful magic of Sharik Hora. They'll be safe there, no matter what.

There's a knock at the door. I open it to find a green-robed *chin* servant bowing his turbaned head as he presents a tray of food. The smell of spiced meat and flatbread would normally set my stomach rumbling, but now it nauseates me.

"I don't want it." I move to close the door.

"But I came all this way." The servant looks up.

It's Darin.

I grab his arm, pulling him into the room so hard he needs to quickstep to keep from spilling the food from his tray. I glance into the hall, but there is no sign of anyone. I shut the door and pull him into a tight embrace. He's gone slippery, but solidifies when he realizes I mean no harm. We hold each other for a long moment.

Then I push away. "What are you doing here?!"

"Came to ask you the same question," Darin says. "We track you all the way across the desert to find you're . . . what? Majah, now? And a boy?"

"I was never a girl," I growl. I've dreaded having this conversation with Darin my entire life, but his accusations and aggressive posture make it easy. "I have the same boy parts you do."

Darin looks at me like I'm an idiot. "Know that. What's that got to do with anythin'?"

I blink. "You know? What do you mean, *you know?* Creator as my witness, Darin Bales, if you were spying on us in the bath . . . "

Darin looks offended. "You might need a fancy helmet for ward-sight, Olive, but I was born with it, along with a bunch of other senses, all keener'n they got a right to be. Knew you had boy parts as well as girl since we were in nappies. Doesn't change who you are."

"And how do you know who I am?" I demand, shocked to hear I was carrying such weight for nothing all these years.

"Know you're a fool, you trust that old man to let us go, no matter what you do," Darin says.

"He swore on the Skull Throne, in front of everyone." I sound defensive, even to myself.

Darin shrugs. "Krasians can find a thousand honorable ways to delay something they don't want to do. Today they won't let us leave till you prove yourself—whatever that means. Then it will always be another Waning, or a coming storm, or the position of the stars. They won't have the right provisions for the journey, or there will be a holiday to prepare for, a ceremony that takes months to plan, and on and on. They'll call us guests and keep us in a silk prison, but now that we know you're here, they will never willingly let us go. So why promise them the sky?"

Now it's my turn to look at him like an idiot. "Don't you get it, Darin? They would have executed you."

"Bah." He waves off my words like a bad smell. "*Damaji* said it himself. We're too valuable as hostages. Somethin' else is goin' on. Think it's got to do with that square-jawed prince you were holdin' hands with."

I was defensive before, but mention of Chadan pushes me to a more aggressive posture. I ball a fist in Darin's face. "I don't owe you any explanations about that, Darin Bales. You and Selen never asked my permission to play kissy, so I don't see why I need yours. I didn't ask you to come rescue me, and I'll stay if I want."

Darin raises an eyebrow at me then crosses his arms. "They never came back."

I'm confused. "Who never came back?"

"Aunt Leesha." Darin bites off the words. "My mam. Wonda. Demons hit their camp not long after they went into the borderlands. Slaughtered Hollow Soldiers and Warded Children, alike."

"Impossible." The word is a reflex, remembering what it was like watching Ella Cutter tear her way through a pack of demons. What would it take to down the whole tribe of Warded Children, along with five hundred of Mother's best armored soldiers? What would it take to bring down the duchess herself, or Mrs. Bales?

Darin shrugs, unwilling to argue. "Whatever you're thinkin', we thought it, too. But the bodies were still smoldering when Selen and I found them. Don't know how it happened, but it happened."

"Bodies?" A chill goes through me. "Did you find . . . ?" Even now, after seeing so much death in the Maze, I can't bring myself to say it. Mother is a force of nature. She can't be dead.

Darin shakes his head. "Couldn't find any sign of your mam, or mine, except . . . " Darin reaches into his robe, sliding free a large and very familiar knife.

Just seeing the weapon cuts me. I know what it means. That knife was like Mother's *hora* wand. Mrs. Bales never let it out of her sight. "Oh, Darin." I reach for him, but it's Darin's turn to push me back.

"Don't want pity," Darin says. "Want to hear you're going to stop all this nonsense and come home."

"It isn't nonsense," I say. "These people need me."

Darin looks at me incredulously. "Hollow needs you. You're heir to the duchy."

I shake my head. "I don't want it. Selen is the duchess' sister. She can do it."

"Doesn't work like that, and you know it," Darin says. "You don't come back, the throne goes to Elona."

I love Grandmum, but we both know she would be a terrible duchess. "At least she'll want the job. How are you expecting us to get home, in any event?"

"They can't hold me," Darin says. "I squeeze through cracks like water, and no one can sneak up on me."

"Don't be so sure of that." I recall the eerie silence of the Watchers who captured me. "And the others aren't as slippery as you."

Darin waves dismissively. "I already know where the guards keep the keys. Give me a few hours and I'll know my way around the harem, too."

"Bet you'll love that," I say, but Darin doesn't rise to the bait the way one of my spear brothers would. He just lets my words hang in the air until I drop my eyes.

"Point is," he goes on as if there had never been a pause, "we can just gather everyone and go. City's huge. Easy to get lost in while we steal supplies and crack open one of the older gates. Fort's meant to keep demons out, not people in."

His plan is so similar to Micha's that I am stunned. Is it really that simple, or are they desperately naïve?

And what if I go? What will happen to my spear brothers if I abandon them to the storm coalescing around Desert Spear? What will happen to the people?

"I can't just leave," I say. "It's complicated."

"See that." Darin takes the pitcher from the tray and pours himself a glass of water. "So explain. Got time. Bet the guards ent even noticed I'm gone yet."

"I don't want to go back to Hollow," I say. "I'm not that Olive anymore, Darin. I don't know that I ever can be again. I don't *want* to be."

"Then don't," Darin says. "Go home and be yourself. Or make a home somewhere else. Night, come to Tibbet's Brook. Folk there love to gossip about their neighbors, but they generally get along. Believe it or not, we've got stranger folk than Olive Paper. Don't need to stay with your kidnappers to be yourself."

"The Majah don't want the real me, either," I say. "But I can't just walk away."

I show him the armlet. "It's a lock only Belina's blood can open. Micha wears one, too. They can track us if we escape, or trigger the bands to contract, and cripple us."

Darin squints at the armlet, studying its magic with his night eyes. At last, he shrugs. "Warding ent really my thing, but magic's magic. Even if we can't get it off, reckon we can muffle it till we get out the city. Bet it ent got a range of more than a mile or two."

"Muffle it?" I was a poor study in Favah's Chamber of Shadows, but it makes sense. Magical energy conducts differently through the elements. There is always loss, but some are more pronounced than others. Gemstones and precious metals are the best conductors. Water is worst.

"I could stick my arm in a bucket of water," I say. It is both simple and utterly impractical for making an escape.

"I was thinking a hogroot paste," Darin says. "Maybe with a plaster cast to hold it in place."

I sigh. "Even if that worked, even if we could just steal away, the Majah need me."

I tell him about the prophecy and what happened on Waning, but he remains unconvinced. "Say it's true," Darin says. "Who's to say what joining blood really means? Could be you've already done that in the Maze. Said yourself there were no attacks last Waning."

Perhaps he's right, except things feel . . . unfinished somehow. Last month felt like the night was holding its breath, and now, with Darin and Selen suddenly in the city with Waning about to fall, the trap is set.

I shake my head. "Something's about to happen, Darin. I can feel it. Our mothers have been missing for months. The Majah are in danger *now*."

"And what if they are?" Darin demands. "They kidnapped you and Micha. You saw what they did to Arick. Creator only knows what they'll do to Rojvah and Selen. Don't owe them anythin'."

"There are sixty thousand people in this city, Darin," I growl. "I won't condemn them all because their leader is a misguided old relic."

I lay a hand on his shoulder. "You said they don't know you're gone. Go back and wait out the new moon. You'll be safe in the Holy City."

"While you go out and fight," Darin says.

I nod. "When Waning is over, I will hold Aleveran to his word. If he won't set you free, we'll escape together." I gesture to some of Chadan's lavish gifts. "I can trade these for provisions to take us across the waste."

"Startin' to think the waste was comin' here in the first place." Darin reaches into his jacket, pulling out the warded cloak my mother gave me on the night she cast the dice. "Brought you this, if you even care."

He tosses the cloak at my head. I catch it, but my vision is blocked for a moment. When I can see again, Darin is gone.

I look at the cloak and am filled with fear. Where is Mother? Is she alive, or is this the last gift she'll ever give me?

I fall to my knees, pressing the cloth into my face, and sob.

———

I'M STILL WEEPING when there's a knock at my door.

"A moment," I call, wiping the last of my tears on the cloak and quickly shoving it into a cabinet. No doubt my eyes are red and swollen, but there's nothing for it. I put on Kai Olive like a cloak, projecting confidence and control in case it is one of my little brothers, nervous about the coming Waning.

If it is Chadan, I don't know what I'll say, but I won't hold back. Not anymore. I have too much at stake.

But it is neither my prince nor one of my brothers at the door. Drillmaster Chikga bows. "Prince Olive. There are battle plans to discuss for tomorrow's Waning, and Prince Chadan is . . . indisposed."

I blow out a breath. "Of course, Drillmaster." I wave the big man into my room and close the door behind him.

I've just started to turn when a steel cable drops over my head and pulls tight, choking me. Something drives into my neck, and I'm shoved hard, stumbling until I hit the heavy door. The cable burns across my throat as I twist to see Chikga holding me at the end of an *alagai* catcher—a hollow metal staff run with a loop of cable at one end that the user can give slack or tighten at will. *Alagai* catchers are designed to negate the strength advantage of demons, keeping them out of striking range while the cable cuts off their air.

I grab the pole before Chikga can crush my windpipe, but already I am unable to breathe. I try to force it back on him, but the drillmaster is ready, dropping into a roll and using his own weight in an attempt to pull me down. I manage to keep my feet, but I'm forced to stumble helplessly along with the pull, feeling my face swell as I struggle for blood and air.

"I knew you were a traitor." Chikga whips me around the room, smashing me into a dresser, a support beam, the wall, the floor. All along he keeps his balance, always moving, always controlling the battlespace.

I curse myself for a fool. Darin might be able to hear the heartbeat of a fruit fly, but one of the first items Favah tried to teach me to make in the Chamber of Shadows was a listening device. A demonbone split into two pieces, each with wards of resonance carved upon it, will carry sound from one to the other, even at distance.

But was Chikga the one listening, or is he simply an agent? I'll never know if he kills me.

I'm whipped by Darin's tray and snatch up the water pitcher, hurling it at Chikga's head. The throw is true, but Chikga yanks at the pole, dragging me along as he lifts his guard to bat it aside.

Blackness begins to creep into the edges of my vision as I watch his feet. When he moves to throw me again, I match him step for step, pulling on the pole and sending both of us stumbling toward the support beam. I roll around it, bracing the *alagai* catcher like a lever and pulling hard. The drillmaster attempts to hold on, but he's thrown into my writing desk and loses his grip as pens and ink rain down on him.

I drop to my knees, pulling the cable from my throat. I draw a hoarse breath and immediately begin coughing, but there is air in the hacks and wheezes—blessed air.

Chikga is unfazed, already on his feet and stalking in with quick punches and kicks meant to break bones, hyperextend joints, and stun major muscle groups—a blunt but effective form of Micha's Precise Strike school of *sharusahk*.

I accept a few blows as the cost of getting the noose from my throat and struggling to my feet, but I still have armor plates in my robes, and I'm tougher than I look. I get my guard up, catching a punch on my rolled-up arm, batting another aside, and rolling under a third.

But my return blows never land. I'm dizzy and slow, still gasping for air while the drillmaster is fresh, his breath smooth and even. Like a dancer he bats aside my blows, more often than not with a stinging counter.

I'm taking more blows than I can evade, feeling like the clapper in a bell as the drillmaster pummels me. Then he sees an opening and hooks my legs, dropping me to the floor and pouncing as he seeks a submission hold.

"Prince Olive!"

The drillmaster and I look up as one to see Faseek standing horrified in the doorway.

"Stay out of this, boy!" Chikga growls, but in that moment of distraction, I heave with all my might. With solid floor beneath me, I have leverage, and Chikga is unprepared for my full strength. I reverse the hold, putting an arm around Chikga's neck, pulling to cut off his air and force a submission, much as he tried to do to me.

But I'm too desperate, too angry, and fighting for my life. I don't hold back, and with my muscles at full flex, the drillmaster's neck breaks with an audible snap. He collapses to the floor, killed instantly.

I KNEEL ON the floor, breath heaving as I stare into Chikga's dead eyes, waiting for Faseek to cry out, to summon our brothers and the palace servants, to call me a murderer.

But he doesn't. Instead, Faseek quietly closes the door and comes over to stand beside me. "What did he do?"

I look up at him in confusion.

"It doesn't matter." Faseek's eyes scan the room. "You would not have killed him without cause. We can restore your room to order, but it means nothing if a dead drillmaster is found here. We must get rid of the body."

The words are such a relief, it is all I can do not to start weeping again. "There is no *we*, Faseek. Killing a drillmaster is a high crime, even for a *kai*. If we are caught . . . "

Faseek cuts me off by spitting on Chikga's body. "He would have let me starve to death, or cast me out in shame. If I have a life, it is thanks to you."

I lay a gentle hand on Chikga's face, closing his eyes. His head lolls bonelessly as I turn it, seeing the resonance ward on one of his earrings. If the drillmaster was spying directly, then I have a chance.

I am numb as we clean the room. I feel the maelstrom of emotion swirling around me only at a distance, focusing my attention on sweeping up shards of broken pitcher and righting scattered furniture. The result is not perfect, but on casual inspection, the room appears normal.

With Faseek scouting ahead, we make our way up to the ramparts. It's forbidden for any save *Sharum* and *dama* to go out at night, and there is no one about save a handful of my brothers, still unaccustomed to patrolling the palace walls.

We wait until there is a gap and take Chikga to a secluded spot on the west wall. Faseek produces a bottle of couzi, pouring some into the drillmaster's mouth and on his clothes, then shoves it into Chikga's stiffening hand before we pitch him off the wall.

We do it so casually, as if we murder people every day. I worry the patrolling guards will hear, but the drillmaster makes less noise than I expect, striking the cobbles at the base of the wall with little more than a muffled thump. Off the west wall, his body will be in the shadow until noon, at least.

We slip back inside with little effort. It was so easy. I killed a man, and it was easy. I want to sick up, but I squash the feeling, reaching out to put my hand on Faseek's shoulder. "Thank you, brother."

"Always," Faseek says. "My life is yours, my prince."

"You should go," I say, wondering how long it will be until they discover the body. The longer he goes without being found, the more his blood will congeal and be less useful to the *dama'ting* in determining his cause of death if foul play is suspected.

And it will be. Chikga wasn't using *hora* magic to spy on me without orders. His disappearance will draw scrutiny, but from whom? He was friends with my brother, but what reason would Iraven have to kill me? Aleveran seems more likely, or Chavis.

I wonder, just for an instant, if it could have been Chadan. Bile rises in my throat at the very idea, but I choke it back down, refusing to believe it.

"What will you do?" Faseek asks.

"Return to my quarters," I say, "but first I will visit the palace harem, and make sure I am seen by the *Jiwah'Sharum*."

Faseek nods. "Good luck, brother."

48

HAREM

THE WARRIOR'S HAREM is much as I had imagined from my broth-ers' descriptions. Dimly lit, the air is thick and cloying with incense and the scented smoke of great water pipes. Women move through the haze in various states of undress from their brightly colored silk robes and diaphanous veils.

They are beautiful, and it is no wonder they hold the men entranced. There is artistry in their movements, clothing, and powder kit, in the music they play and the strength and complexity of their seductive dance.

The men speak of conquests among the *Jiwah'Sharum*, but seeing them with my own eyes, I know the lie. These women have power the men do not understand.

My role is to be seen enjoying the harem as a man, but watching the women undulate and writhe atop small podiums reminds me of laughing with Selen in my chambers as Micha and Kendall tried to teach us the Krasian pillow dance. I remember the steps, and part of me wants to snap my hips to the beat of the music as I cross the room.

With no call to muster, most of my spear brothers have come to the harem tonight, lying in the pillows among pipes and bottles of couzi as they are attended by the *Jiwah'Sharum*.

"Prince Olive!" Gorvan booms. I turn to see him beside a large water pipe with a thinly clad *Jiwah'Sharum* on his lap. Her hand is somewhere in the older boy's robes, and I don't want to think about where.

The other men give a cheer when they see me, Thivan most of all. "I bet Thivan fifty draki you'd never come down here," Gorvan says loudly.

I force a laugh I do not feel. "Then you are a fool, Gorvan, for when would you collect?"

Everyone roars with laughter at that, Gorvan most of all. "Come, my *kai*! Share couzi with us!"

I still can't see the woman's hand. "I don't drink couzi, Gorvan, and I came to watch pillow dancers, not smell your fetid breath."

Again, laughter all around, as Madana appears to attend me. "Welcome, Your Highness. You honor us with your presence. Of course it is beneath you to sit with the *dal'Sharum*." She leads me through a curtain to a more private chamber with a bed of pillows and cool water to drink.

"We are not often honored with princes," Madana says. "What will ease your burdens? A massage, perhaps?"

I shake my head. "Even in the green lands, we have tales of Krasian pillow dancing. I would like to see it with my own eyes."

Madana's eyes crinkle with pleasure. "Of course, Highness. All my brides will take a turn dancing for you, that you may pick your favorites to attend you."

I watch a steady progression of dancers, some more skilled or more beautiful than others. At another time, I might have enjoyed it more—perhaps more than I am comfortable with—but tonight tension sickness drives off any chance of arousal.

I'm less interested in their bodies than I am in their clothes. Their jewelry. The way they paint their eyes and braid their hair. The scents they use.

The curtains they go behind to change and apply their powders.

I LEAVE THE harem close to dawn. No alarms have sounded, so I assume Chigka has yet to be discovered. Drunken *Sharum* dying accidental deaths is a sadly common occurrence, but I am not fool enough to think the subterfuge will buy more than a few hours. Whoever sent Chikga will come for me once he is found. My only hope is to disappear.

I leave Chadan's palace before first light, crossing the city in twilight. Demons tend to return to the Core long before the sky begins to brighten, and it's unthinkable for them to penetrate all the way into the powerfully warded palace districts in any event, but curfew is in effect until dawn. I am thankful for the empty streets, reaching the gates of the Holy City right at dawn.

It is the first day of Waning, and the white-sleeved guards admit me all the way to Sharik Hora without comment. I head for the temple's lavish harem as if I were going to call on Micha, but turn away from the gate and move around the wall instead.

My *nie'Sharum* training and the strength of my fingers is enough to get me over the wall into the private gardens, but my *Sharum* blacks will stand out among all the women in colored silk like a nightwolf among sheep. The sacred harem's eunuch guards wear only tan bidos and golden shackles on their wrists and ankles, but all are powerfully built and trained in *sharusahk*. Stout batons hang from thongs at their waists. They will descend upon me if I move about the gardens like this, and I will quickly be overwhelmed.

Fortunately, I came prepared. My trip to the harem was more than an excuse to be seen. I had my first proper bath in months, and snuck into the changing room, tucking some silks and a powder kit into my robes. I slip into a secluded garden bower to change.

Outside, Krasian women all dress in plain blacks, but within the harem, fashion is power—a sign of one's position and status. The stylish but conservative robes of young unwed girls of high blood and marriageable age are not so different from the dresses worn by well-bred girls at court in Hollow. Brightly colored silks decorated with wardwork, lace, and bangles. Flowing scarves and glittering jewelry. Intricately patterned fans.

These stand in sharp contrast with the provocative—if not outright scandalous—diaphanous robes of young pillow brides still called upon often by their husbands. I catch flashes of bare flesh as their thin veils flow around them like smoke. Their belts tinkle with the tiny finger cymbals used in the pillow dance.

Moving with stately grace among these are the elder *Jiwah Ka*, as dignified and aloof as the high ladies of Mother's court. Their fine conservative robes are thick but colorful, the quality and cut signifying status, wealth, and power over the other women. Pillow wives may have their husbands' favor, but First Wives have his purse, and dominion over his household.

The women of the great harem of Sharik Hora run the full spectrum, especially on Waning, when all are dressed in their finest to receive their husbands, brothers, and sons. Already, many of them await family in visiting chambers just outside the harem proper.

I've chosen the transparent blue silks of a pillow bride. Gossamer cloth the color of clear sky accented with a carefully woven silk bido and short velvet vest the color of deep water.

I feel scandalous, and naked for lack of armor, but it will keep eyes where I want them, and away from places I don't. My thin veil is opaque, complementing the vest and bido, disguising my face without seeming as if I have anything to hide.

A stolen wig covers my short hair with a proper bride's long tresses. I cover that with a blue scarf that softens my muscular shoulders and arms.

The costume jewelry I borrowed from the *Jiwah'Sharum* will not pass close inspection among the rich brides of the great harem, but it is riskier to go without.

Setting a piece of silvered glass on the branches of a flower bush, I take out the powder kit, copying the style of paints favored by young pillow wives, adding a blush to my cheeks and smoky kohl on my eyelids. I extend the lashes and paint my lips, surprising myself at how natural the work is. I haven't touched a paintbox in months, but Grandmum Elona's lessons are ingrained in memory.

Before long the face in front of me barely resembles Prince Olive the *kai'Sharum*, calling back to the fashionable girl I was not a year ago, but with eyes less naïve. My heart aches for that girl, but she isn't me, anymore.

Clean, painted, and perfumed, I step out of the bower a completely different person. I add a sway to my hips as I walk, mimicking the confident, seductive gait of a vain young bride. It feels natural, not so different from how Elona taught me to saunter across a room.

Women glance my way as I pass through the gardens, but I have fallen fully into the role, and do not fear I will be recognized. On the contrary, the looks I receive range from complimentary to jealous.

I hear singing, high and beautiful, and follow the sound, thinking it must lead me to Micha. It is not my sister I find, however, but my niece. Rojvah kneels beside a great fountain depicting four larger-than-life warriors, their muscular bodies clad only in veiled turbans and bidos. They hold their shields above them in a diamond formation, deflecting the spray of the fountain in all directions.

Rojvah is singing as she brushes out her long, auburn hair. She is clad in the robes of an unwed maiden, a mix of reds to complement her hair and complexion, ranging from deep wine to cinnamon. The cut leaves more to the imagination than my pillow silks, but none would call it demure. At her throat is a choker much like the one Micha wears. I wonder why it was not taken with the rest of her *hora* jewelry, but then I see the red stone and realize it is blood-locked, much as my armlet.

"Beautiful singing, sister," I say as I step close to the fountain, glancing this way and that to ensure no one else is about. "Welcome. You are new to the harem?"

Rojvah smiles, and she is stunningly beautiful. "I suppose you could say that. I was *nie'dama'ting*, but Chavis stripped me of the white. I am a captive here, but . . . " She shrugs, running her fingertips over the beautiful red silk robes. "In some ways, I have never felt so free."

"Ay, well I don't," a familiar voice says at my back. I do not start, turning casually to look at Selen over the security of my veil. Her hair is braided with bands of gold, and the edge of her headscarf is trimmed with warded coins. She looks beautiful, but I can tell my tall friend is decidedly uncomfortable in her green maiden robes. They strain against her powerful frame, and she moves awkwardly in the layers of veil.

But while I'm looking at her, Selen takes a good look at me and crosses her arms. "About time you showed up. Least you look more like yourself, this time."

"You know this woman?" Rojvah asks.

Selen snorts. "Rojvah, meet your aunt Olive."

Rojvah's head whips around, eyes narrowing as she scrutinizes my face and body. "Incredible."

"Ay, she's got a real gift." Selen makes no effort to mask the anger in her voice. "As comfy in a frilly nightgown as a suit of armor. Fancy that."

I don't know what to say, so I reach out and grab her instead, pulling my friend into an embrace. She tries to push me away, but I hold fast against her efforts until she gives in and holds me in return. Her voice cracks as she whispers in my ear. "We thought we'd lost you."

"I know." I fight the tears threatening to spoil my eye makeup, but I am no more able to keep the choke from my voice than she is. "I'm so sorry. I thought you were still safe in Hollow."

Now Selen does shove me back. "And, what? You were going to just stay here? Be Prince Olive, and forget everyone who loves you?"

Micha appears, keeping watch near the entrance to the small plaza, and I realize she must have told them everything.

"At first, I had no choice," I say. "I did what I had to. But I found something here, Selen. Something we only tasted when we put on armor and snuck off on the borough tour. I'm not the Olive you remember."

"Demonshit," Selen growls. "Ent been gone three months. None of us are the same since the tour, but I don't buy you're a whole new person just because you had a few weeks of brainwashing."

"It's not brainwashing." I realize the naïveté of the words even as I say them, for of course that is what *sharaj* is. Micha said it herself. Drillmasters break individuals and rebuild them into a unit where every warrior trusts his life to the shield of the man next to him. It worked on the others, and it worked on me. Even now, I would step in front of a pack of demons for any of my spear brothers.

But then the drillmaster tried to kill me.

"I'm not a whole new person," I allow at last. "But I'm not the spoiled, anxious, emotional princess of Hollow anymore, either. I can't go back to being her."

"Don't care about that," Selen says. "Come home whoever you like. Just *come home*."

"Darin told me the same thing," I say. "I wasn't ready to listen last night, but I am, now."

"Glad to hear it," a voice says from above. I look up to see Darin rise from his perch in the shadow at the center of the fountain warriors' shields. He is doused in the fountain's spray, but the water seems to simply slide off him. He leaps down, and his clothes aren't even wet.

"Corespawn it, Darin Bales," I say, but I'm more irritated at myself for letting him get the drop on me again. "I told you to go back to Arick."

"Ay, you did," Darin agrees. "Problem is, you don't get to tell me what to do, Olive Paper."

He's right. I've gotten used to giving orders, but these are not my spear brothers, or my subjects. They're my friends. My family.

"Waning is tonight," I say. "Aleveran has commanded every citizen to seek protection in the Holy Undercity for the next three nights. It will be chaos, and that is where they will search for me. No one will think to look in the harem. I can hide here in plain sight, while we plan our escape."

Micha shakes her head. "They might not look for you here, but if you go missing they will watch the rest of us too closely. There are enough hidden *Sharum'ting* passages and safe rooms in the temple to shelter us through Waning. We simply need a way out of the blood locks."

I look to Rojvah. "Chamber of Shadows was always my worst subject. Is there anything you can do?"

"I am not gifted like Mother and Grandmother," Rojvah says, "but like my brother and his kamanj, I was given no choice but to practice endlessly. Let me see the lock."

Her soft hands are gentle as she examines the armlet, tracing the lines of the wards with the edge of one painted nail. "The armlet is warded to contract if an attempt is made to force the lock, or the wrong blood is used."

I hadn't known that. I think of all the times I've been spattered with blood, all the times I was tempted to sneak into a smith's tent and put a hammer to it. I never had any idea how close I was to amputating my own arm.

"Can you remove it?" I know it's my imagination, but I feel it tightening.

"With a properly sealed Chamber of Shadows to cut off the signal and the right materials, I could disable the wards and free you in . . . " she shrugs, "half an hour?"

Hope kindles in my breast, but Micha looks skeptical. "And here?" she asks. "Now, with the tools at hand?"

Rojvah shakes her head. "Impossible."

I look to Darin. "Any luck finding hogroot and plaster?"

Darin shakes his head. "Hogroot's a wild plant. Ent pretty and smells awful. Not something that grows in a garden like this. Reckon they got some in the Chambers of Healing, but that place is locked up too tight even for me. Give me a few hours and I can sniff out a Gatherer in the bazaar and get what we need."

"Too long," Micha says. "When they notice Olive is missing, Belina will track the armlet and find her here." She lifts the hem of her robe, baring a long stretch of leg. Darin blushes and turns away as she tears off a piece of inner cloth. She lays a hand on Darin's shoulder. "Take this."

Darin looks at the scrap of cloth, and I see it is stitched in a neat, delicate hand with a map of the temple.

"I meant this for Olive last moon," Micha says, "before she . . . decided to stay. We are here." She points at the cloth. "Collect Arick and meet us . . . " her finger slides along passages like she was solving a child's paper maze, "here. Go now."

Darin nods, flitting from shadow to shadow on his way out of the gardens.

"How can he meet us, if we remain shackled?" I ask.

"Because I'm going to find Belina," Micha says, "and get blood to open the locks."

"That won't be necessary," a voice replies. One of the thick hedges that surround the fountain rolls back as if the branches had a life of their own, revealing a woman clad all in white with a black veil, holding a glowing bit of *hora* as she stands in the shadows.

Belina.

49

LOCKED

MUSCLES AND TENDONS bunch and tighten as I watch the *nie'Damaji'ting* emerge. I could cover the distance between us in seconds, and my body screams at me to attack, but I know she will be ready for it. Even if she cannot activate my armlet in sunlight, I do not know if I am up to the task of fighting one of Father's *dama'ting* wives, legendary for their Precise Strike school of *sharusahk*.

"Don't look so surprised," Belina says. "One of the first things the dice told me when I took the veil was that I would need to stand by the *Sharum* fountain in the great harem of Sharik Hora on the tenth Waning of the Year of Everam 3800. It took more than forty years for me to understand why, but I never doubted the path Everam set for me."

"I am weary of dice." I wish I had a spear to put through the witch's heart and have done.

"I am not your enemy." Belina takes a step forward, and unconsciously, I take a step back. Selen has her fists raised, but Rojvah and Micha know *dama'ting* better. Both look ready to get to their knees or flee.

"You are no longer safe in Desert Spear." Belina takes another step.

This time I hold my ground. "That implies there is a time I was."

"There was a time when you were not a liability to Aleveran." Belina is nose-to-nose with me now. My hand shakes as I try to keep from balling a fist. "But he fears your influence on his grandson. He sent Chikga to end it."

The admission isn't really a surprise, but hearing it aloud makes it real in a way it wasn't, before.

The *Damaji* tried to have me killed, even after I pledged myself to him.

"But . . . the prophecy," I say. "He needs me. Krasia needs me."

"To bleed," Belina says. "Chavis believes the prophecy can only be fulfilled with your death. That it is the precondition to turning the eye of Alagai Ka away from Desert Spear."

My blood turns to ice at the thought, but I keep my voice calm. "What do you believe?"

"That it is like blood for the dice," Belina says. "You must choose to bleed willingly, or the prophecy will be . . . corrupted."

I turn to present the armlet to her. "Then free me. Let me choose."

Belina smiles. "No doubt Micha chose this spot because it is close to one of the hidden exits of the harem. Go. When Chavis comes to demand the sympathy bones linked to your shackles, I will provide false ones. She and Aleveran will not be able to find you, or strike at you from afar."

"But you will," I growl.

"One way or another, the prophecy must be fulfilled," Belina says. "I do not wish your death, but if you attempt to leave Desert Spear before the storms pass, you will do it without limbs."

Suddenly, Micha lunges past me, already spinning into a kick that cracks across Belina's face. She does not scream, but a jolt runs through her at what must be blinding pain. Blood soaks her black veil as the *nie'Damaji'ting* stumbles back. Micha follows, pressing her thumbs into the bloody cloth.

But Belina recovers quickly. She seems to float away from Micha's next blow, coming back in to drive stiffened knuckles into my sister's midsection, seeking the precise point where her lines of energy converge. A precise strike to such a spot could paralyze, or even kill.

But Micha is wise to the move, twisting her body to protect the convergence even as she accepts the blow. Then she tumbles away, pressing her thumbs to the blood locks on her anklets. The red stones turn milky white again, and the shackles open with an audible click.

"Well done." Belina removes her veil and wipes the remaining blood from her face. "It seems the fabled *Sharum'ting* of the Damajah live up to their reputation." She carefully folds the veil and tucks it into her *hora* pouch. "I won't underestimate you again."

Micha pulls off the anklets, dropping them to the ground with a clatter as she stalks in. "You can cast no spells here in the sunlight, *Dama'ting*."

Belina frowns, taking a fighting stance. "I do not need them, insolent girl. No doubt you impress the Kaji *Sharum*, but you are no match for the Majah *sharusahk*. And even in sunlight, I can draw strength from my *hora*."

I know she's right. Any *hora* jewelry next to her skin can be drawn upon to make her as strong as I am, as fast as Darin.

Micha knows this, but it does not slow her approach. "It won't help you."

When they come together, I see Belina was not lying. Her limbs are a blur as she attacks and defends, but once Micha attacks, she does not let up. Each move flows into the next, and for a few moments they appear to be at an impasse. But Micha is learning her foe, adapting. Soon she begins to pick apart Belina's defenses, striking convergences that make the *dama'ting* grunt with pain even as her limbs buckle and lose strength.

Belina recovers quickly, no doubt Drawing on the power of her *hora*, but that power is finite in the sunlight. I see worry begin to work its way through the *dama'ting* serenity of her expression, and then fear. No doubt she is wondering how long she can keep this up.

Not long enough, it seems. When their circling puts her back to the opening in the hedge maze, she whips out her *hanzhar*, and blood arcs into the air. Micha skitters back in surprise, clutching a bloody forearm. Before she can recover, Belina turns and flees.

"Do not let her escape!" Micha cries.

Selen and I lunge for Belina, but she's using the last of her stored magic, moving in a blur of white silk too fast to follow. Before we can close the distance, the hedges close behind her. I glance at the hedge maze, but even if I knew it well, I doubt we'd be able to catch her before she can reach a safe space with guards to defend her.

"What do we do now?" I ask.

Micha's eyes are hard as she binds the cut on her arm. "What she wants . . . for now." She leads us down a series of twisting paths through the hedge maze. Twice we squeeze through all-but-invisible gaps in the hedges until we come to a statue that abuts the harem wall. Micha twists a ward on its base and slides open a hidden door. "Quickly. We need to get to the mirror of heroes."

I hurry through, coming out into a quiet hall that seems seldom used. I see why, as it dead-ends at a mirror framed in human skulls that will peer back at any who dare stop to admire their reflection. It's a perfect place for a hidden passage. Even in Sharik Hora, few would have the courage to submit themselves to the judgment of the spirits of heroes past.

But it seems Chadan is one of them. My prince stands in front of the mirror of heroes as if seeking history's judgment. My heart aches at the sight of him.

CHADAN TURNS WITH a start when he realizes he is no longer alone. He takes in the sight of four women in colored silk, and rushes our way.

"Are you women all right?" There is genuine concern in his voice. I can tell he doesn't recognize me in pillow silks, and why should he? "What are you doing outside the harem? Has something happened?"

Another man might avert his gaze when encountering four women out of their blacks, but Chadan is not interested in women, and barely gives our clothes and bodies a glance. He focuses instead on our eyes, and when his meet mine, I freeze as they widen in recognition.

Now he looks at my body. His eyes narrow as he inspects me up and down, then seizes my arms in their gauzy silk sleeves. "Olive?!"

I sense Micha take a step forward. She attacked Belina without warning, but I cannot allow that here. I switch to the silent hand language she had begun teaching me and Selen, making a quick gesture. *Hold.*

Chadan throws his arms around me, hugging me close. "I've been so worried. Drillmaster Chikga has been murdered, and there were signs of struggle in your room. We've had people looking everywhere."

He steps back, eyes running over me once more. "I see it now. It's a wonder I never did before. When I heard you'd gone to the *Jiwah'Sharum*, I thought it was to punish me after our argument, but it wasn't, was it? You went to steal clothes to sneak into the great harem."

"I had to see my family," I say. "I had to make sure they were all right."

"Of course," Chadan agrees. "But they are safer inside."

I shake my head. "Nowhere is safe. Chikga is dead because your grandfather sent him to kill me."

"Impossible," Chadan says. "What does Grandfather gain by killing you when you have sworn yourself to him? Chikga is Iraven's creature."

"Nie'Damaji'ting Belina says otherwise," I say.

"Of course." Chadan sounds ready to spit. "The witch would say anything to protect her son. But it makes no sense. If Grandfather wanted you dead, he would simply have you arrested."

"Unless he thought you would resent him for it," I say. "Easier to use an assassin and keep his own hands clean."

"Ware your words." Chadan's voice hardens. "You speak of my grandfather Damaji Aleveran, direct descendant of Majah, himself, who freed us from bondage to your traitorous brother Asome and restored Desert Spear to glory. He is not some dishonorable dog, striking quietly in the night."

I cross my arms. "Except when he sends Watchers to kidnap a girl with barely fifteen summers from her home while his emissaries are under truce. Forgive me if I do not trust your grandfather's *honor*."

Chadan has no retort, his face taking on the practiced calm façade I know so well. There are times when I can see past it, but not now.

"Put your blacks back on," Chadan says at last. "We'll go before the Skull Throne with your story. I'm sure—"

"Are you?" I cut in. "Are you sure? My life is one thing, but this is my family. What would you do, to protect your family?"

"Anything," Chadan says, and I sense the double edge of the word.

"I thought I was family, too," I say. "Your *ajin'pal*. Your—"

"I want you to be," Chadan says. "But I won't defy the throne. Now put your blacks on so you can stand with dignity while we get to the bottom of this."

The words are the slap I need, a reminder that even my lover is not without prejudice.

I laugh, spreading my arms and giving my hips a shake to rattle the coins around my waist. "What do I care if the *Damaji's* court sees me like this? It's closer to the real me than the beaten, head-shaved boy you met in *sharaj*."

I take a step back. "But it doesn't matter, because we're not going before the Skull Throne. We're leaving."

Chadan takes a step forward, mirroring me. "I won't let you."

I glance at Micha. "Take the others and go. I'll be along in a moment."

"Let me . . . " Micha falls silent as I raise a hand.

"Just go, sister."

Chadan puts a hand out as the others move around him to head for the mirror, but the corridor is too wide for him to block completely. "Do not."

I step into his path. "Go." This time I put the weight of command on the word, and the others obey, moving around my back to head down the hall.

"Olive, you don't have to do this." There is real emotion in Chadan's voice at last. "Please. Do not make me stop you."

There is a tiny crack in his voice, and it almost breaks me. I don't want this any more than he does, but still I set my feet in a *sharusahk* stance, even as my *ajin'pal* does the same. "I am not a terrified girl, whipped within an inch of her life and thrown into your place of power this time, brother."

"What are you, then?" Chadan's voice has gone flat. "My spear brother? Or a pillow dancer, sneaking out of the harem with something that doesn't belong to her?"

I straighten my back at the cold words. They cut, but at the same time, they make what must come next easier. "I am both, my prince. I thought you, of all people, might understand that. Picking one or the other is a false choice, and my friends and I don't *belong* to anyone."

"I . . . " His expression softens as the words sink in. He cares for me still, and I see in his eyes that in a different life, given time and room and liberty, we might have found happiness together.

But we have none of those things in this life. Chadan still thinks he can somehow reason with me, but I know my prince well enough to understand he won't just let me go.

I throw a quick punch in his moment of hesitation. If Chadan is surprised, it does not show. His speed is almost supernatural as he reorients in time to bat it aside. He grabs my wrist, using my own force to yank me hard toward an elbow he puts in line with my throat.

I put up my other arm to block the elbow, and Chadan grabs that arm as well. But this time, he has no force to turn against me, and with two points of contact, I am able to set my feet and lift him clear off the ground, driving him into the harem wall with all of my strength.

His helmet clangs against the stone, and a ripple runs over his *alagai* scales as the armor distributes some of the impact. Still, he is momentarily stunned. With the wall at his back to keep him from skittering away, I land heavy punches, ignoring the pain as the sharp scales lacerate my fists. The loose pants of my pillow silks prove ideal for kicks, and I throw a knee between his legs, doubling him over.

It hurts me to do it, but the pain buys the necessary time as Micha pulls back the mirror to reveal a hidden passage and my friends escape.

Every blow pains me, a betrayal of everything Chadan and I shared. But I can't let up. If I give him even a moment to recover, he's as likely as not to put me on the ground and organize pursuit before Micha and the others get far.

I grab one of his arms and the front of his robes, twisting into a throw that will send my prince tumbling down the hall, giving me time to follow the others through the passage. I hope there's a way to lock it from the inside, if only long enough for us to slip away.

But Chadan anticipates the throw. Perhaps he even invited it. He quicksteps around me, keeping his feet as I heave, and uses my own strength against me for a throw of his own. It's my turn to have my breath blown out as I slam into a wall, cracking the bones of heroes arranged in a sand ward.

Chadan gasps in horror at the sacrilege, and I take advantage of the distraction to rush back at him with rapid kicks and punches, throwing elbows and knees, searching for an opening to exploit.

But Prince Chadan leaves no openings. I fight with the *sharukin* we were taught in *sharaj*, punches and kicks that combine timing and physics with explosive aggression meant to quickly kill or disable a foe. But Chadan was trained by *dama*, famously secretive about their *sharukin*, and it shows in his style.

He stands rooted in space, as if some sixth sense is telling him what I will do before I do it. Subtle twists of his back and hips barely slip the path of my blows as he snatches at the limbs to turn their force against me.

I throw a punch and an open hand meets it, sliding the blow aside as his arm seems to coil bonelessly up mine. I try to rotate in the opposite direction, but he is too fast. When he reaches the desired hold, Chadan stiffens his arm, violently locking the joints of my wrist, elbow, and shoulder.

He pulls me in, and I have no choice but to allow it, lest he break one of the locked joints. Chadan pivots, spine cracking like a whip as he brings his other arm down in a chop to my neck that will leave me stunned. I twist and curl my free arm in its path, catching the blow on the meat of my arm.

The moment his hand retracts, I follow it home with a quick jab at his unprotected face. He avoids the blow, but relinquishes his hold to do so. I step back to create a bit of space, resisting the urge to massage my sore arm.

I come back at him, and Chadan lets me do the work, not bothering to punch or kick in return. Instead he grabs at my punches, trying to lock my wrist and turn them into throws or submission holds. His own wrists are incredibly strong, but I keep a constant motion, flexing my even greater muscles to keep him from getting sufficient leverage. At last, I guide him into position for a powerful spinning kick to the head that I think will end the fight.

If it connected. Again, Chadan is ready for the move, catching the foot and throwing his upper body back as his leg comes up, as quick and dexterous as his arm. He snakes his foot around my knee and into the joint of my hip, then whips himself into a spinning leap. My hip screams and I desperately throw myself in the direction he wants me to go. I hit the floor hard, but it's preferable to a dislocated leg.

My hope for a quick victory fades as I get to my feet, but I can still win this. Chadan is weighed down by armor, and has no night strength to sustain him. I'm stronger, and won't tire as quickly as he will. The twists and throws he's managed are already distant aches, muffled by adrenaline and focus. They come with no loss of strength.

I begin giving ground, keeping my guard in close and offering no free energy for him to use against me.

I can sense Chadan's frustration. His fighting is best when he can calmly channel the aggression of his foes against them. Still, he adapts, keeping on the move, trying to box me into the dead end of the hall while offering little free energy of his own. Always rooted. Balanced.

I back slowly toward the mirror, but it is closed now. The empty eye sockets of ancient heroes bear witness to our fight, but I don't fear their judgment. I'm more afraid that, even if I defeat Chadan, I won't know how to open the passageway.

I push the thought away. That is the victor's worry, and there is no guarantee it will be me. We're in a secluded hall, but sooner or later the sounds of our struggle will draw attention.

So I fight, throwing kicks and punches to keep him moving, but falling short of giving him force he can redirect. It becomes a waiting game, but slowly it starts to tell. A hiss in his breath. A weakness in his blocks. A slight dip in his guard. Even *alagai*-scale armor is heavy, as are the thick robes used to keep the steel scales from his skin. The day is hot, and thick *Sharum* black doesn't breathe like pillow silks.

I move in as if to throw the same probing left punch I've delivered a hundred times, but this time I stop midway and deliver a shallow push-kick instead. Chadan is already moving to block the punch, and reacts too slowly to the kick. The ball of my slippered foot makes solid contact with his thigh just above the knee, forcing the joint to hyperextend.

Chadan cries out in pain and stumbles as I drop low and spin a full circuit, sweeping his other leg.

Somehow he regains a measure of control in the fall, writhing like a snake as he whips himself around to grapple.

I'm ready, and block his attempts to establish a hold that will grant him leverage against my greater strength. We hit the ground with a jolt, and both of us try to turn the rebound against the other, canceling the energy.

We roll around on the floor, grunting and straining, but muscle-to-muscle, Chadan is no match for me. His bones creak under the grip of my powerful fingers as I force my way into a submission hold. For the first time during the fight, I see fear in his eyes as he realizes he cannot stop me.

For some reason, that look hurts most of all. This is a lesson Chadan needed to learn, but I hate being the one to teach it.

Slowly, carefully, I cross the ends of his collar and pull, cutting off the flow of blood to his brain. Chadan kicks and thrashes, but my legs are wrapped around his from behind, preventing him from reaching me or rising to his feet. He throws punches over his shoulder to rain upon my unprotected head, but they are awkward and lack the force to dislodge me as I slowly increase the pressure.

"W-will you kill me," Chadan gasps as his face reddens and swells, "like you did Chikga?"

The question falls as heavily as any blow, and for an instant, my grip loses strength. The opportunity is all Chadan needs to break the hold, pulling in a choked breath as he scrambles away. I can tell from the clumsy, frenetic way he moves that this is the last of his strength, a desperate attempt to create space between us while he gasps and coughs and attempts to recover.

I don't give him the chance, grabbing his ankle and pulling hard. He catches himself with his arms before hitting his face on the floor, but it leaves a gap at the back of his helmet and no way to block as I punch him solidly in the head. Chadan goes down hard, the floor striking a second blow against his forehead as his helm clangs against the stone. Still, his shaking hands move to push him up.

I grab one arm, twisting it behind him into a submission hold as I pull the scarf from my shoulders. I catch his wrist in a twist of the silk, using it to keep control as I loop the scarf around his opposite elbow and yank his arms together, binding them with another twist. Able to control both of his arms with the silk in one fist, I capture his legs in turn until

I've bound all four limbs together. Chadan groans, dazed and breathless, but he doesn't have the strength to stop me.

"I'm sorry, brother." Tears threaten to blur my vision as I pull off my veil, twisting it into a gag. "Chikga attacked me in my quarters. If I had not killed him, he surely would have killed me. You would have done the same."

"Then why did you run," Chadan gasps. "Why didn't you come to me?"

"Because you put your family first," I tell him. "And so must I."

"Your brothers are your family, too," Chadan says. "Will you abandon us tonight, when Waning comes?"

The words cut deep, because I know he's right. The demons are hunting me and Darin. Last moon they did nothing, as if they sensed his approach. Now, with both of us in the city, the *alagai* will strike, killing Everam only knows how many, while Darin and I hide in the catacombs.

But that is only part of the story.

"Majah abandoned me, first," I say. "Never once has your grandfather dealt with me in good faith, and you've done nothing to stop it."

I lay a gentle hand on his cheek, feeling my own face screw up in anguish. "I'm sorry, my prince. I wish there was another way."

"You won't get away," he groans.

I put the veil around his face, forcing the twisted silk between his teeth. I shouldn't say anything. I should just go. But the words are coming and there's no stopping them. "You could have cried for help at any time, but you didn't."

Chadan turns to look me in the eye, his face so expressionless it would do a *dama'ting* proud, leaving me to see only myself reflected in his eyes. Like *sharusahk*, he offers me nothing, turning my own attack against me.

It's more than I can bear and I break the stare. Without looking back, I move quickly to the mirror, but it, too, judges. Like Chadan, I see only myself reflected in the silvered glass, facing the empty stare of heroes' skulls.

I'm forced to meet their gaze as I search for something that might trigger the mechanism to open it.

I needn't have bothered. The mirror opens as I approach, and I see the glass is transparent on the other side, allowing those within to observe the hall and ensure it is empty before exiting.

Micha stands there alone, waiting. "I guided the others to a lower level and returned for you, sister."

"How much did you see?" I ask.

"Enough," Micha says.

"You could have intervened," I say, thankful she did not.

Micha's eyes crinkle as she smiles behind her veil. "You don't need saving anymore, brother."

Brother. It is what Chadan and the others call me, and it feels right. But here? With Micha? It doesn't. Is that what I am to her?

Should I have to choose?

I take her hand as the mirror clicks shut behind us. "Whatever I am to others, we will always be sisters."

Micha squeezes my hand, and I see her eyes are wet. My hand itches for the tiny, tinkling tear bottles that hang at my waist, but Micha surprises me, wiping away the precious tears with the cuff of her sleeve.

"There will be time for tears later. Come, sister."

THE *SHARUM'TING* PASSAGE narrows as it goes, becoming so tight I have to twist to keep my shoulders from scraping the walls. It tapers further, until a big man would not be able to pass at all, making the passage useless to *Sharum.*

That's good news against pursuit, but I've always been broader in the arms and shoulders than other women, and my months in *sharaj* and the Maze have layered muscle over my natural span. At first I am simply unable to move at speed, but soon the press of stone triggers a wrenching fear that tightens my stomach. If the tunnel constricts any more, I could get stuck. Even now, the passage is too tight for me to draw a full breath. I feel suffocated by it.

Micha has no such problems. My sister moves with an efficient, skittering gait I am unable to replicate, and it is clear she is holding back to allow me to keep pace.

"Where are the others?" I ask, trying to keep thoughts of getting stuck from taking over my mind.

"In a safe place," Micha says, "We will join them soon. Release your breath. One last squeeze before the passage widens."

The idea of releasing what little breath I have to squeeze yet further into a crushing tunnel terrifies me, but I trust in my sister and obey, imagining my fear releasing with the air as I blow out my breath and contract my chest and shove myself into a space my body has no business fitting. I expect the walls to scrape against me, abrading my fine silks, but the stone is polished smooth from untold ages of use. Only my armlet grates against the stone, and I think it would be a fitting irony if that were what catches me fast.

But then I pop through the choke point, and movement gets easier. The tunnel widens quickly after that.

50

PASSAGES

I RUN MY FINGERTIPS over the blood-locked armlet, wondering if even now Belina is using it to map Micha's tunnels. At any moment, the *dama'ting* could bring it to life, crippling me where I stand. We are doing as she bade, but it is not in the nature of *dama'ting* to forgive an assault upon their person.

"I can't believe what you did to Belina," I say.

"When we were in *sharaj*, my spear sisters and I were trained to bully the *nie'dama'ting*," Micha says. "The priestesses encouraged it. They called it 'A reminder to be humble before Everam.' *Nie'dama'ting* study *sharusahk* two hours a day. My sisters and I studied for twenty."

Twenty hours a day? Even after months of hard training, the number shocks me. "How is that possible?"

Micha shrugs. "All things are possible, when your sense of self is stripped away in *sharaj*. There were five of us then, nieces and lesser daughters of the Deliverer, too holy for the black, yet deemed unfit for the white. The Damajah took us into the underpalace and gave us to her eunuch drillmaster, Enkido."

"Gave you?" I ask.

"Like dogs to be trained." The words horrify me, but Micha speaks them calmly—a pain long since accepted. "You took orders from

Chikga, but we *belonged* to Enkido. If we were not strong enough to survive his training, we knew we would not be missed."

"Surely Father——" I begin.

"The Shar'Dama Ka only had eyes for the war and his sons," Micha cuts in. "We disappeared for years, and I do not think he even noticed."

I don't know why this surprises me. My father never had time for me, either. "And then?"

"We were beaten," Micha says. "Sleep-deprived. Poisoned. Scarred. Made to visualize death until we lost our fear of it. Enkido took five simpering princesses, reduced us to nothing, and then rebuilt us into Everam's spear sisters."

I want to say something. To lay my hand on her, or offer comfort, but for all our years together, Micha has never needed comfort from me. I don't know how to offer it now in a way she will accept.

"It wasn't all bad," Micha goes on. "In those years I came to know and rely upon my sisters. All of us vied for Drillmaster Enkido's rare words of praise like hounds for scraps. We hated him at first, but he had a father's love for us all, and in time we shared daughters' love for him.

"This is what training does," she goes on. "It is how the clerics take people and turn them into weapons. A brutal start to destroy your old world, then they craft a false world around you, this one with an illusion of stability. It makes you love those hurt beside you more for your shared pain. It makes you love those doing the hurting, for they do it to teach you. To better you. Instead, you direct your hurt at their enemies."

Micha sighs. "I did not question it until I came to Hollow. I was still the Damajah's creature, then, and your mother knew it. She trusted me to protect you, but not to instruct you. But living in Hollow, falling in love, taught me how much bigger the world was than secret tunnels and assassination. I thought you greenlanders soft, but in time I came to see I would kill anyone who tried to make you hard. In this, like so many things, I failed you."

"You could never fail me," I say. "Perhaps fate wanted me hard."

"*Inevera*," Micha says.

"Do you still believe Enkido loved you?" I ask.

Micha is quiet a long time. "In his way, I think he did," she says at last, "but he, too, was stunted by *sharaj*. I am not certain he truly understood what love was. I did not, when I first came to your mother's court."

I wonder if Chadan understands love. If even I do. "Do you love him, still?"

Micha nods. "We filled as many tear bottles as any daughters when he fell to the *alagai*. Even now, I cannot sift who I am from what he made me." She shrugs. "It is too much for me to judge. So I love him as a daughter would, without condition."

I nod, unable to keep my thoughts from drifting back to Chadan, left tied and humiliated in the hall above. Did he ever truly love me? Did I, him? Or were our feelings twisted by what *sharaj* and the *alagai* put us through? Are we ourselves, or what Chikga made of us?

Is it still possible to sift the real me from the result?

After a few twists and turns, Micha stops, lifting a large wardstone from the wall. It is hinged on top, hiding a lever. When she pulls it, there is a thunk in the floor beneath our feet. She replaces the ward and pushes down on a large cornerstone on the floor, opening a hidden trap.

"A secret passage inside a secret passage?" I ask.

"Sharik Hora is riddled with them," Micha says. "Some the *dama* and *dama'ting* have used for centuries, but others were lost to time until the Damajah used the *alagai hora* to divine their locations for her agents."

Even after all I've seen, it's hard to think of Nanny Micha as an agent of my father's mysterious *Jiwah Ka*, but she moves about these tunnels like they are a part of her. There is so much about her I don't know.

"You first," Micha says. "Hang from the lip and the drop is not far."

The room below is dimly lit, but still bright enough that I shield my eyes after moving through the dark tunnel. I do as she says, dropping lightly to a smooth stone floor.

I look up to see Micha follow, tumbling out of the path of the trapdoor as it swings shut by some hidden mechanism. She drops silently beside me as my eyes adjust to the dim light filtering through shuttered windows. There is a firepit, water troughs, buckets and ladle, benches to sit and lie upon.

"It's a sweat room," I realize, but like everything in Sharik Hora, it is built out of human bones in a macabre display. The troughs and buckets are shaped of interlocking bone, sealed with resin to keep them from leaking. The thought of soaking in water ladled from a hero's skull makes me gag. "Creator. Why would anyone come here?"

Micha nods. "Even the *dama* believe it is haunted. They whisper these are the bones of martyrs too anguished to find the lonely path, their souls trapped on Ala. Once, I saw a *dama* come here seeking a vision. Another time, two *nie'dama* stoked the fire on a dare, but lost their nerve at the ladle. Otherwise everyone avoids the place."

"Guess that helps keep it secret," Selen steps into the light with Rojvah beside her, "but it ent a place you want to wait around in."

I rush to her, and this time she opens her arms, squeezing tight. "You've still got a lot of explaining to do," she says in my ear.

"As do you." I crush her tighter against me. For this moment, none of that matters.

Micha moves to a corner of the room behind the piles of sweat stones—stacks of polished obsidian heated with fire to make steam. She shifts a few bones and there is a click as she pushes the corner inward, creating a space wide enough for us to crouch and squeeze through.

We follow as Micha leads us down, down into the undercity. Mostly we travel the secret ways, but occasionally our path leads through seldom-trafficked rooms and halls of the temple proper. I lose track of the twists and turns before she opens one last hidden door, revealing a large room nestled deep beneath Sharik Hora.

Inside, everything is coated in a thick layer of dust, the place doubtless undisturbed since my father led the exodus from Desert Spear almost twenty years ago.

"This is a *Sharum'ting* safe room," Micha says, lighting skull lamps like those I saw above. "The Majah have more space than they require, so there was never any need to search for hidden chambers. There is ancient magic here—centuries of heroes' bones shaping and concentrating its protections." She looks at my armlet. "Belina will no more be able to track you in this place than she might hear a whisper in a room full of shouting warriors. We are safe here."

The words are comforting, but I cannot help but feel unsure. I know something of *hora* magic, but the magic of heroes' bones is still a mystery to me.

"Ay, safe until we starve." Selen looks decidedly uncomfortable amid the bleached bones.

"That won't be a concern." Micha leads us to the back of the chamber, where a door leads to a natural cavern complete with a waterfall and pool. "The oasis is above us. There is fresh water and fish." She gestures beside the pool where a field of mushrooms grow. "Those are safe to eat. There are stores of honey, nuts, and salt, as well."

Indeed, this hidden shelter seems to have everything we need. There is a sleeping area, *Sharum'ting* blacks with plates of fired clay, and weapons . . .

"What are those?" I ask in wonder, moving to the racks. There are standard shields trimmed with what look like ulnae and radii. Arrows and spears with bone heads. A mace, made from what looks like a man's thigh lashed to a large skull.

"Weapons and armor blessed with *sharik hora*," Micha says. "A last resort if the *alagai* ever attack the Holy City."

"Things get that bad, are a few bone spears going to be enough to save us?" I ask.

"It is always the warrior you must put your faith in," Micha says. "Never the weapon. Remain here while I am gone. Protect one another."

"Where are you going?" I ask.

"To meet Darin and find my nephew," Micha says. "I have not seen Arick since he was in swaddling. If the *Sharum* have harmed him . . . "

I think of the swollen, purple bruises on Arick's pale face, and on the faces of his captors. "They were not gentle, sister, but trust that for every bruise, there are three Arms of Everam similarly marked."

Micha grunts, but it is a prideful sound. "I would expect no less from my spear sister Sikvah's son."

Selen and I change into warrior blacks, then set about dusting off the ancient chamber as we gather food and water. Only Rojvah seems at ease amid the leering skulls.

Hours pass, and I run out of work to do, pacing the chamber until at last Micha returns with Darin and Arick, the latter now clad in the white-sleeved blacks of the temple guard. His eyes and hands darkened with makeup, he appears indistinguishable from the real thing.

Arick and I have yet to be formally introduced, but Micha takes her nephew aside as soon as the door seals behind them.

Darin is still clad in what looks like a cross between farmer's denim and Krasian high fashion. He has retrieved his satchel from wherever the guards stored it, and his pipes and his mother's knife are on his belt, along with a sack of what I assume are the other belongings the *Sharum* confiscated.

"What?" he asks warily as he catches me staring.

I smile. "Just thinking you should compliment your tailor. Rare to see you looking so fashion-forward."

"Ay, you know Darin," Selen says. "Moaned and complained the whole time they were measuring him, but don't let it fool you. He loves skulking around in his bespoke denim britches."

I laugh, and suddenly I'm Princess Olive again, ten summers old with my best friends in the world.

Arick has drifted to the rack of ancient *hora* weapons. He lifts a bone spear, putting it through the deft spins of a complex *sharukin*. Micha puts her hand on her heart, and Rojvah joins them, producing a tear bottle for her aunt as tears stream down her face.

Darin sniffs the air, then turns his head to look directly at the hidden door at the far end of the room.

"How about we go fishin'?"

DARIN DOES ALL the fishing while Selen and I sit by the water. I don't know how he does it, but he hooks fish after fish, even as he recounts their adventures on the road south.

You'd never know it to look at him, but when shy Darin has a story to tell, his Jongleur training kicks in. Voices. Accents. Impressions. There's more expression on the faces of his characters than I've ever seen him display on his own.

Selen heckles a bit at first when he forgets something or misremembers one of her favorite parts, but then both of us fall under Darin's spell.

Selen squeezes my hand when he speaks of the remains of Mother's escort, and I bite my lip to keep from crying. A few minutes later, we clutch at each other, howling with laughter at Darin's impression of an innkeeper arguing with her husband, or the way the merchant smelled. He makes himself the butt of half the jokes, giving the impression of a buffoon Selen all but carried on her back, but I can see in the way she looks at him that it's nothing close to truth.

I wonder if they've kissed again, and it's such a normal thought that it seems alien to me. When did I last have time for the luxury of wondering who Selen's been kissing?

It's my turn next. I don't have Darin's flair, but I try to be honest, even when it paints me in poor light.

Parts of the tale feel different in the telling than they did when lived, another skin I've begun to shed. But then I speak of Chadan and my spear brothers, and find some of my feelings are still fresh. Still raw. It will be nightfall, soon. The first night of Waning, when Alagai Ka is said to walk the night. I should be with my brothers, not hiding here amid the bones of true *sharik*.

51

WANING

ICHA IS STILL with her niece and nephew when we return, keeping in perfect harmony with Rojvah's singing even as she and Arick spar with spear and shield. She instructs as they go, and the twins hang on every word.

I know how they feel. Even when she only showed a shadow of her true self, Micha was as much a mother to me as anyone. My own was always occupied. The first time I walked, Micha was there to support me. How could I not have seen that she was so much more?

There's nothing to mark the hours, or tell night from day, but sometime after we have feasted on fish roasted with honey and nuts, Darin cocks his head.

I feel like a coiled asp with nothing to strike. "What do you hear?"

"Fighting," Darin says. "Shouts . . . " He shakes his head as if to clear it, tension lining his face. "Screaming. Shrieking. Pain." He presses the heels of his hands to his temples as if to massage away a headache. "Shattering stone." He covers his ears, flinching at sounds none of us can hear. "It's too much. Can't shut them out."

Selen and I rush to him, but Rojvah is there first. Darin looks like he's having a seizure as she takes him in her arms and dials the sound wards on her choker to put them in a bubble.

After a moment, he calms, going limp in her arms. Selen and I both breathe a sigh of relief, but not before Selen gives Rojvah a look that would do Elona proud. Maybe they haven't kissed, after all.

But even as Darin's tension eases, mine grows ever more unbearable. Far above our heads, my brothers are fighting for their lives. I shift uncomfortably until he gives Rojvah a last embrace and sits up. Rojvah dials her choker warily, but as the bubble bursts, Darin retains his calm.

"What can you tell us?" Micha asks.

"Corelings are in the city," Darin says. "Hundreds. Maybe thousands. Destroying everything in their path."

I shiver, breaking out in goosebumps and a nervous sweat. "They broke the defenses so quickly."

Darin shakes his head. "Didn't hear a thing until a few minutes ago when they were already close. Don't think they went through the Maze at all."

"Perhaps Iraven's Pit Warders didn't seal the last breach as well as they believed," Micha says. "But no matter. They will not penetrate the Holy City. So long as the Majah take refuge behind the bone walls, they will be safe."

"Perhaps," I say. "But will they have anything left to come home to? And what of my spear brothers, out in the night?"

Faseek, who risked everything to help me. Chadan, attempting to lead without me at his side. Gorvan, Thivan, Parkot, Montidahr, and the others. Out fighting while I cower in the Holy City.

"Don't you go thinking anything stupid, Olive Paper," Selen warns.

It's unnerving, how well she knows me, even now. "What's stupid is hiding when I can make a difference out there."

"Or make it worse," Selen reminds me. "You're the one they're after."

"There's no proof of that," I say. "Just dice and guesses. But even if there was, all the more reason I should be with my brothers. If it's me the demons want, they can have me before I use one of my brothers as a shield."

"The Hollow greatward was your shield, until these people stole you off it!" Selen snaps. "The Holy City is the next best thing, and with everyone safe inside, the *Sharum* will see it's hopeless to defend an empty city and retreat."

"Unlikely," Rojvah snorts. "They are men, after all."

Arick spits on the floor. "And why should they? Why should we give the *alagai* even an inch of ground without exacting a price in blood and ichor? What glory is there hiding in the undercity like w . . . "

Micha, Selen, Rojvah and I all fix him with a stare that gives him pause.

"Choose your next word carefully, brother," Rojvah warns.

"Cowards," Arick growls. The word is a knife in my chest, because he's right.

"Doesn't matter." Darin is staring at the ceiling, his senses far away. "They're sounding a retreat."

DARIN GOES OUT to scout before morning comes. I know he's the best suited to the task, but it grates on me to wait while he takes all the risk.

We all jump when he returns. Selen and Rojvah both move to him, but I don't have time for greetings. "What did you find?"

Darin lifts a shopping bag with fresh hogroot stalks poking from the top. "Best you come and see for yourself."

"*Alagai'viran.*" Rojvah gives the plant its Krasian name. "Yes, that will work." She grinds the leaves into a wet paste that she uses to paint over the armlet and mixes into the plaster. She soaks this into strips of cloth, wrapping it in a hardening cast.

The plaster is still wet when Micha and I dress in plain *dal'ting* blacks and blend into the crowd of essential workers waiting to be allowed out of the Holy Undercity to begin assessing the damage. With all able-bodied men called to *sharaj*, women make up the majority of the construction crews and fire brigades. Micha and I do not seem out of place. My sister jostles through the crowd and I follow in her wake to the head of the line. Somewhere along the way, she must have lifted some woman's papers, because she furnishes the gate guards with enough to let us pass with only a cursory glance.

Darin is waiting for us outside. He follows a step behind, for all appearances our *chin* servant. I hate playing the part, but it was Darin's idea. Everyone ignores him, and that's how he likes it best.

What we find is horrifying. Horns blare and brigades rush to combat fires that rage throughout the city. No longer constrained to the *chin* quarter, the *alagai* have cut a path of destruction leaving whole neighborhoods in ruin. The Mehnding Palace, home to thousands, is ablaze. The rubble and smoke and dust reach all the way to the outskirts of the Holy City.

And there are dead. Those who refused to abandon their homes, or stayed in hope of looting when others were gone, now spattered and eviscerated on the streets. We make our way to the Majah Palace and find many of my brothers repairing damaged wards on the wall.

I shudder. If the fighting made it all the way here, things were dire, indeed. I spot Faseek cleaning scorch marks that mar a large clay demon ward, and catch his eye, beckoning him over to stand just out of sight of the others.

My friend looks exhausted, covered in dust, sweat, ichor, and blood. "Apologies, honored *dal'ting*, but I have no time to . . . "

I unfasten my veil, and Faseek's eyes bulge. "Olive! You—"

"I know," I cut him off. "I shame myself with such womanly attire."

"I was going to say you look beautiful." Faseek winks. "If you're looking to evade the guards looking for you, I think you've discovered the right tack. There's a warrant to arrest you for the murder of Drillmaster Chikga."

"What are our brothers saying?" I ask.

Faseek spits in the dust. "Chikga was respected, but he was not loved. Our brothers agree that if you killed him, he must have given you cause."

"And Chadan?" I can't help but ask. Micha and Darin shift uncomfortably, but I need to know.

Faseek seems to understand. It might have been a surprise at court, but everyone in the Princes Unit knows Chadan and I are pillow friends. "He is . . . strained," Faseek admits, "but he will not tolerate anyone speaking ill of you. He tells the men this is a misunderstanding, and their *ajin'pal* will return."

My heart aches at the words. My brothers remain loyal, even though I was not there in their hour of need. Chadan remains loyal, though I did not love him enough to trust.

"*Inevera*, it will be so," I say. "What happened last night?"

"It was like two moons ago," Faseek says. "Our lines did not break. They burst from the streets behind us, countless *alagai*, more interested in destroying the city than fighting. But when we engaged . . . " He shakes his head.

"They were ready for you," I say.

"It was a trap!" Faseek hisses. "They fell on us like a swarm of locusts. We lost seventeen before Chadan called a retreat."

Seventeen. It's like a rock demon punched me in the chest. Seventeen of my brothers died on *alagai* talons while I hid in a temple cellar.

"The Sharum Ka called Prince Chadan a coward, even so," Faseek says. "He would have stripped Chadan of the white veil had the *Damaji* not intervened. Aleveran praised the move, ceding the streets and reassigning our warriors to protect the palaces and holy sites."

I should be relieved that my brothers will be behind fortified walls tonight, but the plan lacks strategy.

"The enemy cannot be defeated by guarding rich men's palaces and letting the demons destroy everything the *chin* and *khaffit* own," I say.

"Prince Iraven agrees," Faseek says. "The Sharum Ka has scouts mapping the city, hoping to find some sort of pattern. But for tonight, we have our orders."

"I will return this time tomorrow," I say. "Will you meet me?"

Faseek punches a fist to his chest, like he did when I was his *kai*. "Of course. Perhaps you will come as yourself."

I nod. "Perhaps."

I turn and head back toward the Holy City. "This is because of us." The words are barely a whisper, but I know Darin hears.

"You don't know that," Micha says.

"Think she's right," Darin says. "This is a hunt and the corelings are just hounds to flush us out of the bushes."

I ball a fist. "We should be the ones flushing them."

"It's the hunter we ought to be worrying about," Darin says. "Until we know where to find him, we're all better off waiting things out."

"Even if they level Desert Spear to get to us?" I ask bitterly.

"Just stuff, Olive," Darin says. "The folk are what matter, and the Holy City is big enough for all of them."

I want to argue, but I know he's right.

———

THAT EVENING I pace the floor, not knowing what to do with myself. Darin sits by the fishing pool, breathing in a steady rhythm and staring blankly at the water. Selen and Rojvah remain in the main chamber, giving him the distance he wants, but both cast worried gazes his way. The fighting will be closer, tonight.

Darin doesn't react as I approach, but I'm sure he smells me coming. I say nothing, kneeling by the water a few feet away. I breathe as Favah taught me, a slow, steady rhythm to relax my body and bring peace to my mind.

Or so she claimed. The breathing could still my body, but it never calmed my nerves or quieted my mind.

And outside, the Enemy is rising.

"They're on the streets," Darin confirms quietly a moment later. "Some are just wrecking everything in sight, but the rest . . . "

He trails off, and I don't press, giving my friend the time he needs even as every muscle and tendon in my body ties a slow knot.

"They're heading for the palaces," Darin confirms my fears.

I LISTEN UNTIL I understand how Darin felt last night. How he feels even now, trying to process so much pain, so much suffering, all at once. The walls are holding, but everywhere there is screaming and death.

When I can't stand any more, I get up, giving Darin some peace as I head into the main chamber. The others look at me, but I say nothing, walking to the weapons rack and selecting one of the sacred *hora* spears. I put it through a series of *sharukin*, amazed at how light the bone spearhead and crosspiece are compared with steel or even warded glass. It appears fragile, a delicate relic better suited to a museum than combat, but when I touch the point with a fingertip, it immediately wells red with blood.

Selen comes over to me. "Know what you're thinking."

I don't look up from the weapons rack. The macabre artistry of it helps keep the real world at bay. I select a sickle and chain, every link carved from *sharik hora*. I imagine throwing this holy chain around a demon's throat and seeing the *alagai's* flesh blacken and smoke.

"Do you?" I ask. "Because I sure as the sun don't."

"You're thinking you can't stand another corespawned second hiding in this cage," Selen says, "while other people fight the demons that are looking for you."

I test a bone blade against my fingernail and it shears like a razor. "Can you blame me for that?"

"'Course not," Selen says. "But you're taking more than your due. Demons have attacked Fort Krasia for three thousand years. You think it's gonna stop if Olive Paper surrenders?"

I flick away the pared nail. "Never said I mean to surrender."

"But it ent just that," Selen says. "You want to go find *him*. Your boyfriend."

I whirl on her. "He's not my boyf—!" I cut off as Selen just raises an eyebrow.

"Ent blaming you," she says. "I had a good look when we left the harem. I'd be smitten too, if I'd spent three months in sweat rooms with a handsome prince like that."

"This isn't some stableboy I had a round of kissy with and ended up in the shit." I turn back to the weapons rack, choosing three thigh bones, connected by short chains. I whip the weapon through the air, imagining the power as the impact wards on the sacred bone strike *alagai* flesh. "Chadan saved my life. And I saved his. Back and forth, more times than I can count. And now he's out there alone, without me to guard his back."

"Ent alone," Selen says. "Got more than a hundred of your brothers with him, and it sounds like he knows how to take care of himself."

I select a punch dagger, testing it with a lunge. "You don't understand." I put the dagger back on the rack and reach for—

There's a thump as Selen puts a hand on my chest, shoving hard. I stumble back, shocked.

"Ay, that's right, Olive Paper," Selen growls. "We've been keeping each other's secrets since we were in nappies, and you will ripping look at me when I talk to you."

I rock back at the force of the words, but Selen isn't done.

"You think I don't know what it's like to love someone?" Selen demands. "To risk everything to protect them? Because if I don't, what in the dark of night am I doing trapped in a tomb in the middle of the corespawned desert?"

I spread my hands. "You're right, Sel. I'm sorry. If it was you up there, you can bet I wouldn't be hiding in a basement."

"It's like that?" Selen asks. "Your prince?"

I can only shrug helplessly. "Ay. It's like that."

Selen blows out a breath. "So how can we help?"

I look at her. "This isn't your fight, Sel."

"Not now it ent," she agrees. "But the moment you step in, it is. We didn't come all this way to let you get cored. But your own brother said you'd be arrested if you showed yourself."

"He said there was a warrant," I say. "But my brothers would not allow them to enforce it, especially if I show up at dusk. All men are brothers in the night."

Selen wrinkles her nose. "Women and children don't count?"

"Women and children are not allowed in the Maze."

"And what will your brothers say, when Micha and I show up at your side with spears tonight?"

I honestly don't know, but that's not what Selen needs to hear. "They will accept you, or I'll knock the sense into them. I won't leave you again."

I know it is a lie. It's one thing to gamble my own life, but quite another to gamble everyone else's.

"I want to come," Selen says, but I shake my head.

"No one is going to question three Arms of Everam on the street, but they'll want papers if we have women with us." Somehow Darin has secured uniforms of the temple guards. Arick has already put makeup around his eyes to disguise his pale skin.

"Fine for you and Arick," Selen says, "but I'm taller and wider than Darin. How come he gets to go?"

Indeed, Darin is swimming in his uniform, cut for a much larger man. He looks up as Selen names him. "Just need a minute."

He closes his eyes, takes a deep breath, and slowly exhales. As he does, he seems to swell, getting taller and thicker until the uniform fits almost perfectly.

Selen forgets her irritation, letting out a low whistle. "That trick's new."

"Looks more impressive than it is." Darin tries to take a step, loses his balance, and stumbles a bit. "Ent any heavier or stronger, just taking up more space."

"It's still early," I tell Selen. "We're just going to scout a bit. We can't show ourselves before sunset."

"And what do we do come morning?" Selen asks.

I shrug. "Let's focus on getting there."

Darin walks a little awkwardly at first, but he's found his stride by the time we march past the gate and into the city. Arick, on the other hand, looks every inch the *dal'Sharum*. His size alone marks him as a fighter to watch, but he moves with an easy grace that hints at skill to match his strength, and the *hora* spear and shield give credence to his uniform as a holy warrior.

It's not uncommon for wealthier *Sharum* families to have a spear or shield enhanced with the blessed bones of a famed ancestor, though they are usually considered too precious for combat.

"Hope you didn't leave anything important in your room." Darin points down the street.

Flames still smolder in Chadan's palace. The outer wall where the barracks were housed is partially collapsed, as if the demons had tunneled under the foundations, but the palace itself appears to have held.

Faseek materializes out of the shadows as we approach the meeting place. "Prince Olive." He puts a fist to his chest and bows deeply.

"Enough of that" The gesture makes me uneasy. I don't deserve it, and anyone who sees it will have an unwanted clue to who we are. "What happened last night?"

"The palace wards were too strong for the *alagai* to attack directly," Faseek says, "so they threw stones and set fires to weaken the warding with soot and ash, while the rest of them trampled the city to dust."

He swallows. "But they were tunneling. They collapsed the supports under a corner of the wall, and everything came crashing down. We lost fourteen in the collapse, and another score before Chadan cut us a re-treat to the palace itself."

Now it's my turn to swallow, though my throat is dry. "Is he . . . ?"

"He's fine," Faseek says. "He just returned from Sharik Hora. But the rest of the men . . . " He shakes his head. "Half are injured, and all are haunted. This is like nothing we've ever seen. The *alagai* are salting the Ala. Giving us nowhere to retreat to. Soon, the Holy City will be all that's left."

But for how long? The demons cannot approach Sharik Hora with-out burning away, but as with Chadan's walls, they can lob stones and debris, slowly grinding heroes' bones to powder before the protections weaken and they can force their way forward.

The only hope is to fight. Now, while we still can.

"What did Iraven's scouts find?" I ask.

Faseek's face darkens. Darin sniffs, perhaps smelling my brother's fear. "A path to the abyss."

My knees weaken. For a moment I fear I will sway, but I hear Moth-er's voice in my head.

Never lose composure, Mother told me a thousand times. *Not when you stub your toe, and not when the whole duchy is ablaze. Your people take their cues from you. If you are calm, they will be calm. If you are brave . . .*

It was easy for her to say. I don't think Mother has emotions the way other folk do. She took her own lessons too well.

But now I am thankful for the words, because they give me strength to look Faseek in the eye, lending him courage I don't have. "Explain."

"When the *alagai* breached the walls in the *chin* quarter two moons ago, they did not leave."

The words hang for long moments in the stunned silence between us. "How is that possible?" I ask at last. "Iraven said he drove them back. Sealed the breach."

Faseek nods. "The Warders repaired the breach in the wall, but the *chin* quarter's undercity was in such disrepair it was condemned. The Sharum Ka had it sealed off, and darkness grew within."

The words are ominous, but Mother's training keeps me focused. "What did they find, precisely?

"The *chin* quarter stands unmolested, even as the demons have leveled every other part of the city they pass through. They went into the undercity and found . . . "

A look of horror crosses my brother's face. Faseek is the bravest warrior I know. Fearless in battle. Yet the very thought of what they found shakes him.

I lay a hand on his shoulder, comforting and firm. I squeeze, looking him in the eyes with a hard shell of calm over my mounting fears. "What did they see?"

"The *alagai* . . . " he swallows again, "are tunneling a greatward."

Acid nausea forms in my belly, spreading out to make my muscles feel shaky, sick. I'm in over my head. We all are. I remember stories of demon warding from the histories of the demon war. If there was any doubt remaining, this proves there is a mind demon controlling the assault.

But I show none of my fear to my spear brother, arching my back the way Mother did when she wanted to be imperious. "So we have a target."

I turn to Darin with the same tone. "Warn Micha. Tell the others to gather the *hora* weapons and armor up. Now. We'll meet you as quickly as we can."

Darin nods and runs off. Faseek looks about to say something, but I hold up a finger, staying him until Darin is well out of sight.

"Your runner is quick," Faseek says, "but he will not be quick enough. We muster in a quarter hour. The Sharum Ka believes it is best to infiltrate the *alagai* tunnels in the day when they will be weakest. The Princes Unit will take point with his personal guard, the Spears of the Desert."

"Of course," I say. "The Sharum Ka needs his best men." And because my brother is wise enough to take his rival to the abyss with him, lest the *Damaji* treat this as yet another suicide mission.

"It is an honor," Faseek says. "We will battle Alagai Ka himself, and be victorious, or die on *alagai* talons, and stand proud before Everam's judgment."

I look at him a long time, wondering if perhaps I have lent him too much courage. It's hard to see the weak, fearful boy he was just a few months ago. He's put on muscle, but it's more than that. Faseek is one of the fiercest fighters we have. First into the fray.

Today, that's likely to get him killed.

A horn sounds out over the city, coming from the training grounds. The Horn of Sharak.

"We are called to muster." Faseek punches a fist to his chest. "Farewell, my prince. I will see you again, in this life or the next."

I surprise him by pulling him into an embrace, but he does not resist. "Do not spend your life cheaply, warrior."

Faseek nods. "If I die, it will be drowning in oceans of ichor."

I kiss his cheek and let him go.

"We don't have much time," Arick says. "You may have fooled Darin, but my sister will see through your lie."

I don't face him. "What do you mean?"

The horn sounds again. "They are blowing the Horn of Sharak," Arick says, "and you mean to answer."

My hand tightens on the haft of my spear. "And if I do?"

Arick stamps the butt of his spear on the ground. "Then we'll do it together."

"Why?" I ask. "This is not your city. Not your tribe. The Majah stripped you of the black."

"The Majah can tear my clothes," Arick sounds pained, "but only Everam can take the black from me. Fighting *alagai* is the only time I've ever truly felt alive. This is not my city or my tribe, but all men are brothers in the night. I won't hide in a tomb to greater men while others shed blood to hold back the forces of Nie."

I look at him at last, putting a hand on his shoulder. "Then come, brother. It is time to be counted."

52

LEFT BEHIND

M Y BODY FEELS awkward, swollen like a balloon to fit the
Sharum uniform, but my legs are longer, and without added
mass to fill the new volume, I feel light as a feather. It takes
a few moments to hit my stride, but when I do, the ruined streets pass in
a blur.

Running is what I've always been best at. Running from my problems or things that overwhelm my senses, running to fetch help when
I'm in over my head.

But if the demons are building a ward here in the city, there's no running from that. It means they're digging in, and will only get stronger.
How can we fight that? There hasn't been a demon greatward since the
war, and from the stories Mam told, they nearly killed her and Da, Aunt
Leesha, Bloodfather, and the Damajah.

What are we supposed to do, in the face of that? Olive sounded like
she had a plan, but I could smell her fear.

I avoid the gate, crowded with folk trying in vain to get permission
to leave the Holy City. Instead I climb the bone-encrusted wall, avoiding the distracted wall guards and making my way to the statue that
hides one of the entrances to Micha's secret tunnels. They have more
twists and turns than a gopher burrow, but I don't need to remember
them when I can just follow my nose.

I'm back in Micha's secret chamber in short order, relaying the news.

Selen slaps her forehead before I even finish. "Darin Bales, you ripping idiot."

I break off in confusion, smelling her annoyance. "What did I do?"

"What was the big hurry to run and tell us?" Selen demands. "We're hiding in the safest place in the city. Olive just ran you off so she could join up and fight."

I stiffen. Could it be? "How's she gonna do that if Arick's with her?"

"Olive Paper can pick up a milk cow and lift it over her head," Selen says. "Arick's tough, but he ent enough to stop her."

"Nor would he try," Rojvah says. "My brother will need no convincing to kill *alagai* again."

I feel sick, because she's makin' a lot of sense. I remember the wild look in Arick's eyes when he was drunk on demon magic, so like Ella Cutter before she tried to kill Mam. And Olive is different now, in ways I still don't understand. But would she lie to my face like that? Olive Paper?

Startin' to wonder if there's anyone I can really trust anymore.

"I'll go after her," I say. "She can't have gotten far."

"If she's rejoined her spear brothers, it won't do much good," Micha says. "I doubt you could force her to return any more than Arick."

She's right, but that doesn't make it any easier to hear. I beat Olive once, but I know it was because I got lucky, and she's come a long way since then. Don't want to fight her for real. Don't even know that it's my business. "So what do we do? Wait?"

"The Core with that," Selen says, going to the weapons rack. "Gonna get herself killed. If she's going into the hive, we're going after her. Then when this is all over, I'm gonna kill her myself for leaving us behind."

The thought of going down into a demon hive scares me so much I have to clench to keep from emptying my bladder. "We gonna be much help, if she's got a hundred spears around her? Micha killed a mind demon, once. Why not Olive?"

"I stabbed a surprised mind demon trapped in a sunlit room," Micha says. "If it had known I was coming—if it had an instant to prepare—it would have sent me down the lonely path."

"And this ent just any mind," Selen reminds me. "Your own mam thought it was Alagai ripping Ka. Demon's been planning this a long time."

The words hang like dread in the air and I stand frozen, even as the others prepare. Micha has already taken a *hora* spear and shield, concealing other weapons in her robe. Rojvah takes a bone *hanzhar* from the rack, slipping it into her belt. Micha and Selen have donned *Sharum'ting* blacks, but Rojvah's still in her pillow silks. It's hard to look at her without my eyes sliding to places they don't belong, and the translucent silk will offer no protection against a coreling's claws.

"Maybe you ought to stay," I tell her.

In response, Rojvah touches her choker and opens her mouth. Micha and Selen hear nothing, but the high-pitched sound she makes drives me to my knees, hands over my ears.

As quickly as she started, Rojvah stops, and the room goes quiet.

"Tell me again, to leave my brother to his fate," she says quietly.

She's right. They're all right. I'm not helping. I'm just the coward holding everybody back. "Ay, sorry."

"The demon hive is in the *chin* quarter," Micha says. "We can travel there without leaving the undercity, perhaps in time to intercept Olive and the *Sharum*."

"Faseek says the demons never left the undercity." I hate to keep arguing, but it has to be said. "With everyone sheltering here in the Holy City . . . "

"We must assume the undercity is compromised," Micha agrees.

I'd already come to the same conclusion, but having her say it makes it all the more real. Again I feel a pressing need to find a privy.

I shrink back to my normal size, the warrior's robes hanging off me like I'm a boy in his father's clothes. "I need to change," I tell them, running to the other chamber.

53

—•—

NIGHT VEILS

THE SUN IS high in the sky, but Arick and I keep our night veils up as we cross the training grounds. The night veil is a symbol of unity, but it is also a functional garment to filter out sand, dust, or a foul stench.

The training grounds has all three. I had become inured to it, but after a few days away, the smell envelops me like a cloud—dirt and male sweat, some fresh on the skin and some long saturated into clothes and leather.

The *dal'Sharum* are focused on their own formations, and not a glance is spared for two warriors hurrying to muster. We approach the Princes Unit, and my heart aches to see our familiar number cut by a quarter, with many that remain in the ranks wearing bandages and slings.

If those men can spear a demon, the feedback magic might heal their wounds, but it makes an already dangerous task near impossible.

"Death stalks us tonight, brothers!" my prince shouts, as if in response to my thoughts. We are at the back of the men, and I can picture him perfectly, pacing in front of them as he gives our nightly speech.

"Close your eyes, and imagine it!" Chadan shouts. I glance to see Arick pause his approach to comply. "The *alagai* that gets past your guard, its teeth sinking into your soft throat. Claws piercing organs and talons rending the flesh from your bones. Imagine your death, and embrace it."

I wait, watching the tense breath he takes in and holds, and the relaxed way he lets it out.

Without thinking, I lower my veil and open my mouth to speak my part, but Gorvan is a hair quicker, stepping into the back ranks of our men. "We are the *Sharum* of Desert Spear! What is our fate?"

"To spend our lives on *alagai* talons!" Arick and I join the men in their thunderous reply as I continue my approach, shadowing Gorvan as he inspects our warriors.

Faseek is the first to spot us. He gives a slight bow, touching his fist to his chest. Parkot notes the move and looks up at me, eyes widening above his night veil. "*Ajin'pel.*"

His voice is low, but Gorvan hears. He whirls angrily, ready to spit demonfire on whoever has the disrespect to speak during the Ka's speech, but then he catches sight of me and chokes on his shout. Heads turn at the strangled sound, and my brothers whisper like girls gossiping in the back of Mistress Darsy's classroom as I advance through the ranks.

"Nie is not like the enemies of the day!" Chadan calls. "She does not fight for land or resources. She does not come to steal our wells or our wives."

Gorvan has fallen in behind me, and my prince is unprepared when I step from the crowd, instead. "What does she come for?"

Those who hadn't seen me yet gasp, and I hear my name run like fire across their lips.

Chadan freezes for a moment, staring. Then he straightens, falling back into our routine. "She comes to exterminate us!" There is renewed passion in his shout. "She comes to undo Creation and return us to the Void! Nie cannot be reasoned with!"

I clatter my spear against my shield and the sound is a thunderclap as Arick and my brothers mirror the move.

"Nie cannot be placated or satiated!" Chadan shouts, and twice more I lead a clash of spears. "Nie can only be fought!" I raise my spear into the air. Chadan matches me, and in the periphery of my vision I see

Arick and 150 of my brothers do the same. As one, we roar so loudly the Creator must hear us in Heaven.

For just a moment, Chadan meets my eyes. I feared what I would find in his gaze, but instead of judgment or accusation, there is a wet glitter in his eyes.

"I will spend my life on *alagai* talons!" He is supposed to look at the crowd, but we could not break this stare if we wanted to. "But I will not spend it cheaply!"

"Prince Chadan's a miser!" I shout, not taking my eyes from him. "Should we help him haggle?"

"Haggle!" The men clash their spears again, relieved laughter passing like a wave through the ranks. "Haggle! Haggle!"

None of them are more relieved than me. Just like that, I am second *kai* of the Princes Unit again, as if everything hasn't changed.

CHADAN LOOKS READY to embrace me, but this is not the time, and we both know it. Instead, he turns to Arick. "This is the half-blood princeling who came with the greenlanders masquerading as a *dal'Sharum*?"

"You are not the only *Sharum* prince unjustly shamed at court," I say carefully. My brothers and I have forged our bonds in blood and ichor, but they may yet reject Arick. "This is my cousin Arick asu'Rojer am'Inn am'Kaji."

Arick lowers his veil. "There are a hundred princes in Everam's Bounty closer to the throne than I. I am no *kai*. I just want to fight."

"Then you have come to the right place," Chadan says loudly for all to hear. "The princes judge our warriors by the ichor they spill, not the blood in their veins."

My relief is short-lived as I hear more gasps behind us. I think for a moment that someone rejects Arick's inclusion, then turn to see it is much worse than that. The crowd has parted for the Sharum Ka and a few of his elite guards, the Spears of the Desert.

Arick steps back, attempting to disappear into the ranks, but the white sleeves of his stolen uniform stand out. Impersonating the Arms of Everam is a crime punishable by death, and both of us stand guilty.

I tense as Iraven approaches, but his spear and shield are slung over his back, his hands held low and open to show me he is holding no secret weapon. "Mother said you would come. It was hard to believe, but I've learned to have faith in her prophecies."

Dama'ting are not meant to have boys, Favah once taught, *because mothers are blind to their sons' failings, and cannot help but scheme and use the dice for their benefit first, and the tribe's second.*

"I know what it's like," I tell him, "to live a life shaped by the dice. Have you come to arrest us?"

Iraven shakes his head. "We march into the eternal night of the abyss. Put your night veils up, and there will be nothing but brotherhood between us."

It's an answer, and an evasion. I want to trust Iraven, but he has never given me reason to. "And if we return and step into daylight once more?"

"To return we must survive," Iraven says, "and any who do will carry such glory that even the *Damaji* would not dare speak against them."

He reaches a hand toward me. "Come. We will march side by side into the Mouth of the Abyss. If Alagai Ka himself is hiding in the ward's eye, how can he stand against four princes of Krasia, bleeding as one?"

Again, Belina's words come to me. *The storms will end when the heir of Hollow joins blood with the Majah, and the princes stand in the eye.*

I begin to feel hope. It seems my whole life has been building toward this moment, and with such a force acting as one, what can't we accomplish?

MOST OF THE time, *kai* command from the rear of their units. It is a prudent tactic, ensuring a view of the battlespace and a stable chain of command, while keeping the strongest fighters in reserve until they are needed.

But it is not the way to win glory and inspire warriors. My father was said to command from the front, showing the men he did not put his life above theirs, and inspiring a loyalty that ran deep in his *Sharum's* hearts.

My brother is the same, and it is clear Iraven expects no less from us. Chadan and I stand on either side of the Sharum Ka, shields locked, as we advance down the narrow, twisting tunnels that lead into the demon greatward.

Our maps of the *chin* quarter's undercity are useless. The demons have been hard at work in the months since it was sealed off, digging new tunnels and using the stone and soil to build walls and embankments to shape the others.

In wardsight I can see ambient magic like heat haze in the air. The symbol is pulling at that power, creating a current as it shapes and circulates magic like a beating heart.

"Where do we go?" Chadan asks.

Iraven starts to answer, but I realize it is simple. "The mind demon will be at the center of the ward. We need only follow the flow of magic to get there."

Iraven gives me a withering look for interrupting him, but he does not argue.

I learn quickly that the very thing that guides us is the first line of defense. As the flowing magic passes the men, it pulls at their auras like a cloud of insects sucking blood. The greatward doesn't form a forbidding that prevents us from entering. Instead, it weakens us like a spider's poison as we attempt to traverse the web.

Our brothers move as if wading through water, hackles raised as they jump at every sound. Many are breathing hard, as if we climb a steep hill instead of the gentle downward slope of the tunnel. They will be slow when they must be quick. Tired when they must be fresh. Anxious when they need to remain calm.

In their powerfully warded *alagai*-scale armor, Iraven and Chadan are shielded from the effect. The olive has been replaced with the spear of Majah on Chadan's breastplate.

My own armor is simple *Sharum* fare, thick robes with pockets for fired clay plates that will shatter on impact, dispersing force. Proof against one blow, but not two in the same place.

Still, I am no more hindered than the other princes. I've shattered the plaster over Belina's armlet—no point hiding when her son fights at my side—but its wards cannot account for this. It is the *sharik hora* trimming my shield. The heroes' bones softly radiate the same golden glow that protects the Holy City. The demon magic cannot touch it, flowing around me like water.

In the row behind us, Faseek and Gorvan have come to the same conclusion, putting Arick with his bone shield ahead of them like a windbreaker. I can see my cousin's pride, and his *Sharum* heart.

The men farther back have neither magic armor nor heroes' bones. We have to slow our pace to just keep them from exhausting themselves, and as they grow increasingly hindered by the insidious demon magic, I worry about their martial efficacy.

The heroes' bones protect me from the demon ward's drain, but they do nothing to alleviate my growing sense of unease. *Alagai* flee sunlight, and are not known to shelter in surface caves or even a dark cellar, but they are creatures of the underground. We are in their domain now, and surely they know it.

The tunnel widens at one point, and I signal the men to widen their line as Chadan, Iraven, and I fall back into the shield wall.

But attack doesn't come from the front. Stone walls on either side of the tunnel shimmer and blur like one of Mother's Cloaks of Unsight, and sand demons appear, leaping to attack our flanks.

"Shields!" Iraven barks, but as I feared, the men are slow to respond. A few fumble, failing to get their shields up in time to prevent being savaged. Even those who manage to turn their shields in time don't have a chance to lock with their neighbors. The demons burst through, running through the ranks in a frenzy of talon and jaw. Warriors scream as they are pulled down. Some of their auras snuff like candles, while others dim rapidly as untended wounds pump blood onto the tunnel floor.

A demon races at me, but I am not slow like the other warriors. I snap my shield into position, and the *alagai* shrieks as it slams into the hero bones. The air fills with a nauseating smoke, and as I throw the creature back, I see its scales are blackened and burned.

I draw back and stab, the bone head of my spear punching through the demon's armor like nail into soft wood. The flesh beneath sizzles, ichor bubbling a froth as the blessed weapon does its grim work.

"Defensive square!" Iraven cries. "Fill the gaps!" Their training takes over, and men from the inner ranks rush to form a shield wall that surrounds us on all sides. A second rank raises their shields high, protecting against ambush from above.

Iraven turns, meeting my eyes, though he speaks to all his lieutenants. "Hunt."

We nod, becoming predators as we scan the battlespace. There is still active fighting, demons that will collapse our defense from within if they are not contained.

I throw my *hora* spear, no longer afraid the bone head might shatter. With one thrust, the priceless relic reverted to its true function— a weapon of war. My aim is true and I skewer a demon that had Parkot pinned. I draw my *hanzhar* and charge to finish the creature off before it can heal, but I needn't have bothered. The demon shrieks and kicks as noxious fumes sizzle from its entry and exit wounds. By the time I cut its throat, the *alagai* is already dead.

I know what to expect from the other hunters, but Arick surprises me. He attacks with wild abandon, matching the demons in ferocity. I would think him magic-drunk, but the bone weapons do not send feedback magic into us the way warded metal does. Arick's fury comes from within.

Sharaj would have drilled discipline into him, but here, he's just what we need. Having never trained with us, he's not missing from our formation, and *Sharum* respect a warrior who gives himself to battle so fully. Like a champion of old, Arick moves from fight to fight, stabbing, hacking, and trampling. He leaves a path of wounded and crippled demons behind him for Gorvan and Faseek to finish off.

Not to be outdone, Iraven and Chadan are blurs of movement, enhanced by their powerful armor as the princes defend their own bodyguard.

It doesn't take long to clear the inner square, but it doesn't feel like a victory. The bodies of my fallen brothers lay scattered on the tunnel floor. I hurry to those with a flicker of aura remaining, but I can do little more than offer a word of comfort before they slip away to walk the lonely path.

"P-prince Olive." The words are a croak. The speaker is Andew, one of my greenblood brothers, brought to Desert Spear as a child when the Majah returned.

I lift the cloth he presses against his midsection, and steel my expression to hide my horror at the deep wound and the damaged organs it reveals. I doubt a skilled Gatherer with an operating theater and assistants could save him, and I dare not even try.

Andew will not recover. He will not be able to walk or fight. But he will not die slow. I glance at Iraven, but he has not noticed us yet. My brother will not be merciful tonight.

But what is mercy to a man dying on the path to the abyss? What can I do for him? I can't even promise we'll be able to bring his body back for his family to mourn before the clerics add his bones to the temple. It is more likely that those that fall in this abysmal place will be permanently lost.

Andew reaches, shaking as he takes my hands. "*Ajin'pal*, my spirit is ready for the lonely path. I have lived an Evejan life, and shown thirteen *alagai* the sun. Everam will add their ashes to the scale when He weighs my soul at the gates of heaven."

Something splashes on Andew's face, and I realize I am weeping. This was a Laktonian boy taken here against his will, much as I was. But the certainty in his words and eyes takes me aback. He has fully taken the ways of his captors as his own. He is a fool, but I envy him. I, too, felt the call of glory in the Maze, but I cannot imagine ever having the same peace in my eyes. The surety that everything is the Creator's plan.

Andew squeezes the wrist below my *hanzhar*, turning the blade toward his heart. "Guide me, I beg."

Guide me. I realize with horror that he is asking me to kill him quickly, before the demons come for him.

I shake my head, tears shimmering as they fly through the air. The idea goes against everything my mother ever taught, everything I've ever believed. It is an unforgivable violation of the Gatherer's Oath. "I can't."

"Please, *ajin'pel*." His other hand joins the first around my wrist. He is not strong enough to budge me, but I feel him pulling the blade toward his chest. "I beg you. Do not leave me to be unmanned by the *alagai*."

It feels as if the blade is piercing my heart instead. I grit my teeth and squeeze the tears from my eyes before my gaze meets his. This is a violation of the Gatherer's Oath, but I am not a Gatherer. I am *Sharum*, and

Andew deserves a death with honor. "Look to the lonely path, brother. Everam will welcome you, for your glory is boundless."

I give a strangled cry as I thrust, watching the light leave my brother's eyes. Then I throw my head back and wail, letting Everam's seraphs know a warrior comes.

A hand lays across my shoulder. For a moment I think it must be Chadan, but I turn to see it is Iraven. "You did the right thing, brother, but it is never easy."

The words sicken me. How many times must Iraven have done this horrid deed, to speak of it with such experience?

We start moving again, having lost more than a dozen warriors. The men keep shields locked on all sides as warriors probe the walls with their spears, searching for more hidden ambush pockets cloaked in demon magic. They find nothing, because the next ambush comes from the front.

Sticky filaments, invisible in the dark, strike the shields of warriors maintaining the wall. Even the rocks belowground have a soft glow of magic, but the webs of cave demons are magic-dead—dark and lifeless. The wards on our shields don't affect their powerful adhesive, and the moment contact is made, *alagai* begin reeling warriors in.

Some of the men sacrifice their shields to keep their feet, but others, be they stubborn or slow, are hauled shrieking up to the crevices in the stone where the demons hide.

Then more of the cave demons drop into our midst. They have the look of spiders, their armored exoskeletons black like polished obsidian, a bulbous body at the center of segmented legs, longer than spears and each ending in a sharp, venomous tip. They snap like whips, and when they find openings, warriors convulse and drop weapons from nerveless fingers. Only those quick enough to throw their spears through a gap in the chitinous legs manage to survive, but they hang, vulnerable as they try to cut themselves free of the webs without their spears.

The air fills with arrows as our archers turn every demon to show itself into a pincushion. Their writhing and kicking bodies land inside our lines, and my brothers quickly move to destroy them.

No sooner have we turned our attention to the new threat than a thundering of taloned feet heralds a stream of demons pouring into the tunnel from either end.

Everything becomes chaos and melee. There's no time to think. No luxury of fear. It's kill or be killed, and I lose track of who I am fighting beside, of who saves my life and whose I save. I move from fight to fight, operating on instinct and muscle memory more than conscious thought. Picking fights where my brothers are in danger of being overwhelmed, I hack off a taloned arm here, a horned tail there.

Still I'm too late to keep Thivan's head from leaving his body. I take a long look, embracing the sight, and then I let it go. There will be time to mourn and blame myself if I survive. I stalk the cave demon that killed him, and as if sensing my fury, it draws back at first. Then it startles, and its eyes turn cold with that familiar recognition. The demon leaps at me, a whirl of stabbing, spearlike limbs.

I sever the points off two on the first pass. The second brings me in close enough to get at the nexus point, and I amputate all four legs on one side in a single blow.

The demon shrieks and collapses, and as it struggles to rise, I smash the center of its thorax with the skeletal fist at the base of my *hora* spear. The black carapace shatters, piercing the cave demon's organs with shards of its own armor.

Even now, the crippled demon might heal the most grievous wounds, surviving to sting some unwary warrior. I whirl the spear again, severing its head.

The demons are fast, smart, and have all the advantages. Feedback magic has given some of the men new strength, but our losses continue to mount.

"To me!" Iraven cries, raising his spear. "Warriors rally to me!"

The men who are able comply quickly, forming a new defensive ring. I remain in the fighting, helping others break free long enough to join the tighter ring of shields.

My dead brothers lay everywhere. Some have been dragged off and are being fed upon by *alagai* safe from the fighting. Others are strewn about the active battlefield, making the ground slick with blood and ichor.

A cave demon spits web in Levan's face while he struggles with bare hands to keep it from tearing out his throat. I impale the demon, leaping into a tumble that uses my spear as a lever to throw it into the path of Gorvan and Faseek. Gorvan puts his spear through the cave demon's abdomen, pinning it to the ground while Faseek severs its thorax with a surgical swipe of his spear.

I turn to Levan. His helmet and some of the skin on his face were torn away when I knocked the cave demon back, but the injury is superficial. He shakes his head violently, perhaps trying to restore clarity, but when he looks up his eyes are unfocused. Still, he seems ready to return to the fight. He's lost his spear, but pulls a warded knife from his belt.

But then Levan thrusts the knife at me, instead. The blade shatters one of my armor plates and I stumble back in surprise. Quick as a cat, Levan follows me in, stabbing again in the same precise spot. This time the sharp blade parts the thick robe and slides between shards of broken plate to pierce my side. It catches in my rib cage, and I feel bones crack like the ceramic plate. Levan pulls the knife back for a third and final thrust into my heart.

I roll, batting the blade away with my shield, and react on instinct, thrusting my spear into his exposed armpit where there are no armor plates. The bone blade slides effortlessly through his chest, and he coughs a gout of blood that knocks off his night veil. I watch in horror as the clouds leave Levan's eyes and my friend stares first at the spear still skewering his body, then up at me, his face a confused mask of betrayal. "P-Prince . . . Olive?"

I reacted on instinct, but the sudden recognition brings me back to horrifying reality, and it is too much to embrace and let go. Levan's shaking hand grips the shaft of the spear, and I realize it is all that holds him upright. The light leaves his eyes, and his aura fades away.

"Olive, what did you do?" Chadan rushes to my side, and I realize how that exchange must have appeared. His eyes hold the same expression now frozen on Levan's face—shock and betrayal.

"He attacked me." The words feel lame and inadequate even as I speak them. Did Levan really try to kill me? Could I have imagined it?

There are shouts from within the re-formed defensive ring. We turn as one to see brother fighting brother. Half a dozen warriors have lost their helmets and turned on the men beside them, attempting to remove theirs as well.

With every helmet lost, another set of unfocused eyes looks up, and then there are two warriors moving to steal the helmets of two more.

"Everam's Beard," Chadan whispers.

"We have to get out of here," I croak. Hot blood seeps through my robes, but there is no way to tend the wound, and little to be done for the cracked ribs in any event.

"Scatter and rally back to me!" Iraven cries. "Shields out! Any man missing his helmet is an enemy. Do not hesitate to kill them if they approach."

The words are so cold and ruthless I do not know if I could have given the order, but there is no choice and we all know it. Three hundred of my brothers entered the demon ward. Less than thirty are able to form around us, all of them bleeding and breathing hard.

Our corrupted brothers mass before us, shields up and spears leading. Many are wounded, but they pay it no mind. More than one appears to be ignoring life-threatening injuries. Still they press in.

Iraven looks at the advancing warriors and our weak defense. Chadan and I do the same. The tunnel is wide enough to surround us, and from there, the outcome will not be in doubt. The fear I've been pushing to the side finally seeps in as I realize this is likely the end.

My brother reaches the same conclusion. "Run!"

54

MIND GAMES

DEMONS CLUSTER IN one of the tunnels, staying out of the fray but blocking our path. We cannot go through our corrupt brothers without killing them, and so we do the only thing we can, racing deeper into the demon ward.

We've been such fools. This was never a surprise attack on the mind demon. He invited us into his web. Now we're being herded like livestock, and it's my fault. I brought Alagai Ka here, and I was woodbrained enough to think I could fight him with my spear. I'm just glad the others aren't here to pay the price for my arrogance.

The tunnel narrows and opens above and to one side into an enormous cavern. A sense of hopelessness fills me as we continue to run across what becomes simply a ledge on the steep cavern wall. Countless stalactites hang from the cavern's roof, some little more than texture, and others big enough to build a manse inside. I look down, but even in wardsight, the bottom is too deep to see, save for a few stalagmites jutting taller than Sharik Hora's minarets.

The ledge narrows until we are running single file, becoming little more than a shelf of rock and soil clinging to the cliff face. Ahead of me, Chadan runs with the lightness and speed of magically enhanced strength, but his steel armor is still heavy. The shelf gives way, collapsing beneath his feet.

"Chadan!" I reach out, catching one of his pinwheeling arms. I throw myself back, heaving, and might have pulled him to safety, but Arick is not able to pull short against my sudden stop, slamming into me from behind. He falls onto his backside, and I watch him stare in horror as my prince and I tumble down into darkness.

I AWAKEN IN a pile of loose stones kicked up on our descent. I remember tumbling head over heels, striking the stone slope of the cliff again and again, then blackness. I groan, putting my hands under me. I have no idea how long I've been unconscious. Seconds? Minutes? Hours?

Chadan lies a few feet away. I pull shattered ceramic plates from my robes, dropping the shards to the ground as I go to him. I slip shaking, filthy fingers under his veil, feeling for a pulse. He's alive, but unconscious. No doubt the charged *alagai*-scale armor protected him from the fall, and even now its *hora* and wards work to speed his healing. He looks better than I feel, battered and bruised with cracked ribs that scream every time I take a full breath.

I don't know how far we fell, but it was a long way—removing us from the demon ward entirely. Even without my spear and shield, I don't feel the pull of its flow at my aura. There's no way to know what happened to Iraven and the others, or even how to get back to where we were. The cavern wall quickly becomes too steep to climb.

With the wards on my helmet I can still see, and I retrieve our weapons and shields from where they lie amid the rubble. Even if we're off the demon ward, we are not safe. I don't know if the sun is still shining above, but here beneath the Ala, night is eternal, and the *alagai* will not withdraw and give us time to regroup or escape.

I still have my satchel, and open my robe to clean and stitch the worst of my wounds while I wait for Chadan's armor to restore him. When he groans, I go to him, giving him a sip of cool water.

"Olive?" His voice is a harsh rasp. "Where are we?"

"We fell from a ledge," I tell him. "I don't know where we are, but the *alagai* still hunt us. Can you sit up?"

He nods, allowing me to support him as he wobbles to a sitting position. "I'm all right. I just need a moment."

I hear a clatter of stones from behind a mound of stalagmites and get to my feet, spear and shield at the ready. "We don't have a moment."

"Olive." Iraven appears from around the bend before Chadan can attempt to rise. "Thank Everam I've found you."

I cannot deny my relief, but still I tilt my head. "How?"

"The armlet." Iraven holds up a tiny sphere of warded glass. Inside, a gold arrow floats in its center, no doubt containing a sliver of the demonbone that powers my armlet.

The arrow is pointing at me.

"Mother made this to locate you," Iraven says. "She gave it to me after you . . . escaped the harem. It seems you found a way to evade its signal for days, but *inevera*, it was working after you fell. Come, I will take you back to the others."

"Are they all right?" I ask.

"Safe, for now," Iraven says.

Chadan struggles to his feet, but after a moment, he looks steady and determined. "They will not survive long without us."

Iraven waves a hand at me. "This way, sister."

Sister? Iraven has never called me that—not since the night I was taken from Hollow. I look at him again, suspicious. How exactly did he find us? The compass would not have navigated the tunnels for him, and with his two greatest rivals fallen from a cliff, why search for us at all?

I remember the story Mother told me, about how the corelings tried to assassinate her. *I was lured from the wards by a mimic demon that took the form of a friend, calling my name.*

Iraven seems himself. His helmet is in place, and I can clearly see its mind wards. His armor is covered in blood, ichor, and filth, but it is as I remember. Could a mimic demon duplicate his wards?

With his spear and shield on his back, Iraven's hands are free. "Hold this a moment," I say, tossing him my shield. Iraven catches it instinctively, unaffected by the touch of the heroes' bones.

"This is a sacred item," Iraven growls as I make a show of fixing my robes, rearranging the remaining armor plates for maximum balance and protection. "You should treat it with more respect."

I nod and our eyes meet as he hands it back. They are not clouded like Levan's were. It's just my imagination.

"This way." Iraven gestures to one of many paths leading deeper into the crevasse. Chadan follows.

"That's not the direction you came from," I say.

Iraven does not slow. "It's faster."

"How can you know that?" I ask.

"I've been wandering around down here for hours," Iraven says, "trying to find you."

It makes no sense. The Sharum Ka left his warriors hiding in a demon hive to spend hours searching for us by himself?

I'm not the only one who notices and comes to the same conclusion. "You sent Chikga to kill Olive, didn't you?" Chadan's voice is calm, but I know his spirit is nothing but.

Chadan is ready for an attack, but Iraven is quick. The hidden blade he pulls from under his vambrace is long and thin, perfect for slipping between the scales of Tazhan armor. Chadan tries to block, but before he can fully react, Iraven has buried the knife in his lung.

I scream as Chadan coughs blood, his breath a wet wheeze. He falls to his knees as I charge, *hora* spear leading the way. Iraven leaves the knife buried in Chadan to the hilt, turning to face my charge. In one smooth motion, he rolls the shield off his shoulder and onto his arm, taking his spear from its harness.

"I'll kill you!" The words escape my lips before I realize I mean them. Twice now, my brother has taken everything from me. I won't give him a third chance.

But my attack is undisciplined, born of anger, rage, and surprise. Iraven turns it against me, twisting out of my path even as I am tripped and sent sprawling. I try to regain control, but take a bash of his shield to the head instead. I keep moving, trying to create space while I recover my senses.

"Do you think Mother and I spent the last fifteen years working to regain power," Iraven growls, "only to let you steal my glory and give it to your *push'ting* prince?"

"His family has led the Majah for three thousand years," I say. "What gives you the right to take it from them?"

"My father is the Deliverer," Iraven says. "My mother was called by the dice to be Majah *Damaji'ting*. It is my birthright to rule our tribe, and if I reclaim it, I can hand Desert Spear back to Father on an electrum platter, without a drop of blood spilled."

"Then you will be handing him a lie," I say. "Chadan bleeds here with us, and Chikga and Thivan and the hundreds of brothers we brought to bleed in this forsaken place."

"Still nothing," Iraven says, "compared with the ocean of blood that will wash over the sands if Father takes the city by force. But it isn't a price you have to pay, sister. You are not Majah. You owe no loyalty to Aleveran or his scion."

I spit at his feet. "I have already paid. You made me a pawn in your schemes and bled me with the alagai tail on the sacred floor of Sharik Hora, before the Skull Throne, itself. Will you tell Father that, as well?"

"Tell him yourself," Iraven says. "When we deliver Desert Spear to him side by side."

The image flickers across my mind's eye. Meeting Father—really meeting him—for the first time, presenting him something he has sought for fifteen years—the reunification of the tribes of Krasia.

Father would *notice* me. He'd have no choice.

Desire, long repressed, wells in me. Dreams of my father coming to Hollow to see me, or visiting him in New Krasia. Dreams of being someone he was proud of, and not just one of seventy children he was too busy to know.

My spear starts to dip. Behind me, Chadan lets out a hoarse gasp.

"I've waited my whole life to be noticed by Father," I say.

"It is in your grasp." Iraven's voice is all charm. "If we escape this place together with the same tale, none will doubt us, or question it when I take you into my house and make you *kai* of the Spears of the Desert."

"No." I lift my spear again. "If this is the price for Father to notice me, then I have overvalued his attention."

Iraven looks genuinely disappointed, but he nods and begins to advance. "I promise a quick death with honor."

"I can't promise the same," I tell him. "You sold your honor long ago."

———

I DODGE A thrust of Iraven's spear, swinging my own in an arc to knock him off balance with a whack across the back.

It never connects.

Iraven whips his spear up over his shoulder to block my swing, then reverses the move, cracking me atop the helm with the butt of the weapon.

Again I stumble back, but this time Iraven follows me in, his spear pumping as rapidly as a hummingbird's wings.

Loath as I am to admit it, Iraven is an amazing fighter. Better than me. Better than Chadan. Our father was said to be the greatest living *sharusahk* master, and he instructed his sons personally. I was a fool to think myself a match for him.

In his *alagai*-scale armor, Iraven is as strong as I am, and less vulnerable. My own armor is missing several plates, and having watched me position them, my half brother knows where the vulnerable spots are.

I focus on defense, keeping out of range when I can, blocking with my shield when I must, and parrying when I have no other choice.

It makes no difference. Every move I make, Iraven finds a way to turn against me. When I step, it is in the direction he wants me to go. When I parry a blow, he twists it into a new line of attack, forcing me to defend rather than counter. When I attack, he turns the force of it against me, guiding me into position for a counterstrike that more often than not hits home. Two more of the plates in my robes are shattered. Soon they will offer no protection at all.

"I'm disappointed, Olive," Iraven says. "You are blood of the Deliverer. For all the glory you've garnered, I expected you to fight better than this."

He's right. Not for the first time, I curse the years wasted on herb lore that could have been spent learning the spear.

I want to blame Mother, but I know she did her best. Hollow needed Mother's healing hand after Father and the Deliverer purged the demons from our lands. Preparing me to succeed her meant pushing aside who I was and trying to make me into her mimic, that I might carry on her steady rule.

But the war wasn't really over. The enemy was still out there, regrouping. Hollow needed a healing hand fifteen years ago, but it's time that hand held a spear once more.

I growl and charge in, seemingly more reckless than before. I know what Iraven will do. How he will turn it into a circle to redirect the force.

At the last moment, just as he begins to move, I shift my weight, throwing my body away from my target.

And into the path of his step.

My thrust is perfect, with the full weight of my strength driving the spear into his chest, a blow even warded armor cannot withstand.

At least, it would have been, if I'd carried a properly warded steel spear. Against the *alagai*, its *sharik hora* magic made my weapon all but indestructible. Against Iraven—a hero himself—it is only bone and lacquer. The speartip shatters against his Tazhan armor like it was made of glass.

Still, Iraven is driven back by the force of the blow. I seize the advantage, grabbing the shaft of his spear and delivering a push-kick to his midsection that folds him over and sends him reeling back, weaponless.

I have the initiative now, pressing him with quick thrusts of his own spear, driving him away from Chadan.

But even disarmed, Iraven is dangerous, and incredibly fast. He bats away my thrusts with his shield to create openings for kicks, punches, and shield-bashes. He gets in close, snaking his arm around the spear shaft, then throws himself into a tumble that pops it from my grasp.

I'm sent sprawling, and Iraven might have ended it there, but instead he tosses the spear aside, dropping his shield, as well. I think to keep mine, but I realize too late a shield is a disadvantage in *sharusahk*. It makes me slow, throwing off my balance. Iraven grabs the edges, and by controlling the shield on my arm, he controls me. He lifts it out of the path of knees he throws into my unprotected midsection, blasting the breath from me, then he somersaults, and I am forced to yank my arm from the straps before it's broken.

I have a moment's hope things might be better hand-to-hand, but Iraven fights with a *dama's* skill and a *Sharum's* ferocity, turning my own moves against me to amplify his already enhanced strength. One of his punches connects so hard it shatters one of my few remaining armor plates and drives the shards into my thigh.

His takedown happens a moment later, and my leg buckles as I try to stop it. We hit the ground hard and Iraven drives my face into the rock, stunning me as he works his way into a death hold. He increases the pressure, cutting off the flow of blood to my brain.

Worse than suffocating, I feel like my head is swelling, face growing hot. I slap helplessly at his arms, struggling to get to my feet, but Iraven has his legs wrapped around mine, shifting his weight to drop me back down every time I start to rise.

Blackness forms at the edge of my vision, closing with alarming speed. This is it. This I how I die. I twist to look my brother in the eye. I tell myself it's because I want him to remember his betrayal, and not so I won't be alone in my final moments.

Instead, I see Chadan tackle Iraven off me. The impact makes my head spin, compressing my chest when what I need more than anything is to breathe. My vision goes dim, but then the weight is off, and I pull a heaving breath, and then another, watching the battle as if through a distance lens.

Iraven kicks Chadan away as they tumble across the cavern floor. The knife is no longer sticking from my prince's chest, but that is not necessarily a good thing.

Iraven rolls to his feet, but then his leg buckles under him, and I see Chadan returned my brother's blade in the pass, burying it in the gap between *alagai* scales on the Sharum Ka's thigh.

Iraven does not cry out. He looks Chadan in the eye as he regains his balance, standing tall as he pulls the blade out. The impairment will be short-lived. The stored magic in his Tazhan armor will speed the healing.

But my prince is not so fortunate, his breath still a stunted wheeze. No doubt he counted on a similar restorative effect when he pulled the knife from his chest, but even Tazhan wardwork and *alagai hora* aren't quick enough to keep a collapsed lung from filling with blood once the blade is pulled free.

Chadan is on his feet, but only barely. His ragged breaths are long and shallow, his face pale and sweaty. I can see his aura dimming. He might be able to exchange a few weak blows, but win or lose, it will be his life.

I try to cry out to him, but I have no voice. An attempt to sit up met with equal failure. I heal as quickly as they do, but Iraven came closer to killing me than I want to think about. For now, all I can do is watch as both men assume *sharusahk* stances.

Suddenly a high-pitched keening sound echoes through the ravine, and something happens to Iraven. He stiffens, then removes his helmet and the protection its wards offer his mind.

I've lost track of how many times I've watched Mother's herald Kendall spin tales of mind demons in Mother's salons. Part of the act was pulling willing victims into a plush chair at the center of her circle, where she would mesmerize them with a combination of soothing words and the music of her fiddle. Then she would suggest they do things not in their nature, like shouting animal sounds, or planking between chairs so Kendall could stand on their backs.

Like those party guests, Iraven's eyelids grow heavy and droop closed, but there is a twitch in the skin as his eyes move rapidly beneath. After only a few seconds, he relaxes, opening them to offer me a flat stare I know instinctively does not belong to my brother.

"Long have I waited for this moment," Iraven says, but it is no longer him speaking. From out of the shadow of a stalagmite mound, something stirs.

Delicate, compared with the *alagai* I've seen—this demon is small and slender, no larger than Faseek when I met him in *sharaj*, with a large, conical cranium. Its eyes are giant, pools of polished black, alien and unreadable. A ring of short, vestigial horns poke through the tough, charcoal-colored flesh to form a sort of crown about its brow. The horns become ingrown as they run down its body, creating jagged ridges in the leathery flesh.

Demon drones, like those we kill in the Maze, lack sex organs of any kind. This one presents with a small penis hanging in the shadows of its slender, bipedal legs. The talons at the ends of its fingered hands look more like manicured nails than savage weapons, but I have no doubt they are sharp.

But most overwhelming is the glow of its magic. So powerful I have to squint as if from bright light until my warded eyes can adjust.

I know him on sight, as would anyone raised in Hollow. There are paintings of the Father of Demons in both the cathedral and Mother's keep, illustrations in the histories of the demon war, even a statue in Gatherers' University of my father, Arlen, and Renna Bales leading him chained down into the Core.

Alagai Ka, the demon king.

55

DOMINATION

THE MOMENT STRETCHES long, and Chadan slumps, his last reserve of strength leaving him. I crawl to him as he drops to his
knees, wheezing shallow, rapid breaths through a mouth spattered with blood.

Iraven paces me as I move, holding position between me and the
demon king. My brother's eyes are not clouded like Levan's were. They
regard me with cold dispassion, like a student studying ants under glass.

I cradle Chadan in my arms, presenting no threat in an attempt to
buy time as I gather my strength.

"I didn't . . . " Chadan coughs, ". . . stand . . . frozen."

I hold my prince tighter, touching his face. "No, you didn't." I kiss
him gently, tasting his blood on my lips.

I look back at Iraven. "You never sealed the breach, did you,
brother?"

Iraven throws his head back and laughs. "You speak as if this grunting ape had a chance. Everything was according to my design."

I look over his shoulder at Alagai Ka, standing aloof and unreadable
a few paces back. My brother isn't here at all, anymore. Revulsion shudders through me as I realize he speaks with the demon's voice.

"The leaders of this breeding ground are barely drones," Iraven
says. "Even if they had doubts about our breach, none had the courage

to investigate for themselves. They were cowed into trusting this puppet and his men, who only remember what I wish them to of our first encounter."

So the demon corrupted my brother a month ago, at least, planting suggestions in his mind that held even under the light of day.

"You made him send Chikga to kill me," I guess.

"Your clutchmate was already entertaining the thought," Iraven says. "It was a simple matter to stoke his feelings of resentment and fear into action."

"Why?" I ask.

"To drive you out of the Holy City," Iraven says. "The training drone was no match for you, but I knew it would force your hand and bring you and the Explorer's son to me."

Darin.

"That isn't going to happen," I say. "He is safe in the Holy City."

Iraven clucks his tongue. "He and your other clutchmates approach even now, thinking they can save you. But we have time enough to feed before they arrive."

More of the demon's human slaves appear, almost all those that remained when I was separated from the group. Their helms removed, my brothers are puppets of the demon king.

Arick is not among them. If his *hora* shield protected him even after his helm was removed, he may have been able to escape. Or they may have been forced to kill him. There is no way to know.

Gorvan and Faseek separate themselves from the group. Once, the sight of my spear brothers would give me hope, but these are not my brothers. Like Levan, their eyes are glazed and blank. Alagai Ka hasn't had time to corrupt them fully, as he has with Iraven. If I can kill the demon, they will be free.

Still, I am unprepared when Faseek takes the last few strides at a run, leaping to kick me in the head. The powerful blow knocks me onto my back, stunned, as they grab Chadan.

My prince's aura is cooling as life ebbs from his oxygen-starved blood. He gives Faseek a sad look, then his head lolls as he rolls it around to regard Gorvan. "I forgive you, brothers." His words are a dry croak. "I know this is not you."

Our brothers say nothing. Faseek pulls off Chadan's helmet and Gorvan drops him unceremoniously to the ground. Chadan stiffens, and then gets to his feet, his injury seemingly forgotten. He turns to me, but the serene face I am so used to is gone, replaced with an open mask of fear, helpless to stop his body as it marches over to where the demon king stands.

"Resist," I growl. My ears are still ringing, but I know which way is down, and that's halfway to balance. I stay limp, hoping Alagai Ka will underestimate me one last time.

"I cannot." Tears run down Chadan's cheeks, streaking the blood and grime. "He's too strong."

I choke back a sob, instead meeting his eyes with all the love and determination I can muster as I speak the words we've shared so many times.

"We are the *Sharum* of Desert Spear. What is our fate?"

Chadan swallows hard, but he seems to draw strength from the words. "To spend our lives on *alagai* talons."

"Indeed," Iraven says as Chadan is made to kneel before the demon king. Alagai Ka raises a finger, and what looks like a woman's black manicured nail grows into a hooked talon three inches long.

I've gathered my strength long enough. I tuck my feet under me while the attention is on Chadan. Alagai Ka is only a few strides away. I can cross that distance in a second and butt him in the head with the mind wards on my helmet. That should stun him long enough for my *hanzhar* to finish the job.

I flex my muscles, but just as I start to rise, Iraven darts in, tripping me before I halve the distance. My own strength is used to twist the knife from my hand and slam me back down into the stone floor. Iraven puts a boot between my shoulder blades, pinning me facedown to wail helplessly as Alagai Ka slices my prince's head open like a gourd, removing the top to sink his claws into the wet meat within. He stuffs the disgusting mass into his maw, masticating with three rows of sharp teeth.

I stop screaming long enough to sick up, but pinned to the ground, most of it gets on me. Iraven and my spear brothers look on impassively as the demon king feasts on Chadan's brains and my heart is torn to pieces.

Right until this moment, I expected some miracle. Some sign the Creator is watching, and would send help or give us strength to prevail. Like a fool, I saw what I wanted to see in the prophecy, and believed it beyond sense. I shouldn't have followed Chadan here. I should have dragged him into Micha's safehold with me.

Iraven makes a slurping sound in my ear. "He loved you, you know. And died in anguish, knowing you would share his fate. The pain gives exquisite flavor to his mind."

Gone is any last vestige of my dignity. I moan and strain against his hold, but Iraven knows more than me about pressure points and force. He keeps me pinned, forcing me to watch as Alagai Ka finishes feeding and casts my prince's lifeless body aside. Only then does he let me go.

I crawl to Chadan, shaking and weeping. My heart feels like it's trying to climb my throat, and all I can manage is a toneless moan as I take his cooling body in my arms.

I look up and see the demon king watching me with his black, lidless eyes. I can sense his pleasure, drinking my suffering as he licks Chadan's blood from his claws like Baroness Emelia pairing wine with fine Angierian cheese.

The realization breaks despair's hold on me. I harden my heart and set Chadan's body on the ground, taking off my night veil to wrap the ruin of his head. Blood quickly seeps through the cloth, and my hands come away sticky with it. I am not laying just my prince to rest, but a part of myself—a life that could have been, for both of us, snuffed out before it had a chance. My tears are for both of us, but I have no time for tear bottles, and let them streak my face. "I will see you in Heaven, brother."

Then I fall into the rhythmic breathing of *sharusahk*, which Chadan used to maintain when he wanted to suppress his emotions.

Alagai Ka loses interest when I look up, heart cold. He turns instead to my kneeling brothers, remnants of the Princes Unit and the Spears of the Desert. Waves of magic emanate from the demon, washing over them like ever-expanding ripples in a pond. As those ripples touch the men, they stiffen, then begin to writhe, moaning in pain as wave after wave runs through them.

I watch as their auras begin to change, the demon editing their minds the way Mother rewrites a speech.

"They will have no recollection of what really happened this night." Iraven's voice is a low, mocking whisper. "They will return to the light with tales of valor and heroism, of how their brothers martyred themselves to give Iraven, Majah son of the Deliverer, the opening to finish his father's work and destroy Alagai Ka."

The demon has its back to me, so I turn to face Iraven, or at least the thing that wears his body. It looks like my brother. Sounds like him. Walks with the same swagger. Speaks with the same condescension. But it isn't him. Just another extension of Alagai Ka, a conduit to speak to while the demon king divides his attention between us and the hundreds of minds he's editing.

"Your surviving spear brothers will be distraught at the loss of their princes," Iraven predicts. "They will blame the *Damaji* for creating the rift between you, and for stripping the men of their pride and unit crest right before Waning. They will don the spear and olive in your honor, and assassinate Aleveran, paving the way for a civil war the 'hero' Iraven can ride to the throne. And then the city is mine."

I get up, shaking my head. I will spend my life on *alagai* talons, but I will not spend it cheaply. "The storms will end."

Iraven snorts. "You humans and your dice. All these centuries, trying to look at infinity through a pinhole."

I think of Grandmum Elona. The way she could cut her enemies apart without even touching them. I throw Iraven one of her most withering looks. "If you mind demons see the future so clearly, how is it humans exterminated all your brothers fifteen years ago?"

A vein throbs on Iraven's forehead, and he flashes a dangerous smile. "My brethren were fools. But I am still alive, and my vengeance has already begun."

He paces in front of me, moving in close. I can smell spiced lamb on his breath. "The storms will end not because you won, but because there is no point in continuing them once I have you and control the city from within. It will be a safe larder for the new queen."

A chill runs through me, but I keep the rhythm of my breath. Let the demon see the fear in my aura. "The queens were all killed."

"They were, and they weren't." Iraven winks. "I will show you personally, after you lure your friends to me and help subdue them, just as your brother did to you."

Iraven is in close, but the demon thinks me cowed and is a trice too slow to react to my quick punch to the throat. I advance as he staggers back, delivering a stomp to the side of his knee.

Even the finest armor offers scant protection to the knees unless the fighter is willing to sacrifice mobility, and only a fool would sacrifice mobility in the Maze. His leg snaps like a dry twig.

I'm already moving as Iraven collapses, out of reach of his grasping fingers before he realizes he cannot pursue. The demon still has his back turned as I sprint two steps and cross the remaining distance between us in a leap. None of my enslaved brothers are close enough to stop me.

I crash into Alagai Ka from behind, expecting to bowl him over. The demon king doesn't budge, and I feel as if I've thrown myself into a stone wall. Stunned, I grasp the sharply ridged shoulders and throw back my head to slam the mind wards on my helmet into the back of his skull.

Without turning, Alagai Ka reaches out almost casually to catch one of my arms. He rolls his midsection, yanking my arm to redirect the force of my attack into a perfect *sharusahk* throw.

I hit the ground hard, but there can be no hesitation now. I won't get another chance at this. I bound back to my feet and continue to attack. The demon tries to draw a ward in the air, but I ruin it with a high kick, then whip around to throw my opposite leg into his midsection.

It's like kicking a goldwood tree. Again, I expect my smaller foe to be knocked aside, but his feet seem rooted to the ground by more than mere talons. He hits me with a backhand blow to the face that nearly dislocates my jaw. Alagai Ka may be no bigger than a small man but with terrifying strength he bats my punches away and seizes me by the throat, lifting me clear off the ground.

I choke and pull helplessly at his wrist. The demon king's arm is longer than mine, and my punches fall short. With no ground to offer leverage, I throw my hip forward to generate momentum for a kick to the demon's head.

He might have parried with his other arm, but Alagai Ka lets it happen, accepting the blow without flinching. The many vestigial horns that form a crown around his brow are still sharp, and my leg comes away torn and bloody. I try to cry out, but only a crushed squeak escapes my lips.

Unable to draw breath, I lose the calm I maintained with its rhythm. I thrash desperately as Gorvan and Faseek come forward to unfasten my helmet and pull it off my head.

The demon's grip loosens slightly, and I draw a half breath as his cranium throbs.

I FLINCH, EXPECTING sudden pain or some psychic struggle, but there is nothing. I feel a sudden warmth on my arm, and the demon king hisses. Gorvan tears the white sleeve away to reveal Belina's armlet, but he and Faseek fumble with it, unable to so much as find the latch. They strain and pull at the little spear to no avail.

"It's a blood lock," I croak. "Your slaves cannot open it, and you and your drones cannot touch it."

"I could cut your arm off," Iraven is sitting up, calmly holding his broken knee in place while the *hora* in his armor speed the healing, "but I wish to present you to the queen unspoiled."

He gets to his feet, though his left leg still bends unnaturally as he strides over to me. The pain must be intense, but under the demon's sway, Iraven shows no sign of pain or discomfort.

"And why bother, when we have the blood to open it right here?" Iraven presses his thumb against the tip of the little spear, offering his own blood instead of his mother's. Whatever magic discerns such things accepts the substitution, and the red drains from the gem, leaving it clear as the spear slides free and the latch pops open.

I have a flash of panic, and then my synapses catch fire as the demon slips inside my mind.

MEMORIES FLIP PAST my mind's eye, the demon going through them like the pages of a scrapbook. My shame as Mother dressed me down for disappointing her with a less-than-perfect test score. Selen forcing a submission from me in the practice yard. The first time I insisted on making my own dress for the Solstice Festival and looked like a fool because I made those *stupid* ruffles in an attempt to soften my shoulders. Having to cover myself in baths and privies and sweat rooms my entire life, even as others walked around nude without a second thought.

All the nights I cried myself to sleep.

I sense Alagai Ka's pleasure at my suffering, but these small moments are not enough to satisfy the monster's hunger. He burrows deeper, clawing past my defenses with ease as he violates my most private thoughts.

Dropping my guard on the borough tour to kiss Lanna, only to have demons exploit that one moment of vulnerability to kill half the children in the camp. The realization that Micha and Mother had been lying to me my entire life.

These the demon savors, feeding in a way meat and blood cannot satiate. Still it is not enough.

"A lady doesn't eat with her fingers," Mother said at the table.

"A lady sits with both feet on the floor . . ."

"A lady doesn't use language like that . . . "

A thousand half-forgotten moments forming an endless litany from my mother as she attempted to make me pass in polite society, to shape me into the duchess she wanted me to be.

But I am not a lady. I don't even know what the word means, anymore. Grandmum was a lady, and so was Captain Wonda, and neither of them ever had much use for Mother's school of lady's manners.

"You are my daughter, but you are also my son."

Alagai Ka sucks at my memories like a baby at the breast, forcing me to relive moments of childhood through adult eyes. Did I tell Mother I wanted to be a girl because it was what I wanted, or did I just say what I thought she wanted to hear? What she spent the first five summers of my life coaching me to say? I was too young to truly understand the choice she was giving me, or the ramifications it would have on my life.

Instead, Mother took a child's promise as tacit consent to guide me away from masculine pursuits, even those I had aptitude for, redirecting me to others she found more suitable. She gave me the sewing kit that brought me so many hours of pleasure to keep me occupied because she wouldn't let me go hunting with Selen and the general. She scowled and pressured me from wearing breeches, even as Selen gave up dresses almost entirely.

I've never allowed myself to dwell on it, to truly let myself get angry with Mother. I've told myself she loved me. That she tried and meant her best, but did not have the time she would have wished with me.

But caught in the demon's will, I have no choice but to wallow. An acid burn of anger builds in my chest as I watch it all unfold—the big lie of my life built on countless smaller ones, starting since birth. Every moment manipulated by the duchess and the surrogates she sent to mother me. Grandmum Elona and her powder kit. Darsy and Favah with their endless lessons. And Micha, the living weapon she planted beside my cradle in the guise of a nanny.

Selen was no less a girl than me, even as she hunted and strutted around in leggings and kissed anyone she liked. Part of me hated her for it. Part of me still does. Selen was allowed to be herself. To find that self on her own terms and in her own time. I never had that chance.

I try to pull away from the feeling. Selen is my best friend. It isn't right to blame her for my problems. But I feel the demon's will guiding my thoughts like Mother did my life, keeping my pain, my confusion over who I am, at the forefront. Keeping me distracted and off balance as his tendrils snake and burrow through my brain.

Does it matter who I am, when a demon is in my mind?

But I can't deny it matters to me. Everything changed when the Krasians thought I was male. Who knows what they would do if they learned the truth? Who knows what it would do to my friendships at Gatherers' University or with my spear brothers? What the royals from other duchies trying to broker marriage with me would do if they knew?

The only person I ever risked confiding in lies cooling on the ground because of me. Because I wasn't strong enough. Because I was a fool.

I try to shake my head, but my body is frozen. It's the demon's doing, just like these spinning thoughts. They are mine, but he is creating a whirlwind of them to hide how incomplete a picture they make. Perhaps these memories are true, but that does not make them Truth. What does it matter, who I was raised to be? What does it matter, who others see me as?

A seventh sense comes into focus, beyond the human five, or even the infinite complexity of wardsight. This sense abandons the physical entirely, existing in the invisible space between. I sense Alagai Ka in my mind, feel the vibration in the air, connecting us.

I am Olive, I tell him. *That is all that matters.*

Then I lash out with all my strength. Not the strength I have always relied on—my arms, my muscles. That is meaningless here. What matters is my will, my sense of self. But abandoning the boxes others have sought to put me in has given me power unlike anything I have ever felt.

I seize the connection with my mind like a wrist in *sharusahk*, pulling it taut and letting it guide me along my return strike.

Alagai Ka is powerful, but he is arrogant, and unprepared as I shrug off what had been an overwhelming assault a moment ago. Like an opponent caught off balance, his defenses are not fully in place, and I force myself into his thoughts, seeking answers of my own.

56

METAMORPHOSIS

I WAKE FROM HIBERNATION with a start. After nearly a turning, my greatward has restored me to strength, but even here at my center of power—a safehold far from the remains of the hive—I no longer feel secure. After millennia of domination, I am . . . hiding. From surface stock.

The idea disgusts me, but though my flesh has healed, it still tingles with the memory of the symbols of power forcibly inked into my body, using my own magic against me. Of the burning chain that bound me.

Not since I was a hatchling had any creature, even the most powerful of my brethren, dared touch my body, or made me fear for my life. Yet these filthy mammals, no older than a blink of my eye, struck me. Bound me. Tortured and mocked me. Forced me to debase myself to survive. To lead them to the hive, that they might attempt to destroy it.

With no way to refuse, I twisted their goal and made it my own. Once, the hive queen had been a sleek killing machine, radiating power and intellect. It was a pleasure to serve her. But queens grow with each laying, and she had grown so bloated she could no longer leave the birthing chamber. Millennia trapped there atrophied her mind.

After thousands of turnings, none wished to be free of her more than me. Free of her constant need for the security of my presence, her constant hunger, her irresistible psychic demands. I had been her slave too long.

If the humans failed to penetrate the hive, I needed only take care not to die with them. And if they succeeded and killed the queen, I would be free of her, and a new, hatchling queen would be free to take over and strengthen the hive under my guidance.

So I led them to the hive, and escaped amid the confusion as my captors battled the queen's bodyguard. I was less than an ember of the flame I had once been when I fled to my Safehold.

Now, after many cycles bathed in the power of my greatward and nourished by my personal stock, I am restored, and can once again turn my attention outward. I do not know the outcome of the battle, but whatever the new power structure of the hive, none of my brethren remain who are powerful enough to challenge me. I will kill the new consort and regain primacy, and then I will seek my revenge.

It is true night on the surface, when there is no satellite to reflect the day star and the flows of magic are strongest. Even in hibernation, I sensed it. I need information before I act, and now is the time to seek it.

I concentrate, pulling currents of magic into my greatward and Reading them. The human cities on the surface are thriving, each protected by greatwards that cast forbiddings over vast areas. My kind have been pushed to the edge of their territory, a scattered remnant of lesser castes, abandoned by their minds and too stupid to realize they have lost.

The queen is dead, then. She would never have tolerated this from the surface stock. It tells me the new queen and consort are weak, and regaining primacy will be as simple as killing whichever of my lesser get has bound his mind to hers.

I reach further, easily finding the Draw of the hive's three-dimensional greatward—formed of caverns and waterways and tunnels cut into living stone. It is my life's work, a nexus of incredible power. Greater by far than the smaller greatward hidden beneath Safehold. The hive calls to me. Sings. But the song is hollow, like wind through a stalagmite field.

There is no life within.

My colony is gone.

Safehold's greatward responds to my sudden terror, feeding me vast amounts of magic, enough to sunder a mountain.

I concentrate, restoring my calm and releasing the excess power. Such a display is a beacon my enemies will sense, and they will send armies to destroy my greatward and hunt me down while I am weakened.

Even now I am loath to leave Safehold, but I do not hesitate to enter the between-state, shedding my physical form to become pure energy and will. I strengthen the probing tendril that connects me to the hive and use it to leap the distance, materializing at the center of the greatward at almost the exact moment I vanish from Safehold.

The hive ward holds a great well of power, and I drink deep of it, becoming connected to every part of the massive symbol at once.

All I sense is death. Echoes of psychic screams as minds and queens and countless drones died. Their scorched bodies have rotted where they fell, for even now, no predators are bold enough to enter our territory.

I have underestimated the humans again—this time to the extinction of the entire colony. The hive greatward remains intact, but without drones and a royal caste, there is nothing to give it life. Even the livestock has fled.

But here at my center of power, time can be peeled back like layers of flesh as I Read the imprint of the hive's magic.

The divergence is easy to find, and I absorb it, reliving those last moments as if I were there myself. I see the Explorer touch the Core and harness a power too great for any physical body to conduct. He was consumed like all that touched the Source before him, but an indomitable will can work a fraction of the Core's near-infinite magic, if only for a moment before they are destroyed.

My sire taught me that.

A fraction of infinity is still without end. The victory was near-total, destroying every demon in the hive and thousands on the surface. Only the drones at the farthest reaches of the hunting grounds survived.

A change in hierarchy I could navigate, but without a queen, there is no way to rebuild the colony. What good is it to rule over a grave?

There are other hives, but they are in faraway places, and will have powerful consorts of their own.

Desperate, I extend my senses, amplified by the greatward, and search. The ichor in my veins grows colder as I sift through the pathetic dregs of drones that escaped the surge more by fortune than fate. Only on the sands of the ancient lands are there drones in abundance, and those of the weakest, least useful caste.

I am reaching the edge of my perception when I sense it, still guarding the ruins where I was captured. A lone mimic demon, one of the bodyguards I brought to that hated place. It was stranded when our mental connection was severed and has not fed in a turning, but still the creature brims with power.

I touch it with a tendril of magic, and the mimic enters the between-state instantly, rushing to me like an excited pet. I run a hand over its liquid black scales, shivering with pleasure at their latent power.

I can feel my body changing. Without a queen to suppress me, I begin emitting triggers, both pheromonal and magical, that the mimic absorbs.

I divide my consciousness and take control of its body to flee to Safehold, but we are unable to enter the between-state. Already the triggers have set off a chain of events that cannot be interrupted.

Instead I climb on the mimic's back as it takes the form of a giant wind drone. I draw wards to cloak our passage through the night sky, but still I clutch the precious drone tightly until we reach Safehold and I feel the greatward's protections envelop us.

The magics here are strong, the location remote. We are nestled in stone beneath my secret larder, a breeding ground of human stock who have no contact with the outside world, no defenses against my kind. I am a god to them, and they willingly deliver sacrifices for our repast.

The mimic feeds voraciously. The changeling drones can take the form of almost anything, but this is no ordinary transformation. It is becoming something greater than either of us.

When we are sated, I lead it to the well of power at the center of my greatward, and there we curl together and fall into a deep sleep, unmoving for many cycles.

When I wake at last, the mimic has left my embrace and spun its cocoon. I hiss in pleasure, gliding a talon over the soft silk, feeling the life inside, pulsing as it pulls vast amounts of Core magic from my well.

Already the power of the young proto-queen is overwhelming my senses, bonding me as her consort. I am in ecstasy as she dominates my will, making her needs my own. She is not a true queen, but still she is above my caste, and I want nothing more than to be her slave. After thousands of turnings, I had forgotten how it felt. The vitality and power that can only come from a hatchling queen giving me true purpose.

I stand spellbound for cycles more, waiting for the metamorphosis to complete. When it does, the proto-queen slashes open the silk of her cocoon with a swipe of the deadly stinger atop her powerful reticulated tail.

I have human stock ready, marching them to her by the dozens. She is savage in her hunger, and it is a glory to behold.

The proto-queen notices me when her hunger is momentarily sated. She emits an irresistible trigger, and arousal subsumes my being. My male organs have swollen to many times their normal size during my vigil, even as my limbs have frozen. I am immobile, defenseless as she pulls me in.

Her mating is nearly as savage as her feeding, but I offer no resistance. I am helpless before her, our minds linked. If she wished to feed on my body—as mating queens often do to lesser consorts—I would offer her my throat without hesitation.

Even without feeding, she nearly kills me. All the power I have been absorbing these many cycles upon my greatward is sucked away with my issue, leaving me with barely a flicker when I am cast aside.

Again she spins a cocoon, falling into a deep sleep as a single egg forms within her. A true queen.

The hatchling queen will gorge first upon her mother, flesh and magic alike, then she, too, will need human stock to sate her hunger before compelling me to mate once more.

Then she will spread her great wings and return us to the hive, where she will feed endlessly, her abdomen distending as she births a new colony.

ALAGAI KA'S TERRIBLE will fixes on me then, yanking me from his memories. I emerge disoriented. I realize only a moment has passed, but in that time I feel as if I lived years in the demon king's body.

Minds still bound in twisted tendrils of will, I can feel Alagai Ka's anger at my invasion, his . . . indignation at being probed by a *human*. He bats me from his mind as easily as one might swat a fly, slamming my consciousness back into my own body, still caught in the demon's iron grip.

The demon's face wears a recognizable expression at last—open fury. But we were linked, and I know his true anger is at himself, humiliated to once again be humbled by a mammal.

I've found his weakness.

Maybe it's not just the queen that was getting old and weak? I cannot speak the words with the demon's clawed hand grasping my throat, but he is in my mind, hearing the thoughts like a mocking whisper.

Alagai Ka's charcoal lips pull back, revealing rows of razor-sharp teeth. I can see the hate in his reflective black eyes—feel it thrumming all around me.

This time the demon doesn't need Iraven to speak. His words resonate in my mind, exploiting my own weakness.

My new queen will need a repast worthy of her glory. One that proves my strength and loyalty. It is customary for a consort to feed his hatchling queen his enemies.

The demon's long tongue snakes out over the rows of teeth to lick my cheek. Try as I might, I cannot hide my revulsion, and I know that gives him pleasure.

The first flesh she feasts upon will be your parents. Then you, and Darin Bales.

I struggle. Against his grip. Against his will. Both are overwhelming.

And then the Woodcutter will come, and the Pillow Queen. All my enemies, compelled to seek us out as I guide them to the open maw of my queen, that she may feast and make their power her own.

And when there are none strong enough to threaten our return, we will return to the hive in swarm.

His crushing will closes on my mind, even as he squeezes shut my throat. I try to fight, but all I manage is a weak convulsion before oblivion takes me.

57

PIPER

THE DAMAJAH'S RESONANCE wards pulse in time with my pipes,
filling the air with music. Micha rests her voice as she leads us
through the vast undercity as assuredly as she did the hidden
passages and shortcuts of Sharik Hora. Her scent is steady. Focused.

Angry.

Everyone smells of it. Micha and Selen at Olive, Rojvah at Arick.

Maybe something in me is broken, but I don't understand why. I
only know how to be angry with myself.

Ay, Olive was wood-brained to try to fight a mind demon alone, but
given the choice of running off alone or taking my friends along with me
into a likely slaughter—I wish I had the stones to do the same.

It's what Da did, when he left us behind and touched the Core.

I could have left Selen, that first night on the road. Night, I *should*
have. Without her slowing me I could have caught the Majah before
they got Olive anywhere near that boat. Maybe I couldn't have fought
them, but reckon I could have snuck around and figured out a way to
open whatever locks they had on Olive and Micha. With an hour's head
start, even *dama'ting* dice couldn't have caught us before we got back to
Hollow.

Creator, even if they caught us, it's Olive and me the demons want.

Selen and Rojvah and Arick could be safe behind the wards right now if I'd had half as much sack as my da.

But I was scared and didn't want to go alone, and now we're all going to die.

What's the point of being mad at Olive and Arick when I should be mad at myself?

The feeling makes its way into my music, as they often do. *There is no worthy prey here*, my pipes tell any coreling that might chance to hear them, gently guiding their attention elsewhere with my own feelings of inadequacy.

It doesn't take long before I can sense the demon greatward. Its power is so great it glows on the horizon like a coming dawn. Even the others can't miss it.

"How could this have grown unnoticed inside the city?" Rojvah asks.

"The Majah don't have enough Warders to maintain the entire undercity," Micha says. "Easier to close it off and use the Holy Undercity. It's more than big enough."

"Ay," Selen agrees. "But that doesn't explain why the *Sharum* never noticed."

Micha has no reply to that, but there is worry in her scent, and she increases the pace.

Ent much of a Warder, but I've seen magic whorl in the symbols for as long as I can remember. Power will flow to its center, and like a spider in a web, that's where the demon will set.

All of us have blessed *hora* weapons and shields, but Selen and I have Cloaks of Unsight, as well. Rojvah and Micha have no such protection. Da would have given his cloak to one of them, but the cloak and the knife are all I have left of Mam, and I ent got the stones to give either of them up, especially here.

Micha seems to come to the same conclusion as we enter the demon greatward, lifting her voice to harmonize with my pipes. Immediately, Rojvah does the same, the three of us taking the song's power to new heights.

Our trio has only played together a little, but already Micha and Rojvah weave their voices like sisters with a lifetime of practice. Both are more skilled than I am, but they let me lead, probably because they don't think I could keep up.

Our spellsong transcends anything I could effect alone, creating a halo of sound to keep us invisible to corelings while subtly nudging them out of our path like water flowing around a stone in a brook.

The cloaks and music and blessed bone shields have a cumulative effect, but there are demons everywhere. Enough to put everyone on edge. Wanderers patrol the tunnels openly, and regulars hide around corners and behind stalagmites, or in crevices in the stone above our heads. Twice I sense hidden ambush pockets, warded like the ones *Sharum* use in the Maze. Even I can't see or hear the sand demons clustered within.

But I can smell them. Taste them on the air.

I suck in, knowing it will hide my own scent, but I can do nothing for the others. The demons smell us, as well. I see the wanderers sniff the air, probing with their snouts as they vainly try to pinpoint the source.

But smells are not enough to spur the demons into action. We pass without incident, continuing to wind deeper along the ward with every step.

I add a sharp note to my piping, and everyone stops short. Across the tunnel in front of us are thick strands of clear, sticky silk. It is invisible in wardsight and hidden from the natural spectrum here in the darkness.

Mam loved to tell stories about Da by the fire at night, and one of the most exciting was the time he walked right into a cave demon's web.

But I don't need much light to see. The dim glow of the wards is more than enough for me to spot the heavy thread. Da had powers like I could only dream of, which is probably why it never occurred to him to just turn slippery. No need for a coward's trick when he could just light up his wards with power and burn the webs to ash.

But in my slippery state, I pass through the sticky silk easily as a bead curtain, gently holding some of the strands aside for the others to slip through. Above I can hear the cave demons shifting, but with nothing adhering to the thread, there are none of the sharp motions that would trigger an attack.

No sooner are we past this latest defense than I pick up the scent I've been dreading since this began.

Blood.

A FIGURE DETACHES itself from the shadow of a large stalagmite. The others tense, but I know who it is before he even moves.

For the first time I've seen—perhaps the first time in his life—Arick is wrapped in his father's motley cloak with the hood drawn up. I can see the magic dancing along its concealing wards, hiding him much as Mam's cloak does me.

Arick is covered in sweat, ichor, and blood, but little of the latter seems to be his own. He's lost his *hora* spear and shield, but has scavenged others, still sticky with the blood of the Majah warriors they once belonged to.

Rojvah rushes to her brother, embracing him without missing a note of her song. Her eyes are wet with tears.

"What happened?" Selen asks, while the rest of us maintain the musical shield.

"We were ambushed," Arick says. "They knew we were coming. Expected it. When the melee turned chaotic, men lost their helmets, and the mind took them."

"Took them?" Selen asks. "What do you mean *took* them?"

Arick makes a spitting noise. "They became slaves to Alagai Ka, and turned on us. We were not prepared to defend against our own spear brothers. It was all the opening they needed."

"Night," Selen breathes. We've all heard tales of mind demon possession, but it's one thing to hear an ale story and another to live one. I wonder if there's still time to run away.

"Where's Olive?" Selen demands.

Arick takes us down a narrowing path. "We had no choice but to flee, and the *alagai* herded us this way." The tunnel opens up on one side to a great cavern. The way ahead is a narrow ledge clinging to a high cliff face. Ahead, part of it has collapsed.

"That is where Olive fell," Arick says. Selen slaps a hand to her mouth at the words and I miss the next few notes, fumbling to find harmony again.

Olive can't be dead. Could we have come all this way, only to lose her because I was gullible and let her go down here without us?

All of us look over the edge, peering into the darkness below. It's a long way down. Even with wardsight, it drops farther than any of us can see.

"There was no way to go after her." Arick's voice is cold, but I can smell his shame. Indeed, the slope is too steep for an armored warrior to climb without proper gear. I could do it, but I'd have to leave the others behind. It would take time to do it safely, and Creator only knows what's waiting down there.

"What happened to the others?" Selen asks. "Why were you alone?"

"Taken," Arick says. "Iraven was one of the demon's slaves all along. Perhaps before he led us down here in the first place. He turned on us, pulling helms from the strongest fighters and trapping us on this ledge. Before long, half the men had lost their helms, and the rest were driven over the edge. I . . . " He swallows, breathing deep to steady himself. "I killed my spear brothers."

Selen reaches out, squeezing his shoulder. "That wasn't them, Arick. Ent your fault."

Arick nods, but still there are tears in his eyes. "When I was the only one who had not been taken, I hid in Father's cloak, and the demon looking through their eyes could not see me." He points farther down the tunnel. "After they gave up the search for me, Iraven marched the others below."

Rojvah stops singing at that. "Ever do you speak ill of our father, but here on the road to Nie's abyss, his spirit protects you where your grandfather's strength of arms could not."

I hear it before I see it. A slight breeze blows through the cavern, hitting Arick's face and exhaling through a tear in his hood. I walk around him, as if to peer again over the edge, but glance at the back of his hood as I do. The large embroidered mind ward is torn.

Rojvah has resumed her song, but now I stop playing, tucking my pipes away in my satchel. Rojvah and Micha turn to me in surprise as I drop out of our trio. "Hiding doesn't sound like you."

"Even I am not fool enough to fight an entire hive alone," Arick says.

The words make perfect sense, but there is something wrong about them. I remember the night Arick fought in the desert, the berserk rage that consumed him, blinding him to all sense of self-preservation in his drive to kill.

Red curls have fallen onto his brow, though I watched him carefully tuck and bind them with turban cloth so there would be no chance of them coming loose while he masqueraded as a full-blood *dal'Sharum*.

Looking closer, I can see from the shape of his hood that his helm is missing from beneath the black wrappings. My eyes flick back to Arick's scavenged spear and shield. Without hood or helm or hero's bone . . .

"What really happened to Olive?" I demand.

Something changes in Arick's eyes. "You'll see her soon enough."

Arick lunges for my head, attempting to knock my hood and helm askew. Fast as he is, I am faster, and expecting the attack. I turn slippery, quickstepping to the side. His grasping hand misses, so he attempts to tackle me, instead.

In my slippery state, the second attack is as simple to avoid as the first, but then Arick whips the spear off his back and into my path as I slide out of the way. I step back to avoid it, and my feet meet open air. I try to grab the shaft of his spear, but my hands are still slippery. I solidify, and Arick uses the grip to pull me close and grab my helmet before push-kicking me off the ledge.

"Darin!" Selen screams, dropping her spear to reach out her hand to me. Arick moves to take advantage of her distraction, but I don't see what happens next as I slam against hard stone and tumble end over end, picking up speed as I bounce down the slope.

58

LONG WAY DOWN

MOVING TOO FAST to stick, I draw a sharp breath and suck in, pulling the particles of my body closer together. I shrink, becoming tougher, harder, as I am battered and bashed.

My spear snaps and the bone tip shatters, tearing my robes but unable to penetrate my toughened skin. The shoulder strap of my shield is designed for quick removal, and cannot withstand the rigors of the fall. It clatters away long before I hit bottom, slamming to a hard stop.

My ears are ringing, and the ground seems to spin beneath me as I try to work the dirt from a mouth gone dry. I smell blood, but it isn't mine. I expect most folks would have broken a couple of bones in that fall—if not their necks—but I'm just dizzy and a little achy. Olive is tougher than most folks, but if she came down this same way, she might be hurt.

When I am able I put my hands under me and push up, seeing a bright glow of ambient magic flowing through the cavern. Wherever I am, it is close to the center of the ward. Ahead I hear a ruckus, but I'm still too disoriented to sift out the sounds.

I throw on the hood of Mam's cloak, wrapping myself in its protective folds. Still I keep to the shadow of the stalagmites as I get my feet under me and creep silently toward the noise.

The space opens up around a bend and I find the source of the blood smell. Prince Chadan lies in a pool of blood on the cold stone, aura snuffed.

After the slaughter of the Warded Children and Hollow Soldiers, I should be able to look on a dead body without losing my lunch, but the prince's head is cracked open, his brains scooped out like a soft-boiled egg.

Close to a hundred *Sharum* are on their knees, with Prince Iraven standing at their head in full armor. None of them wear their helmets, just as Arick said, though many still carry them.

A few feet away, Olive is in the grasp of the mind demon—a creature even more terrifying in reality than in paintings and Mam's ale stories. I can sense the demon's age, his overwhelming power, and I know in my heart this is the coreling Mam and Da kept prisoner all those years ago. Alagai Ka, the Father of Demons, who tried to kill me while I was still in Mam's belly. The very sight of him makes me want to run far away.

But the demon has Olive.

Slowly, I draw Mam's knife beneath the folds of the cloak, inching my way across the floor.

Prince Iraven laughs. I glance his way, seeing the prince looking right at me, even wrapped in my cloak. "Do you think yourself invisible?" Iraven asks incredulously. "Even if I cannot see you, my slaves can."

"Rippin' idiot!" I curse as Iraven leaps for me, surprisingly quick in his scaled armor. Arick told the truth about the *Sharum* and their helmets, but lied about the protection of the cloak. I've walked right into the demon king's waiting talons.

The father waits below.

I go slippery and slide past Iraven, bolting for Alagai Ka. If I cannot sneak, I will trust to blind speed and Mam's blade. Indeed, the hilt throbs in my hand as if hungry to avenge her.

My hood falls back in the mad dash, along with its protective wards. Immediately, I feel the demon's will try to latch on to me, much like Mam does when she forces me to dissipate and drags me into a vent. I can see the power rippling from Alagai Ka's throbbing cranium wash over me.

Warded Children have a rule—no one with less than sixteen summers can be inked. In part because young bodies can distort the tattoos as they grow, but mostly from the belief that folk should consent as adults before making a permanent choice.

But Mam was never one to follow rules, especially where I was concerned. As soon as my skull bones fused, she used her special electrum ink to tattoo a mind ward atop my head and touch it up over the years as I grew.

The silvery ink is nearly invisible, and hidden beneath the thick curls of my hair. Most wards won't activate when hidden, but mine Draws power from my own innate magic, and is always charged.

I feel the demon's will hammering against the forbidding around my mind. The ward grows warm, then so hot it burns. I fear my hair will smolder, but the barrier holds. The mind demon can no more force his way into my mind than Ella Cutter could punch her way out of the Bunker.

I pick up speed. The wards on Mam's knife glow fiercely as I lunge for Alagai Ka's bulbous head.

Fast as I am, I ent fast enough. I nick the flesh of his forehead and feel the blade come to life in my hand, but before it can penetrate far, the demon tosses Olive at me. I've gone solid to attack, and she hits me hard. I fumble the knife, trying to keep from stabbing her.

I remember cowering as Mam told stories about fighting Alagai Ka. How every moment they survived seemed a miracle.

Underestimate a mind, it's the last thing you'll ever do, Mam said. *Might look scrawny, but they've magic enough to be as strong or fast or tough as they want. Anything doesn't kill 'em, they can heal in a blink.*

Olive and I hit the ground in a tangle, but I can't waste time on her. The only hope we have is to kill Alagai Ka here and now. I roll away and spring back to my feet, ready to charge again.

Olive grabs me from behind, putting me in a submission hold and twisting me back down. I go slippery and pop from her grasp like a leapfrog.

I rush the demon before Olive can catch up. He seems more than willing to meet me head-on, batting Mam's knife away with a slender wrist, then swiping with sharp claws. I twist away, but somehow the demon's talons find purchase, cutting deep into my flesh.

I stumble back and cry out, as much in horror as pain. Nothing has ever caught me like that when I'm slippery, but this monster has been using magic for thousands of years. My tricks must seem like a hound rolling over and playing dead.

Mam's knife is glowing fiercely. I draw an impact ward in the air with the point and watch the knife's wards dim as the power forms and streaks through the air toward the demon.

Alagai Ka remains unimpressed. Holding up a clawed hand he absorbs the magic without effect, advancing on me with malice in his black eyes.

I fumble for my pipes, and the demon hisses as I put them to my lips. He ceases his approach, covering his earholes and opening his maw to let out a piercing keen. His human slaves get to their feet at the sound, and I shiver in fear.

They ent as quick as Arick was. The mass of warriors shuffles slowly, like marionettes in a Jongleur show. They're blunt instruments, but there's a hundred of them, and they quickly form a circle, cutting off any chance of escape as Iraven and Olive advance on me with grace and speed the others lack.

I'm forced to drop my pipes to hang from their strap as the *Sharum* charge. I turn slippery, but they've stopped trying to grab me. Punches and kicks glance off me, but though I can lessen the impacts, I can't avoid them entirely. Not with a ring of spears and locked shields tightening all around me.

I'm out of tricks as the noose closes, but then a scream pierces the din, and again Alagai Ka puts his clawed hands over his earholes, shrieking.

THE *SHARUM* STOP advancing and go limp, dropping bonelessly to the ground. Even Olive and Iraven slump to their knees and tip over.

"Darin!" Selen appears, shield-bashing her way through the collapsing ring that surrounds me. Warriors tumble like tenpins as she makes it to my side. "You all right?"

"Ay." I throw my cloak over the bloody slashes the demon left across half my chest. This ent the time for distractions. "But none of us are all right for long. Demon's already got Olive and the others."

Arick stands before Micha and Rojvah, a new helmet secured around his chin with turban silk. The women are singing with power and passion, the wards on their chokers glowing brightly in the darkness. Arick's spear and shield shine once again with the protection of heroes' bones, and the demon hisses at their advance.

But Alagai Ka does not flee. Like I did a moment ago, he sketches impact wards in the air. I cover my ears as the ground explodes at Micha and Rojvah's feet. They are knocked to the ground as their singing turns to shrieks, and then silence.

The impacts kick up a cloud of dust, and the demon draws another ward, blowing it in their faces. As Micha and Rojvah attempt to resume the song, both get a mouthful of dirt and choke on the words.

Arick's veil is up as he charges through the cloud, but with the singers silenced, the mind demon's slaves reanimate. Iraven leaps to his feet, and Selen pushes in front of me, spear and shield at the ready.

Iraven ignores her, rushing to block the path to the Father of Demons. The other *Sharum* are a little slower getting to their feet, but they mass around the rest of us, closing in once more.

"Show no mercy!" Micha's voice is hoarse as she hooks one of the shuffling warriors' legs and twists, sending him stumbling into a pair of his fellows. She kicks herself upright, bashing in another of the *Sharum's* knees and darting through the opening as he falls away.

She slips a hand in her robes and pulls out a sickle of hero's bone. Her movements are precise as she locks the blade into fighting position with a flick of her wrist, and uses it to open the throat of the next warrior to face her. "Whether they will it or not, these are servants of Nie. We must not let Alagai Ka escape!"

59

SHEDDING BLOOD

ICHA'S SCREAM PIERCES the void, bringing me back from whatever corner of my mind Alagai Ka imprisoned my consciousness.

I hear the demon king's shriek in response as he pulls back from my mind to face this new threat. For a moment, I feel safe. Micha has come to rescue me, as she has so many times in my life. My loyal nanny, looking out for me no matter how awful I am in return.

My eyes open as I hit the ground, and the bubble of safety bursts. Inches from my face, Iraven stares back at me. I signal my limbs to move, but they are stiff and numb, coming back to life as slowly as my thoughts.

Iraven, too, spasms without getting hands and feet under him. The withdrawal of Alagai Ka's will is like being shaken from a deep sleep.

"Darin!" Selen cries, shield-rushing through my brothers, equally disoriented by the demon's sudden lapse of control. I look up as she leaps over my body, seeing Darin standing right in front of me.

What is he doing here? How did he get so close? What was Alagai Ka forcing me to do to him?

I feel sick at the thought. I don't think the demon had time to alter my mind, but he had complete control of my body. Could I ever forgive myself if he made me hurt my friends?

Alagai Ka lifts a delicate talon, drawing impact wards in the air like Mother with her *hora* wand. Micha, Rojvah, and Arick are scattered, and I realize even together, we are outmatched. What hope do we have, when even our mothers and fathers failed to kill the demon king? He took over my will effortlessly. Any moment now, he will turn his attention back to me, and I know I will not be able to resist.

But then I see it, lying on the cold ground.

My armlet.

At first a bauble, then a shackle, now it is an instrument of hope. A chance to finish what our families started, all those years ago. A chance to take a step closer to fulfilling their dream of a world without demons. Without Alagai Ka, the queen will no longer be able to mate. We can find Safehold and end the hive once and for all.

But then I am struck by the demon's mental command to rise, and I cannot resist. Like a loyal hound, Iraven springs to his feet and leaps to the demon king's defense. My spear brothers rise less gracefully, but already their spears and shields are rising to point at my friends.

Alagai Ka has directed me to rise and confront Darin, but his attention is divided. I feel his irresistible will, but he is not in control of my limbs, or inside my head. I put my hands under me, crawling as I stumble to my feet. Not so far as to appear suspicious, but far enough to hook the armlet with a finger as I rise. I twist slightly to hide my arm from the demon's sight as I clasp the armlet about my biceps and press my thumb against the tip of the little spear, shedding blood to seal the lock.

I can sense the demon's injunction, but now the ward keeps his will at bay. Still I obey, feigning the same glassy look I've seen on other *Sharum* under demon control.

Alagai Ka wants me to smile at him. To reassure him. To draw him close, and then . . .

I shudder. What if the demon has already corrupted part of me, like he did Iraven? My brother did not know he was the demon king's agent in the day. What if Darin lets me in close, and my body betrays me?

It's a risk I have to take. By using Alagai Ka's plan, perhaps I can buy just a few seconds more before the demon realizes he no longer controls me.

"Dar, it's me." My words are the barest breath, but even through the din of battle around us, I know he can hear them.

Darin remains wary as I take a step forward. He skitters back a step, lifting his mother's knife, razor-sharp and hot with magic. "Think I'm stupid?"

I smile and spread my arms to show my empty hands—and the armlet. I see his eyes flick to it, and he relaxes slightly, but he does not lower the knife.

"I didn't respect you like I should have, Darin Bales, but I never thought you were stupid." I smile, giving him a secret wink. "Smart enough to make this look good."

I ball a fist, but give him time to slip aside, revealing the game. I don't pull the next blows, but I don't need to. Slippery and at full speed, I can't lay a knuckle on him and we both know it.

"Give me your knife." I whisper the words under the sharp breath I blow out with my next punch.

Darin dances back, suddenly wary again. "Not a chance."

Around us, the fight is raging. Selen puts a spear into Gorvan's thigh, but if the big warrior even feels it, he gives no sign. He leans into the blow, whipping his shield across to crack her in the temple.

She stumbles, and my brothers bear her down, tossing aside her *hora* weapons and pulling off her helmet.

"Darin, please," I breathe. Our window is fast closing. Soon all of us will be overwhelmed.

Arick is a strong fighter. Given a few years' experience, he could be truly great. But he is no match for my brother. Iraven is through his guard in two moves, burying his spear in my cousin's guts. Arick falls onto his back, desperately trying to keep his insides from spilling out.

Iraven raises his spear to finish the job, but Micha lets out another shriek, checking him. The grit must be shredding her throat to produce that grating wail, but it has the desired effect. Alagai Ka keens, and for a moment, his human drones waver.

Micha wastes no time, sprinting for the demon king, but even as the others under Alagai Ka's control hesitate, Iraven intercepts her. The keening sound the demon is making must trigger commands planted deep in his subconscious to defend his master from harm.

Micha cannot maintain the cry as she moves to defend against this new foe. There is a chain at the end of her sickle, weighted at the end with a clenched, skeletal fist. She tangles it around Iraven's spear, pulling it aside and moving close to strike with the sickle, but Iraven catches the blow easily on his shield.

Alagai Ka recovers, and so, too, do his human slaves. Rojvah catches the arm of the first to reach for her and strikes him in the throat with stiffened fingers as she twists to throw him into a stalagmite.

But the next is upon her before she resets. Her bone *hanzhar* takes his hand off at the wrist, but the crippling wound does nothing to stop him as he throws his arms around her, and more add to the press, pulling away her protections against the Father of Demons.

Darin sees it, too. He glances at Selen, on her feet and part of a wave of warriors coming for us. For a moment, his defenses waver, and I tackle him to the ground.

He's slippery as ever, but I'm not trying to hold or harm him. Just to get through. "Pipes," I grunt as we roll in the filth. "Give me the knife and play your pipes."

Darin says nothing, but he solidifies, offering little resistance as I twist the knife from his grip. I reverse my grip, hiding the blade with my forearm, away from Alagai Ka.

Micha has managed to divest Iraven of his spear. It lies a few feet from them, tangled with her sickle and chain. She fights instead with a bone flail, but it is ineffective against Iraven's shield. I see his arm dart behind his back, pulling a punch dagger from his belt.

I want to cry out as he bats her weapon aside and moves in, but Alagai Ka is watching their battle, and I dare not draw his attention as Darin raises the pipes to his lips.

The sound comes just as Iraven drives his punch dagger into the center of my sister's chest. A jarring series of notes, impossibly loud, drown out my scream as I take two steps forward and throw the knife with all of my strength.

Alagai Ka again puts his taloned hands to his head, twisting to look our way. As the blade sails end over end toward his bulbous head, Micha coughs blood, dropping to her knees.

The demon's eyes widen, and he reacts faster than I would have thought possible, sketching a glowing defensive ward in the air before him. A normal weapon would bounce off it as surely as striking a wall.

But Renna Bales' knife is no ordinary weapon. Powerful wards are etched along the blade and its bone handle, which glows like the blessed weapons of *sharik hora*. It flies through the barrier as easily as air, burying itself in the side of the demon's head.

Alagai Ka's mental whispers, vibrating in the air all around us, suddenly cease. Selen and my spear brothers, closing in on us, fall limp again.

Even Iraven comes back to something of himself. "Sister?" He reaches a hand out to Micha, but she slaps it aside. The gesture is enough to take her balance, and she falls over, aura dimming fast as blood continues to pump from her body.

Every fiber of my being wants to go to her, to stem the flow of blood, or simply to hold her close.

My nanny, my tutor, my true sister, is dying, and I should be with her.

But Alagai Ka isn't dead, yet.

I try to embrace the pain, but it is impossible, so I let it out, screaming as I turn away from her, charging the demon king as he staggers backward, grasping blindly for the handle of the knife. His leathery fingers sizzle and smoke as they close around the warded bone. Still he perseveres, hissing and snarling as the ash-gray flesh on his hand chars black.

The knife doesn't come free with the first tug, and I am there before the second, punching the demon hard in the head. He reels from the blow and I turn a full circuit, smashing the armlet against the opposite side of his skull. There's a satisfying impact and a flash of magic as the mind ward connects.

I press the assault, hitting as hard and fast as I can, always focused on the demon's conical skull. The only hope I have against this creature is to keep him dazed and off balance until I can get hold of the knife and cut off his head.

Already, Alagai Ka is adapting. Bone and leathery skin thicken, toughen, protecting his brain from new blows while his innate magic heals the contusions from the old.

I catch hold of the knife handle, blade still stuck lengthwise in the thick bone of the demon's skull. I yank the handle back and forth, and feel a rush of pleasure as Alagai Ka shrieks in agony. Feedback magic kicks up my arm, driving off the pain and exhaustion as I step around the demon to put him in a submission hold.

Darin circles us, wrapped in his warded cloak as he plays his pipes. The demon shrieks and thrashes, jerking the blade loose from his skull. I bury it in his throat, instead, but lack the leverage to sever his neck.

Rojvah lends her voice to Darin's pipes. Again the demon tries to keen, activating Iraven's conditioning, but he chokes on steel and ichor, instead.

I glance at Iraven, on his knees, staring down numbly at Micha's cooling form.

With renewed strength, I push the blade deeper into Alagai Ka's throat. The price of killing him is already too high, but anything less dishonors my sister's memory.

The demon's burned hand latches on to my wrist, his grip grinding the bones against one another. I bite down, channeling the pain into power as I resist his pull, muscles vibrating with the strain.

But even with the knife stealing some of the demon king's magic and feeding it to me, I can no more match this ancient creature's strength than I can his will. Slowly, he draws the blade from his body.

It doesn't matter. Alagai Ka cannot see Selen, wrapped in her Cloak of Unsight, enter the fight. She charges in from the side, the point of her blessed spear aimed at the demon king's jutting ribs. I need only hold him a moment more. When she strikes, I will stop resisting the demon's pull, tearing the knife free to cut off his head once and for all.

But whether by a sixth sense or one of the five, again the demon senses the attack in time to react. He twists with savage strength, putting me right in the path of the oncoming spear.

Selen attempts to pull the blow, but there's too much force and too little time. I feel it punch though my robes and deep into my side.

"Night, Sel!" I cry.

"Sorry!" Selen shouts, but she doesn't lose focus, letting go her spear and dodging around me to press the attack before Alagai Ka can escape. She balls a fist, and I see she is wearing the chained bracelet of warded rings that she bought in the Majah bazaar all those months ago. Her punch strikes like a thunderbolt, shattering the demon's jaw before he can keen again.

The bone spearpoint in my side doesn't hurt, but there is a . . . wrongness to its presence in my body, like a pebble in my sandal. I dare not pull it out. Even if I don't bleed to death, it may have struck something vital. Like Micha and Chadan, I may be a martyr to this cause.

The *Sharum* pray for a glorious death fighting *alagai*. They dream of it. We lost ourselves in the fantasy of it every night before charging into the Maze. But now that I am faced with one, I don't want it. I want to kill Alagai Ka. I will die in the attempt if I must. But in my heart, I want to live.

I twist the knife, doing as much damage as I can as Selen pummels the demon. Alagai Ka is stronger, but I have leverage in my hold, and keep his hands from covering his ears as Darin and Rojvah continue their musical assault.

My spear brothers are recovering from the demon's control, groaning and fumbling their helmets back on. Some have already gotten groggily to their feet.

There is no time to coddle them. "To arms, warriors of Majah! Sharak Ka is upon you! We have Alagai Ka! Kill the Father of Demons, and earn everlasting glory!"

The words snap them to attention, awakening the hope that lies at the heart of all warriors—to be remembered in deed long after they have taken the lonely path.

Many still have their spears. Others pull secondary weapons—warded knives, batons, hatchets. Some have only their fists. But all of them move toward the mind demon, and my hopes begin to rise.

Just a few moments more, and it will be over. But still the demon forces out my wrist, inch by agonizing inch, until at last, Renna's knife slips free. The moment the weapon's point is drawn from its flesh, Alagai Ka dissipates, slipping into the greatward and riding it to Creator knows where.

Selen and I collapse into each other as the demon vanishes. I scream as the spear tears from my body and we hit the ground.

"Sorry, Olive!" Selen says again, holding me close as she puts pressure on my wound. Charged with magic, the wound clots quickly, but I don't know what internal damage there might be.

All of us cast about, searching. The demon might still be close, or he could be licking his wounds a thousand miles away in Safehold.

A sound rises in the void between stalagmite mounds, like autumn leaves blown by a hurricane. A flight of wind demons the size of barn owls swarms out of the darkness, filling the air with leathern wings and lashing talons.

Selen covers us as a demon slams into her bone shield. It gives a piercing cry, scales scorching black, and before it can escape, I sever one of its wings with the knife.

A clatter of talons is the only warning as a storm of sand demons flow around the stalagmites like water.

I pass Selen the knife and take up her spear, the tip still wet with my blood. "Warriors of Majah, form around me!"

My brothers know their work, forming a shield wall with me at its center, surrounding Darin, Rojvah, and the wounded. Those without shields cluster inside the shell, ready to assist as warriors fall, or *alagai* get through. Selen takes my right side, Faseek and Gorvan my left. Even Arick is on his feet, makeup running from his ashen face as he holds his wound closed and adds his shield to the wall.

Only Iraven keeps to his knees, cradling Micha in his arms inside our wall.

I am not the only one to notice. Prince Iraven is Sharum Ka. He should be commanding this group, not me. But there is no time to question it. No time for anything, as the wind demons circle around the cavern for another pass and the sand demons reach the shield wall.

"Everam is watching, brothers and sisters!" I cry as the killing begins. "Make Him proud!"

60

CORRUPTED

THERE IS A clash of talons and sparking magic as the sand demons launch themselves at our shields. I strike over the edge of Selen's shield, skewering the *alagai* and threatening to tear open my wound. I didn't much feel the cut, but my nerves scream at the ripping of flesh just begun to knit.

Braced against the impact, Arick groans and staggers a step, but he does not yield. My brothers work their spears over the wall, killing more of the demons, but it will not be enough.

We're going to die here. All of us. Alagai Ka has failed to turn us into his willing slaves, so he will wipe us out, that none might betray what really happened here.

But then, rising above the shouts and shrieks, I hear Darin's pipes and Rojvah's voice. The two entwine their music with rising power, but it isn't the *Song of Waning*, or some other composition I know. I don't think it's a composition at all. It's something improvised to meet the moment, and without the demon king's influence, his drones cannot resist it.

Wind demons shriek as they fly to echolocate objects around them, and the presence of their fellows. They bank in perfect formation, beginning another dive. The duo take those sounds and reflect back a corrupted version.

The effect is almost instantaneous. Demons begin colliding in midair and instinctively lashing out with teeth and claws. Others miscalculate their flight paths, crashing into walls, stalactites, the ground, at high speed. A handful bounce off the shield wall, but none make it over our defenses.

My warriors are quick to finish off the stunned and wounded demons as Rojvah changes her song and Darin continues to improvise around it. They turn their power to the sand demons, and the *alagai* scrabble back from us in terror, turning to flee into the many tunnels leading into the cavern.

The remaining wind demons are next, sent flocking back to wherever they came from. Before long, there isn't a living demon anywhere in sight. This, more than anything, convinces me.

I turn to Gorvan and Faseek. "Alagai Ka has fled the field. Make litters for the wounded. We must return to the Holy City before he can gather strength to return."

My brothers punch fists to their chests. "Your will, Prince Olive," Faseek says. "It is a great victory."

I say nothing, and the men get to work.

"They ent wrong," Selen says. "Just getting out alive is a win."

I spit on the ground, watching Rojvah continue her song even as she tends her brother's wounds. Chadan and Micha have gone cold, just like hundreds of my brothers since we entered this Creator-forsaken place.

"There's no win, Sel," I say. "We paid in blood and have nothing to show for it but loss."

"We could have killed him," Selen says. "We were close. I felt it."

I nod. "I felt it, too. But now he's gone, and he ent stupid enough to expose himself again. He'll wait, and plot, and come at us when we're not looking, from a direction we don't expect."

Selen gives me a doubtful look. "How can you know so much about what that thing was thinking?"

"Because I was in his head."

"Get away from my sister," I tell Iraven, who still kneels with Micha's cold body across his lap. His bloody punch dagger lies on the stone beside them.

My brother does not move. "She's my sister, too."

"It didn't stop you from killing her."

"Nor were you able to resist putting your arm around Darin Bales' throat." There is no fight in Iraven's tone, only a weary resignation.

"The Father of Lies made all of us into slaves." Drillmaster Zim of the Spears of the Desert is Iraven's closest lieutenant. He stands close by and others are listening, a reminder that though the men follow me for the moment, Iraven is Sharum Ka, and they are sworn to serve him.

I don't look at the drillmaster, eyes fixed on my brother. "Were you the demon king's slave when you kidnapped her? When you took Micha from her wife—her life?"

The words give Iraven pause, and it is a long time before he speaks. "I don't know."

"Not good enough!" My *hanzhar* is back on my belt, and I grip it now, hand shaking with rage. "You ruined her life! *Our* lives! All this blood and pain, and for what?"

Iraven nods. "You said once I owed you a blood debt, little brother, and so I do. But Everam is listening, and I cannot say before Him that Alagai Ka took me last moon, or if the Father of Lies planted seeds of evil in my mind long ago. It seems bringing you and your friends here was always his infernal plan."

He looks up, meeting my eyes at last. "It would be easy to blame the Father of Lies, but I was the second son of a second wife, exiled from our father's court. The most hated member of the most hated tribe. The Damajah foresaw that I could achieve glory still, and for that I would have given anything. Even if Alagai Ka took no part, I cannot say I would have done differently."

He reaches into his armor and I stiffen, ready to defend. But Iraven remains on his knees as he pulls off his *alagai*-scale shirt and tosses it at my feet. "Take it."

A suit of Tazhan armor is a princely gift, but I kick it aside like a filthy rag. "I don't want your armor."

"I no longer need it." Iraven's robes are soaked with sweat, the black hair matted to his chest as he pulls these open, as well.

"It is one thing to do Alagai Ka's bidding in the dark of new moon." Iraven picks up the punch dagger. I half draw my *hanzhar*, but he turns the blade on himself, pressing the point into the flesh over his heart. "It's another to learn that you carry that bidding into the day."

The *Sharum* all begin murmuring at once, but I am frozen. Iraven opens his fingers, presenting the hilt to me. "Olive asu Ahmann am'Paper am'Hollow. The time has come to collect your debt."

The *Sharum* go silent, staring at me, but I make no move to take the blade. "I've had enough blood."

"You are my brother," Iraven says, "and I am your Sharum Ka. You cannot honorably refuse me."

I shake my head. "You of all people cannot dictate honor or familial loyalty to me, brother."

"I beg you," Iraven whispers, a reminder of Andew, left dead at my hand. "Do not leave me unmanned by Alagai Ka."

I cast about helplessly. The *Sharum* all have the blank stare of men who have accepted death. None of them will raise a hand to stop me. Indeed, Iraven is right that they will count it against my honor if I refuse.

Darin takes the pipes from his lips to protest. "Olive, you can't."

"Ent your decision, Darin," Selen says.

Darin looks like he wants to say more, but he takes his pipes back up, instead. Time is wasting, and the longer we stay down here, the greater the chance Alagai Ka will return.

I look to Rojvah. She is holding a groaning Arick's hand as warriors lift him onto a litter, but like everyone she watches me. Iraven is her blood, too, but she looks at her uncle sadly then nods at me.

Trembling, I take a step forward, then another, until I am close enough to kneel beside Micha. My vision blurs as I look into her eyes one last time, then gently close the lids, laying a tearful kiss on each. I reach into her robes, searching until I find one of the tiny tear bottles she always carries. Awkwardly I scrape the sharp edge against my cheeks, filling the vial with several drops. I close it in her hands. "Let my love guide you on the lonely path, sister. You died a warrior, and will sup at Everam's table in Heaven."

Then I turn to Iraven, still presenting the handle of the punch dagger. I slip my fingers into it, closing my hand so the blade becomes an extension of my fist.

A surge of adrenaline runs through me, but I embrace the feeling, breathing in the steady rhythm that kept Micha and Chadan so calm.

My heart is cold as I look into Iraven's eyes. "Is your soul ready for the lonely path?"

"No," Iraven admits. "But I will walk it all the same, and accept Everam's judgment. I am no longer fit for this world. I cannot ask our brothers to trust in my leadership when I do not trust myself. Better to end it now, with honor."

Honor.

Does he even know the meaning of the word? Do I?

Iraven tore apart my life, my very sense of self, for his own selfish pride. Micha would be alive now, if not for him. Chadan would be alive. Chikga and Andew and countless others. I would be safe in Hollow, and none of this would have come to pass.

Just as Andew did, Iraven lays a gentle hand over mine, pulling slightly to push the blade deeper into his flesh. "Do it, brother."

I scowl. Am I his brother? Our relationship began with him kidnapping me because he thought I was only a sister—a thing to be possessed. It was not until he thought me a man that he treated me with anything resembling dignity, but even then I was kept like a prize.

Chadan, Faseek, and the rest of my classmates in *sharaj* earned the right to call me brother. Iraven did not.

"I'm not your brother, Iraven." I shove hard, driving the blade into his heart, as he did to Micha. "I'm your sister."

Iraven nods, not breaking eye contact as he falls forward, leaning his weight on me. "I am sorry . . . sister."

Horror fills me as the light leaves his eyes. It's easy to tell myself he deserves this. That he kidnapped me and killed Micha. That he betrayed us all.

But I was in Alagai Ka's head. None of us have ever been anything but pieces on a board to him. Iraven slumps in my arms, and I throw back my head and howl.

Drillmaster Zim approaches, and I wonder if he is duty-bound to arrest me, or exact vengeance for killing his master. Instead he lays a heavy hand on my shoulder and gives a paternal squeeze. "It took courage for him to take the lonely path, my prince. And it took courage for you to send him on his way. You did him great honor."

"He didn't deserve it," I say.

"*Inevera*." The drillmaster shrugs. "That is for the Creator to judge. We cannot admit him to Heaven, but for his sacrifice, I will carry his body back myself, and petition the *Damaji* to bleach his bones for Sharik Hora."

I nod. "Chadan and Micha, as well." The other fallen are too numerous to carry, but I won't leave my sister and my prince for the demons to scavenge.

"Of course," the drillmaster says.

61

FINAL AUDIENCE

I WALK BETWEEN THE litters bearing Micha and Chadan, feeling un-
moored. Micha was caring for me before Selen was even born. I
have no memory of life before her. And any joy in Prince Olive's
life came from Chadan. Without them, everything is shattered.

I want nothing more than to be alone, to mourn, but the men look to
me, and we are still in the enemy's territory. I keep my back straight and
my eyes up, wary of danger. Some part of me, detached from the anguish and pain, keeps talking, listening to reconnaissance and issuing
orders, but enveloped in the protective shroud of Darin and Rojvah's
music, nothing threatens us as we leave the demon greatward.

All of us hiss and hold up hands to block the morning sun as we
emerge from the undercity. Time was meaningless in the eternal night
below. It feels like we were underground for weeks, but the *Sharum* carried no provision, and none of us have eaten, or seem hindered by the
lack. I'm not even hungry.

It's the morning after Waning.

The city is in ruin. Dead *Sharum* litter the streets next to stinking
piles of ash—*alagai* who have seen the sun. Buildings that stood for a
thousand years and more are reduced to rubble, the domes of great palaces cracked like eggs.

But the storm is over. I intend to be far from Desert Spear by the next full moon, and without us, there is little reason for Alagai Ka to return.

Only the Holy City remains untouched. It is bigger than the remaining Majah require, and the oasis at its center can feed thousands. The clerics will have no choice but to share its luxury now, with the rest of the city destroyed.

The Arms of Everam lower their spears at our approach to the holy gates. "Prince Olive, by order of the *Damaji*, we place you under arrest."

Drillmaster Zim lets out a low growl, and my spear brothers cluster around me. "Prince Olive put a blade into Alagai Ka himself, and saved us all."

The guards glance at one another nervously, but I've seen enough conflict.

"It's all right," I step past the soldiers guarding me, gently easing their spears aside. "I will stand before the Skull Throne one last time."

BELINA WAILS WHEN Iraven's body is brought before the Skull Throne. She breaks away from the council of *dama'ting* to throw herself upon the litter bearing her son, weeping openly as her sisters in white collect her tears. Even Chavis kneels beside her, as Aleveran and the council of *dama* look on impassively.

The ritual is both performative and sincere. Runners delivered a list of the wounded and deceased to the throne hours ago, but it is a tradition for Krasian mothers to hold their tears until they see the remains of their fallen sons in the flesh.

The Evejah says souls on the lonely path can lose their way on the mist-cloaked path from the mortal realm to the gates of Heaven. A warrior with tear bottles in his hands is said to have a lighted way, and can add them to the balance when Everam weighs his spirit.

Iraven needs all the help he can get. He will arrive in the wake of the far nobler souls he sent down the lonely path before him.

My companions and I stand patiently through the display. At one point, Belina's eyes flick our way, an invitation to join her. Iraven was my brother, and Rojvah's uncle. Arick's relation is more removed, but there is blood shared. Tradition dictates we mourn as family, but Rojvah and Arick do not budge, taking their cues from me.

It would be easy to join the performance. Crying on command was a trick Grandmum taught me early, but as a man, I am not expected to give even that much. All it would take is some small act. A bow, or a single knee. A hand on Belina's shoulder. Night, I could just look sad and stare at the floor.

But I can muster no emotion for my brother. His last moments were perhaps the only sincere ones we ever had. Alagai Ka's influence or not, I cannot bring myself to mourn the man who murdered Chadan and Micha. Who led my spear brothers into the waiting talons of the *alagai*.

I keep my head up and my eyes straight ahead, refusing even the barest gesture. It is a deep insult, and I can feel tension rising in the room the longer it goes on.

At last, the wailing and crying dies down, and Aleveran signals Dama Maroch to approach the litter bearing my prince's shrouded form.

Chadan's *dal'ting* mother is not allowed at court, so the wailing will come later. I wonder what Maroch will do when he sees his only son lying dead, but the *dama* has too much dignity to show emotion like a woman. He lifts the shroud, examining the body without a hint of emotion. He turns to Aleveran and bows. "It is him, Damaji."

Sitting on high, Damaji Aleveran acknowledges the death of his grandson with little more than a solemn nod.

I want to scream. To wail like Belina, and force them to honor him. Chadan did everything these men ever asked. He was a perfect son and they did not deserve him. If this is what it means to be a Krasian man, I don't understand why I ever wanted any part of it.

But it doesn't matter if his own family did not love him enough. Chadan already has my tears to guide him to Heaven.

When the last tear is scraped from Belina's cheek, she rises from her knees with a viper's grace, gliding two steps until we lock stares. "You can pay your brother no honor, even with him dead at your hand?"

I consider denying it, but Belina's hand drops to her *hora* pouch, a reminder of the dice within. "Do not lie. Everam has already whispered me truth."

"Dama'ting Favah taught me the dice whisper only a fraction of truth," I say loudly. "Did they tell you Iraven asked me to help him onto the lonely path? The blade was the honor I owed him, and it was paid."

"Tsst!" Belina's hand darts into her *hora* pouch, removing the small replica of my armlet. Before she can begin to squeeze, I reach over and prick my finger on the little spear, opening the blood lock. I cast the armlet to the floor, but pocket the spear, still wet with my blood.

Belina's brows tighten. "The cuff can be replaced."

"Try it," I growl, "and the beating Micha gave you will feel like a gentle massage."

The other *dama'ting* tsst and gasp at that, eyes flicking to Belina. News of the defeat will shame and weaken her in the estimation of her fellow priestesses—the only estimation that truly matters to a *dama'ting*. It might even cost her the black veil.

The only way to save face would be to meet my challenge. Indeed, Evejan Law allows a *dama'ting* to kill any *Sharum* who offends her, and if I were to fight back, the sentence for striking a Bride of Everam is death.

Still, Belina is wise enough not to take the bait. Aleveran is the real power here, and he has not given her leave. I am playing a dangerous game, making an open enemy of her, but like her son, Belina was always my enemy. The time for pretending otherwise is over.

"Enough." Aleveran's left finger gives an irritated flick. Belina steps back to join the *dama'ting* counsel, but her hate-filled eyes do not leave mine. I turn away instead, dismissing her as I turn to face the *Damaji*.

"We were lenient the last time you stood before us, Prince Olive," Aleveran says. "But instead of keeping your word and your honor, you murdered Drillmaster Chikga, ran from justice, and now both the princes of Majah are dead. Tell me why I shouldn't execute you here and now."

Prince Olive? Is that who I am? Not always, perhaps, but here before the Skull Throne it feels right. Krasian men only truly respect their own, and now that I have their respect, I will accept nothing less.

I return his cold appraisal with a lofty gaze to do even Mother proud. "You're not going to execute me."

"Still insolent." Damaji'ting Chavis has taken her customary place atop the sixth step. "You—"

"Tsst!" I cut her off, and have to suppress a smile as the old woman's eyes go wide. If they want me to be a man, I will be one. "I speak of *alagai'sharak*, Damaji'ting. This is *men's* business. While you waited in the safety of the Holy City, I went to the abyss and put a knife in the Father of Demons. I will tolerate no more of your disrespect."

The silence that follows is heavy. Chavis shakes at my audacity, but I am right and she knows it. Even the most powerful woman in Krasia must be respectful of a warrior bathed in glory.

At last, Aleveran raises a finger and the *Damaji'ting* steps back. "Why is that, young prince?"

"Because you cannot afford another war," I say. "If you hold my friends and me, or harm us in any way, the armies of Thesa and New Krasia will descend upon you. The great gate is breached, Damaji. Your city is in ruins. Even if the oasis can feed those who remain, you do not have the warriors to defend the Holy City. The only logical recourse is to supply us for a desert crossing, and let us go."

The *Damaji's* eyes narrow. "Why would Iraven ask for death?"

"Because he never sealed the breach two moons ago," I say. "He was taken by Alagai Ka, and became the Father of Demons' agent in the day."

"Impossible," Aleveran says. "The power of the Holy City would have broken even the hold of the *alagai* king."

I shake my head. "The Father of Lies can implant suggestions that bind his victims' will even when their minds are returned to protection."

Dama Maroch scoffs. "How can you know this?"

I want to punch him in his condescending face. If he had half the courage of his son, he would know firsthand.

"Because it is in the accounts of my father," I say instead, "Ahmann asu Hoshkamin am'Jardir, the Shar'Dama Ka. Written into the sacred texts after his victory in Sharak Ka and return from Nie's abyss."

The words are a reminder of who I am, but more important, they are a reminder of who the *Majah* are—the tribe that abandoned the Deliverer's army before the final sallies of Sharak Ka.

"And because I threatened to interfere with Alagai Ka's plans," I add, "Iraven sent Chikga to kill me. Then, yesterday, the Sharum Ka led his warriors into a trap."

"Lies," Maroch says. "What proof do you have that it wasn't you who took the chance to rid yourself of rivals?"

I turn to look at Zim. The drillmaster waits for a nod from Aleveran, then steps forward and kneels before the Skull Throne, placing his hands on the floor.

"Rise, honored Drillmaster Zim," Aleveran says. "Speak your truth for Everam to judge."

Zim rolls smoothly back onto his heels, rising to stand at full height before the *Damaji*. Like all of us, he is covered in blood and ichor, marks of great honor in the temple of Heroes' Bones. "The Sharum Ka was like a brother to me, Damaji. His glory was boundless. But I swear by Everam and my hope of Heaven that he deceived us and led us into ambush. It is only because of Prince Olive that any of us returned alive. It was Olive who struck Alagai Ka down, while the rest of us lay beaten."

It's not precisely true, and I feel Selen bristle beside me as her own contribution is erased, but no one contradicts Drillmaster Zim.

"Will the other men attest to this?" Aleveran asks.

Zim nods. "They will, Damaji. And if Olive asu Ahmann is not their next Sharum Ka . . . " He chooses his next words carefully. "I do not know who else the *Sharum* will accept."

That surprises me. I know it is true of the Princes Unit, and perhaps what remains of the Spears of the Desert, but I did not realize my name carried such weight among the *Sharum* at large. A lump forms in my throat.

Aleveran scowls. "They will accept who the Skull Throne decrees, Drillmaster, and no other."

Zim bows again. "Of course, Damaji. I meant no disrespect, only to convey what Prince Olive means to his spear brothers."

Aleveran nods, dismissing the drillmaster with a flick of his finger. "It appears the prophecy was true, Prince Olive."

"Perhaps," I say. "Or perhaps you made it true by stealing me from my home and bringing me here. Regardless, my fate is fulfilled, and I call upon you to keep your promise and give back the life you stole."

"What could your greenland life offer," Aleveran asks, "to tip the balance against the white turban and throne of Sharum Ka? As the drillmaster says, there is no other warrior to match your glory and lineage, and Desert Spear requires a First Warrior, now more than ever. Stay, and enjoy the fruits of your victory."

For a moment that life flashes before my eyes. It is a life of honor, but it is not my life. I don't want the Spear Throne, or any throne, though one awaits me at home, as well.

"No," I say, drawing breaths of surprise from around the room. Has any warrior in history ever turned down the Spear Throne?

I keep my eyes on Aleveran. The others do not matter. "Alagai Ka is not dead, Damaji. I do not think any mortal can truly kill the Father of Demons. I must look to my homeland, as you must yours."

Rojvah takes a step forward, standing just behind me. As we rehearsed, I take a step back to match her.

Aleveran raises a brow. "You have something to add, girl?"

Rojvah takes two steps forward, bowing. "My grandmother, the Damajah, sent me with a message. Had we been received with civility, I would have conveyed it then, but I will offer it now."

The lines on Aleveran's face deepen as he flicks a finger in permission. Chavis looks like she has just sucked a lemon.

"The Damajah hereby divorces Dama'ting Belina, expelling her from her circle of sister-wives."

The news is enough to make even the *dama'ting* gasp. With that decree, the last tie of blood between New Krasia and Old is severed, weakening Belina's power even further.

"If the *Damaji* wishes to send new ambassadors to the Deliverer's court in good faith," Rojvah adds, "they will be welcomed, and can begin negotiations for trade and military support."

"What makes you think the Majah need the traitor's court?" Maroch asks.

As I did before, Rojvah never takes her eyes off Aleveran, responding as if it had been the *Damaji* who spoke. "I leave it to your wisdom, Damaji, to decide what is best for your people. I bear the offer, only."

The *Damaji* stares at her for a moment that seems to stretch in time, and then at me. At last he whisks his hand like Mother excusing me from the dining table. "Go, then."

Dama Maroch betrays a hint of emotion now, as he turns to face his father, but the *Damaji* turns a palm to him, and any protests die on his son's lips.

"You will have whatever is required for your journey," Aleveran says, "and our thanks."

I nod, but I do not bow before turning on my heel and striding out of the chamber, my friends following behind.

MICHA'S BODY WAITS outside in the hall, not "worthy" to have been taken before the throne.

Part of me wants to bring her body back to Hollow and her wife Kendall, but I think in her heart, Sharik Hora is where my sister would want to be interred. Here in the place she was raised, the halls and passages she knew like her own body. Her bones, and Chadan's, bleached like those of their ancestors, added to those of countless generations of heroes before them, protecting the holy temple with their golden magic.

The blood I share with my sister is enough to open the blood lock on her choker. I cannot sing as she did, but I claim it—all that I have of hers. I take her marriage earring as well, to give to Kendall when I return home.

Selen puts an arm around me, and I lean in as she squeezes. "Can't believe she's gone."

"Hard to believe anything that's happened, these last months," I say. We may be going home, but nothing will ever be the same. Not who we are, nor the place we'll return to. With no one left to define me, I will have to define myself.

"I think your mum was right," I say.

"Ay, don't ever say that," Selen says. "What about?"

"The time for secrets is over," I say. "We're going to have to make some changes when we get home."

Selen squeezes me tighter. "High time."

62

THE FATHER WAITS

"So Mam and the others are still alive?" I ask, when Olive finishes recounting what she experienced in the demon king's mind.

We've been given lavish chambers to await preparation of our caravan home. The *Damaji* has put servants in the walls to spy on us, but Olive and Rojvah's chokers keep us in a bubble of silence.

Selen lays a hand over mine as the thought takes root. Mam and Aunt Leesha ent dead? Part of me refused to believe it was possible for them to die, but news they may still be out there is no easier to accept.

"It stands to reason," Olive agrees. "The demon told me he was going to feed them to the hatchling queen, so she could absorb their power."

"You cannot trust the word of the Father of Lies," Rojvah says.

"Maybe not," Olive agrees, "but I was in his head, if only for a second. I believe him."

"Master Hary used to say the best lies are always true," I say. "Aunt Leesha's prophecy was *The father waits below in darkness for his progeny to return*. Thought it meant my da. That he was still alive. But Ahmann Jardir is my bloodfather, and your da. Maybe the dice were tryin' to tell us he's waitin' on a rescue."

Olive sighs. "Core if I know, Darin. Creator as my witness, I've never had a throw of the dice make sense to me. Even in hindsight, I still don't entirely understand my own."

"He'll keep coming for us," I say. Just the memory of that creature makes my hands shake and my bladder tighten. "Mam says Alagai Ka can heal any injury just by dissipating and re-forming. Din't go to all this trouble to leave us free."

"Ay," Olive says, "but by the next new moon I mean for us to be safe in Everam's Bounty. A moon after that, on the Hollow greatward. Alagai Ka won't have another chance to strike at us, and why bother when he knows we'll come to him?"

"How, when we don't know where he is?" Selen asks.

But we do, I realize, as more of Leesha's prophecy becomes clear. We've known all along where the mimic neo-queen is. "The city in the mountains."

Olive nods. "Safehold."

OUT ON THE terrace, I am alone with my thoughts, or as close as can be. Sounds from all over reach my ears as folk salvage what they can before moving to the Holy City. After a time they settle into a background din I can ignore.

That is, until Arick comes and joins me. The Majah have not stripped him of his *Sharum* blacks, earned this time with blood and ichor. Even with his orange hair and pale skin, the armored robes suit him.

I don't turn from my view of the city, but Arick knows I sense him. "You didn't tell her the demon possessed me, too."

He's right. I left that part out when we filled Olive in on what happened after she left us to rejoin her unit.

"Neither did Selen, or your sister," I say. "Or you, for that matter."

"Why?" Arick asks. "Was Iraven's betrayal any worse than mine?"

"Ent the Creator, Arick," I shrug. "Not my place to judge. Demon didn't have you that long. Reckon it takes time to remodel someone's head."

"It doesn't need to remodel to leave the door unlocked," Arick says. "I pushed you off that ledge. I couldn't control myself. Who knows what else I might do?"

"Then why didn't you tell her?" I ask.

"Because I am a coward who is not ready to die," Arick says. "Why didn't you?"

I spit over the terrace rail. "Because we *ent* cowards, Arick. Won't turn on my kin 'cause I'm scared of somethin' that might or might not've happened. If Alagai Ka's got your stones in a vise, I say we're better off killing him than you."

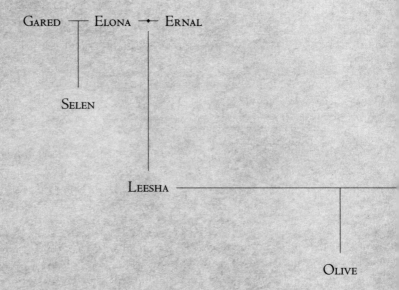

FAMILY TREE

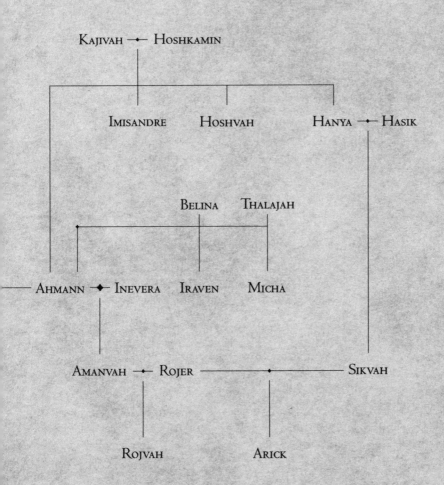

KRASIAN DICTIONARY

———•———

Ajin'pal/ajin'pan: Blood brother/blood sister. Name for the bond that forms between a mentor and a young warrior fighting their first *alagai'sharak*. An *ajin'pal* or *pan* is considered a blood relative thereafter.

Ajin'pel: Blooded to many. A warrior of such renown that they have blooded many an *ajin'pal* over the years. *Ajin'pel* are very influential among the *Sharum*.

Ala: (1) The perfect world created by Everam, corrupted by Nie. (2) Dirt, soil, clay, etcetera.

Alagai: Corelings (demons). Direct translation is "plague of Ala."

Alagai hora: Demonbones used to create magic items, such as the warded dice *dama'ting* use to tell the future. *Alagai hora* burst into flame if exposed to direct sunlight.

Alagai Ka: The mind demon consort to Alagai'ting Ka, the Mother of Demons. Also known as Father of Demons, the Father of Lies, and the demon king. Alagai Ka and his sons were said to be the most powerful of the demon lords—generals and captains of Nie's forces.

Alagai-scale: Special Majah armor technique guarded by the powerful Tazhan family.

Alagai'sharak: Holy war against demonkind.

Alagai tail: A whip consisting of three strips of leather braided with sharp barbs to cut into a victim's flesh. Used by *dama* as an instrument of punishment.

Alagai'ting Ka: The Mother of Demons of Krasian myth, also known as the Mother of Evil and the demon queen.

Alomom: Powder that Watchers use to hide the scent of their sweat.

Arms of Everam: Guards of the Holy City in Desert Spear. They wear white sleeves with their *Sharum* blacks, symbolizing their arms in service to the *dama*.

Asu: "Son" or "son of," often used as a suffix or prefix in a boy's name.

Baba: Grandfather (informal term of affection).

Bido: Loincloth worn by both men and women under their robes. A youth who has not yet earned vocational robes is referred to as "still in their bido."

Bloodfather: Godparent, used most often for *ajin'pal* of a deceased father.

Chin: Outsider/infidel. Anyone who is not at least half-blood Krasian. *Chin* is derogatory, synonymous with coward.

Chi'Sharum: Greenbloods who go through *Hannu Pash* and are raised to warrior status with all of its rights and privileges. Their caste remains below that of the Krasian-blood *dal'Sharum*.

Couzi: A harsh, illegal liquor filtered with cinnamon. Because of its potency, couzi is served in tiny cups meant to be taken in one swallow.

Dal: Prefix meaning "honored."

Dal'Sharum: The Krasian warrior caste, which includes the vast majority of the men. *Dal'Sharum* are broken into smaller units answerable to individual *kai'Sharum*. *Dal'Sharum* dress in black armored robes with a black turban helm and night veil. All are trained in hand-to-hand combat (*sharusahk*), as well as spear fighting and shield formations.

Dama: Clerical caste, which is above warrior. *Dama* are both religious and secular leaders. They wear white robes and eschew the spear in favor of alagai tail whips. All *dama* are masters of *sharusahk*, the Krasian hand-to-hand martial art, including secret techniques not given to the *Sharum*.

Damajah: Singular title for Inevera, the First Wife of Ahmann Jardir, the Shar'Dama Ka. The Damajah is both spiritual and secular leader of every woman in New Krasia.

Damaji: The male religious and secular leader of one of the twelve tribes of Krasia.

Damaji'ting: Female religious and secular leader of a tribe with dominion over its women.

Dama'ting: Female clerical caste, holy women who also serve as healers and midwives. *Dama'ting* hold the secrets of *hora* magic, including the power to foretell the future, and are held in fear and awe. Harming a *dama'ting* or hindering them in any way is punishable by death.

Desert Spear: Known in the North as Fort Krasia, an enormous fortress city built around the oasis and ancient Holy City of Sharik Hora.

Draki: Krasian unit of currency.

Drillmasters: Elite warriors who train *nie'Sharum*. Drillmasters wear standard *dal'Sharum* blacks, but their night veils are red.

Evejah, the: The holy book of Everam, written by Kaji, the first Deliverer, some three millennia past. The Evejah is separated into sections called Dunes. Each *dama* pens a copy of the Evejah in his own blood during his clerical training.

Evejan: Name of the Krasian religion, "those who follow the Evejah."

Evejan law: Militant religious law imposed on general citizenry.

Everam: The Creator.

Everam's Bounty: Formerly the Free City of Fort Rizon, it was conquered in 333 AR with its vast farmland and became the capital of New Krasia in the green lands.

Ginjaz: Turncoat, traitor.

Greenlander: One from the green lands. A less derogatory term than *chin*.

Green lands: Krasian name for Thesa (the lands north of the Krasian desert), a large swath of which has become New Krasia.

Hannu Pash: Literally "life's path," this represents both a ceremony and a period of training and religious indoctrination to determine a young Krasian's vocation.

Hava: Spice to flavor and preserve food. Hava is foundational in Krasian cooking.

Heasah: Prostitute.

Hora magic: Any magic using demon body parts (bones, ichor, etcetera) as a battery to power spells.

Horn of Sharak: Ceremonial horn blown to begin and end *alagai'sharak*.

Inevera: (1) Krasian word meaning "Everam's will" or "Everam willing." (2) A common name for women in the Kaji tribe.

Jiwah/jiwan: Wife/husband.

Jiwah Ka: First Wife. The *Jiwah Ka* is the first and most honored of a Krasian man's wives. She has veto power over subsequent marriages, and can command her sister-wives.

Jiwah Sen: Lesser wives, subservient to a man's *Jiwah Ka*.

Jiwah'Sharum: Literally "wives of warriors," these are women who live in *Sharum* harems during their fertile years. It is considered a great honor to serve. All warriors have access to their tribe's *Jiwah'Sharum*, and are expected to keep them continually with child, adding warriors to the tribe.

Kai'Sharum: Krasian military captains. *Kai'Sharum* receive special training in Sharik Hora and lead individual units in *alagai'sharak*. *Kai'Sharum* wear *dal'Sharum* blacks, but their night veils are white.

Kaji: The name of the original Deliverer and patriarch of the Kaji tribe, also known as Shar'Dama Ka. More than three thousand years ago, Kaji united the known world in war against demons, ushering in millennia of peace.

Kamanj: A bowed string instrument similar to a fiddle that ends in a spike planted on the ground or a player's leg to steady it.

Khaffit: Lowest male caste in Krasian society. Expelled from *sharaj*, *khaffit* are forced to dress in the tan clothes of children and shave their cheeks as a sign that they are not true men.

Lonely path: Krasian term for death. All warriors must walk the mist-shrouded road to Heaven, with temptations on the path to test their spirit and ensure that only the worthy stand before Everam to be judged. Spirits who venture off the path are lost.

Nie: (1) The name of the Uncreator, feminine opposite to Everam, and the goddess of night and demonkind. (2) Nothing, none, void, no, not. (3) Prefix for trainees in line for a vocation.

Nie'dama: *Nie'Sharum* selected for *dama* training.

Nie'dama'ting: *Dama'ting* in training. Also known as Betrothed, they are promised Brides of Everam. Men laying hands on them is punishable by death or loss of the offending limb.

Nie Ka: Literally "first of none," a term for the head boy of a *nie'Sharum* class, who commands the other boys as sergeant to the *dal'Sharum* drillmasters.

Nie's abyss: Also known as the Core. In Evejan scripture, it is the seven-layered underworld where *alagai* hide from the sun. Each layer is populated with a different breed of demon.

Nie'Sharum: Warriors-in-training.

Night veil: Veil worn by *Sharum* during *alagai'sharak* to hide their identities, showing that all men are equal allies in the night.

Oot: *Dal'Sharum* signal for "beware" or "demon approaching."

Princes Unit: Olive and Chadan's *Sharum* unit, composed of *nie'Sharum* of various castes blooded young due to crisis. Derided by older warriors as the "Princess" Unit, they top the kill counts almost every night, taking on the most dangerous missions.

Push'ting: This can refer to people who are homosexual, transgender, or who otherwise challenge gender norms. Same-sex relationships are common in Krasia, but *push'ting* is used in the derogatory for those who refuse even a symbolic marriage for the purpose of children.

Scorpion: The scorpion is a giant crossbow using springs instead of a bowstring. It shoots thick spears with heavy heads (stingers) and can kill sand and wind demons outright at a thousand feet, even without wards.

Sharaj: Barracks for young boys in *Hannu Pash*, much like a military boarding school. The *sharaji* are organized by blood. Full blood for the sons and daughters of pure-blooded Majah warrior families. Half blood for the sons of *dal'Sharum* and *chin* women. Coward's blood for the sons of *khaffit*. Green blood for the sons of *chin*.

Sharak Ka: The First War. The final battle of *alagai'sharak*, when the Deliverer will lead Everam's armies to victory or defeat.

Sharak Sun: The Daylight War, during which humanity must be conquered and united into Everam's army for Sharak Ka.

Shar'dama: Dama who fight *alagai'sharak* in defiance of Evejan law.

Shar'Dama Ka: First Warrior–Cleric. The Krasian term for the Deliverer, who will come to free mankind from the *alagai*.

Sharik Hora: The great temple in Krasia made out of the bones of fallen warriors. Having their bones lacquered and added to the temple is the highest honor that warriors can attain.

Sharukin: Warrior poses. Practiced series of movements for *sharusahk*.

Sharum: Warrior. The *Sharum* dress in black robes inlaid with pockets for fired clay armor plates.

Sharum Ka: First Warrior. A title for the secular leader of *alagai'sharak*. The Sharum Ka is appointed by the occupant of the Skull Throne, and all *Sharum* answer to him and him only from dusk until dawn. The Sharum Ka has his own palace at the head of the training grounds and sits on the Spear Throne. He wears *dal'Sharum* blacks, but his turban and night veil are white.

Sharum'ting: Female warriors, mostly serving as personal guards to the *dama'ting*.

Sharusahk: The Krasian art of unarmed combat. There are various schools of *sharusahk* depending on caste and tribe, but all consist of brutal, efficient moves designed to turn an opponent's strength against them to stun, cripple, and kill.

Shield team: Small teams of two to five warriors subdividing *Sharum* units.

Skull Throne: The traditional seat of power for Krasia's leader. Since the split with the Majah tribe, there are now two Skull Thrones. The one in New Krasia is the original—made from the skulls of deceased Sharum Ka and coated in electrum, the throne is powered by the skull of a mind demon, casting a forbiddance that prevents demons from entering the inner city of Everam's Bounty. The one in old Krasia is newly made from the skulls of fallen warriors and sits in the holy temple of Sharik Hora.

Spears of the Desert: Sharum Ka Iraven's elite bodyguard unit.

Spear Throne: The throne of the Sharum Ka, made from the broken spears of previous Sharum Kas.

Stinger: The ammunition for the scorpion ballistae. Stingers are giant spears with heavy iron heads that can punch through demon armor on a parabolic shot.

Tikka: Grandmother (informal term of affection).

'ting: Suffix meaning "woman."

Tribes: Reference to the twelve tribes of Krasia—Anjha, Bajin, Halvas, Jama, Kaji, Khanjin, Krevakh, Majah, Mehnding, Nanji, Sharach, Shunjin.

Undercity: Huge honeycomb of warded caverns beneath Desert Spear where women, children, and *khaffit* are locked at night to keep them safe from demons while the men fight.

Vah: "Daughter" or "daughter of." Often used as a suffix or prefix in a girl's name.

Waning: (1) Three-day monthly religious observance for Evejans occurring on the days directly before, on, and after the new moon. Attendance at Sharik Hora is mandatory, and families spend the days together, even pulling sons out of *sharaj*. Demons are said to be more powerful on Waning, when it is said Alagai Ka walks the surface.

Wardwork: Scrollwork on clothing or items consisting of ward patterns with real potency.

Watchers: Watchers are *dal'Sharum*, primarily of the Krevakh and Nanji tribes, trained in special weapons and tactics. They serve as scouts, spies, and assassins. Watchers carry and fight with iron-shod ladders six feet long as well as smaller, close-combat weapons. The ladders have interconnecting ends so they can be joined together. Watchers are so proficient they can run straight up a ladder without bracing it and balance at the top.

WARD GRIMOIRE

PROTECTION WARDS

Protection (defensive) wards Draw magic to form a barrier (forbiddance) through which demon corelings cannot pass. Wards are strongest when used against the specific demon type to which they are assigned, and are most commonly used in conjunction with other wards in circles of protection. When a circle activates, all coreflesh is forcibly banished from its line. A mixed group of demons is referred to as a host.

BANK DEMON

Description: Also called frog demons or froggies, these demons appear much like common fly frogs, but they are large enough to swallow humans whole. They lie in wait in shallow water, springing only when prey comes within range. They lash out with long, powerful tongues, catching victims and dragging them into their wide maws. Bank demons will then return to the water, drowning their struggling prey. A group of bank demons is called an army.

CAVE DEMON

Description: Cave demons, also known as tunnel or spider demons, have eight segmented legs and can run at great speed. Cave demons excrete a sticky silk that is magic-dead—invisible to wardsight and immune to wards of protection. They will prepare traps and lie in wait for the unwary. These demons seldom rise to the surface unless summoned by a mind; they are more commonly found in deep caves and the tunnels of a demon hive. A group of cave demons is called a clutter.

CLAY DEMON

Description: Clay demons are native to the hard clay flats on the outskirts of the Krasian desert. They are perhaps three feet long, but heavy with compact muscle and thick, overlapping armor plates. Their short, hard talons allow them to cling to most any rock face, even hanging upside down. Their orange-brown armor can blend invisibly into an adobe wall or clay bed. The blunt head of a clay demon can smash through nearly anything, cracking stone and denting steel. A group of clay demons is known as a shattering.

FIELD DEMON

Description: Sleek and low to the ground, with long, powerful limbs and retractable claws, field demons are the fastest thing on four legs when they have open ground to run and can leap great distances. Tough scales on their limbs and back can turn aside most weapons, but their underbelly—if exposed—is more vulnerable. A group of field demons, also known as fieldies, is called a reap.

FLAME DEMON

Description: Flame demons have eyes, nostrils, and mouths that glow with a smoky orange light. They are the smallest demons, no larger than a cat. Like all demons, they have long, hooked claws and rows of razor-sharp teeth. Their armor consists of small, overlapping scales, sharp and hard. Flame demons can spit fire in brief bursts. Their sticky firespit burns intensely on contact with air and can set almost any substance alight, even metal and stone. A group of flame demons is known as a blaze.

LIGHTNING DEMON

Description: Though lightning demons are nearly indistinguishable from their wind demon cousins, their spit is charged with electricity that can paralyze a victim. They spit as they dive, snatching up their helpless victims to devour them alive. A group of lightning demons is known as a thundercloud.

MIMIC DEMON

Description: Mimics are the elite bodyguards to mind demons. Less vulnerable to light than their masters and more intelligent than the lesser breeds, mimics serve as lieutenants and are able to summon and exert their will upon coreling drones. Their natural form is unknown, but they are able to assume the form of nearly anything they encounter, from inanimate objects to creatures, clothing, and equipment. One of their favorite tricks is to learn the names of their prey and take the form of a friend, feigning distress and calling to their victims to convince them to leave the safety of their wards. A gathering of mimic demons is known as a troupe.

MIND DEMON

Description: Also known as coreling princes, mind demons are the generals of demonkind. The only male-sexed caste among demonkind, minds are physically weak and have little in the way of the natural defenses of the other corelings, but they have vast mental and magical powers. They can read and control minds, communicate telepathically, and implant permanent suggestions. They can draw wards in the air and power them with their own innate magic. Coreling drones follow their every mental command without hesitation, and will give their lives to protect them. Sensitive to even moonlight, mind demons only rise on the three-night period of the new moon cycle, in the hours when night is darkest. A gathering of mind demons is known as a court.

ROCK DEMON

Description: The largest of the coreling breeds, rock demons, also known as rockies, can range in height from six to twenty feet. Hulking masses of sinew and sharp edges, they have thick carapaces knobbed with bony protrusions, and their spiked tails can shatter stone. They stand hunched on two clawed feet, with long, gnarled arms ending in talons the size of butcher knives, and multiple rows of bladelike teeth. No known physical force can harm a rock demon. A group of rock demons is called a quake.

SAND DEMON

Description: Cousins to rock demons, sand demons are smaller and more nimble, but still among the strongest and best armored of the coreling breeds. They have small, sharp scales that are a dirty yellow almost indistinguishable from gritty sand. They run on all fours but can rise to two legs in combat. Their short snouts have rows of sharp teeth, with nostril slits just below large, lidless eyes. Thick horns curve upward and back, cutting through the scales. Sand demons hunt in packs known as storms.

SNOW DEMON

Description: Similar to flame demons in size and build, snow demons are native to frozen Northern climates and high mountain elevations. Their scales are such pure white, they scintillate with color if caught in the light. Snow demons are nearly invisible in the snow, and spit a liquid so cold it instantly freezes anything it touches. Steel struck with coldspit can become brittle enough to shatter. A group of snow demons is called a blizzard.

STONE DEMON

Description: Smaller cousins of rock demons—who form through faces of pure rock—stone demons feature armor with the mottled appearance of conglomerate rock. They tend to be squat and slow, but are among the strongest and most indestructible of demons. Requiring less specialized environments to rise, stone demons are more common than rock demons. A group of stone demons is called a conglomerate.

SUCCOR

Description: The succor ward is a general ward of protection taught to children. Not as powerful as wards keyed to individual breeds, succor wards create a general field of discomfort that is enough to drive most corelings away unless prey is in sight. Very large or powerful wards can form a forbiddance. The ward is used in the Thesan dice game Succor, as well as its Krasian variation, Sharak.

SWAMP DEMON

Description: Swamp demons are native to swamps and marshy areas, an amphibious form of wood demon at home both in the water and in the trees. Swamp demons are blotched green and brown to blend into their surroundings, and will often hide in trees, mud, or shallow water to spring on prey. They spit a thick, sticky slime that rots any organic material it comes in contact with. A group of swamp demons is called a muck.

WATER DEMON

Description: Water demons are seldom seen. They come in various forms and sizes. Some are man-sized, sleek and scaly, with webbed hands and feet, tipped with sharp talons. Others are large enough to pull ships beneath the surface with their thick, horned tentacles. Others are bigger still, leviathans able to leap above the water and splash down to create tremendous waves. Water demons can only breathe underwater, though they can surface for a short time. A group of water demons is called a wave.

WIND DEMON

Description: Wind demons stand as tall as humans at the shoulder, but have head fins that rise much higher, topping eight or nine feet. Their sharp-edged beaks hide rows of teeth. Their skin is a tough, flexible armor that can turn most any spearpoint or arrowhead. It stretches out from their sides and along the underside of their arms to form the tough membrane of their wings, which can span three times their height. Clumsy and slow on land, wind demons have tremendous power in the sky. The thin wing bones are jointed with wicked hooked talons. Their preferred attack is a silent dive, opening their wings with a great snap just before impact, severing a victim's head before grabbing the body in their hind talons and flying off. A group of wind demons is called a flight.

WOOD DEMON

Description: Wood demons, also called woodies, are native to forests. Next to rock demons, they are the largest and most powerful demons, averaging from five to fifteen feet tall when standing on their hind legs, the smallest sometimes referred to as stump demons. Wood demons have short, powerful hindquarters and long, sinewy arms, perfect for climbing trees and leaping from branch to branch. Their claws are short, hard points, designed for gripping trees. Wood demons' armor is barklike in color and texture, and they have large black eyes. Wood demons cannot be harmed by normal fire, but will burn readily if brought into contact with hotter fires, such as firespit or liquid demonfire. Wood demons will kill flame demons on sight, and hunt in groups called copses.

COMBAT WARDS

Combat wards repurpose magic for offensive effects. Some Draw power directly from the demon they strike, while others are powered by batteries such as demonbone, also known as *hora*.

COLD

Description: Cold wards reduce thermal energy, rapidly dropping the temperature of their target area to below freezing. Powerful cold wards can shatter steel or even rock demon armor.

CUTTING

Description: Cutting wards, when etched along the length of a blade, siphon power from demons as they strike, weakening armor, strengthening the weapon, and sharpening the blade down to a near-molecular level, allowing the weapon to cut through even coreling armor and flesh.

FIRESPIT/COLDSPIT

Description: These wards are used as defense against flame demons, turning their firespit into a cool breeze. When drawn in reverse, they turn the coldspit of a snow demon into a warm breeze.

GLASS

Description: When etched on glass and charged with magic, these wards effect a permanent change, making glass harder than diamond and stronger than steel without changing its weight or appearance. Warded glass is widely used to create near-indestructible windows, vials, weapons, and armor.

HEAT

Description: Heat wards increase thermal energy, converting magic directly to heat. Objects painted with heat wards are consumed when the wards activate unless highly resistant to extreme temperatures.

IMPACT

Description: These wards turn magic into concussive force. They can be used alone, or to augment the blow of a blunt weapon. When used to strike a demon, they siphon magic like cutting wards, weakening armor even as they multiply force. The stronger the original impact, the more power is generated.

LECTRIC

Description: These wards convert magic directly into electricity that can be directed at an object or creature. The wards can also be linked to form circuits.

MAGNETIC

Description: Magnetic wards charge their target area, drawing ferrous materials like a powerful magnet. They are sometimes used to increase the accuracy of iron cannonballs.

MOISTURE

Description: Moisture wards attract moisture from the air or nearby bodies of water. They can be used to ensure that plants get the necessary water without human care, to fill a small reservoir, or to quench a flame demon. Powerful moisture wards can drown or, if reversed, dehydrate a victim.

PIERCING

Description: Piercing wards Draw from the point of impact on a demon's body, weakening coreling armor even as they focus magic into a weapon's point for maximum penetrative power.

PRESSURE

Description: Pressure wards exert a crushing force that builds in heat and intensity the longer they remain in contact with a demon.

PERCEPTION WARDS

Perception wards create magical effects that can alter the senses of demons and sometimes humans.

BLENDING

Description: Blending wards pull from their surroundings to camouflage their target area. Unlike unsight wards, which only work on demons, blending wards can hide things from human senses, as well. Sudden or quick movement can negate a blending ward's power.

CONFUSION

Description: Confusion wards radiate a field of disorientation that can cause creatures to become dizzy and lose their sense of direction. Unless prey is in sight, affected coreling drones will often forget what they are doing, wandering away harmlessly.

LIGHT
Description: Light wards convert magic to pure white light. Depending on the power source, the light can be anything from a soft glow to a blinding glare.

PROPHECY
Description: Carved into the *alagai hora* of the *dama'ting*, prophecy wards read the currents of magic to make predictions about the future. Their magic pulls the demonbone dice out of their natural trajectories to answer questions spoken in prayer to Everam. The processes used both to make the dice and to read them are closely guarded secrets of the Krasian priestesses—it is death to share them with outsiders.

RESONANCE
Description: Resonance wards can affect the flow of soundwaves, disrupting them to create areas of silence, or strengthening them to amplify sound. A demonbone broken into two pieces and carved with wards of resonance can effect communication over great distances.

UNSIGHT
Description: Wards of unsight can make objects invisible to demons, provided those objects keep relatively still. Wards of unsight in conjunction with wards of confusion are used to make Cloaks of Unsight that protect humans in the naked night.

WARDSIGHT
Description: When worn around the eyes and charged, these wards can allow surface creatures to see in the magical spectrum. Creatures with wardsight can see in complete darkness as easily as clear day, watch the flow of ambient magic, judge the relative power of wardings, and see the auras given off by all living things. A skilled practitioner can Read these auras to tell what others are feeling or thinking, and sometimes to gain a sense of their past or even their future.

ACKNOWLEDGMENTS

———◆———

The Desert Prince proved to be my most ambitious and difficult novel to date, in part because much of it was written in 2020 (amid the global Covid-19 pandemic and a time of unprecedented social and political unrest), but also because of its own unique challenges. Creating a new Demon Cycle series that is welcoming to new readers while still keeping canon with the old series was a heavier lift than expected, and Olive and Darin proved to be the most unique characters I have ever had the pleasure of writing. Finding their voices was a journey in itself, but there was treasure at the end.

Thanks as always to my endlessly supportive partner, Lauren, and my daughters, Cassandra and Sirena. I was so lucky to quarantine with such amazing women.

To my editors Tricia and Natasha, and my sensitivity reader Rebecca, thank you for multiple edit passes as we ensured this book was the best it could be. Your input was invaluable.

To my author friends, Alina, Katherine, Naomi, Myke, & Wesley, who listened with patience and understanding whenever I needed a friendly ear and professional advice, a special thanks.

Recognition once again to Dr. Bill Greene for being a resource on combat medicine, and appreciation to my beta reader Amelia for her empathy. Love always to my biggest fan, Mom, who always finds a typo everyone else missed.

To all the other heroes, the production teams at Del Rey Books and Voyager, the publicists, artists, art directors, and translators, not to mention the booksellers—none of this would be possible without you.

Next round's on me.

ABOUT THE AUTHOR

PETER V. BRETT is the internationally bestselling author of the Demon Cycle series, which has sold more than three and a half million copies in twenty-seven languages worldwide. Novels include *The Warded Man, The Desert Spear, The Daylight War, The Skull Throne,* and *The Core.* He lives in Brooklyn.

petervbrett.com

Facebook.com/PVBrett

Twitter: @PVBrett

Instagram: @pvbrett